The Bad Boy Trilogy

Shandi Boyes

Copyright

Also by Shandi Boyes

Perception Series

Saving Noah (Noah & Emily)

Fighting Jacob (Jacob & Lola)

Taming Nick (Nick & Jenni)

Redeeming Slater (Slater and Kylie)

Saving Emily (Noah & Emily - Novella)

Wrapped Up with Rise Up (Perception Novella - should be read after the
Bound Series)

Enigma

Enigma (Isaac & Isabelle #1)

Unraveling an Enigma (Isaac & Isabelle #2)

Enigma The Mystery Unmasked (Isaac & Isabelle #3)

Enigma: The Final Chapter (Isaac & Isabelle #4)

Beneath The Secrets (Hugo & Ava #1)

Beneath The Sheets (Hugo & Ava #2)

Spy Thy Neighbor (Hunter & Paige)

The Opposite Effect (Brax & Clara)

I Married a Mob Boss (Rico & Blaire)

Second Shot (Hawke & Gemma)

The Way We Are (Ryan & Savannah #1)

The Way We Were (Ryan & Savannah #2)

Sugar and Spice (Cormack & Harlow)

Lady In Waiting (Regan & Alex #1)

Man in Queue (Regan & Alex #2)

Couple on Hold (Regan & Alex #3)

Enigma: The Wedding (Isaac and Isabelle)

Silent Vigilante (Brandon and Melody #1)

Hushed Guardian (Brandon & Melody #2)

Quiet Protector (Brandon & Melody #3)

Twisted Lies (Jae & CJ)

Enigma: An Isaac Retelling

Bound Series

Chains (Marcus & Cleo #1)

Links (Marcus & Cleo #2)

Bound (Marcus & Cleo #3)

Restrain (Marcus & Cleo #4)

The Misfits (Dexter & Megan).

Russian Mob Chronicles

Nikolai: A Mafia Prince Romance (Nikolai & Justine #1)

Nikolai: Taking Back What's Mine (Nikolai & Justine #2)

Nikolai: What's Left of Me (Nikolai & Justine #3)

Nikolai: Mine to Protect (Nikolai & Justine #4)

Asher: My Russian Revenge (Asher & Zariah)

Nikolai: Through the Devil's Eyes (Nikolai & Justine #5)

Trey (Trey & K)

The Italian Cartel

Dimitri

Roxanne

Reign

Mafia Ties (Novella)

Maddox

Demi

Rocco

Clover

Smith

RomCom Standalones

Just Playin' (Elvis & Willow)

Ain't Happenin' (Lorenzo & Skylar)

The Drop Zone (Colby & Jamie)

Very Unlikely (Lennox & Summer)

False Start (Cash & McKayla)

One Night Only

Hotshot Boss (Mr. Carson & Octavia)

Hotshot Neighbor (Caleb & Jess)

Bobrov Bratva

Wicked Intentions

Sinful Intentions

Devious Intentions

Deadly Intentions

Short Stories

Christmas Trio (Wesley, Andrew & Mallory -- short story)

Falling For A Stranger (Short Story)

Dedication

To all the people who have supported me from book one, I wouldn't be here without you.

I appreciate you.

Shandi xx

Want to stay in touch?

Facebook: facebook.com/authorshandi

Instagram: instagram.com/authorshandi

Email: authorshandi@gmail.com

Reader's Group: bit.ly/ShandiBookBabes

Website: authorshandi.com

Newsletter: https://www.subscribepage.com/AuthorShandi

Spy Thy Neigbor

Chapter One

"Holy mackerel! Is she an Olympic gymnast?" I mumble to myself while chewing on the end of my pencil with teeth marks gnawed along the edge. "Now that just looks painful."

I wasn't aware you could bend like that without distorting at least one muscle in your body. I wonder if she's a contortionist because that's not natural. No woman should be able to bend like that.

I certainly can't bend like that.

After straying my eyes away from the sweat-producing visual in front of me, I add a few key pointers on the brunette's back-breaking position to my extensively documented notepad.

My neighbor, whom I've nicknamed Archer, has been entertaining his most recent guest for the past hour and a half. By entertaining, I mean he's undertaken sheet-clenching, core-clustering, screaming-at-the-top-of-her-lungs sexual activities.

This type of entertaining is nothing new for Archer. He has a new bed companion a minimum of three to four times a week. He doesn't seem to have a preference for his bed-hopping friends. Blonde, brunette, Asian, African American, Caucasian, it doesn't matter to him. The only preference he seems to have is 'the louder they scream, the better.'

Although the women I've seen him with are undoubtedly gorgeous, they don't have an intellectual bone in their entire body.

Well, that's my personal assumption.

Considering I've never met my mysterious neighbor or his bevy of bed companions, I can't give a fair opinion on the capacity of their brain power. So, instead, I'm callously judging a book by its cover because even with me knowing every precise detail of Archer's well-formed physique, we are perfect strangers.

But even being a stranger, I still know Archer very well. It's not just the rigid panels of his stomach that carve into his formidable V muscle, the way the veins in his arms pulse during exertive activities, or how his sixth ab muscle is slightly larger than the other five that I can divulge to you. I can also tell you what his face looks like in the middle of ecstasy, how he always gets a smear of peanut butter on his top lip every time he eats three pieces of toast for breakfast, and that he doesn't drink coffee or tea.

How do I know this if we've never met?

I've been stalking him relentlessly over the past six weeks.

My mysterious bearded neighbor lives in a glass house perched on the edge of Bronte's Peak. With his bathroom the only room finished with sturdy walls, every detail of his life is on display for all to see. Like one big performance for the prying eyes of strangers—for people like me.

I was desperate, on the verge of a nervous breakdown, and incredibly close to missing an important deadline when I spotted Archer for the first time.

Ever since that night, my life changed...

I've been staring at the screen of my Mac Notebook for three hours straight. The incessant blink of the cursor on a blank white page has my nerves rattled and my conundrum intensifying. I have a deadline. A very strict deadline. Three months are all that remain for me to pen a three hundred and sixty-five-page document.

With fingers that type at the speed of lightning and more free time on my hands than I've ever had, you'd assume the deadline will be an easy feat. It isn't. I'm suffering from the worst case of writer's block I've ever experienced. Not just writer's block. Writer's. Block. I haven't penned a single word in over a month. Not even something as simple as a grocery list. But I have no choice. I must finish my novel.

Writing is my bread and butter. It is my sole source of income. Without it, I'll soon be a pauper who can't afford the luxury of flying over to the other side of the country to a beachside cottage for a writing vacation. If I don't pen my latest creation, I'll lose contracts well into the six figures and royalty payments even more lucrative than that. So, no matter how much my heart is decimated into tiny shreds, and I want to live in the shadow of a dark cloud, I must write a bestselling romance novel. It isn't an option. It is a requirement.

I'm so desperate, I'll happily accept a bad rendition of the manuscript I wrote as a senior in high school. Heck, I will even accept the childish novel I penned on my fascination with Joseph Gordon-Levitt, star of 3rd Rock from the Sun. It might be rubbish, but it was something, and I have nothing. My brain is blank.

"Words? What are words?" are the only phrases flowing through my overworked brain.

Once another hour ticks by, my usually calm composure cracks. With a grunt, I push away from my makeshift desk, stand from my old leather chair, and start pacing.

Pacing is never a good thing. If you ever see me pacing, I suggest you run far far away from me. I only pace when I'm on the verge of snapping or sitting dangerously on the edge of normality.

And that is precisely where I am tonight.

I've reached breaking point.

With a hard yank on my laptop, I pull its charging cord out of the power plug and bolt down the wooden steps. My heart thrashes faster with every thump of my feet on the rickety old stairwell. I trudge through the impeccably clean kitchen and living area. It's spotlessly clean since I have the obsessive habit of scrubbing surfaces until they sparkle when I'm seeking writing inspiration.

I grasp my laptop for near death, strangling it as it has done to my *creativity. A blast of humid, sticky air momentarily distracts my pursuit of introducing my laptop to the cruel, wordless world I am a part of. The smell of a fall night filters through my nose, lightening my senses as the refreshing scent of salt and sand from the beautiful, blue-watered beach below calms some of the rage boiling my blood.*

I raise my arm into the air, ready to send my laptop and its annoying blinking cursor into the pitch-dark ocean. My throw suspends mid-air when a ragged scream shrills through my ears.

The glass-shattering squeal is so ear-piercingly loud, it rattles through my hand, loosening my death-tight grip on the laptop. I fumble, curse, then fumble some more when my much-loved electronic device slips from my hold and plummets to the ground.

My teeth grit when my laptop crashes onto the stained wooden deck with an almighty thud.

While bending down to survey the damage inflicted on my beloved Mac, an even more riveting sight enters my peripheral vision. My throat becomes scratchy, and a surge of excitement dashes through me when my eyes lock in on a couple in a lust-filled lovemaking session.

Heat inflames my cheeks as I snap my gaze to the ground, beyond mortified that my temper tantrum has interrupted their intimate gathering.

With my wide gaze locked on the wooden floorboards, I gather up the broken pieces of my laptop with the hope I can salvage some of the unpublished manuscripts from the hard drive.

My pulse quickens when the female's cries of ecstasy intensify partway through my scavenger hunt. Although I can't see the woman's face, her ear-piercing screams tell me she's close to climax.

I'm not proud to admit this, but it's been a while since I've heard anything remotely like the pleasurable groans seeping from her lips.

Actually, I don't ever recall hearing those noises come from my mouth.

While vainly endeavoring to keep my focus on the black night sky with its sprinkling of stars peeking out from the darkness of storm clouds. I step back until my sweater-covered torso connects with the outer wall of my bungalow. My heart is wildly racing, and my body is covered in a dense layer of sweat. It is reacting the same way it did when my research for erotic novels found me visiting websites much steamier than the sweet young-adult romance I am accustomed to writing.

I turn my torso and sneakily slip through the glass sliding door I'd only exited mere seconds ago. I'm almost in the clear, then my quick steps halt when I catch the quickest glimpse of a perfectly round, muscular, booty-luscious, drool-over-for-months male ass.

I'm not lying when I say it is the most spectacular male ass I've ever seen.

My eyes bulge as the moisture accumulating on my skin moves to a much lower region of my body.

I should look away.

I should respect my neighbor's privacy.

But I'm in such awe of the fluidity of his movements I can't force my eyes away.

I've never witnessed anything so primal, raw, and awe-inspiring...

I used to watch Archer for a few minutes each night. Then, as the days crept on, my stalker obsession grew. If I'm not watching Archer, he invades my thoughts—always—even while I'm sleeping.

This will make me sound like the character Glenn Close played in *Fatal Attraction*, but I assure you I am not a psychopath. I'm perfectly sane.

Well, I was until I traveled to the other side of the country and started a slight obsession with my tattoo-covered neighbor. But my fascination isn't what you think. I'm not some crazy stalker who wants to sink my claws into Archer and never let go. I don't wish ill harm to his female companions, nor am I secretly plotting their demise.

I stalk him as if he's my savior.

My inspiration.

My Yoko Ono of the book-writing world.

He's my current series alpha male book boyfriend.

Without him and his busty bevy of companions, I'd still be staring at the blinking cursor on the blank screen of my monitor, praying for a string of words to magically appear. I would have never penned half of my latest, no doubt, *New York Times* best-selling novel.

The way Archer moves his hips with such fluidity and ease, how every muscle in his body ensures his female companions' cries of ecstasy are heard over the crashing of waves in the distance, and the way his perfect Adonis ass constricts and releases with each precise thrust has inspired magic.

Pure book alpha male magic that's flowing onto the pages more quickly than I can write them.

My editor is in love with the first one hundred pages of edits she has completed. My agent is using snippets of my newly created masterpiece to secure book spotlights on major television programs for the three months following my scheduled release, and my publisher and I are in negotiations about a new three-book deal on the intriguing life of Archer Boyd—my mystery neighbor's pseudonym I created.

A grin curls on my lips when I lock my eyes back on Archer. His nickname is highly fitting, considering how well he's had his latest companion arched over his couch the last twenty minutes. His moves should defy physics, but somehow, he makes it look easy.

I stop taking dot points of his impressive technique when my cell phone dings with an incoming text. After drifting my eyes back to Archer and his companion and taking note that their romp has moved from the couch to the fur rug in front of the roaring fire in the living room, I set down my pencil and pad onto the side table, then move into the kitchen to grab my phone.

A grin curls on my lips when I spot who the message is from.

PEPPER:

Did you get the package?

I chuckle so loud, I snort.

ME:

Yep! I'm using it right now.

That's a lie. I opened her package the instant it arrived, but it's been sitting on the wooden bench near the entryway door for the past three days.

After quickly checking Archer's status, I devote my attention back to my phone.

PEPPER:

Are you shitting me? Does it work? Hook a girl up with some army man porn!

ME:

Army porn??

PEPPER:

Yeah, army porn. Any images you take with the night vision lens will be green, but from what you've been describing, I'll happily accept Archer in any color I can get him.

I giggle even louder than earlier. Pepper is my best friend. We've been friends since preschool. Her real name is Quinn, but everyone calls her Pepper after her disastrous karaoke rendition of the Salt-N-Pepa song "Shoop" at my twenty-first birthday party four years ago. Ever since that drunken night, Pepper's nickname has stuck.

ME:

No images. It's against the law to photograph people without their consent. Isn't it?

PEPPER:

And stalking them for the past several weeks is entirely legal?

I grimace.

ME:

True…

My breath hitches when I raise my eyes back to Archer and

discover he's vanished from the large living room at the back of his residence.

ME:

BRB. My target has slipped the net.

PEPPER:

Go get him, Tiger!

ME:

Roar!!

Laughing, I place my phone onto the kitchen counter then tiptoe closer to the window. I have the shades open, but all the lights in the three-bedroom rented wooden bungalow are switched off. I'd hate for Archer to catch me spying on him before I've finished penning the first draft.

When I fail to locate Archer within his house, I head for the back deck. I've noticed over the past few weeks that he has a slight fascination with outdoor activities.

The coolness of a late fall night blasts my face when I step onto the patio's wooden deck, but my temperature rises instead of plummeting. The hunch I was running with is accurate. Archer and his companion have taken their lusty twist to a more scenic location. Although, I have no clue why. Neither of them are looking at the spectacular scenery.

Even in the darkness of the night, I can recall the marvelous views that distracted me from my writing goals for the first four days after I arrived here. Crystal blue waters, pristine white beaches, and little pockets of caves hidden throughout like treasured gems make Bronte's Peak a spectacular destination.

It's so beautiful that millions of tourists invade its pristine beaches at all times of the year. Luckily for me, the beach below is for the private residents who live in this elite gated community.

That reason alone was why I chose to rent this bungalow. I wanted seclusion and privacy. My plan had been to hide away from the world. No social media, no television, and no mobile devices to distract me as I finish my fourth book in a five-book series.

My well-thought plan lasted a total of three hours.

Thank God I stumbled upon Archer. Otherwise, I have no clue where I'd be right now.

The night I first spotted him, I sat down and scribbled relentlessly on an old notepad I found in the kitchen drawer. I'd always been an electronics girl when it came to writing, even jotting down book ideas on my iPhone while standing in the line at the bank, but with words flowing from my brain faster than my hands could write them, I couldn't risk the chance of losing my inspiration since my Mac was broken.

I had to get every word down while they were fresh, and thus began the fictional story of Archer Boyd—an alpha male billionaire who lives in a crystal house.

Although I've been using my backup laptop for the past five weeks, my notes and sketches on Archer have continued as they did the first night I spied on him. Such as now, when Archer curls his female companion's torso over the glass railing of his back patio, I sketch their position in my trusty notepad.

Surprisingly, his companion's cries of pleasure are only just heard over the scribbling of pencil to paper. Usually, I can't hear my pulse over the volume of his date's squeals.

A smile tugs at my lips when I finish my rendition of Archer and his companion's lust-filled pose. To call this piece 'art' would be a grave injustice to the art community. It's horrific. Many people class writing as an artistic craft, but you can be safely assured it's the *only* creative bone I have in my body. My sketch looks more like two dogs having fun at the local dog park than the romance novel cover I was aiming for.

My immature giggle dampens when a disappointed moan jingles through my ears. I've not once heard that type of response from one of Archer's companions. Even with him kicking them out immediately after the deed has been done, displeasure has never been voiced.

When I raise my eyes from my notepad, I discover the cause of the brunette's devastated cry. Archer is no longer tangled in a mind-hazing adult-only game of *Twister*. He's angrily storming down the glass stairs and stomping across the small patch of sand that divides our patios.

Oh crap!

I plaster my back to the outer wall of my cabin, cowardly trying to hide. I don't know why I bother. From the expression crossing Archer's face and the white-hot glare beaming from his eyes, I have no doubt he has spotted me spying on him.

If I were smart, I'd scurry into my cabin, lock the doors, and book the first flight home. Unfortunately, my brain has never been able to think on the spot. So instead of scurrying, I remain glued to the glass door, watching Archer's quickly advancing form span the distance between us.

The veins in my neck pulsate when I catch sight of his... umm... package that's generally hidden from view in numerous female crevices. Even though I've been watching him for weeks, I've never seen him this up-close and personal. The hardness of his cock is as firm as his fists are clenched, and it's an even more spectacular view than I've witnessed from a distance.

My throat dries when Archer stops in front of me. His hasty movements stir up an intoxicating smell of salt and sweat-slicked skin, accelerating my pulse. I'm taken aback when my eyes float up from the hairless ridges of his tattooed torso to his face. I've always imagined his eyes were light brown, so I'm somewhat surprised by their unique dark-blue coloring.

His heavy-hooded gaze roams over my face, absorbing the blush blooming on my cheeks before locking in on my wide grayish-blue eyes. "Are you only a voyeur, or do you also participate?" he asks with his lusty eyes burning into mine.

Even in the intense circumstances of our meeting, a dash of euphoria pumps through my veins from the husky roughness of his voice. It reminds me of Tom Hiddleston—rough and gritty but as smooth as chocolate.

Archer stares at me with his brow bowed high, reminding me that I've failed to answer him.

"Am I a what?" The shakiness of my voice makes it more seductive than normal.

My already wildly beating heart hastens even more when a smirk tugs on Archer's lips. "Are you a voyeur?" he repeats.

I shrug, truly unsure. "I don't know what that is." My voice is as weak as my reply.

My body temperature rises as the battle to keep my eyes on Archer's face moves into dangerous territory. Even standing in the briskness of a fall night, wearing nothing but a cocky grin, the thickness of his cock hasn't subsided a bit. If anything, it's become firmer.

He is primed and ready to go.

I snap my eyes up from his impressively large cock to his face when he advises, "A voyeur is a person who gets sexual satisfaction from watching others have sex." He's not the slightest bit embarrassed he's explaining a sexual term to a virtual stranger. "Do you only watch people have sex, or do you enjoy participating as well?"

You'd think his question would have me blushing like a naïve virgin, but it doesn't. I've watched him enough the past six weeks that he's more like a close acquaintance than a stranger. Second only to Pepper, he's one of my dearest friends—even without me knowing his real name.

Okay, Paige, I think it's time to seek professional help.

When Archer continues staring, I swallow to relieve my parched throat before saying, "I participate too."

Holy crab cakes, I can't believe I openly admitted I've been watching him.

Any concern about him calling the police to report me for stalking fades when a brash grin etches on his kiss-swollen mouth. He has an outrageously gorgeous smile. It is almost as breathtaking as his cock— which is ripped from my vision when he pivots on his heels and stalks back down the stairs without another word seeping from his lips.

When he reaches the bottom step, he cranks his neck and stares me straight in the eyes. "Are you *coming?*" His tone couldn't be laced with more sexual innuendo if he tried.

I remain frozen like a statue, more confused than ever. "Coming where exactly?"

Now I'm blushing like an idiot.

My heart thrashes against my ribs when Archer replies with a salacious grin, "To join us." He nudges his head to the brunette splayed over the patio railing, patiently awaiting his return during the 'us' part of his reply.

My eyes pop out of my head as my throat works hard to swallow, then I shake my head. Although I've been extremely deviant the past six weeks watching him in a range of lust-driven exchanges, I'm not adventurous enough to participate in a threesome.

No way in hell.

Archer's blazing eyes scorch my skin when he rakes them up my body. He drags them from my French-tipped toenails, past the frilled edges of my mid-thigh denim shorts, to the white knitted one-shoulder sweater. When his heavy-lidded eyes lock with mine, my breath hitches. This is the first time in six weeks I've spotted disappointment in his candid eyes. "If you change your mind, you know where to find me."

After a brazen wink, he continues his journey.

Chapter Two

The instant Archer steps foot on his glass and steel patio, I slip into the bungalow. As my heart hammers my ribs, I keep my eyes glued to my bare feet scuttling across the wood floors. The shake of my hand runs up my arm when I yank on the blinds covering the large window spanning the living room. When my harsh pull on the cord causes the mechanism to lock into place, a quiet squeal emits from my lips.

I can't hide my shameful face from the world if I can't get the damn blind to slot into place.

After a few inaudible swear words and a couple of gentle tugs, the blind finally lowers into position, concealing Archer and the busty brunette from my view.

After dashing into the kitchen, I snatch my phone off the counter, then scurry into the makeshift writing cave I created in a room in the upstairs attic. While taking the stairs two steps at a time, I log into Skype and connect to Pepper's account.

"Wow, that's an all-time low for Archer. I don't think you've ever called me within half an hour before," Pepper says down the line, not bothering to issue a greeting.

"He busted me spying on him," I confess with a grimace.

Pepper's pupils enlarge to the size of dinner plates as her mouth gapes. "During..." She stops speaking, allowing the shocked expression on her face to ask the question her mouth is failing to produce.

"Yep! Right in the middle of the deed," I respond while entering the darkness of my writing cave. The trembling of my heart is apparent in my tone.

After flicking on an overhead light, I stroll to my old, cracked leather chair stored behind an even more outdated desk.

"Are you sure he saw you? Maybe he was just *peering* in your direction?" Pepper asks, her tone laced with humor.

A massive creak bounces around the small, dingy space when I slump into my old writing chair. "I'm certain he busted me." I spin my office chair around to look at the extensive collection of notes and sketches I have of Archer taped around my office space. "He didn't just bust me, Pepper, he walked over and invited me to join him."

My attention turns from the inaccurate description of Archer's eyes I have in his profile to my phone's screen when Pepper's loud chuckle thunders down the line. She's laughing so hard her face is nothing but a blur as she rolls around on her bed in her apartment.

I huff at her absurdity before standing from my chair and heading to the storyboard on my right. "He asked if I was a voyeur," I inform her while scrubbing out the light brown coloring of his eyes and switching it to a murky blue.

When Pepper's laughter settles, she wipes under her hazel eyes, removing her cackling-induced tearstains. "Technically, you *are* a voyeur, Paige."

My eyes narrow into thin slits.

"You've been watching a man sleep with a range of women over a six-week period. If that isn't voyeurism, then I'm Mother Teresa," she argues, her words brittle with laughter. When I roll my eyes, she inches closer to the screen. "Did you just roll your eyes at me?" Her tone switches from playful to a deep, commanding voice. "If you roll your eyes at me one more time, young lady, I'll take you over my knee and spank you until you beg me to stop."

My laugh bounces off the sea-scented walls. "You've been reading my manuscript."

I sent Pepper the first half of my draft two days ago, hoping she'd beta read it for me to ensure the storyline was heading in the right direction. I'm surprised she's already begun reading it. Normally, she does anything in her power to avoid perusing my rough drafts. Once, she even faked having pancreatitis—hospital stay and all—just to get out of reading my months of hard work.

It isn't that she doesn't enjoy reading, she just prefers smut and erotic novels, not clean young- adult-only reads.

Pepper waggles her brows and nods. "Damn, Paige, when you said you were switching your genre from young adult to steamy romance, I didn't think you'd pull it off."

I stick out my tongue and roll my eyes again.

Pepper cocks her brow high into her rich, chocolate-brown locks. "Come on. The hotness scale of your last three novels was pathetic. I've seen kindergarten kids get more action than your characters did."

Even though my ego is stung by her catty remark, a smile pulls at my lips. I'll be the first to admit I've never felt comfortable adding sex scenes to my storyline.

Don't take my admission the wrong way. I lost my V card only a few weeks after my eighteenth birthday. Unfortunately, it was with the same guy who stabbed my heart with a spear gun twelve weeks ago. The same guy who was the cause of my decision to fly to the other side of the country.

Trying to ignore the twisted mess of confusion in my heart, I flop onto my office chair and spin around to face my outdated laptop screen. Stream upon stream of beautiful words reflect back at me. Although Riley tore my heart out of my chest, I'm still grateful he was a part of my life. If it weren't for him, I would have never stumbled upon Archer.

I have no doubt the words displayed in front of me are pure brilliance, an absolute best seller. That would have *never* happened without Riley, my first high school boyfriend, my one and only sexual conquest, and, until three months ago, my fiancé.

My focus returns to my phone screen when Pepper taps her finger on her iPad speaker, dragging me from my dreary thoughts with a loud doink. "Oh, you're still there. You went all stiff and robotic. I wasn't sure if it was a glitch or if you let that *asshole* invade your thoughts again."

Other than huffing softly, I remain quiet. I can't argue with Pepper. She knows me well enough to know where my mind strayed. We've been friends since the day we started preschool, and at times, I swear, she knows me better than I know myself.

Pepper adjusts her position, folding her legs under her bottom before lifting her mischief-filled eyes to me. "Why are you spending your Thursday night thinking about he-whose-name-will-never-be-spoken-of-again when Mr. I'm-going-to-spank-your-ass-until-you-beg-for-mercy offered you a chance to join him for a night of crazy monkey sex? I know what opportunity I'd be taking, and it most certainly wouldn't be recalling memories that aren't worth rehashing."

"It isn't that simple, Quinn." I sink deeper into my chair. "Riley and I were together for nearly seven years. I can't just simply forget him and jump into bed with a random stranger."

"Uh, yeah, you can," she responds with a brisk nod. "And don't think pulling out my real name will change the facts. Riley is an *asshole.* You deserve ten times better than he could ever give you. I can see it. Everyone in our hometown can see it. The only person who doesn't see it is you, Paige." She leans in closer to the monitor so her head engulfs the entire screen. "I love you, Sweet Pea, but it's time for this momma bear to bring out the big guns."

A grin curls on my lips, loving her use of our favorable nicknames.

"You need to get your skinny derriere off that hideous writing chair you dragged across the country, march your pasty white butt over to the Adonis-assed male specimen living next door, and climb aboard his sex train for the ride of your life. You're well overdue to cash in your earth-shattering climax ticket." Any pain festering in my heart eases from the playfulness in her tone. Pepper can always bring me back from the ledge.

"I love you, Pepper." My tone relays the truth of my statement.

"I know you do. But right now, I only want to see your back end walking away from me."

I screw up my nose. "I can't. Even if I wanted to ride Archer's sex train all the way to climax station, he isn't alone. His brunette friend has been happily keeping the neighborhood awake the past two hours."

"And? What's wrong with that?" Pepper interrupts with her brow arched high.

My heart beats triple time. "I could never do... *that*."

"It's called a threesome, Paige. Look it up the next time you're googling research for your *steamy* romance novel."

A set of heavy lines groove into my forehead. "Whatever," I scowl. "I'm writing steamy contemporary romance, not ménage. My readers don't want to read about my heroines doing the deed with other people. They want a loving, heartfelt connection crammed with the warm and fuzzies."

Pepper gags. "No, they don't. They want mind-hazing, multi-climaxing, sheet-clawing, can't-walk-straight-for-days sex! Trust me, if you're going to dip your toes into this genre, you need to go in deep. Hard-cock-thrusting-to-the-brim deep."

I roll my eyes and shake my head. Pepper's arched brow becomes lost in her dead-straight hair as she stares at me, daring me to negate her claim. Everything she's saying is true. Steamy contemporary romance readers want steam—it's the whole reason they pick that genre. But I don't necessarily believe I have to practice what I preach. I've never stepped foot in an ice hockey rink, but I penned a very sweet hockey romance two years ago that's still selling well today.

My eyes drift between the numerous notes pinned to the wall about Archer. "Even without having a bucketload of sexual experience, I have enough encounters between Archer and his female companions to pen *at least* ten steamy novels."

"It's not the same," argues Pepper with a brisk shake of her head. "Not even close."

"I thought you liked the first half of my draft?"

"I didn't like it," she replies, still shaking her head.

My heart slithers into my gut.

"I f'ing *loved* it! Why? Because you haven't reached the sex scenes yet. You're at the crazy flirty stage every reader loves devouring." Her lips quirk. "But I will admit, you have me hooked. I'm dying to know who will bring Archer to his knees."

I giggle, loving the eagerness in her voice. "I'm still working on the final scene. I'm not exactly sure how it will end for Archer just yet."

Normally, I plot the entire storyline before I commence writing the first chapter, but even with more notes than I've ever compiled for a novel, the second half of Archer's story is void of an ending.

"Maybe you could go through my notes and help me choose an ending?"

"I don't need to see your notes. Archer falls head over heels in love with a novelist named Paige, and they have numerous Kindle-melting sex scenes. He then uses his endless bank balance to pay for Paige's wannabe-actress best friend to star in her own movie. Then they all live happily ever after in a lust-driven relationship filled with multiple orgasms and sheet-clawing sex. The end."

My eyes bug. "We all live happily ever after *together?*"

"No," Pepper interrupts dramatically. "Archer and Paige live happily ever after. Pepper becomes famous and has sex with cabana boys while holidaying in the Caribbean six months out of the year."

I giggle. "I'm glad to hear your cabana-boy infatuation won't end when you become famous."

"There's no possibility my cabana-boy fascination will *ever* end. Have you seen the cabana boys at some of the resorts? My god!"

I laugh even louder, but it isn't strong enough to miss gravel crunching under tires. "Archer is on the move. I'll call you back," I say into the screen.

"No," Pepper squeals before I have the chance to disconnect the call. "Just the quickest glimpse. Please," she shamefully begs. "Then I can make sure you're describing him right."

I run my teeth over my bottom lip while I contemplate her suggestion. She's been begging me relentlessly for the past six weeks to snap a sneaky picture of Archer. I've denied every one of her requests. I don't know why, but photographing Archer seems like it would be crossing the line I drew in the sand to ensure my stalker fixation with him didn't become manic.

Like stalking someone is sane to begin with.

After a beat, I say, "Okay, but I don't have much zoom power on my iPhone."

"It's fine. I'll grab my glasses," Pepper retorts, giggling.

While she searches her bedroom for her glasses, I tiptoe to the only window in my writing cave. The beat of my heart kicks up the closer I get to the small arched opening. I've never considered writing suspense novels, but the range of emotions I've been experiencing the past six weeks while stalking Archer has me contemplating penning something suspenseful and mysterious.

When I reach the window, I pull back the lace curtain and peer down at the driveway in front of Archer's house. His brunette companion is dressed back in her tight black pencil skirt and fire-red satin blouse, and her arms are flung around Archer's shoulders. An odd feeling hits me hard and fast when I notice she's nuzzling his neck. Considering what they were doing only moments ago, I shouldn't find a goodbye cuddle so upsetting.

"Perhaps red week is closer than I thought."

After shrugging off my comment, I return my focus to Archer. The further the yellow and black taxi rolls down the driveway, the tighter the woman's grip on Archer's shoulders becomes. My jaw gains a spasm when she encloses her red-painted lips over his lipstick-smeared mouth to kiss him farewell.

From the excitement on her face and the length of her embrace, she has no clue this will be her one and only encounter with Archer. I've seen him with a range of women the last six weeks, but not once has he slept with the same woman twice.

My heart leaps out of my chest when Pepper reappears on my phone's screen, loudly declaring she's back. After apologizing for giving me my first gray hair, she requests I turn my phone's camera to Archer. When I do, we watch the unnamed brunette naïvely blow a kiss to Archer as she slips into the back seat of the taxi. Archer remains standing on the front porch, barefoot and in a pair of jeans and plaid shirt rolled up at the elbows—his attire of choice.

"Wow, your description is pretty accurate, Paige. Although he's wearing a little more clothing than I've imagined the past week." Pepper's voice is barely a whisper. It seems as if she's afraid Archer might hear her.

I giggle, shocked she's rattled. Usually, nothing lowers the volume of her voice, not even my father.

My laughter dissipates when Archer cranks his neck to the side and peers straight at the window I'm gawking at him from.

"Move, move, move!" Pepper barks out like a TI drill sergeant breaking in a bunch of rookie recruits.

"He can't see us," I assure her while maintaining my original position. "It's a mirrored window. I can see out, but no one can see in."

"Are you sure?" Pepper's usually smooth voice shakes with unease. "Because he looks like he's staring right at you."

"I'm sure." The weakness of my tone dampens my certainty. "The same thing has happened a few times over the past week. I swear he's staring straight at me, but he can't see me. I've checked. *Numerous* times."

Several heart-thrashing seconds pass with Archer peering at my window before he scrubs his hand across his beard then enters his house, switching off every light on his way.

Chapter Three

The crispness of a late fall afternoon causes goosebumps to form on the nape of my neck. While adjusting my position, I pray for the sun to emerge from the cloud it snuck behind. I've spent most of the last hour lazing on the pristine beach of Bronte's Peak, relishing in the unusually warm conditions for late fall.

When the glare reflecting off the white pages of the novel I'm reading becomes too much for me to bear, I bookmark my current page, set the book down on my towel, then roll over. My lips purse when the sting of a sunburn tingles my shoulders from my abrupt movements.

With it being fall, I stupidly forwent my sunscreen. From the warmth spreading across my shoulder blades and down my back, I can tell my complacency will cost me dearly. It's fair to say I have pasty white skin. It takes mere minutes for the sun's rays to have my skin switching from Alaska snow white to pastel pink. Within an hour, I'm almost as red as a lobster.

Although I flew across the country solely to finish my novel, after being busted by Archer last night, my desire to write is waning. I've never penned a single sentence when my mood is woeful. Last night was no exception. I figure if I bask in the sun for a few hours and enjoy the splendor of the scenery surrounding me, my mood will improve, closely followed by my word count.

A dog's bark echoing in the silence gains my attention. After shifting onto my backside, I peer over the sand dunes to the flat beach below. A gorgeous golden retriever is charging along the water's edge. His coat becomes saturated when he dives into the waves barreling onto the shore.

My eyes dart in all directions when he vanishes under the no doubt frigid water. The beat of my heart increases when he fails to emerge from the pounding waves. After snapping up from my sandy seat, I rush to the dune's edge. With a hand covering my eyes from the rapidly setting afternoon sun, I scan the ocean's horizon, seeking any signs of the dog in the dark blue waters.

I release the breath I'm holding in when the golden retriever emerges from the sea with a large stick dangling from his mouth.

That darn dog nearly gave me a heart attack.

While clutching my erratically beating chest, I slump back down onto my towel and watch the drenched dog race across the sand. He's not the slightest bit concerned he had me on the verge of heart failure.

My chances of falling into a coronary attack amplify when I discover who the golden retriever runs back to.

Archer.

What is he doing here? He's rarely home during the day, and if he is, he's not once stepped foot onto the sand beyond his back patio in the six weeks I've been watching him.

After slumping low into the dunes to conceal myself, I drink in every inch of him. Unlike the other times I've seen him dressed, his legs aren't covered by designer jeans and a plaid shirt. He's once again barefoot and wearing black knee-length board shorts with a plain white t-shirt. His long dirty blond hair is pulled off his face, exposing more of his scruffy beard, defined cheekbones, and piercing eyes. He looks incredibly delicious.

If I squint, he reminds me a lot of Jax from *Sons of Anarchy*. Although he's more built than Charlie Hunnam, and he has a much more extensive tattoo collection, they do have a lot of similarities.

My pupils balloon as my heart freezes.

Archer couldn't be Charlie Hunnam, could he? He does live in an extremely elegant-looking glass house in an exclusive neighborhood. I've also noted numerous flashy cars in his four-car garage at the side of his driveway.

Shit! Imagine how much trouble I'd be in if I were caught spying on a celebrity?

Stalking is a big no-no in general, but I'd be ridiculed for life if I was found to be spying on someone famous. The press would have a field day.

Through shaky hands, I snag my iPhone out of my Nordstrom beach bag, open the Safari app, and type 'Charlie Hunnam' into the search app. I sigh loudly when the first bit of information I stumble over is Charlie's eye color. His eyes are hazel. After staring into Archer's heavy-lidded gaze last night, I can recall with the utmost certainty that his eyes are as blue as the ocean when the sun sets over it.

Thank goodness.

After gathering my belongings, I contemplate trudging through the dunes back to my rented bungalow. Although I've reached my quota of sun for the day, I don't want to risk Archer spotting me sitting here. If he thinks I'm spying on him during the day, it might be the final push he needs to switch me from a nosy neighbor to verified stalker.

My attempts at a quick getaway are foiled when a cold wetness runs down my bare thigh. I spring into the air, my heart leaping out of my chest as quickly as my legs leave the sand. A giggle escapes my lips when I realize what caused my third heart stutter of the day. It's the gorgeous golden retriever who was also the cause of my earlier panic. My laughter bubbles in my chest when his bumpy tongue tickles the skin between my fingers as he licks off the sticky remnants of the Boston bun I devoured for afternoon tea.

After running my hand through the gloriously smooth fur on the top of his head, I dig the leftover bun from the paper bag at my side and hand it to him. I swear he swallows the entire half without chewing. Although grateful he enjoyed the sugary treat as much as me, my heart constricts when I catch sight of the name engraved on the bone-shaped pendant dangling from his leather collar.

Charlie.

"Please tell me your name is Charlie?" I gaze into his big adorable brown eyes pleading into mine, no doubt begging for more bun. "Because I know people create fake identities all the time. Hair color, eye color, none of that matters if you have the right amount of money. Trust me. I wear contact lenses all the time."

I've *definitely* reached my quota of sun for one day. I'm talking to a dog for crying out loud, and if that isn't bad enough, I'm waiting for him to reply.

My pulse speeds up when a chocolatey smooth voice rumbles over the padded cell, quietness swamping me from all sides. "Charlie, come on, boy," calls out the male voice I usually only hear during sexual activities. "Come on, Charlie, it's time to head home."

Charlie's head cranks to the side when he hears Archer calling him.

"Go on, boy," I say, encouraging him to leave before he blows my cover. "Go to Archer."

Charlie peers at me with his tongue dangling out of his mouth. Even being a dog, I can't miss the confusion on his adorable face.

"Do you not like the name Archer? I thought it was very fitting." I lean in close and whisper, "You've obviously missed the number of times he *arches* women over his couch."

My blubbering ends when the top of Archer's head pops over the sand dunes. I inwardly squeal before flopping to the ground. My crouched position finally alerts me to Charlie's interest. The stick he lugged from the bottom of the ocean is resting against my beach bag.

Charlie's eyes dance between me and his beloved stick when I stretch out to grab it. The instant my hand wraps around the slobber-covered branch, he jumps up from his seated position, ready to play fetch. He wags his tail excitedly, spraying me with splatters of salty water from his wet coat.

"Here you go..." I grunt while throwing the stick as far as I can from my hidden position.

When Charlie takes off for the stick, I get hammered by the sand his eager sprint kicks up. My mouth, nose, and unfortunately, my eyes are invaded by the grittiness of fine white particles.

I'm still rubbing the sand from my eyes when a cold wetness brushes my thigh for the second time. It is closely followed by a drool-covered stick.

After furrowing my brows together, I glare into Charlie's big brown eyes. "You're meant to take the stick back to Archer." Although my words are meant to come out as threatening, neither Charlie nor myself are buying my attempt at sternness. How could I be angry at a dog as beautiful as him?

I freeze like a statue when "Who's Archer?" comes from a voice at the side.

A voice I immediately recognize.

A voice I only hear in the middle of ecstasy.

I snarl at Charlie for blowing my cover before shifting my eyes to the side. Archer is standing to my right. His heavily tattooed arms are braced in front of his well-formed chest, and his unamused eyes are firmly fixated on me.

"Charlie's owner." My voice is as unconvincing as my perplexed expression. Can you blame me? This is the second time I've been caught snooping on him in not even twenty-four hours.

Archer's murky blue eyes glare straight into mine as he asks, "You know Charlie's owner?"

I purse my lips, feigning ignorance before briefly shaking my head. "No. I just like naming strangers."

If he doesn't call the looney hospital after that line, I might consider calling them myself.

Shockingly, Archer finds my attempt at humor more entertaining than my woeful shot at anger. But even more shocking than that is the stir of emotions that twists in my stomach when awarded his deep, throaty laugh. I didn't think anything could sound as provocative as the carnal moans he grunts during sexual activity, but his laugh has made a quick liar out of me.

Once Archer's chuckles ease, he uncrosses his arms then offers me his hand to shake. "Hunter," he introduces while grinning a smile that does stupid things to my insides.

"Paige," I reply while endeavoring to keep surprise out of my introduction.

Although his name isn't exactly Archer, I was pretty darn close.

After standing from the ground and wiping the sand from my hand, I accept his handshake. His eyes rake my barely covered body as he displays his beard isn't the only manly part about him. His shake is very masculine as well. Thankfully, I'm wearing a gorgeous gold and black sequined O-ring side-tie monokini I purchased on a shopping spree last summer. Unfortunately, my chest doesn't resemble *any* of the busty ladies I've seen Hunter with in the past six weeks. That whole more-than-a-handful-is-a-waste platitude is one I regularly use when describing my less-than-stellar female attributes.

When Hunter's eyes return to my face, I smile, appreciating the glint of lust in them. "Enjoying the last few rays of sun?"

I nod. "I like taking advantage of anything I'm offered."

He tries to conceal it, but I don't miss the corners of his lips tugging into a wry grin. "Then why didn't you take me up on my offer last night?"

As I blubber out the first response that pops into my head, my cheeks turn the color of my sun-kissed shoulders. "Brunettes aren't really my thing."

When my comment comes out both witty and intelligent, I bite the inside of my cheek, fighting to keep my smile at bay.

I've never been overly good at flirting, but I seem to be a quick learner.

My attempt to hide my smile is worthless when a broad grin stretches across Archer's face.

Shit! I meant to say Hunter.

"I'll keep that in mind for next time." He clips a lead onto Charlie's collar before guiding him back toward the beach. "I'll see you around, Paige?"

Since his statement sounds more like a question than a declaration, I nod.

Once he's halfway down the dunes, it dawns on me what he said. I cup my hands around my mouth to ensure my girlie voice projects down the dunes, then shout, "Sexually cavorting with women isn't really my thing either." My reply is as embarrassing as it comes, but I need him to understand my objection had nothing to do with his female friend being a brunette.

I cringe when my loud voice echoes in the quiet of the late afternoon, then my face turns a shade of crimson when a group of teenage boys at the water's edge respond to my declaration.

"You don't know what you're missing out on."

"Give it a go. You may just like it."

"Don't knock it till you've tried it."

I wave my hand in the air, silently thanking them for their recommendations, but even with their snickers bellowing into my ears, I don't miss Hunter's hearty chuckle.

While grimacing at my stupidity, I gather my bag and towel from the sandy ground then head back to my bungalow.

"If you learn to laugh at yourself, life will become a whole lot funnier," I mumble to myself.

That was one of my mom's favorite quotes, and I've lived by it as often as possible in the past twelve weeks.

Chapter Four

"No!" I glare at the blank screen of my laptop, certain I'm not seeing what I think I'm seeing. "Don't you dare, you son of a bitch." I shake the monitor, begging for the words I just finished typing to magically reappear. "No! Oh god, you can't do this to me now."

I push away from the desk then start pacing in the small confines of my writing cave. Hours upon hours of hard work just vanished in an instant. I don't know what happened. I was eagerly typing away, then the screen glitched before it plunged into blackness.

After roughly yanking on my hair, I snatch my phone from my desk and FaceTime Pepper.

"Jake, I'm taking a quick break," she shouts to someone in the distance before switching her focus back to me. "Hey, Sweet Pea. Any sand-stuck-in-crevices stories to share today?"

A broad grin stretches across her face when she weaves through the coffee bean chain store she works at.

"I broke my laptop." My voice is high as devastation dangles on my vocal cords. "Not a little broken. The screen is black! I-lost-every-thing broken."

Pepper's flawless face gets a new wrinkle when she screws up her nose. "Show me."

As I twist my phone to show her my blank laptop monitor, my hand trembles.

"Did you try a hard reset?"

Even though she can't see me, I nod. "Yes. I've turned it off at the wall, begged to the writing gods, and I even promised not to write smut on it if it would turn back on. Nothing has worked." Groaning, I flop onto the writing chair I salvaged from a dump site over three years ago. It is hideously ugly, but it's my good luck charm. I penned my very first best-selling novel on it. "Hours of hard work, gone. I'll never get the entire first draft rewritten before my deadline." I burrow my head into my shaking hands before stammering out, "God, Pepper, what am I going to do?"

"First, you need to take a deep breath."

I suck in a deep, nerve-cleansing gulp of air.

"Second, you need to remember you've never missed a deadline. Not once in three years."

"This is different. I didn't have a computer malfunction weeks before my final draft is due." The crackling of my voice displays I'm on the verge of crying.

"That's where step three comes in." Pepper moves in close to the screen. "Grab that piece-of-shit computer I told you to get rid of years ago and get your tushie to the local IT shop. Upon entering, fall to your knees, cry like you're a baby who had its binky stolen, and beg for them to save the hard drive."

"Save the what?" Although my mood is dire, it seems nowhere near as bad just from talking to Pepper. She has a way of bringing me off the ledge.

"Just because the outside of the laptop has gone kaput doesn't mean the inside is worthless. But if you don't get your backside out of that revolting chair and to the computer store, you'll never know what data can be saved." I jump from my chair like my ass is on fire when Pepper screams, "Move, Paige! Move, move, move." Her demanding voice bellows down the line like it did four nights ago when she thought Hunter had spotted us spying on him.

I yank my laptop off the desk then charge down the stairs. "I love you, Pepper."

"I know you do, Sweet Pea."

After air-kissing her goodbye, I disconnect FaceTime and call an Uber.

* * *

By the time I make it to Ravenshoe, I'm sweating like a pig. Unfortunately, perspiring is one of the many side effects I endure when nervous. I'm not normally a bumbling idiot, but when something stands between me and a deadline, all my normal traits vanish, and a naïve, fumbling imbecile takes over my body.

"Thank you," I mumble before slipping out of an SUV in front of an IT shop called *Mr. Fix It*.

Once I've gathered my belongings, I scan the unfamiliar street. Ravenshoe is busier than I was expecting. The sidewalks are packed with residents, and the roads are clogged with traffic that's nearly thicker than the sweat slicking my body.

After shrugging off my surprise that Ravenshoe is a bustling hive of activity compared to the serenity of the private beach at Bronte's Peak, I saunter through the single glass door of the computer shop. A bell above the entryway chimes when I pull open the heavily weighted door.

I scrunch my nose when burning wires and *toast* stream through my nostril cavities. Upon spotting a gentleman in his mid-fifties with a rounded stomach and a comb-over, I adjust my bag before making a beeline for him. My brisk pace slows when the quickest glimpse of a profile freezes my heart. Hunter is darting through the moderately-sized store, grabbing a selection of computer parts and accessories. A grin curls on my lips when I discover his outfit has returned to his much-loved combination that consists of a pair of designer jeans and a plaid shirt.

After watching him in silence for a few minutes, mentally taking note of his finer quirks I could use for Archer, I continue with my original pursuit.

"Hi," I greet the computer repairman with a large smile. I'm hoping my over-the-top friendliness will have my laptop pushed to the front of the line.

The gentleman sets down a weird-looking green and silver contraption before joining me at the counter. It's a hard-fought battle to maintain my smile when his sullied eyes rake my body, not once, not twice, but three times. His depraved stare is so inappropriate, it's downright unprofessional.

"What can I do for you, honey?" he asks, his voice as slimy as his greasy hair.

I place my laptop on the glass counter, which houses small camera devices and a collection of pens. "I've broken my laptop."

He shifts his dark brown eyes from my not-that-impressive bosoms to my laptop. "Hardware malfunction or malware issue?"

I shrug. "Ah... you tell me?"

The grooves indenting my head amplify when he cranks open the laptop screen and pushes the power button. I look a little ridiculous sweating in the coolness of a November day, but I'm not a complete idiot. I know how to turn on a laptop.

After a short deliberation, he grunts out, "Fixing an old girl like this is pointless. You're better off purchasing a new device." He tosses my laptop to the side like trash before moseying to a shelf full of fancy laptops.

"Oh no, I don't want a new laptop. I need the documents stored inside this one." My voice squeaks as panic sets in. "Very important documents are hidden somewhere in this laptop. Very *very* important documents."

The repairman's lips quirk into a cunning smile as he strolls back to me. "That important, hey?"

I eagerly nod, willing to do anything to get him on my side.

Well, almost anything.

Sweat forms on the top of his shiny head as his eyes scan my laptop for the second time. "I'm sure I can get your *important* documents off this device for you."

"Really?" My excitement is as high as my voice.

"Sure, the hardware in this old girl would survive a house fire. Even if you've fried the motherboard, I'll still be able to retrieve some data." He lifts his dark eyes to mine. "It will cost you, though."

"That's fine. Charge any amount you want." *I'm sure it won't be as high as the advance I'll lose if I don't get this draft handed in by the end of the year.*

"Alright, leave it with me, and I'll have it back to you in around eight weeks."

My heart slithers into my gut. "Eight weeks?" I squeak out.

"It's only six weeks until Christmas, honey. My schedule is fully booked."

Tears prick my eyes as a sweat mustache forms on my top lip.

"Oh, don't go crying on me. I can't stand seeing a girl cry." He yanks two tissues out of a box on his left and hands them to me. "Maybe we can make a deal. I could have it back to you by the end of the week."

My tears dry from the sheer relief scorching through my veins.

The blessing doesn't last long.

"For the right incentive, of course," he adds after pushing his protective glasses up his blackhead-covered nose.

My suspicious eyes dance between his. Even though his covetous gaze is already horrifyingly displaying his true intentions, I want him to spell it all out, as clear as day, so I *fully* understand the agreement he wants me to sign up for.

When my arched brow doesn't give him the hint, I ask, "What's the condition?"

Without pause for consideration, he blurts out, "You have to go out with me."

While awaiting my reply, he peers at me like Hannibal Lecter stared at Clarice in *Silence of The Lambs* when they first met. All he needs is a slithering tongue, and the scene would be set.

"On just a date?" I clarify with a suspicious stare. "No *extracurricular* activities required?"

My stomach churns when the corners of his mouth tug into a sly smirk.

I grit my teeth before snarling through a tight jaw. "No deal. I'll take my laptop to another computer shop."

After snatching my laptop off the counter, I charge for the door. My brutal pace slows when the computer repairman shouts, "I'm the only repair shop within a hundred miles of Ravenshoe!"

"Then I'll stop by the local high school," I snap back after spinning around to face him. "I'm sure any teen there will have better computer skills than you and your hideous comb-over." A blast of cool air hits me in the face when I yank open the door, but before I merge into foot traffic on the sidewalk, I crank my neck back and give the repairman one final serve. "And just for the record, *buddy*, I wouldn't care if the map for Pablo Gaviria's buried billions in Columbia was on this computer. I'd rather go poor than slap skins with a man like you."

My sassy attitude dampens when a deep, rumbling laugh barrels through my ears. I'm taken aback when I switch my narrowed eyes from the slack-jawed computer repairman to my right. Hunter is responsible for the laughter booming around the repair shop, and my angry face only makes him chuckle harder.

After hitting him with the same stink-eye I gave the repairman, I spin on my heels and charge out onto the sidewalk. Halfway down the block, I'm still rambling incoherently under my breath. Even if it forces me to walk straight into a shitstorm without an umbrella, I'd rather miss my deadline than be a random guy's side platter for the night.

I also despise when men use a woman's desperation as a way in. If they were smart, they'd realize most women would pick the helpful geeky, glasses-wearing guy over a Calvin Klein underwear model any day. Because at the end of the day, looks vanish. Brains don't.

My fast strides down the bustling sidewalk slow when I hear my name being called over the hum of activity. When I spin on my heels, my heart beats double time. Hunter is weaving his way through the throng of people mingling on the sidewalk. My lungs struggle to secure a full breath just from the way the muscles in his thighs stretch and expand as he endeavors to bridge the distance between us.

"Hey," he greets me, still smirking the same smile he wore in the computer store.

"Hey." My breathlessness makes my single word come out as a long pant. "Sorry about that." I nudge my head in the direction he just came from. Even though I was irate, he didn't deserve my knee-shaking stink eye.

Hunter's smile enlarges. "It's all good. Bosco deserved it."

I don't refute his claim. Bosco should be glad his nuts are still attached to his body.

As his shrewd eyes bore into mine, Hunter scrubs his hand along the edge of his scruffy beard. I return his stare with just as much vigor, loving the chance to study a side of him I can't access from a distance.

When I commenced writing about Archer, I placed him in his mid-thirties. But from the youthfulness of his eyes and the fact his face is void of any wrinkles, I need to lower his age range to late twenties, making him closer to my twenty-five years. He has a straight, defined nose, sharp cheekbones partially hidden by a maintained but full beard, and intelligent eyes.

He's handsome in a unique, masculine way.

After Hunter finishes his assessment of my body and face, he announces, "I can fix your laptop for you."

I curve my brow before giving him the same dubious stare I gave Bosco. "At what cost?"

His chuckles gain him the attention of a handful of residents walking by. Upon noticing we've acquired unwanted eyes, he places his hand on my elbow and guides me into a small bakery at our side. His simplest touch causes a surge of awareness to prickle my skin.

Thankfully, the loud grumble of my stomach distracts Hunter from my body's reaction to his closeness. The yummy smell of freshly baked goodies and pastries slams into me when he moves us to the corner of the bakery. Peering down at my watch, I note it's a little after two. No wonder I'm hungry. I haven't eaten since breakfast. I have a terrible habit of forgetting to eat when I am writing.

Hunter draws my attention away from the delicious goodies on display in the glass cabinets when he says, "It won't cost you anything." I stare at him, confused by his offer. It's only once he continues speaking does it dawn on me what he's talking about. "It will make up for the rudeness of my... *approach* the other night."

My brows become lost in my hair. *I* was busted watching *him* during a sexual encounter, yet he's worried about his rudeness.

"It will only take around an hour. Easy work," he assures me after spotting my angst-ridden face.

I peer into his wholesome eyes. "Are you sure you don't mind?" Although I hate asking for help, especially from a stranger, I'm in a real pickle.

"Certain," Hunter responds without a snip of hesitation, easing my guilt about taking up his valuable time.

"Alright. That will be great. When can you do it?"

I send a silent prayer to the writing gods that he says sometime within the next week.

My prayers are answered when he replies with a grin. "Now."

My eyes bulge, but I play it cool. "Okay, great," I stumble out through the tumbleweeds in my throat. "Let me grab us a couple of treats first, then we'll get this show on the road."

Chapter Five

My dropped jaw gains leverage the more Hunter's Hellcat rolls down the driveway of his residence. Although most of my time the past six weeks has been spent spying on him, I never paid much attention to the splendor of his home. Let me tell you, I've been missing out. This place is enormous. Panel upon panel of multi-hued glass, meticulously joined with thick steel beams painted the color of the ocean backdrop creates an awe-inspiring architectural delight.

When Hunter parks his car in front of a four-car garage, I toss open my door. The gravel crunching under my feet matches the rhythm of my thumping heart when I follow him up a small flight of stairs to a set of double glass doors. I don't know who this guy is, but he's obviously stinking rich. His residence screams of wealth. I'm not talking Ivanka Trump asked daddy for a loan. I'm talking about Eric Berry signing his deal with the Kansas City Chiefs rich.

I rub my hands together like a kid in a candy store when an electronic face fills the computer panel once it notices our approach.

"Are you shitting me?" My voice is equally eccentric and high. "You have a computerized security system?"

Hunter smirks at my giddiness but remains quiet. My eyes bulge even more when a female voice booms out of the speakers. "Welcome home, Mr. Kane... and *guest.*"

My eyes rocket to Hunter as my mouth falls open. "Is that a computer program, or is a real-life person watching us?" I'm putting bets on it being a real-life person because I swear she sneered when she said, "Guest."

"She is a computer." Hunter turns his eyes to the panel on his right. "Patricia, this is Paige. Add her face to your database for future recognition."

"Yes, Mr. Kane," the computer program replies.

Even though Hunter has declared Patricia is a computer, I stand by my original statement. There's no doubt she's sneering.

Ignoring my bug-eyed expression, Hunter pushes open the thick glass door and enters the opulent foyer of his home before offering to take my jacket. His house has a cold, sterilized feel with stark white cabinets and marbled floors, but it's surprisingly warm.

After shrugging out of my red bomber jacket, I hand it to Hunter. While he hangs our coats in the coatroom at the side of the foyer, I step deeper into the space. I inwardly chuckle when my eyes absorb the nude paintings adorning his pristine walls. They're a similar color to the ocean backdrop, but unlike the disastrous pieces I've sketched of Hunter and his companions over the last six weeks, these resemble humans.

With my laptop slung under his arm, Hunter gallops down the three stairs to the living area at the back of his residence. As my eyes categorize every inch of his home, I closely shadow him. A ten-seater dining table sits on my right, an expansive and adeptly decorated white marble kitchen is on my left, and a vast living area is directly in front of me.

From this vantage point, there are uninterrupted views of the pristine beaches below. It's nearly as spectacular as the scenery I've witnessed in this space numerous times over the past six weeks.

My eyes stray from the beautiful vista when tinkering sounds through my ears. Spinning around, I spot Hunter seated on a glass barstool at the breakfast bar where he eats his three slices of toast every morning. The back of my laptop is removed, and he's fiddling with stuff inside my computer that is way over my technical knowledge.

Curious, I step closer to him. "Do you work with computers?"

The corners of his lips crimp before he shakes his head. "It's more a hobby I stumbled into."

My brows stitch. "But you know what you're doing, right? Because I wasn't joking when I said *very* important documents are stored in that laptop."

Every crude joke I've ever heard filters through my brain when Hunter throws back his head and laughs. I'll dish out more one-liners than Chris Rock at the Comedy Cellar if it guarantees he'll laugh like that again.

When his chuckles settle down, his glistening eyes lock with mine. "I've got you covered, Paige." After a lengthy stare, he returns to tinkering with my laptop. "I work for a telemarketing company in New Delhi."

My brows stitch together. "As in you own the company? Or..." My words trail off when I can't think of a plausible reason why a guy who works in telemarketing would live in a house worth well into the millions.

When he chooses not to answer my question, I head for a small selection of photo frames on the fireplace mantel. The photographs cross a broad span of years in Hunter's life from a young teen to a college graduate.

"Have you always had the beard?" I pick up a photo of him I'd guess was taken four or five years ago. Although his beard isn't quite the thickness it is now, it still covers most of his jawline.

I hear Hunter's nod more than I see it. "Yeah... pretty much since I could grow one."

My lips twist before I return the photo to its rightful spot. I've never really been a fan of beards, but Hunter's has grown on me. When I first began writing about Archer—the fictional character based on Hunter—I initially removed the detail of his beard. But after a few paragraphs, something felt off in the story. It was only after I added his beard back in did the storyline progress with a natural flow.

Archer is the very first character I've penned with a full beard.

"Is this your mom?" I ask after taking in an image of a lady with sandy blonde hair and blue eyes. She is grinning broadly, and her arm is wrapped around Hunter's waist. She's quite short, the top of her head only just reaching Hunter's shoulder.

Hunter's eyes drift from my laptop to the photo I am holding. "Yeah, that's my mom and my little sister," he informs me, his tone gruff and reserved.

"Your sister is very young," I respond, my voice high in surprise.

The girl in the photo appears to be around the age of four or five, so I didn't consider that she'd have some type of family connection to Hunter.

"She was five in that photo," Hunter announces. "She's ten now."

I place the picture frame back on the mantelpiece before moseying closer to him. "How old were *you* in that picture?"

He cocks a brow and eyes me curiously. "Are you trying to find out how old I am?"

Smiling, I nod.

My smile slips when he mutters, "Then why don't you just ask how old I am?" Although his tone has an edge of annoyance associated with it, the twinkle in his eyes doesn't relay any anger.

I prop my elbows on the counter and gaze into his dark blue eyes before asking, "How old are you, Hunter?"

His almost hidden smirk really has a way of doing stupid things to my insides, especially when it follows his gravelly voice that's full of mischief. "Old enough to know from the sparkle in your eyes, it wouldn't matter if I were twenty-five or fifty-five, you'd still want to jump my bones."

My mouth gapes open. Nothing against Hunter, he has the body of an Adonis and many other impressive attributes, but he's the opposite of the men I've dated. I like my men clean-shaven and smooth. Hunter is rough and a little too edgy for my liking.

He couldn't be more opposite of Riley if he tried.

Riley is as stiff as the overly starched ties he wears every day behind his crisp, perfectly laundered suit. The only time I saw him out of a suit was when he was returning from a soccer match. He shaves his face every morning at precisely seven and polishes his shoes every Thursday night while sitting on our bed watching *Scandal*.

Unlike Riley, I've not once seen Hunter in a suit. He favors designer jeans and a range of plaid shirts over stiff, restricting material. Most of his handsome face is covered by a thick beard, and his hair is a little too long for my liking.

If you saw Hunter and Riley standing side by side, it would be like comparing night and day. Riley looks like a cut-throat businessman, whereas Hunter looks set to cut down a tree.

I stop smiling about my comparison portfolio when Hunter announces, "I'm twenty-eight." His rough tone demands my attention. "I'm a Capricorn, don't like long walks on the beach, am allergic to shellfish, and have one sibling." His lips perk as his brows furrow. "I think that about covers it. Unless you have any other questions you'd like me to answer?"

Now his eyes are sparked with annoyance.

Obviously, he isn't a fan of being interrogated... *or holding a conversation.*

I plop onto the stool next to him. "Nope, we're good."

Several minutes pass in silence. It's awkward and highly uncomfortable. If my laptop weren't in a million pieces across his kitchen counter, I would have snatched it from his grasp and went and hid, only emerging when the devil-horn-wearing Hunter disappeared.

It sucks to admit this, but I prefer the fictional Hunter I've created on paper to the one sitting next to me.

After cursing under his breath, Hunter sets down a small screwdriver and scrubs his hand along his scruff-covered jaw. "I'm sorry. I'm not used to... *this*." He gestures his hand to me.

"*This?*" I ask through arched brows.

He rakes his teeth over his lower lip before muttering, "Interacting with girls."

I bow my brows even higher while glaring into his eyes. That's a blatant lie. I've seen him *interact* with plenty of women over the past six weeks. Other than sleeping, that appears to be the only thing he does in his pretty glass house.

"Interacting with them while they are stilled clothed," he adds when he notices my contemptuous face.

"Oh, well, in that case..." I stand from my chair while fumbling with the buttons on my crushed linen shirt. When he fails to acknowledge my attempt at humor, I flop back onto the barstool then cross my arms in front of my chest. "I'm not getting naked just for you to feel comfortable."

His murky blue eyes lock with mine. They're sparked with amusement. "Oh... was that for my benefit? I thought it was part payment for fixing your laptop."

My mouth forms an 'O.' "Part payment? Believe me, *buddy*, if I were going to strip naked for services rendered, you'd be stamping the invoice paid in full."

Hunter chuckles a full-hearted laugh.

It once again does stupid things to my insides.

After several long, tedious minutes, he snaps his mouth shut and mutters, "I like you, Paige." He sounds surprised by his admission, but not as much as I am stunned about my pleasure from his compliment. Anyone would swear he told me I'm beautiful.

Another length of silence passes between us. This time, it's void of the earlier awkwardness. Hunter continues dismantling my laptop into hundreds of tiny pieces, making it look like a giant jigsaw puzzle I'd never have the chance of putting together while I watch him in awe.

After a beat, he raises his eyes to mine and asks, "What do you do for a living, Paige?"

I won't lie. I like the way he says my name. He adds a tinge of huskiness to it, giving it a sexy feel.

"I'm a... *writer*?" I half-inform, half-question.

I don't know why, but even with fourteen books penned under my name, I still feel like a fraud when I tell people I 'write' for a living. I've never had any other occupation. I started writing short stories for the high school newsletter when I was a junior, then I went to college to study my craft.

With the ease of self-publishing, my first novel was listed for download the month I started college. And as they say, the rest is history.

Now don't read my admission the wrong way. It's often quoted that being a writer is hard work. It is. To gain traction in this industry, you must see it as a marathon, not a sprint. It took a good two years to upgrade my dinner selections from ramen noodles to microwave meals. Only once my 'work' was put into the right hands did I see substantial readership growth.

But if I don't continue producing new novels every couple of months, I'll lose my vivacious audience, which, in turn, means I'll lose revenue. Since I don't want to go back to eating peanut butter sandwiches for lunch and ramen noodles for dinner, I must hand in my draft by the end of next month.

When the smell of burning skin streams through my nose, I shift my eyes to the side. Hunter's face is lined with anger. His nostrils are flaring, and his ferocious gaze is burning a hole in the side of my head.

His voice is vicious when he snarls out, "You're a reporter?"

You'd think the panic I felt when he stormed toward my bungalow last week would be my most fearful moment with him. It isn't. The way he's glaring at me and the furious tick his beard-covered jaw is failing to hide has me shaking in my boots more now than when he busted me spying on him in the middle of a lust-hazed romp.

"No." Locks of hair fall into my face when I shake my head. "I write books."

In a flash, the natural beige coloring of Hunter's face returns, closely followed by the normal width of his eyes.

Once the crinkles in his brows smooth, he asks, "What type of books?"

I balk, flabbergasted by the sudden change in his demeanor. He's gone from looking like a man who wants to scoop out my liver and eat it for dinner to the humble boy next door... *if you can look past his tattoos and rough exterior.*

When I remain quiet, he shifts his gaze from my laptop to me. His eyes roam my flushed cheeks, wide eyes, and O-formed mouth before he asks with a cheeky grin, "Do you write mommy porn?"

My dropped jaw gains leverage. "What? No!" *Although some scenes I've written about you are borderline mommy porn.* "I write *romance.*" My tone is as unconvincing as the ruffled expression on my face. It isn't my fault. Adult romance is a new genre I decided to test out last month. It's going well—for the most part.

Hunter's brow cocks. "*Fifty Shades of Grey* was classed as romance."

Now he has me by the throat.

"Did you read it?" I ask as my writer-fighting spirit emerges.

Hunter angles his body to face me. "What? *Fifty Shades?*"

When I nod, his tongue delves out to lick his lips before he turns his attention back to my laptop.

"Well? Did you?" I ask again when he remains as quiet as a baby sleeping. When his bushy beard fails to hide his wry smirk, I tap my boot against his. "Then you can't really call it *mommy porn*, can you? Because I'm reasonably sure you don't have any mommy parts."

My insides do the cha-cha from discovering that he reads. There's nothing sexier than a brute of a man with panty-wetting good looks holding a book in his hand. I'm part of numerous Facebook groups solely dedicated to hunting down sexy man readers. Now I wish I'd packed paperbacks of my books. It could have been a stellar marketing move on my behalf. Although my clean, sweet romance reads may not be up to Hunter's mommy-porn standards.

Another stretch of silence passes between us. Unlike the previous two times, there's a weird sensation impinging the air around us. It's similar to the connection I felt when Hunter peers up at my writing cave window. It's heart-pumping and intense.

Our bizarre kinship dampens when the shrill of a cell phone fills the void of silence. Hunter places parts of my laptop onto the white countertop so he can retrieve a cell out of his pocket. My brows furrow when I notice how outdated his phone is. With a computerized house and obvious wealth, I'm shocked he's carrying a phone similar to the one I had when I was a teeny bopper.

After drifting his eyes to me, Hunter flips open his phone and presses it to his ear. "Boss," he greets. "Hmm, weird... okay, I'll take some equipment to your apartment this afternoon and complete a search." He stands from his chair and walks to the large door at the back of the living room. "What type of devices am I looking for?" he asks before slipping out the glass door.

Surprisingly, all noise stops when he closes the door behind him. I know for a fact that his house isn't soundproof, but his lips are moving, and I can't hear a peep, so I'm going to assume he made his house soundproof from outside noise.

This man just keeps getting more intriguing as the weeks move on.

Once Hunter finishes his call, he returns the phone to his pocket and joins me back by the kitchen. "I have to run a few errands," he informs me, his tone back to its initial gruffness.

"Okay, no worries."

As I slip off the barstool, I glance at my dissembled laptop. Upon noticing my nervy expression, Hunter says, "I'll finish repairing your computer as soon as I get back, and I'll drop it off later tonight."

"That will be great, thanks," I reply, smiling.

I lean in, preparing to kiss him goodbye on the cheek before remembering we're practically strangers. So instead of a friendly kiss goodbye, I wave like a gullible idiot.

I swear I look like a twelve-year-old.

While cringing about my idiocy, I make a beeline for the glass door Hunter just entered. Even with waves crashing to shore and my pulse shrilling in my ears, I still hear his faint laughter as I sprint across the patch of sand separating our patios.

Chapter Six

"Oh my god. I think I'm in love!"

Hunter smirks to hide his grimace from my overly loud voice. "It was nothing major. Just a fuse short-circuiting the tantalum surface mount capacitor, causing..." He stops talking when he notices my baffled expression. It's safe to say computers and I have never been close friends. "It's fixed," he advises in a term I can understand.

I place the switched-on laptop on my entryway table then fire up my Scrivener writing program. I snap my eyes closed and send a prayer to the writing gods for guiding me to Hunter when my manuscripts, both current and old, pop up on my once-again-functioning screen.

"Thank you so much!" I squeal with dramatic flair. "You have no idea how much this means to me."

Caught up by my excitement, I throw my arms around Hunter's torso, then press my lips to his cheek. I smile when his prickles tickle my nostrils. I can't believe how soft his beard is. I was anticipating for it to have a steel-wool feel to it, where it's as soft as a cashmere sweater.

An interesting fact I'll note for future reference.

While doing my best to ignore his noteworthy smell, I pull back from our impromptu embrace and peer into his still mischief-filled eyes. "How much do I owe you?"

Hunter waves off my question as if money isn't an issue for him. "It's fine. No payment is required."

"Come on, I have to pay you something." I drift my eyes to his palatial home while contemplating an appropriate method of payment. When I realize nothing of monetary value would interest him, I mutter, "What about a beer?"

My lips hurt from the vast smile that stretches across my face when Hunter nods. "A beer sounds great."

"Awesome." I clap my hands together like I'm still that annoying twelve-year-old he was introduced to earlier before gesturing my head to the paper-covered two-seater sofa in the middle of the living room. "You take a seat, and I'll grab us a beer."

After gathering bundles of handwritten notes off the couch and coffee table, I sashay into the kitchen to snag two bottles of beer from the sparsely stocked refrigerator. While strolling back into the living room, my heart does a funny flutter. Although Hunter isn't overly large, standing at approximately six feet tall with a moderate build, he swamps the homey living room in my modest rented cabin.

While smiling at the rarity of seeing a woodsy man in the flesh, I hand Hunter a beer before filling the empty seat next to him with my backside.

"Cheers." I clink the neck of my beer against his before downing a generous mouthful.

Malted liquid spurts out of my mouth, drenching Hunter and me when he unexpectedly asks, "How long have you been a voyeur? Just the six weeks you've been here, or is it something you've done before?"

I cough and wheeze while fighting to breathe through the beer now sitting in my lungs instead of my flipping stomach.

"Are you okay?" Hunter asks while gently whacking my back.

Although mortified with embarrassment, my panic doesn't linger for long. Not an ounce of anger reflects from Hunter. He appears more concerned about my near choke than my incriminatory activities the past six weeks.

Once my mini-meltdown simmers, I lock my eyes with the murky blue ones staring at me with worry. "You knew I was watching the whole time?"

A cunning grin etches onto his sinful mouth before he bobs his chin. "For future reference, when you're standing in pitch-black darkness, an iPhone screen can illuminate an entire face."

I gulp loudly.

I have no other defense, so silence reigns supreme.

While eying me over the rim of his beer bottle, Hunter takes a generous sip. I set my beer down on the coffee table, then fold my hands together in my lap, hoping to conceal their shake from Hunter.

When several long seconds pass in silence, I can't help but blurt out. "Why aren't you mad?"

My heart beats double-time as I impatiently wait for him to answer my question. Although he lets me stew for several tortuous seconds, he eventually lets me off the hook. "Your interest gave me a slight curiosity in Martymachlia."

"Marty what?" The tremble of my heart is evident in my voice.

Hunter licks the beer from his lips before explaining, "Martymachlia is sexual arousal from having others watch their *activities*."

My pupils dilate to the size of dinner plates, but in all honesty, even shocked he admitted he gets turned on by people watching him during intimate moments, I'm also incredibly aroused. It isn't the fact he's a little more deviant than expected causing the tingle between my legs. It's because he's so comfortable with his sexual preferences.

It's a refreshing change from what I am used to.

Riley refused to talk about anything relating to sex—in or out of the bedroom.

After swallowing to dislodge the brick in my throat, I ask, "So instead of being angry about me spying on you, you *liked* it?"

He smirks but remains quiet with his eyes locked on me. I inwardly gasp when a warm slickness coats my panties from the hungry look that materializes in his eyes the longer he stares at me.

I've watched him in compromising situations for weeks, and my body has never reacted this way.

I begin to wonder if he can read my inner thoughts when he smiles a cocky grin before he takes another swig of his beer. I return his ardent stare, blinking and confused. The *friendship* I created with Hunter's pseudonym, Archer, is a little crazy, but this is ten times weirder. Hunter and I are virtually strangers, but we're sitting in my living room—that now seems two sizes too small from the stifling heat bouncing between us—talking about his sexual preferences as if we're discussing the difference between full cream and skim milk.

Although a little weird, I will admit, I appreciate his frankness. It's rare to find a guy willing to discuss anything these days, let alone sex.

After adjusting my position so my body is facing Hunter, I ask, "How did you discover you had this *marty* condition?" I try to keep my tone neutral and friendly like this is something I discuss regularly.

My efforts are poor. Hunter glares at me over the rim of his beer bottle before muttering against the glass, "Please don't say it like that. It makes it sound like I'm some sort of *freak*."

I arch a brow and stare at him in a sadistic, jeering type of way.

He scoffs. "Who are you to talk?" He returns my leering stare. "You were the one getting *horny* while watching. *I* at least had a partner."

"Part*ners*." I draw out the S with a sneer. "And I wasn't getting *horny*." My voice sounds like a pre-pubescent teen during my last word. "I was getting inspired."

"Come on, Paige. I'm being honest, and you're spitting out lies like Richard Nixon during the Watergate scandal."

I sneer at him before drifting my eyes to the coffee table to contemplate in peace. I can't look at his handsome face and maintain rational thoughts. I honestly didn't find the interactions between him and his bevy of female companions sexually arousing. I viewed their exchanges as if they were one of the nudes hanging on his walls. I appreciated the smooth lines and fluidity of their connection but didn't get any stimulation from it.

Well, other than mental.

I snap my eyes back to Hunter when he misunderstands my quietness as embarrassment. "There's nothing to be ashamed of, Paige. If watching people is your *thing*, then it's your *thing*."

"I'm not a voyeur."

He slants his head and quirks his lips. "How long have you been staying here? Six weeks now?"

I nod. Nearly seven but close enough.

"Not once have I seen a *visitor* here that entire time." Hunter freezes with his beer resting against his plump lips, his pupils dilating. "Please, for the love of God, don't tell me you've gone six weeks without..." My eyes dance between his, wondering why he suddenly stopped talking.

When I see the mortified look on his face, the rest of his sentence slaps me hard in the face. "No! I'm fine." My roar bounces off the wood-lined walls and shrills into my ears on repeat. "I'm good. I promise."

He glares into my eyes, blatantly calling bullshit.

"I'm *fine*," I assure him again. "I've taken care of *business*." I snap my mouth shut, mortified I said that out loud.

Hunter's pupils dilate even more. "Fuck," he mutters under his breath while adjusting his crotch. "Now *that* is something I'd turn into a voyeur for."

I don't deny his accusation that I'm a voyeur.

I'm too muted by shock to compile a reply to his false statement.

As he scratches his beard, his eyes blaze into mine. "Damn, Paige. You can't tell a guy something like that and not expect some sort of reaction." He licks a droplet of beer from his top lip before muttering, "I could bounce a nickel off my cock just thinking about you touching yourself."

My insides clench, turned on by his admission, and shockingly, the temperature in the room becomes roasting. I'm stunned by my body's reaction to his white-hot gaze, but there's no doubt the tingling in my womb is compliments of his yearning watch.

I can't remember the last time my libido has been this stimulated. I'm fairly certain it's *never* been this intense.

I know people's tastes change. I used to hate eggs when I was younger. Now I'd donate a kidney for eggs Benedict on a lazy Sunday morning. But can your preferences alter so much in a short period? Hunter is *nothing* like Riley, not in the slightest, but I can't deny the prompts of my body. Even though my mind is a jumbled mess of confusion, my body wants Hunter. *Badly.*

Our core-clutching stare-down ends when a cell phone breaks through the silence. Hunter grits his teeth before he fishes his outdated cell phone from his jeans pocket. After locking his eyes back with mine, he flips open the screen and squashes his cell to his ear. "Boss," he greets before waiting a beat. "Alright, I'll head there now. What type of information do you want to unearth?"

I try in vain to keep my interest away from his private conversation, but my efforts are futile. Uncovering the real Archer Boyd is becoming a riveting experience. It is stimulating my mind with more storylines than I can comprehend.

"I'll see you in a few." After disconnecting his call, Hunter places his phone back into his pocket, then stands from the couch. "I have to go."

And just like that, our intense connection is lost.

Chapter Seven

With a huff, I plop into my writing chair and spin around to face the new Mac I purchased earlier today. Stream upon stream of beautiful words are displayed on the screen in front of me, but nothing can overcome the woeful mood I've been in the last five days. And no, my bad temper has nothing to do with that time of the month and everything to do with the bearded man who lives in the glass house next door.

I haven't seen Hunter in days. Not a single smidge of him. From the number of *activities* he undertook in his private residence the previous six weeks, I can only assume he is avoiding me, or he's taken his lust-crazed romps to another location.

Although I have plenty of inspiration to pen a decent novel, I can't help but be a little peeved.

I don't fully understand what I'm annoyed at, but I am utterly blindsided by my odd behavior of late. I've stated on numerous occasions that Hunter isn't my type, and I'm in no way obsessed with him, but my writing is swaying in the opposite direction. Pages of angst-filled drama and jealousy are the heart of my current masterpiece. Either my subconscious is sounding alarm bells, or I've completely jumped ship from my usual style of writing.

I guess I could rationalize it as a painter working without a muse. I'm sure Leonardo da Vinci didn't paint the *Mona Lisa* without having Lisa Gherardini displayed in front of him, so how am I expected to bring Archer to life on the pages without assessing his finer quirks in full detail? Any artist will tell you it's the minor details that create the biggest impact on any art form.

Oh god. I sound like a grade-A lunatic.

My stern reprimand on the consequences I could face for being charged with stalking is interrupted when a quick tap bellows up the wooden staircase. I save my red editing pen from being gnawed to death by my chattering teeth by using it as a clip to secure a messy bun on my head while trudging down the stairs. My slow pace quickens when I discover who is standing behind the glass door of the wooden deck.

With a broad grin stretched across my face, I unlatch the lock and slide open the door. The smell of the salty ocean and bottled cologne smacks me in the face from my hasty movements.

"Hey, Hunter," I greet, my tone way too high for my liking.

Even with a large scruff of hair on his chin, Hunter can't hide his smile at the eagerness in my voice. He returns my greeting while bouncing his eyes between mine. After a beat, he asks, "Can I come in?"

"Umm... sure." I move out of the doorway to allow him entry, mortified I forgot my manners.

The scent of yummy cologne amplifies the further he enters the cabin.

I close the door to settle the winds whipping inside, then spin around to face Hunter. "Giorgio Armani or Tom Ford?"

His brows furrow as he stares at me in confusion.

"Your aftershave."

I've smelled his scent before, but I can't pinpoint the exact brand of his cologne.

The corners of Hunter's lips curve upwards before he mutters, "Neither."

Not bothering to ease my curiosity, he ambles into my kitchen.

It's only when he places a plastic bag full to the brim with Chinese takeout on the tiled counter do I realize he's carrying goodies. My eyes were too invested in the vibrant sparkle in his gaze to notice he was bearing gifts.

"Hungry?" he asks, his voice smoother than melted chocolate.

The instant his murky blue eyes lock with mine, the sweat-producing visual of him in various stages of intimacy smack into me. Unlike the times I watched him have sex in person, the reruns cause a hot trickle of desire to heat my blood and cluster in my womb.

Upon spotting my shocked expression, Hunter asks, "Is eating against the writing code?"

I shake my head, forcefully removing the images of his nakedness from my mind before replying, "No. I'm always up for eating."

I enter the kitchen, happy to use food as a distraction from my out-of-character awkwardness. Hunter eyes me curiously as I move through the compact space, gathering plates, cutlery, and two beers from the refrigerator. The flips of my stomach smooth to a slight twinge when the smell of Chinese food and Hunter lingers through the air, spurring on my rampant hunger... *for food.*

Over the next hour, we devour a wide variety of delicious dishes without speaking a peep. Unlike the last time we undertook a silent stance, it's void of any awkwardness. Hunter has an aura that demolishes my usually impenetrable walls I raise when in the company of the opposite sex.

Normally, I'm more reserved with my food selection. I don't want to appear like a pig at a trough, but I feel comfortable enough around him that I devoured more than my share of the Chinese food he bought without a single qualm crossing my mind.

Stuffed and requiring a nap, I slump low into the two-seater sofa I'm sprawled on and rest a hand on the curve of my now protruding stomach. "That was... *scrumptious.*"

I make a mental note to ensure I mention the way Hunter's eyes reveal he's smiling without his lips needing to move when a bright shimmer beams from his eyes during my grateful comment.

While gathering our stained plates off the coffee table, he asks, "Full?"

I leap up to help collect our used dishware, mortified that my food-induced coma once again had me forgetting my manners. "I'm more stuffed than my grandmother's overcooked turkey at Thanksgiving." With dishes balancing on my palms, I shadow him into the poky kitchen.

Hunter smirks before he places the dishware into the sink and commences washing them like he's always belonged here. Grinning like a cat staring at a fishbowl, I snag a dish cloth off the kitchen counter and dry the bubble-covered plate he thrusts at me.

"For someone who doesn't know how to *interact* with girls, you're doing a stellar job," I quip, loving that he doesn't see the kitchen as a 'woman-only zone' like Riley quoted numerous times the past three years.

Hunter continues washing dishes like he was born to do it while relishing the peace. On the other hand, I have been cooped up in this cabin for the past five days with no real-life adult interaction, so I'm feeling a little chatty.

We couldn't be more opposite if we tried.

"So where have you been the past couple of days? I haven't seen you around." My pupils widen to the size of the dinner plate I'm grasping. "Not that I've been looking."

As fiery heat creeps across my cheeks, Hunter's breathy chuckle fans a little scattering of hairs curling on his top lip. He must have been busy the past five days because his usually well-kept beard is more bushy than usual. "I've been busy at work."

He hands me the final dish like five little words will ease my curiosity.

It doesn't.

Not in the slightest.

I wait for the gurgling noise of the sink water draining away to vanish before continuing with my interrogation, "Did you go to New Delhi?"

Hunter shakes his head. "No, Paige, I didn't go to New Delhi."

"So where were you?"

After placing the cutlery in the kitchen drawer, I move to the refrigerator for more beer. A whiny groan purrs through my lips when I discover there's only one beer. Not speaking a word, Hunter gathers a glass from an overhead cupboard, snags the beer from my grasp, then pours half of it into the glass before handing it to me.

After a prolonged stare, he mutters, "I've been *working*, Paige." His tone is back to the same edgy one he used during my last interrogation.

"I do not mean to interrogate you. I'm merely being neighborly," I bite back before taking a swig of my beer, desperately needing something to soothe my ravaged throat.

Hunter's nose screws up as he eyeballs me. His ardent stare has my pulse quickening and my pussy throbbing. I freeze when my inner monologue reaches my head.

What the hell is wrong with me? I can't think about Hunter in this manner.

I stop reprimanding myself when he repeats, "You were being *neighborly?*"

The froth in my mouth doubles in size when I rapidly shake my head. "Yeah. It's what neighbors do. We keep an eye on each other to make sure neither of us ends up in any trouble."

A cocky grin etches on his mouth. It's more concerning than the earlier unwanted throbs of my vagina. "Is that why you've been *watching* me for the past seven weeks? Are you making sure I'm not getting into any *mischief?*"

I kick him in the shoe, unappreciative of the humor in his tone. "Not that type of trouble," I say with a roll of my eyes.

Look at me acting all high and mighty when that is *exactly* why I eyeballed him for weeks on end.

"What if I saw a bandit stealing one of your nude paintings? I wouldn't have any way of telling you. I don't even know your full name, let alone your phone number," I gabble out while walking into the living room, saying anything to get the heat off me and my snooping.

I guzzle down the rest of my beer, praying it will stop the word 'vomit' spilling from my lips. I pretty much just asked for his number by dropping hints.

Can anyone say "Loser?"

Hunter runs the back of his hand over his mouth, removing a smidgen of beer from his top lip before he answers, "I have the world's most advanced security system. I'm not the slightest bit concerned about being robbed."

"Good to know." I vainly try to hide the snarl in my tone. I miserably fail.

With a silent huff, I plop onto the rock-hard sofa. My movements are heavy, weighed down by the harsh blow of rejection.

The sting only burns for a second when Hunter mutters, "But for peace of mind, I guess we could always exchange phone numbers?"

A broad grin stretches across my face as my insides break into a jig. "Sure, if you want."

I shrug, hoping it will conceal my happiness.

Just like all my ploys tonight, my attempt at aloofness is woeful.

Chapter Eight

"Hey, Hunter." I pull open the back patio sliding door before gesturing for him to enter.

When he does, my eyes rocket down to the plastic bag in his hand, eager to see what meal he's arrived with today. For the past four days, he's arrived at precisely nine o'clock with a bag full of scrumptious food. The first night was Chinese, the second Italian, and the third was burgers and fries.

At the start, it felt a little odd accepting his generosity. I'd never had a male friend before, so I was a little unsure of the protocol. But as the days move on, our odd kinship is rapidly merging into a close bond. I've only known him in person for a little over a week, but I feel like I've known him for over half of my life. He is the close confidant I once thought Archer was.

"Looks a little plain today," I jest when a loaf of bread is the only distinguishable item in his bag of goodies.

When I lean in to press a kiss to his cheek, Hunter's cheekbone rises under my lips. "I thought we could go back to basics today."

After taking a moment to relish the warmth of his breath on my cheek, I close the door then follow him into the compact kitchen. As he moves around my kitchen, gathering supplies and unpacking the ingredients from his bag, I leap onto the tiled countertop to watch him in awe.

The Hunter who stated he found it troubling to interact with women while clothed has been nowhere in sight the past four days. He's calm, relaxed, and carefree.

Don't take my admission the wrong way. The sparks of attraction flying between us the night he returned my laptop are still firing, but I'm giving it my best shot to keep them at a dull flame instead of a raging, out-of-control wildfire.

It has been a very hard feat.

Hunter pulls a skillet off the pot rack dangling above the gas cooktop, places it onto the open flame, and dumps a tablespoon of butter into it. After pulling out eight slices of bread, he sets to work on making grilled ham and cheese sandwiches.

When he wordlessly announces the final ingredient, a jar of pickles, I launch off the bench. "No pickles for me, please," I request, my voice high with disgust. "Pickles are gross. Just the thought of their salty ghastliness sliding down my throat makes me gag. Much to my father's dismay, I've never been a fan of pickles."

A smile stretches across my face when memories of my dad sneakily hiding the occasional pickle in my sandwich when I was in junior high creep into my mind. Although he doesn't have the rough and rugged appearance Hunter has perfected, he has no qualms making a mean grilled cheese sandwich. His sandwiches are now just served on a gold-edged plate.

When Hunter flips over the sandwiches, revealing a beautiful golden covering, I remove two beers from the refrigerator. We've quickly slipped into a routine the past four nights. Hunter supplies the food, and I provide the alcohol and conversation. Although Hunter probably wishes I wasn't so fond of the articulate side of my offerings, considering I do most of the talking.

With a stack of grilled sandwiches balancing on a plate, Hunter follows me into the living room. After dumping the beers onto the coffee table, I snag two scatter cushions off the couch and place them on the floor, and hey presto, our makeshift dining area is complete.

Just like the previous four nights, our meal is shared in silence. Too much quiet generally irritates me, but surprisingly, I enjoy small moments of silence when I am with Hunter. So many of his characteristics are exposed through actions more than words. I've added a vault load of mental notes on his finer quirks to my already extensive collection. Like how the small crumbs of bread from his top lip drop onto his beard and become nonexistent, how he wipes the back of his hand over his mouth after every third bite, and how his gulps of beer are so large, he drinks half of the bottle with only one swig.

Once there's nothing but crumbs left on the plate, I crank my elbow onto the couch and rest my cheek on my hand. "So... did anything exciting happen in the telemarketing world today?"

Hunter smirks against the rim of his beer bottle before taking another large gulp. Once his tongue has cleared away a droplet of beer from his top lip, he shakes his head. I inwardly sigh. I've asked him the same question every day for the past four days, and he responds the same every time I ask.

"What about you? Did you smash your word count?"

I smile while nodding. After telling him about my strict deadline the first night we dined together, each day when he leaves, he assigns me a word count I must strive to reach the following day. Since I am super competitive, I give it my all. Yesterday he assigned one of the biggest targets to date—ten thousand words in a day.

Shockingly, I hit my goal by six, meaning I added another two thousand before I showered in preparation for his arrival.

"It may end up being nothing but a whole heap of word vomit, but I smashed it," I inform, my tone high and eager.

Hunter awards me with a playful wink before placing his beer on the coffee table. I eye him curiously when his hand delves into his jeans pocket to remove a small black camera-like device. "I have something that may assist with your writing," he explains to my bemused expression.

After snatching my iPhone off the table, he connects the device to the speaker port of my phone. My brows shoot up to my hairline when he logs into my phone without asking for the lock code. While making a mental note to check the security of my phone, I lean in close when he snaps a picture of one of my many random scraps of paper lying around the living room. "With this device, you can scan your notes and upload them to your phone."

"Kind of like notes to PDF?"

He shrugs. "Not really. This is similar to a scanner, but instead of scanning the documents as an image, it takes your handwritten words and types them into your pages app."

My eyes bug to of my head. "So I can edit the documents?"

When Hunter nods, a massive surge of euphoria pumps into my veins. This will be an ingenious device for me. Normally, I have to rewrite my handwritten notes. This device will save me hours of work.

"Thank you so much," I praise before accepting my phone from him to test how the device works.

The low hang of my jaw increases when I scan one of my hideous sketches, and it converts it to an image below the typed text Hunter just scanned.

Like a kid with a new toy, I continue scanning anything I can get my hands on.

Within minutes, I have pages of notes stored on my phone that would have taken me hours to type.

"This is brilliant. Where did you find it?"

My brows form a small 'v' in the middle of my forehead when a wash of apprehension crosses Hunter's face. After coughing to clear his throat, he quietly mutters, "I designed it."

I stare at him with shock and disbelief tainting my face. "You made this?" I question while jerking my head to the device I'm clutching like it's worth a million dollars.

His eyes flick down to the device before they lift and lock with mine. "Yep," he says with an apprehensive dip of his chin.

I remain quiet, silenced by shock. After he fixed my laptop last week, I knew he had impressive computer skills, but I had no idea his knowledge was this extensive. This isn't an odd-looking homemade contraption. It looks like Apple or Toshiba manufactured it. I'm not ashamed to admit, I am in complete awe that he made this.

After a beat, Hunter mistakes my silence as ungratefulness. "I can take it back if you don't like it."

"No." I shake my head while yanking my hand away from him so he can't make true on his threat. "I love it. Thank you so much."

When I plant a kiss on his cheek, any chances of keeping the flame in my belly to the size of a match head disappear. His delicious smell engulfs my senses. It is unique and intoxicating—a mixture of freshly showered skin, soap, and another smell I can't quite distinguish.

After discreetly inhaling a final whiff of his mouthwatering scent, I pull back from his cheek. When a sparkle in his eyes reveals he caught my sneaky appreciation of his alluring smell, I bounce my dilated eyes around the room, seeking anything but his gaze.

The color of my cheeks nearly matches the vibrancy of my hair when my endeavor not to have my ardent stare witnessed has me stumbling onto another fervent watch. Hunter is watching me from the corner of his eye. His hooded gaze is full of zeal and covetousness.

The mariachi beat of my heart kicks up even more when he leans in intimately close to my side. His unique scent and the grilled cheese and pickle sandwiches he consumed linger in my nose when he props one arm on the sofa while the other one brushes away a bunch of my wavy red hair from my face. Time comes to a standstill when he skims his index finger down my scrunched-up nose.

Before my brain has time to compile an objection, I blurt out, "How come I've never seen you with a redhead?" One of Hunter's heavy brows slants in confusion, but I continue on as if it didn't. "I've seen you with blondes, brunettes, and once you even had a girl with a pink stripe down the side, but not once have I seen you with a redhead." My words come out in a flurry before my brain can stop them. "Do you not like redheads?"

His eyes dance between mine. "I offered, Paige. Remember? It was *you* who turned *me* down."

I shake my head, denying his claim. "I didn't turn you down. I turned down a *threesome*." I squeak on my last word.

Hunter remains quiet, no doubt dazed into silence. My brain is begging me to return his passiveness, but my impulses override it. I scoot across the floor, filling in the minute speck of space between us. I've never been so bold, but I'm fortified and more than ready to begin a new chapter in my life. I want to move on from the stigma of a broken-hearted woman to have an adventure. Hunter seems like the type of guy who could offer me the no-commitment, fast-paced thrill ride I'm seeking. He could invigorate me as I rediscover the Paige I lost years ago.

The muscles in Hunter's thighs flex as his eyes drift between mine. Although he doesn't aid in filling the gap between us, he doesn't pull away either, confirming to my brain that I'm making the right decision with my newly gained boldness.

Just as Hunter's breaths tickle my puckered lips, he mutters, "We can't, Paige. Not now."

I hold back the windless groan his brutal rejection inflicts on my lungs while flopping onto my backside. Even with his cold, hard slap to my ego stinging like a bitch, I'm not desperate enough to request an explanation for his lack of interest.

I threw myself at him.

He denied my advances.

No explanation is needed.

While lifting my half-empty beer to my suddenly parched mouth, I once again seek anything but Hunter's gaze. Although I'm not desperate enough to demand an explanation, it doesn't mean I don't need a few minutes to soothe the sting.

My back molars grind together when Hunter removes the nearly empty bottle from my grasp and dumps it back onto the coffee table. Before any words can spill from his hard-lined lips, I blubber, "I get it. It's cool. You don't have to explai—"

"Shut up, Paige," he interrupts before he pinches my chin between his thumb and index finger and angles my head back to face him.

My mouth gapes, shell-shocked by the bluntness of his reply. Although at times, his moods swing toward grumpy, but he's never been this blunt before.

"If I didn't consider you a friend, my cock would be filling that hole in your mouth."

I snap my mouth closed, equally shocked and turned on by his crude statement.

"But since you're my friend, my cock will stay in my jeans and not in your pretty little mouth where it really wants to be."

I roll my eyes skyward. "Please. We are *not* friends. I hardly know you. You're practically a stranger." My eyes bulge out of my head, stunned that the words I was meant to say inside my head spilled from my mouth.

Hunter coasts even closer to me, absorbing any sense of normality I had left. "We're not friends?"

"Not even close."

My trembling voice gives away my deceit, but Hunter acts ignorant. "So you don't have any concerns about being another notch on my extensively serrated bedpost?"

I cross my arms in front of my chest to hide the quiver of my hands before shaking my head.

His top lip forms into a snarl, but he continues playing it cool. "You wouldn't be at all devastated when I dressed you and walked you to the door the instant I had my fill of your no doubt tight pussy?"

A barrage of emotions smacks into me at once. I'm excited about his dirty words but also devastated by their callousness. I've seen Hunter in his element. I know without a doubt he'd rocket my core to the next galaxy, but I can't comprehend why he believes our kinship requires a no-sexy-time stipulation.

Even with my heart warning me against it, I shake my head, once again denying his claim.

Hunter's hooded eyes blaze into mine, searing my soul from the inside out as he mutters, "And I *never* called you again."

The shake of my head comes to a standstill as does the beat of my heart.

Never?

Upon spotting my shocked response, Hunter mumbles, "Yeah, that's what I thought. I like you, Paige. Surprisingly enough, I don't want to touch you." He waits for our eyes to meet before finalizing his reply, "Because I don't want to hurt you."

My heart recommences beating so it can accommodate the mass surge of blood pumping through it. Although being rejected dents even the world's biggest egos, it's admirable he's being upfront with me. It takes a lot of guts for a man to be honest, let alone to a virtual stranger.

"So... we're going to be just *friends*?" The cheekiness in my voice hides my confusion. I like Hunter more than I probably should, but I also like the idea of being his friend.

Hunter nods. "If you want?"

I lick my lips before replying, "Alright. I think I can handle that."

I hope.

Chapter Nine

"Do you want to go for a swim?"

Hunter's eyes drift from the suds-filled sink to me. Our routine hasn't altered the past two weeks. He arrives every night at nine bearing scrumptious gifts. We dine together on the floor of my living room, he washes while I dry, and then we snuggle on the couch and watch a movie.

I want to say the fire in my belly has been kept at a dull flame, but that would be a lie. It's expanded to a decent, winter-warming fire, but it's normal for friends to snuggle on the couch every night. *Isn't it?*

I'd also like to say our conversations have exposed sides of Hunter I didn't discover while stalking him, but unfortunately, they haven't. For the most part, he listens while I blubber incessantly, but even with us having an oddly imbalanced friendship, I enjoy spending time with him. I can be myself around him, which is a refreshing change after spending years pretending to be someone I'm not.

Hunter snatches the dish cloth out of my hand to dry his suds-covered one. "You don't have a pool," he replies to my suggestion as his eyes float to the window of my cozy kitchen. "Or a hot tub," he adds when the coolness of a winter breeze sneaks through the cracks of the wood paneling.

I expand my arms to the expansive view of the blackened ocean of Bronte's Peak behind me. "Who needs a pool when you have an entire ocean?"

He eyes me dubiously but remains quiet when I step away from him, walking backward. When I hit the glass sliding door of the back patio, I toe off my shoes and toss them to the side of the cramped living space.

When my hand darts down to the button in my jeans, the glint in Hunter's gaze augments from curious to disbelief. "You're not?" he questions, his usually prominent voice barely a murmur.

His earth-shattering timbre incites my boldness. After flashing him a quick smirk, I hotfoot it across the patio. By the time I make it down the three stairs of the back deck, my jeans have been shimmied off my legs and dumped onto the sandy ground. Sand squishes between my toes as I make a mad dash for the water's edge. I throw off my sweater and long-sleeve shirt on the way.

The coolness of a late fall breeze whizzes through my hair when I increase my speed. My hammering heart nearly blocks out Hunter's wolf whistles and catcalls as I race across the sand like a mad woman on a mission. My smile is as large as the surge of adrenaline pumping through my veins. I hit the edge of the dunes wearing nothing but mismatched cotton panties and a satin bra.

After squealing the loudest squeal I've ever screamed, I charge for the waves crashing on the foreshore. My cheeks burn from the mammoth grin stretched across my face, and my lungs heave as they struggle to fill with air, but I've never felt more free.

When I reach the water's edge, I crank my neck to the left before sliding it to the right. Satisfied no one is watching, I spin around to face Hunter. "Close your eyes, Hunter. Things are about to get scandalous," I warn, my voice dramatic.

With a broad grin on his face, he continues strolling down the sand dunes. When I arch a brow at him, another silent warning on how far I'm willing to stretch my antics tonight, he throws his forearm over his eyes. As my heart hammers my ribs, I unhook my bra and slide my panties down my legs.

If I risk being arrested for public indecency, I plan to give it my all.

Goosebumps prickle the surface of my skin, and a swear word seeps from my lips when I dive into the bitterly cold water. But even with the possibility of getting frost bite increasing by the second, nothing can wipe the grin off my face.

Salty water pummels me when I collide with the waves breaking to shore, but I continue with my mission, fighting against the surge of water trying to sweep me back to reality.

A sense of achievement washes over me when I reach the serene of the flat ocean. "Come on, Hunter!" My high-pitch squeal echoes in the eerie quietness of the almost midnight sky. "It's so beautiful out here!"

The moonlight glistens on my wet cheeks when I spread my arms out wide and float on the surface of the frigid water. I snap my eyes closed then surrender to the calmness of the ocean. My weightlessness adds to the invincibility I'm feeling.

I am unstoppable.

After enjoying the tranquility of being swept away for a few minutes, I slowly flutter my eyes open. The sky is bright with a dusting of stars, and the moon is full. It's truly a beautiful image I'll treasure for years to come.

My stargazing comes to a halt when my name is called out in the distance. While treading water, I crank my neck to the foreshore.

"Paige!" Hunter calls out again, his voice so loud it bellows over the crashing waves in the distance.

As my eyes lock onto a small black speck approaching from my right, I shout, "I'm over here."

The crazy beat of my heart overtakes Hunter's swimming strokes when the visual of a drenching wet and completely naked Hunter swamps my vision.

Jesus Christ!

Even hidden under the rippling of water, I can see every spectacular inch of his scrumptious chest, bumped abs, and killer arms. It's been weeks since I've seen the glorious visual of a naked Hunter, and boy, I've missed it.

"Holy fuck. It's fucking freezing!" Hunter's chattering teeth don't dampen the deepness of his tone. "I'm pretty sure I won't recognize my dick when we exit the water."

I throw my head back and laugh. Not a slight, dainty giggle, but a full-hearted chuckle that exposes sides of my wittiness I often hide.

Hunter glares at me, his face marred with both shock and concern. I'm sure I look like a grade-A lunatic, but after the day I've had, I needed this. Finding out your fiancé moved his mistress into your shared home ten days after you left him is a shattering blow to any ego.

Memories of the conversation I had with Pepper earlier today make quick work of my laughter. As I battle to hold in the tears I've kept at bay for most of the day, my face scrunches up. Upon sensing a change in my composure, Hunter runs his index finger down the grooves in my nose before drawing me into his chest.

I plaster my body as close to him as I can. I don't allow an ounce of air between us while accepting his comfort.

Sometimes a good hug is the only cure needed for the deepest heartache.

A stretch of silence passes between us as we tread water. It isn't awkward. We're both happy to take a breather from reality to stare at a star-filled sky. It's surreal to think I only met Hunter weeks ago, and I'm already comfortable enough around him to strip naked and dive into a frigidly cold ocean, not to mention snuggle into his bare chest.

And although I try to ignore it, I can't miss certain parts of his body rubbing against mine.

It is unmissable.

After a few more minutes of silent stargazing, Hunter runs his hand down my goosebump-riddled back. "Are you going to use this for a scene in your book?"

I smile, loving that he isn't the slightest bit fazed by my erratic behavior. If I'd pulled this type of stunt with Riley, he would have had a coronary and shipped me off for extensive therapy. Hunter not being concerned shows he gets me and my quirkiness.

"Yeah... it could work," I reply, still smiling. "What do you think? The heroine dives into the water after an argument, and the hero takes off after her. He then shows her what she means to him by making love to her under the stars in the middle of the ocean." I stop talking, and my lips purse. "Although from what you said earlier, I may need to rework the scene. I don't want to factor in shrinkage."

My heart warms when a hearty chuckle rumbles out of Hunter's blue-tinged lips. "It wouldn't matter if they were swimming in Antarctica, Paige, if the woman is who the man desires, shrinkage won't be a problem."

The veins in my neck pulsate when his eyes lower to absorb portions of my naked body plastered to his. Just like my weirdness doesn't daunt him, he has no qualms about openly ogling me without fear of reprimand.

When his eyes lift and lock with mine, after a few seconds of long gawks, the energy between us shifts. It fires the night sky with a cluster of invisible fireworks. "Trust me." His hungry eyes bounce between mine. "He will have *no* problems getting hard."

My heart beats out a rocking tune, beyond smitten by his compliment. "I'll be s-sure to take note of that." The jitteriness of my tone relays my wavering constraint. The energy teeming between us is too great to ignore. It is hammering into me as badly now as it was when he gifted me his latest mastermind invention.

Hunter's eyes shift from a murky blue to a navy blue as they bore into mine. They show so much hunger, I'm shocked by the words he speaks next. I thought they would have been far less tamed. "Now can we get out of here before my cock snaps off?"

Desperate to hide my devastation, I take off for the shore. A winded grunt escapes Hunter's lips when I use his body as a springboard during the commencement of my mad dash. "Loser gets dirty dishes duty for the next week," I yell out between swimming strokes.

"Challenge accepted," I hear Hunter shout over my frantic splashes.

Even with Hunter's rock-hard abs garnering me a decent lead, he overtakes me halfway to shore then emerges from the water before me. When it dawns on me that my defeat is more a victory than a loss, I slow my strokes, giving my eyes plenty of time to drink in every inch of his panty-wetting body when he cups his cock in his hands and races for his jeans and shirt dumped at the water's edge.

His ass—my god. It needs its own entry in the dictionary to explain how scrumptious it is.

The crisp night buds his dark nipples into firm peaks, and goose-bumps prickle his torso. His lack of clothing showcases his yummy Apollo belt and spectacular Adonis ass I'll never grow tired of ogling. The visual of him wet and naked is a core-clenching image that makes me completely forget I'm currently submerged in a bitterly cold ocean.

I only continue swimming back to the shore when Hunter's legs slip into his favorite pair of jeans.

Air hisses from his lips when I emerge from the water. Unlike me, he doesn't hide the fact he's eyeballing me. He categorizes and absorbs every inch of my body as I did him without the slightest bit of intimidation. He notices the way my small breasts bounce beneath my forearm as I pad across the sand, the extra swing his hooded gaze instilled on my hips, and that not all the shimmering between my legs is from the water.

"What are you doing to me, Paige," he mutters under his breath before he wraps his plaid shirt around my shoulders. It engulfs me with his delicious scent and makes the throb of my clit even more noticeable.

Since his words come out more as a statement than a question, I don't respond. I merely watch him button up the three buttons on his shirt, gather my panties and bra from the sand and stuff them into his jeans pocket, then guide me to the cabin by curling his hand over mine.

Even the walk up the sandy path between our properties is done in complete silence. Not only has the chattering of my teeth rendered me speechless, so has the tension bristling between us.

When I reach my patio, I press a kiss to the edge of Hunter's mouth. "Thanks for joining me for a swim."

I feel his mouth raise against my lips. "It was my pleasure. But can we do it in summer next time?"

Laughing, I nod while trying not to look too deeply into his suggestion there may be a next time.

After flashing him a quick smirk, I walk up my patio steps. Just as I'm about to yank open the glass door, Hunter calls my name.

I tilt back to face him. "Yeah?"

"Do you have any plans for Christmas Eve?"

While keeping my excitement concealed behind a neutral expression, I shake my head.

A broad grin stretches across his face. "Do you want to come to a party with me?"

My heart rate skyrockets, but I continue playing it cool. "A family thing or just us?"

Hunter throws back his head and laughs. "You just went skinny-dipping on a public beach without a smidgen of concern, but you're freaked about the prospect of meeting some friends of mine?"

I snarl at him, baring teeth. "I'm not *scared*. I was merely making sure this is the type of things *friends* did." I cross my arms in front of my chest, hoisting my little bosoms higher. "It could be because my brain has frozen over, but this kind of sounds like a date to me?"

Hunter smirks while shaking his head. "It's not a date. It is just two *friends* hanging out." His eyes drop to his plaid shirt curled around my body. "It's so casual, you can wear jeans and a plaid shirt if you want."

I tug his shirt in close to my body while stating matter-of-factly, "You're not getting this back."

He smirks a deliciously wicked smile. "Good. 'Cause you're not getting your panties back either."

My jaw drops. I completely forgot my panties are in his jeans pocket.

After propping my hip onto the wall of the cabin, I stare into his jeering face like my heart isn't racing a million miles an hour. "Will you give me back my panties if I go to this party with you?"

"Nope," he replies without a delay, his eyes as scorching as his reply made my body temperature.

Battling to lessen the rush of desire swamping my pantyless crotch from his gleaming gaze, I cross my legs before saying with a snarl, "Then I guess you're going to the party dateless."

I push off the wall and mosey into the cabin, my pace only slowing when Hunter murmurs, "What about a compromise?"

I smile, smitten he isn't giving up without a fight. My nipples tighten when I step back onto the patio. The perkiness of my breasts isn't from the chilly breeze blowing in from the west. It's from the hankering gleam in Hunter's eyes as he dangles my satin bra from his index finger.

"You keep my shirt. I'll keep your panties. You get your bra. I get a date," he negotiates.

My teeth rake my bottom lip while I pretend I wasn't two heartbeats away from spinning around and accepting his date before he suggested the compromise. I won't lie. I love the way sweat beads on the top of his brow from my delay in replying. Even if it's only for a minute, it's nice for the shoe to be on the other foot in our odd *friendship*.

Once I believe he's sweated it out long enough, I say, "You have yourself a deal."

Chapter Ten

My leisurely pace up the sand-lined path halts when my eyes lock in on a raw, earth-shattering visual. Hunter is in the shower. Not the shower in his overly priced, pristine glass house. The outside shower nestled in the privacy of his glass and steel patio.

The early morning sun glistens on his wet torso as water from the shower head drenches the long hair framing his face. A breathless moan ripples from my lips when I follow the torrent of water slithering past his smooth pecs and bumps of his six-pack before it gushes over his fisted manhood.

His parted lips release quick pants in a rhythm matching the strokes on his cock.

No matter how much my conscience tells me to look away, just like the first night I discovered Hunter in a lust-crazed romp, I can't pry my eyes from him. The visual is too primal, raw, and utterly carnal not to devour. His head is lolled to the side, his plump lips are split, and the sexiest groans I've ever heard are rumbling from his throat as he brings himself to the brink of ecstasy.

I lick my parched lips as my eyes drink in every delicious inch of him—his carved, prominent muscles, smooth hairless torso, and a gorgeous face covered by a scruffy beard.

The beat of my heart grows wild when my eyes drop lower. Even his large, manly hand fisting his cock can't take away from the sheer girth and length of his thickened shaft. It's panty-wetting, delicious, uncut, and jutted with the slightest shimmering of pre-cum at the tip. Just watching him pleasure himself brings new understanding to the world of voyeurs. If the visuals I could encounter are this entertaining, I may consider altering my opinion on my voyeurism status.

My throat struggles to swallow when Hunter's pace quickens. He leans deeper into the shower as his hand works his cock from the base to the tip in precise, perfect strokes. I curve my knees inward, battling to ease the crazy pulse surging through my womb when his thumb slides over the crown of his impressive dick to gather a drop of pre-cum beading at the end. Slickness coats my swimwear when I squeeze my thighs together. I am unable to harbor my excitement any longer.

The throb between my legs turns lethal when Hunter hears a moan I fail to stifle. His weighted eyelids pop open before his heavily dilated eyes lock with mine. Another throaty moan topples from my O-formed mouth when the pace of his strokes strengthens from staring into my lust-crazed eyes.

His hips thrust as he guides his magnificent cock in and out of his clenched fist. I stare at him, wide-eyed and open-mouthed, shocked beyond comprehension at the rapid surge of my libido. Just watching him unravel is bringing my climax to the surface at a frantic velocity.

Just as his nostrils flare and the veins in his cock bulge, an annoying buzz blasts my ears.

A rough, tormented groan simpers through my parched lips when I emerge back into the land of the living. Even knowing the glorious visual was nothing but a dream, the wetness between my legs doesn't dampen any. I'm beyond saturated.

I want to say my X-rated dream was the first I've had of Hunter, but that would be a lie. Ever since our skinny-dipping adventure four nights ago, I haven't stopped dreaming about him. And like a sex-deprived nympho, every one of my dreams features Hunter in the middle of a sex act, nude, alone, and handsy.

While endeavoring to ignore the throb of excitement thickening my blood, I throw my legs over the side of the bed and mosey into the bathroom for my fourth cold shower this week.

* * *

Pepper's eyes flick between me and a program she's watching on Netflix. "Do a Google image reverse search on him."

I place my bowl of half-eaten cornflakes on my desk then curl my legs under my bottom. "A what?"

"You upload an image onto Google, and it searches for similar images. Maybe it will find him?" she advises after drifting her eyes back to her phone's screen.

We've been FaceTiming the past thirty minutes while watching a recording of our favorite sitcom, *Empire*. We're usually inseparable, spending a minimum of two to three hours together each day, but since I flew to the other side of the country, we've had to resort to FaceTime to keep our unique closeness firmly tethered.

"If he's someone famous, it will find him quick smart," Pepper adds.

I consider her suggestion for as long as it takes me to remember that I don't have a photo of Hunter.

After sharing my dilemma with Pepper, she says, "If you didn't hold out on my request for army porn weeks ago, that wouldn't have been a problem, would it?" Suddenly, her shoulders square and her pupils enlarge. "What's the name of that town near Bronte's Peak? The one you visited to get your laptop repaired?"

"Ravenshoe?" I scrunch up my face, unsure why an unknown town on the other side of the country would be of interest to her.

"Yes!" She jumps from her chair and ruffles through a collection of gossip magazines at her side. Once she finds the article she's looking for, she saunters back to the computer desk and plops into her leather chair. "You know that song blowing up the charts? Umm... what's it called... it's by that group of hotties?"

"Oh... umm... Surrender something?"

""Surrender Me!" That's it," Pepper interrupts, startling me when her loud roar thunders down the line. "I was reading a little article written in a magazine about them this morning. What would you say if I told you the band members of Rise Up live in Ravenshoe?"

My eyes bulge out of their sockets. "Are you serious?"

Pepper waggles her manicured brows while nodding. "Fancy-schmancy house, nice cars, obviously wealthy. Maybe all those women you saw coming and going from Hunter's home those first six weeks were groupies?"

My heart painfully twists during the last part of her statement. Before we became friends, seeing the troop of women come in and out of Hunter's life like a revolving door didn't bother me the slightest. Now... now it stings a little.

"Does the article tell you their names?"

Pepper's eyes scan the document. "Noah Taylor, lead singer. Marcus Everett, bassist. Nicholas Holt, guitarist. And the drummer is Slater Scott."

I slump deeper into my seat. "It's not Hunter then."

"Why?"

My brows inch as high as my voice. "Because he introduced himself as Hunter."

"And? What name did you use when you introduced yourself?"

My heart slithers into my gut. "Paige."

Pepper smirks a winning smile. "Exactly. Maybe you aren't the only one using an alias?"

Keystrokes resonate out of my iPhone speaker as I sit in silence, muted by guilt.

"He isn't the lead singer. Noah is smoking hot but has a dark and moody appearance."

I pull my phone closer to my face. "What are you doing?"

"Googling the Rise Up band members," she reports like it's no big deal she's invading Hunter's privacy. After a small stretch of silence, she turns her eyes to me. "Do you need a visitor? Because I need to see if Marcus is this hot in real life. If he is, I'm giving up my dreams of becoming an actress and taking up the role of Marcus's lead groupie."

I giggle softly. "Better than any cabana boy you've seen?"

"Ah… much better." She returns her eyes to her laptop. "Check your email. I sent you a picture."

I lower the phone and log into my email account. "Wow," I mumble when Marcus pops up on the screen. He has a gorgeous face and seducing green eyes. "I have to write a character with his bedroom eyes."

Pepper laughs. "Hell, yeah. But I think it's safe to say he isn't Hunter. Even with the lack of zoom on your phone, I'm fairly sure Hunter didn't have ravishing African American skin."

I laugh. "No, he's nearly as white as me."

"So that leaves two possibilities. Nick, the guitarist, or Slater, the drummer. Although Nick has similar length hair and coloring, his frame is too small, and his skin is void of any tattoos." Pepper angles her head to the side as she assesses her laptop screen with vivid accuracy. "Does Hunter have dreads?" When she gawks at me through my iPhone screen, I shake my head. "Darn it. I could see a resemblance between Slater and Hunter, but with how tight Slater's dreads are, that's not something he does just for when he's on the road. They're permanent." With a loud sigh, she leans deeper into her chair. "I thought I was onto a winner. I guess you'll have to ask Hunter who the hell he is the next time you see him."

My nose scrunches. "He isn't a fan of sharing personal information."

"What man is?" Pepper shrugs. "I emailed you a photo of each band member. If you see them, be a doll and grab me an autograph. There's a big buzz around them at the moment."

"Alright. I'll keep my eye out," I reply with a cheeky wink.

My attention turns from Pepper's grinning face when a rumbling engine resonates in the silence. I leap out of my chair, eager to see if it's Hunter. I haven't seen hide nor hair of him for the past three days. After spending every night with him for nearly three weeks, I've noticed his absence.

With my phone in my hand, I move toward the arched window of my office.

"Show me," Pepper whispers down the line.

While keeping my eyes planted on the three people emerging from a candy apple red muscle car, I twist my phone around. I'm stunned into silence. In the nine weeks I've been here, this is the first time I've seen a male visitor arrive at Hunter's house, let alone two of them.

"Where the hell are you visiting? Are only hot people allowed to live there?"

I laugh even though I wholeheartedly agree with Pepper's assessment. The brunette standing between the two men is gorgeous. She has light beige skin and luxurious dark hair falling in waves around her shoulders. Even wearing a simple pair of jeans and a long-sleeve shirt, she is stunning. A large brute of a man a good four to five inches taller than Hunter takes the stairs two at a time while the brunette and a handsome blond gentleman lock arms and shadow closely behind him.

A smile tugs on my lips when I spot the brunette's shocked expression from absorbing the enormity of Hunter's house. She looks like a stunned mullet.

"Do you think we should call the police?" Pepper whispers.

I shake my head. "No. Look, the hunky brute is putting in a security code."

Just as I finish speaking, Patricia's computer voice sounds through the quiet.

"That's cool." I can hear Pepper's smile in her voice.

"I told you."

The way the three of them walk through Hunter's residence with wide eyes and open mouths, I can tell this is their first time visiting. Although his house will always be impressive, nothing replicates the first time you've been captivated by something. Their faces display that they're newbies to the grandeur of Hunter's house.

My attention reverts from the beautiful brunette emerging onto the glass deck at the back of Hunter's house to the front of his property when a sports car rolls down the driveway. My heart rate kicks up a gear when a gentleman in a three-piece suit exits the car after parking it next to the shiny muscle car.

"Damn," Pepper draws out in a long, husky drawl. "I'm living in the wrong neighborhood."

She leans in close to her iPhone, ensuring she doesn't miss a thing as the impeccably dressed man makes a beeline for the large glass door. His hair is dark, thick, and luxurious. His body is a similar size to Hunter's, but his choice in clothing accents his god-crafted assets.

Like he can sense us watching, his long strides come to a halt in the marble foyer of Hunter's house, and he cranks his neck to peer at my window. Even knowing he can't see me, I take a step back, unnerved by his powerful gaze.

"Mafia?" Pepper suggests, her voice barely a whisper.

"What? No!" I reply dramatically. "Do you think?"

"He's obviously wealthy, has an edge of darkness to him, and even through your phone, his allure demands my attention. He's either in the mafia or my next sugar daddy."

"Every rich guy is your next sugar daddy," I retort, laughing so hard, I snort.

"Yeah, true. But even if he were as poor as dirt, I'd still let him leave his toothbrush at my place." Pepper's giggling stops when the suit-clad gentleman's intense stare-down of my window is interrupted by a cute blonde wearing a red Chanel suit. "Oh, interesting. It's like watching Lucious and Cookie from *Empire* going to battle," she mumbles when the two engage in a heated argument.

Their discussion is cut short when the dominant one of the duo spots the brunette standing on the glass patio. My insides sigh when the two race to each other. They crash into each other's arms in the middle of the living area. The suit-clad man pulls the brunette into his chest before he takes a seat on one of the white leather sofas in Hunter's living room.

"You need to record that," mutters Pepper, her voice sounding as transfixed as my eyes are. "The sparks firing off those two would make a heart-stopping read."

I nod, even though she can't see me. There's no denying the attraction between the two gorgeous specimens. It's earth-shattering. I've never been much of a crying Nancy, but their closeness is compelling tears to form in my eyes.

"I have to go." I turn my phone screen back to me. "I can't record them and talk to you at the same time."

"Go!" Pepper overemphasizes, excitement heard in her voice.

After air-blowing her a farewell kiss, I disconnect the call and activate the record function on my phone. The blood pumping through my body thickens with excitement, knowing without a doubt I'm in the process of capturing a unique moment between the starring couple of my next alpha male romance.

Chapter Eleven

"Check the hidden compartment inside your suitcase."

I press my phone nearer to my ear as I saunter to my half-unpacked suitcase in the main suite of my rental cabin. A clink of laughter spills from my lips when I slide open the zipper of the hidden compartment in my bursting-at-the-seams suitcase. "Pepper!" I scoff, my tongue clicking against my teeth. "I think a rodent got into my suitcase on the flight over as most of the material on this *outfit* has been compromised."

"It's supposed to be like that." Just from her tone, I can tell she's rolling her eyes. "It's a crotchless lace teddy."

"Yeah... I worked that out when I noticed the *entire* crotch was missing." I flop onto the bed. "Why in the world did you sneak *that* into my suitcase?"

I turn my eyes to the ceiling when Pepper's contagious laughter barrels down the line. "Because I knew after seven years of dating Riley, that may be the only thing to clear the cobwebs between your legs."

"Thanks for the confidence boost, Pepper."

"Hey, I'm not saying you need any help in being sexy, Paige. You've got that shit covered. But... you've been living the past three years as if you're my mother. It's time to slip out of the granny panties and add a touch of naughtiness to your ensemble. Wearing sexy clothing isn't about how you look in it. It's how you feel while wearing it."

I remain quiet, contemplating what she's saying.

I can't even remember the last time I wore anything remotely sexy, so she could be onto something.

"Besides, that little number will have Hunter tripping over his feet."

"We're *friends*, Pepper," I quote the same saying I've said to myself numerous times over the past several weeks.

"Friends who eat dinner together nearly every night, go skinny-dipping, and plan dates a month in advance. Yeah... *friends*." Pepper's tone is full of sarcasm. "I've never skinny-dipped with a *friend*." My mouth opens in preparation to dispute her claim, but she cuts me off. "College parties don't count. Your dip in the ocean was only with two people. That's a lot more intimate than a bunch of horny college kids doing a naked swim at Lake George."

Unable to negate her claim, I jump up off the bed and walk to the antique dresser in the middle of the room. My friendship with Hunter has been going great guns. Other than his disappearance for three days earlier this week, we've dined together most nights the past three weeks, have watched a range of movies while snuggling on the couch, and he set up some fandangled thingy on my laptop so my manuscripts will automatically store to my iCloud account, meaning I'll never have to worry about losing any work if my laptop goes kaput again.

It's been a great few weeks that has exposed sides of Hunter I didn't know existed even after weeks of stalking him. He's a great guy —kind, funny, and a little moody. I just wish I could learn to control my libido around him. He wants to be friends, and in all honesty, I want the same, but for some absurd reason, anytime he's around, my sexual appetite rushes to the surface like an out-of-control tidal wave.

I'm beyond flabbergasted by my body's reaction to Hunter. He's *nothing* like the men I usually lust over, but a different side of Paige emerges in his presence. I don't know if my newfound personality is a forced change from leaving a seven-year relationship or a revamp I've been endeavoring to undertake the past three years. Either way, I'm loving it. A change is as good as a holiday.

"Silenced by the truth, hey?" Pepper snickers, reminding me I still have my cell attached to my ear. "If Hunter is only your friend, why can I hear you fluffing your hair? And was that your Sisley Phyto-Lip Gloss being opened? You only wear that brand when you want to get *lucky*."

I screw the stick of my Sisley lip gloss back into its container and throw it into my makeup bag. "God. Am I going crazy, Pepper?" I spit out the only logical reason for my sudden shift in personality. "Maybe I'm attracted to Hunter because he's the only guy within a ten-mile radius?"

"Please," Pepper overemphasizes in a thick drawl. "You like him because he's a hot brute of a man with an Adonis ass. It has nothing to do with loneliness." Even though her tone is friendly, it has an edge of bitchiness attached to it.

"Hunter is *nothing* like Riley."

"Exactly!" she interrupts. "That's what makes him even more attractive." The creak of her leather office chair sounds down the line, closely followed by the padding of her tiny feet. "When you see Hunter, does your heart beat faster?"

I bite my lip and nod.

Even though she can't see me, she continues with her quest, intuiting my reply. "Do your palms get a little clammy and your tummy jittery?"

"Yes," I say in barely a whisper. *Every single time I see him.*

"Those things don't happen because you've been hiding away from society in your writing cave penning your next novel. It's because you dig him. Hunter isn't Riley, not even close, but you're assuming it's Hunter who is the odd man out. Are you sure it wasn't Riley all along?"

My brows furrow, baffled by her statement.

"You started dating Riley when you were seventeen. Did you

even know then what your preferences were, or did you alter them to suit the guy shining a light on you?" Pepper questions my silent musing.

I take a minute to consider what she is saying.

"Riley didn't wear a suit until he started working at Leimans," I mumble as the logic of Pepper's statement crashes into me.

Over the seven years I was with Riley, his hair went from a long, wispy style to a short back and sides cut. The stubble on his chin was cleared away, and his clothing selection altered from slacks and printed tees to expensive business suits. But since he was still Riley, I never put much thought into the alteration of his appearance. He was my partner, so I just took it in stride.

"That's right. But for some strange reason, you have it in your head that you're only attracted to business-looking men. If you were to look past Hunter's caveman attire, what would you see?"

I gulp loudly.

"Exactly!" she squeals, scaring the living daylights out of me. "Don't take this the wrong way, as you are in no way ready for a relationship, but that's the brilliance of a friends-with-benefits agreement. You get an award-winning novel, and you may even get your pent-up sexual frustration taken care of."

My nose screws up. "And what does Hunter get out of this?"

Pepper expels a large, frustrated breath. "You, Paige. He gets the pleasure of spending time with a woman as beautiful and as kind-hearted as you."

A misting of fluid hampers my vision. I am pleased as punch by her compliment. After my ego copped a severe pounding last week, her littlest compliment has a huge impact on my faltering esteem.

Before I can respond to Pepper's praise, a knock sounds through my ears. My heart beats triple time when I pop my head into the hallway and discover who is knocking. "I've got to go, Pepper. Hunter is here." Excitement laces my voice.

"Go get him, tiger," she jests.

Her full-hearted chuckle booms down the line when I roar before disconnecting the call. After yanking open the top drawer of the dresser, I ditch the meager scrap of lace material inside before strolling down the hallway. My steps are hurried, surprised by Hunter's impromptu visit. Even though we've hung out numerous times the past three weeks, he's never arrived in the morning before.

"Do you have a dress?" he asks the instant I open the door, not bothering to issue a greeting.

"Hi, Hunter," I retort, my tone jokingly snappy.

He spins on his heels to face me. A grin curls on my lips when he scrubs at his beard. That's a telltale sign that he's nervous. "Sorry. Hello, Paige." His eyes sparkle with candor when he leans in to press a kiss to the edge of my mouth. "Do you have a dress?" he mumbles against my mouth, his beard tickling my lips.

I scrunch up my face and cock my hip. "Not in your size."

Euphoria pumps through my veins when his boisterous chuckle booms into my ears. "Not for me. For you," he retorts between laughter. His cologne I still can't distinguish engulfs me when he stops laughing and takes a step closer to me. "I need your help."

"Okay," I reply without hesitation.

What? It's the neighborly thing to do.

"I need your help in a dress." When I slant my head and stitch my brows, Hunter asks, "If I were to turn up to a high-priced charity function, would I gain unwanted attention?"

I run my eyes over his scruffy jaw, jeans, and plaid shirt-covered body before nodding. Although I've grown accustomed to his unique ruggedly handsome look, the pretentious people who typically attend such events may not appreciate his ruggedness.

"But if I turned up with a beautiful woman on my arm, they'll assume you dragged me there against my wishes, and I'll remain inconspicuous," Hunter continues.

A broad grin stretches across my face, not because his statement is accurate, but because he thinks I'm beautiful.

"That sounds like a great theory, but I don't have a dress," I inform him, cringing.

He stares at me like I just told him I'm not a woman. "You don't have a dress?"

"Nope. I came here to write. You're lucky you see me out of my pajamas." *And with my hair brushed.*

Hunter's sinful mouth curls into a grin.

"But if I have enough time, I could probably rustle something up?" I suggest, eager to do anything to put a smile on his face. My plan works when his grin enlarges to a full, heart-stopping smile. "How fancy?"

Like it could get any bigger, his smile widens even more. "Ten thousand dollars a plate."

My heart fails. "What?" I shake my head, clearing my ears of any congestion to ensure I can hear him properly this time around. "How much?"

"Ten thousand a plate," Hunter repeats.

I swallow the brick in my throat, sending it straight to my swishy tummy. "And how long do I have to prepare for this 10K event?"

"An hour," he states matter-of-factly while curtly nodding.

I double balk. "Are you serious?"

While rubbing his hands together, he nods.

"Well, I guess you better call in a favor from your fancy-schmancy friends to get me a reservation at an overpriced boutique because this doesn't sound like a drop-into-Target-on-the-way type of function."

The smile that etches onto Hunter's face nearly causes me to have a coronary. "Deal." He yanks a smooth black cell phone out of his pocket. His fingers move swiftly over the screen before he squashes it to his ear. "Hey, Cormack, I need a favor," he says into his fancy phone I didn't know he owned.

And just like that, an appointment is made.

Ten minutes later, I've zipped up my half-unpacked suitcase, stored it in the trunk of Hunter's car, and am heading to a dress boutique in the middle of Ravenshoe for an impromptu shopping splurge. This is one of the reasons I love my industry. I can just up and leave on a dime. No excuses needed and no pleading with the boss for time off. Complete control.

My attention shifts from the scenery flying by when the smooth, rich voice of Hunter sounds through my ears.

I crank my neck to peer at him. "Sorry, what did you say? I spaced out a little."

He scrapes his hand along his hairy jaw, making my fingers twitch with envy. "The shopping attendant at On Point Boutique needs to know your cup size." His tone is unwavering, not the slightest bit embarrassed about the sensitivity of his question. "I said a little more than a handful, but for some reason, she doesn't appreciate my candidness."

A feverish heat follows the path his eyes make when they indecently roam my body to gauge not only my cup size but every fine hair on my body as well. When his ardent eyes settle on my face, I cock my brow and return his sweat-impinging showdown. Although our *friendliness* the past few weeks has occasionally stepped over the friendship barrier, he's never taken it this far before.

He must think because we are stuck in traffic and surrounded by cars that he's safe from an attack by a horny writer.

He isn't.

The pegs of his teeth stick out of his bearded face when he asks, "So... what is it? They look like a ten out of ten to me."

I grit my teeth to hide my smile before punching him in the bicep. After mustering a fake snarl, I hold my hand out, requesting his phone. His brash grin enlarges to a shit-eating smile when he secures a device from jeans pocket and hands it to me. My brows furrow when I peer at a small glass bead nestled in my palm. It would be no bigger than half an inch in size.

"Put it in your ear," Hunter instructs to my baffled expression. "It will pick up the vibration of your voice from your inner eardrum."

"So I'll sound like a robot?" I mimic the noises of a robot to enhance my statement.

He chuckles. "No. You'll still sound like you. Trust me."

Grimacing, I place the small bead into my ear. My eyes widen when a nasally female voice shrills down the line, barking orders at someone on the other end.

"Hello," I say, my voice shaky. My heart stops hammering my ribs when my voice sounds eerily similar to how I normally sound, if not more refined. "Umm... Hunter said you needed my cup size?"

The female attendant huffs. "Yes. Due to the *unendurable* short notice we've been given, we will have *no* chance to alter the dress you chose, so we need to ensure we have your correct measurements."

"Okay," I mumble, annoyed at the rudeness in her tone. I cup my hand around my mouth and swivel to face the window. "I'm a B cup," I barely whisper into my hand.

"I'm sorry, I didn't catch that," she replies, her pitch snarky.

I cough to clear my throat. "I'm a B cup," I repeat, slightly louder.

"Nope, still didn't get that."

"B for bonnet," I mutter through clenched teeth.

"You need to talk up."

"I'm a B cup!" I shout, my temper spurred on by the rudeness of her tone.

Because of the loudness of my voice, there's no way in hell Hunter missed my comment.

"Thank you. We will see you in thirty minutes," the boutique assistant snarls before disconnecting the call.

I shake the bead out of my ear. The roughness of my shake matches the grinding of my teeth. The only way that could have been more embarrassing was if I had Hunter pull over and take my chest measurements himself.

My eyes rocket to Hunter when he says, "I don't know how she didn't hear you the first time. It was crystal clear from my end."

I glare at him, more confused than ever. He grins cockily while tapping on his right earlobe. When I look closely, I see the smallest shimmer of a black bead sitting in his ear. "You were eavesdropping on my *private* conversation," I squeal, shock evident in my voice.

He shakes his head. "No. Eavesdropping means I was spying. I wasn't snooping. I was *observing*." His tone is a mix between facetious and factual.

"How can you hear anything with your ear clogged up by a

bead?" I ask in an endeavor to shift the focus of our conversation away from my less-than-stellar chest region.

Hunter purses his lips. "It's no different than a hearing aid. With a microphone on the end, sound waves travel through the amplifier and exit via the speaker. With echo reduction, this device makes everything crystal clear."

"So even if I whispered that you were an asshole under my breath, you'd hear me?" I mumble ever so quietly.

"Yep," he replies with a chuckle.

I roll my eyes and return them to the scenery whizzing by. "Adonis-assed asshole."

"Heard that too."

That was the point, I silently chant to myself.

Twenty minutes later, we pull into a fancy-looking dress shop in the middle of Ravenshoe. Just like the last time I visited this town a few weeks ago, it's a bustling hive of activity. Exhaust fumes linger in the air, and the hum of vigorous activities sounds through my ears. I love the serenity of Bronte's Peak, but if it weren't for Hunter saving me from the solitude, I'd be strapped into a straitjacket by now.

"You're not going to feed the meter?" I ask when he curls out of his car and walks straight past the expired meter.

"Nope," he says with a shake of his head before he pulls open the boutique's heavy glass door for me. "My boss owns this town, so I'm not concerned about getting a ticket."

"Telemarketing my ass," I mumble under my breath while ambling into the opulent surroundings.

Even without his fandangled listening device in his ear, I can be assured Hunter heard my statement because I said it loud enough to ensure he would.

Chapter Twelve

Much to the dismay of Melinda, the dressing hostess from On Point Boutique, I groove out of the dressing room like one of Flo Rida's female entourage, wearing a low-cut dress that shows more of my stomach than my swimwear does.

Just like the movie montage in *Sweet Little Things* with Christina Applegate and Cameron Diaz, I work the immodest dress like it is Julia Roberts's hooker outfit from *Pretty Woman*. While ignoring Melinda's disgruntled snickering, I shake my tushie in front of a wall of mirrors, knowing without a doubt I'd never be caught dead in an outfit as skimpy as this.

Once I've finished checking myself out, I spin around to face Hunter, fully anticipating the thumbs-down signal he's given for the last dozen dresses I've tried on.

Even more shocking than the amount of collagen in Melinda's top lip is discovering his thumb is pointing to the ceiling.

Hold on, make that thumbs.

I cock my hip and glare into Hunter's dilated eyes. "Unless this ten-thousand-dollar-a-plate gala is for the Adult Video Awards in Vegas, I'm not wearing this dress," I snarl out before pacing back to the curtain to try on another dress.

Hunter leaps off the press-studded chaise and hotfoots it after me. "Come on, Paige, take one for the team. If you wear that dress, no man in the room will pay me any attention."

"The men may not, but I'll be the target of every woman in the room." I spin around, soundlessly requesting he release the hook on the hideous *outfit* I'm wearing. "You may as well stick a bullseye on my back to make sure their daggers have something to aim at."

Hunter chuckles as he slides down the zipper of my dress. The simplest of tasks causes a shift in dynamics between us. It's quick and absolute. We've gone from two friends playing hooky from work to feeling like we're about to star in one of the productions crowned winner at the Adult Video Awards.

I clutch the material of the dress to my less-than-stellar cleavage before spinning around to once again face him. My steps are shaky since I'm balancing on wobbly knees. I stare into his eyes, gauging if he can feel the zapping in the air as well.

His eyes are expressive but not enough for me to garner an answer to my silent interrogation. "Tell me you feel something?" I mutter, my voice barely a whisper, no longer able to harbor my need to know if he can feel the energy in the air or if I'm simply going insane from lack of human contact.

All writers are a little bit quirky. Heck, I'm beyond quirky, but I'm still stumped by the vibrancy that sparks the air when I'm in Hunter's presence. I've never felt anything like this. I've read about it but always assumed it was an overly dramatic way to describe two characters' connection. But this isn't just a feeling in my core. It's real, and it is heart-stopping.

Hunter's top lip twinges as his eyes bounce between mine. Just when I think he's going to say something, his eyes drift past my shoulder to the dark emerald-green satin gown hanging in the middle of the monstrously sized dressing room. It has a gorgeous tight cross-over fitted bodice and mermaid tail. Although it's divine, there's no way in hell I'm paying the excessive amount on the price tag for *one* dress. It costs more than all the royalties I've collected from my first novel thus far.

"That one." Hunter's eyes spark with zeal. After pressing his finger to his lips, his fervent gaze turns to Melinda. "We are taking that one."

When he points to the ridiculously overpriced dress, Melinda's eyes flare with excitement. *Obviously, she works off commission.*

Her eagerness doesn't last long when I shake my head. "No. I'm not paying for a dress that costs more than the first car I owned. We will take the azalea guipure-lace illusion dress, but instead of navy blue, I'll take it in cobalt blue and one size smaller." My tone is surprisingly firm, not just spurred on by Melinda's rudeness the past hour but from another brutal rejection by Hunter.

When he attempts an objection, I press my index finger against his lips. "Shut up." I use the same tone he did when he rejected me weeks ago. "I know you didn't like the knee-length skirt, but with the right stiletto heels and a few accessories, it will be a knockout. Trust me."

Not giving him the chance to protest any further, I snap the curtain closed and slip out of the exorbitantly priced stripper dress before sliding back into my stretchy yoga pants and one-shoulder long-sleeve shirt.

Hunter remains quiet as we shadow Melinda out of the dressing room. I vaguely try to pretend I'm not cringing at paying a little over five hundred dollars for a dress. Don't get me wrong, the dress is pretty, but it still isn't worth that price point. The crinkles impeding my forehead deepen when Hunter pulls his wallet out of the back pocket of his jeans when we arrive at the cashier station.

"What are you doing?" I query, my voice snarky.

I need to eat something. I always get a little bitchy when I'm hungry.

His eyes drift between Melinda and me. "Paying for your dress?" His tone is as dubious as his facial expression.

My brows hit my hairline before I ask, "Do I look like a hooker to you?"

My pulse speeds up when his eyes leisurely run the curves of my body. "No. Not a low-end one anyway."

My bitchiness falters from the jaunty gleam in his eyes.

I kick him in the ankle before handing my credit card to a scowling-faced Melinda. "You're *certainly* not Richard Gere, and I'm no Julia Roberts," I mumble under my breath.

From the crass grin that stretches across his face, I can be assured he heard my witty comment.

After gathering my boutique bag from Melinda, I return my credit card to my purse and follow Hunter to his car. The midday sun beaming off the charcoal black coloring gives me a brilliant idea. "I want to drive," I shout, probably a little loud since a little old lady walking by jumps in fright. After issuing an apology to the lady now one step closer to her grave, I lock my eyes with Hunter. "I want to drive your Hellcat. Just the first twenty miles."

"Nope. Not happening," he replies, his tone curt.

I stop my brisk pace to his car and cross my arms in front of my chest. "Then I'm not going to the gala."

"Bullshit," Hunter retorts, not the slightest bit concerned about my threat. "You wouldn't have bought a dress if you weren't planning on coming."

Little does he know acting is another one of my creative arts.

"I can wear that dress to any function," I say, wiping his smug grin right off his face. "Besides, what am I getting out of this deal? I'm helping you out, yet I'm the one being handed the short straw."

I should feel threatened by the glare he's directing at me, but it doesn't hold any heat. The twitching of his lips as he suppresses a smile gives away his true feelings.

"I have to consume food only rabbits should eat and squeeze into a dress two sizes too small so some old geezer can skip his little blue pill for the night. Sounds like a rip-roaring night of fun. *Not.* I'd rather wax my eyebrows and watch re-runs of *Mash.*" I spin on my heels, preparing to walk down the cracked concrete sidewalk. "Bye, Hunter."

My brisk pace halts again when the snappiest "Fine" comes out of a pair of stern-lined lips.

I quickly spin on my heels, not wanting to give him the opportunity to recant his statement. His eyes glare into mine as I span the distance between us. "If you get one scratch on my car—"

"You'll spank my bottom?" I interrupt while grinning a victorious smirk before I snatch the keys out of his hands.

"I'll do far worse than spank your ass, Paige," he rebuts, his tone grumbly.

I munch on my bottom lip, feigning that I'm a little sex fiend who has no qualms about a playful spanking. "Oh, well, in that case," I purr, my voice extra throaty.

Not appreciating my attempts at sarcasm, he snatches the keys back out of my grasp. While doing my best to ignore his noteworthy scent, I balance on my tippy toes and brush my lips on the shell of his earlobe. "I promise I won't scratch your car… unless you want me to?"

* * *

It takes ten miles for Hunter to release the deathly tight grip on his thighs and another twenty miles before his tight jaw loosens. By the time we're fifty miles out of Ravenshoe, the strain encumbering his gorgeous face slackens, and the standard pre-terrified Hunter re-emerges.

I drift my eyes from the road to Hunter. "What's your interest in the charity gala?" Nothing against him, but he doesn't appear to be a charity function type of guy.

He scrapes his hand along his beard as a smirk stretches across his mouth. "What is it with women judging me this week? First Izzy. Now you."

I smile, loving that he can read my real intentions when I've only spoken six little words. "I'm not judging you." I twist my lips to lessen the size of my smile. "Just *clothed,* you don't seem like the type who'd like this kind of event."

His grin enlarges, either smitten by my compliment or agreeing with it. I haven't worked out the difference between his musing smile and his amused one yet. When I catch the impish gleam in his eyes, I know he's taken my ribbing as playful, not bitchy.

"You, of all people, know you should never judge a book by its cover," he quips.

"Ha," I interrupt with a loud shriek. "That's one of the most inaccurate statements in the writing world. Writers are always judged. Too many commas, not enough commas. Too much sex, not enough sex. Too much description, not enough description, and don't even get me started on the cover. Unfortunately, we live in a world full of critics."

"So you judge a person based solely on the clothes they are wearing?" His tone is a cross between curious and blunt.

"Not all the time, but for the majority, yes." *Wow, that even sounded snobbish to me.*

Hunter briefly nods. "So, what was your first opinion of me?"

"You weren't exactly clothed at the time, so it doesn't count."

The grin on his face turns titanic. "So my nakedness did ignite your stalker obsession?"

I swallow the brick that lodged in my throat from rehashing memories of his nakedness before replying, "Not exactly... it was your Adonis ass."

The stranglehold on my throat lessens when Hunter's chuckle booms around the car's interior. "I like you, Paige," he chokes out between laughter.

"Yep. We've already established that." *That's the whole reason you won't touch me.*

With the fire forming in my belly from his idolatrous glare, I wish I had more of a bitch gene. I like Hunter. He's a great guy. But I've never had this type of obsession with a man before. It's consuming my every waking moment.

Maybe it's the thrill of the chase? I've never been turned down before, so I don't have anything to compare it to. Since I was with Riley from the age of seventeen, it was normally me turning away tempting invitations, not inciting them.

My attention reverts from planning ways to make myself less appealing to Hunter when he says, "I'm not in the telemarketing industry."

I stray my eyes from the road to him but remain quiet, leaving my interrogation cap where I removed it weeks ago—on the kitchen counter in my rental cabin.

While keeping his gaze planted straight ahead, he elaborates, "My boss has a very important asset attending the gala tonight. I'm to ensure she remains safe." My pulse quickens when his eyes turn to me. They are full of qualm and worry. "I fucked up last month, and the consequences of my actions could have ended up a lot worse than they did. I'm endeavoring to make it up to my boss, but I can't do that without your help."

An inappropriately timed smile etches onto my face. I do not love that he made a mistake, but I'm delighted he needs my help. "So you work in security?" I keep my tone low, feigning disinterest.

Hunter's lips twist as he hesitantly nods.

"Do you carry a gun?" I flick my eyes between the road and him.

He takes his time figuring a response before he mutters, "Yes."

"Cool," I drawl out extravagantly. "Can I see your pistol?"

When he chuckles, the concern hampering his face fades. "Are we still talking about my gun?"

I sock him one right in the arm. "What happened to us being *friends*?" My playful tone hides my excitement.

Hunter smirks while running his hand over his jaw.

After a short moment of silence, he asks, "So what's your deal, Paige? Why books?" completely ignoring my *friends* reference.

I twist my lips. "Name one other profession where you can talk to the voices in your head and not get thrown into a looney bin?"

His brows bow. "True," he says with a nod, not fazed by my reference I am a little loopy. "I also guess you're an only child?"

"What makes you say that?" I ask through furrowed brows. Although his statement is accurate, I'm interested to find out how he reached his conclusion.

My pulse thrums in my neck when his murky blue eyes lock with mine. "We've been driving for nearly an hour, and you haven't stopped fidgeting. You're either an only child or the youngest member of your family. They always have the ants-in-the-pants type of personality."

"Or maybe I'm just horny," I shoot back, my tone teeming with wit. "And all this squirming isn't to settle the ants in my pants. It's to stop the throbbing your sexy car is causing the lower half of my body do."

Damn! Where did that naughty devil come from?

The beat of my heart merges into dangerous territory when Hunter's thick fingers grasp my nape. I freeze like an ice sculpture when the softness of his beard tickles the shell of my ear. "Just like my cock, you stiffen when you're horny. You fidget when you are excited," he murmurs into my ear ever so confidently.

My eyes stray from the road to him. "How do you know that?"

What he's saying is true. I'm not a person who fidgets when nervous. I only do it when my insides are bursting with excitement. But the instant I step into the bedroom, my confidence falters, right along with my movements.

Time stands still when he mutters, "Because you're not the only one who's been watching, Paige." My breathing returns in shallow pants when he removes his hand from my neck and slots his Adonis ass back into the passenger seat. "There's a gas station a quarter of a mile out. Pull over, and we will swap places," he instructs, seemingly unaffected by our riveting exchange.

With my mouth refusing to articulate speech, I nod.

* * *

Two hours later, we pull into the long driveway of a posh hotel. Although our trip was filled with conversation, we never ventured back over the friends' line Hunter drew in the sand weeks ago.

A grin curls on my lips when a valet opens my door and assists me out. "Welcome to the Wiltshire Hotel, madame," he greets me.

"Thank you," I reply.

After lifting my eyes, I take in the impressive surroundings while shadowing Hunter to the check-in counter. A few dozen people are milling around the expensive-looking checked marble floors and antique furniture. It only takes a matter of seconds for Hunter's attire to gain us the attention of numerous pairs of eyes. Even with the sleeves of his plaid shirt rolled down, the vast collection of tattoos on his hands and the one on the side of his neck are still prominent.

Even being eyeballed like he's a circus act and not a man, Hunter's confidence doesn't falter the slightest. He's so comfortable in his own skin, he doesn't give two hoots about other people's opinions. That's a refreshing change in a world full of judgmental people, and it makes me like him even more.

My eyes bounce between Hunter and the desk clerk when she advises him his room is ready. "Was I supposed to book my own room?" I query, panicked I didn't consider this earlier. I hope the hotel has a vacancy.

"My room is a two-room suite," Hunter advises my baffled expression. "If you don't feel comfortable, I can book you your own suite."

Smiling, I shake my head. "No, it's fine. I'm more than happy to share your suite." My words come out hoarse, strangled with excitement at spending more one-on-one time with him.

"It's a beautiful room," the desk clerk explains while turning her concerned eyes to me. "It has views of the skyline from both rooms, and the doors are *lockable,* so I'm sure you and your *friend* will be very comfortable and *safe.*"

When her eyes return to Hunter, they narrow into tiny slits. While returning the hotel clerk's sneer, he snatches the keycard off the polished counter and makes a beeline to the elevator. Unable to come up with a reply to the hotel clerk's bitterness, I give her the stink eye before shadowing Hunter to the elevator banks.

My jaw slackens when we enter the enormous apartment-size suite two minutes later. "Wowsers, this place is huge," I say, my eyes bugging as big as my mouth.

I grin like a kid in a candy store when Hunter flicks a button on the console at the side, and the blinds covering the windows lift. My jaw drops lower the further the blinds rise. The gorgeous city skyline scatters for as far as my eyes can see. Various size buildings of architectural wonder fill my vision. As the lateness of the evening creeps up on us, smog hovers between the buildings. It's both an eerie and beautiful visual.

My attention diverts from the architectural wonder to Hunter when he says, "I've got to run an errand. Are you okay if I leave you here for an hour?"

I nod. "Sure. What time is the gala?"

A clink of laughter topples from my lips when Hunter pulls up the sleeve of his plaid shirt to check the tattooed Rolex on his wrist. After witnessing the grandeur of his house, car, and now this splendid hotel suite, I have no doubt he could afford a real Rolex if he wanted one, but this way, in his eyes, it's always knock-off time.

"It starts in around an hour." He slides his sleeve back down then locks his eyes with mine. "Your room is the one on the right." He points to a set of double doors. "I'll be back in enough time to get ready before we have to leave."

I stiffen when he presses a quick peck to the side of my mouth, but my rigid posture slackens when the hairs on his top lip tickle my nostrils. *Imagine what it would feel like in more sensitive regions of the body?* My stiff stance resumes.

"I'll see you in a few."

Hunter grins before he spins on his heels and strolls out of the room without a backward glance. I kick off my shoes in the entryway then make my way to my bedroom. My toes dig into the plush carpet when I cross the expansive sunken living area. If I hadn't seen the sign in the elevator advising the presidential suite was located on the top floor, I would have assumed this suite was it. It's massive. Body-hugging sofas are scattered through the living area, thick, luxurious furnishings are draped over the floor-to-ceiling windows, and each piece of furniture looks like it was shipped here directly from France. It's gorgeous.

After lowering the gold-embossed door handle, I swing open the white French door of my room. My breath snags halfway to my lungs when the enormity of the space smashes into me. It isn't just the sheer grandeur of the French-designed room that has my breathing faltering. It is the beautiful emerald-green dress from the boutique store in Ravenshoe carefully strewn across the king-size bed.

My heart beats double-time as I pad across the room. I run my sweat-slicked hands down my legging-covered thighs before snagging a small envelope off the high thread count silk. I catch my lower lip with my teeth when my eyes speedread the card.

Wear this tonight.
Hunter.

My eyes roam over the dress, searching for the price tag. If it still has the tag attached, I could return it and get back the exorbitant four-figure price Hunter paid for it.

A sting of pain inflicts my bottom lip when I fail to locate the price tag, but before I can fully register the pain, my cell phone unexpectedly dings, indicating I have received a text message. Because my leggings don't have any pockets, my phone is tucked into the waistband of my pants, which added to my heart attack status from its unexpected ding.

After gathering my heart off the floor, I yank out my phone and peer down at the screen.

HUNTER:

Don't even think about it. They have a no-return policy.

A ridiculous grin stretches across my face. *How does he already know me so well?*

ME:

I don't have the faintest clue what you're talking about.

The monstrous bed dips when I sit on the edge of it.

HUNTER:

The dress.

I smile.

ME:

Dress? What dress?

He only walked me to the foyer, so I make him sweat a little. That's what he gets for paying a ridiculous amount of money for an article of clothing.

HUNTER:

The one in your room.

ME:

???

HUNTER:

The one you're sitting next to.

My eyes snap to the door. When I fail to locate Hunter, I scramble off the bed and walk back into the living area of the suite. Sweat slicks my skin as excitement overwhelms me.

HUNTER:

Warmer...

I pace deeper into the living room.

HUNTER:

Colder...

Twisting my lips, I change my direction and head for the foyer.

HUNTER:

Warmer...

A broad grin stretches across my face as I quicken my pace.

HUNTER:

Hot…. HOT! Scorching hot!

Laughing, my eyes scope the premises. The smell of freshly cut flowers filters into my nose from the gorgeous bouquet of lilies, roses, and lisianthus on the entryway table. When I stop to admire the beautiful arrangement on the antique rotunda table, my phone vibrates in my hand.

HUNTER:

Bingo.

My heart thwacks against my ribs as my eyes scan the floral arrangement. The beat turns dangerous when I spot the smallest speck of black on one of the lilies' petals. Not long after I screw up my nose, a message arrives on my phone.

HUNTER:

That's not a good look for you.

Holy hell! Is that a camera?

My eyes rocket between the floral bouquet and my bedroom door. The camera is facing the wrong way, so there's no way he could have seen me sitting on my bed from this angle. I stiffen, and my pupils widen as an improper thought pops into my head.

As I type out a message on my phone, my teeth grit.

ME:

Did you put a camera in my room???

My face reddens as anger envelops me. The living hell is scared out of me for a second time when my cell phone suddenly rings.

After exhaling a calming breath, I hit the call button and press it to my ear.

"Who's the voyeur in this *friendship*?" Hunter's rich chocolatey voice sounds down the line.

I glare at the tiny camera attached to the bouquet while snarling,

"Voyeurism and being a peeping Tom are two completely separate entities. Believe me, I've researched them both."

Hunter laughs. "Don't believe everything Google tells you, Paige. Most of the stuff on there is fiction, not fact."

"I don't believe everything I read, Hunter." I draw out his name as he had done to mine. "But even a noob knows you can't photograph someone without their consent."

"Ah... that's where you are *very* wrong. I've not only informed you that you're under surveillance, but the device is also not in a public place or a restroom, so I'm free to invade your privacy as much as I see fit."

"See this." I yank the small black device off the petal and throw it into a bin at my side.

My brazenness freezes when Hunter's growl sounds down the line. "You're even sexier when you're angry."

Frozen from the sexy ruggedness of his voice, my eyes shoot in all directions, searching for more camera devices.

My eyes slant when he says, "You'll never find them all."

Gritting my teeth, I disconnect the call and switch off my phone. You'd think my first reaction would be to grab my bag and request another room, or better yet, the first flight home, but for some reason, unbeknown to me, my feet remain firmly planted on the floor.

It may be imprudent of me, but I already trust Hunter, so I don't believe he'd ever purposely set out to hurt me, let alone spy on me.

I suffer my third coronary failure of the day when the smooth richness of Hunter's voice sounds out of my switched-off phone speaker mere seconds later. "If you don't want me to see you naked, close your bedroom door. The cameras are only in the living areas."

I slide my index finger across my phone's screen, ensuring it's turned off.

It is.

"Then how could you see I was sitting on the bed?" My voice is rickety, confused about how he can talk to me using a switched-off phone.

"Your image was reflecting from the mirror hanging in the entryway."

My eyes rocket to the large gold-embossed mirror hanging in the elegant foyer. The quickening of my pulse settles when I see the emerald-green dress lying on the bed in its reflection.

My bewildered eyes shift back down to my phone when Hunter says, "Paige?"

"Yes," I reply, my voice croaky.

"Stop biting your lip. You're making my teeth jealous."

I release my bottom lip from my menacing teeth as I stare at my phone, incredulous that this is happening. "Who the hell are you?" I barely whisper.

"I'm the man your momma warned you about," he mutters before a click sounds down the line.

"Hello... Hunter?"

When he fails to answer, I dump my phone onto the entryway table and sweep my eyes around the room. My heart is hammering against my ribs, and a fine layer of sweat is misting my skin, but even beyond baffled, I'm also incredibly thrilled. I've never had this absurd amount of excitement thickening my blood before. I feel like an entirely different person around Hunter. I'm not the highly-educated and well-spoken daughter of a much-respected pillar of the community. Nor am I the trophy fiancée on the arm of a cutthroat businessman who only speaks when spoken to and never airs her political objections in public. For the first time, I'm just me. Paige, the quirky novelist.

Squealing, I charge across the monstrous living room and dive onto the enormous bed. The thickness of the fluffy duvet swallows me whole, swamping me with its heavenliness that's nearly as soft as Hunter's beard.

I turn my eyes to the ceiling to silently ponder.

After ten minutes of musing, I reach the same conclusion over and over again.

I may not know who the real Hunter Kane is, but for the moment, I don't care.

Chapter Thirteen

After telling myself to relax, I release a big breath then flutter my eyes open. The dress is worth every penny just for the way it hugs me in all the right places. The ruched bodice and built-in bra make my less-than-stellar breasts pop, and the fan of the skirt hides my less-desirable assets. Today isn't the first time I've dressed up in a lovely gown, but it's the first time I've wanted to.

Leaning over, I snag a few extra bobby pins from the dresser and pin back a wayward tress of hair that has fallen from my side-swept hairstyle. My lips are a vibrant red, and my eyes have been done with a thick coat of eyeliner and mascara. The darkness gives me the alluring, sex-kitten look I was aiming for while also being classy.

I smile while wondering what Hunter's reaction will be when he sees me. I'm a far cry from the sweatpants-wearing novelist he's used to seeing. My pulse leaps with excitement when a tap sounds on the wooden door of my room. After checking my lipstick in the mirror and ensuring my wavy hair has been wrangled into smooth, glossy locks, I head for the door.

The inane smile stretched across my face dampens when my eyes lock in on Hunter. I cock my hip, wordlessly demanding the focus of his eyes, which are absorbing every inch of my skin. When they finally lock with mine, I observe, "I'm wearing a dress that cost more than my first car, and you're wearing *that?*"

My eyes lower to absorb his long-sleeve button-up shirt and stiff jeans. I appreciate that he at least went to the effort of changing his plaid shirt to a dress shirt, but he isn't even close to being dressed as formally as I am. I look like Cinderella about to attend the ball. He looks like he's a college student heading to a Cold Play concert.

Upon catching my non-amused glare, he scrapes his hand along his jaw then shrugs. "I don't own a suit."

"Then go buy one." I wave my hand around the elegant surroundings. "I'm sure you can afford it."

A spark ignites in his eyes, but he remains as quiet as a graveyard at midnight.

"If I have to wear this get up, so do you," I respond to his silence. After spinning him on his heels, I nudge him toward the door. "Go down to the lobby and ask the concierge for directions to the nearest suit store. I'll grab my purse and meet you at the taxi stand out front."

"It's eight o'clock on a Saturday, Paige. All the shops are closed," he argues.

As my brisk pace halts, I suck in numerous deep breaths while my muddled brain tries to think of a solution to our situation. It wouldn't matter if I wore more diamonds than Elizabeth Taylor owned in her lifetime. If I turn up to a ten-thousand-dollar-a-plate function with Hunter dressed how he is, he will gain the attention of everyone in the room. Considering his rationalization for bringing me here was to ensure he remained incognito, he needs to wear a suit. There is no other viable option.

"You need to wear a suit," I explain as kindly as possible. I love that Hunter is who he is, but if he wants to fix the mistakes he made with his boss, he needs to do this. "If you want to make things right with your boss, you need to look the part."

"I don't own a suit." He stares into my eyes so I can see the truth in his statement.

"Can you borrow one?" I suggest while returning his sweat-producing stare.

After smiling a traffic-stopping grin, he nods.

Ten minutes later, we enter the presidential suite. My breath hitches when he enters the suite without bothering to knock. I'm at a complete loss for words when my eyes take in the grandeur of the room. I thought the views were spectacular from Hunter's suite, but these are ten times better.

My dress swishes on the pristine marble tiles as I shadow him deeper into the suite. Three large plush leather sofas line the space of the sunken living room. A baby grand piano sits in one corner, and a crystal bar is in the opposite one. The suite screams of wealth and superiority.

The heels on my stilettos snag in the thick carpet when we step into the sunken living area. When we round the corner, my leisured pace comes to a complete halt. Standing in the corner of the room, talking on a cell phone is the dark and mysterious stranger I spied on in Hunter's glass house three days ago.

When he notices Hunter and me approaching, the alluring stranger finalizes his call and places his cell into the breast pocket of his suit jacket. In contrast to Hunter, he looks dressed to impress in a full black tuxedo, white dress shirt, and bowtie.

My eyes rocket to Hunter when he asks, "Hey, boss, can I borrow a suit?"

So this is Hunter's boss?

Hunter's boss arches his brow and peers at Hunter in shock. My heartbeat quickens when an ostentatious smirk etches on his mouth before he nods. After gesturing his hand to a set of double doors on the other side of the suite, he says, "Help yourself to anything you like."

Hunter's brows bow. "Don't even think about it." His tone is laced with cheekiness. "After tonight, you won't catch me in a suit *ever* again." While ignoring the jeering look stretching across his boss's face, he shifts on his feet to face me. "I'll be back in a minute."

I smile and nod, relieved he's finally accepted there's no other viable attire for him tonight than a suit. When he struts into the room, his boss moves to stand in front of me. The smell of expensive cologne smacks into me. Unlike Hunter, I can recognize his scent. Clive Christian 1872.

He offers me his hand to shake. "Isaac Holt."

"Paige," I introduce before accepting his handshake.

Isaac is gorgeous in a dark and mysterious way. His eyes are dark gray in color, and his hair is thick and luxurious. I smile when I notice he has a cleft chin hiding behind a few days of stubble.

I've always wanted to pen a book with a male lead who has a dimple in his chin.

"How do you know Hunter?"

Isaac strides to a crystal bar set up in the room's corner. After pouring himself a generous helping of whiskey, he dips the tumbler toward me.

I wave my hand in front of my body, denying his offer of a whiskey before answering, "I'm his neighbor."

A smirk etches on Isaac's mouth before he downs the generous helping of whiskey in one hit. After running the back of his hand across his lips, he questions, "You're the tenant staying in my cabin?"

My eyes balk with surprise. "You own the cabin?"

He smirks while pouring himself another whiskey. "Yes. I own most of the houses in that gated community."

From the way he carries himself and the aura of wealth permeating from him, I'm not astonished by his admission. "Do you own Hunter's residence as well?" I ask curiously.

"No." He places the decanter of whiskey onto the bar and ambles closer to me. "Don't let Hunter's appearance deceive you, Paige. Under his ruggedness is a man with a brilliant mind and even sharper ethics."

"Then why do you have him working your security? Why not put his brilliant mind to good use?" I blurt out before my brain can cite an objection.

Just from Isaac's demeanor alone, I know he isn't a man I should spar against, but I'm curious as to why he'd say Hunter is a brilliant man but then only use him as a protective detail. Let alone the fact Isaac doesn't seem like the type of man who requires the aid of a bodyguard. He looks more than capable of taking care of himself.

"Hunter told you he works for me?" Isaac's brow is arched, and his words are clipped.

After swallowing to relieve my parched throat, I nod.

Isaac huffs, seemingly stunned Hunter shared that information with me, but before he can configure a response, Hunter strides back into the room. Every limb in my body becomes immobile as he spans the distance between the master suite and the sunken lounge. When his murky blue eyes lift from securing the button on the cuff of his midnight black suit, an asinine grin tugs on his lips, no doubt loving my muted reaction.

I'm speechless and utterly flabbergasted, unable to relay the core-crunching visual in front of me. My body slicks with sweat as a frenetic rush of desire swamps the lower regions of my body. The suit he chose to wear fits him like it was tailored specifically for his body shape. The darkness of the crisp blue dress shirt makes his eyes more effervescent, and the cut lines of the luxurious fabric showcase his body as if he were standing before me naked as the day he was born.

It's a riveting visual, and it has my heart racing.

Hunter winks cockily as he glides past me to join Isaac by the bar. I stand frozen at the side of the living room, muted by rampant horniness. Isaac's eyes flick to me, glaring at me and my awkwardness for several uncomfortable seconds before he turns his gaze back to Hunter. I'd normally respond to an inquisitive stare, but I'm too stunned at the desire coursing through my veins to form words.

Blood floods my heart when Hunter says, "She's okay. You can speak in front of Paige. I trust her."

I smile, beyond pleased I'm not the only one who's issued the trust card so early in our newly formed friendship.

Isaac curtly nods. "Although my empire has contributed a significant amount of money to this foundation, my focus is not on business tonight."

"You're going in for Izzy," Hunter intuits.

"Yes," Isaac answers. "Hugo has advised she's en route. Even though she will be in my sight at all times, I still want eyes surrounding her. Until we know who is following her, everyone around her is to be treated as a threat."

"I understand," Hunter replies with a nod. "Unfortunately, the hotel the gala is being held at has top-notch security. I can only access the data center from the server in their security office. Once I infiltrate their system, I'll have complete access to their security feeds and monitoring stations. Anyone arriving or leaving will be caught."

Relief fills Isaac's expressive eyes. "Good."

My expression changes from curious to excited. When Hunter said he worked in security, my first thoughts drifted to Kevin Costner in *The Bodyguard*. But the mention of servers and other computer gobbledygook I've never understood makes his job sound a lot more integral than merely protecting an asset from overzealous fans. It has my interests immensely piqued on exactly what he does for a living.

My eyes stray from the ground to Hunter when he says, "I also have an extra set of eyes that have agreed to help me tonight."

My heart beats triple time when he swings his eyes to me and smiles. Giddiness clusters my brain as I return his smile.

"Okay. Good." Isaac's tone is slightly reserved as his eyes bounce between Hunter and me. "Then let's head out. I want to arrive before Isabelle."

With a nod, Hunter encloses his hand around mine then guides us back into the elegant hallway. My excited fidgeting becomes distracting when we enter the elevator behind Isaac. I've never had so much energy coursing through me.

"Stop fidgeting," Hunter mutters while ushering me to the back of the elevator.

Leaning in close to his side, I mumble, "I can't help it. I'm too excited."

I bounce on my heels as my eyes drift between the elegantly dressed men and women in the car with us. Even with the dense aroma of wealth hampering my senses, eagerness beams out of me.

The tick impinging Hunter's jaw gains intensity when he catches the curious glare Isaac is directing at me. His brows are furrowed. He appears utterly baffled. I can understand why. I'm sure I look like an absolute twit.

Hunter and Isaac's moods are somber and brooding, whereas I have a gigantic smile stretched across my face, and my eyes are full and bright. The intrigue, mystery, and vibrancy are too much for me to handle. I have more storylines swirling in my mind than I've ever had. If I didn't have the curious eyes of Hunter and Isaac eyeballing my every move, I would have whipped out my phone and jotted down some notes, but not wanting to encourage more curious rubber-neckers, I keep my cell in my clutch and my eyes straight ahead.

After lessening the size of my smile, I inwardly battle to get my childish antics under control. My fidgeting only halts when a warm hand heats the skin high on the back of my thigh. All cogent thoughts disappear when it glides up the silkiness of my dress, stopping once it hits the curve of my backside. A breathless moan ripples through my O-formed mouth when my ass cheek is squeezed by a rough hand. It kneads away my giddiness and replaces it with rampant horniness.

While keeping my head facing the front of the packed car, I shift my eyes to Hunter. He's also facing forward, seemingly unaware of the sweat-forming friskiness happening right next to him, but the gleam in his eyes and the twitching of his top lip leaves me no doubt that it is his hand feeling up my backside.

"I thought you wanted us to be friends?" The tremble of my voice shamefully exposes my excitement to his tease.

"We *are* friends, Paige," Hunter replies with his eyes planted straight ahead.

"So groping my ass is your idea of friendship?" I strangle out quietly, shocked I can articulate speech. Usually, it isn't just my body that freezes during sexual contact. My words fail as well.

I grimace when the lady standing next to me takes a step forward. *Obviously, my quiet declaration wasn't that quiet.* Then I freeze like a statue when Hunter's fingers dip lower, inching closer to the one region of my body that's paying careful attention to every movement he makes.

The heat in the car turns rife, and it feels like the walls are closing in on me when he continues his endeavor of ceasing my childish fidgeting. Through heavy pants, my eyes drink in Hunter's handsome face. I have no idea how he's maintaining his calm, cool demeanor. The slickness that coated my panties when he walked out of the suite wearing a tailored suit has doubled, and my throat is hoarse from the blazing heat warming my body. I'm an utter wreck.

"All this to stop me fidgeting?" I choke out, my voice strangled by arousal.

The corners of Hunter's lips tug higher. "That, and the fact I couldn't resist seeing if your ass felt as good as it looks in that dress." The exultant smirk curving my mouth turns into a full grin when he mutters under his breath, "It does."

My attention sidetracks from his teasing hands when the elevator dings, announcing we've arrived at the lobby. As a congregation of people exit and enter the elevator, I stand still, frozen in place with desire. If Hunter didn't relinquish my bottom from his magic hand, I would have spent the remainder of my night riding the elevator. That ride was more enthralling than any rollercoaster I've ever been on.

The trip to the gala is made in complete silence, my mind too baffled to configure speech. The confusion about my friendship with Hunter has reached a level of weirdness even someone as quirky as me can't comprehend. Hunter is giving me different signals, left, right, and center. He pulls out the friend card but then lavishes me with more attention than Riley ever gave me. He denies my advances but then gets friendly with my backside in an elevator full of strangers.

He's confusing the heck out of me.

By the time we arrive at the hotel thirty minutes later, my excited fidgeting returns, although not as paramount as it was earlier. It is still weighed down by the lust thickening my blood from Hunter's earlier tease. After a quiet word with Isaac, Hunter crooks out his elbow in offering.

See? Mixed signals.

Smiling to mask my confusion, I accept his offer. Excitement sparks my veins, but I ignore the wooziness his touch caused to my brain as I glide into the hotel foyer. The aroma of overpriced champagne lingers in the air as he guides us into the heavily populated space housing hundreds of well-dressed patrons.

Just as Hunter predicted, numerous gala attendees turn their eyes to him when he graces them with his presence. Once their judgmental eyes finish assessing him in great detail, they study me with just as much depth.

Although most of the eyes he gained are from snobbish, prudish people, a handful of the women's gazes don't loiter on him because of his tattooed hands and rugged appearance. They appreciate the core-tightening view.

I can't blame them. There's nothing as sexually stimulating as a stealthy brute of a man in a refined suit. Hunter's aura no doubt implies he's a man of great stamina, but his eyes expose his true self. Underneath his rugged appearance is a soul worth exploring. *A soul I plan on unearthing.*

"I told you..." Hunter leans in close to my side, "... they're either assuming you're a little rich girl who is out to make Daddy mad, or I'm some rich schmuck with a trophy wife on his arm."

"So which one am I? Rich bitch with Daddy issues, or money-hungry trophy wife?" I jest, trying to lighten the somber mood encroaching our intimate gathering.

His eyes swoop down to mine. "Yeah... I'm not falling for that one." He guides us to the corner of the room. "No matter which way I answer, I'd be digging my own grave."

I elbow him in the ribs but don't bother refuting his statement since it was acutely accurate. When we reach a small alcove in the corner of the space, Hunter relinquishes me from his side. While holding back the whine his loss of contact compelled, I eye him curiously. He digs his hand into the breast pocket of his suit jacket and produces a diamante-encrusted black satin mask.

"It's a masked gala," he explains before spinning his finger, wordlessly requesting me to turn around.

Excitement thickens my blood when I twirl around as requested.

After tucking a stray tress of hair behind my ear, Hunter slips the mask in front of my eyes and fastens the straps at the back of my head. I smile when I feel the heat of his body on the smooth coolness of the satin material.

Once the mask is secured, I spin back around to face him. I wobble in my stilettos halfway around. He also put on a mask similar to mine, minus the diamantes. The blackness of the mask on his already concealed face makes his blue eyes even more sharp-witted and bright.

My grin tugs higher when I remove a frayed strand of silk off his cheek, and his muscles twitch in response to my touch.

Maybe he's a sexual fidgeter?

The twitch impinging his cheek grows when he slips his hand into the pocket of his trousers and produces a silver necklace. The chain is so thin, it's nearly invisible, but the gorgeous murky emerald-green stone clasped in the middle of a twisted silver design is mesmerizing.

Warmth glows on my cheeks when he places the pendant on the curve of my pushed-up breasts before fastening the clasps at the nape of my neck. His citrus-smelling mouth fans my lips when he says, "There you go," under his breath.

I'm honestly at a loss for words. Not just at his generosity, but the way he instills it—no fanfare, no groveling, not even a jewelry box. He just presents it as if he placed a vending machine prize around my neck and not a precious gem.

"Thank you." I adjust the pendant so it sits in the middle of my chest. "It's breathtaking."

My words come out weak, strangled by emotions. I'm not used to being awarded gifts without a penance attached to them. If I were smart, I would have realized sooner why Riley always arrived home from weekend meetings with a gift in tow.

"You're welcome." Hunter cups my jaw to lift my downcast head. "It's a necklace, Paige, not an engagement ring."

"Yeah, but with the dress, you don't think it's all a little too much?"

"No." He shakes his head. "But if it makes you feel better, you can class it as a partial payment for your *services* tonight." His voice is jam-packed with sexual innuendo.

When I kick him in the ankle, he chuckles a full-hearted laugh.

There's no sexier sound in the world than Hunter's chocolatey-smooth chuckle.

Chapter Fourteen

"If they would just leave their post for twenty seconds, I'd be set," Hunter grumbles.

We've spent the last thirty minutes in the opulent foyer of the hotel, waiting for two security officers to move away from the only door housing the server room for the hotel security. I've downed four Long Island iced teas during the sweat-mustache-producing surveillance. I needed something in my hands to stop my fidgeting. Now, I'm more jittery from the alcohol pumping in my veins than euphoric.

"We have to do something." I slide off the barstool. "Because they look settled in for the night, and I've reached my quota on iced tea." My voice slightly slurs, exposing the truth of my statement.

I yank Hunter off the barstool by the lapels of his suit. His delicious aftershave swamps my senses, adding to the giddiness clustering my brain and twisting my stomach. Once I have the lapels of his suit jacket smoothed back where they're supposed to be, I lock my eyes with his amused gaze. A smug smirk is etched on his face. Even hidden under a beastly beard, his smile makes my knees weak and my panties moist.

As his eyes bounce between mine, the grin on his face turns

mocking, no doubt perceiving what has instigated my recent bout of stiltedness. Hunter isn't reserved or shy, which isn't surprising. A man with his stamina requires a sense of assertiveness and dominance. If he lacked either of those, the skills I witnessed many times in my first six weeks at Bronte's Peak wouldn't have been as fire-sparking as they were.

The twisting of my stomach winds up to the base of my throat. Before Hunter and I became friends, his *liaisons* never bothered me. Now they sting a little. Not at all similar to the heartbroken angst Riley pummeled me with, but the sting of a paper cut—small but still painful enough to feel.

"Paige," Hunter mutters, his tone flat like he can sense where my thoughts drifted to without a word spilling from my lips.

He's so much like Pepper.

He doesn't know about Riley, but I may have been a little snarky to him last week about his *numerous* female companions. I didn't mean to get snippy at him, but with it being that time of the month, the occasional bitchy comment slipped from my lips before I had a chance to rationalize my jealousy. Thankfully, Hunter took my snide remarks in stride by completely ignoring them or changing the course of our conversation, but only now am I wondering if my bitterness is why I haven't seen any visitors at his place the past few weeks?

Ignoring the outlandish beat of my heart, I return Hunter's flirty smile before saying, "I'll give you thirty seconds, but any longer than that, you're on your own."

Feeling brazen from the buzz of alcohol warming my blood, I press a kiss to the side of his mouth before sauntering away from him.

I don't need to turn around to know his eyes are on me. I can feel it in my bones.

With a vivacious smirk, I greet the security officers guarding the door as I saunter by with an extra swing to my hips. I roll back my shoulders, hoisting my bosoms out further. Their small size is at least two cups bigger, thanks to the aid of a strapless silicone-padded bra.

I inwardly cheer when my prance gains me the two extra sets of eyes I was endeavoring to secure. Just as I reach the middle of the foyer, I inhale a nerve-cleansing breath before throwing my arm up to my forehead and collapsing to the ground.

Half of the grimace crossing my face is thanks to the acting classes Pepper dragged me to during our college years, but the other half is from the rigid hardness of the marble floor.

I think I'll be sporting a bruise for that effort in the morning.

Stomping feet boom into my ears as the security officers and Hunter rush toward me. I lock my eyes with Hunter and squint before inconspicuously nudging my head to the security office the guards just left unattended. When a smirk peeks out from beneath his newly trimmed beard, I switch my small whimpers to a pained howl.

Upon hearing my devastating sobs, the security officers increase their already brisk pace, whereas Hunter slips into the office undetected.

"Oh dear, they must have over-polished the floor," I sob, my voice as pathetic as my excuse for falling on the world's most level surface.

The security guards fuss over me and request I remain on the floor as they call in assistance from the medical team on the radios strapped to their shoulders. I continue with my over-the-top performance for nearly thirty seconds, giving it my all. I even manage to pick up a southern accent I've never had merely to increase the authenticity of my Oscar-worthy performance.

Just as I've finished giving the security officers a rundown of my clumsiness the past twelve months, Hunter emerges from the security office. The smile on his face when he taps two fingers on the breast pocket of his jacket is the largest I've ever seen. After jerking his head to the ballroom entrance at my nine o'clock, he returns to his original station at the bar.

"Stay on the ground, honey. We have confirmation the medic is close by," one of the security officers with gorgeous dark skin says when I scurry onto my hands and knees.

"Oh, I'm fine. It was just a little tumble." I scamper to my feet, which is no easy feat in a dress that weighs nearly as much as I do. "See." I step forward three paces before spinning around and sauntering back. "I'm perfectly fine. It must have been all the wonderful help you fine gentleman issued. How could I possibly thank you?"

The cheeks of the second officer with pasty white skin and rich hazel eyes turn a shade of pink, but I don't give him the chance to issue whatever reward he's formulated in his wicked mind when I say, "I'll be sure to fill in a guest comment card at the reception desk for the pleasing service I have received before leaving this evening." My southern accent is still in full effect.

While sweating like a pig on a stick, I make a beeline for the double doors of the ballroom the fundraiser is being held in. A blast of fresh air from the over-door air conditioning gives my sweat-slicked skin a small moment of reprieve as I glide into the room. My eyes shoot in all directions, eager to absorb the grandeur of the space. Mirrored balls, crystal vases, and black long-stemmed roses give the room a sleek, masculine appearance.

The squeal rippling from my lips is only just heard over Rhianna's song "Love on the Brain" being played over the speakers when my elbow is suddenly grasped. After muttering an apology for scaring me to death, Hunter guides me toward a set of concealed doors on my left.

On our journey, I catch the quickest glimpse of Isaac dancing in the middle of the dance floor with the beautiful brunette I saw at Hunter's house earlier this week.

Once we enter the room, Hunter pulls down two white catering chairs from a wooden tabletop, removes his suit jacket, and dumps a hemp bag I didn't realize he was carrying until now onto the table.

"Where were you hiding that?" I ask while watching him set up a mini surveillance site.

He takes a seat behind a clunky-looking laptop. "I had a contact in reception hold it for me." He removes his mask before his luminous eyes lift from the monitor to me. "How many chips will that riveting performance cost me?"

I nudge him with my hip. "Ask me after the bruise on my ass heals."

He chuckles before turning his eyes back to the computer, where his fingers move across the flat silicon keyboard at lightning speed. I watch him carefully, categorizing every expression that crosses his face as he merges into a world I've never seen him in before.

Now I understand what Isaac meant about not letting Hunter's outward appearance deceive me. He's in his element, and it's a spellbinding visual. In minutes, he has a state-of-the-art security monitoring station set up on the catering table. All the attendees mingling at the gala or within the hotel have their faces captured, even the couple getting a little handsy in elevator number six.

"They are a cute couple." I wave my hand to an image in the corner of one of the screens capturing Isaac and his female date. "Is she the asset you were referring to earlier?"

Hunter nods. "Yes, that's Izzy. Isaac's Aphrodite."

"So who is Isaac? Hephaestus, Aries, or Adonis?"

He smirks. "You studied Greek mythology?"

I screw up my nose. "Not really. I attended a handful of lectures while waiting for the creative writing class to have an open seat my first semester in college. It wasn't my thing."

Hunter laughs again, but his focus remains arrested on the computer monitors. I'm shocked he can maintain a conversation while working. I've never been able to work and communicate at the same time. More often than not I found myself typing the conversation around me instead of the scene my characters were acting out.

"Isaac would like to say he's Poseidon, the ultimate protector, but I'd say he's Aries, her one true love," Hunter says after a short stint of musing.

My mouth gapes, surprised by his extensive knowledge. "Greek mythology major?"

"Nope." He shakes his head at my arched brow. "I just have a bad habit of reading something once and never forgetting it."

I giggle while nudging his broad shoulder with my elbow, assuming he's pulling the wool over my eyes. It's only when he locks his truth-bearing eyes with mine do I realize he's being serious.

"You remember everything you read?" Disbelief taints my voice.

Hunter's lips tug higher in one corner as he nods.

"How many floors are there at the hotel we are staying at?"

"Sixty-eight," he answers without delay. "The pool, gym, and sauna are located on the twelfth floor, and there was a pamphlet for a Thai restaurant at 1917 Markwell Street sitting on the entryway table of the presidential suite when we entered."

My mouth gapes. "What was the hotel check-in clerk's name?"

"Mischa."

My lips twist. I wasn't paying much attention when we checked in, so I have no way of gauging his accuracy.

"Did you want to dance?"

His eyes rocket between mine, and astonishment from the sudden change in conversation is evident all over his face. Since I've secured his devotion, I snatch the piece of paper sitting next to his silicon keyboard and hold it close to my chest.

"What's the first sentence of this document?" I ensure my hands are covering the document from both sides just in case the paper is see-through.

Hunter's lips quirk as he stares into my musing eyes. "I can't answer that."

The rough grittiness of his voice sets my pulse racing, but it won't stop me from saying, "Ha! Proof you were telling porkies!" My loud voice booms around the room.

My earlier dizziness comes rushing back to the surface when his cloudy blue eyes stare steadfastly into mine. Even having a mask covering most of my face, I feel exposed, almost naked from his greedy gaze. "I can't answer... as there are no words on that paper. It's all code."

I furrow my brows together before I sneakily pull the paper away from my chest.

The groove in the middle of my forehead deepens when Hunter recites, "55321667A2245B."

It is the exact code on the first line of the document.

I place the paper onto his makeshift desk. "That's cool and a little bit freaky."

"Kind of like you penning a novel about a bearded billionaire living in a crystal house?"

I cringe, but my panic is kept at bay when I realize he doesn't seem the slightest bit angry. "You know about Archer?" My voice is scratchy, hampered by the barrel of emotions pummeling into me at once.

He smiles before nodding.

"And you're not angry?"

"No, Paige. I'm not angry. Although the billionaire title is a *slight* exaggeration," he replies with a chuckle.

My mouth gapes further. "What the hell is wrong with you? I'd be beyond pissed if I discovered someone was invading my privacy."

"I live my life as an open book." Hunter's tone isn't hindered by the slightest bit of anger.

I cross my arms in front of my chest, faking annoyance. "Then why did you give me the telemarketing line the first day we met?"

"I live my life as an open book. He doesn't." He nudges his head to Isaac and Izzy floating across the computer monitor as they move toward a set of double doors similar to the ones we're hiding behind.

Too shocked by his latest revelation to remain standing, I take the spare seat next to him and watch him work in silence. Although I am surprised by his admission, I'm not totally stunned by it. Hunter has been nothing but forthright the past few weeks. He has the type of personality that people are either drawn to or repelled by. Grouchy Hunter scares me, but frank Hunter sucks me right into the Hunter vortex. He should come with a warning because once you've been swept into the Hunter vortex, there's no possibility of breaking free.

"Where are they going?" I ask when Isaac and Izzy slip behind a set of doors.

Hunter doesn't need to reply. The crass grin stretching across his face is all the answer I need.

My pulse quickens, surprised by their audacity to get *friendly* in a public place.

"Is Izzy really in danger or is Isaac being overcautious?" My voice is weak, strained by excitement.

Hunter's lips twist. "I wish he was."

"Is it your job to protect her?"

"For now, yes, it's my main priority."

"Sounds like an exciting job?" I'm an outsider to this uniquely dynamic group, but my heart is still hammering my ribs.

"It is, for the most part," he answers, his tone reserved.

I eyeball him, silently demanding further explanation.

"I like the parts where I'm not forced to wear a suit," he explains, unamused. "Isaac has been trying to get me into a monkey suit for years."

"Well, I think you look very handsome," I add an extra dose of sugar to my voice. "You look an intriguing mix of mountaineer and—"

"I look like Wolverine stuffed in a suit."

"Exactly! What woman doesn't want a rough and rugged Hugh Jackman in a suit? Roar!"

His laughter bellows over the music streaming through the double doors.

A small stretch of silence crosses between us. It isn't awkward or stuffy. I just don't feel the need to fill the void with noise.

After a few more minutes of quiet, I nudge him with my elbow. "You never answered my initial question."

"Which one?"

From the gleam in his eyes, I know he's acutely aware of which question I'm referring to, but feeling playful, I play along with his little ruse. "Did you want to dan—"

"No," Hunter interjects before the whole sentence spills from my lips.

"Why not?" I shoot back.

His brows bow. "Because I don't dance. Period." He sounds disgusted that I even suggested it.

"We can dance in here where no one will see us," I suggest with a shrug.

"No."

"Hunter—"

"No, Paige."

"Dancing is just like sex, you just keep your clothes on," I continue to argue.

"No, Paige."

"I've seen you move your hips. You could totally work it on the dance floor."

"Paige," Hunter drawls out in a long angry snarl, his frantic pace on the keyboard halting. "I don't dance."

I huff and cross my arms in front of my chest, hoisting my small bosoms higher. He's discreet, but I don't miss his quick glance at my chest region. My insides sigh from his adroit glimpse.

When his eyes return to my face, his thumb twangs my lower lip. "Suck your lip back in. Pouting isn't sexy when you're..." He stops talking, and his face screws up. After a brief shake of his head, he turns his attention back to the computer monitor.

I watch him in silence, confused as to why he stopped midsentence.

Then it dawns on me.

He doesn't know how old I am.

Smiling at the memories of the time I asked him his age, I mumble. "I'm twenty-five."

Hunter peers up at me. "What?"

"I'm twenty-five, a Virgo, love long walks on the beach, and have no siblings." I lock my eyes with his amused gaze. "I think that about covers it. Unless you have any other questions you want me to answer?"

"Only one," he replies, which shocks the contemptuous look right off my face. "What's your opinion on going undercover?"

My eyes widen until they're nearly as large as my mouth.

* * *

"So all I have to do is walk around the room?"

"Yes." Hunter adjusts my hair so the bead in my ear is concealed. "I'll keep in contact with you by the listening device. If you think

126

someone is acting suspicious or you feel uncomfortable, scratch your right collarbone, and I'll move in."

"Should I be concerned for my safety?" I question after swallowing a lump in my throat.

He shakes his head. "No. But you'll garner some attention."

My heart rate increases. Not just from the way his eyes rake over my body but from the increase of adrenaline pumping through my veins.

This is more exciting than watching the Super Bowl.

After he finishes his avid assessment of my body, Hunter locks his eyes with mine. "In that dress, you'll gain the devotion of a lot of old geezers who want to skip their little blue pill for the night."

Grinning, I kick his borrowed polished black shoes with the toe of my stilettos. Hunter smiles and returns my kick with a gentle nudge to my pumps. "I appreciate you doing this, Paige." He adjusts the pendant on my necklace. "I have twelve cameras uploaded from the hotel's main server in the ballroom, but with the blind spots and poor lighting, I can't get everyone's faces. You doing this will ensure I capture every attendee in the room."

"And you call *me* a voyeur," I jest, my tone drenched in wit. When the entirety of his statement hits me, I freeze. "Hold on, how will you capture everyone's faces just from having me wandering aimlessly around the room?"

Hunter's lips quirk as he returns his focus to the computer equipment. After a few quick strokes on the keyboard, the side of his well-formed torso fills the main screen of his security monitor.

A groan I've never heard before rumbles from my throat when I realize where the new image is projecting from. "You put a camera in my necklace?" I squeal, sending my voice ricocheting off the white-washed walls. "What if I wore it in the shower?"

The shit-eating grin on his face enlarges. "I could only hope."

This time when I kick him, I aim for his shin, and I add more force. "*Friends* don't see their *friends* naked."

The scowl on my face fades when Hunter says, "I was just evening the score between us."

Although his voice is full of playfulness, I remain quiet, muted by guilt.

Not even the world's best lawyer could win this case.

After a beat, he mumbles, "Don't feel guilty, Paige. If I didn't want you to see me naked, you wouldn't have." He locks his eyes with mine so I can see the honesty behind them. "You saw what I wanted you to see."

"You wanted me to see that you're a manwhore?" I query with my nose scrunched up tight.

He laughs. It isn't his usual boisterous chuckle, being more reserved and apprehensive. "No. I wanted you to see me at my worst."

My brows furrow. "Why?"

Hunter sets a contraption down on the desk and shifts on his feet to face me. He fiddles with my necklace while muttering, "Because I didn't want you to like me."

He's so quiet, if I didn't have his listening contraption in my ear, I wouldn't have heard him.

"You didn't have to be a manwhore for that. I don't like you." Even I can hear the deceit in my voice.

He chuckles again. This time it's his proper laugh. "That's good to know," he mumbles under his breath as he places his palm on the curve of my back and guides me to the set of double doors. "Remember, scratch your collarbone if you're worried," he instructs, his tone more serious than earlier.

I exhale a deep breath and nod. "Let's do this." I lean in to press a kiss on his hairy cheek. He spins me on my heels and shoves me toward the mass gathering of gala attendees when I guess, "Creed Aventus?" When I twirl back around to face him, the fan of my skirt flares out. "One day I'll learn what your scent is," I quip, walking backward. "Then all your greatest secrets will be exposed." I make my voice super dramatic like I'm the voiceover for the newest sci-fi movie about to hit the cinemas.

He winks before closing the door between us.

After running my sweaty hands down the front of my dress, I

mosey around the room filled to the brim with sparkling gown-wearing ladies and gentlemen dressed to the nines. The room has the distinct aroma of wealth and superiority, which isn't surprising considering the required donation per attendee.

I've attended numerous functions similar to this in my lifetime, but not one the past two years. Nothing against the organizers, but it doesn't seem like I've been missing out on anything. These types of events aren't about having fun. They are either to network or drain your bank balance for a worthy cause.

My heart leaps out of my chest when Hunter's chocolatey-rich voice unexpectedly sounds through my ear. "That's a good pace, Paige, just be sure to circle the entire room."

"Okay," I barely whisper, ensuring I don't look like a loon talking to herself.

By the time I've made it halfway around the room, I've dipped my chin in greeting to many inconspicuous gawkers and altered the course of my direction when a few inquisitive stares lasted longer than I was comfortable with.

As I make my way toward a bar set up in the corner of the ballroom, I freeze, and my hand clamps over my chest.

"Everything alright?" Hunter asks not even two seconds later.

My lips quiver when I begin to speak. "Yes. Everything is fine."

I can hear Hunter running his hand over his beard. "Are you sure everything is okay? Your pendant isn't responding."

"Everything is fine." My voice jitters as I track two females crossing the space between the bar and the dance floor.

"Paige," Hunter drawls out in his smooth, rich voice. "What's going on?"

From his tone alone, I can tell he isn't buying the explanation I offered.

I huff. "Two Victoria's Secret models are walking by."

"So you covered your pendant to stop me from seeing them?" he asks with amusement in his tone.

"Yep," I snarl, the 'P' having an extra pop to it.

"I have at least another ten cameras in your region alone. Covering your pendant was utterly pointless."

Upon hearing the laughter in his voice, I lower my hand from my chest. Alessandro Ambrosio graces me with her perfect smile as she saunters by. Just from the way her god-gifted assets jiggle, I have no doubt she didn't need the help of silicone to achieve her alluring curves. She's downright gorgeous.

"Although I don't quite have the angle you do," Hunter growls, his voice low and clearly aroused. When my hand snaps back up to cover the pendant, his chuckle jingles through my ear and clusters in my core. "I'm joking, Paige."

Even with hearing the truth in his tone, his little taunt bruised my ego.

Any concerns about my faltering esteem diminish when he says, "There's only one girl my eyes are tracking in that room."

"Izzy," I respond after recalling why I'm aimlessly wandering around like a loser without a date.

"No, Paige. *You*," Hunter replies. The beat of my heart shrills in my ears, and I have no chance of hiding the smile spreading across my face when he says, "Now hurry up so we can get out of here. This bowtie is cutting off my circulation."

Grinning like an idiot, I continue with my original endeavor.

Chapter Fifteen

Hunter's eyes track me when I enter the room and glide across the floor. Although his gaze spurs a rush of goose-bumps to prickle my skin, the usually frozen stance a coveted glance like his would incite is surprisingly void.

I tug on the untied bowtie dangling around his broad shoulders. "Get too restrictive?"

His smile makes me giddy. Something has changed between us this weekend. I don't know if it stems from his generous gifts or the honesty he's bestowed upon me, but whatever it is, I like it.

"What will you do with these images?" My voice is high with excitement as image after image flicks across the multiple monitors in front of him.

"I'll run them through facial recognition. If anything triggers a flag, I'll run an additional search on a more advanced program," he replies with his gaze locked in on a dark-haired gentleman sitting on a barstool.

"Have you done that to me?" I endeavor to keep suspicion out of my voice. I fail.

His eyes drift to mine. "No." He shakes his head. "You're the first girl I've propositioned *before* running a background search." A cheeky glimmer shimmers in his eyes. "And look where that got me."

I rib him with my elbow. "I'm not the one who pulled out the *friend* card."

My nipples harden when he quietly mutters, "Biggest fucking mistake I ever made."

Not willing to let his little comment slide, I ask, "Not running the background check? Or the friend card?" I tap on the listening device in my ear, ensuring he's aware I heard his sneaky comment. "And by the way, I'm keeping this. It's nearly as good as having eyes in the back of my head."

He chuckles. "It's only a prototype at the moment, but once I have them manufactured, I'll be sure to give you a friend's discount."

"There you go with the *friend* card again," I say with a roll of my eyes. Heat pulses through the middle of my legs when Hunter laughs. When his focus returns to the bank of computers, either refusing or choosing not to answer my earlier question, I ask, "Is skirting questions a hobby of yours or more of a career?" My tone is full of wit.

"There's only one skirt I like getting into, sweetheart, and it isn't an interrogation." When I screw up my nose and snarl at him, he runs his index finger down the grooves indenting my nose. "I like that you're a mystery, Paige. That's why I didn't run a background search on you. It kind of sucks knowing everything about someone. You're an unknown. A little onion I'm unraveling one layer at a time."

Warmth blooms across my chest. "Oh, that's so sweet, except for the smelly onion reference. You couldn't have said I was a beautiful rose you're removing one petal at a time?"

The covetousness in his murky blue eyes spears me into place. "Are you asking me to deflower you, Paige?" he asks, his voice rough and gravelly.

I stare at him, blinking and confused. From the impish glimmer in his eyes, I have no doubt there's a whole heap of hidden innuendo in his statement, but I'm wholly stumped at what it is. Even after watching him in meticulous detail for months, I still haven't learned how to read his prompts yet. Unless he lays his cards out on the table for me to see, I have no clue what he's thinking.

It's only when the corners of his lips flitter and his rascal eyes lock with mine does the sentiment of his question slam into me, closely followed by a fiery heat.

I swallow, feeling the warmth pumping through my veins extending to my cheeks.

"And Paige finally clicks on," he mutters, tapping the heel of my stiletto with his boot. Before any response can dribble from my mouth, Hunter's attention turns back to the computer monitor. "Isaac is on the move. It's time for us to go."

He stands from the chair and rapidly gathers his equipment. I'd offer to help him, but I don't want to impede his technical-looking dissembling, so I just stand to the side and watch him in awe.

In record time, he has everything stored back into his hemp bag left slouched on the floor during his surveillance.

After ensuring everything in the room is back to its original configuration, appearing as if we've never been here, he holds his hand out in offering.

It's the simplest of gestures, but it causes the biggest dose of excitement to heat my blood.

* * *

My head lifts from the extensive room service menu when Hunter walks into the living room of our shared suite twenty minutes after we've returned. A grin curls on my lips when I notice he's back in his usual attire—jeans and a blue and black plaid shirt. His hair is wet and flopped to the side, and he smells freshly showered.

"Going to work?" I ask while trying to ignore the drumming of my heart from his invitingly wet appearance.

He shakes his head. "Not yet. Knowing my boss, he'll be a while."

I freeze. "Twice in one night? Lucky girl," I mumble under my breath.

"You hungry?" Hunter jerks his head to the menu in my hand.

I nod. "You?"

He smiles while housing a black firearm in the drawer of the entryway table. "Yep. But not for anything they're selling." He snatches the menu out of my hand and throws it onto the coffee table. "No pickles, right?"

I smile and nod.

"Alright. Let's get you fed." His fingers fumble over his phone's screen. Not even ten seconds later, he returns his phone to his jeans pocket. "Done."

My brows meet my hairline. "Did you order us dinner or get directions to the closest deli?"

He runs his hand along the edge of his jaw, infusing the air with his scent I still haven't distinguished. "I not only ordered dinner, but I also arranged to have a case of Richart chocolates delivered for dessert and sold half a million in stocks."

My eyes bulge, but I maintain a silent front, incapable of articulating a response.

"I'm joking," he jests, hurdling over the couch and slipping into the spare seat next to me. "I didn't order the chocolates."

I stare at him, more confused than ever. I really need to work on unlocking his many facial expressions because I can't tell if he's joking or not.

The groove in the middle of my forehead smooths when Hunter playfully yanks on a wayward curl of my wet hair. I've also showered and changed, wearing my standard attire consisting of a pair of stretchy black pants and a loose t-shirt.

"Have you ever shopped online?" he questions after lifting his gaze from my beaming lips to my eyes.

I stare at him in a sadistic jeering type of way.

He grins. "How many websites do you normally visit before you finalize your purchases?"

My lips quirk. "Depends. Sometimes one, but if it's an expensive purchase, I normally shop around to make sure I'm getting a good deal."

"Well, if you download my app, you'll never have to search for the best deal again," Hunter states matter-of-factly.

"You develop apps as well?"

He grins as he digs his cell back out of his pocket and opens an app. "Name one thing you really want right now, and I'll have it delivered within twenty minutes and at the lowest price guaranteed."

My eyes rocket to his. "No way. Are you serious?" Lucidity smacks into me. "Is that how you got my dress here so quick?"

Hunter waggles his brows as a chortling grin etches behind his shaggy beard. "Although don't tell Melinda. She won't be impressed with the loss of commission."

"Serves her right," I mumble under my breath.

While he chuckles at my snide comment, I tap my index finger on my lip, trying to think of something I could order that will stump Hunter and the egotistical glint brightening his handsome face. "A signed copy of *The Weekend Romance* by Rachel Maloney." My voice is weak from struggling to conceal the rush of emotions pummeling into me.

Hunter's grin enlarges as his fingers fly across his phone's screen, completely unaware I just assigned him an impossible task.

Not wanting to be the cause of his disappointment when he fails to procure my eccentric demand, I say, "Hold on, scrap that. Umm..."

My eyes scan the room while thinking of something unusual for an online order.

My pulse quickens when I think of the perfect item.

"Schweddy Balls," I squeak out, my voice high. "Vanilla ice cream—"

"Loaded with fudge-covered rum and malt balls," Hunter interrupts, his tone as playful as the cheeky grin on his sinful-looking lips.

The smile on my face turns cataclysmic. "It went to Ben & Jerry's ice-cream graveyard back in 2011, so I don't like your chances of getting it here in twenty minutes."

"Done," he states, his tone condescending.

"Bullshit," I retort, shocking myself with my foul language.

Hunter winks before swiveling his phone screen around to face me. My pupils enlarge when I see he has purchased a one-pint limited edition batch of Schweddy Balls for two hundred and thirty-eight dollars.

"Two hundred and thirty-eight dollars is *not* the best deal," I mock.

"It's for an ice cream flavor that's been defunct since 2011," he disputes.

I giggle. "It's probably out of date."

My small giggle turns into a full-hearted laugh when Hunter says, "I don't care if it's covered in mold. For two hundred dollars, you're going to eat every spoonful."

In sync, our necks crank to the door when a doorbell rings through the suite.

Hunter's eyes drop to the phone in his hand. "Wow, that's a new record."

After snagging his wallet off the coffee table, he heads for the door. My brow cocks when he walks back into the living room with a plastic bag in one hand and a bottle of Dr. Pepper sarsaparilla in the other. The grumbling of my stomach intensifies when the smell of creamy pasta and freshly baked bread ignites my senses.

Remaining quiet, Hunter moves his computer equipment, which is still scanning faces, off the coffee table to place it on the six-seater table in the dining area. Once the coffee table has been cleared, he nudges his head, requesting me to join him on the floor for supper.

This is nothing out of the ordinary for us. All the meals we've shared the past few weeks have been on the living room floor of my rented cabin.

Smiling, I slide off the leather couch and plop my backside onto the floor next to him. With a cheeky expression on his face, Hunter pulls out two Styrofoam containers from the plastic bag. "Just remember, you can't judge a book by its cover. It looks disgusting, but it tastes so fucking good." He slides a container with a Gray's Papaya logo on the top to me.

He watches me curiously as I lift the lid. "What is it?" I slightly gag. It looks like someone's stomach overloaded on mac and cheese and *dispelled* the excess pasta onto a hotdog.

"Trust me. It's the bomb."

I giggle over his eccentric pronunciation of the word 'bomb.'

"A carbohydrate bomb."

Hunter doesn't grace me with a reply. He merely lifts the sticky mess from the container and inches it toward my lips. My mouth hesitantly opens. I'm not eager to taste something that looks like it belongs in the bottom of a spew bucket.

"Come on, Paige. I know your mouth opens bigger than that," he jests.

My mouth dangles open larger, more from the cheekiness of Hunter's statement than his request. After pinching the bridge of my nose, I take a large bite of the unappealing feast. My mom always taught me that plugging your nose dulls your taste buds. I used to think she was fibbing just to force me to eat my vegetables at dinner, but after testing her theory on a Brussel sprout, I realized it had some legitimacy. Although I could still taste their horrid flavor, they weren't as potent as normal.

Hunter shakes his head at my eccentric behavior but remains quiet, waiting for me to express an opinion on his meal of choice.

When the messy concoction hits my taste buds, my first response is hesitance, closely followed by shock.

Hunter cocks his brow when a deep moan rumbles from my stuffed mouth. "Good?" he asks.

I don't issue a reply. I'm too eager to devour another bite than spark a conversation.

Removing the bun from his grip, I take another mouth-filling bite of the unique-flavored meal. I moan even louder. My taste buds love it just as much the second time around.

"Told you." Hunter flops onto his backside. "That shit is the *bomb!*"

For the next twenty minutes, we sit on the floor eating ourselves into a carbohydrate coma while sharing the Dr. Pepper sarsaparilla he ordered—minus any glasses. I smile every time Hunter takes a swig before handing the bottle to me, not the slightest bit concerned our lips are sealing over the same rim.

Upon noticing only a mouthful of soda left in the bottom of the bottle, he kindly offers the bottle to me. I screw up my nose and shake my head. "Google says the last five percent of a bottle is pretty much just backwash, so I'm good."

He laughs. "So you're saying your spit is in this bottle?"

"Not just mine, yours as well," I reply, holding back a gag.

"Our spit combined? Sweet."

Heat slides through my veins, warming my pussy when he downs the remainder of the soda with a deep moan. His Adam's apple bobs up and down in an erotic way, quickening my pulse. When a bead of pop shimmers on his top lip, an overwhelming desire to crawl into his lap and lick it off his plump lips smashes into me.

For every second that passes, my restraint falters more and more. I can imagine how delicious his mouth will taste. Creamy goodness from the pasta, sickly sweet from the soda, and a taste that belongs solely to him because he's unique in every possible way—his smell, his looks, and his personality.

A groan rumbles from my lips when Hunter runs his hand over his mouth, gathering the small droplet of soda my tongue was begging to lap up.

With my fantasy crashing to oblivion, his curious eyes bounce between mine. "You alright?" The smoothness of his voice adds to the dampness of my panties.

I swallow to relieve the dryness in my throat before replying, "Uh-huh."

While he gathers our rubbish, I battle to calm the crazy pulse surging through my body. Earlier today, I rationalized to Pepper that my attraction to Hunter may be based on being isolated at Bronte's Peak. Tonight, I realized it isn't. Not the slightest. My eyes absorbed hundreds of well-dressed, handsome men at the gala this evening, but my interests never wavered from the smooth chocolate voice in my ear. He's different from every other guy I've met. Not just his appearance, but his personality as well, and I really like that about him.

Just as Hunter dumps our trash into a bin in the entryway, a ringing cell phone shrills from his jeans pocket. My breathing levels when I realize it's the ringtone on his ancient 'work' phone. Delving his hand into his pocket, he pulls out his cell. His eyes lift and lock with mine as he flips the screen and presses it to his ear. "Hey, Hugo," he greets, his tone jovial.

I release the breath I'm holding in, grateful he seems carefree. I've noticed the past few weeks that Hunter's moods swing toward the negative after he takes a call on that phone.

My relieved breath is quickly redrawn when a fretful mask slips over his face, and he scrapes his hand along the edge of his jaw. "Alright, I'll go and check on him," he mutters, his tone concerned.

He disconnects the call without issuing a farewell to his caller. I remain quiet, watching his throat work hard to swallow.

After a short period of contemplation, he asks, "Are you alright if I leave you here for a few?"

I nod. "Yeah, sure. Is everything okay?" I ask, my tone reserved. I don't want to force him to open up to me, but I'm worried about the unease clouding his eyes.

"I'm not sure," he replies. "Hugo asked me to go check on Isaac. Something is going on between him and Izzy."

My eyes dance between his. "Did you want me to come with you?".

The darkness of the cloud in his eyes lightens from my offer. "Thanks for the offer, but Isaac's a pretty guarded man, so he wouldn't appreciate an audience. I'm also not too sure what I'll be walking in on."

When he gathers his pistol from the entryway drawer and houses it in the back of his jeans, I step closer to him while nodding. Most men I've met are guarded.

Hunter takes a step closer to me, standing so close, the garlic from the creamy sauce on our hotdogs filters through my nose. "Are you sure you're alright staying here by yourself?"

"Yep. I'm going to write," I reply with excitement in my voice.

All day I've had a truckload of storylines bouncing around in my head, dying to be let free. But not wanting to be rude, I left my laptop stored in my suitcase instead of on my lap where it really wanted to be.

He smirks at my excitement. "Alright, I'll see you in a few."

My pulse quickens when the lips I'd been fantasizing about earlier incline closer to me. Unable to harbor the desire to find out if his lips have their own unique taste, I adjust the tilt of my chin, forcing his lips to land smack bang on mine. Air hisses out of his mouth, fluttering my lips with the flavor of the meal we just shared and a tangy citrus scent.

Elation swamps me. Even though he doesn't increase the intensity of our kiss, he doesn't pull away either. We stand still, completely motionless in the middle of the foyer with our lips joined and our hands fisted by our sides. I don't know how much time passes. I'm too busy fighting the urge to run my tongue along the seam of his mouth to keep time. Although our kiss is as basic as an innocent schoolyard peck, it's still heart-stopping. It is also our very first kiss.

Only after enough time passes that our lips have nearly become one does Hunter pull back. His massively dilated eyes bounce between mine, reflecting a range of emotions. Shock and apprehension are there, but the one making me giddy is the yearning. I just hope it isn't there because of his lack of female contact the past few weeks.

I know from experience he's a sexually motivated creature, but ever since our friendship formed, his female *visitors* have become extinct. I'm not sure if all contact has ceased to exist, but he certainly doesn't bring them back to his glass house anymore.

"I'll be back as soon as I can." Hunter's voice is deeper than usual. When I nod, he places another kiss on the edge of my mouth. My laughter vibrates on his lips when he mutters, "Not going to pull another fast one on me?"

I draw back and peer into his eyes. "It's no big deal. *Friends* kiss *friends* on the lips all the time. It is only once tongue gets involved does it cause issues."

I'm so full of shit. If the hot trickle of desire dampening between my legs isn't enough of a clue to my deceit, the galloping of my heart is a surefire indication.

A bolt of lightning shoots through my pussy, aiding my eagerness when Hunter responds, "So I could have been tasting your lips the entire time I've been friends with you?"

The smug grin on his face enlarges when I nod. "If you wanted to?"

My heart beats wildly when he says, "Fuck Isaac. I think a night in is on the cards."

I laugh even with my insides twisting in excitement. "Go and do what you need to do." I nudge him toward the door. "I'll be here when you get back."

I'm not going to lie. I love that he seems hesitant to leave.

Once he slips behind the door, I bolt back into the living room, eager to FaceTime with Pepper.

* * *

I've only just finished replaying every event that has happened for the past twelve hours to Pepper when a doorbell buzzes into the room.

Pepper inhales a quick breath as her mouth forms an 'O.' "Do you think it's Hunter?"

"Why would he ring the doorbell?" I ask through scrunched brows.

She shrugs. "Only one way to find out."

"Do I look okay?" I check my hair and face in the small video of me in the top corner of my phone.

"You look gorgeous! Go get him," Pepper replies.

After air kissing her farewell, I place my phone on the coffee table, leap off the thick woolen rug, and head for the door. The pulse between my legs thrums more the closer I get to the foyer. My excitement is short-lived when I swing open the door to find a bike messenger in a super tight pair of bike pants and a reflective vest standing in the hallway. His outfit is so tight I can see every detail of his body.

Every.

Single.

Detail.

"Hi," I greet him with unease in my voice.

After the bike messenger finishes absorbing my flushed expression, wide eyes, and panting chest, his gaze shifts down to a clipboard in his hand. "Paige?" he asks.

"That's me," I reply, smiling.

He stores his clipboard under his arm, then digs his hand into the backpack resting at his side. "I'm sorry it took us longer than quoted, but your order was a hard one to fill."

A small giggle spills from my lips when he hands me a one-pint serving of Schweddy Balls ice cream with a silver catering spoon dangling on the top. I giggle loudly when I read the gift tag attached to the spoon.

Eat this.

Hunter.

"A man of many words," I mumble to myself. I return my eyes to the bike messenger. "Thank you."

My interest piques when the bike messenger holds his index finger in the air, requesting a minute before he goes digging through his bag again. My nose gets a twinge when he pulls out an item covered in brown paper and twine. I can tell from the shape alone that it's some type of book.

Moisture forms in my eyes as my heart rate climbs astronomically. While juggling the ice cream and spoon in one hand, I attempt to open the package with my other.

"Thank you," I mumble to the bike courier when he removes the ice cream from my unstable grip.

Through shaking hands, I untangle the twine and tear a large section of brown paper away from the middle of the parcel. Tears prick my eyes when a familiar ocean side cover of a first edition copy of *The Weekend Romance* comes into my vision.

After running the back of my hand over my cheeks to remove my tears, I crack open the pristine cover. A whizz of air parts my lips when I see Rachel's signature scribbled across the front page. Although Hunter found a signed first edition of the book I wanted, it isn't the exact one I've been searching for over the past three years.

Chapter Sixteen

"He opens the petal of her flower, searching for the sweet nectar of her rosebud. What the fuck is that?"

My heart leaps out of my ribcage. "Oh my god, Hunter, you scared the shit out of me!" I shriek while clutching my chest with my hand. "You can't do that to someone. Jesus Christ." I sink deeper into the reclining chair I'm sitting on and suck in deep breaths to calm the mad beat of my heart. "For future reference, never sneak up on a writer when they're in the zone. It could end up very poorly for you and your package."

Hunter moves around the reclining chair to sit on the coffee table opposite me. When his eyes lift to me from the devoured ice cream container I licked clean, I rub my stomach. "It was *sooo* good," I drawl out. "I was planning on saving you some, but I got a little bit eager."

He chuckles, but it isn't his full-hearted laugh. It's reserved and with a bit of hesitation. I return his passiveness while I study him in great depth. Although his eyes are still sparked with their normal vivacity, it isn't as potent as normal. His brows are hanging a little lower, and his aura points to his mood swinging more toward the moodier, grumpy Hunter than the chipper one who left here earlier.

When my eyes drift to the clock hanging in the middle of the living room, I balk. He has been gone for a little over three hours, and I've been writing nonstop for two.

After returning my eyes to Hunter, I ask, "Is everything okay with Isaac and Izzy?"

"Only time will tell," he answers while rubbing a kink out of the back of his neck.

From his short response, I know he doesn't want to continue our conversation, so I flash him a quick smirk, silently relaying I'm here if he needs to talk before returning my focus to my laptop. I don't type. I just pretend to work on my novel as I keep an eagle eye on him over my Mac screen.

His eyes remain planted on his black boots for several minutes before they lift and lock with mine. "If you're writing a story about a bee falling in love with a human, it's already been done."

I slant my head and cock my brow. "What?" I query with a screwed-up nose.

"*The Bee Movie*, starring Jerry Seinfeld," he elaborates.

I snarl at him. "I know what movie you're referring to, but what does it have to do with my WIP?"

"Whip?"

"WIP. W. I. P. It means work in progress," I advise after remembering that most people don't understand author talk.

Hunter's hand drops from his neck, and he scoots a little closer to me. "If this is a romance book, what's the whole petal-rosebud referring to?"

Heat creeps across my cheeks. "It's the beginning of a *bedroom* scene I'm working on."

I endeavor to keep my voice confident.

I miserably fail.

"Scrap it and start again." Hunter's tone is blunt and straight to the point.

I balk. "No way! I've been working on that scene for over two hours," I blubber out. "You only got one small snippet of it. You can't judge an entire scene from one line."

He props his elbows onto his knees and tilts his torso closer to me. "Read it to me then."

"Ah... no," I reply with a brisk shake of my head.

"Paige."

"No, Hunter. I'm not reading it to you." I snap my laptop screen shut and hold it in close to my chest.

Hunter cocks his brow and bores his eyes into mine. "Read it to me... or I'll hack into your cloud backup and send your manuscript to every email recipient in the country."

My mouth gapes. Shock is all over my face. I don't need time to deliberate if his threat is idle. The frivolous look on his face is all I need to know he intends on doing as pledged if I don't read it to him.

Snarling, I huff, "Fine!" After opening my Scrivener program, I commence reading the steamy scene I just created. "He lays her on the bed, her hair a rich molten waterfall crescent on the pillow. He eyes her delicately, absorbing the softness of her skin, smooth and velvety like a plucked rose petal. His lips press on her neck, collarbone, and right rib before they lower even further. Her breath stiffens when he reaches her lady parts, brushing his fingers on the undergarments hiding the petals of her flower."

I stop reading and glare at Hunter when his body shakes as he fights to hold his laughter.

Upon spotting my furious glare, he coughs, clearing his throat. "Sorry. Please continue."

After snarling at him, I stray my eyes back to my laptop. "Her insides sigh in happiness, like a child making a snow angel in an abandoned field when he slides her modest underwear down her legs. She moans his name in a soft whisper when he opens the petals of her flower, searching for the sweet nectar of her rosebud. He wants to taste the sweetness of her pollen, devour the nectar of her delicate flower."

My teeth grit, and I slam my laptop shut when Hunter's loud chuckle bellows through my ears. Even copping the wrath of my knee-clattering stink eye doesn't lessen his uproarious laughter.

"You're an asshole," I mutter before dumping my laptop on the coffee table and storming into my room, slamming the door behind me.

When he doesn't attempt to follow me, I make my way into the bathroom, deciding a nice hot shower may be the only thing to lessen the anger boiling my blood.

I take my time in the ginormous double shower attached to my room, letting the steaming hot water drain away the negativity of Hunter's response. I'm sure with a bit of tweaking and some word alterations, the scene will be beautiful and poetic, a real justice to the connection my characters have.

I stop lathering my breasts with body wash as a whiny moan spills from my lips.

There's no saving that.

It's rubbish.

Total rubbish.

This is the reason I penned young adult romance—to avoid the stupid sex scenes.

After dumping the shower puff onto the tiled marble floor, I step under the spray. Water gurgles in the back of my throat when I let out a long, deep scream, expelling the negativity choking my writing inspiration. I wouldn't have any issues writing a half-decent sex scene if I had some real experience. I'm not saying Riley was a dud in the bedroom...

... actually, yes, I am.

Riley was as plain as they came. Missionary every Tuesday night, lasting for approximately fifteen minutes, give or take a minute or two. I'm fairly sure Riley didn't understand the meaning of the word *foreplay*. His routine never altered the entire three years we lived together, so I wasn't at all surprised when I walked in on him and Beth Millner in the obligatory missionary position in the bed I only emerged from an hour earlier.

If my neighbor, Mrs. Peters, hadn't stopped me that morning for a friendly chit-chat on my way to have brunch with Pepper, I have no doubt I'd still be unaware of Riley's indiscretions to this day. Our impromptu chat meant I caught sight of Beth's car pulling into the driveway of the home I shared with Riley.

Although Beth and I were friends in high school, we rarely saw each other since senior prom, so I knew in that instant she wasn't there to visit me.

"The same time, every Sunday morning," Mrs. Peters muttered while tapping my forearm gently.

Even seeing Riley's affair firsthand, it still took four weeks of deliberations before I built up the courage to leave him. It wasn't a lack of self-esteem that had me delaying the inevitable. It was because it was seven years of my life I was walking away from. That may not seem like much time over an eighty-year lifespan, but when you're only twenty-five, seven years seems like a lifetime, and when every detail of your life is played out in public, a failed relationship is the last thing you want to add to your list of achievements.

After crashing at Pepper's house for three weeks, plotting my next move, she suggested I rent the cabin and get away from it all to solely concentrate on my writing. And that's exactly what I've been doing the past few months.

Although this weekend away was never figured into my plans, I would have never said no to Hunter's request. That, in itself, is truly astounding considering how long it usually takes me to make a decision, but I owe Hunter a lot. Without him and his bevy of female companions, I'd still be penning my own rendition of *Basic Instinct*, ice picks and all. So even though Hunter thinks my sex scenes are laughable, I appreciate his honesty.

I'd rather have one person laughing at me than an entire reading community.

I step out of the shower, wrap a towel around my body, and finger comb my hair before wandering into my room. My brisk pace halts when I walk into the main area of my room and find Hunter leaning on the doorjamb. His shoulder is propped on the wall, and my Mac is balancing precariously on his palm.

Sensing my presence, his head lifts from the screen of my laptop. "This is really good, Paige." My chest swells, honored by the praise in his voice, but my happiness is short-lived when he continues, "It's just the sex scenes."

"What's wrong with them?" I ask, my tone hesitant.

Hunter's brows furrow together. "They are good, just too... *flowery.* You have these two amazing characters who have fire-sparking passion that dulls the instant they step into the bedroom."

"That's life," I argue as my eyes bounce between his. "Sometimes that's just the way it is."

He shakes his head. "No, it isn't." His tone is blunt and without hesitation.

I cross my arms in front of my chest. "Maybe not for you, but for *real life* relationships, they can be just like that. Not every guy is an Adonis in the bedroom. Some are just... *duds.*"

Hunter places my Mac on the dresser to his left before his eyes lock with mine. "You need to write from experience, Paige. Write what's in your heart."

"I'm trying," I snarl through gritted teeth while battling to keep my tears at bay. "But when you've got nothing to go off, it makes it a little hard."

Hunter eyeballs me. Not just a general stare—he *stares* at me for numerous heart-clutching seconds. When his eyes drop, reality slams into me. I'm standing in front of him in nothing but a fluffy hotel towel with a wet, shaggy mane. *Like my night could get any worse.*

My throat struggles to swallow when he pushes off the wall and prowls toward me. Even with the air conditioning set to a reasonable level, it becomes muggier with every step he takes. I attempt to speak, but the fervor in his eyes renders me speechless. My mouth moves but refuses to relinquish any words.

"The sexual connection between a couple should increase the closer they get to each other." His voice is smoother than melted chocolate. "The sparks, the desire... they should grow with every minute they spend together until neither can resist the urge any longer."

He cups my jaw, redirecting the mad pulse surging through my body to my aching-with-desire pussy. "They fight their attraction for as long as possible, but when the pull becomes too great, they stop fighting and give in to their desires."

A speckling of goosebumps follows the trail his beard makes across the corner of my mouth, past my inflamed cheek until he stops at the shell of my earlobe. "If you want to write about the connection a couple feels during sex, you have to experience it. *Taste* it. *Devour* it. *Feel* what they are feeling."

Excitement darts down my spine when he repositions himself to stand behind me. He's standing so close I feel the heat of his thickened cock against the curve of my backside. Air puffs from my lips when his hand slithers up the planes of my stomach to unknot the twist in my towel, sending it toppling to the floor.

You'd think my first reaction would be to dive for the towel or the bathrobe sprawled on the monstrous bed I'm standing next to, but it isn't. I stand still, frozen in place with both desire and shock, and for once, allowing my body to overrule my head.

My pulse shrills in my ears when he curls his hands over mine and guides them over the silky smoothness of my skin that's still damp from the shower. My heart thrashes against my ribs, matching the pulse of my clit when he uses my hands to cup my breasts. He kneads and caresses them until my nipples bud painfully.

"A woman's body was created to be worshiped, Paige. Your body was created for pleasure. To both give and take."

My mouth waters, turned on by his words and the softness of my hands fondling my breasts. Although I told him weeks ago that I'd "taken care of business," it was a lie. I've never brought myself to climax. But with his rich, velvety voice whispering in my ear, the roughness of his beard scratching my neckline, and the way my breasts feel larger and sexier in my smaller hands, I'm already tiptoeing to orgasm station.

My thighs shake when Hunter glides my right hand away from my breast, directing it toward the wetness dampening the insides of my thighs. A breathless, throaty moan simpers from my lips when he places his boot between my bare feet to spread them with a gentle kick. My pupils dilate when he cups my drenched pussy with my hand. When he guides my index finger over my pussy, coating both of our fingers with the evidence of my excitement, the quiver of my thighs intensifies.

"This is not a flower. It's a gift. Every drop of liquid is an unspoken promise of impending pleasure." His voice sends a surge of red-hot desire to my already slicked pussy.

I rest my head on his shoulder when the weight of my legs becomes too much for me to handle. My muscles are exhausted from fighting to stay upright as all the energy in my body focuses on more needy regions.

"Touch your pussy, Paige. Feel the way it clings to and massages your finger. What makes it wetter. Learn what it likes, then work harder to unravel its greatest desire. What it loves. No man can tell you what *you* want, crave, or desire. Only you can."

When my knees falter at his words, he releases my hands from his grasp and secures them around my waist, keeping me upright. Unashamed and on the brink of ecstasy, I use him as an anchor while I continue fondling my breasts and playing with my pussy.

Normally, I'd never be so bold, but with his head buried in the crook of my neck and us surrounded by nothing but cream-colored walls, I feel no embarrassment or shame. Oddly, I feel desired and sexy.

The heat in the room becomes stifling when I thrust my finger in and out of my clenching pussy in rhythm to Hunter's heavy breaths hitting my neckline when he bombards me with a flurry of dirty compliments. He says my body deserves nothing but perfection, how good it feels against his, and how I should never let another person's opinion alter my own on what is or is not right for my body.

The heaviness of my breasts increases as the first signs of an orgasm rises. My thighs shake, and my breaths become more labored.

"Do you feel it? The spark? The loss of control?" he mutters in my ear, intuiting that I'm close to the brink.

"Uh-huh," I pant between breaths.

"That's what you write about, Paige. What you're feeling right now. How good you feel. How desirable your body is."

The warmth of his breath on my ear sets me off. I moan as an orgasm rushes over me. It buckles my knees and sends a noise I've never heard before into the silence of the night. Hunter groans as he tightens his grip on my hips. His probing fingers add even more strength to the climax shimmering new life into my emotionally drained body. My body shatters, sexually satiated and emotionally appeased at the same time.

The blissful haze of an orgasm keeps me floating on cloud nine when Hunter gathers me in his arms and strides toward the large bed. While keeping his heavily dilated eyes arrested on my idyllic face, he yanks back the thick duvet cover and places me beneath it. The fog of my climax slowly dissipates when he lifts the covers, presses a kiss on the edge of my temple, then he ambles to the door.

I lurch from the bed, exposing my naked breasts to his view. "Where are you going?" My voice is hoarse, scorched from the erotic screams that shredded from my throat during climax.

He doesn't spin around.

He doesn't grace me with a reply.

He just stalks out of the room without a backward glance.

Chapter Seventeen

Awkward.

That's the only word I can use to describe the thick stench plaguing the air between Hunter and me as we make the two-hundred-and-fifty-mile journey home. He's barely spoken a word to me since last night. And since I don't know exactly how to apologize for bringing myself to climax in front of him, I've also maintained a quiet front.

He is mere inches from me, but it feels like we're worlds apart.

* * *

For every mile we travel, my annoyance firms. I didn't ask Hunter to touch me last night. *I didn't stop him either.* But we're grown adults, so the fact he's acting so childish is irritating the shit out of me.

* * *

Huffing, I turn my attention away from the scenery of Ravenshoe whizzing by and focus it on Hunter. "Who is watching Charlie?" I ask, endeavoring to spark some type of conversation between us before I die of asphyxiation from the tension depriving the air of enough oxygen to maintain life.

His eyes drift from the road to me. "Who?"

Even though his reply is short, I'm grateful I've pried a response from him.

"Charlie. Your dog."

His shoulders stiffen. "Oh... umm... he isn't my dog."

"Huh?"

Hunter scrapes his hand along the edge of his jaw. "I kind of borrowed him."

My brows furrow. "You borrowed a dog? Why?"

His eyes drift between the road and me. "Because I saw you sitting in the sand dunes."

"And you wanted to talk to me, so you used Charlie as a way in?" I interrupt, wanting him to hurry up and get to the heart of his story. I'm not a sitting-on-the-edge-of-your-seat suspense type of girl. I like to get straight to the nitty-gritty, often jumping ahead in any books I'm reading just to find out what happens before going back and reading the entire chapter.

"No, Paige." When hunter shakes his head, confusion swamps me. "I wanted to *fuck* you. So I used Charlie as my way in," he clarifies, his voice stern. "I wanted to fuck you from the very first day I spotted you."

I'm shocked, not just from the crudeness of his reply but his admission as well.

To be honest, I don't know whether to be pissed or happy.

"So everything... Charlie, fixing my laptop, the app, the gifts were all because you wanted to get into my panties?" I ask, my tone a cross between curious and astounded.

If his sole purpose was to get me between the sheets, why didn't he take advantage of the opportunity last night?

He swallows before turning his eyes back to me. "Charlie was a ploy. The rest was me. I like you, Paige. The stuff I've given you is because I wanted to, not because I want to fuck you."

His statement should bristle my spikes, but they don't. Because he didn't say he *wanted* to fuck me. He said he *wants* to fuck me.

My happiness doesn't last long when he mutters, "But what happened last night won't happen again. I was supposed to show you the connection your characters should feel. To explain the dynamic, not do it. I took it too far."

"No, you didn't." My squeal bellows through the thick stench of awkwardness plaguing the air. "You didn't even touch me."

Technically, I was the only one doing the touching.

Hunter's face lines with anger. "Oh, but I fucking wanted to," he mutters under his breath. After firming his grip on the steering wheel, he turns his hardhearted eyes to me. "Do you have any idea how hard it was for me to walk away last night? Seeing how your eyes spark and your lips part when you're about to come? It fucking killed me walking away."

"Then why did you?" I reply, both angry and confused. Angry for the way I felt when he walked out without a word escaping his lips and confused as to why he keeps fighting this unique draw we have toward each other.

"Because a girl like you doesn't belong with a man like me!" His angry roar rumbles through my heaving chest.

I laugh in disbelief, a crazy cackle that exposes my nuttiness. "Are you seriously giving me that line after spending weeks telling me how I should never let another person's opinion alter my own?"

"It's not a line, Paige. It's the truth. I have nothing to offer you."

"Bullshit, Hunter. You blew my mind last night. Made me achieve something I've never done before."

"As you said earlier, that was all you, Paige. I didn't touch you." His voice is a vicious snarl and full of maliciousness that maims my heart.

My back molars smash together. "Oh. Okay. I guess my opinion on you has changed," I retaliate before swinging open the passenger door of his car with brutal strength, forcing him to slam on his brakes halfway down his gravel driveway. "Because here I was thinking you were a *smart* man. Obviously, you're more *stupid* than I initially perceived."

I grit my teeth, suffocating a squeal when he snarls, "And quick-witted Paige *finally* clicks on."

"Fuck you, Hunter," I snarl before curling out of his car.

After slamming his door shut, I storm toward the back deck of my rented cabin. Hot, salty tears are threatening to spill down my face at any moment, and the only thing keeping them at bay is the potent anger boiling my blood.

My frenzied pace falters when gravel crunching under feet sounds through my ears as Hunter chases to catch up with me. "You saw how many women I've fucked, Paige! You witnessed it firsthand, yet it still isn't enough to scare you away from me." His fury is easily heard over the crashing waves in the distance. "Then what the fuck will it take?"

"You don't need to ask for help, asswipe! You're doing a stellar job right now!" I retort as I continue with my brisk pace, not bothering to turn around and face him. "You want to scare me away? Guess what, you have!"

While willing myself not to cry, I rush into the cabin. I grab everything and anything I can get hold of before shoving it into my half-packed suitcase. My movements are chaotic and filled with devastation.

Once I have my clothing packed, I drag my suitcase into the small living area. I don't need to lift my eyes to know Hunter is present. I can both sense and smell him.

"Where are you going?" he asks, his voice gruff.

I place my suitcase next to the entryway table before locking my tear-glistening eyes with his. His face is stern and lined with anger, but his eyes give away his true self.

They are full of worry.

"I can't do this anymore, Hunter. You keep drawing me in, then pushing me away in the same breath. You need to either let me in or let me go," I plead as my heart cracks along with my voice.

His stern mask momentarily slips, revealing a flicker of panic he rarely exposes. I hold his gaze, ensuring he's aware my words aren't an idle threat. I can't keep doing this pulling and pushing routine of the past four weeks. It's exhausting, and I'm burned out.

"Do you feel anything for me?" My heart hammers against my ribs. "Anything at all?"

His jaw muscle ticks when he begins to speak. "Of course I do, you're my friend—"

"Stop giving me the stupid fucking friends' line," I interrupt, my voice rising in anger. "You know as well as I do that you're using it as a barrier between us because you're too scared to admit your true feelings."

My firm stance eases when anger floods Hunter's eyes. He glares at me, issuing me the same threatening stare he gave me during my last round of interrogations, but even with my heart hammering against my ribs, I maintain a strong front, pretending his ardent glare isn't affecting me.

In reality, it's causing a sick feeling to spread through my stomach.

When the dense stretch of silence passing between us becomes too suffocating to ignore, I spin on my heels and gather my suitcase. My steps are frantic as I battle to hold in the tears threatening to spill down my face. Hunter has openly expressed on numerous occasions that he hates talking about himself, but now is different. This weekend shifted our relationship out of the friendship zone, and I'm no longer willing to hide my feelings.

I did it for years with Riley.

I refuse to do it with Hunter.

Hunter's indistinguishable smell hits my senses the closer I get to him. My steps are hurried since I'm desperate to escape the room that's shrinking by the minute. My chin quivers when I dip it in farewell while racing to the door. I need privacy before I'll allow my tears to fall.

Just as I hit the edge of the patio door, Hunter catches my wrists. A whimper scuttles from my lips when he pins me to the wall with his imposing body. I go from steaming in anger to frozen with desire in seconds from being trapped by six feet of pure man.

His eyes are wide, his nostrils flaring, and his whole composure screams of nothing but fury, but instead of being unnerved by his intimidating stance, I'm excited and incredibly turned on. My breasts are heavy, my clit is throbbing, matching the mad beat of my heart, and my body is acutely aware of every inch of him pressed up against me.

I'm not the only one aroused by our closeness. Hunter's cock is thick and hard against my stomach. "Do you have any idea what you're fucking doing to me?" The hotness of his breath adds to the intense heat radiating from my cheeks. "You've sent me into such a tailspin, I can't think straight anymore. I fucked up at my job as I was too fixated on you, yet you feel the need to ask if I have feelings for you. I can't breathe, sleep, or eat without thinking about you. You're driving me fucking crazy."

"Good. It's about time you joined the crazy club because I've been here for weeks." My words come out fast, spurred on by the desire to unravel him, to force him to finally admit the undeniable connection between us.

"I've been there from the fucking start, Paige. From the moment I saw you." He steps closer, pinning me more firmly to the wall. I feel the surge of his pulse streaming through his body via his hands clamped around my wrists. "The instant I saw you, I wanted you. The way the moonlight caught your hair, your smooth, soft skin, your beautiful face. I wanted it all."

My breaths come out in ragged pants, my chest not able to fully expand with how close he's standing. "Then why did you throw down the friend card? Why have you kept me at arm's length?"

"Because I knew you'd ruin me," he mutters, his words hurried.

My pupils widen as shock spreads across my face.

"For over ten years I've kept everyone at arm's length. I tried to do that to you as well. For weeks, I kept my distance, but the pull became too great. It became too much."

I nod in full agreement. Even shocked beyond hell at how quickly my feelings have developed for him, I can't deny the draw between us. We're magnetized to one another.

He stares at me, his gaze smoldering with lust and anger. "I don't just want to *feel* you, *taste* you and have you beneath me, Paige. I want to have *all* of you."

"Then have me," I mumble, unable to understand why he's holding back.

He angrily shakes his head. "That's not me, Paige. I don't want a relationship. I've never wanted that."

"That's because you hadn't met me." My voice is low, overcome by the barrage of emotions barreling into me. "I want you to *touch* me, *feel* me, *taste* every single inch of me, Hunter. I want you to have *all* of me."

Incapable of moving my arms since he has my wrists pinned at my side, I flex out my chest, urging him even closer, giving him that final push. A brutal grunt escapes his lips when my budded nipples crash into his firm pecs, and his tightness around my wrists firms.

I moan, incredibly turned on by the roughness of his hold. Upon hearing my shameful response, the anger lining his face lessens, and a new glint brightens his eyes. As though he could find any more space between us, he leans in even closer. "Don't destroy me, Paige."

"Never." My voice is shaky, shocked he'd ever think I'd hurt him while also wondering who already has.

His eyes search my face, seeking any untruth. When he fails to locate any deceit, he slowly and possessively seals his lips over mine. I gasp out the word, "Finally," when his tongue delves into my mouth, stepping us over the friendship line he drew in the sand weeks ago.

The roughness of his beard is unlike anything I've ever experienced, but it heightens my excitement, adding more giddiness to his heart-twisting kiss. The inside of his mouth has the same citrus freshness as his lips, a scrumptious mix of flavor and heat.

He relinquishes my wrists from his rigid grip to band his arms around my waist, drawing me nearer. Every nerve in my body goes haywire, incapable of grasping what to do first. I want to run my fingers through his thick mane and nibble on his lips. I also want to grind against his thick cock rubbing the seam of my panties while he holds me against the wall, devouring every inch of my mouth in perfect, lengthened strokes.

There are too many choices, and my mind is fritzed on which item to select first.

Why can't I do them all?

So I do exactly that. I run my fingers through his hair, securing his mouth to mine so I can nibble on his delicious tangy lips while I grind my throbbing pussy on the impressive thickness in his jeans.

When he tries to pull away, I hold on, refusing to relinquish his mouth from mine. It's taken him this long to revoke the friendship card he issued, and I haven't had nearly enough time to ensure he never wants to use it again.

"I want you in bed so I can take my time with you," Hunter mutters against my lips. "Screaming my name in a place where no one else will hear it."

My nipples bud even harder as a needy moan topples from my lips. "My bed, not yours." I suck his bottom lip into my mouth. *He can't dress me and walk me to the door if it isn't his house.*

He's walking through the living room of my cabin before I even realize he's moving, too engrossed with sampling every inch of his mouth to maintain rational thoughts. Just like he made himself at home in my kitchen and living area the past few weeks, he enters the cabin's main bedroom, not needing to ask for directions.

The thick duvet cover on my bed feels cold against my feverish skin when he places me down on the edge. A cringe crosses my face when I catch my reflection in the full-length mirror in the corner of the room. My hair is mussed from his large hand tugging it during our kiss, my lips are swollen and red, my eyes are wide, and my pupils are heavily dilated. But even looking the most frazzled I've ever been, I also feel incredibly desirable. That probably has something to do with the way his dark, possessive eyes are scanning my face, adding to the thickness his jeans are failing to conceal.

"You shouldn't let me touch you," he mutters, his voice deep and raspy. "I shouldn't be allowed to fucking touch you."

My breathing sharpens, panicked he hates what he's seeing.

When my hands dart up to my hair, vainly trying to smooth the frazzled pieces into manageable locks, Hunter mutters, "You're fucking beautiful, Paige. Don't ever doubt it."

"Then why did you say that? Why would you say that?"

"Because if I get one taste of you, I'll never let you go." His voice is low and full of worry. "You don't need a man like me, Paige. You deserve someone better than me."

"What are you saying? I need a man in a suit, clean-shaven, and with no tattoos?"

My teeth grit when he nods.

"Been there. Done that," I snap, my tone brittle like cracked glass. "Didn't make him any better of a man."

His murky blue eyes flash, and his nostrils flare as jealousy swamps him. The raging beat of my heart speeds up when he removes his gun from the back of his trousers and places it on the table at his right. His eyes scorch into mine as his fingers make quick work of the buttons on his red and black plaid shirt. The wetness between my legs multiplies when the smooth ridges of his torso become exposed, closely followed by the bumps of his stomach.

I moan, a needy, raspy groan when his shirt falls off his shoulders, puddling around his boot-covered feet. When he steps toward me, my eyes devour how his muscles flex with every long stride he takes.

When he reaches the end of the bed, I glide my eyes from the band of his jeans to his vehement gaze. "I warned you," he mutters while staring straight into my eyes.

I nod. "And I didn't listen. Lucky you seem to like my defiance."

A ghost of a smile sneaks out from behind his beard. "I like you any way I can get you," he barely mutters before clasping my hand in his and hoisting me off the bed.

"Lucky me, 'cause I don't like you at all." The laughter spilling from Hunter's mouth simmers when I grip his erect crotch and squeeze it in my hand. "This, on the contrary, I think I could *really* like this."

His lips quirk. "Nah. That won't happen anytime soon."

I stare at him with alarm on my face. I thought with the removal of his shirt I was making headway in my endeavor to have him stepping over the friendship line. Now, I'm not so sure my ploy is working.

Any concerns about my lack of seduction vanish when Hunter says, "You won't like it. You'll *love* my cock by the time I'm finished with you."

Chapter Eighteen

Just like the carefree Paige who only emerges in Hunter's presence, a new, unstiffened Paige surfaces in the bedroom as well. It might have something to do with the way his eyes devour every inch of me as he removes my shirt. Or how he loosens the elastic holding my hair so my wavy locks can spring free. Or the fact the thickness in his jeans gets larger with every second that passes as he wrangles my skin-tight jeans down my quivering thighs.

Whatever it is, I'm loving the newly found, relaxed Paige.

For the first time, I feel desired.

I'd even go as far as saying I feel sexy.

The warmth of Hunter's breath adds to the misting of sweat on my skin when he stands from his crouched position. His trek is slow since he stops at several intimate spots on the way to press a kiss or a nip to my heated and aching skin.

Just like last night, he moves to stand behind me before pressing his body firmly to mine, engulfing me in his hot, manly form. Shivers rack my body when the bristles of his beard tickle my neck a mere second before his teeth sink into my shoulder blade. Excitement surges through my blood when his tongue lavishes the spot, both soothing my skin and adding to my lightheadedness. One of his hands grips my neck, securing my body to his, while the other curls around my chest to cup my breast. He teases and caresses my nipple until it puckers in desperation.

Desire pummels through me when Hunter mutters on a breathy groan, "I love your fucking tits, Paige. I knew they'd be ten out of ten. I can't wait to see my cum smeared all over them."

His clever fingers work me into a frenzy while his crass words add to the dampness of my panties. As his lips pay dedicated attention to my neck, his hand moves away from my breast to follow the path he guided mine down in our hotel room last night. Goosebumps follow the trail his hands make over the small swell of my breasts, down the smooth plains of my stomach before stopping at my aching-with-desire pussy.

A hiss of air parts his lips when his fingers run over the dampness of my panties. My core tightens with every soft stroke he makes. When he slips his hand inside my panties, breaking through the small cotton barrier between us, my nails bend while securing a rigid hold of his thighs.

"You're so fucking wet." He rolls his hips so his thick cock grinds into my backside. "Are you dying to *feel* this, *taste* it, *fuck* it?"

Unashamedly, I nod. "Yes... so what's taking you so long?"

His beard scratches my neck when he smiles at my eagerness. "In time, Paige." He pushes his finger inside me in a slow and unbridled thrust. "First, I'm going to make you come like you did last night, but I'll use my hands this time. Then, I'll make you come again... *on my face.*"

I moan and buck against him, turned on by his promise. My entire body is pulled taut, aroused, and close to the brink. The combination of his words and the way he is finger fucking me has me racing to climax. I am ready and eager to topple into oblivion.

The buildup of tension in my core strengthens when he squashes the pad of his palm firmly onto my throbbing clit. Then, when he adds another finger into the mix, my race for release becomes frantic, almost uncontrollable.

"Open your eyes, Paige. See how beautiful you are when you come," Hunter mutters into my ear.

When my eyes flutter open, heady desire scorches through my veins. My knees buckle, and my orgasm comes to fruition as I catch sight of our reflection in the full-length mirror in the corner of the room. Hunter's manly body overpowers mine as he arches over me. He sends me to the brink with nothing but a talented pair of hands and a dirty, wicked mouth.

I climax with a hoarse cry, shameless and free of doubt. Hours of tension is swept away in an instant when my body is engulfed by a mind-shattering orgasm, stronger than any before it.

I've barely had time to emerge from the clouds when my feverish body is swamped by the softness of a cloud. My panties are snapped off, and an eager mouth dives onto the cleft of my trembling pussy. I secure a firm grip on Hunter's hair before trying to pull him away. I'm too sensitive, too overcome, too spent for my pussy to handle this type of attention so soon after a mind-hazing climax.

He pins me to the mattress by my hips before his tongue delves inside me. He laps up the residue of my orgasm while also adding to my wetness.

"I warned you, Paige," Hunter mutters against my drenched lips, forcing a tremble to roll down my spine. "I told you what I was going to do."

I come for the second time when his lips circle my pulsating clit, and he sucks down hard. As my body shakes, I scream his name. Every muscle contracts while battling through an orgasm even more intense than the one before it.

Hunter's deep growl ripples through my pussy when he places a final set of teasing licks to my swollen clit before he stands from his crouched position. His beard is wet and glistening, shamefully exposing the power he has on my body. His torso is slicked with sweat, and the front of his jeans is extended and taut.

When my eyes lock with his, a shudder runs through my exhausted body, invigorating it with renewed excitement from the hankering look in his eyes.

One of his hands runs over his beard, clearing away the evidence of my arousal while the other gathers it from my pussy. "How long has it been?" he asks while lowering the zipper of his jeans so he can transfer some of the slickness on his hand to his cock.

The deepness of his voice makes my insides clench, not to mention the imminent removal of his impressive cock from his trunks, but not enough for me not to seek clarification to his question. "Since?" My voice is scarce from the loud screams torn from my throat during my climax.

"Since you've been fucked?" he replies, not the slightest bit ashamed.

I swallow the brick suddenly lodged in my throat. "Umm... I don't... ah..."

"So a while?" he fills in.

While biting on the inside of my cheek, I briefly nod. Deep down inside, I knew something wasn't quite right with Riley, so our Tuesday night schedule came to a grinding halt a good six months before I discovered him in bed with Beth. Although I'm certain Riley blames my 'lack of interest in sex' as the downfall of our relationship, rumors are Beth wasn't the first affair he undertook during our seven-year relationship.

My mind snaps back to the present when Hunter asks, "Doggie? Or do you want to ride on top, cowgirl style?"

My eyes bounce between his, shell-shocked he's seeking permission as to what position we're going to do. Even with our sex life replicating a married couple in their eighties, Riley never once asked for my input.

While ignoring the nerves hampering my boosted self-esteem from two mind-blowing orgasms, I suggest, "Missionary?"

Locks of Hunter's sandy blond hair fall into his face when he shakes his head. "No. It's not a good position for getting reacquainted with sex. Doggie is a good angle to loosen your pelvis a little, or if you're on top, you can control how much you can handle."

You'd expect me to be annoyed at his comment, considering he's pretty much throwing it in my face that he's more sexually experienced than me, but I'm not. He only stopped touching me mere seconds ago, and my body is already missing his touch.

"You pick," I blurt out, too embarrassed to admit I don't know which position would be most enjoyable.

A smile creeps across Hunter's face before he mutters, "Cowgirl, it is." His tone is as thick and rugged as his cock. "Then I get to see your beautiful face while I'm fucking you."

When his jeans clatter to the floor, my eyes widen and drop, eager to see him in his full naked glory. I frantically assess and categorize every delicious inch of his body. Although I've seen him naked on numerous occasions, it's never been this personal. Tonight, I not only get to see his body, but I also get to feel it as well.

Above me.

Beneath me.

Inside me.

A crass grin etches on Hunter's face when he notices my ogling eyes. He stares straight at me, all rugged, primal, and one hundred percent masculine as he releases his cock from his cotton briefs. I squeeze my thighs together, vainly trying to lessen the dampness puddling there when I'm confronted with the full and gloriously satisfying visual of his naked package. His cock is just as impressive, if not more so than I remember—thick, lengthened, uncut, and rugged—just like its owner.

A condom wrapper being torn open diverts my attention from his thickened shaft. After awarding me with a cocky wink, Hunter rolls the condom down his girthy cock before he prowls toward me. My lungs burn as they strive to secure a full breath when he places his knee between my legs before gliding his body along mine. His hair is wet at the ends, and he smells musky and intoxicating.

Every inch of my skin he touches sets on fire. His touch moistens my skin with more perspiration as it battles to calm the raging heat shooting through it.

I wrap my legs around his waist and guide his head down to mine, more eager to taste his delicious lips again. The smell of my arousal mixed with his unique scent intensifies when his lips inch closer to mine. A throaty moan roars from my throat when he seals his lips over mine and spears his tongue in my mouth. I buck against him, loving the heat of his cock nestled between the wet lines of my pussy.

Every brush the crown of his cock makes to my aching clit has me tugging his hair harder.

He doesn't seem to mind. The more I tug, the more his crotch pins me to the mattress.

After quickening the thrusts of my hips, I run my hands over the ridges of his back. I love feeling his heated skin under mine. His back is as bumpy as his muscular midsection, and it sets my pulse racing.

When Hunter flips us over, swapping our position so I am on top of him, a squeal abruptly leaves my lips. With a grin, he bands his arms around my back, then scoots up the bed until his torso is resting on the headboard, and my thighs are straddling his wide hips.

I angle my chin down low so my thick red hair acts as a shield for my aroused face. Normally, my face was buried in the crook of Riley's neck during sexual encounters, so this feels very open and unguarded.

We are face to face, mere inches from each other.

Hunter grips my chin and jerks it higher. "No hiding, Paige. I want to see your beautiful face while you fuck me."

When he rocks his hips, stroking his cock along my wetness, my head flings back, and a husky moan spills from my mouth.

"That's it, baby," Hunter coaxes, his throat a sexy purr. "Sex is just like dancing, remember? Now we're dancing. Dance with me, Paige."

I unclench my fists and roll my shoulders back to ease my stiffened posture. "Sex is just like dancing," I mutter to myself before moving my hips in a similar rhythm to Hunter.

One grind of my pussy against his stiffened shaft has my next chase to climax ramping up a gear. He is so thick and heavy beneath me, I'm suddenly a little wary of taking a man so adequately hung.

Before my worries can get the better of me, Hunter takes my pert nipple into his warm and inviting mouth. He nibbles on the stiffened peak, making it even harder before he circles it with his tongue. The talents of his mouth are mind-blowing. He only lathers my breasts with core-shattering devotion for seconds, yet I'm already on the cusp of climax again.

Moaning, I rock my hips faster, needing something to lessen the insane throb between my legs. My breathless whimpers turn into feral groans when the crown of his cock connects with my clit. With his mouth and hands on my breasts and his fat cock stimulating my clit, I'm on the verge of free-falling into ecstasy again at any moment.

After leaning back, I balance my hands on his thighs before increasing my pace even more. I'm not the slightest bit ashamed I'm about to get off like a teen at prom. I rub myself along his hard-as-stone shaft in a rhythm so fast, my topple into climax occurs quicker than I'm expecting.

When an orgasm crashes into me, I moan a long and shuddering groan. None of my usual stiffness is present—not a single ounce as I shudder and shake above Hunter. I scream his name over and over again as white-hot passion overtakes my body.

Once the tremors racing through my body simmer, I flutter open my eyes and stare into Hunter's heavily dilated gaze. Any concerns tempting to surface vanish when he says, "Holy fuck, that was the sexiest thing I've ever seen. Now you need to do it again with my cock inside you."

I lift myself off the bed on a pair of shaky knees, gaining the height needed so the crown of his cock can nestle between my legs. Desire shoots through me when I slowly lower down to take in the first inch of his thick shaft.

"Slower," Hunter demands, his voice strangled with lust.

My breath hitches as I continue lowering myself down. Even with experiencing countless orgasms and being drenching wet front to back, his girthy cock still causes pain to rocket through my core as much as ecstasy.

"You need to relax, Paige. Breathe and relax."

While licking my parched lips, I nod before inhaling a deep breath of air.

Just granting my body permission to breathe loosens the walls of my clamped vagina, and I glide down another two inches.

"That's it, baby, nice and slow."

When my pussy hits the base of Hunter's cock, I gasp in a deep breath. I didn't think I had it in me.

A smile stretches across my face, pleased as punch that I've taken him all the way to the root. Although painful, it's also incredibly arousing.

I've never felt so full.

When my eyes lock with Hunter, I see that he is also smiling. I understand why when he twitches his cock to ensure I know exactly how deeply seated he is.

He throws his head back and groans when I swivel my hips to return his tease.

"Fuck, Paige. Unless you want me to come this instant, you better not do that again."

As my smile enlarges, I swivel my hips again, wordlessly denying his request. When his eyes snap open and bore into mine, my pulse hastens. His gaze is greedy and wanting and solely devoted to me. With a wicked smirk on his ruggedly handsome face, he props his hands at the side of his splayed hips before he swings his legs over the side of the bed.

I cry out when he thrusts into me again. He's even deeper this time around.

My pussy ripples around him, squeezing him tight when he drags his hips back before launching them forward again. "You're so fucking tight," he mutters, his voice rough and one hundred percent sexy.

My head lolls to the side, and my lips part when he increases the tempo of his pumps. Even though I'm riding on top and am technically supposed to have control, my playful tease has switched things up. The reins have been handed to Hunter.

After a handful more mind-hazing pumps, one of Hunter's hands guides my shoulders back, opening me to him even more while the other lowers to the region where our bodies are connected in the most intimate way. Any pain I'm experiencing is voided when he rolls his thumb over my throbbing clit. He stimulates it at the same teasing pace his cock consumes my pussy.

As my body temperature rises, a musky smell invades my senses. My skin is covered with a fine misting of sweat, and my heart is beating wildly. It almost matches the insane throb of my pussy.

My eyes snap shut when Hunter's tongue delves out to lick a bead of sweat rolling between my breasts. I thrust my chest out, loving the sensation of his beard scratching the stiff peaks of my nipples.

"Oh god," I pant when he scrapes his beard across my chest, firmly tightening my coil. "Again. Please. Do it again." When he does as requested, blistering lights shatter in front of my eyes. "Oh. Oh. Oh."

"Ah. Fuck. Christ," he mutters when his cock gets strangled by my pussy from another climax shimmering through my body.

His fingers dig into my nape as his pumps grow wilder. He pushes me over the edge, his wordless demand for me to scream his name as brutal as my hazy head. I become lost in an orgasm as his lunging thrusts have the crown of his fat cock hitting the tender spot inside me. My core spasms, launching a pleasurable pulse to every region of my body, spurring all the fine hairs on my skin to bristle.

While fucking me senseless, Hunter holds my gaze. He watches me unravel, absorbing and categorizing every shudder he instigated.

His ardent stare lengthens my orgasm before catapulting it to a never-before-reached level. It is a beautifully long climax that zaps every bit of my energy.

Just when I think the shudders will never end, my body goes lax, and I slowly come down from the blessedness. I lean into Hunter, unable to hold up my head, let alone continue fucking at the ruthless pace he's undertaking.

I take a few minutes to breathe before the wondrous circumstances of our exchange pulls me out of the trenches. After regaining control of my wild heart, I push off Hunter's torso then meet his pumps thrust for thrust. I bounce on and off his cock at the same speed he pounds into me. I feel him get thicker as his chase to release deepens.

I sling my arms around his damp shoulders then lock my eyes with his, desperate to see him lose control as I had. To watch him come undone.

His gorgeous face constricts as his hips jerk faster. He slams into me with brutal force, causing another tidal wave of excitement to scorch through my exhausted body.

While moaning a feral groan, he does one final thrust, impaling me to the very base of his fat cock before the tremors of my body extend to his. "Fuck, Paige," he roars. "Fuck, fuck, fuck!"

My pussy ripples around him, squeezing and massaging every drop of cum firing from his throbbing cock. Once every bead has been expelled, he draws me in closer then nuzzles his damp head into the nook of my neck. I smile when his breath hits my neckline in hard, ragged pants. It is similar to his twitching cock as it endeavors to deflate.

He's still hard enough to drill a mine, and although round two shouldn't be on my mind right now, it appears as if my once misplaced libido has other ideas.

"Jesus Christ, Paige," Hunter mutters against my neck when I slowly commence rocking against him. "You're going to fucking destroy me."

Chapter Nineteen

My taps on the keyboard stop when I sense another presence in my writing cave. When I lift my eyes from the stream of words in front of me, I discover an even more awe-inspiring visual than an almost completed novel.

Hunter's shoulder is propped on the doorjamb. He's wearing nothing but a pair of unbuttoned jeans and a cocky grin. The low hang of his jeans means his scrumptious Apollo belt is on full display, his drool-worthy tattooed pecs, and the breathtaking bumps of his impressive six-pack.

After giving my eyes plenty of time to absorb the panty-wetting visual, I lock my eyes with his face. Guilt smashes into me when I notice how tired he looks. His eyes are plagued with dark rings, and his beard is more unkempt than normal.

I grimace when I realize it's a little after four in the morning. "Did my typing wake you?"

With a shake of his head, he pushes off the doorframe and enters my writing space. "No. Just a cold bed."

"I figured you'd be used to that with how quickly you kicked your conquests out." I snap my vindictive mouth shut before lifting my apologetic eyes to his. "I'm sorry," I mumble, my voice sincere. "I get a little bitchy when I'm hungry."

His plump lips not hidden by his scraggly beard tug into a smirk, silently accepting my apology. He plucks me out of my hideous writing chair, takes a seat, then pulls me down to sit on his lap. Any concerns about him being upset by my snarky comment vanish when the bristles of his beard scratch my neck. He nuzzles into my side then presses a succession of feather-like kisses to my jaw.

The softness of his prickles reminds me of a tabby cat curling up against its owner. The only difference is I'm the one purring instead of Hunter.

The past two weeks have been crazy. Yeah, I know what you're thinking—*Paige, my dear, you were already crazy*—but it's been a different type of crazy. After the gala, Hunter's work schedule turned hectic, meaning I only see him when he crawls into my bed in the wee hours of the morning, and more often than not, he leaves before I'm awake.

Our regular dinner dates have become nonexistent, meaning I've resorted back to jam and peanut butter sandwiches to get me by. But even with our conflicting schedules, I wouldn't change a thing.

The past two weeks haven't just been crazy. They've been staggering as well. Our budding relationship is unlike anything I've ever experienced. It's filled with moments of discovery and Hallmark-movie cheesiness. I don't know if Hunter classes us as a friends-with-benefits arrangement or something more, but whatever it is, it is wonderful.

"What are you working on?" Hunter's voice isn't as smooth as normal due to the early hour.

When I close my notes on my Scrivener writing app to bring up the draft of my current manuscript, Hunter wheels in close to my desk. He props his elbows onto the edge of my writing chair then speed-reads my rough first draft.

I don't breathe or make a sound while scrutinizing every expression crossing his face. He's reading a newly created bedroom scene I just penned, and I'm nervous as hell he is going to tear it apart like he did the last naughty scene I wrote.

I can tell the exact moment he reaches the raunchy part of the story just from how his lips twitch, but he remains quiet, reading the three-thousand-plus word scene in absolute silence.

Even with his response hard for me to gauge, this is ten times better than sending my draft to a group of beta readers. This way I get to see how a reader may react while reading my work. It's an exceptional experience, one I'm sure authors would pay bucketloads of cash to experience.

Once he finishes reading the scene, Hunter slumps back into my chair, taking me with him. I wait impatiently for him to give his feedback. Although his expression doesn't allude to the humor he experienced the last time he read my raunchy scene, I'm still braced for impact. It isn't that I haven't put my heart and soul into this piece as he suggested—I have—but my writing skills are lacking in the steamy romance department, so I'm expecting some type of negative rebuttal.

Which I don't get.

"It's really good, Paige." Hunter locks his glistening-with-pride eyes with my shocked ones. "Really, *really* good."

I search his eyes for any untruths. When I fail to discover any, I suck in a large breath that puffs my chest out. "You're not just telling me that because you want to get into my panties, right?"

He throws his head back and laughs. "No, Paige. But if I'd known I only had to compliment your writing to get into your panties, I would have done it months ago."

I rib him in the elbow, pretending not to love his playfulness. Once his chuckles die down, he pulls me deeper into his chest. His raging heart confirms my story has the impact I'm looking for. "They have it all... spark, intrigue, fire-heating passion. It's a good scene. You should be proud," he says a short time later while running his hand down my back.

I pop my head off his chest. "I can't take all the credit." I waggle my brows while peering into his lust-filled eyes. "I kind of stole a lot of the scenes from what we've created the past two weeks."

My heart beats double-time when an impish gleam brightens his murky eyes. "Do you want to add another scene to your book?"

He bucks his hips so I can't mistake that he's primed and ready to go. While biting my bottom lip, I nod. A girlie squeal topples from my mouth when he abruptly stands, taking me with him. My ear-piercing shriek turns into laughter when he snags the open jar of Nutella off my writing desk. I don't eat it while writing. That would just create a mess. It's merely there so I can sniff it. It's a weird approach, but it keeps my hunger at bay long enough I can get down a chapter or two between breaks.

Tiny, breathless pants ripple through my lips when Hunter gallops down the stairs with me still in his arms. The frigidness of the tiled counter cools my backside when he places me down before moving to the refrigerator. Just like the past six weeks, he moves around my kitchen with ease.

The puffiness of my chest, compliments to his accolade about my writing, increases when I watch him prepare eggs Benedict. It only took me ordering it at the hotel the morning after our first *interaction* for him to know it's my favorite breakfast food.

Hunter stops stirring the hollandaise sauce when I dig my finger into the jar of Nutella and scoop out a large chunk. My Nutella-loaded finger freezes halfway between the jar and my lips when I catch his cajoling gaze. He isn't a man of many words, but his eyes alone are sweet-talking enough. He doesn't even need to speak, and I'm willing to do anything he requests.

After removing the saucepan from the heat, he places it onto the wooden cutting board then prowls my way. My pulse quickens to match the throb awakening in my clit. "I was planning on serving you breakfast before eating mine." His voice is smoother than the hazelnut spread dripping off my finger and onto my thigh. "But you've convinced me to revise my tactics."

When my eyes snap to the counter next to the open-flamed cook-top, my heartbeat intensifies. Only one plate is sitting next to the discarded saucepan. When I return my eyes to Hunter, the meaning behind his comment crashes into me.

Food isn't on his breakfast menu.

I am.

After stopping to stand in front of me, he pushes my legs apart so he can slot between them. My knees hit the hard curves of his waist when he pops my Nutella-covered finger into his mouth and sucks down hard. As he licks off the nutty goodness on my finger, he makes quick work of the satin tie cinching my knee-length dressing gown to my waist. Air hisses from his lips when he discovers I'm completely bare under the smooth material.

"You can never be too prepared for late-night visitors," I murmur, wanting to ensure he's aware I'm only dressed like this for him.

Although his late-night visits are every night, he rarely wakes me, believing I'd be too tired for extracurricular activities. What he doesn't realize is that I'd refrain from sleeping for a year just for the energy his contact invigorates me with. Even the simplest of gestures, like how he runs his index finger down my scrunched nose, sparks my body with renewed hope. He gets me like no one else ever has. He understands me, and the depth of his knowledge is both shocking and exciting, especially when another reality smashes into me.

I'm falling in love with him.

I tried not to fall for him, but with every day that went by, I fell harder and harder. I often joke with Hunter that I don't like him. But I do. I like him a lot—a *real* lot.

I also love him.

Mistaking my stiffened stance as nervousness, Hunter mutters against my heated skin. "Dance with me, Paige."

Although I am nervous, this time, it isn't from sexual contact. It's being scared to death that I'm placing my heart on the line again only to risk it being shattered.

After recalling the words he spoke to me only two short weeks ago, I whisper, "Don't destroy me, Hunter."

"Never."

His warm breath fans my earlobe before he tugs it with his teeth. I melt into his embrace, purring even louder than I did when he drew me into his chest in my writing cave. The way my body reacts to him is genuinely terrifying. My nipples bud painfully, my pussy aches for him, and my entire body pulls taut, dying to be consumed by him. I always knew he'd rocket my core to the next galaxy. I just had no clue it would be this profound. He hasn't just rocketed my core, he's demolished and destroyed it for any man who may come after him.

As his fingers travel up the grooves of my ribcage, Hunter's lips suck, nibble, and bite on my neck. A moan spills from my lips when his exploring hands stop at the swell of my breasts. While sucking on my neck firm enough to mark, he fondles and tweaks my nipples until their hardened peaks.

I thrust out my chest, loving how his big manly hands swamp my less-than-stellar anatomy. Even though his previous companions were big-breasted ladies, he's never once shown a lack of appreciation for my smaller assets.

For that alone, I *like* him even more.

With devotion focused on marking my neck with his touch, he curls his arms around my waist and lifts me from the counter. A broad grin stretches across my face when he murmurs, "Grab the Nutella," into my ear a second before he whisks me out of the kitchen.

As his big hands knead and caress my ass, he moves through the cabin. His steps are as slow and lazy as the teasing kiss he gives after sealing his lips over mine. My stomach grumbles when his citrus-flavored mouth combined with the Nutella he sucked off my finger hits my taste buds.

It's the perfect combination, ensuring I'll never eat Terry's Milk Chocolate Orange Balls again without getting horny.

A grin tugs at my lips when Hunter deposits me onto the bed right in front of the mirror. He even angles my backside so not even the wide span of his shoulders can hide the glistening wetness between my legs.

After giving both our eyes enough time to enjoy the scandalous image in front of us, Hunter mutters, "I still shouldn't be allowed to touch you, but fucked if I can stay away. You've put me under a spell, Paige. Every minute of every day is spent thinking about what I've done to you, what I want to do to you, and for exactly how fucking long I'm planning to do it."

"Yet, you're still making me wait."

The flare darting through his eyes heats me up everywhere. "I'm just making sure you know what you're getting."

"I know what I'm getting…" I drop my eyes to his impressive crotch. "And then some."

His growl activates every one of my hot buttons. With his eyes fixed on mine and the rock behind his zipper growing larger for every second we stare at each other, Hunter lowers the fastener in his jeans, then frees his dick from its tight constraints. "Are you sure you're ready for this, Paige? Ready to *taste* it, feel it—"

"And be thoroughly *fucked* by it." My crudeness should shock me. I should be scampering across the mattress and hiding under the bedding, but for some reason, I'm not. Hunter's attention has done wonders for my self-esteem over the past two weeks. I feel confident and beautiful and one hundred percent sexy. "So, once again, what are you waiting for?"

When Hunter wedges his knees between my legs, air whistles between my teeth, stopping their press mid-squeeze. "I was just waiting for your fantastic tits to be fully exposed. I think it's about time I see them covered in my cum."

I don't care that his knee is wedged between my legs. They're squeezing together no matter the firmness of the obstacle between them. His voice was too knee-quaking for a nonchalant response, and it was even hotter than usual since it occurred at the same time a droplet of pre-cum beaded on the end of his fat cock. "What do you say, Paige, a tit fuck for breakfast?"

I almost reply, *I doubt there's enough there to satisfy your hunger,* but I hold back. The image of Hunter stroking his cock is already mesmerizing, but it is even more perverse when I notice the direction of his hooded gaze. He's staring at my chest, and nothing but admiration is beaming from his lusty eyes. "A tit fuck then reverse cowgirl on the edge of the bed. That way, we both get to enjoy watching each other's face in ecstasy without bringing boring missionary into the equation."

Hunter's voice is rough when he mutters, "Missionary isn't boring when you're doing it with the right person." His change in tone isn't because he's worried he is once again reminding me about his previous promiscuity. It is from me scooting closer so the droplet of pre-cum that's about to drip from his cock can fall onto my breasts.

Desire surges through me when Hunter gathers the drop of pre-cum with his thumb before he transfers it to my nipple. The sticky goodness aids in his endeavor to have my nipples standing at attention and ready to be devoured.

Once the second nipple is coated with the same gooey substance, he nudges my shoulder. His shove doesn't have my back bracing the bedding, but I'm far enough away from him, my shoulder blades touch and my breasts push forward.

"Such perfect tits, Paige. They're going to look so good with my cum smeared over them."

There's enough pre-cum leaking from his cock to lube up the small gulley between my breasts, but Hunter acts as if there isn't. With a smirk as panty-wetting as it is playful, he dips two fingers in the jar of Nutella, scoops out a generous serve, then raises it to my chin.

It feels like lava scorches my veins when he drags his Nutella-covered hand down the pulse in my throat and between my thrusting chest before he pops his fingers into his mouth to lick up the leftovers.

"Hmm..." he groans in a throaty moan. "Paige and Nutella, my new favorite combination."

Either forgetting his pledge of a tit-fuck or blindsided by the same rampant horniness making a mess between my legs, he drags his tongue up the path his fingers just took, only stopping when he reaches my mouth. "Want a taste?"

I barely breathe out, "Yes," when he spears his tongue between my lips and drags it against the roof of my mouth.

Good lord, he tastes good. Sweet and chocolatey—just like his scrumptious voice.

By the time he pulls back from his arousing kiss, his beard is as dark as the mess between my breasts and as matted as he makes my heart feel.

There's no denying my earlier assumption. I am in love with a man I barely know even with me knowing almost all his infamous quirks.

It's incredible what you can unearth when you stalk someone for weeks.

"That's it, baby, dance with me," Hunter groans as his lips drop from my mouth to my neck before they eventually lower to my chest.

He sucks my nipple into his mouth, not the slightest bit confronted that he smeared his pre-cum on it only seconds ago while he rocks his cock in and out of his clenched hand. The visual of him jacking off is so enticing, tingles race to the lower half of my stomach as my hips begin to naturally rock. We move as one for several long minutes, my pace only slowing when Hunter's rocks between my breasts bring the crest of his cock to within an inch of my mouth.

He grunts an undecipherable word when my tongue delves out to lick up the sticky goodness pooling at the end, then he doubles the shimmers sparking every inch of my body by instructing me to roll my shoulders forward.

"Yes... just like that," he murmurs when the slightest movement causes my breasts to cup his thrusting shaft. "Now squeeze them together for me. Milk my cock with your tits like your pussy does every time I fuck you."

I almost fall back onto the bedding when I do as instructed, but before my shoulder blades get close to the duvet, Hunter bands his arm around my back and holds me in place.

"I got you," he mutters between the long plunges of his cock, both the roughness of his voice and his pace picking up. "I got you real fucking good."

When I drop my eyes to the scene causing his murky blue eyes to become the color of the ocean in the dead of night, rampant horniness clusters low in my stomach. My breasts are less than impressive, they barely fill a B cup, but the image of Hunter's cock sliding in and out of them is panty-wetting delicious. Not even the odd coloring of our lubricant of choice detracts from the awe-inspiring visual. It has me on the cusp of ecstasy in an embarrassing amount of time and desperate to witness the contrast of Hunter's milky white cum against the darkness of the Nutella.

"Fuck, Paige," Hunter grunts between grinds when each rock of his hips has my tongue connecting with his enlarged knob. "If you keep doing that, I'm going to come in your mouth instead of over your tits." His threat excites me more than it scares me, and he knows it. "If that's what you want, I'll have to even the score. I'm all about fairness."

With my breasts no longer on his radar, he scoots forward until more than the tip of his cock encroaches my lips. Several inches break past the barrier I'd never keep fully shut from him.

My moan vibrates down his silky shaft when the combined taste of Hunter and Nutella activates my taste buds. It is a manly, virile palette that has me forgetting I have a gag reflex.

"Sorry."

He isn't sorry. He's as desperate for me to swallow him down as I am for him to make true on his promise to return the favor. The rock of his hips as he stuffs inches of his cock down my throat assures me of this, not to mention his firm hold of my hair. Even if I wanted to pull back, his hold would never allow it.

Hunter gives fantastic head, and a part of his skills is directly attributed to his hairy chin. Even if I hadn't added back the detail of Archer's furry face, I would have eventually written about a character with a full beard because there's nothing more appealing than a rough and rugged man with his head between a woman's legs other than evidence of their exchange still lingering on his face hours later.

Hunter's beard often smells like me, and I like that almost as much as I love the salty liquid pumping onto my tongue.

"This is your final warning, Paige," Hunter warns between big breaths. "If you don't want to eat me for breakfast, I suggest you lay back and thrust those fantastic tits into the air." When I grip his Adonis ass and yank him forward until my eyes are on the verge of popping out of my head, he curses into the cool morning air before he surrenders to the sensation keeping his balls close to his tattooed thighs.

It takes his torso rising and falling several times in a row before his chin eventually balances on his chest, and he smiles a deliciously wicked smirk. "Now it's my turn for breakfast," he mutters before he hooks my ankle out from beneath me and yanks me down the bed.

When my hands shoot to his hair, the sensation of his mouth on the cleft of my pussy almost too much to bear, he snatches up my wrists and pins them to my sides. As he holds me hostage to the bed with both his strength and the desire making my limbs double their weight, he stabs his tongue between the lines of my pussy before he drags it up to my clit.

"Do you feel it, Paige?" he murmurs against my aching-with-need skin before he hits my clit with back-to-back flicks of his tongue. "The desire. The connection. The uncontrollable urge to fuck like nothing else in the world matters."

"Yes," I reply with a faint bob of my head. "I feel it."

I feel it so much, I rock against his mouth without a care in the world and dance on his face void of a single qualm. Then, not even a minute later, I shimmer through an orgasm so strong, the scream that rips from my throat could be heard in Ravenshoe.

"One more," Hunter growls against my dripping center a mere second after I've descended from blessedness.

I shake my head, certain I don't have another orgasm in me today. That one was the strength of three, so I could possibly be out of cum for another hour or two.

"One more," Hunter growls against my throbbing pussy again before he locks his eyes with mine over the goopy mess between my breasts. "Then I'll show you that the magic has nothing to do with your chosen position and everything to do with how a woman's body was created to be worshiped. Doggy, cowgirl, or missionary. It doesn't matter when the fireworks start long before a couple enters the bedroom." He licks my cleft, pokes his tongue inside me, then gently grazes my clit with his teeth before muttering, "I should know. I felt them the moment I saw you. The nerves. The butterflies. The desire to make you mine. I felt them all with one fleeting glance."

His confession sets me off. With an arched back and a moan unlike any I've heard leave my mouth, I come with a hoarse cry. Hunter groans when my wetness soaks his lips. After holding down my bucking hips to make sure he doesn't miss a drop, he drags his beard along the cleft of my pussy, coating it with my scent.

His bristles push my orgasm into a record-breaking shimmer. I shake for several long seconds, equally exhausted and ecstatic that nothing inside me is broken. It was merely the wrong man holding the key to my greatest desires.

Pepper was right.

Hunter isn't the odd man out.

I just didn't know what I was looking for until his naked backside was thrust into my peripheral vision. But now that I do, I won't let it go for anything.

Not even a *New York Times* No. 1 best seller.

Chapter Twenty

I'm lying in the crook of Hunter's arm, sexually satiated and gorged. After we feasted on each other's bodies for breakfast, he made an extra-large helping of eggs Benedict for us to share in my bed. Even feeling like a sticky mess from the smears of Nutella still covering my body, I am content and happy.

Who wouldn't be after numerous mind-altering orgasms?

After lifting my head off Hunter's chest, I peer into his eyes. He's drinking in the popcorn ceiling of the cabin, seemingly deep in thought. Even with his warm hand running down my back, a chill runs through my body, bristling every fine hair. Upon feeling the quiver racking my body, his eyes drop to mine. They're more clouded than usual, and his demeanor is swaying toward Grumpy Hunter instead of the Dominating Hunter I was handling only an hour ago.

"Rough week?"

I keep my question wide open so he can answer any way he chooses, which he does two seconds later. "More like one shit storm after another."

I prop my elbow next to his naked torso and balance my cheek on my palm. With a playful smirk, I say, "I've heard the telemarketing industry is pretty cutthroat."

My tease has the effect I'm aiming for when a hearty chuckle rumbles out of his stern lips. His laughter is so boisterous, it vibrates through my body, warming both my heart and my pussy.

When his laughter eventually dies down, he says, "That it is... that it is."

"Then why do it?" My tone has not an ounce of probing associated with it. I want to ensure he knows I'm not interrogating him into revealing guarded secrets. I am genuinely interested to learn why he stays in an industry that exhausts him so much. "With your skills in app development and all your other computer knowledge, your career possibilities are endless."

Just from his assets alone, I'm reasonably sure he doesn't work for Isaac for a monetary value, so it must be something greater keeping him there.

"I've considered leaving," Hunter replies, his tone still somewhat apprehensive. "Mainly after I screwed up last month."

I nod but remain quiet.

"But after talking to my mom, I realized I don't work for Isaac for the money. I work for him because I like him."

I run my thumb over the groove in the middle of his forehead. "Enough that it's worth all this heartache?"

His eyes drift between mine before he curtly nods. I smile, appreciating his honesty and understanding what he's saying. My job is not nearly as important as his, but I sacrifice a lot to do it. I often canceled engagements when my characters were talking or wake up in the middle of the night to jot down notes, so I can relate.

Hunter scoots down the bed so we come face to face. Air whizzes through his lips when his shuffle causes the sheet to fall to my waist, and he spots the smallest portion of my side boob.

"My eyes are up here, *buddy*," I jest while pulling the sheet up to cover my chest.

Although I'd love nothing more than to spend a few more hours with Hunter between the sheets, I don't want anything to interrupt the conversation we're undertaking. Even knowing him for months, there's still so much about him I haven't unearthed. I don't know what month he was born, let alone why he hates tea and coffee.

I run my finger past his slanted brow, over the scruffiness of his dark beard before stopping at the tattoo on the side of his neck. "What does this say?" I trace the word *traicion* integrated into his tattoo. "It's not English, is it?"

Hunter's throat works hard to swallow as he shakes his head. "It's Spanish." His tone is back to a sternness I haven't experienced in weeks. "It translates to 'betrayal.'"

My nose scrunches up, and dread swishes in my stomach. "Why would you have that tattooed on you?" I blurt out before I can stop myself.

When the heat in the room turns stifling, I lift my eyes to Hunter's face. He's glaring at me like he's silently daring me to continue with my interrogation. His gaze is so furious, my pulse quickens and my pussy throbs.

After wearily smiling, I scoot down the bed and burrow my head into his chest, not game enough this early in our... *friendship*... to confront Grumpy Hunter. I'm not a confrontational person as it is, but sparring against a man like Hunter when he's tired and withdrawn seems like a stupid move to make.

"I'm not saying I don't like your tattoo. I'm simply trying to understand why you'd mark your skin with such a hurtful word," I mumble into his chest a short time later. "Betrayal is a terrible thing. No one should ever have to experience it." *I most certainly wish I never did.*

Hunter exhales a deep breath of air that rustles my already tousled hair. After a few moments of silence, he slips out of bed. My heart thrashes against my chest when he throws his legs into the jeans he discarded on the floor earlier. Tears prick my eyes as my panic skyrockets, but in my distressed state, I've lost the ability to articulate speech.

If I'd known he'd have such an adverse reaction to my wish to know him a little better, I wouldn't have done it. I don't want to know all his secrets—I just want to know him better than anyone else.

"Hunter, I'm sorr—"

"Shut up, Paige."

My mouth gapes, not solely shell-shocked by bluntness but also surprised when he lifts me out of bed and dresses me in the satin dressing gown I was wearing earlier. His movements are fast and efficient, the tie knotted around my waist within a matter of seconds.

I will not cry. I will not cry, I silently chant to myself.

"This is my house, so you can't kick me out," I mutter as my voice quickly converts from devastated to anger.

My chin quivers when Hunter cups my jaw and lifts my downcast head. "Don't." His tone is a cross between stern and apologetic, and it sends my head into a tailspin.

After enclosing his hand around mine, he exits the cabin's main bedroom. Since he's clutching my hand to near death, I follow him.

My panic simmers when we walk toward the stairs that lead to my writing cave instead of the back patio door. My heart pounds my ribcage with every step we climb as does my curiosity.

When we enter the space that now seems two sizes too small from the awkwardness plaguing the air, Hunter sits on my writing chair then pulls me onto his lap. After wrapping his hands around mine like he did weeks ago at the hotel, he fires up the Internet Explorer program on my laptop. His pulse is surging through his body so rapidly, it pulverizes my hands.

The heavy pants of his breath blast my neck when he types a long string of code into the search bar using my index fingers. I know from experience he can type faster than this, but by going slow, I can memorize every keystroke he makes.

Once the search engine bar is filled with code, he releases my hands, grips my waist, then swivels me to face him. "I don't like talking about my past." He coughs to clear his throat. "I don't like talking about my life in general."

"Okay," I faintly murmur.

"But that doesn't mean I don't want you to know me, Paige. I want you to know me."

A small grin curls on my lips, glad he realized I wasn't trying to interrogate him. I merely want to know him.

Hunter's eyes flick to the monitor of my laptop before he returns them to me. "If you hit enter, every detail of my life will be displayed on your laptop's screen." His grip on my hips tightens, sending a ping of pain through my body. "*Every* detail, Paige. The good and the bad."

He tries to hide away the flare of emotion tainting his face, but he isn't quick enough for me to miss it. Just from the concern clouding his eyes, I know he's worried I'll discover something about him I don't like.

I hold his gaze for several minutes, waiting for his panic to pass before asking, "Is this similar to the search you typically conducted on your... *dates?*" When he curtly nods, I ask, "Will you run this search on me the instant I hit the enter button?"

His head bob switches to a shake. "No. Because unlike me, you don't have any issues communicating."

Even in the tenseness of our conversation, a small giggle rumbles up my chest.

The strain hampering Hunter's face eases when I hold down the delete button on my laptop until every digit and letter of the code is removed. After shifting my eyes from the now blank screen to him, I say, "I don't want to find out about you from anyone but you."

"That could end up being a very long time, Paige." His tone exposes the truth of his statement, much less his candid eyes.

I shrug. "Then I guess that just means you'll have to keep me around a little longer than originally intended."

A trace of a smile peeks out from behind his beard when he mutters, "And Paige finally clicks on."

Chapter Twenty-One

A chilly winter wind sifts through my hair as Hunter and I walk down a bustling sidewalk in Hopeton. For Christmas Eve, the streets aren't as jam-packed as they usually are, but there are still a notable number of people mingling in the space.

I lean in close to Hunter's side, craving his body heat while also happy to have him standing beside me. I thought the first two weeks of our relationship was a crazy rollercoaster ride, but they had nothing on the past week. Hunter's work meant I didn't see hide nor hair of him the five days following our exchange in my writing cave, but he didn't need to explain the extenuating circumstances of his absence.

The media handled every aspect of it.

Isaac's partner, Isabelle, the asset Hunter was assigned to protect, was kidnapped. If that wasn't already daunting, it was by a well-known and much-feared mob boss.

I remained glued to the broadcast the entire day of Izzy's kidnapping. I searched every station for a play-by-play rundown of the events that transpired that afternoon. For the most part, I was seeking any signs if Hunter was a part of the operation that killed Col Petretti and the arrest of two of his assailants, but a part of me was watching purely for storylines.

Even tragedy can appear beautiful to the right eyes.

The news of Isabelle's kidnapping wasn't solely contained to the local news channels, though. It spread across the country, even reaching Pepper.

"I told you he was mafia!" she screamed down the phone when Isaac's face was blasted across multiple channels while carrying an unconscious Izzy out of an abandoned warehouse in Harbortown.

My heart was maimed when I saw Isaac's devastated face as he placed Izzy onto a medical responder's stretcher. I've only ever seen that look once before. It was when my father said his final goodbye to my mother before she slipped into her unconsciousness a little over three years ago after a brief two-year battle with ALS.

My mother was a beautiful woman. A true gift from God. I miss her every single day, but for the past three months, I've been following the pledge I made to her in her final days—I'm living my life how I want to live it instead of what is expected of me.

My brisk strides down the cracked concrete path slow when we pass a small bookshop. It won't matter how many copies of *The Weekend Romance* I purchase, I won't stop looking until I find the exact one I'm searching for.

Upon sensing my slowed pace, Hunter stops then peers down at me. His eyes drift between the bookstore and me for barely a second before he jerks his head to the glass entry door, wordlessly encouraging me to enter.

"Are you sure we have enough time?" I don't want to be late to the Christmas party we've been planning to attend for the past six weeks.

Hunter places his hand on the curve of my back and guides me to the single door of the bookshop. "We have plenty of time."

When he opens the door for me to enter, the smell of vanilla and almonds smacks into me. My eyes shoot in all directions, absorbing the lines of bookshelves that fill the small space before they lock with a lady with black ringlet hair greeting us with a broad smile. "We're twenty minutes from closing. Are you looking for anything in particular?" she questions, stepping closer to us.

Hunter shakes his head at the exact moment I say, *"The Weekend Romance* by Rachel Maloney."

As his eyes snap to me, confusion mars his ruggedly handsome face. Oblivious to his odd expression, the owner directs me to a large section of romance books near the front window of the bookstore. Tears well in my eyes when I see over two dozen books with the familiar coastal cover in a prime position in the romance section. Even decades after it was released, it continues to be a favorite amongst readers.

My hand shakes when I remove the first book off the shelf and crack open the pristine condition hardcover. When I fail to locate an inscription inside, I pop it back on the shelf before pulling down the one next to it.

After my third removal and replacement, Hunter mutters, "You're looking for a particular signed copy?"

I bite the inside of my cheek in warning for my tears to stay at bay before nodding. "My mom wrote a message inside a first edition copy. I didn't realize its importance until it was too late. During a move from college to my family home, it became lost in transit."

Hunter moves to the other end of the bookshelf housing first edition copies of *The Weekend Romance* before pulling down a copy. "What does the inscription say?"

Heat creeps across my cheeks, closely followed by a large grin. "Be yourself. No matter what. Some will adore you, and some will hate everything about you, but who cares? It's your life. Make the most of it. I love you, Pookie Bear."

Hunter places the book back onto the shelf then moves to stand next to me. His eyes shift between my tear-welling ones as he promises, "You'll find it one day, Paige." He drags his eyes over the impressive collection before adding, "It may even be here."

* * *

Twenty minutes later, we've checked every copy of *The Weekend Romance* on the shelves. Unfortunately, none had the inscription I was searching for. Feeling slightly deflated, I nuzzle into Hunter's side before continuing our original journey.

Music blasts into my eardrums when we enter the head office of Destiny Records in Hopeton half an hour later than planned due to an impromptu stop at the bookstore. Compared to the gala we attended weeks ago, this event has a relaxed, cheerful vibe. The women are still dressed elegantly, but their hemlines are a little riskier, and instead of wearing tuxedos, the men are wearing suits—some with jackets, some without.

After slinging off my coat, I offer it to the attendant standing by the door as my eyes scan the room. Hunter's brows furrow when he witnesses an exchange between the tall brute of a man I saw at his home weeks ago and a gorgeous African American man near the bar.

"I'll be back in a minute."

He presses a quick kiss on the edge of my cheek before he strides closer to the two men. He doesn't interrupt them. He just stands to the side, scrutinizing their confrontation.

After a minor bout, the African American man puts on his suit jacket and strides to the door, tipping his chin in greeting to me on the way by.

"Everything okay?" I query when Hunter returns by my side.

His brows slant. "Maybe ask me in a year or two... because with all the shit that's been happening the past two months, I honestly don't know how to answer."

I fight to hide my delight that he believes I'll be around in a year or two to ask.

My brow bows when Hunter runs his shaky hand along his beard. This is the first time I've seen him genuinely nervous.

A grin curls on my lips when the reason for his nervousness is revealed. "Do you want to dance?"

There's no chance of hiding the grin attempting to stretch across my face, so I set it free before nodding.

My smile sags when Hunter directs us away from the dance floor.

I shoot my eyes between his amused gaze and an office door marked *Boardroom* when he swings open the door before gesturing for me to enter before him.

"There's no chance in hell I'm going to make a fool out of myself, so we either dance in here, or we don't dance."

I drag him into the boardroom before he can change his mind. "Here is great."

As I wrap my arms around his broad shoulders, I inhale a large breath of air through my nose, drinking in his delicious scent.

"Million by Paco Rabanne."

Hunter smirks before shaking his head.

Darn it! One day I'll guess his scent.

"Ready?" Hunter asks while curling his arms around my waist.

I smile and nod, hopeful some playfulness will ease the tension fettering his face.

We're dancing, not swimming with sharks.

* * *

I smile to hide the cringe attempting to cross my face when Hunter stomps on my foot for the third time in the past ten minutes. I'll be honest. I now understand his hesitation to dance. He has two left feet and absolutely no dancing abilities whatsoever. He's stiff, robotic, and the look on his face is anything but pleasant. But since I appreciate that he went to the effort of attempting to dance with me, I'm going to keep my big mouth shut.

Well, I would have if the tempo of the song didn't change.

When the techno crap booming out of the speakers in the ceiling changes to a faster beat, I unwrap my arms from Hunter's girthy shoulders then take a giant step backward.

"Moving out of the danger zone?" he questions.

Since half his words were chopped up by laughter, I gabble out, "Something like that."

After recalling Hunter gently guiding me through my awkwardness weeks ago, I interlock our hands and sway them into a wavy pattern.

"If you start doing the sprinkler, I'm fucking out," he warns, chuckling.

I hit him with a frisky wink before spinning around and plastering my backside to his crotch. I sway my hips in beat to the music but in a slower, more sensual pace to ensure Hunter can keep up.

"Dancing is just like sex, remember. I've experienced your moves. I know you have no problems swinging your hips."

Hunter's citrus-scented breath hits my neckline when he laughs, but as the song progresses, the stiffness of his hips relaxes. He bends his knees, aligning our bodies better before adding a grind to my sensual sways. Although his feet remain planted on the floor like concrete, his hips, torso, and hands loosen up.

One hand lingers on my hip, keeping me firmly attached to him while the other conducts an in-depth frisk of my body. Even with our bodies flushed with heat, my nipples tighten like a chilly wind is blowing into the enclosed room when he briefly brushes past them.

As the music overtakes me, I lean deeper into Hunter. I mold my body as close to his as possible, loving his sweat-slicked skin wrapped around mine. We dance so near, not even air exists between us. The sweat dampening me from head to toe causes my dress to cling to my skin, but nothing can dull the excitement thickening my blood.

My dance moves become more sensual, almost sultry when Hunter mutters, "God, Paige. Will I ever get enough of you? I just had you before we left, and I already want you again. I want to *feel* you, *taste* you, *devour* you." He grinds up against me, ensuring I can feel his thick, hot rod behind his zipper.

"Here?" The breathy deliverance of my question divulges my excitement about his inability to reel in his eagerness in my presence. I love that he craves me as much as I do him. It is a nice change.

"Would you let me?" His beard scrapes my cheek when he drags his lips from my ear to the base of my throat. "Would you let me fuck you here?" His warm breath on my neck and the roughness of his beard as he nibbles my skin dampens my already slicked panties.

When I attempt to spin around to face him, he firms his grip on my hips, both keeping me facing the front and denying me access to his truth-revealing eyes. "Answer me, Paige. Would you let me fuck you here, where you could get caught with my cock between your legs, pounding your sweet, tight little pussy? Would you let me scandalize you that much?"

My eyes snap to the frosted glass wall sheltering us from the other partygoers. Although no one has disturbed us in here, I've heard numerous muffled voices walking by the past thirty minutes, and considering the glass door doesn't have a lock, the possibility of getting caught is credible.

When Hunter leans in closer to me, the vicious shudder that racks through my body gives me the answer I'm seeking.

"Yes," I murmur, allowing my body to overrule my astute brain.

When he releases my hips from his grip, I spin around to face him. My movements are slow and unbalanced, compliments to a wobbly pair of legs.

The quiver of my thighs intensifies when my eyes lock with Hunter's. His gaze is sparked with unbridled hankering that is brightening his eyes beyond their normal murkiness.

I peer into them while declaring, "I'll take you any way I can get you."

The music dulls to barely a hum when I'm overwhelmed by hands, teeth, salivating lips, and the roughness of a full beard. Just like every other kiss we've shared, this one is dominating and skilled. Its wildness makes me forget that we're in a glass box surrounded by partygoers, and it proves I made the right decision.

A disappointed groan spills from my lips when Hunter pulls his talented mouth away from mine. I'm panting, dying to secure a full breath, and every nerve in my body is sparked.

His eyes flick between mine, his face a cross between confused and aroused. "Not here." His voice is as strained as the zipper in his jeans. "I don't want anyone to see you."

I stare at him in utter shock. He never voiced a single qualm about having spectators during the sexual rendezvous he hosted at his house, so what's changed now?

"They weren't you, Paige," Hunter replies to my quiet ramblings. "I didn't care who saw them, but I don't want anyone seeing you."

Even though my bitchy spikes should be hackled from his comment, they aren't. The fact he isn't treating me as if I am one of the numerous notches on his bedpost keeps my anger at bay.

After leaning up on my tippy toes, I press my lips to the shell of his ear. "Then take me home."

Smiling, he encloses his hand over mine and guides me back out of the boardroom. Even though we only arrived at the party forty minutes ago, and I haven't been introduced to any of his friends or work associates, I'm too horny to care.

There will be plenty of time to mingle with his friends at a later date.

The suspicious eyes of the lady who housed my coat earlier bounce between Hunter and me when I hand her my ticket. Clearly, we haven't done a good job concealing the lusty gleam in our eyes.

With the feverish need still warming my body, I don't bother putting on my coat when she hands it back to me.

I'm still trying to reel in a sense of normality when Hunter pulls his Hellcat away from the curb and commences our thirty-minute trip home. Hoping some music will distract my lust-riddled mind long enough to rein in my unbridled horniness, I switch on the radio.

Nothing works.

I can smell Hunter's delicious scent, taste his tangy flavor on my lips, and feel the slickness between my legs.

When Hunter slows his speed for some pedestrians crossing the road, he shifts his eyes to me. They expose he's fighting the same struggle, walking down the same beaten path.

His grip on the steering wheel tightens when I unlatch my seat belt and reposition myself so I'm kneeling on the seat instead of sitting, then he holds it even firmer when I say, "I can't wait any longer." As my hand slithers down to the crotch of his trousers, I nibble on his hairy jaw. Desire twists in my stomach when I discover he's already hard, heavy, and thick. "I want you now."

The excitement heating my skin intensifies when he pulls down a deserted side alley, yanks his seat back, then pulls me into his lap. My dress bunches around my waist when my knees wrap around his bulky hips, then he steals the moan escaping my mouth when he seals his lips over mine. I groan when his delicious taste and smell engulf my senses. Then I moan some more when he rubs his cock against my aching pussy in a rhythm to match the pace of his tongue in my mouth.

An exciting mix of speed and skill builds the tension in my womb rapidly. As one of his hands fists my hair, holding it to his mouth, the other gropes my breast. He pinches my nipple into a tight, hardened bud before doing the same to my left side.

While keeping my mouth arrested with his, I fumble with the buttons on his shirt. I'm dying to feel his firm, tattooed skin under my hands again.

Just as the last button on his shirt is undone, Hunter yanks down the front of my dress, fully exposing my breasts. He groans a rough grunt when he realizes I'm not wearing a bra. After tearing his mouth away from mine, his eyes lower to my chest. I feel the twitches of his cock when he drinks in my small yet still adequate breasts.

The dampness of my silk panties increases when he mutters, "Fuck, you're beautiful. I don't know what I ever did to be able to touch you, but I am sure damn fucking grateful I did it."

"You're not too bad yourself," I say as we engage in another long, lingering stare.

He flashes me a flirty grin when I drag my damp panties down the length of his thickened shaft. I go extra slow to ensure he feels the effect he has on me.

"If we weren't trapped in the confines of my car, I'd be laying you out and devouring that sweet pussy of yours until you begged me to stop."

I thrust against him harder. "You make me want to whip out my notepad and take notes. My readers will love this scene."

He laughs, not at all shocked by my comment. Lucky because I wasn't joking. Many of the bedroom scenes I've written in the past few weeks are based on my interactions with Hunter.

"Then we better make sure it's a good one." After slipping my panties to the side, he strokes my drenched pussy. "As I know how much those romance readers love a good mommy-porn book."

Once the dampness he gathered from between my legs has been gobbled up by his mouth, Hunter adjusts the rearview mirror so it is elongated and faces us, then he weaves his hand through my hair and tugs my head back.

The unsteady rhythm of my heart breaks into a new beat when the reason behind the adjustment of the rearview mirror comes to light. Even with my head thrust back, I can see Hunter's face as clearly as he can see mine.

"I know how much you love throwing your head back and howling while riding my cock. This way, I still get to see your beautiful face."

My nostrils flare in an attempt to cool my skyrocketing body temperature when he removes a condom from his jeans pocket before he guides the rigid material over his glorious backside.

"Can I?" He stares up at me with the condom wrapper between his teeth and a curious stare. "I've just never done it before. It would be good for research."

"Research?" he double-checks, his voice as raw as my throat feels.

I lift my chin. "For the book I'm writing." I snatch the condom out from between his teeth, grinning when it rips open before adding, "Although they may be a little lax on protection from time to time, Archer would never be so foolish."

An unknown glint darts through Hunter's eyes, but I don't have the time to ask what it is. His eyes drop to the panties doing a poor job of hiding my throbbing pussy from his hooded gaze a mere second before I pinch the tip of the condom and roll it down his veiny shaft.

"Make sure it goes all the way down," he murmurs when I stop rolling the latex half an inch from his balls tucked up underneath him.

I can barely breathe through the brutal grunt that rumbles in my chest when he raises his ass out of his seat, exposing another two inches of his cock. I've ogled him naked more times the past couple of weeks than I did when he was unaware I was watching, and it still isn't enough. I'll never grow tired of watching the veins in his cock throb harder the longer I stare or how the tip becomes wetter with only the slightest brush of my thumb. I could stare at him for twenty-four hours a day and not grow tired.

"What did I tell you, Paige?" Hunter mutters as the smell of my arousal filters in the air. "I said you'd love my cock once I was done with you, and you do."

"I do," I concur. "Very much so." Before I can utter another declaration far too early to express, I lock my eyes with Hunter's, then murmur, "But once again, you're leaving me hanging."

He mutters something under his breath, but I don't quite hear what he says. My ears are too battered by the throaty groan whimpering from my lips when he snaps my panties off after only the quickest glance of our surroundings.

He wasn't lying when he said he didn't want anyone to see me. He wants our escapades solely between us, and I can't fault him for that. I've only just stopped clamming up, so I'll never do anything to have my adventurous side backtracking for even a second. Heck, Pepper will burn me on a stake if I slow down the climax train now. She said it would be a long, satisfying track since it was decommissioned for so long.

I'm beginning to believe her.

When he mistakes my shock about my unexpected happiness as worry, Hunter assures, "You don't need to worry about anyone seeing you. In two clicks, I had surveillance shut down three blocks over before I pulled down the alleyway."

"Three blocks over?" I spit out, shocked. When Hunter jerks up his chin, I giggle. "Your cock is impressive, but three blocks is a little overkill, don't you think?" I peer around the car's cab, certain the confident, carefree voice I just used doesn't belong to me. I've never sounded so liberated from responsibilities.

Hunter's beard can't hide his smile when he mutters, "If I had done it just to conceal my dick, perhaps... but not for your screams." After opening me up for him by spreading his thighs as far as they can go, he braces the head of his fat cock against the entrance of my pussy before disclosing, "They could be heard three towns over, but since I'm planning to suffocate them with my tongue, I figured it was best not to break every one of Isaac's protocols."

He displays precisely what he means when he jerks his hips upward, impaling me with one breathless thrust. My moan only rolls halfway up my throat before Hunter's tongue licks it up. He scoops it into his mouth with a long, greedy lick before he swallows down the rest as effectively as my pussy chokes his cock.

His kisses are always overwhelming, growing better and better the more we do, but this is different. It is almost too much. He's assaulting my pussy and mouth with the same level of savagery, and it has me on the brink of climax in a short time.

When the sensation becomes too much, I pull back so I can secure a full breath.

It is a tragic waste of time when Hunter drops his devotion to my breasts. The instant his beard scratches over my puckered nipple, I moan like I'm possessed.

"Keep them down," Hunter pleads a mere second before the flicks of his hips have me on the verge of screaming.

While biting my lip hard enough to mark, I shake my head, silently advising him that his request isn't possible. I can't have the best sex of my life and be quiet. That is absurd even to consider.

With a smirk that has me wondering if I said my thoughts out loud, Hunter curses under his breath. I join him when he stills the thrusts of his hips. The tingles low in my womb are still paramount, and my body is coated with a misting of sweat, but I need more than the scratchiness of his beard as he leans across my body to fiddle with the console in the dashboard to freefall into ecstasy.

I need every inch of him.

Mercifully, whatever Hunter is doing only takes him a minute. After a handful of keystrokes and the silencing of his cell phone, the rocks of his hips return more potent than ever—as does the gleam in his eyes.

"What did you do?" I query, sure there's more to the glint in his eyes than an impending orgasm. Mischievous Hunter has arrived a day early, and I'd be a liar if I said I was upset by the prospect.

"Nothing." He is a terrible liar. His chest shudders as he strives to hold in his chuckles exposes this, much less the drop of my jaw when an ear-piercing siren almost bursts my eardrums.

"You activated the tornado warning system?" When he nods, unaware I wasn't asking a question, I shout, "It's December! No one is going to believe there is a tornado in December. They're going to come out to investigate, and when they do..." I gulp. My breasts aren't extraordinary, but I still don't want them eyed by random strangers.

I'm lost for words, but Hunter picks up the slack for once. "They'll see a car parked down an alleyway but not hear a single peep of what's going on inside." His lips tug at one side when I arch a brow in confusion. It is settled when he mutters, "Patricia, activate central command security for my vehicle."

"Yes, Mr. Kane," she answers half a second before the windows of Hunter's ride blackout completely. The tint is so dark, the only visible objects are my white breasts and cheeks.

"None one can see us."

"No, they can't," Hunter agrees as he takes my budded nipple back into his mouth. "And thanks to the siren, no one can hear us either."

I won't lie. The thrill racing through my veins gives credit to Hunter's claims that my watch gave him a slight fascination with Martymachlia. The risk that we could be caught is already thrilling, much less knowing we're possibly surrounded by people none the wiser about the scandalous activity occurring next to them.

Hunter moans against my aching breasts when I squeeze the walls of my pussy around his still hard shaft instead of yanking away from him. "I should have known not all the heat on your cheeks when you were watching me was because of voyeurism. You like the idea of being watched as much as I loved knowing you were watching me."

Jealousy is the only thing heard in my tone when I reply, "I didn't like watching you with th—"

Hunter squashes his index finger against my kiss-swollen lips. "I wasn't talking about them. I was referencing the times I was alone, doing the most mundane things."

"Eating peanut butter toast every morning isn't mundane," I mutter against his finger. "Sometimes it is the littlest detail that makes the biggest impact."

"Mm-hmm," he murmurs again before he drops his finger from my lip to my less-than-ample breasts. "Because these exposed your desires long before your mouth."

He brushes the back of his hand down each of my nipples before doing the last thing I expect him to do. He covers my chest with my dress, lifts me off his cock, then deposits me onto my seat like the stretchy rubber at the end of the condom isn't digging into his throbbing cock.

"Hu—"

Before I can get half his name out, he interrupts, "Your body was designed to be worshiped, Paige. I can't do that in a car parked down a dirty alley."

After tucking away his cock, he pushes a handful of buttons on his electronic console before demanding Patricia to deactivate the security program she had only just implemented. I try to lessen the redness on my cheeks when the tint on the windows clears away enough to spot a handful of residents milling outside of the apartment buildings Hunter's Hellcat is wedged between.

I shouldn't have bothered to act cordial because more than my cheeks heat up when Hunter finalizes his sentence, "But on the beach responsible for re-sparking some of the life in your eyes, I reckon I could worship you there." As he guides his car between the residents, grateful the siren was a false alarm but still peeved about the inconvenience, Hunter strays his eyes to mine. "What do you say, Paige? Shall we test out if shrinkage will be an issue before placing it in your next novel?"

Too horny to care about how many sand-loving crevices my body has, I nod.

Chapter Twenty-Two

After lifting my arms out of the duvet covering my bed, I have a long, leisurely stretch. My muscles are delightfully sore from hours of lovemaking on the beach that went well into the wee hours of this morning. Christmas morning will never be viewed in the same light again after my magical night with Hunter.

When I lower my arms, crinkling paper catches my attention. A grin curves onto my mouth when I discover a handwritten note sitting on the spare pillow next to me.

My grin enlarges to a full-toothed smile when I read what it says.

Call me.

Hunter

Hunter is understandably spending the day with his mother and sister two towns over. Most of my adult life I've returned home for Christmas, but it doesn't feel right this year with a failed relationship under my belt. I also agreed to go to the Christmas Eve party with Hunter last month, and I planned on keeping my word. My dad and I will have a belated Christmas celebration when I return home in mid-January. Although he was disappointed I decided not to come home, he said he understood.

After placing the note on the bedside table, I scoot up the bed until my back rests on the headboard. The happiness twisting my stomach increases when I dial Hunter's number and squash my phone to my ear.

I smile when his rich, chocolatey voice sounds down the line. "Good morning, Sleeping Beauty."

"Good morning, Hunter. Merry Christmas." My voice is husky, still raw from the erotic screams torn from my throat last night.

"Merry Christmas, Paige."

Hunter scrubbing his beard is the only noise that sounds through my cell for the next several minutes.

"Umm..." My heart rate climbs astronomically when I'm unable to miss the nervousness in his voice even with him only speaking one little word. "My mom wants me to invite you to her place for dinner tonight. I told her you might have plans, but she made me promise I'd ask, so I'm asking. There... I asked."

A giggle spills from my lips when a young female voice says, "She won't come if you ask her like that." When she makes a *tsking* noise, I imagine his sister from the photo on his mantelpiece crossing her arms in front of her chest and tapping her foot. "Ask her again and do it properly this time."

My cheeks burn from the size of the smile etching onto my face when Hunter asks, "Will you please come to my mother's house for dinner tonight, Paige?" His voice is the smoothest I've ever heard it. "My mom and little brat of a sister would love to meet you." I laugh when a rough groan sounds down the line, closely followed by, "I'll get you back for that, squirt." Hunter's stomping feet sound down the line before quiet encroaches. "She kicks harder than you." His voice has a hint of laughter behind it. After coughing to clear his throat, he mutters, "I understand if you don't want to come, Paige, I know it's ear—"

"I'd love to come," I interrupt, my smile radiating through my voice.

"Okay." His voice is deeper than normal but just as pulse-quickening. "I'll pick you up in a couple of hours?"

I smile larger. "Alright. I'll see you then."

"Bye, Paige."

"Bye, Hunter."

Just as I pull my phone away from my ear, I hear Hunter call my name.

"Yes." I squash my cell back to my ear so fast, I bet I get a bruise.

My eyes bulge when Hunter mutters, "Stop biting your lip. My teeth are getting jealous."

Stealing me the opportunity to reply, he disconnects our call. I stare at my phone, blinking and confused before remembering a time when something similar happened. My eyes rocket around my room as my suspicions pique.

When I fail to locate any type of electronic device hidden in the wooden walls, I scoot across the bed, adamant a more avid inspection is required. The sun beaming in the open curtains warms my chilled skin as I pad around the room, seeking anything that could house a small camera.

During my third trip past the large window stretching across the entire wall of the bedroom I catch the quickest glimmer reflecting from the corner of Hunter's property. After sheltering my face from the blinding sun's rays, I adjust my eyes. My heart beats triple time when I realize there is a black security dome mounted on the corner wall of Hunter's home, but before half my shock can register, my cell phone unexpectedly vibrates in my hand, scaring the living daylights out of me.

When I peer down at the screen, the insane beat of my heart climbs even more.

HUNTER:

Bingo.

I screw up my nose then turn to face the camera. Instead of the lens facing Hunter's property, it's pointing directly at my bedroom window. My mouth gapes when the camera swivels a few seconds later like it's being controlled remotely.

After sticking out my tongue, I yank the thick curtains shut.

My phone dings not even two seconds later.

HUNTER:

Killjoy.

I smile while my fingers fumble over the screen.

ME:

Peeping Tom.

Hunter must text as fast as he types code because his next message comes through remarkably fast.

HUNTER:

Only for you, Paige. I'll see you soon.

Smiling, I reply.

ME:

Yes, you will. In person.

A happy sigh fills my chest when his reply pops up on the screen.

Hunter:

Can't wait.

* * *

I spent the first hour of my morning preparing for my dinner date with Hunter. Then the next two hours are spent in front of my Mac, adding a decent number of words to the already impressive word count of my manuscripts.

Usually, I only pen one novel at a time, but with the range of storylines hammering me since I arrived at Bronte's Peak, I'm currently juggling two manuscripts. One is a contemporary romance piece on Archer Boyd, and the other is a romantic suspense novel about a millionaire businessman and his Aphrodite.

When the sound of the cabin's back sliding door opening bellows up the stairwell, I hit save on my manuscripts. "Hey, Hunter, I'm in my writing cave," I shout while impatiently waiting for my program to save everything before shutting it down. With a threat of a storm looming, I don't like leaving my imperative electronic devices plugged in.

A smile sweeps across my face when big stomps echo through my ears.

Someone's a little eager.

After powering down my laptop, I yank the cord out of the wall and spin around to face Hunter. My breath snags halfway to my lungs when I run smack bang into a solid, suit-covered chest. I linger my eyes on the well-formed chest for several heart-thrashing seconds so my heart has a chance to settle down before I hesitantly lift them to a face I can recall in photographic memory.

"Merry Christmas, Candace." Riley swoops down and plants a kiss on my O-formed mouth.

If he'd slapped me in the face, he couldn't have shocked me more.

When I yank away from him, I stumble over my feet and fall into my leather writing chair.

"Woah, careful there, darling. You'll hurt yourself." He thinks he sounds endearing, but all I hear is the condescending tone of a horrid man.

"What are you doing here, Riley?" I stammer out through the mad beat of my heart.

When he takes a step closer to me, I hold out my hand, demanding for him to stop.

He doesn't.

"It's Christmas, Candace. I've spent every Christmas with you the past seven years. I didn't want to miss one." He shoves his hands into his pockets. "Unfortunately, I've arrived late because it took me this long to track you down." He rocks on his heels, his entire composure screaming of superiority and arrogance.

Oh my god, is that how Hunter saw me the first time? As a rich, condescending snob?

When he interprets my silence as an open invitation, Riley takes another step closer to me. "God, I've missed you, darling."

My spikes bristle. "Oh, I'm sure you did while you had Beth sleeping in my bed."

His pupils widen, and he gasps in a quick breath, seemingly shocked I knew about his affair with Beth, let alone him moving her into our shared home.

"Yeah, I knew all about Beth. Why do you think I left?"

His smug smirk weakens as he swallows bleakly. "It was a mistake, Candace. I love you. I realize that now. It won't happen again," he replies, his pitch as arrogant as the pompous look on his face.

He actually believes I'll forgive him just from hearing that one pathetic apology. If you can even call it that. It was more a statement than an attempt of pleading for forgiveness. He didn't even say he was sorry.

My teeth grit when he hoists me from my writing chair with a firm grip on my wrist. Air hisses from my mouth when my chest crashes into his. Unlike the times I've collided with Hunter, this is a hiss of anger, not excitement.

Riley's cagey eyes bounce between mine. Even though he only turned thirty last year, he looks at least five years older. *Deceit does age you.* "I promise you, Candace, there's no other woman in the world for me but you."

When he tightens his grip around my waist, I attempt to yank away from him, but the more I fight, the harder he holds me. "You have to believe me, Candace."

The air is vehemently removed from my lungs when Hunter's rich, chocolatey voice sounds through my ears. "Who is Candace?"

When I swing my eyes to the entrance of my writing cave, I spot Hunter standing at the stoop of the stairs. One of his arms is hanging at the side of his body, his fist clenched tightly, while the other is slipped behind his back, no doubt bracing the gun he houses in the back of his jeans.

His ticking jaw intensifies as his eyes dart between Riley and me. After pushing off Riley's chest, I take a giant step backward, wanting to ensure Hunter doesn't misconstrue our position as intimate.

I breathe a sigh of relief when Hunter's eyes lock with mine before he silently asks if I'm okay. When I nod, his hand slides deeper into the back of his jeans before his eyes shift to Riley. His jaw is tense, and his gaze is dangerous. "Who are you?" he asks, his voice rough and brimmed with anger.

"Riley," Riley responds cockily, his arrogance not as tarnished as it should be for a scorned man. "Candace's fiancé." He cranks his neck to me. "Candace, who is this guy?" His voice is as uneased as the mask slipping over Hunter's face.

"Who the fuck is Candace?" Hunter snarls, his loud voice booming through my ears, startling me.

I stand still, frozen in shock. I demand my mouth to work but seeing Hunter and Riley side by side has muted me into silence. I knew it would be like comparing day to night, and it is, but every point is being awarded to Hunter even with him wearing a plaid shirt and a pair of ripped designer jeans. His feet are covered with the black motorcycle boots he regularly wears, and although his beard was recently trimmed, it covers a vast majority of his gorgeous face. His hair is longer than when I first spotted him, hanging an inch below his ears. Whereas Riley is decked out in a navy-blue pinstriped suit with a ghastly Christmas-themed tie. His shoes are so polished, I can see my reflection in them. His model-inspired face is void of any type of facial hair, and his hair is cut in a short back and sides style.

They couldn't be any more different if they tried, but Riley's smooth, sophisticated look isn't winning him any brownie points this time around.

I step between Riley and Hunter when Riley steps up to Hunter like he regularly did our gardener when he trimmed our lawn shorter than he liked. "I'm Riley," he advises again like Hunter is hard of hearing. After gesturing his hand to me, he says, "Candace's fiancé."

Hunter balks, physically impacted by his lie. His pupils widen, swamping the corneas of his murky blue eyes. I shake my head, soundlessly denying Riley's statement, but before Hunter spots my silent response, Riley asks, "And you are?"

My heart shatters into a million pieces when Hunter answers, "I'm Hunter. Candace's *friend*." He glares at me over Riley's shoulder with nothing but resentment reflecting from his shattered eyes. "Just thought I'd come check on my *friend* since it's Christmas, and she was alone. You know, it's the *friendly* thing to do." He locks his shattered eyes back to Riley. "But you look like you've got this covered."

"That I do."

I'm desperate to slap the haughty expression off Riley's face, but a far more dire situation demands my utmost attention. "Hunter," I squeak out when he spins on his heels and gallops down the stairs. "Wait! Hunter, please."

I yank my arm out of Riley's firm grip when he tries to stop me, then barge him out of the way. My heart races a million miles an hour as I chase after Hunter. I beg my legs to continue moving as a barrage of emotions slams into me at once—fear, resentment, confusion. It all smashes into me.

"Hunter, wait," I call out again when I catch him in the driveway of his home, my words trembling through the fear clutching my throat. "Give me a chance to explain."

A small moment of relief washes over me when his furious pace slows. After inhaling a big breath to replenish my lungs with air, I span the distance between us. The pain in Hunter's eyes matches mine to a T. His fists are balled just as tight, and his facial expression is anything but pleasant.

"That wasn't what it looked like—"

"Is your name Paige or Candace?" His raspy tone is full of warning that his anger is rapidly surging.

"It isn't that simple."

"Yes, it is," he sneers, once again cutting me off. "Is your name Paige or Candace?"

"If you'll give me a chance to explain—"

Hunter's eyes scorch into mine as he shouts, "Answer the fucking question! What is your name? Your *real* name."

As I fight back tears, I faintly murmur, "It's Candace."

The anger projecting out of Hunter strangles the oxygen out of the air. It makes it hard for me to breathe. Even with his jaw covered by the thick beard I've grown to love, I can't miss the furious tick inflicting it. He glares at me for numerous heart-pounding seconds before he turns on his heels and continues his original journey without speaking another word.

I try to go after him. I want to, but my legs refuse to move. They're weighed down by the pain stabbing the middle of my chest.

"I'm sorry, Hunter," I strangle out a second before he curls into his car and slams the door shut.

His car fishtails out of control, barely missing the large steel gate at the entrance of his property when he flattens his foot onto the accelerator.

Burning rubber lingers in the air for several minutes after his dramatic exit. I remain motionless in the driveway while desperately striving to find a way through what just transpired. I am truly at a loss, both dazed and confused.

I snap back to reality when an arm unexpectedly curls around my shoulders. When I recognize the bottled cologne I've grown to hate infiltrating my nostrils, I brutally yank out of Riley's embrace.

"Oh, come on, Candace, if I can get over you sleeping with a lumberjack, you can get over my affair with Beth," Riley snaps, his voice back to the normal condescending tone I was accustomed to hearing the past seven years.

I spin on my heels. My movements so quick and manic, my hair slaps my face. After pointing to a dark gray rental car sitting at the front of the cabin, I sneer out, "You need to leave."

"Candace—"

"Stop calling me that! No one calls me Candace anymore."

He glares at me. "It's your name, isn't it?"

My sadness about Hunter's abrupt departure is overtaken by anger at Riley's sudden arrival. "You don't call me Candace because it's my christened name. You use it for the social status associated with it." Anger burns through me when he doesn't attempt to negate my claims. "That's why you came back, isn't it? It's just dawned on you the extent of your unfortunate timing." When a mask of panic slips over his face, a cunning grin curls on my lips. "Well, now that we have that settled, let's hash out a few more points. This..." I gesture my hand between us, "... will never happen again. As far as any media is concerned, we never happened to begin with. And for every second you delay leaving, you're lowering your political chances more and more." My tone should alert him to the fact I'm not joking. The Candace he remembers is long gone, and I plan to show him that.

Riley's eyes slit like he can cut down my determination with a stare. "The bitterness of a scorned woman will have no influence on my future candidacy bid."

"I may not, but what about my father?" I cross my arms in front of my chest. "I'm fairly confident when he hears about the extracurricular activities you've undertaken the past three years of our relationship, he'll be more than happy to have a friendly chat with your campaign supporters." The panic in his no-longer slit eyes increases with every syllable that seeps from my lips. "And what's that saying you've always quoted?" I tap my lips, pretending I've forgotten the quote he cited numerous times over the past three years. "Without power, you'll never have money, but without money, you'll never have power." I straighten my spine and stare him straight in the eyes. "You'll have neither money nor power if you don't leave this instant!"

He glares at me with nothing but unbridled disdain on his face, but I don't back down. I am a stronger, more determined, kick-ass Paige than he knows, and I'm not putting up with his shit anymore.

Air wafts me in the face when Riley finally gets the hint that he isn't wanted. He storms by me and marches to the rental car sitting in the driveway.

I try to hold in my smile, to show a small snippet of the class my mother ingrained in me, but no matter how hard I fight, I can't stop a victorious grin from etching onto my face. Victory is too good to contain.

"I hope your fall into the gutter doesn't hurt too much," Riley snarls before curling into the car.

Incapable of letting him have the last word, I shout, "It couldn't any more than it did with you."

Chapter Twenty-Three

Vying to stop the winter chill blowing in from the west, I tug my knitted cardigan in tighter. I've been sitting in the sand dunes in front of my rented cabin, watching the waves tumble to shore over the past two hours. Bronte's Peak is the quietest it's been since I arrived here months ago.

Usually, too much silence makes me crazy, but I needed fresh air. I was hoping it would lessen the swirls hampering my stomach the past six hours. Although the cramps encumbering my tummy have eased, the crisp winter air has done nothing to reduce the pain inside my heart.

I shouldn't be surprised. Even a pep talk from Pepper didn't settle the pain.

I've been calling Hunter's cell nonstop for the past six hours, and every one of my calls have gone directly to his voicemail. When I text, I get an automated response saying my text has bounced and to try later. The only godsend I have is knowing I'm his neighbor. Sooner or later, he will have to return home, and when he does, I plan to beg for the chance to explain why I lied.

My little fib isn't as heinous as Hunter thinks it is. When he gives me the opportunity to defend myself, I am sure he'll see the funny side to it.

The Weekend Romance by Rachel Maloney is a loosely based fictional story of how the governor of New York City's daughter—my mom—fell madly in love with the gardener's son—my dad. The story includes numerous real-life facts about their relationship, like the first day they met when my dad fell off a ladder pruning the bushes at my grandfather's estate when he spotted my mom sauntering by the large, elegant windows to the precious words they spoke to each other when they discovered they were going to become parents.

My mom penned *The Weekend Romance* as a gift to my father for their tenth wedding anniversary. My dad was so impressed with her work, he encouraged her to have the book published. He never expected it to be a *New York Times* number one best-selling book for eight weeks in a row, be translated into thirteen foreign languages, and made into a blockbuster motion picture.

If he had known, he might have pleaded harder with my mom to reconsider her decision to leave the characters' names as the original names she used in the manuscript.

Actually, scrap that.

I don't think he'd change a thing.

I was only a child at the time my mom penned *The Weekend Romance*, and even I knew she was creating brilliance, so I'm sure my dad was even more aware.

For the six months following the novel's release, my father playfully called me by my middle name—Paige. As the months went by, the name stuck.

Those nearest and dearest to me call me Paige. The only person in my inner circle who hasn't the past fifteen years is Riley, and that was purely for political gain. He used me as I am sure Hunter thinks I used him.

The twisting of my heart amplifies when an engine rumbles through the quietness surrounding me. I leap up from the sand dunes and crank my neck to Hunter's house. When I spot Hunter's Hellcat gliding down the driveway of his home, I sigh in relief.

I knew you'd eventually come home.

After gathering the picnic blanket from the ground, I wrap it around my arm before urgently striding up the sand-lined path between our properties. My pace quickens when the rich smoothness of Hunter's voice slides through my ears. It's like melted chocolate on a hot summer day.

I've just cleared the opening of the sand dunes when a light in his house flicks on, illuminating his property with an artificial glow. My heart skips a beat when I catch the quickest glimpse of him moving toward the bi-fold doors at the back of his living space, then it completely stops beating when my stalking gaze captures another person in his presence.

Jealousy twists my stomach before winding up to my throat when a beautiful woman with waves of red hair enters the living area. Her eyes are zipping around the surroundings with eagerness, absorbing the enormity and grandeur of Hunter's house.

I stand frozen, hidden in the shadows of his patio when the cute redhead removes her shoes and jacket. She looks set for an extended stay.

When my pulse races, sending my heart rate to a dangerous level, I attempt to suck in some deep breaths. It is a woeful waste of time. Nothing can settle the morbid fear crippling me from the inside out.

I beg for my eyes to look away when a set of privacy curtains I didn't know Hunter owned roll down the large panels of glass his house is designed with. Even though the blinds slide fluidly into place, they aren't quick enough to conceal the image of the redhead slinging her arms around Hunter's shoulders and nuzzling into the crook of his neck.

When the pain becomes too much for me to handle, I throw the blanket to the ground and scream bloody murder. I thought walking in on my fiancé in the midst of an affair hurt, but this is ten times more. I trusted Hunter. I showed him the real Paige, a side hardly anyone gets to see, and he still betrayed me.

That hurts more than anything.

After angrily flinging a rogue tear off my cheek, I rush into the cabin and crank the stereo as loud as it will go. I refuse to hear another moan of ecstasy screamed from my neighbor's house.

The pain knotted in my throat intensifies when I enter my writing cave to hide from the image I know will rip my heart straight out of my chest. When I slide down to sit on the wooden floor, my eyes catch sight of my storyboards of Archer Boyd—the bearded billionaire who lives in a crystal house. Even though most of the board is made up of handwritten notes, I've studied Hunter in so much depth during the past three months, I can physically see each expression I jotted down.

Like a movie playing before my eyes, each scribbled note is displayed in graphic detail.

The storyboard causes even more anger and despair. I leap up from the floor and yank down every shred of paper from it. I rip them into tiny specks that float into the air like snowflakes falling from a darkened sky. Even though I am destroying hours of hard work, the triumphant feeling is worth the loss in research.

Once the storyboard has been destroyed, I focus my attention on removing every bit of information about Hunter from my laptop. I delete the scanned handwritten notes and sketches I placed on there with the app he created for me, then I trash any notes and references in my writing applications.

My manic behavior only ends when I open the nearly finished manuscript about Archer Boyd. I've been working on it nonstop for the past three weeks and only have the final chapter and epilogue to go.

When my eyes scan the beautiful words in front of me, a new idea formulates in my head. After twisting a red editor's pen into my hair to hold it off my face, I pull my writing chair in close to my desk and set to work. Everything I'm feeling is put down on paper, and every word I type loosens the restrictive hold Hunter has placed on my heart.

I type and type until I have nothing left to type, and six hours have ticked by on the clock, then I sink into my writer's chair and stare at the incessant blink of a black cursor on a white screen.

Since my manuscript is finished, my writing application requests that I fill in the title page. My heart beats wildly as the events from the day I arrived at the cabin until now roll through my head. When the scene stops on the day I spotted Hunter on the back patio of his glass house, the perfect title smacks into me.

While exhaling a big breath, I type the name of my newly penned novel:

Spy Thy Neighbor

The smell of warm paper and fresh ink filters through my nose when the inkjet printer at my side sets to work on printing the one hundred and fifty A4-sized pages of my manuscript. I save the one and only original copy onto a spare USB before deleting it from my writing application.

I only have one plan for this book.

It isn't publishing it.

Leaving the printer to do its job, I trudge down the stairs and head to the main bathroom. I shed my clothes on the way, not wanting to waste any time. The thought of a heavenly, hot shower is the only thing keeping me motivated.

As I lather my body with soap, I try to keep my focus off Hunter, but it's a fraudulent mission. I've showered with him numerous times in this very shower.

It's crazy to think how much things have changed in twenty-four hours. This time yesterday, I was waking up sexually satiated, and now it feels like I haven't been touched by him in months instead of hours.

God, I am pathetic.

I thought the weeks it took to leave Riley were pitiful, but this beats that tenfold. Hunter only betrayed me mere hours ago, and I'm already missing him.

I am better than this.

I am stronger than this.

And it isn't just Riley about to learn this.

After remembering the promise I made to my mother three years ago, I switch off the water and step out of the shower. Once I have a towel wrapped around my body, I walk into my bedroom. My steps are more determined than they were before I entered the shower. After dressing in a wool skirt, lace-topped stockings, and a cashmere two-piece cardigan, I call for a taxi before I commence packing my belongings.

It's time for me to go home.

Unlike the time I packed in a frenzied haze only weeks ago, this time, I ensure I collect every item I arrived with. My clothing and laptop will travel with me on the plane, but my writing chair, printing equipment, and storyboards will be collected by a transport company later in the week.

A grin curls on my lips when I open the top drawer of the dresser and discover the crotchless teddy Pepper snuck into my suitcase three months ago. "I don't think I'll need you anytime soon," I mumble to myself while placing the lingerie onto the unmade bed in the middle of the room.

I inhale deeply, gathering the quickest scent of my last sexual encounter with Hunter still lingering in the air before making my way to the taxi parked at the front of the cabin.

"Thank you," I say with a smile when the cab driver with kind eyes removes my suitcase from my hand to place it into the trunk.

I race back into the cabin to gather the freshly-inked manuscript from the printer and the USB from my writing cave before making my way back outside. "Could you please start the meter? I'll only be a few minutes," I request to the driver.

His eyes connect with mine before he curtly nods. I leave my laptop and handbag in the taxi's backseat before sauntering toward Hunter's house. He isn't home. One of the garage doors of his four-car garage has been left open, and his Hellcat is nowhere in sight.

A swear word seeps from my lips when I bob down to place the manuscript on the doormat and Patricia's computerized voice sounds through my ears. "Welcome, Paige."

My eyes dart to the security panel at the side when it flashes up a message stating that the front door has been unlocked.

"Thank you." I catch my eye roll halfway that I'm communicating with a computer program before pushing open Hunter's heavily weighted front door. I shouldn't be entering his residence unattended without permission, but curiosity killed the cat.

My heart bleeds more with every step I take. Cheap floral perfume is trapped in the space since the privacy blinds are still lowered, and no windows have been opened.

I feel physically ill when I enter the living area and see that the couches are askew. The thick Persian rug is indented from where the sofas used to lie. The coffee table is upturned, and some of the paintings adorning the walls are crooked.

It looks more like a fraternity house after a raging party than a private residence.

After pushing aside a champagne glass that has a coating of red lipstick on the rim, I place the manuscript and USB for *Spy Thy Neighbor* onto the counter Hunter eats his three slices of peanut butter toast at. While ignoring the pain splitting my heart in two, I snag a pen from a computer desk in the corner of the room and write an inscription on the title page of the one-of-a-kind book.

In true Hunter style, I keep my message brief:

Enjoy.
Paige Turner
New York Times Best-selling Author

The hairs on the nape prickle when I sense a presence standing behind me shortly before cruel words are spoken by a voice I'll never forget. "What are you doing in my house, *Candace*?"

Chapter Twenty-Four

A shiver moves through me from the anger projected in Hunter's low, sharp tone. I don't need to turn around to know he's angry. The terse crackling in the air makes me acutely aware of the anger flowing out of him in tiny, invisible waves.

He isn't the only one angry, though. My blood hasn't stopped simmering since last night, adding to the pain festering in my heart. He betrayed me and played me for a fool. He doesn't deserve an explanation for my intrusion. He deserves nothing.

After squaring my shoulders, I pivot on my heels and make a beeline for the front door. I keep my head low, using my hair as a shelter to ensure he doesn't see the pain not even the world's most scalding shower couldn't remove from my face.

The smell of hot, sweaty skin and alcohol increases the further I move as does the knot in my stomach.

I jerk to a halt when my wrist is suddenly seized, and I'm pinned to the wall by Hunter's imposing frame. Furious heat sweeps through my body when I realize he's shirtless and barefoot, wearing nothing but his favorite pair of jeans. His hair is wet and flopped to the side, his face is sleepless, and the other half of the almost empty bottle of liquor he's grasping is seeping from his pores, suffocating his normally alluring smell.

Even knowing I'll never budge a man of his size, I push on his torso with my hands while barging my hip into his waist. His stance remains firm, not the slightest bit intimidated by my fight. His eyes are wild, and his nostrils flare with every breath he takes.

His boozy breath flutters on my overheated cheeks as his furious eyes scorch into mine. "What are you doing here, *Candace?*" he asks again, his voice just as vicious as it was the first time he interrogated me.

"I came to say goodbye." My lips thin with annoyance, hating that my voice came out in a quiver.

Hunter's furious mask slips for the quickest second before it returns stronger than ever. When he sucks in a deep breath, he pushes me into the wall more firmly. His fierce gaze sears into mine, pausing the frantic beat of my heart. "You had your fun, and now it's time to leave?"

My stomach recoils from the bitterness of his words. "Yeah, I had my fun," I sneer as my anger steamrolls back in from catching the quickest whiff of the floral perfume still lingering on his skin. "Because being *betrayed* is a rollercoaster ride every woman lines up for."

He takes a step back, balking at my allegation. I use his unsteadiness to my advantage. After pushing on his chest with all my might, I slip under his arm and race to the door.

Just as I grasp the steel bar door handle, Hunter commands, "Patricia, commence security lockdown."

"Yes, Mr. Kane," replies the computerized voice of Hunter's home security system.

The clicking of locks overtakes the shrilling of the pulse in my ears. I furiously yank on the door, endeavoring to open it. It remains shut, locked tighter than Hunter's mouth during interrogation.

While grinding my back molars together, I twist around to face Hunter. "Let me out." The quiver of my words is more from anger than devastation. My body is shaking and slicked with sweat, and my eyes are welling with tears as every emotion I've ever felt hammers into me.

"Patricia, play the surveillance of my arrival home last night," Hunter instructs, completely ignoring my request to be released.

"Yes, Mr. Kane," Patricia replies.

I blink, reeling back the tears looming in my eyes when I am confronted with the image of Hunter arriving home with the pretty redhead last night. The gut-wrenching video is projected onto a white screen that has lowered from the ceiling in his living room. It's so large, it covers the entire span of the window in Hunter's living area. Unlike last night, this visual gives a bird's eye view of the incident captured by the surveillance cameras installed in Hunter's house.

Blood roars in my ears when the pretty redhead removes her coat and tosses it onto one of the leather couches in Hunter's sunken living area. I try to tear my eyes away. I beg them to look at anything but the screen, but no matter how hard I plead, my eyes refuse to budge.

My throat tightens painfully when the redhead slips off her shoes and pads closer to Hunter. Eagerness beams out of her when she curls her arms around his neck. My breathing halts, preparing for the brutal blow I am about to be dealt.

The commands of my lungs are fruitless. The event unfolds differently than I imagined hundreds of times last night. Hunter doesn't return the redhead's embrace. He pulls away from her before stalking toward a bar in the corner of the room.

After his fingers punch something into his phone, he places it on the counter and snags a liquor bottle from the small selection in front of him. Undetermined, the redhead pouts before she prances after him. My brows furrow, utterly mortified that she can't take a hint.

Even with her ego copping a hard blow, she continues with her endeavor of seducing Hunter. After molding the generous curves of her body with Hunter's side, she runs her fingers through his beard. I clench my jaw before snapping my eyes to Hunter. That may not seem like an intimate act to most people, but to me, it hurts like a million bee stings.

Hunter watches me with dark, troubled eyes while guzzling down mouthfuls of the amber liquor from the bottle he's clasping but remains quiet.

Against the suggestion of my smart head, I turn my eyes back to the video. The Hunter in the surveillance video replicates the one standing at my side. He's gulping down large swigs of brown liquid, but he's using a glass instead of a bottle.

The swirling in my stomach intensifies when the redhead loosens the buttons of his shirt. When inches of his smooth, tattooed torso are exposed, and her efforts shift to the belt holding up his jeans, it lurches into my throat.

Confident I've seen enough, I snap my eyes closed. The brisk movements of my eyelids send a couple of tears rolling down my cheeks, but I brush them away without fear, certain no woman could watch such a horrifying image and not be upset.

My eyes pop back open when glass smashing filters through my ears. Brown liquid seeps down one of the nude paintings lining the walls, pooling around the shards of glass sprawled across the floor.

When I lift my tear-swamped eyes from the bottle of alcohol Hunter broke on the wall to him, my heart cracks. He looks so broken, both angry and hurt.

"Watch it," he demands, his tone flat and brimming with anger.

I shake my head, which sends more tears dropping onto my cheeks.

Either blind to my rejection or fuming mad about it, Hunter quickly spans the distance between us. His furious pace helps him reach me in under a heartbeat. After curling his body around mine, enveloping me with his feverish heat, he grips my chin and forces my head back to face the projector screen. "Watch it," he commands again, his hot breath fanning my earlobe.

His furious pulse adds to the quiver of my chin when my eyes return to the projector screen. I flinch in the same manner as the redhead in the video when Hunter upends one of the couches in his living room and sends it sailing across the room. It hits the wall with such force, one of his nude paintings topples to the floor.

Hunter snaps his eyes closed and inhales numerous big breaths as the redhead stands to the side of him with her mouth gaped open in surprise. Once he's reined in some sort of composure, he flutters open his eyes and locks them with the redhead. I can't hear any of the words he speaks, but I can tell he's apologizing. His mortified expression displays his remorse for scaring her, not to mention the shame in his eyes.

After doing up the buttons on his shirt, he gathers the redhead's coat from the untouched couch, places his hand on the curve of her lower back, then walks her to the door.

"Patricia, play the surveillance video from the Dungeon nightclub at sixteen times the speed from four o'clock this morning," Hunter requests, his words slurred but still crammed with anger.

"Yes, Mr. Kane," Patricia complies.

Even though my gaze remains fixated on the screen, Hunter keeps his hand wrapped around my throat and his index finger and thumb pinching my chin. Although his hold could be construed as aggressive, my body isn't registering it like that. It's excited by his domineering nature.

My heart was shredded last night, but as the footage of Hunter downing drink after drink, alone, at a bustling nightclub filters before my eyes, the uncontrollable thud in my chest transfers to another region of my body. This one is much lower.

"You didn't sleep with her?" I mumble more to myself than Hunter.

"I fucking wanted to, but I couldn't," he responds to my silent interrogation. "She wasn't who I wanted."

The sweat rolling down his torso is absorbed by my cardigan when he molds his body to mine. I try to suppress it, but the faintest moan topples from my gaped lips. Even being angry that he purposely set out to hurt me last night, my body melts when his beard scratches my neck. When he sinks his teeth into my shoulder blade while his erect cock grinds my backside, my panties dampen.

"Can I have you, Paige? Can I scandalize you some more?"

When I nod, the hand wrapped around my neck lowers to my breast while the other one slides beneath the hem of my skirt. When his thick fingers brush over my panties clinging to my pussy, my knees shake. I grind down on his hand, my earlier pain a forgotten memory.

I throw my head back and pant when his finger slips inside my panties before he slowly enters my clenching core. As his thumb and index finger roll my budded nipple, his finger fucks me at a rapid yet also leisurely pace. He curls his fingers at the tip, making sure he gets the tender spot inside me while his mouth lavishes my neck with bites and kisses.

The tension bristling between us is incredible, and within a short time, I'm on the verge of a climax.

Just as I'm about to announce that I'm close to detonation, Hunter mutters, "One last fuck before you run back to your country club friends to tell them how you spent Christmas slumming with the less fortunate."

My orgasm comes to a screeching halt—as does my heart. I lurch away from him, both disgusted and shocked by the callousness of his words.

When I spin around to face him, I nearly lose my footing. I'm dizzy from the closeness of a climax and the anger roaring through my veins. Heat rises from my gut to my cheeks when I catch sight of his mocking smirk. His eyes are blazing, and his entire composure screams of arrogance.

He is the ugliest I've ever seen him.

"Candace Paige Maloney, daughter of Gerald Maloney, Senator from California." His tone is dangerously even. "Prestigious granddaughter of Richard Breene, ex-governor and oil tycoon with an estimated worth of over three billion dollars." He drawls out my grandfather's worth like he's announcing the jackpot in the lottery. "Her major at college was political science before she changed it to creative writing after her mother was diagnosed with ALS."

Tears prick my eyes at the mention of my mother's name. The only thing keeping them at bay is the remorse that flashes through

Hunter's eyes for the tiniest second before he continues his malicious drunken tirade. "Candace's best friend since kindergarten is Quinn Peters, crowned Miss Daisy Beauty Queen in 2017. She currently works at a local coffee bean chain while attending audition after audition after audition, as she, along with the other eighty-eight percent of Los Angeles residents, is an aspiring actress. Surprise. Surprise."

I cross my arms in front of my chest. My anger is so paramount, my face is red, and steam is nearly billowing out of my ears. "Are you done?"

"Just one last thing." He lifts his index finger into the air—the same finger still glistening with evidence of my near arousal. "Patricia, bring up the last-searched item on my home server," he requests, his words slurring.

My pulse is pounding in my ears so efficiently, I don't hear Patricia agreeing to his command. I am beyond ropable that he invaded my privacy like this. He had no right to do this. I don't care how angry he is.

The fevered heat slicking my skin with sweat intensifies when image after image of my engagement to Riley fills the projector screen. Most are magazine articles, but the occasional random picture from attendees who came to our small and highly unrated engagement party pops up. Even the obligatory newspaper announcement Riley's mom placed in the local paper of her hometown has been included.

"I find it interesting I could locate hundreds of articles on your engagement to Riley Smith, but I failed to find one mention of it ending." Hunter's slur doesn't affect the maliciousness of his words. They're as stinging as ever. "So what was I, Paige? The cold feet before the wedding fuck? Or the shmuck you used to get back at your daddy for spending too many hours in the office playing sergeant to his little minions?"

"Neither," I say with a shake of my head.

The quickest spark of relief brightens Hunter's eyes.

It's short-lived.

"You were the stupid fuck I used to fill my scrapbook with storylines." My tone matches his earlier maliciousness. "You were the one who said I had to write from experience. And boy did I experience it. I *felt* it, *tasted* it, *devoured* it. I took every inch you were willing to give *all* just to fill the blank pages of a book."

When Hunter balks as if my words physically slapped him, I smirk a grin I've only ever been on the receiving end of before strutting to his front door. I keep my eyes straight ahead, ensuring he won't see the hot, salty tears threatening to spill down my cheeks. I've never been a confrontational type of person, but after what I've endured the past twenty-four hours, my claws are bared, and my inner bitch has been unleashed.

After inhaling a big breath to rid my voice of nerves, I say, "Let me out so I can go share my newly-discovered mommy-porn stories with my rich country club friends."

The cracks in my heart enlarge when Hunter snarls without pause for thought, "Patricia, disarm all security locks."

The heat of the midday sun does nothing to lessen the dampness of my cheeks as I race down the stairs of Hunter's residence and hotfoot it to the taxi still idling at the front of the cabin. As I slot into the back seat, I tell the driver to take me anywhere but here.

He does precisely that without seeing hide nor hair of Hunter.

Chapter Twenty-Five

"Wow. Swanky view." Pepper peers out of the supersized double windows of my hotel suite at Oceana Beach Club Resort in Santa Monica. The dull hum of tourists chatting filters into the room when she opens the bi-folding doors and steps onto the patio. The sun setting in the distance bounces off her dark chocolate hair, haloing her in a luminous glow. "Have you spent any time out here?" She cranks her neck back to peer at me, her eyes rolling when I shake my head. "Miles of beautiful beaches and even more pristine men, and you've cooped yourself up in a hotel room. If you wanted to spend your days looking at ugly, bland walls, you could have just stayed at my apartment."

I shrug and turn my eyes to the makeshift writing cave I created in the living area of my suite. I've rarely ventured from my laptop the past five days, only leaving it to shower and have the occasional bite to eat.

"I came here to write, not look at the scenery," I blubber, blurting out the same excuse I gave her when I shut myself off from any form of communication.

I've spent the last five days doing what I was supposed to do while at the cabin. I finished penning a steamy romance novel. I switched off all electronic devices, completely hiding away from social media, and kept my focus solely on my manuscript.

I'm not saying my mind didn't stray to Hunter numerous times the past five days, but I vied to keep it as irregularly as possible, deciding nothing but my work would be my primary focus.

When Pepper saunters back into my room, leaving the patio door open, I push off my chair and close it. Usually, too much quiet is my archenemy, but for the past few days, I've discovered the enjoyment you can achieve from little bouts of solitude.

Sometimes the most powerful thing you can say is nothing at all.

Pepper snags a stone-cold French fry off the room service tray before padding to my makeshift writing cave. "Did you get your manuscript in on time?"

I nod. "Yep. I emailed it to my editor this morning. The hero is no Archer Boyd, but I think the storyline will keep my readers enthralled."

"I told you you've never missed a deadline," Pepper replies, her brow arching high.

I narrow my eyes at her. "I only made it by the skin of my teeth. I've hardly slept a wink the past five days."

She tugs on a strand of my hair that hasn't been washed in nearly a week. "Even without your deadline looming, you wouldn't have been getting any sleep. You know it, and so do I."

I plop into the hard office chair the hotel chain supplies, hating the way my backside doesn't mold into the deep crevices of the padded chair as did my old writing chair.

At my request, the transport company shipped my favorite chair back to my father's residence. Until I can decide on my next move, I'm technically homeless.

"Now I just have to think of a title," I mumble after returning my focus to the only thing that will ensure I don't end up homeless and jobless.

I spin around to face the blank white page I've been staring at for the past two hours as Pepper's bare feet move soundlessly across the plush carpet. With a huff, she props her hip onto the side of my desk and purses her lips. "Do you have any idea what you want to call it, or are you just sending me into this bad boy blindfolded?"

I smile, loving that she can drag my mind away from any negativity attempting to surface in it. "I've been tossing around a few ideas, but nothing has stuck. I want the title to be mysterious and intriguing."

"Mystery Man!" Pepper pipes up, scaring the living daylights out of me.

I shake my head. "Already done by Kristen Ashley."

"Oh yeah, I love that book," she replies, smiling.

I waggle my brows. "Me too."

Pepper taps her index finger on her red-painted lips. "Mad... *man?*" I cock my brow and glare at her. "No?" she asks with a shake of her head and a cheeky grin.

When she snags my iPhone off the table and switches it on, I ask, "What are you doing?"

This is the first time my phone has been switched in the past five days. I cut off all communication after receiving a three-word text message from Hunter the night I left the cabin.

It simply said, *I'm sorry, Paige.*

I try to pretend my lack of electronic communication is to spite Hunter, but in reality, I know he's capable of reaching me, switched-off phone or not. I merely turned it off to stop myself from messaging him.

I've undertaken numerous personal battles the past few days about whether I should contact him to negate the false statement I gave him the last time we talked. The only thing that has stopped me is my pride... and perhaps a little bit of bitchiness.

When my phone fails to ding, indicating it has a new voicemail or text message, I slump deeper into my chair as rejection maims my already disfigured heart. Half of me tries to pretend I don't give two hoots about Hunter, where the other half—mainly the writing half— is dying to know if he read the manuscript for *Spy Thy Neighbor.*

I poured my soul into that book. The promise I made to my mom to live the life I want to live, not the one I felt compelled to live because of my family name, Riley's betrayal, and the most important of all—how I fell in love with a bearded man who lived in the glass house next door.

If I did my job as a writer, Hunter would no longer have any doubts about my intentions. He'd realize his assumptions were wrong and that I was with him because I wanted to be with him.

He also should have manned up and apologized in person.

Obviously, my writing isn't quite the caliber I thought it was.

"Oh, here we go," Pepper says, drawing my thoughts back into the present. "Dr. Google has supplied us with a broad range of words matching mystery. We have puzzle, conundrum, riddle, enigma, problem—"

For the first time in days, my heart beats faster. "Enigma," I say, testing the word out for size. "I like that. It's mysterious, dark, and alluring... just like my main character."

A broad grin etches onto Pepper's mouth. "It has a sexy feel to it too. Like you're expecting to meet Mr. Dark and Handsome between the pages."

I smile. "That is the *exact* response I want from my readers, so I guess that's it. *Enigma.*"

"And who says Google is hopeless?" Pepper places my phone back onto my desk just as a knock taps on my suite's door. Her face brightens as excitement sparks in her eyes.

"Don't get too excited. Cabana boys don't do house calls. It's probably just room service coming to collect their cart."

With a pout, she pushes off the desk and moseys to the entryway. I gather some small bills from my purse in the desk drawer before following her.

My steps falter, closely followed by my breathing when my eyes lock in on a pair of murky blue eyes I'll never forget. *Hunter.*

His eyes are plagued with dark circles and crammed with remorse, and his beard is scruffy and unkempt. Even heartbroken and still harboring anger at him, I hate seeing him hurt.

Pepper's eyes bounce between Hunter and me like she's

watching a tennis match between Roger Federer and Novak Djokovic. When she catches Hunter's curious glare, she mumbles. "I'll be... *downstairs.*"

She snags her purse off the entryway table, glides past Hunter, and slips out the door. My lips struggle to hold back a smile when she silently mouths, "He's so hot," behind Hunter's shoulder while hooking her thumb at him.

After doing an impromptu grind-up behind a completely oblivious Hunter, she disappears down the hall. I shake my head. Only Pepper would find time for banter during a heart-strangling confrontation.

Once she's no longer in sight, I return my focus to Hunter. When I spot a glint of amusement in his eyes, I realize he's aware of Pepper's spontaneous dance-off.

As his intoxicating smell quickly swamps the suite, I roll my shoulders while remembering the pledge I made to myself five days ago. Quirky. Eccentric. A little nutty. I'll happily accept any of those names, but doormat is one I'll no longer tolerate. Not from Riley and most definitely not from Hunter—the man who taught me I'm more than enough.

A bout of silence stretches between us, neither willing to show their hand first. It's thick and heavy, which weighs down my already crippled heart. Hunter isn't a communicator, but this should be different. Why come all the way here to continue with the same tactic that divided us to start with? If he'd just given me the chance to explain that afternoon, things wouldn't have gone as far as they did.

No longer able to stand the quiet, I mutter, "What do you want, Hunter?"

He digs his hand into the front pocket of his beloved jeans before taking a step closer to me. "I wanted to give this back to its rightful owner."

My heart whacks my ribs when he pulls out the USB I left on his kitchen counter. It holds the only digital version of *Spy Thy Neighbor.*

"Did you read it?"

He nods. "Every word, Paige." He licks his dry lips before adding, "It's *really* good. Although your readers may kill you if you blindside them with that cliffhanger." His tone is aiming for cheeky, but it still sounds pained.

Air escapes my nostrils, my body's only visible response to the hurt stabbing in my chest. "Well, I didn't know how it would end," I answer truthfully. "I hadn't planned on an ex-fiancé crashing back into the picture."

He tries to tuck it away, but I don't miss the quick flash of anger crossing his face.

"Riley isn't my fian—"

"I know. I read that," Hunter interjects as his remorseful eyes bounce between mine. "I'm so sorry, Paige. For not giving you time to explain. For the hurtful things I said."

When he cups my jaw, I beg for my body to pull away, to reject his touch, but I can't. My body doesn't care how angry he makes me, it will never deny his touch.

As his sorrow-filled eyes silently plead for forgiveness, he murmurs, "I fucked up, Paige."

"Yeah, you did." I wipe away a tear dribbling down my face from my quick head bob. "You hurt me, Hunter. Even if you didn't betray me like Riley, you still purposely set out to hurt me... that's something I don't know if I can forget." My words come out rough, hampered by the sob sitting in the back of my throat, dying to break free. "Then you invaded my privacy. You didn't need to do that. I would have answered any questions you had, all you had to do was ask."

"I know. I made a mistake, but I'm here trying to make it right."

"Don't," I plead when he presses a kiss on the side of my mouth. "Don't," I beg again when I lean into his second kiss instead of repelling from it. "You hurt me." The pained sob of my words exposes the truth of my statement. "You're still hurting me."

An unexpected whimper seeps from my lips when his beard inches away from my cheek. Although it is what I wanted, the disappointment roaring through my body would have you believing the opposite.

With his hand still curled around my jaw, he pleads, "Tell me how to fix this. I want to fix the mistakes I made."

More tears spill from my eyes when I shake my head. "I can't tell you how to do that, Hunter. Only you can work out how to fix the wrongs you made."

After faintly cursing under his breath, he removes his cold hand from my face, scrubs it across his beard, then speaks a bunch of truths I never thought he'd share. "I thought you made me my father. That you forced me into a twisted love triangle I would have never chosen to be a part of." I try to deny his claims, but he keeps speaking before I have the chance. "For the first four weeks of my sister's life, I thought she was my daughter." His devastated laugh sucker-punches the wind out of my lungs. "Turns out the girl I had been dating since junior high was more interested in the refined Mr. Kane than me."

Instinctively, one of my hands fists his shirt while the other flattens against the area just above his heart. "They had been having an affair for a year prior to my sister's birth. The confusion about April's paternity was only discovered when she required a blood transfusion shortly after birth. Her blood type was A negative... just like my dad. That was the beginning of a bitter paternity battle."

He stops talking, and his throat works hard to swallow. "When the results came back exposing my father as April's biological parent, my mom sought the aid of a divorce attorney. I supported her all the way, more concerned about the pain she was experiencing than my own." His words are hurried like they're spilling from his mouth before he has the chance to stop them. "When my mom's lawyer filed the official divorce papers, she discovered my dad had taken everything my parents had accumulated in their twenty-year marriage and signed it all into his mistress's name months earlier. He was not only planning on leaving my mom heartbroken but broke as well."

The thick beard covering most of his face is unable to hide the tick of his jaw. "It was the night I arrived home to my mom crying over an eviction notice that my true hacking abilities became unearthed. I'd dabbled in hacking in my early teens, but nothing more than issuing free cinema tickets for my friends and me or changing the grades of some college friends' papers." A smile tugs on his lips when he continues to talk, "Within three hours, the house my parents purchased a year after marrying was returned to my mother's name, and my dad's bank accounts were wiped clean. I took every penny he had." His wild smile enlarges. "The look on his face when I told him I was the one who cleaned him out was priceless. The sweetest revenge."

He exhales a big breath before relocking his eyes with mine. "But the downfall of youth is being too cocky. I was sloppy, leaving a paper trail a mile long. I paid for the consequences of my actions. Two years in county jail."

I try to speak, to say something, but for once in my life, I'm truly at a loss for words.

After a small stint of silence, the smile Hunter was wearing earlier returns. "But even with me leaving a massive paper trail behind, they still couldn't find where I hid his money. That's when my dad got desperate. He gave me two options. Either tell him where the money was, or he would have me prosecuted."

"You chose option B," I whisper when my mouth finally cooperates with my brain.

Hunter nods. "I hated him so much, to me, there was only one option." His chest expands when he inhales a large gulp of air. "I got served a four-year sentence. I was out in two for good behavior."

"Did they ever find the money?" I query when my curiosity gets the better of me.

"No," he replies with a shake of his head. "It's been hiding in plain sight for over ten years, but since my dad is so blinded with rage, he can't see the signs flashing before his eyes."

I stare at him, shocked and confused.

"It's in a trust fund in my sister's name," he elaborates. "The interest from her sizable bank balance gets deposited into my mom's account every month. If my dad had any concerns for the welfare of his youngest child, he might have realized an unemployed divorcee left penniless after her husband fleeced her for every dime couldn't raise a small child without assistance. But since his gaze has been rapt on the wrong child the entire time, he's none the wiser to the substantial trust fund his daughter now has."

"Does he not see her?" I ask, my voice pained for April growing up without a father.

Hunter shakes his head. "No. Last I heard, my dad is in Cuba living off the money he swindled from a group of investment bankers."

"What about April's mom?"

He once again shakes his head. "She hasn't seen her since the day she left her on my mom's doorstep with a note pinned to the blanket wrapped around her."

"So your mom raised April as if she's her daughter?"

The smile that etches onto Hunter's mouth makes my knees weak. "Yep," he breathes out. "Even though April doesn't have my mom's blood running through her veins, she has part of mine, and that's enough for my mom."

"Sounds like an incredible lady," I murmur as fond memories of my mom pummel into me.

"She is."

Another stretch of thick silence greets us. Although heartbreak is still heating my blood, it isn't as potent as it was when Hunter first entered the room. It has simmered from his honesty.

After a short stint of contemplation, Hunter locks his remorseful eyes with mine. "When I read your manuscript, I realized how fucking stupid I had been. But I was hurting, Paige. I thought I'd finally allowed someone in, only to have the door slammed in my face." His eyes float between mine. "I was wrong, and I'm sorry for that."

I nod, soundlessly accepting his apology. I had forgiven him the instant the first "sorry" spilled from his lips. The final quote my mom gifted me before she passed has been running on repeat in my mind for the past five days. "You've got to take the good with the bad, smile with the sad, love what you've got, and remember what you had. Always forgive, but never forget. Learn from mistakes, but never regret."

Although I am angry at how Hunter handled the situation, I can't say I don't understand his reaction. He was hurting, believing I had betrayed him. But if he had talked to me instead of relying solely on the false documents in front of him, he would have realized I never betrayed him.

I guess I can't talk. I knew the cruel words fired off my tongue during our argument had no factual basis, but I still spat them out, forgetting that two wrongs don't make a right. If anything, I'm not the only one who deserves an apology. Hunter does as well.

"Hunter, I'm so—"

"Don't," he interrupts, his tone both stern and remorseful. "I unleashed my anger about what had happened ten years ago on the wrong person. Don't apologize for reacting the way you did, Paige. I deserved it. Hurting or not, I was in the wrong."

This time when he cups my jaw, I don't pull away. I relish it.

Another stretch of silence passes between us. It isn't riddled with anger and pain like earlier. It's filled with forgiveness and another feeling I can't quite recognize.

My eyes bounce between Hunter's as I try to comprehend what the unidentifiable glimmer in his eyes is.

When it smacks into me, I inhale a sharp breath while stepping backward. It isn't his remorseful eyes that have my heart stuttering. It's the glint he's trying to conceal with a repentant look causing my greatest concern. "You're expecting me to run."

"No, I'm not expecting you to run," he denies with a shake of his head. "But I want you to."

"Why?" My words strangle in my throat as my eyes shimmer with new tears. "And don't you dare give me the same pathetic excuse you did last time about me deserving a better man." When grimness thins his lips, I know that's the exact line he's planning to issue. "Stop, Hunter! Haven't we been through enough? Did you not read a word I wrote?"

"You wrote that before you knew I spent time in jail, before you knew of the viciousness I unleash when angry." His hard-set eyes are incapable of concealing the hurt he's feeling. "Your dad's biennial election is also looming, so it would be an injudicious time for you to expose your connection to a criminal."

"What happened to not judging a book by its cover? You don't know my dad, but you're judging him by his outward appearance. He didn't become a senator for the title or the fanfare. He did it because he loves his state and country. You might see him as a sergeant playing with his minions, but underneath the suit is a man who has many similarities to you."

Unlike Riley, my dad never used my grandfather's influence to secure his position. It was years of hard work and the love and devotion of a dedicated partner that made him the man he is today. I can see so many likenesses between my dad and Hunter. That's one of the reasons I was myself around Hunter so quickly.

And why I fell in love with him even faster than that.

I cup Hunter's jaw similarly to how he held mine. A grin tugs at my lips when his cheeks twitch from my briefest touch. "You use your appearance as a shield, but you can't fool me. Just like you saw the real Paige, I see you, Hunter. The *real* you." The cracks in my heart are filled by the massive surge of blood pumping through it. "You might have an Adonis ass and a body crafted to make my knees shake..." a smirk etches on his mouth from my playful comment, "... but it is your insides I fell in love with. Not the cover of your story. The heart of it, cheeky Hunter, playful Hunter, mysterious Hunter, and even grumpy Hunter... I love them all the same."

He draws in a long, shaky breath, showcasing that hearing my feelings in person has more impact than reading them off a sheet of paper.

The repairs to my heart increase when I notice the painful glimmer in his eyes dampens with every second we stand across from each other. I've only known him for a few short months, but I can't deny the prompts my heart is relaying.

I love him.

Unequivocally and without a doubt.

I've never had these types of feelings before. Not even for a second of the seven years I was with Riley. I knew from the moment I saw Hunter he would be my greatest risk. I just never knew it would also be so substantial.

The stranglehold that's been crippling my heart for the past five days eases when Hunter murmurs, "Don't destroy me, Paige."

"Never," I reply before sealing my lips over his.

Chapter Twenty-Six

Two hours later, I am beyond exhausted and content. After requesting VIP cabana status for Pepper and booking her own room, Hunter spent the next ninety minutes issuing his apologies with his body.

It was the most riveting apology I've ever been given, and it's seen me spend the last ten minutes working out a way to make him need to apologize again and again.

The lazy beat of my heart quickens when Hunter enters the suite's main room. He's shirtless and barefoot, and his cell phone is attached to his ear. Just like five days ago, his body is glimmering with wetness, but it isn't from a shower. It's from the exhaustive activities we've just undertaken.

A chill runs down my spine when I realize he's talking into his untraceable cell.

After scampering off the sweat-dampened sheets, I pad across the floor. The muscles in Hunter's back tense when I mold the curves of my body with his.

He tugs my arms around his waist firmer before he mutters, "Can't. He's in Vegas helping Parker secure Isaac's asset."

Once I've wrangled my hands free from his painless clutch, I slither them down the damp ridges of his abdomen before slipping past the waistband of his unbuttoned jeans. He inhales a quick, sharp breath when I stroke his cock through his jeans, priming him for round two.

The vibration of Hunter's chuckle rumbles through my chest when he says, "I'm a little *indisposed* right now."

Oh, yes, you are.

I curl around to the front of his body and stare into his murky blue eyes while lowering his zipper. He smiles a heart-stopping grin but continues with his conversation like nothing scandalous is about to occur.

I have news for him.

"That means you're fifteen hundred miles closer to Izzy than me. I've tried everyone, but being New Year's Eve, I'm running out of options. Besides, you're the only man Isaac trusts with Izzy."

His thighs prickle with goosebumps when I lower his jeans down his legs, then my eyes bulge when I realize he isn't wearing any briefs.

After lifting my hunger-filled eyes to Hunter, I whisper, "Hurry up. I want to suck your cock."

Pre-cum pools on the tip of his fat cock before he says with urgency, "I've got to go. Can you do this or not, Hugo?"

I lower myself onto my knees before wrapping my hand around the base of his throbbing shaft. His musky, manly scent deepens when I hover my lips over his glistening knob.

"I'll add it to the long list of favors," Hunter pushes out, his words so fast they sound like cracks of a whip.

Stealing his caller's chance to reply, he disconnects his call, throws his phone onto the crumpled bed, then secures my hair into a loose ponytail by using his fist as a band. A feral groan leaves his mouth when I suck down hard. I'm more than eager to see the expression that only crosses his face when he's coming.

A pleasurable shudder darts through me when his delicious cock swamps my taste buds. He tastes tangy and salty, and he smells intoxicating. It's a unique scent of cologne, soap, sweat and... *me.*

I work him hard and fast, loving the thick veins throbbing under the smoothness of his skin that's taut, jutted, and hot. When my sucks become more forceful, he rubs his thumbs over the hollows in my cheeks, softening them for the exhaustive activity they're undertaking.

I take him deeper and harder, moaning through every drop of pre-cum expelled onto my tongue.

I can't get enough. I love that I can make him so open and raw. That I can unravel him.

Tasty drops of salty goodness spurt onto my tongue as I pump him faster. My jaw is aching from sucking him so furiously, but my pace doesn't slow in the slightest. I take him to the very back of my throat before swiveling my tongue around his veiny shaft.

A rough groan tearing from his throat has Hunter's grip on my hair tightening. He's getting close to the end, and the knowledge has my nipples budding with excitement and my pussy slicking with moisture.

"Fuck, Paige." His hips jerk forward, ramming even more of his cock into my mouth. "You suck dick so good." After another three rocks of his hips, he murmurs, "In or out, baby? I can't hold back much longer." My eyes bulge when I grip his Adonis ass and thrust his hips forward. His cock is jammed down my throat, but the pain is worth the smile that etches onto his ruggedly handsome face when he says, "In it is."

The muscles in his stomach contract and his head drops back as the first spurts of cum explode onto my tongue. I struggle to swallow the thick stream pumping from his engorged knob, but I continue working my throat until every drop has been consumed.

When I slowly glide his still hard cock out of my mouth, I lift my eyes to Hunter's face. He grins a deliriously delicious smile before banding his arms around my waist and hoisting me off the ground. "My turn for dessert," he mutters into my ear while making a beeline for the bed.

I squeal into delight when he tosses me onto the springy mattress. It switches to a moan when his beard is scratching the cleft of my pussy before I've even done one whole bounce.

"Mmm," he growls against my aching slit when he discovers how aroused I am from sucking his dick. I'm dripping back to front, and despite a tinge of modesty demanding I close my legs to a ladylike width, I sweep them open so they can accommodate the wide span of Hunter's shoulders. "Do you feel it, Paige?" he asks before spearing his tongue between the wet lines of my pussy and dragging it up to my clit. "The excitement? The rush? The desire?"

Incapable of speaking, I nod before weaving my fingers through his hair that's damp at the tips.

Even with his eyes on my breasts instead of my face, Hunter must intuit my reply. "That's why your story was so good. It has the connection a couple should feel. The bond that can't be made up on a whim." He peers at me over the blobs of flesh he admires as if they're far more luscious than they are before muttering, "The love."

Before I can identify the glimmer in his eyes or demand him to spell it out for me, he bombards my clit with back-to-back rapid-fire hits. I scream his name as my body shakes through a long, revitalizing orgasm.

I've barely returned from the blessedness when Hunter crawls up my body. His beard is glistening with evidence of my arousal, and the cutest gleam is brightening his dark eyes.

"Nuh-uh," he murmurs when my spent body naturally rolls to locate a more enjoyable position. "Stay right where you are." He snags a condom from the box on the bedside table, rips it open with his teeth, then rolls it down his fat cock all the while returning my stare.

We've never done missionary.

Not once.

"Don't look so surprised, Paige. I said missionary isn't boring if you're doing with the right person."

After curling my legs around his sweat-slicked waist, he lines his cock up with the entrance of my pussy, then lifts his eyes to mine. When I jerk up my chin, silently granting him permission to enter me, he slowly notches inside me.

I dig the pads of my feet into his perfect ass when his hips sink low enough, his Apollo belt rubs my overstimulated clit. "That shouldn't feel so good."

Good lord, he brought out his shy smirk.

As he sinks my body into the mattress with perfectly constructed pumps, Hunter lowers his forehead to rest on mine. "Now I can't miss a single expression that crosses your beautiful face."

I can smell my arousal on his beard and breath, but since it's mingled with the musky scent of his overheated skin, it's almost enticing.

We breathe as one for the next several minutes while he makes love to me like actions will always speak louder than words. Since I believe that, I bestow the same amount of devotion on him that he's awarding me. I run my hands down his back before gripping his ass cheeks and giving them a gentle squeeze. He soundlessly laughs like he can't understand my obsession with his butt, but his cock also throbs, which gives away his true response.

He loves that I am as smitten by his cock and ass as he is my breasts and pussy.

He may even love something more than them.

"Slower," Hunter barks out when my excitement gets the better of me. "Nice and slow, baby. We're not fucking. *We are making love.*"

I don't know if he speaks his last four words or if my lusty head made them up, but they are the final push I need for the wave in my womb to spill over.

That, along with the words he speaks next, "You ruined me, Paige. You fucking ruined me for eternity. But despite that, I promise to love you even longer than that."

Chapter Twenty-Seven

Incapable of leashing my curiosity for a second longer, I pop my head off Hunter's chest, bend an elbow, and peer into his sexually satiated eyes. "When did you read my manuscript?"

"The day you left," he answers while scraping a hand over his unshaven jaw.

"Five days ago?" I try to keep bitchiness out of my tone. It's a waste of time. My words are smeared with annoyance.

When Hunter nods, I climb out of bed and pace the room. "Then why are you only arriving now? Why did it take you five days to realize you were wrong?" He tries to interrupt me, but I keep rambling. "You knew I did nothing wrong, yet you left me wallowing in self-pity and stupidly feeling guilty for lashing out when *you* were the one being an unreasonable asshole." My hair swishes against my naked back when I twist around to face him. "I've barely slept or eaten the last five days because of *you*. And don't think it was just my writing stopping me from ordering the biggest burger on the room service menu. It was the twisted, sick feeling in my stomach. I was lost. Hungry. Pissed off! How could you leave me hanging like that? That's the mother lode of all cliffhangers. The ultimate betrayal."

I get ready for a second tirade when Hunter slips off the bed, enters the living room of the suite, and gathers up his hemp bag he dumped near the entryway table. If he thinks he's walking out on me, he has another thing coming. I don't care what obstacles come at me, after the words he spoke last night, I will fight for us. It won't be fair, and it won't be clean, but my god, I will fight.

My clenched fists unfold when Hunter strides back into the room, his cock swinging with every step, to place a heavy rectangular object into my palm. "This is why it took me five days to get here." He nudges his head to the wrapped product. "It took a lot longer to find than I was anticipating."

Tears well in my eyes as they roam the brown paper and twine-covered parcel. From its size and weight alone, I can easily derive that it's a book.

I bite the inside of my cheek before carefully tearing open the top corner of the parcel. Time comes to a standstill when the spine of *The Weekend Romance* peeks out from behind the paper.

A tear rolls down my cheek as I lift my eyes to Hunter. He's watching me with a reserved yet poignant stare. He looks more fearful now than he did when he first arrived at my door.

After wiping away the tears from my ashen cheeks, I continue removing the paper covering my mom's book. My chest heaves up and down when I crack open the spine to discover her handwritten inscription inside, the one she wrote for me.

As a sob tears from my throat, I hug the book in close to my chest before slinging my spare arm around Hunter's broad shoulders. "You found it," I barely whisper, my lips quivering against his neck.

My body shudders in the shock that he found something I've been searching for years to find. Not trusting my legs to keep me upright, Hunter gathers me into his arms, then sits on the bed. He doesn't speak. He simply runs his hand down the curve of my back, silently supporting me.

While endeavoring to get my sobs under control, I listen to the frantic beat of his heart.

It takes several tedious minutes, but once again, it doesn't feel awkward.

It just feels right.

By the time I've settled my emotions, Hunter's torso is wet with my tears, and his eyes are more pained than earlier. "I wanted to give it to you earlier, Paige, but I didn't want you to think I was using it as leverage to force you to forgive me."

"I know," I interrupt, not requiring further explanation.

Hunter is the first person I've met who gives gifts without any stipulations attached.

That's another reason I fell in love with him so quickly and the sole reason I'll love him for eternity as well.

Epilogue

Six Months Later...

Hunter's fingers fly over the keyboard. His brows are knitted, and his concentration is solely focused on the laptop in front of him. He is in his element.

I don't mind that he's distracted. I'm too busy drinking in the way his crisp black suit showcases his Adonis ass in panty-wetting detail to worry about his focus being on anyone but me.

His beard is neatly trimmed, and both his hair and his tattoo collection have grown the past six months. He looks so scrumptiously delicious, if we weren't in a church about to attend the wedding of his work colleague and friend, Hugo, I'd have a hard time keeping my hands off him.

The past six months have been staggering.

Day after day is filled with nothing but joy and adventure.

The morning following Hunter's reappearance, we traveled back to the cabin.

What? I had two weeks remaining on my lease so it would have been heinous of me not to take advantage of the spectacular views of Bronte's Peak.

Once my contract expired, and against Hunter's wish, I begrudgingly returned to my hometown. I lasted all of three days before I stood on the stoop of my neighbor's glass house with a suitcase in one hand and delivery slip for my writing chair in another.

I'll never forget the smile that etched onto Hunter's face when Patricia announced my arrival. It's a memory that will remain ingrained in my mind until the end of time.

Only one other memory comes in a close second. It was the day Hunter and my dad met. To say I was surprised when my dad introduced himself to Hunter like he already knew him would have been an understatement. I was flabbergasted.

When Dad noticed my shocked expression, he simply said, "Did you really think I'd let you fly to the other side of the country without first checking who you may be associating with?"

I wasn't the only one stunned by his admission. Hunter looked mortified, and while I am being forthright, he looked a little scared. Not a single spark of hesitation crossed my dad's face when he accepted Hunter's handshake, proving what I already knew. My dad would never judge a book by its cover.

My focus returns from reminiscing when Hunter says, "Done." He lifts his eyes from the laptop screen covered in code to me. "Are you sure this is what you want to do, Paige?"

I nod without hesitation. "Yep. He deserves it." I kick his black polished dress shoe with my pricy pumps. "Don't tell me you're backing down. Riley is a cheater and a retiree bank swindler. He's the very epitome of your dad."

When Hunter and I left my hotel in Santa Monica, we were inundated with reporters. Malicious questions regarding my so-called 'affair' with Hunter fired off their vindictive tongues as Hunter guided me from the hotel's foyer to an awaiting town car.

Just from the range of questions, I could tell Riley leaked news of my connection with Hunter, but instead of acknowledging that our engagement ended four months prior, he made out as if I was the adulteress in our relationship.

While I sat in the back seat of the town car, stunned like a fish out of water, Hunter hacked every newspaper in the country, endeavoring to remove the false reports made about me.

My shock at the reporters' inaccurate statements turned into awe as I watched him work his magic on a small handheld device he created. Within forty minutes, he shut down every article regarding my alleged affair for the eastern side of the country and was rapidly making his way through the west. It was only once I scooted across the leather seat and curled my hand over his did his mission stop.

"Let them run the story," I said while peering into his eyes.

Hunter's lips thinned. "No, Paige. He's making you out to be the one who betrayed him."

"So?" I shrugged. "We know that isn't true, and that's all that matters." My eyes danced between his. "Besides, I've always believed in Karma." I grinned a sly smirk. "Once the dust settles, Karma can step in." I dropped my eyes to Hunter's large black boots tapping the floor of the town car. "With a boot that big, I'm pretty sure Karma's kick will hurt."

That day was a little over six months ago. Today, Karma will finally see sunlight. Not just for me but for the hundreds of retirees Riley fleeced of their retirement funds before he relocated his financial services business to Spain.

Hunter's eyes lock with mine. "I'm not backing down. I'm just making sure you're aware once I push the enter button, everything he has will be gone. I can't bring it bac—"

His words stop when I lean over his shoulder and hit the enter button, wiping Riley clean of every penny he has. "Oops," I breathe out like my insides aren't dancing with happiness that half of Riley's money is being returned to its rightful owners while the remaining half is being distributed to numerous orphanages around the world.

Within ten seconds, Riley's *supposed* hidden bank accounts go from high seven figures to one. Three *measly* dollars.

"I had to leave enough so he could pay for a balance slip." Hunter's smooth as chocolate tone is incapable of hiding the hilarity in his voice.

After closing his laptop screen, he places it into his hemp bag before standing from the pew he's sitting on. I purr like a cat when he wraps his arms around my torso and burrows his head into my neck.

I purr louder when his beard scratches my earlobe. "You're a bad girl, Paige. I think I like this new naughty side."

Cranking back, I peer into his eyes. "Really?" I query as my hands move for the buttons of his suit.

He smiles as lust fires in his eyes. "What are you doing?"

"Research for my next novel." I walk backward, silently praying the confession chamber is unlocked and empty.

Hunter bows his brows, but it can't hide the girth growing behind the zipper of his fancy-schmancy trousers. "In a church?"

My teeth munch on my bottom lip before I nod. "I'll take you any way I can get you."

And I did. Not once but twice in the little white church in the middle of Rochdale, New York.

* * *

The next story in the Enigma series is a brand-new character, Brax.
You can find his book here:
The Opposite Effect

The Opposite Effect

Prologue

Feet scuffling on a tiled floor steal my focus from my half-eaten cheesesteak sandwich. Even with me requesting they hold the relish, my hands are covered in the ghastly orange liquid that makes me gag just thinking about eating it.

When I lift my gaze from my partially dissected dinner, I spot Diesel standing in the lunchroom's doorway. His shoulder is propped against the doorjamb, his extensively tattooed arms are crossed in front of his broad chest, and a look of terror is stretched across his face.

After pushing back from the lunch table hidden out back, I dump my unsalvageable sandwich into the trash, then head to the sink to get cleaned up. Diesel is a cutthroat take-no-shit-from-anyone type of guy, so I'm surprised his cocky personality is a little off.

"What's up, man?" While washing my sticky hands in the kitchen sink, I mutter a string of profanities under my breath.

How the fuck can you mess up a cheesesteak sandwich?

Diesel waits for me to snag a dishcloth off the drying rack before announcing, "Got a client out front requesting to speak to the manager." My lips quirk when he air quotes 'manager.' Although I've held the title for the past two years, it's rarely used by my crew.

Once I hang the damp towel onto a hook above the microwave, I gesture for Diesel to lead the way. Buzzing tattoo guns and the groans of idiot kids who walk through our doors the day they turn eighteen sounds through my ears when we stride through Inked Tattoo Shop.

When I spot Charity tattooing a Pokémon figure onto a kid who looks barely old enough to drive, let alone permanently mark his skin with the latest fad, I rake my fingers through my shoulder-length hair.

It will take a tattoo four times its size to cover up Pikachu or whatever the fuck Pokémon character that is. By the look on his face and the tears staining his cheeks, I'm confident having it covered won't be a walk in the park for neither him nor the tattoo artist assigned to the job.

When we reach the foyer out front, I scan the area, seeking the bozo who interrupted the 'manager' during his measly half-an-hour lunch break.

Upon failing to locate the irate face I regularly see when a client realizes their home-botched tattoo will cost over a grand to fix, I shift my eyes to Diesel. "Where is he?"

Diesel smiles a grin I only see when he's wrapping his arm around a bar bunny at the end of a Saturday night shift. "It isn't a he. It's a *she*."

Still grinning, he points to the far corner of the room. When I tilt my head, only just clearing Johnny's wide shoulders, I catch the quickest flurry of an enticing body. My heart rate kicks up a gear—*as does the pulse in my cock*—when I drink in the slender blonde sparring with Johnny like backyard brawls are a regular event on her schedule.

Her platinum locks roll past her shoulders like a satin waterfall, and her expensive threads showcase every curve of her fit body. Her face is fresh with only a slight sprinkling of makeup, and every strand on her faultless head has been meticulously placed.

Although I can't hear a word she's speaking, I know she's giving Johnny as good as she's getting. If the crossed arms under her ample breasts and stiffened stance aren't enough indication, her resting bitch face is a sure-fire sign.

This woman is two seconds from exploding.

Since I don't want a bomb detonated in my shop on a busy Saturday night, I pat Diesel on the back before heading for the attractive blonde. A rich floral scent with a hint of spice filters into my nose when I stand next to Johnny. I'm fairly sure the flowery scent is coming from the blonde, but I can't one hundred percent testify to that. Johnny is generous with the discount he offers female clientele. If the loss comes from his takings, I have no concerns about him accepting payments for services rendered in the form of extra-curricular activities.

"I'm pretty sure you're sitting at around two seconds," I interrupt when I overhear the blonde telling Johnny she's five seconds away from having his "moronic ass fired."

"Great." Her eyes snap to mine. They're as dazzling as the diamond bracelet circling her delicate wrist. "Another beast added to the mix. What is this, a poorly scripted rendition of *Beauty and the Beast?*"

Three females standing behind her break into an ear-piercing drunken cackle, but surprisingly, the blonde maintains eye contact. I'll give it to her. I'm impressed at her ability to keep her eyes on my face. Most women absorb my face before dropping to sample the rest of the package. It doesn't matter if they're screaming nothing but wealth like the princess standing before me, or they don't have a nickel to their name, the routine never alters. So yeah, I'll admit it, she gets credit where credit is due.

After propping my elbows onto the counter, I lean over it, which brings my six-foot-two height down to her at-a-guess five-foot-seven stature. "What can I do you for, Princess? Unlike you, some of us have to work for a living."

She rolls her eyes before saying in a snooty twang, "Not according to..." She gestures her hand to Johnny, sending a multi-hued shimmer of light across the cabinet from her diamond bracelet. "Him—"

"Johnny," I interrupt.

She rolls her eyes again. "Whatever you call him. No one cares. I came here to get a tattoo." She points to the tube light hanging from the shop's awning. "This is a tattoo parlor. But..." she snaps her eyes back to Johnny, "... *he* is refusing to serve me. I don't know about you, but in any other industry, that would call for instant dismissal."

I smirk, not shocked by her attitude but most definitely stunned by my positive response to it. Normally, I would toss out a berating client before giving them the chance to explain. Instead, I slot into the 'manager' role I'll never completely fill. "Lucky for Johnny, we aren't just any *other* industry." My voice has an edge of annoyance to it even with me being most entertained by the change-up in clientele. "If Johnny is refusing to tattoo you, it will be for a reason. So, what is it?"

With a huff, she digs her hand into the front pocket of her designer jeans that look like they cost more than my entire wardrobe. "Other than Johnny being a moron, I have no clue why he's refusing my request."

"It's beca—"

I slice my hand through the air, cutting Johnny off. His wife packed her bags and headed to Reno nine months ago, leaving him the sole guardian of their two children. He wouldn't refuse the chance to make a quick dollar without a legitimate reason. Just the blonde's overpriced shoes, designer handbag, and perfectly swept hair leave no doubt he could have charged her triple the regular hourly rate, and she'd have been none the wiser.

He'd never turn down an opportunity like this without a solid reason.

I lock my eyes with Johnny. "Why don't you head out back and work on those sketches you started last week? I'll man the counter. Next client who enters is yours."

Johnny nods before sauntering to the manager's office stationed next to his cubicle. Once he passes through the battered wooden door, I return my focus to the blonde. Victory is etched on her face, and the bitch pose she's already perfected escalates.

I stand from my slouched position, then shoot my eyes to a sign attached to the side wall of the foyer. "We have the right to refuse patrons under the influence of alcohol, drugs, or peer pressure." I tap my fingers on the big black letters scrawled across the sign. Even someone with their eyes as thinly slit as hers can still read it.

After speedreading the sign three times, she scoffs. "I'm not drunk," she denies while crossing her arms under her chest, hoisting her impressive rack higher.

It takes everything I have to drag my eyes away from her fantastic tits to peer at her intoxicated friends behind her, but I manage— somewhat. The blonde's snarky beast comment was delivered over five minutes ago, but her friends are still cackling like a bunch of overly botoxed biddies holding an annual meeting at a members-only country club.

My curved brow arches higher when I notice the only brunette in the trio is clasping an open bottle of champagne.

While running a hand over my jaw, which is marked with a few days of stubble, I shift my eyes back to the blonde. When I twist my lips, a deep rustle escapes her nose before she cranks her neck to her friends.

Even smacking them with a furious stink eye doesn't dampen their laughter.

If anything, her actions increases it.

Realizing her friends won't help me believe she isn't under the influence, she gestures to them that it's time to leave. Just before she emerges onto the sidewalk, she peers back at me and narrows her eyes. I smile and wink at her, more than happy to add a sprinkling of salt to her freshly opened wounds.

When a black town car slides up to the curb at the front of the shop, I swing my eyes to Diesel. "What was so hard about that?" My tone is dripping with cockiness. "You need to stop entertaining bar bunnies on your days off and wrestle a few rich chicks. They give a bit of lip, but since it's from the same mouth that will be screaming your name later that night, you put up with it."

After lifting my arms to protect my face, I throw a handful of rapid-fire jabs into Diesel's T-shirt-covered torso. A grin tugs on his fat lips before he spars up, priming for an impromptu spar in the foyer.

Usually, we box in an old gym at the back of the shopping complex in Ravenshoe. It's rundown, but the guy behind the rusty equipment is a brilliant trainer.

In just a few short weeks, Hank has switched Diesel from a back-yard brawler to a low-ranking fighter.

Fighting isn't something I'm interested in, but I turn up every session to show my support to Diesel. Although I will admit, the energy boost after going a few rounds in the ring with Diesel has aided in my bedroom antics. I have stamina by the miles and more than a dozen bar bunnies willing to exhaust me of resources.

When Diesel uses my distraction of the shop's bells to his advantage, my neck snaps to the side, and my jaw pops under the force of his knuckles. After working my jaw side to side, I lock my furious eyes with Diesel's.

With a grin that announces he isn't sorry, he holds his hands in the air in a non-defensive manner. "Sorry." The shortness of his apology can't hide his laughter.

While rubbing my hand along my now throbbing jaw, I drift my eyes from Diesel to the door. "Welcome to Inked..." My greeting falls short when I'm confronted with the same pair of icy-blue eyes that stormed out of here mere minutes ago.

The bitch is back.

When the blonde completes her surveillance of the rest of my package, I wait for her eyes to return to my face before giving her a cocky wink. "Back for round two?"

My jeans tighten when she laughs. It's a dainty giggle full of poise and perfection—*just like its owner.*

"Unlikely." Her words are as cool as the color of her eyes. "I don't *wrestle* with Neanderthals."

Ouch. If my ego wasn't stroked by a pretty blonde out back thirty minutes ago—the same blonde who brought me my sandwich—this blonde's taunt may have bruised my ego.

Lucky for me, I have a gigantic shield protecting my even bigger ego from spoiled princesses with vindictive tongues.

"Unless your daddy found a cure for drunkenness, your *desires* will not be granted in this fine establishment this evening."

Her eyes narrow at the mention of her father, exposing her first flaw of the night.

"I'm *not* drunk." The crispness of her words adds strength to her statement.

Holding my gaze, she saunters closer, allowing me to see the frankness in her eyes. Her hardhearted eyes aren't truth-exposing. It's the fact there isn't a single speck of life in her eyes, let alone the drunk shimmer most inebriated people get, exposing her sobriety. Her eyes replicate staring into an empty pit. They're void of any type of soul.

"I adhered to your rules by requesting my *tipsy* friends to leave. Now your *fine* establishment has no reason *not* to serve me." She tries to make her voice sound sincere. Her attempts are fruitless. I don't think she has a sincere bone in her body.

I grit my teeth, loathing that I'm about to overrule one of my guys, but just her take-no-shit stance exposes she won't leave until she gets what she came here for, so I may as well give it to her. "Do you have a design in mind, or are we going into this agreement freestyle?"

My dick knocks at the zipper in my jeans when she grins a traffic-stopping smile.

Yeah, not happening, buddy.

When she pulls out the sheet of paper she was clutching for dear life earlier, I only just hold in a swear word. She wants a man's name inked on her skin.

Don't ask me why, but the thought of *any* man's name on her skin that isn't mine pisses me off, and considering we've only just met and have spent most of our confrontation defusing her callousness, simply having a thought like that irritates me even more.

After running my eyes over the guy's name in thick black ink smack bang in the middle of the intricate design, I drop them to the blonde's left hand. Upon noticing it is void of a ring—engagement or wedding—I lock my eyes back on hers. "Is this your father's name?" I nudge my head to the tattoo design in my hand.

Lines indent her forehead before she shakes her head.

"Your grandfather? Brother? Deceased uncle? Any type of male relation?" When she shakes her head again, I say, "Sorry, Princess, I can't do your tattoo."

Her eyes slit more with every syllable I speak. "You just agreed to do it."

"Yeah, so?" I shrug like backtracking is on my resume. "That was before you showed me the design."

"What's wrong with the design?" She crosses her arms before arching a perfectly manicured brow. "Not *tacky* enough for you?"

"There's only one *tacky* person in this tattoo parlor, *Princess*." I draw out the word usually used as a term of endearment as if it is a derogative word instead. "It ain't me."

She huffs, her irritation growing by the second. She isn't the only one annoyed. My cock's thickness hasn't lessened from her feistiness. It stiffens with every snarl she hits me with.

"Look. I want to get this tattoo done. You're a tattoo artist. Do whatever you need to do to make this happen."

I nudge my head to the piece of paper. "Are you giving me permission to make alterations to this design as I see fit?"

"Yes!" She throws her arms into the air. "Can we just get this done, then I can get back to—"

"Prince Charming waiting for you in a crystal palace?" I turn my eyes to the clock on the wall displaying it is a little after eleven. "It's okay, Princess, you still have a good fifty minutes before you'll get turned back into poor, defenseless Cinderella."

She glares at me with shock all over her face.

Of course, a real-life princess wouldn't understand a fairy tale.

When I head to the drawing board to transfer her design onto tracing paper before adding the change I require to feel comfortable tattooing a lifetime commitment onto her no-doubt virgin skin, she stands to the side, glaring at me while swiveling her diamond tennis bracelet around her wrist.

Once I'm happy with the design, I amble back her way. "I've altered the design—"

"Yes, yes, whatever," she interrupts, her tone obnoxious.

With a tight jaw, I place the tattoo contract and a copy of the newly designed trace onto the glass cabinet in front of her. "If you're happy with the design, sign here, here, and here." I point to each section of the contract she's required to sign.

Snatching the pen out of my grasp, she signs each section in a frenzied hurry. After storing the contract in the locked drawer under the cash register, I gesture for her to follow me. As we walk through Inked, her eyes bounce in all directions, strengthening my assumption that this is her first tattoo.

The width of her pupils increases when we enter a private cubicle at the back of the shop. When she spots my tattoo gun sitting on a sterilized stainless-steel table, her face pales.

After closing the door behind me, I ask, "Where do you want your tattoo?"

Heat creeps across her cheeks before she points to her lower right hipbone.

"Then you're gonna need to remove your jeans," I advise before moving to the station to set up my instruments.

When her eyes snap to mine, wordlessly demanding clarification of my request, I nod.

I might be a fucking great tattoo artist, but I'm not a miracle worker.

She hesitates for a moment before doing as instructed. I'm not at all surprised to discover she's wearing a pair of panties I've only seen in the Victoria's Secret catalogs Charity peruses during her lunch break.

After ensuring my gear is in order, I nudge my head to my tattooing chair, silently demanding she sit. As she saunters across the room, I try to keep my eyes planted on her face. I miserably fail. Even with her bitchometer rocketing to the next galaxy, she has a tight, fit body that would only look better if she removed the massive chip off her shoulder.

After sitting in my swivel chair, I roll in close to her side. She stiffens when I lower the band of her panties to prep the area she wants inked. When our eyes briefly lock, her stern mask falters for the slightest second, exposing a side of her I'm confident she hasn't seen in years.

"First time being tattooed?" I query while placing the used alcohol prep pads into a bin at my side.

When she fails to answer my question, I lift my eyes from the stencil I've placed on the creamy skin covering her hip to her.

Four simple words and her stern mask has slid firmly back into place.

"Do we have to do the small talk?"

"I'm just trying to be friendly."

"Well, I'd rather you didn't. You're *not* my friend. You will *never* be my friend. So, I'd prefer if you stayed *quiet* and did the *job* I'm paying you to do."

My back molars smash together before I grind out through clenched teeth, "Then let's do this, Princess." *Before you give me a motherfucking headache.*

It takes all my strength not to dig my tattoo gun into her delicate skin deeper than necessary. The only thing stopping me is my professional obligation. As much as my client is a malicious cow, my name will forever be associated with this piece of artwork on her body, which ensures I'll tattoo nothing but the best, even if I want to send her out in the world with a stick figure of me flipping her the bird.

* * *

Because of the intricate design she selected, the tattoo takes a little over two hours to complete. Princess Stuck-Up didn't speak a word the entire time. I won't lie. I loved the way her knuckles went white from her death grip hold on the armrest when I tattooed the skin near her hip bone.

"While it heals, it'll itch like a bitch, but if you keep applying the ointment as per these instructions, you shouldn't face too many issues." I hand her a pamphlet on taking care of freshly inked skin.

When she snatches it out of my hand, I drop my eyes to my newly created masterpiece. My lips purse. It is a sleek design, feminine with the inclusion of a tiger lily, but not overly girly. If it didn't have a name smack bang in the middle of it, it would have been a nice tattoo.

After wiping the excess ink off her hip, I wrap her tattoo with a protective covering and then assist the unnamed blonde from the chair.

A grin curls on my lips when a grimace crosses her face as she bends down to collect her handbag off the floor. "Run that while I get dressed."

Heavy grooves indent my forehead when she hands me an American Express Centurion card. I've heard rumors that this card costs a quarter of a million a year just to have it. I shouldn't expect anything less from a woman who looks like she uses Benjamin Franklins as toilet paper.

"It's a credit card. You've seen one before, haven't you?" she snarls, her tone condescending.

"Yes, madame," I reply while fighting the urge not to salute her pompous attitude with my middle finger. I jerk my head to the bathroom attached to my cubicle. "There's a full-length mirror in there if you want to check out your new tattoo." When she smirks a condescending grin, I mutter under my breath before slipping out the door, "I hope you like your new tattoo, Princess."

* * *

I've only just run her credit card through the terminal and placed the credit of her sale into Johnny's account when the blonde storms out of my cubicle. She barely notices a group of fraternity brothers getting matching tats wolf-whistling and catcalling at her as she charges across the room in nothing but a pair of cream panties and a long-sleeve shirt. Her face is red with anger, matching her vibrant lipstick, and her pupils are massive.

"You son of a bitch!" she yells while raising her hand in the air.

A chuckle topples from my lips when her wildly flung slap fails to connect with any part of my face or body since I took a step back, moving out of the firing zone.

When she preps for a second swing, I point to a sign hanging next to the one I read earlier. "We also have the right to remove any clientele deemed to be abusive to our staff or clients." My tone is as mocking as my expression. "If you try to strike me again, I'll have no other option than to place you on the curb." I lower my eyes to her scarcely covered body. "Panties and all."

The anger lining her face increases. "Where is the sign that says you can tattoo whatever the hell you see fit onto a person's body without first seeking their permission?"

The grin tugging on my lips breaks free. "In the top drawer." I point to the drawer I stored her contract in. "It's on the same contract *you* signed stating the design of your tattoo was left at the discretion of your tattoo artist. AKA... me."

I can see her scream work its way from her stomach to her lips. For every second that ticks by, the fury blackening her eyes grows significantly, but she detonates with only the slightest bit of carnage.

After releasing a window-shattering scream, she storms back to my cubicle, rambling incessantly under her breath about how she's going to sue me for every penny I have.

If I were a good man, I'd tell her I don't have many pennies.

Pity I'm not.

After redressing in her skin-tight designer jeans and four-inch stiletto boots, she saunters out of my cubicle, slamming the door behind her. Her nostrils flare when she snatches her credit card and receipt out of my hand, but she doesn't murmur a peep as she scrambles for the door.

"Have a wonderful day."

She slams the front glass door so harshly, the gust of its closure knocks the two signs I'd referenced earlier off the wall.

Upon hearing the commotion her abrupt exit caused, Ryder the owner of Inked, exits his office. "Everything all right?" His eyes bounce between the blonde standing at the curb shrieking into a cell phone and me.

I lift my chin. "It's all good."

Although I'm telling him everything is fine, I really need to start considering the consequences of my actions. If I knew I was going against a woman who has more money than sense, I may have considered taking a different route.

Oh, who am I kidding? Nothing would have changed.

Ryder nudges his head to the door. "So what's the deal? She didn't like the terms of your agreement?"

I laugh at the insinuation in his voice. "You know as well as I do, Elvis, nothing but money is exchanged for my services."

Ryder's heavy brow slants at my use of his infamous nickname. His son, Slater, let it slip a few months ago when he was here adding more ink to his already vast collection. I've been keeping it up my sleeve, waiting for a prime opportunity to use it. Tonight seems like the ideal time.

When the blonde curls into a black town car pulled to the curb in front of her, I shift my eyes to Ryder. "I may or may not have changed her boyfriend's name to Princess."

A lewd grin curves onto his lips before he shakes his head in disbelief. "Did you get her to sign the contract?"

"Do you think I got this handsome by lining up for brains? I cut that queue and went straight back to the looks department. Who needs smarts when you look like this?" I run my hand down the front of me while smiling a shit-eating grin.

Any humor in Ryder's face vanishes, replaced with nothing but pure anger.

"I'm joking, Ryder. Of course, I got her to sign the contract. I even stenciled her tattoo with the name adjustment included," I inform him while rocking on my heels. "She signed that too."

A chuckle escapes Ryder's no-longer stern lips. "Then we're all good."

"Yes, we are," I reply, grinning.

Although I have an inkling this won't be the last I'll hear from Ms. Clara McGregor.

Chapter One

The doorman at Vipers greets me with a fist pump before opening the large wrought iron door. Pricy leather, warm bodies, and the scent of alcohol filter into my nose when I enter the main section of the strip club.

My eyes divert from a pretty redhead with gold tassels on her breasts to the entryway bar when a distinctive throaty voice sounds through my ears. "Brax, it's been too long." Keke saunters around the bar to wrap her arms around my neck.

I return her embrace. "Hey, Keke, what are you doing over on this side of town? The prim and proper get too dull for you?"

She laughs before scraping her lengthened French tip nails down my forearm. "I'm always on the lookout," she purrs while skimming the full-to-the-brim club.

"For clientele or new staff members?"

Keke winks before she continues scanning the room. She is the manager of a very exclusive club on the other side of Ravenshoe. *Maison du Sexe* (French for House of Sex). Although she refers to her establishment as a bordello, every male on this side of Ravenshoe calls it a brothel. An incredibly high-priced, invited-members-only exclusive brothel. Though if you're friendly with the manager, even guys from my side of the tracks can dip their toes into the high-caliber services Keke offers.

Does that mean I've accepted the numerous offers she's bestowed upon me? No, it does not. Even though I only accept cash payments for my services, that doesn't mean I'm willing to cough up my hard-earned cash for services I can get without money exchanging hands.

Although with my dick on hiatus the past few weeks, I may need to consider other options.

Keke curls her arm around the crook of my elbow and leads me toward the main stage. She stops in front of a beautiful brunette doing an aerial ribbon routine with a set of black satin ribbons suspended from a bolt shackled to the ceiling. Her outfit selection, although skimpy, is more conservative than the clientele at Vipers is used to seeing. It could be deemed more as a gymnast's outfit than a stripper's ensemble.

My heart leaps out of my chest when the brunette rolls down the satin ribbon, her stomach-churning tumble only stopping a mere inch from the stage. One wrong move and she would have been splattered on the highly-polished wooden stage.

After loosening the satin material from her slender thighs, the brunette curtseys to the wolf-whistling crowd before the stage lights are switched off, plunging the entire area into blackness.

"Beautiful. Yes?" Keke questions, her fake French accent fully exploited.

Smirking, I nod. Even with the brunette having her god-gifted assets hidden from view, her routine was provocative and entertaining. No doubt a rare treat for any male clientele in a strip club.

"The clients at Maison's speak fondly of her very often, but no matter how much money I offer, she never accepts my proposition."

My shoulders lift into a shrug. "Showing your body for money is one thing. Selling it is entirely different."

When Keke scoffs, I turn my brown eyes to her and arch a brow. The longer I stare into her rich, chocolate eyes, the more her refined posture slackens. The persona she displays when working is a completely different Keke than the one you see behind closed doors.

Keke is from Fredericksburg, Virginia. She rides horses bareback, drinks beer by the gallon, and when she comes, her voice reverts to its original country twang. *Y'all* included. How do I know this? We've messed around a few times in the past year.

Now don't take my admission the wrong way. Keke may be the manager of a brothel, but she has never once *worked* in that industry. Like the pretty brunette who just finished her ribbon performance, Keke refuses to sell her body for profit. Her firm stance on the issue ensures her staff at Maison's are treated with the utmost respect and dignity. For the industry she works in, that is no easy feat. Luckily for Keke and her staff, she's backed by an exceedingly notorious man— Mr. Henry Gottle, Sr.—mob boss of New York City.

"Have you thought about asking her to do a routine at Maison that excludes a bedroom?"

Keke's face brightens more with every word I speak. "Brax, you little devil. That could work. Get her in the door and convert her once she's signed on the dotted line."

"That wasn't what I meant."

Keke doesn't hear a word spilling from my lips. She simply smiles and presses a kiss on my cheek before sauntering to the roped-off backstage area. Once she enters through the dark red velvet curtains, I swing my eyes around the space, seeking Damon. His rift with his big brother is the sole reason I've rocked up to a strip club at one in the morning on a Sunday.

While adding three hours to his back tattoo earlier today, Damon suggested we meet up for a few beers with his brother. Considering his brother is my best mate, I readily agreed. I had no clue at the time that his watering hole of choice was a strip club on the outskirts of town.

I will admit, though, my initial assessment of this establishment was a little off track. I thought it would be a seedy establishment with dingy lighting and cracked vinyl booths. It isn't. The owner has pumped some serious coin into this place, giving it a nightclub atmosphere.

The booths are high-end with varnished wood trim and black

leather upholstery. The lighting setup is impressive, with it being incorporated into the music pumping out of the speakers shackled to the ceiling. From the caliber of staff I've seen serving clients and dancing, the standard is high. *Incredibly high.* It feels more like I've walked into the dressing room of a Miss Universe swimsuit competition than a seedy strip club.

My aimless wandering comes to a halt when I hear "Brax!" shouted by a profound voice in the distance.

Cranking my neck to the side, I spot Damon in a booth in the back corner. Surprisingly, he is alone. I dip my chin in greeting to numerous scantily clad women as I make my way across the room. The scent of sweat-slicked skin intensifies the closer I get to the back of the club. Damon stands from the booth and greets me with a slap on the back and a man hug.

He grimaces when I return his gesture.

"Sorry, still fresh?"

He nods. "I haven't drunk enough whiskey to lessen the sting of my new ink," he replies, laughing.

"Where's your brother?"

Just as the final syllable escapes my lips, I spot Ryan making his way through the throng of people mingling in the vast space. A smirk etches onto my lips when I see the disappointing glare Ryan is directing at Damon. Ryan and Damon are brothers cut from two entirely different cloths. Ryan was born and raised in Ravenshoe. The week after he graduated high school, he applied to join the police force. He was immediately accepted. He's spent the last nine years working at the Ravenshoe Police Department.

Damon was also born and raised in Ravenshoe, but unlike Ryan, he left the instant he turned eighteen. Although it's never been fully disclosed, there are rumors circulating that Damon and a certain member of the law enforcement office don't see eye to eye. That may be the reason this is Damon's first visit home in over eight years.

My brows lower when Ryan and Damon greet with a shake of hands. Anyone would swear they were strangers meeting for the first time, not brothers.

While issuing my greeting to Ryan, I mutter into his ear, "It's been eight years, man. Time to let bygones be bygones."

Ryan pulls back and peers into my eyes. "You know why he picked for us to meet here, don't you?"

I smile. "Yeah, I know. But there's nothing wrong with an off-duty detective spending his weekend looking at some fine ladies."

Damon picked this establishment as he knew Ryan would hesitate to show up here. Ryan works hard at keeping his reputation as an honest detective sparkling clean. It is a well-known fact that certain business entities in this area pay for the privilege of keeping their establishments off the local enforcement radar. I'm pretty sure this is one of the clubs that kept Ryan's dad's bank balance in the positive during his twenty-year stint with the Ravenshoe Police Department.

Within forty minutes, I've downed three overpriced whiskeys, Ryan and Damon haven't spoken a word to each other, and Damon has secured himself not one but two lap dances.

I nudge Ryan with my shoulder. "What's the deal? Why is he back?" I gesture my head to Damon during my last question.

Although Damon and Ryan have personalities on opposite ends of the spectrum, their looks are nearly identical. Both have glacier blue eyes, cut facial features, and they're extremely popular with the ladies. I've never had any problems pulling in the ladies, but my looks are often referred to as laid-back compared to Ryan's. He has the cutthroat-businessman appearance, with his attire of choice being suits and polished shoes. My outfit selection rarely strays from ripped jeans and designer shirts.

Ryan tosses back a mouthful of the whiskey the waiter just sat in front of him before answering, "I don't know. He sent Ma a message a few days ago saying he might head back this way in a few months. He turns up on her doorstep the very next day."

My lips quirk. "You think he's running from something?" I query, noticing a mask of concern slipping over Ryan's face.

"Something or someone," Ryan mutters before taking another gulp of his drink. He runs the back of his hand over his mouth before locking his blue eyes with mine. "So what's the deal with you? I've seen you turn down three girls since I arrived. That's not the Brax I know."

After shaking my head in disgust, I down my entire nip of whiskey in one hit. "I think my cock is broken."

Ryan coughs, splattering the countertop with the whiskey he was in the process of swallowing. "What?"

I nudge my head to the gorgeous blonde prowling past our booth for the fourth time in the past three minutes. "Beautiful ass, a sinful body, and a rack I'd love to bury my face in." I drop my eyes to the crotch of my jeans. "Nothing. Nada. It's fucking broken."

Ryan throws back his head and laughs. I'm glad he can find amusement in my life-threatening situation. I've never faced this type of *issue* before. Normally, I'd just mumble the word 'pussy' and *schwing*! My cock is ready to pounce. But for the past two months, it's like my cock packed up and went on holiday, no notice given to me or my lust-riddled brain.

Ryan signals to the waiter for another round before aligning his eyes with mine. "Maybe things have just gotten too easy for you?" His voice is more sincere than his leering expression as he runs his eyes over my face and shoulder-length brown hair. "You need to mess up that pretty face of yours. Make it more of a challenge. Your dick has gotten bored with the ease of the game."

While rolling my eyes, I punch him in the arm. When he chuckles, I shake my head and turn my eyes back to the crowd to silently ponder. There are beautiful women as far as my eye can see, yet my cock feels nothing. Not a twinge. Not even a slight fucking throb. As much as Ryan thinks I'm joking, I truly believe my cock is broken.

But I'm twenty-eight for fuck's sake. I'm not even close to the age most men seek help with this type of situation.

Maybe Ryan is right? Maybe the game has gotten too easy?

My wallowing over my broken appendage stops when Ryan asks, "You still buying into Inked?"

I nod, happy to change the course of our conversation. "Yeah. With everything going on with Ryder's boy, he doesn't want to spend as much time at the shop. It's kind of a win-win situation. He gets time with his family. I get to dig my fingers into ownership."

Ryder's son, Slater, was admitted to rehab earlier this month. Slater's band, Rise Up, started smashing the charts late last year with two singles off their debut album. The week following the band's massive success, the band's lead singer, Noah Taylor, was involved in a traffic accident which resulted in him spending three months in a coma at a local private hospital. Ryder was worried about his boy, but Slater seemed to be handling the situation well... until his friend recovered. Then it all went downhill.

Ryder was suspicious a few weeks before Slater's best mate, Marcus, arrived at the shop, but he was giving his boy the benefit of the doubt. Once Ryder had solid proof Slater was dabbling in a wide variety of recreational drugs, he dragged his son's ass to rehab. After some heavy discussions with his missus, Ryder decided to put Inked on the market so he could spend more time with his family.

After losing their daughter a few years ago to leukemia, Ryder and Lucia weren't going to sit back and watch another illness claim the life of their child. Although I have enough coin saved to fully buy Ryder out, the fifty percent buy-in I suggested is a better situation for us both. Inked gets to keep Ryder's honorable name associated with it, and once Ryder's boy gets his head back in the game, Ryder will have Inked to fall back on if home life becomes too dull.

"So when will I make you a customer at Inked?"

Ryan smiles against the rim of his glass. "When you stop accepting cash only for services."

I laugh. "That will *never* happen."

"Then I guess I won't be under your inking gun any time soon."

I waggle my brows. "You keep talking like that, and it won't be an inking gun you'll need to be worried about."

Ryan chuckles. "Lucky I can handle myself," he replies, his tone full of cockiness. "Because I'm not just a good detective. I'm the best—"

"Fucking detective Ravenshoe has ever seen." I noogie his head, messing up his hundred-dollar haircut. "Better watch out. Your head might not fit out the door with how fucking big it's getting."

He grins a smile that causes the girls fluttering around our booth to move in closer. He gestures his head to the crotch of my jeans. "You better watch out, or your severe case of blue balls might not fit in your jeans anymore."

When my eyes narrow in on a pair of rich chocolate eyes emerging from a set of dark velvet curtains, any concerns about my blue-ball status are on track to be decimated.

"I'll catch you around," I say to Ryan while lifting my chin in agreement with Keke's suggestive finger crook. "I've got some *business* to take care of."

Ryan stands from the booth to say goodbye in the same way he greeted me an hour ago. Upon noticing that Damon is indisposed with a pretty blonde, I issue him my farewell by paying for his tab before ambling to the door.

Keke interlocks her arm with mine when we emerge onto the bustling sidewalk outside the club. "My place or yours?"

My brisk pace falters.

"I'm just playing with you, Brax," she purrs, her voice quickly reverting from French madame to the Keke who only emerges behind closed doors. "I know you don't take girls back to your place." She spins on her heels and walks backward while undoing the buttons on her black trench coat. "Although, when you spot what I'm wearing underneath this coat, you may change your mind."

When she does the quickest flash, exposing inches of a baby pink lace teddy she's wearing under her coat, I snap my eyes closed and send a prayer to God for leading me to Keke tonight. Because not only did my eyes bulge when awarded with a visual of her naughty little ensemble, so did my cock.

It's back, baby! Primed and ready to go.

Chapter Two

The annoying shrill of my cell phone wakes me from my slumbering state. Shifting my eyes to the alarm clock, a disgruntled groan rumbles from my parched lips.

Who the fuck is calling me at eight in the morning on a Monday?

Sundays and Mondays are the days Inked's doors remain closed. Although we could trade seven days a week, from the beginning, Ryder scheduled his staff on a five-day roster to ensure a good work-life balance.

After running my hand over my newly clipped hair, I snag my phone off the bedside table. My sleepy eyes pop open when I discover who was calling me.

Fuck, what has she done now?

I dial a number I know by heart before pressing my cell close to my ear.

"Caramine Care, Daniel Beckett speaking."

"Daniel, it's Brax Anderson. I just missed your call. Is everything okay?"

He sighs down the line. "We had a few *issues* occur this week that I'd like to discuss with you in person."

Great.

"All right." I swing my legs off the bed. "I'll be there in around forty minutes."

After disconnecting the call, I enter the bathroom to get ready while my brain tracks the events that transpired since the last time I received this same phone call.

* * *

Two hours later, I'm walking out of Daniel's office.

"I'll have a word with her before I leave, but I assure you the incident that occurred earlier this week won't happen again."

Daniel curtly nods before offering me his hand to shake. "She certainly keeps us on our toes. No one could ever accuse your grandmother of not having enough spirit."

Laughing, I spin on my heels and stride down the hall. A lack of spirit isn't something my grandma could ever be accused of having.

I'm not at all surprised when I walk into my grandma's room at the assisted living home she's a resident of to find her going toe-to-toe with an orderly unpacking her recently packed suitcase.

"You better not steal any of my panties. I've had those panties for four years and don't want some young grub like you stealing them."

She's aiming for her voice to be vicious, but I hear slight laughter in her words. The orderly—who would be in his mid-thirties—cranks his neck to my grandma. Shock and a slight bit of horror are marring his face.

"Don't look at me like that, young man. I know all about men and their weird fetishes these days. My navy-blue striped sailor boy legs vanished last month. Poof. Gone. Not seen hide nor hair of them in over a month." Her words come out with a husky lisp since she doesn't have her full set of dentures in place.

"Grandma, stop giving the staff a hard time. You know as well as I do that you've never owned a pair of boyleg panties."

She huffs, crosses her heavily wrinkled arms under her chest, then strays her rheumy gaze to the gardens outside her window. "I'd own a pair if they let me out of this hellhole," she mumbles under her breath.

Today has been my grandmother's fourth attempt to break out of her assisted living facility the past three months. She only moved into this facility as the staircase in my apartment became too much for her to handle. Although we considered moving to a more suitable location, with me buying a share in Inked and the housing market rocketing in this area, we both agreed there was no viable option other than her moving into an assisted living facility.

We visited numerous aged care facilities the four weeks following our decision. Caramine Care was the last facility we visited. With its approach on free living, a bustling social calendar, and the fact it isn't referred to as a facility for seniors, it seemed like the ideal residence for my grandma.

Obviously, we were wrong.

After gesturing to the orderly that I will finish unpacking the suitcase, I span the distance between my grandma and me. "What am I going to do with you, Grandma? Mr. Beckett said you nearly gave some of the other residents a coronary." I crouch in front of her and peer into her shimmering blue eyes. "He said it took over two hours to get Mr. Peter's heart rate back under control after the stunt you pulled earlier this week."

She rolls her eyes but maintains her resilient stance, her lips as tight as her silver ringlet hair.

"Mr. Beckett would like me to inform you that although the hydrotherapy pool is set to a warm eighty-two-degree setting, it is not a bath." I cough, clearing my throat. "Grandma, if you wish to remain living at Caramine Care, you must wear swimwear at all times while using the facilities."

I try to keep my voice serious, but when the corners of my grandma's red-painted lips curl into a cheeky smirk, any chances of me keeping this situation within chiding territory falters.

"If they don't want their residents using the bathing facilities for their intended design, they should have clear signs displayed throughout the premises for old girls like me."

Quirking my lips, I glare into her mischief-filled eyes. She tries to use her age as an excuse for her erratic behavior, but I know her better than that. She might have Daniel believing her seventy-eight-year-old brain thought the hydrotherapy pool was a bath, but I'm not at all convinced. Why? Because much to the horror of my neighbors, my grandma skinny-dipped in the pool in my apartment building in January last year. Her excuse was "If the twenty-something-year-old residents of your apartment building can do it, why can't I?"

"Besides. It wasn't Mr. Peter's heart that took two hours to control," my grandma mumbles under her breath.

Ignoring her snide comment for fear of it giving me nightmares, I say, "Even if you didn't realize the hydrotherapy pool required a swimsuit, what's the deal with packing your bags? I thought your escapee days were over?"

Although she's tried to escape three times previously, those attempts were during her first two weeks of *incarceration* at Caramine Care. For the past two months, she seemed to have settled in nicely, so I'm somewhat surprised by her sudden attempt to flee.

Before my grandma gets the chance to answer my questions, a commotion at the door secures my attention. A pretty nurse in a tight white uniform and sheer black stockings stands in the entryway of my grandmother's room. She has platinum-blonde hair, peachy painted lips, and an enticingly curvy body.

The more the nurse's eyes wander over my face, the more her pupils dilate. A smirk tugs at my lips when her eyes lower to assess the entirety of my package.

The routine never alters.

Well, except that one time.

After the nurse finishes her avid assessment of my body, she aligns her green eyes with my grandmother. "I'm sorry, Mrs. Anderson, I didn't realize you had company. I'll come back later," she says before spinning on her heels.

Her quick departure is halted when my grandma says, "No. It's fine, Penny, come in and meet my grandson, Brax."

My brow arches, surprised at the chirpiness in my grandma's

voice. She is an entirely different lady compared to the one sparring against the orderly mere minutes ago.

When Penny hesitates for several seconds, unsure if she's coming or going, my grandma kicks me in the shins and nudges her head Penny's way.

"Hi, I'm Brax, Grace's grandson," I greet before offering her my hand to shake.

Heat creeps across Penny's cheeks as she accepts my gesture. "Hi, Brax. It's a pleasure to meet you. Your grandmother has been telling me a lot about you the past two weeks."

"I'm sure she has."

I turn my gaze back to my grandma. Her excited eyes are bouncing between Penny and me. Air escapes my nostrils when the reasoning behind my grandma's sudden interest in escaping smacks into me.

For the past year, she's made it her mission to see me shacked up and married. I lost count of the number of times I arrived home from a shift at Inked to find a female in my living room lying in wait, ready to pounce.

My grandmother's tactics were so convincing, most of my *dates* believed I had personally invited them over.

No matter how often I tell my grandmother that it's not true in this day and age, she's convinced if I'm not married by the time I'm thirty, I'll live the remainder of my life as a childless bachelor.

Although she means well, her matchmaking is driving me crazy. It isn't her lack of taste that has my appreciation waning. The quality of the women she finds is excellent. It's the fact she lures my dates into my home with the promise of matrimony and a family. Considering neither of those items are on my agenda anytime soon, my newly acquired *friends* don't hang around for long after the initial greeting.

After a few more minutes of awkward silence, Penny checks my grandmother's blood pressure and temperature before excusing herself from the room.

The instant she slips into the corridor, I drift my eyes back to my grandma. "Stop trying to set me up with the nurses and doctors."

"Why? Penny seems lovely, and you need a smart girl in your life," she replies in the same tone she uses whenever we argue about her poor matchmaking techniques.

I arch my brow. "You're setting me up to fail."

"*Pfft.* I'm doing no such thing. Penny is single. You're single. How could that turn into failure?"

With a shake of my head to hide my smile, I say, "Grandma, you know as well as I do. Penny might be good for a bit of fun, but even if I were interested in something more than a few nights between the sheets, she will *never* take me home to meet her parents."

Grandma waves her hand in front of her face like she's shooing away a fly. "We're in the twenty-first century, Brax. Parental permission is no longer a necessity."

I shake my head to loosen the invisible noose she slung around my neck, but since I'm not willing to roll over without a fight, I say, "So when the fun is over with Penny, and she ends up brokenhearted, what do you think will happen to your secret candy stash the nursing staff knows about but ignores?"

Panic floods my grandma's eyes when she locks them with the top drawer, which is full to the brim with every candy bar you could imagine.

"Is meddling in your grandson's love life worth the risk of losing your beloved chocolate binge?"

Without hesitation, she shakes her head.

I crouch down so my eyes are level with hers. "I appreciate your effort, but my love life is fine as it is. Especially since I can take my dates to my place now that my grandmother isn't sleeping in the room next door."

My grandma tries to hold in her laughter, but the littlest giggle topples from her lips. She may be seventy-eight, but she has the dirty mind of a twenty-year-old male.

Chapter Three

"Do you want me to head out or stay and see what card she's going to play?"

I shift my gaze from the blonde princess I tattooed three months ago, pacing the cracked sidewalk at the front of Inked to Diesel standing at my side. "Nah, man, you head out. I've got this," I assure him, my tone as unconvincing as my facial expression. "I'm locking up and heading out myself in a few, anyway."

Diesel snags his jacket from the counter and slings it over his shoulders. "She signed a contract, Brax. There's no coming back from that. No matter what her fancy lawyer told her," he reminds me after reading my concerned expression.

"Yeah, I know," I reply with a chin jerk. "But I'm still curious as to why she's been pacing out front for the past two hours."

Diesel bows his brow. "Maybe she's hoping to get you alone?" He waggles his brows. "Your tattoo might have convinced her she needs to sample your other gun. The more magic one."

I pick up a cash register roll at the side of the register and peg it at his head. A grin curves on my mouth when my fluke shot has perfect aim, hitting Diesel just above his left brow.

With a cheeky grin and while rubbing his brow, Diesel lifts his chin in farewell before striding to the door. Clara jumps in fright when the deep rumble of his Harley kicking over booms through her ears. Her eyes track Diesel as he executes a U-turn and rides past her.

Once he's no longer in eyesight, she runs her hand down the front of her jeans then saunters toward the entrance door of Inked. After dropping my eyes to her stilettos, I rake them up her body. Although she still screams of wealth and superiority, her outfit and jewelry selection aren't as elaborate as they were three months ago. Her fitted jeans cuddle the slender curves of her swinging hips, and her body-hugging jacket doesn't have a chance in hell of hiding assets most men would happily ignore her poor attitude to sample.

As the bells above the door ring into the front entrance, I stand from my slouched position and cross my arms over my chest, prepping for round three in our vicious battle. Clara's brisk pace falters when her eyes stop scanning the premises and connect with mine. A grin curls on my lips when she mumbles "Shit" under her breath before she continues her journey, acting like she isn't shocked to see me standing behind the counter.

When I tattooed her three months ago, I had long wavy brown hair that sat an inch below my shoulders, but after Ryan's little jab about my pretty-boy status, I had my hair clipped two weeks ago.

If I'm being totally forthright, it wasn't just Ryan's taunt that had me visiting the barber. It's the fact I've had the same haircut since I was a senior in high school. I was also hoping an update might inspire the same thing to happen between my bedsheets.

I'll do anything if it will fix my broken cock.

Did my plan work? No, not really. Unless you count Clara's sudden arrival? She's only standing before me because the glare on the shop windows hides my new haircut. When she saw Diesel leave, I have no doubt she thought she was clear from running into anyone who'd remember her long-winded tirade the last time she visited the shop.

How fucking wrong was she?

"Did your lawyer stand you up?" I ask, believing that is the only reason she's been pacing out front for the past two hours this late at night.

She freezes like a statue before cranking her neck back. Upon failing to locate anyone behind her, she returns her eyes front and center. "Lawyer?"

I nod. "Yeah, to sue me for your tat. If I recall correctly, you were planning to take every penny I had," I say, quoting part of the rant she evoked the last time she was on these premises. "You signed an agreement, Princess. It is a binding contract—"

"I'm not here about my tattoo," she interrupts, her voice surprisingly strong. "I'm here about that." She points to a display in the shop window.

"You need to be a little more specific," I say when the direction of her finger points to numerous tattoo displays. "There are hundreds of tattoo designs in that window." Suddenly, I freeze, and my brows scrunch. "If you want another tattoo, I suggest you find another tattoo artist."

She shakes her head. "I don't want another tattoo." Locking her icy-blue eyes with mine, she mutters, "The one I have is *more* than enough."

I smirk, loving her edge of feistiness.

I've always appreciated a woman who calls it as she sees it.

After expelling a deep breath, Clara paces to the shop window. "I'm here about this." She pulls down the 'Help Wanted' sign that's been displayed in the window for the past six months. It is so old, the thick black ink has faded to a murky gray color. While spinning the sign around to face me, she says, "I'm here to apply for the position you have advertised."

I throw back my head and laugh. I'm not talking a slight chuckle. I'm talking a full belly-clenching, I-won't-need-to-do-a-sit-up-for-a-month laugh. Tears spring into my eyes, and my body slicks with sweat.

The only thing that dampens the intensity of my laughter is catching sight of Clara's furious glare. Her gaze is scorching, and her strong stance is even hotter than that.

I stop laughing and take a step backward.

She can't be fucking serious. Surely.

Confident I'm being pranked, I shoot my eyes around the deserted shop, fully anticipating one of the guys from my crew to be lying in wait because there's no way this shit is real.

When I fail to detect another body in our presence, I shift my eyes back to Clara. "You're serious?" Disbelief taints my words.

She strengthens her take-no-shit stance before nodding. "I need a job. You have a position advertised." She places her hand on her cocked hip. "Hire me, and it will be a win-win for us both."

I bite on the inside of my cheek, hoping it will hold back a second bout of laughter that's dying to break free.

It's a pointless effort.

The instant my lips tug higher, the grim expression on Clara's face firms. "Is this how you treat all your applicants?" she grumbles, clearly unimpressed.

Smirking, I shake my head. "But I've never had an applicant who looks like you."

Most women would take my reply as a compliment. Clara doesn't. The angry spark in her eyes brightens as the groove between her brows deepens.

Feeling playful, and since I have five minutes until I can officially close up the shop, I play along with her little game. "Can you tattoo?" I use the same tone I used when handling an inquiry from a junkie for the same position earlier today.

Clara's throat works hard to swallow before she shakes her head.

"Do you know how to sterilize tattoo equipment?"

"No," she replies, her tone as abrupt as her pose.

"Do you even know how to clean?"

I am no longer able to hold in my smile when she once again shakes her head. I'd never tell her this, but her honesty does rate her application one point higher than her earlier competitor. That guy couldn't lie straight in bed. Even with her outscoring previous applicants, not only does she not hold the skills necessary to fulfill the position, but I'm also not buying her story about why she's suddenly arrived at Inked.

Playing my part of manager, I connect my eyes with Clara. "As part of the management team at Inked Tattoo, I thank you for your interest in working with us, but unfortunately, you have been unsuccessful in acquiring the position advertised." I try to keep my tone neutral. My attempts are borderline.

Clara takes a step closer to the counter, engulfing my senses with her rich floral scent. "I may not know how to clean or tattoo, but I have no concerns maintaining a vigorous schedule, and I most certainly know how to handle money."

A ghost of a smile cracks my lips. "I'm sure you do, Princess, but we are not seeking a bookkeeper. We're after an all-rounder."

After snagging my keys from the glass display cabinet, I make my way around the counter. Clara balks when I curl my arm around her shoulders to guide her to the door.

I flip the sign to closed, open the front door of Inked, then gesture for Clara to leave. I'm not at all surprised to spot a steel gray Audi parked a few spots up from Inked.

Only a princess would apply for a minimum-wage job with a chariot idling at the curb.

"There's a tattoo shop two streets over called Gunned. I'm sure its owner, Tommy, would *love* to hire a woman of your caliber to count his money."

Tommy is a great tattoo artist—his shop is Inked's number one rival—but he is a fucking sleaze and an even bigger idiot. If anyone on this side of Ravenshoe will be fooled by Clara's sudden desire to get dirt under her French-tipped nails, it would be Tommy.

Clara's eyes bounce between mine. She appears to be considering citing an objection to my request for her to leave, so I'm somewhat surprised when she releases a quiet huff before stepping onto the concrete sidewalk.

After securing the deadbolt, I check that everything has been shut down in the shop, grab my jacket off the coatrack, then head out the back entrance of Inked.

With it being February, a nippy wind prickles my torso with goosebumps when I enter the poorly lit parking lot. I throw my arms into my jacket before locking the chained security door.

Happy everything is secure, I spin on my heels and walk to my custom Harley Davidson Fat Boy parked three spaces up.

My eyes roll skyward when clicking heels on concrete jingles through my ears. I don't need to shift my eyes to know who is shadowing me. The smell of expensive floral perfume and the way the hairs on my nape prickled is all the indication I need to know who is tailing me.

The bitch is back.

"I can keep things in the shop running, freeing up your precious time so you can... *doodle* on more people."

I stop walking to inhale a lung-filling breath of air. After calming down the mad beat of my heart, I turn around to face my newly acquired stalker. "Doodle?" I arch my brow as I glare into Clara's stormy eyes. "You think I *doodle* on people?"

Even though a pinch of fear clouds her impressively stern eyes, she ignores the grim expression on my face and nods.

"It's called art, Princess. It's not fucking doodling."

"Stop calling me that," she snaps, glaring at me with her well-worn bitch façade firmly in place.

"Why? Don't you like your name, *Princess?*"

She crosses her arms under her chest, hoisting her mouthwatering breasts higher in her tight, fitted shirt. "I'm not a princess, so why call me one?"

I shrug. "It's either Princess or Stuck-Up Bitch... The choice is yours."

The veins in her neck thrum as anger lines her face. "My name is Clara. Why don't you just refer to me as Clara?"

"I gave you your choices." My tone warns of my wavering constraint. I'm close to blowing my top.

Her mouth gapes, no doubt shell-shocked at my bluntness.

While scraping my hand over the stubble on my chin, I fight to rein in my anger. Although I've reached my quota of dealing with idiotic people for one week, Clara doesn't deserve to solely cop the wrath of my fury. She may have an icy personality, but my poor mood was lingering hours before she arrived on the doorstep of Inked.

"Look, you've had your fun, so can we please cut the shit? It's been a long-ass week, and I'm too fucking beat to be dealing with more crap right now." I try to keep my tone sincere, but when her eyes slit into thin lines, I realize she isn't buying my attempts at sincerity.

Deciding I'll never win a battle of words against a woman with a fierce tongue like Clara's, I issue my farewell with an emotionless smirk before continuing with my original endeavor.

I make it halfway to my bike before I hear, "What time do you want me to arrive on Monday?"

Fuck me, this woman is worse than a leech.

I don't bother turning around. "I'm not hiring you."

My hands shoot up to massage my throbbing temples when she asks, "Isn't it illegal to advertise under false pretenses?"

After exhaling a large puff of air, I spin around to face her. "What have I falsely advertised?"

"Your sign said you needed help." She stares into my eyes while running her hand down the front of her body. Even in my irate mood, I can't miss her budded nipples braced against her fitted shirt. "I'm here, willing to help, but you're refusing to hire me. I'm not a lawyer, but that sounds illegal to me."

While dragging my eyes away from her chest, I clench my fists into tight balls. It's the only defense I have to fight the urge to scream my frustration into the street. "You're not qualified for the position advertised. If you were, I'd hire you," I reply through gritted teeth.

"Then give me a chance to prove I'm qualified."

I arch my brow. "And how exactly can I do that?"

"Put me on a trial basis. Day-to-day agreement. No contracts. No paperwork." She impresses me with her on-the-spot negotiation skills.

I nearly take a minute to contemplate her recommendation before reality smacks into me. I don't owe her a damn thing. She should feel lucky I didn't have her ass thrown to the curb the instant she stepped foot into my shop after the less-than-stellar rant she unleashed during her last visit.

I lock my eyes with hers. "You're not qualified to work at Inked, but we thank you for taking the time to submit your application," I quote, giving her the same comment I've given every unqualified applicant before her.

She cocks her hip out and glares into my eyes. "You either hire me now, or I'll show up every day until you do."

After straddling my bike, I drift my eyes back to the teeming-with-sass blonde. "So no matter what I say, you're gonna rock up here Monday, ready to work?" When she smiles and nods, I inwardly chuckle. "All right. Good luck on Monday." When her plump lips lift into a broad grin, I realize my attempt at sarcasm was lost on her. "We aren't open on Mondays. If you had done your research on Inked before applying for the position we have advertised, you would have realized that."

Clara balks for the quickest second before stuttering, "Tuesday, then."

I scrub my hand over my clipped hair. "I get it, all right. You're on some soul-searching mission, hoping a few good deeds to those less fortunate will fix some of the fucked-up things you've done in your life, but you're barking up the wrong tree." I twist my body to the side and point down the street. "There is a women's shelter three blocks over. Go and offer them your charity."

She mumbles something under her breath, but she's so quiet, I missed what she said. After rolling her shoulders, she fixes her icy-blue eyes with my dark brown gaze. "I'm sorry for wasting your precious time. I hope you have a pleasant evening," she says before spinning on her heels and stalking back to the street.

A pleasant evening? Is she fucking serious? That proves she would have never survived working in a place like Inked. If the staff didn't scare her off, the clients soon would have.

Maybe I should have hired her and let my crew work their magic?

After snagging my helmet out of the saddle bag on my bike, my eyes scan the nearly pitch-black alleyway. Other than a couple of heavy-breasted bar bunnies bouncing around hoping to secure a warm bed for the night, the parking lot is empty, which isn't surprising considering it is well past midnight on a Saturday night.

The two heavy-breasted ladies' large smiles dampen when I dip my chin in farewell, denying their silent offerings. With Inked's regular schedule, the bunnies know the prime time to show up when they're after a night of adventure. Although their offer is tempting, after my run-in with Princess Stuck-Up, I'm not in the mood for the antics a pair of bunnies would bring to my weekend.

I also can't guarantee my dysfunctional cock will be up for the task.

The profound rumble of my bike echoes through the quiet night when I kick over the engine. After gliding it down the alleyway, I shift my eyes up and down the street, scanning for an opening in the dense flow of traffic that always clogs the streets of Ravenshoe. It doesn't matter if it is one in the morning or three in the afternoon, Ravenshoe's roads are always congested.

During my endeavor to find a break between vehicles, my eyes spot a flurry of blonde standing in the shadows of the bus shelter a few doors up from Inked.

What the fuck is she doing standing at the bus stop?

Unable to leash the moral compass my grandma embedded in me from a young age, I roll my bike away from the pavement and switch off the engine. After storing my helmet on the ape hangers of my bike, I stride to the bus shelter Clara is standing at. Although she frustrates the hell out of me, this side of town, at this time of night, is no place for any woman to be milling around unaccompanied.

"How far out is your ride?"

I rake my eyes along the street to seek the gray Audi I saw earlier.

It's nowhere to be found.

While finalizing the last few steps between us, I tug my jacket in tighter, blocking out the crisp breeze blowing through my thin long-sleeve shirt.

Clara's eyes stray from the street to me. Her pupils widen as a look of surprise washes over her face. "I'm not waiting on a car. I am taking the bus home."

"What?" I ask, certain I didn't hear her right. The roads are clogged with noisy motorists, so my hearing may be a little off.

"I'm waiting for the bus," Clara advises again, her voice stronger this time around.

"You're waiting on the *bus?*"

She huffs loudly. "Yes! The *bus*. You know that big metal thing on four wheels that clangs past here every twenty minutes or so. It's called a *bus*. That's what I'm waiting for."

She rolls her eyes before turning them back to the street. I stare at her in utter disbelief. She must be a fucking lunatic. It is well past midnight on a Saturday. She's decked out in designer threads and wearing more bling than the jewelry store three blocks over stocks, and she's planning on taking the bus. Clearly, she doesn't know this side of Ravenshoe after dark like I do. It isn't a place for anyone to be wandering alone, let alone a woman with the dick-twitching looks she has.

Upon noticing a bus approaching my right, my naturally engrained protective instincts kick in. "You don't need to take the bus. I'll give you a ride home." I nudge my head to the portion of my bike poking out of the alleyway.

"No."

Her abrupt response dumbfounds me.

"Excuse me?" Surprise is clear in my voice. "When someone offers you a ride, you're supposed to say, 'Thank you. That will be lovely.'"

Clara's eyes snap to mine. "Not when you don't want a lift. I'm happy to take the bus."

"You're not taking the fucking bus. Get your ass on my bike."

She steps closer to me as her thinly slit eyes bounce between mine. "Do you have a problem with your hearing? I said *no*."

I return her leering stare. "Do you think saying 'no' to a bunch of punks on the one a.m. express will stop them? You're swimming out of your depth here, Princess. This isn't fucking Kansas."

The smell of exhaust fumes filter into my nose when a rusted old bus marked with '57' on the side pulls in front of the bus shelter.

"I can take care of myself." Clara glares at me with the same fiery spark she wore three months ago. "If I can handle a *beast* of a man like you, I'm sure a couple of *punks* will be no hard feat."

After issuing me a final stink eye, she climbs aboard the bus, completely snubbing my request for her not to.

I stand frozen at the bus stop in absolute shock. I'm not just surprised by her stubbornness but astounded by how fucking hard her feistiness has made my cock.

I've never been so damn hard.

Yeah, not happening, buddy. You'd need a cool million in the bank to ever get the chance of unclamping those legs.

Clara's smug eyes glower into mine when the bus chugs down the road, leaving a throat-clogging puff of smoke in its wake. She thinks she can take care of herself, but she's swimming way out of her depth. But fuck it. If she wants to be stupid, so be it. It isn't my place to play babysitter to a spoiled little rich bitch who would cut off her nose to spite her face. Besides, although the bus company advises their drivers not to engage in any domestic situations, the moral obligation of any man would outweigh corporate propaganda, wouldn't it?

While cursing under my breath, I charge for my bike and throw my leg over it. The big rumble of my engine scares a group of feral cats out of the dumpster at the side when I kick over the motor. My heart beats double time when my departure from the alley has me narrowly missing a handful of motorists. When they honk their horns and yell obscenities out their windows, I flip the bird before pulling back on my throttle. My excessive speed has my front tire lifting off the pavement and the coolness of a late February wind pelting my chest.

Weaving my bike in and out of the heavy traffic, I locate bus 57 a mile out from Inked. When I pull my bike along the right-hand side of the bus, I scan the seats lining the edge, seeking any signs of Clara. When I fail to locate her, I lower my speed and slip my bike to the other side. A moment of reprieve pummels into me when I spot her sitting two seats behind the male driver.

At least she was smart enough to sit close to the driver.

Ignoring the absurdness of the situation, I continue to follow the bus as it makes its way across Ravenshoe. Even though she acts like she hasn't noticed my presence, I catch Clara occasionally glancing my way.

I'll admit, even pissed beyond hell that I've rode ten miles in the wrong direction and am wasting precious minutes of my days off tailing a lady who infuriates me more than any woman before her, the hardness of my cock hasn't lessened a smidge. If anything, her blatant refusal to acknowledge my presence has increased its thickness, not lessened it.

"What's wrong with you? You want some Grade-A pussy?" I mumble to myself while peering down at the crotch of my jeans.

My attention diverts from reprimanding my cock for its unattainable goals when I notice a group of gangbangers at the back of the bus have locked their sights on Clara. If I had to guess their ages, I'd say late teens, early twenties. I've seen them hanging around Inked a few times the past month, but we haven't officially met.

After doing a hand gesture with two of his pimple-faced friends, the approximately six-foot boy with pasty skin and a red bandana wrapped around his grease-slicked hair moves down the aisle, his gangbanger swagger in full force. His wonky grin enlarges the closer he gets to Clara, as does his grip on his crotch.

Blood roars into my ears from the gleam in his eyes. I slam my hand on the bus's window, endeavoring to secure his attention. The glass rattles under the impact of my fist, but he doesn't look my way. My heart rate climbs into dangerous territory when I glance sideways to check my location.

Fuck!

I'm two seconds away from being splattered onto the back of a four-thousand-pound sedan.

Gritting my teeth, I release the throttle and pull back on the brake before veering my bike onto the sidewalk. A delivery driver stacking the morning papers on the curb squeals like a girl when I narrowly miss hitting him. Scraps of newspaper fly into the air, and the scent of fear filters into my nose as I zip past a newspaper stand.

Once the delivery driver gathers his scattered composure, he yells out a string of obscenities. His voice is as shaky as my hands.

I raise my arm into the air in silent apology before continuing with my original endeavor. A rutted grunt escapes my lips when my bike leaves the sidewalk with an almighty thud. I pull back the throttle and catch up with the bus, swerving in and out of the traffic like a mad man.

When I glide up next to the bus, my jaw muscle tenses. The young gangbanger is sitting in the seat behind Clara, twirling a lock of her glossy hair around his index finger.

I bang my fist on the glass once more. My thump is so hard, the glass wobbles under my force. Hearing my commotion, the gangbanger twists his neck to the side and eyes me curiously. His ostentatious grin amplifies when I stare him straight in the face while pointing to Clara.

After removing his hand from Clara's hair, he grabs his crotch while mouthing, "She's fine."

His cocky grin is wiped straight off his face when I use the same finger I pointed at Clara to make a throat-slitting gesture, wordlessly warning him if he touches another hair on her head, I will ruin him.

He balks as his eyes widen. He nudges his head to Clara as if to ask, "Is she yours, Brax?"

When I nod, he holds his hands out in front of his body like he didn't mean her any harm before he stumbles back to his original seat.

If I didn't arrive when I did, I'd hate to think of how far he was planning to take this. The good kids in Ravenshoe are slowly outweighing the bad, but there's still a bunch of rotten eggs tainting the batch.

The tick impinging my jaw lessens when the fear-faced teen returns to his original spot at the back of the bus. Although I've never been an overly violent man, I was born and raised in this area of

Ravenshoe. That alone warrants me a fierce enough reputation that I'm not to be messed with.

When the gangbanger takes a seat next to his two male compadres, I swing my eyes back to Clara. For the first time in the past twelve miles, she isn't facing the front of the bus. Her eyes are locked on me, and all the smugness on her face has vanished, replaced with a look of a woman who is acutely aware of how close her stubbornness had her treading into shark-infested waters.

After issuing me a hesitant smirk, she returns her eyes front and center. Thankfully, the last ten minutes of her brush with the wild side is made without incident. I won't lie, a conceited grin curls on my lips when the young gangbangers bolt off the bus at the stop following our exchange.

Without a backward glance, they hightail it down the alleyway as quick as their quivering legs can take them. If Clara wasn't still sitting two seats behind the driver with a terrified gleam in her eyes, I would have had a good *talk* with them. But since my priorities remain with Clara, that *talk* is being held for a later date.

The instant the bus rolls into the good half of Ravenshoe, I could stop following Clara, but for some reason unbeknownst to me, I continue tailing her for the next five miles.

I've already come this far, so what's a few more miles?

When the bus comes to a halt in front of a fancy apartment building on the most expensive street in Ravenshoe, I pull my bike onto the curb behind it. I'm not at all surprised when Clara hops off the bus. Just seeing her in this expensive setting strengthens my belief that she was attempting to prank me earlier tonight.

Keeping her chin held high, she saunters toward the guarded doors. Just before she enters the heavily manned foyer, she spins around to face me. Her pupils are wide, exposing that she's rattled from her brief encounter with the rough side of Ravenshoe, but even frightened, she holds herself with a sense of dignity and class. She has the type of poise no etiquette class could teach. It is infused in her blood.

"Thank you."

A grin tugs on my lips. From the look on her face, you'd swear it was the first time she's ever said thank you.

I inwardly chuckle. *It probably is.*

"You shouldn't catch the bus at any time, let alone this late at night. It was a stupid thing to do."

Even though her lips thin in grimness, she nods. "I'll add it to my long list of things I'm unqualified to do." Her snarls reveal her stubbornness is still loitering in the shadows. "I've found out today I can't work at a tattoo parlor, a café, or even clean the gas station toilets on the outskirts of town." The hardness of her lips is firm. "Who would have thought you'd need a degree from Harvard to clean a washroom?"

My brows furrow. "You're that desperate for a job you're willing to clean toilets for a buck?"

With her gaze planted straight ahead, she briefly nods.

My heart freezes. I honestly hadn't expected her to say yes.

"Fingers crossed, biker bars and strip clubs aren't as demanding because at the rate I'm going, they'll be my only viable options," she mutters before spinning on her heels.

Strip clubs? Even knowing she's most likely goading me, and I don't know her from a bar of soap, I hate the thought of any woman working in a sleazy club just to make a dime. My momma did it, and I swore I'd never let any woman I know follow in her disastrous footsteps.

Going against my better judgment, I blurt out, "You start Tuesday at two," before my brain can compile a rejection.

Clara freezes halfway into the entrance of her building. Her shoulders rise as she gulps in a deep breath before her eyes snap to mine. "Really?"

When I nod, she smiles a heart-stopping grin that has my cock stiffening all over again.

Don't even think about it. She's way above your paygrade.

"You have a two-week trial to prove yourself. If you fuck it up or scare away any of my customers, your ass will be out on the curb faster than I can snap my fingers."

"I won't. I promise," she guarantees, her assuring eyes adding to the strength of her words.

I arch my brow. "And you're not to take the bus," I warn while glaring into her eyes. "This is not a negotiable term. If you turn up to Inked on the bus, turn around and get straight back on it because your ass will be fired."

Her face pales, and her breathing shallows. She looks more concerned now than she did when I began inking her virgin skin. "I don't have any money to put gas in my car," she mumbles, her quiet words relaying her embarrassment.

Jesus Christ! What the fuck am I getting myself into?

I dig my hand into the back pocket of my jeans to pull out my wallet and snag a twenty from the small selection of notes inside. I hold the note a few inches from my chest before locking my eyes with Clara.

If she wants my money, she'll have to come and get it.

A stretch of silence passes between us as her eyes dance between the crumpled note in my hand and my face. After exhaling a deep breath, she spans the distance between us, her steps shaky and reserved.

Just before she removes the twenty from my grasp, I pull it out of her reach. "This is not a loan. It's an advance. I'll be taking it out of your first paycheck."

She fights her hardest battle, endeavoring to keep her tears at bay before curtly nodding. "Okay. Good," she says, her voice stronger than the weakness in her eyes.

She removes the twenty from my hand, folds it up, then places it in the pocket of her jeans. "Thank you," she murmurs before walking into her apartment building, not once glancing back at me sitting on my Harley, shocked into silence.

Even though I could see the defeated look in her eyes when she accepted my money, I hope she just played me for a fool. No matter how much she irritates me, I'd rather have her pranking me than be so desperate for a job she turns up to Inked on Tuesday morning.

Chapter Four

Knocking distracts me from the tattoo I've been drawing for the past hour. It is a sleek design I've been working on for a long-time client. Although he doesn't have much prime real estate left on his torso for my artwork, this piece is just as important to him as the numerous other tats I've placed on his skin.

When I hear another knock, I slide the sheet of tracing paper to the side and check my watch. My lips quirk when I notice it is a little before one in the afternoon. Considering the shop doesn't open until two-thirty, I ignore the eager patron.

All my best-laid plans go straight to the gutter when the tapping grows louder and louder. Once it hits a point I'm no longer capable of ignoring, I push back from my desk and march to the door. I clasp the stainless-steel door handle, preparing to unleash a verbal tirade on the moron who can't read the hours displayed in thick red ink on the eye-level sign hanging from the door. My plan goes to shit for the second time in under a minute when I swing open the door and am smacked in the face with a rich floral scent.

"You really need to get your hearing tested. I've been knocking for ages," Clara says with her heat-scorching eyes blazing into mine. "Are you going to let me in?"

I nearly step to the side before reality pummels into me. This wasn't our plan. "What are you doing here?"

She freezes. "You said I have a two-week trial," she replies with her icy-blue eyes bouncing between mine.

"Yeah, Tuesday at two."

Her eyes roll skywards. "It *is* Tuesday, Brax."

I only just hold in my surprise that she knows my name. I shouldn't be shocked, though. I'm sure she spent her entire weekend digging for dirt on the guy she's playing tricks on.

"Yeah, it is Tuesday, *Princess*," I say her nickname with the same disdain she said mine with. "But it isn't even one yet. You're way too early."

Her brows furrow. "My brother previously told me being early shows you appreciate the opportunity bestowed upon you." Her hands fist the fabric on her jacket before she stammers, "I appreciate the opportunity."

After leaning against the doorframe, I cross my arms in front of my chest. "First job?" My deep voice only just conceals my laughter. "How old are you?"

She smooths the crinkles her determined hold created in her jacket before locking her eyes with mine. "I'm twenty-five, and yes, it is my first job." Her tone is full of warning that this subject is not up for further discussion.

Deciding it is too early in the week to engage in World War III, I remark, "Arriving fifteen minutes before your shift will be more than adequate to show your appreciation."

Clara briefly nods before asking, "So can I come in?"

Her eyes narrow when I shake my head. "I'm assuming that's yours?" I gesture my head to the white BMW convertible parked in prime position at the front of the shop.

A ghost of a smile creeps across her plump lipstick-covered lips. "Yes."

"Then you need to move it. There's an employee parking lot located at the back of the shop."

Her eyes rocket to mine. The gleam brightening her gaze from absorbing her expensive pride and joy dampens as the seconds tick by. "Is the parking lot secure?"

I throw my head back and laugh. "No, but it is where all *employees* park their vehicles."

"Then my car is fine where it is," she snaps out before crossing her arms under her ample chest.

"If you think your ride is safer parked in the street in clear view of thieving eyes than the parking lot, Princess, you've underestimated this side of Ravenshoe. No gangbanger will dare touch your *precious* pride and joy if it is parked at the back of Inked." She snarls, baring teeth, either hating my use of her nickname or me calling out her stupidity. Either way, I don't care. "If you're planning on walking into this premises as an employee, move your piece-of-shit car into the parking lot. If not, have a *pleasant* evening."

A winning grin stretches across my face when Clara rolls her arms in front of her body like she's curtseying the crowned Prince of Denmark before she walks backward. She just needs to remove the crown from her head and place it on mine, and her performance would be more realistic.

Smirking, I nod when she points to the alley at the side of the shop after unlocking her car doors. "Down the alley and around the back." She rolls her eyes at the arrogance of my reply.

"I'll meet you at the *employee* entrance," I add, rubbing more salt into her freshly cut wounds.

Not waiting for her to reply, I close and lock the door of Inked and head to the employee-only entrance at the back of the shop. I still can't believe Clara McGregor—Princess-Fucking-Socialite—wants to work at Inked. I took a bit of time the past two days running our prior confrontations through my mind. Other than hitting a late case of teen rebellion, I'm at a loss as to why someone like Clara would want to work at Inked, let alone anywhere. It honestly doesn't make any sense. Just her tennis bracelet alone is worth more than my annual salary, and her pride and joy I just insulted no doubt cost more than my apartment.

But even knowing she has more money than sense, I'll follow

through with my pledge. Why? Because I'm a man of my word. I'll play along with Clara's little ruse for as long as she wants as I doubt she'll last a few hours, let alone a few days.

After snagging a spare key for the back door off the key rack, I push open the heavily weighted steel door at the back of Inked. Like a shadow I can't shake, Clara is standing under the rusted awning waiting for me.

"The lock can be a bit stiff, just jimmy the key a little, and it should pop right out," I instruct while pinching the key between my index finger and thumb.

Clara snatches the key out of my grasp and cocks her brow. "Why give me a key if you want me to jimmy the lock? Seems like a pointless task."

Ignoring her cattiness, I continue as if she never spoke. "You should also consider removing your bling. It doesn't fit in around here, and it will only lead to trouble." I clutch the diamond pendant dangling around her neck and hoist it into the air.

She snatches the pendant out of my grasp. "You should consider removing your attitude because it doesn't fit in around here," she snips under her breath.

I smirk. "Will it be like this the entire two weeks? I say something, and you fire back with a bitchy comment?"

"Depends," she replies with a shrug.

I glare into her stern eyes. "On what exactly?"

"On if you keep saying stupid things."

I back her into the outer wall of the shop and press my hands on each side of the brickwork next to her shoulders. The veins in her neck thrum, but she maintains my eye contact, trying to act as if my intimidating stance isn't affecting her. "If you want to work here, you need to lose the attitude. If you can't do that, I suggest you slide your pretty little ass back into your pretty little car and drive your stuck-up princess routine back to the pretty side of Ravenshoe. Because that side of town may see your hard-ball approach as determination, where I just see it as a spoiled little bitch hiding behind a pile of money."

Her lips thin into a hard, disapproving line. "I'm just giving as good as I'm getting, Brax," she replies after locking her challenging blue eyes with mine.

I'll give it to her. This time around, she's got me played. I've given her just as much attitude as she's been bestowing upon me. So much, I'm certain if my grandmother ever catches wind of my interactions with Clara, she'll have my head placed on the guillotine block.

She's quoted numerous times during the past twenty-eight years of my life that, "No matter if they're richer than a queen or poorer than a struggling artist, every woman has the right to be treated with dignity and respect."

But I can't help it. Clara riles me up. Not just my hackles but my cock as well. The first half of my weekend was filled trying to work out what her deal was. The second half was spent striving to release the stranglehold her feistiness placed on my cock.

Just like I came up stumped on why a socialite like Clara would want to work at Inked, nothing could ease the throb of my cock. Not even the pretty little blonde with icy-blue eyes I picked up last night.

For some strange, unknown reason, my cock has set his sights on a little temptress with a scornful mouth and even more sinful lips. I can't say I don't understand his fascination. Clara is so much of a sexpot she only needs to breathe to excite a red-blooded guy. Just the way she's staring up at me now, panting hard with her painted lips pursed, makes her so tempting all I want to do is wipe the sass right out of her mouth with my fucking tongue.

Knowing that will never happen, I drop one of my hands from the wall and scrub it over the few days of scruff on my chin. "I don't think this is a good idea. This agreement isn't going to work."

My cock is already aching to sink into her, and she's only been here for five seconds, so imagine how bad it will be in an hour?

Clara releases a long breath while crossing her arms in front of her chest. "I'm not going anywhere until my trial is over. I may not have signed an official employment document, but a verbal contract is just as binding as a written one. Believe me, I checked."

"Then I'll pay you two weeks of salary, and we'll call it a day."

After glaring at me, she slips under my arm and saunters into the shop like she owns the place. Her shoulders are straight, and her head is held high as she slings off her jacket and hangs it on the coat rack before heading to the foyer. For the first time in her three visits to the premises, she's standing on the opposite side of the counter. "Are you going to show me where everything is? Or am I going to figure it out on my own?"

I grit my teeth and take three steps toward her. "Did you hear anything I said? I'll pay you your two weeks owed."

"Yeah, I heard every word that spilled from your lips, *Brax.*" She spits my name out like it is a piece of trash. "Unlike you, I don't have any concerns about my hearing."

"Then why are you still standing in my foyer? I'm a man of my word. I'll follow through on my agreement. You'll get your money."

She places her hands on her hips and stares me straight in the eyes. "You *agreed* to give me a two-week trial. I'm here to begin my two-week trial. I'm *not* a charity case." Her words come out shaky during the last part of her statement. "Now, are you going to show me where everything is? Or am I going to figure it out on my own?" she requests again, glaring at me.

I stare at her, looking like a slack-jawed idiot. I've never had someone with enough gall to spar up against me on my turf before, let alone a woman my cock wants to wrestle with beneath the sheets. Even giving her a stare that would make most men cower, she doesn't yield the slightest. If anything, her determination strengthens. She came here to start her two-week trial, and she isn't leaving until that happens.

Realizing that arguing with a woman like Clara is utterly pointless, I eat humble pie before spending the next thirty minutes giving her a general rundown on how the shop operates. I explain how she will be left in charge of booking all the appointments, taking clients' payments, and pretty much doing anything the crew requests her to do.

She's quick, but I don't miss the tiniest flare of anxiety that crosses her face when I mention she has to do anything the crew demands.

"Other than Charity, the rest of the crew won't be overly demanding."

She nods as she follows me to the hallway.

"Charity can get a little handsy, but don't let it bother you. She's harmless." I stop talking and run my eyes over Clara's body. "Although, for you, she may be extra grabby."

The spark of worry tainting her face explodes into a full flare.

"If it gets more than you can handle, holla, and I'll have a quiet word with Charity."

Her throat works hard to swallow before she shakes her head. "It's okay. I can take care of myself." The shakiness of her words undermines the strength of her statement.

When we enter the manager's office, I take a seat behind my old scratched-up desk. "If you stay out of my hair, I'll stay out of yours. Then this arrangement might work out for both of us."

An uncharacteristic smile spreads across Clara's face. Although she looks out of place in my small, poorly furnished office, the careful consideration she paid while I explained her position shows she isn't walking into this job lightheartedly. Surprisingly, she appears as if she actually wants to be here. *Unsurprisingly, her smile has the front of my jeans tightening.*

My body's reaction to her pisses me off. Not because I'm ungrateful my cock appears to be back in working order but because the goal it is striving for is unattainable. I hardly know the woman standing before me, yet she already has me wanting to cross out the number one rule I swore I'd never break when I signed on as a partner at Inked.

Never mix business with pleasure.

The fact she already has me wanting to break my rules pisses me off more than the hardness in my jeans.

After she finishes absorbing the outdated office space, Clara connects her glistening eyes with mine. "Where's my desk?"

I laugh while pushing my chair away from my desk. "There's only one seat in this office, Princess. So you either take my knee, or..." My eyes stray to the faded red couch pushed up against the wall.

"The sofa it is," Clara fills in, moving toward the couch.

I have a feeling this will be the longest two weeks of my life.

Chapter Five

"Still can't believe you made Ms. Fancy Thing a member of the Inked family," Diesel says while walking into my office. "You gonna keep her around?"

I drift my eyes past his shoulder to Clara manning the front counter before lifting my shoulders into a shrug. "She seems to be doing all right."

Clara has slipped into her makeshift role at Inked surprisingly well. She's a little uptight, but the male clientele has had no complaints—they're too busy enjoying the view to be angry about her occasional smart mouth. The female customers, on the other hand... they're not as appreciative of the qualities Clara brings to Inked.

Thankfully, our male-to-female ratio at Inked sits at around seventy to thirty.

I turn my eyes back to Diesel. "Have any of the guys said anything? Got any concerns if we keep her on?"

He lowers himself onto the couch, crumpling the paperwork Clara has sprawled across her 'desk' before locking his eyes with mine. "I wasn't talking about keeping her around as an employee." He stares at me with a jeering grin etched on his face. "I was talking on a more *personal* level."

A whizz of air parts my nose. "The only reason Clara is standing behind that counter is because she's here for the dollars. Hell would freeze over before anything *personal* happens between us."

The mocking grin on Diesel's face enlarges. "Don't go acting like your cock hasn't stood to attention every time she greeted you with a bit of lip. You've always liked them with attitude. That's why you're always hiding out in your office the last two weeks... so your desk can conceal the stiffness in your jeans."

I smirk but don't refute his claim. Diesel and I have been friends since fifth grade, so he'd see through any ruse I dangled in front of him. I'm also not one for lying. Even with Clara giving me as good as I've been dishing the past two weeks, she just needs to nibble on the end of her pen, and my cock is paying careful attention to every move she makes.

I'm endeavoring to keep my head in the game—*the head on my shoulders, not the one between my legs*—which ensures our little tit-for-tat routine will never be anything more than an employee and employer having a difference of opinion. *Now I just need my cock to get the memo.*

Diesel cranks his neck to the side just as Clara bends over to gather a register roll from the lower shelf of the cabinet in the foyer. "Damn! I'd even take a bit of lip for an ass that fine."

I sink deeper into my chair. "You've got to get the bar bunnies out of your bed before you'll ever have the opportunity to get a woman of Clara's standards between your sheets. Besides, Inked has rules on the crew not messing around. When that happens, shit gets complicated."

Diesel chuckles. "Fuck the rules. We've never had a woman like Clara work for us. If we did, the rules would have been broken years ago. And while I'm being totally fuckin' forthright, you would have been the first to break them. You had a fondness for bending the rules before you were out of diapers."

I smirk. What he's saying is true. Not just on my rule-breaking, but on the previous female employees of Inked. Other than Charity, none had Clara's sexpot beauty. They were interesting and had great personalities, but they were hired solely based on their credentials.

Does that mean I only hired Clara because she makes my dick twitch? No, not at all.

What? For someone who doesn't like lying, you're doing a mighty fine job of it, Brax.

In all honesty, at the start, Clara was offered a position solely because she's beautiful. But she remains a member of Inked because she has a strong work ethic. Her looks are merely an added bonus. What Clara said during her impromptu interview was true. This situation is a win-win for us both. By keeping our clients happy, they will return again and again.

The visual of Clara prancing around the shop in skintight designer dresses keeps my clients happy.

I scrub my hand over the few days of stubble on my chin while saying, "There's a difference between bending the rules and breaking them. Tapping Clara would be demolishing them."

"She'd be worth the hassle. You've always said it is the rich girls who are wilder in the bedroom. Clara is making me want to test your theory." Diesel's voice is a mix between playful and determined.

I glare into his hanker-filled eyes. "Are you gonna make a move on Clara?"

He rubs his hands together as his mocking grin switches to eagerness. "You got any objections if I do?"

The first thought to enter my mind is, *fuck yes, I mind.* The second is, *why do I even care?* Although I've been using the no-messing-with-the-crew clause as my excuse to stay away from Clara, it isn't set in stone for my crew. It's not in their employment contract, and it is not mentioned during the hiring process, so Diesel is well within his rights to ignore it. But even knowing this, I still don't want him touching Clara. She isn't mine, and she will most likely never be mine, but for some reason, unbeknownst to me, the thought of Diesel treating Clara like she's a bunny annoys the shit out of me.

Before I can reply to Diesel's question—or compile a reason as to why I object to his request—a flurry of blonde scurrying past my office door catches my attention.

After rolling my eyes at her imperfect timing, I say, "Come on in, Princess, you've never been concerned about knocking before, so what's changed now?"

Clara's red pumps enter the frame first, closely followed by the rest of her enticing body. "It's the first time I've ever seen a look of concentration on your face. I wasn't sure if you were holding a serious discussion or needing to use the bathroom."

Diesel's deep laughter fills the office.

"You'll be cleaning the bathroom if you don't watch it," I grumble, glaring at Diesel, my mood still edgy from his disclosure of interest in Clara.

"Un-fucking-likely," Diesel replies while sinking deeper into the couch.

After leaning back in my chair, I intertwine my fingers, striving to ignore the way Diesel's eyes roaming over the dark green dress clinging to the curves of Clara's body has caused a tick to impinge my jaw.

The clicking of heels bounces off the wall when Clara pushes off the doorjamb and ambles deeper into the space. "Charity has secured a walk-in, and Johnny has advised he will be *indisposed* for an hour." A ghost of a smile stretches across my face from the disgruntled cloud her eyes got when she referred to Johnny's unavailability. "The remainder of the crew don't have any clients arriving for another hour, so I'm going to grab a quick bite to eat."

My brow arches. "You're advising me that you're going to lunch?"

My eyes follow her hands when she runs them down the front of her dress before she nods.

"Why? You've never bothered the past two weeks, so what's changed today?" I question after dragging my eyes away from her petite frame. It's a hard-fought battle.

She stiffens. "I was just trying to be polite." Her brows stitch together tightly. "I guess it was imprudent of me to believe manners held any place in a tattoo parlor." With a sigh, she spins on her heels and saunters to the door. Just before she exits, she peers back at me. "You need to make a decision about converting my trial basis to a permanent position soon. It is highly unprofessional to leave such an imperative decision until the last minute." Although her words come out stern, the bitchy smear of her tone can't hide the desperation in her eyes.

"Actually, Diesel and I were just discussing your inclusion in the Inked family." I gesture my hand to Diesel, who hasn't taken his eyes off her ass since she entered my office.

Although my statement is slightly deceitful, it isn't a total lie. Before our conversation veered off course, Diesel and I were discussing the possibility of extending Clara's appointment at Inked.

Clara's breathing quickens, but she remains as quiet as a church mouse as her wide eyes shift between Diesel and me. "And?" she eventually squeaks out, unable to harbor her curiosity any longer.

I quirk my lips. "I haven't reached a decision yet. How about we extend your trial to a day-to-day basis until I've had time to decide?"

Anger spreads through Clara's veins, giving her skin a red hue. The veins in her neck pulse so furiously, they nearly burst. When she glares at me in disdain, I'm primed and ready to cop the wrath of her fury, so you can imagine my surprise when she holds back her usually bitchy retaliation and storms out of the office without a single word seeping from her lips.

I balk and turn my shocked eyes to Diesel. "What the fuck did I just miss?"

"A prime opportunity." Standing from the couch, he stretches his legs before striding to my open office door. After closing the door, he twists to face me. "She just gave you an in, and you shot her down like she has the clap."

I stare at him with bewilderment all over my face. "She didn't give me an in. She's just sucking up as she's worried about her position. Today is the last day of her trial."

Diesel throws his head back and laughs. "Yeah, right." He steps closer to my desk. "'I'm grabbing a quick bite to eat' is a bunny's way of saying, 'will you please fuck me over the lunch table?'"

I can't help the smirk that crosses my face at the way he changed his voice to mimic the women he usually spends his weekends with.

"Maybe for a bunny that might be true, but Clara isn't a bunny."

There's no way in hell Clara is a bunny. That name is solely reserved for girls who have no problems hopping from bed to bed. I may have called Clara a few choice names the past two weeks, but a bunny will never be one of them.

Diesel glares at me like I've grown a second head. "I knew you were off your game, man, but I had no clue it was this bad. Every woman is a bunny. Rich or not." He shifts his hazel eyes to mine, his expression changing from cheeky to serious in a nanosecond. "How long has it been since you graced a woman's womb with your seed?"

While glaring at him, I pretend I don't have a clue what he's referring to.

Not believing the phony look on my face, he continues, "I haven't seen you take home a bunny once the past two weeks. Not even one of the high-class ones I saw sniffing around last week."

"That's because the shit's gotten old. The game is overplayed," I interject with an edge to my voice. "My dysfunctional cock has nothing to do with the fine tail that just left this office. It's just tired of the game."

Diesel bows his brow. "The only shit that's gotten old is you, Brax. The game will never get old. Your dick gets cold, a bunny warms it. Your dick gets lonely, a bunny cuddles it. Your dick gets—"

"Yeah, yeah, I get it. A bunny on my cock is the answer for everything."

Diesel nods. "You've just got to decide if you want the high-class bunny your dick has set its radar on, or if you're going to settle for something a little less fancy but a shitload less complicated."

"My cock and its goals are no concern of yours."

He continues talking as if he didn't hear a word I said. "If you decide it isn't the latter, let me know, and I'll take a step back. But if a diamond-encrusted pussy isn't what you're chasing, step aside and let a real man show you how to seal the deal."

Not giving me a chance to reply, he strides into the corridor, closing my office door behind him.

Chapter Six

"Charity, I'm heading out to grab some food," I advise while striding down the hallway at Inked.

Charity lifts her brown eyes from the lotus tattoo she's drawing on the shoulder of a long-time client and locks them with me. "Bring me back something sweet."

"If you want pussy on a platter, you should go visit Keke," I suggest with a cheeky wink.

Her pupils widen. "I've already tried to tap that, but for some reason, she's adamant her dinner dates must have dangling bits between their legs." She shrugs. "But, hey, I gave it my best shot."

I stop dead in my tracks. "I meant Keke's *establishment*. Not Keke herself."

Although the crew at Inked has no problems swapping bunnies, we draw the line at any other type of sharing. Since Keke isn't a bunny, I'm somewhat shocked by Charity's admission.

A bead of sweat forms on Charity's brow when she notices my surprised expression. "Oh, sorry, man. My bad?" Her eyes dance between mine. "I thought things between you and Keke had cooled since you've got Ms. Sweet Thing over there." She nudges her head to Clara standing behind the counter drinking some funky green concoction.

What is it with everyone assuming I'm knocking boots with Clara? I'm not knocking boots with anyone, let alone Clara, and my cock is not fucking happy about it.

Charity sighs loudly before drifting her eyes from Clara to me. "Why do all the beautiful women in this town only like cock?"

Any anger bubbling in my veins dampens from her assessment. Charity has the mouth of... well, a tattoo artist, but she's downright gorgeous—dark hair styled in an alluring short cut, rich brown eyes, and flawless skin accentuated with a collection of tattoos I designed specifically for her. She's proof not all the beautiful women in this town are solely cock lovers.

I shake my head, bringing my thoughts back to the present. "Something sweet?" I confirm, deciding Charity's attempts at seducing Keke aren't worth burning the solid bridge we've formed in the two years Charity has worked at Inked. Although Keke is a great girl, we both know our kinship isn't going any further than two sexually compatible companions sharing a bed for a few hours.

Charity grins a knockout smile as she nods.

"All right. I'll be back in a few."

Charity returns her focus to her client as I stride to the counter.

"You'll turn into a vegetable if you keep drinking that shit."

Clara lowers a glass of ghastly green liquid from her mouth. "There could be worse things I could turn into." Her icy-blue eyes lock with mine. "I could end up like you."

While smirking at her horrified expression, I say, "I walked straight into that one, didn't I?"

She screws up her nose before nodding. "Yeah, but you can't win them all. Especially when you're fighting a battle you'll *never* win."

A breathy chuckle rumbles up my chest as I continue for the door. Just as I'm about to exit, Clara calls out my name, halting my fast escape. When I crank my neck, I balk. For the first time ever, she appears genuinely nervous.

"Have you given any more thought to extending my position here?"

The bells above the door chime when I close it and amble back to stand in front of her. Her stance is solid, but her eyes are giving away her real concern. She's petrified.

"Yeah, I have. Why don't we discuss it over dinner?"

Holy fuck! Did I just ask her on a date using her employment at Inked as leeway?

I'm so getting sued for workplace harassment.

Clara freezes. "I can't... I don't think that would be a good idea, Brax."

"Why not?"

Her refusal to dine with me has more impact on my gigantic ego than the time she tried to strike me months ago. Especially since I've caught sight of Diesel watching our exchange from the corner of the room. His face is laced with humor, and his whole demeanor screams of arrogance.

"I don't think we should mix business with pleasure," Clara replies, dragging my focus away from Diesel's smug face.

"It is a meal, Princess. There's nothing pleasurable about it." I rake my eyes over the curves I've been ignoring for weeks. "Unless certain *items* are on the menu?"

Yep, I'm definitely getting sued.

Clara's lips thin into a harsh line. "There's no chance of that *ever* happening."

When she glares at me through squinted eyes, hot anger warms my blood. "Then it's lucky we're just grabbing a bite to eat, isn't it?"

My sudden decision to invite Clara to dinner has nothing to do with her employee contract and everything to do with Diesel's admission that he's interested in having her warm his sheets, but I can't help it. The instant Diesel shone his torch on Clara, it was like the possessive switch in my body was turned on. And now that it has been flicked on, I have no chance of turning it off.

Diesel has kept his distance from Clara the past week to give me the opportunity to decide on his suggestion. But he's eyeballing her now like she's a prime piece of steak he can't wait to sink his teeth into. To say my feeling of ownership kicked into overdrive would be an understatement. It's turned calamitous.

In my head, I know I don't have any claim to Clara, but it is like I've stepped back to my high school days, and I'm letting my competitive side overrule my rational-thinking head. I'm so far gone, I'm willing to make a fool out of myself in front of my crew simply to ensure I have the upper hand in the little black book competition Diesel and I have been running since our teen days.

Clara's eyes track me as I walk around the counter. Even though her stern gaze appears to be protesting, not a word spills from her lips when I curl my arm around her tiny waist, hoist her against my body, and guide her toward the front entrance of the shop.

I don't look back at my crew or Diesel to seek confirmation that I've secured their attention. I can feel their curious gazes burning a hole in the back of my head.

The hum of chatter filters into my ears when we merge onto the sidewalk. I swing my eyes to the left before drifting them to the right, seeking a suitable location I can take Clara to eat.

Upon realizing nothing on this side of Ravenshoe will be up to her impeccable standards, I make my way to Betty's Burgers two blocks over from Inked.

You can't go wrong with burgers and fries.

"You're nothing but a brute." Clara's words are barely audible over the scuffling of her stilettos on the concrete sidewalk. "You know I can walk, don't you? That's what legs were invented for. One foot in front of the other. I guess *beasts* like you might not understand the concept since you spend half of your day dragging your knuckles on the ground."

I stop walking and drop my eyes to hers. "If I release you, will you keep walking?"

When I spot the spark of rebellion brightening her light-blue eyes, I continue walking, dragging her along with me. Clara huffs when we enter Betty's Burgers, and her incoherent blubbering continues when I walk her to the booth at the back of the restaurant and place her on the cracked vinyl seat. I smirk when she shuffles across the plastic cladding to sit in the furthest corner of the booth. Her mouth is protesting that she wants to leave, but her actions are speaking louder than her words.

I greet Marnie—the regular waitress at Betty's—with a wink as I snag two menus from her grasp as she saunters past. "I'll be back to take your order soon, sugar," she mutters, her voice as sweet as the term of endearment she regularly calls me.

"Kale, poached salmon, carrot smoothies, or whatever other shit you usually eat isn't available here, but the burgers are good, and the cheese fries are even better," I advise while handing Clara a menu.

Her pupils widen more with every item she reads off the menu. "I can't eat anything here. My trainer, Pierre, would have a coronary." She lifts her eyes from scanning the menu to me. "Who eats a burger with four deep-fried beef patties? That's just asking for a heart attack."

"Are you kidding me? You're nothing but skin and bones. You could handle adding at least four of those burgers to your weekly diet."

That is a total lie. Clara is a slim build, but she has curves in all the right places. Her tits and ass have been the hot topic of many adult-only discussions in my tattoo chair the past three weeks. And I'm fairly certain she has been the source of many self-induced orgasmic experiences for the younger patrons of Inked. Even with her having perfected the princess-resting-bitch-face pose, her body is... *Jesus.*

I slide into the booth before every patron in the restaurant sees *exactly* what I think of Clara's desirable assets.

When a burning pain scorches my skull, I shift my eyes to Clara. Her face is lined with anger. "Did you just insult me?"

I shake my head. "No. Not at all."

Her brow arches. "I work my ass off in a gym for an hour every day before my shift at Inked. I watch every minute portion of food I eat, and I skip the dessert menu six nights a week, all to have a guy who shoves calories into his mouth like they're nothing but air tell me I look like a bag of bones."

"I didn't mean it like that."

"Then what did you mean, Brax? I'm not sure how you can mince words like that."

When she stands from the booth, her slit eyes silently demand that I move.

I don't budge an inch.

"Let me out," she snarls through gritted teeth.

When I shake my head, her anger hits an all-time high.

My cock is definitely broken. The instant her spikes hackled, it turned to stone.

"You honestly can't expect me to stay here after you insulted me! Only a fool would continue to associate with someone who ridicules them."

"That's sweet coming from the lady who has called me a beast on numerous occasions the past two weeks."

She crosses her arms in front of her chest. "If the name fits, use it."

I glare into her eyes. "Then sit the fuck down, *Princess.*"

Her nostrils flare as the anger lining her face deepens. "Let. Me. Out. I'm not dining with you after you insulted me."

"I didn't insult you," I fire back, my loud voice gaining us a handful of spectators.

"Then what do you call it? You pretty much insinuated that you don't find me attractive."

Ignoring the dozen pairs of curious eyes bouncing between Clara and me, I lock my eyes with her and mutter, "Do you want to know the impact your hours of calorie counting and gym workouts have on me?"

The tightness of her arms braced in front of her chest strengthens before she curtly nods.

"Then look down, Princess."

Her brows scrunch as confusion washes over her face. After delving her tongue out to replenish her dry lips, she drops her gaze.

She inhales a sharp, quick breath when her eyes zoom in on the hardness my jeans don't have a hope in hell of hiding.

Feeling the heat of her furious gaze, the thickness of my cock grows.

Yep, it's definitely broken.

When Clara's massively dilated eyes return to mine, I say, "You need to stop acting so defensive. Not everyone is out to get you. Although I could have chosen better words, I didn't mean to insult you. If you look more deeply into what I said, it could be taken as a compliment."

When she huffs and rolls her eyes, I stand from the booth and move out, giving her a clear exit. "If you want to go, go. If not, let's sit down and have a meal together. No stipulations. No expectations. Just two friends enjoying each other's company."

Clara's eyes dance between mine for numerous heart-clutching seconds before she queries, "If I leave, will my position at Inked be on the line?"

My jaw muscle gains a quiver. "No. I may be a *beast*, but I'm still a man under this beastly disguise. I can't offer you a permanent placement at Inked as those positions are reserved for tattoo artists, but your current position is yours for as long as you want it on a casual basis. Take it a day at a time and see where this shit takes you. Once you've had your fill of Inked, just let me know you're ready to move on with a few days' notice."

For the first time ever, a genuine smile sneaks across her thinly slit lips. "Thank you."

I won't lie, my heart slithers into my gut when she slides out of the booth to stand next to me. "I like you, Brax, and I appreciate the opportunity you have bestowed on me, but we are not friends, and because we come from two entirely different lifestyles, we'll most likely never be friends. So why don't you stop pretending you actually like me and let me get back to the job you're paying me to do?"

She doesn't wait for me to reply.

She simply strides to the door and exits without a backward glance.

Chapter Seven

"How are you finding the move? I bet your boy is growing up fast?"

Hugo, one of my regular clients at Inked, smiles a beaming grin. "Yeah, Joel is..." He stops talking as his eyes sheen with moisture. "He's good. So much like his mother."

I pull my tattoo gun back from the rainbow rose I'm adding to his vast collection of tattoos on his right rib and inspect my work. "So what's the deal with this tat? Most of your pieces have some sort of connection to Ava, but this is the first time I've ever inked a flower on your body." My voice comes out shaky, hindered by a small bout of laughter dying to break free.

Nothing against Hugo. He's a tall brute of a man who could easily put any guy on his ass, but the majority of his torso is covered with a range of oddly chosen tattoos. Although his ink selection is one-of-a-kind, every one I've placed on his body has a significant meaning to his life before he moved to Ravenshoe. It didn't take a genius to realize his tattoos revolved around one woman.

If the hidden inclusion of the name Ava in most of his tattoos didn't give enough of a hint, the stories he shared while I added to his collection were a surefire indication. Tattoo artists are the male equivalent of hairdressers for women. The stories clients have shared while sitting in my tattoo chair could fill at least a hundred books.

After wiping the freshly-inked skin with my cloth, I lift my eyes to Hugo. He's grinning a smile I've only seen on his face once before—when I inked his son's name onto his chest. It sits just above his heart.

"I asked Ava to marry me," Hugo admits, his smile enlarging.

My lips curl into a broad grin. "Shit, man, you work fast," I jest. He only moved back to Rochdale three months ago.

He laughs. "That's only the beginning. We are having a baby at the end of the year."

I cock my brow. "Damn, you better watch out. You'll run out of skin to ink with all those memories you're creating." I nudge my head to the bathroom while pulling off my latex gloves. "Go tell me what you think. You'll have to switch off the light to see Ava's name since you went with the invisible ink again."

Hugo stands from my tattoo chair, filling my cubicle with his six-foot-five frame. I clean up my station while he checks out his newly inked piece in the bathroom attached to my cubicle.

He emerges thirty seconds later with a broad grin on his face.

"Good?" I query, already knowing his answer.

"Perfect." No more words are needed. His face tells the entire story.

Hugo throws his shirt over his head while shadowing me to the counter to ring up his purchase. I've worked at Inked for over ten years, and he is the only client I've agreed to tattoo a name on without seeing a wedding band wrapped around his finger. I didn't need to warn him about the lifetime commitment that comes with having a person's name inked onto your skin. His eyes relayed he was well aware of the commitment he was making. The fact he's getting married proves I didn't misread his loyalty to Ava.

My brisk pace to the cash register slows when "Brax" sounds from a pair of lips that can cause my dick and spikes to bristle at the same time.

Things between Clara and me the past three weeks have followed a similar path they did the weeks prior to my disastrous attempt at sharing a meal with her. Although she's a little standoffish with both the staff and me, she does exactly what she's paid to do. And she does it well.

The only thing that has changed is our game of tit for tat. It came to a screeching halt the instant she exited the restaurant three weeks ago. I guess finding out your scornful tongue gives your boss a raging hard-on would dampen anyone's eagerness to take part in a bit of friendly banter.

Clara walks out of my office balancing a planner in one hand while twirling a pencil in the other. "Your seven o'clock appointment just canceled. Did you want me to bump up one of your following appointments? Or…" Her words stop when they lift from the leather-stitched planner to the enormity of Hugo standing beside me.

The longer her eyes roam Hugo, the more the raging tornado in her eyes grows. I can see her short temper flaring, dying to break free.

I'm not the only one who has noticed her blazing reaction to Hugo's presence. The buzzing of tattoo guns quiets down, and the usual hum of conversation dulls to barely a whisper.

The longer Clara glares at Hugo, the more attention she garners from her colleagues.

After sucking in a deep breath, Clara finally shifts her widened gaze to me. "You're busy. I'll come back."

I balk, staggered by her odd behavior.

She's never been concerned about interrupting me before, so what's changed now?

"No, let's do this shit now, Princess. The quicker I get these appointments over with, the quicker my weekend will start."

Her throat works hard to swallow before her narrowed gaze rockets back to Hugo. She stares at him as if she's daring him to say something while I bounce my confused eyes between them, trying to work out how they know each other. From the dazed expression on Clara's face and the shit-eating grin on Hugo's, it doesn't take a genius to realize they've met before.

My back molars smack together as my mind runs through various scenarios of how well they could know each other. All my skits follow along a similar path—Hugo and Clara naked together.

"Yeah, come on, *Princess*," Hugo says, his voice a thick drawl. "Brax hasn't got all day."

My brow cocks. Just from the contempt displayed in Hugo's words, I think my initial assumption of his friendliness with Clara may have been wrong. But even with having my unwarranted jealousy checked, my mood is still woeful. I've been working with a massive headache the past two hours.

Actually, make that weeks.

She's standing right in front of me.

The biggest fucking headache of my life.

Like my crippling headaches aren't irritating enough, my cock's stint in segregation has become even more severe since Clara arrived on the doorstep of Inked. Nothing kills a man's good mood quicker than losing his mojo.

Clara's narrowed eyes shift from glaring at Hugo to me. "We'll continue this later," she instructs, her tone smeared with superiority like the princess she is.

My eyes drift around the handful of the Inked crew watching the exchange between Clara and me with eagle eyes. Charity's mouth is gaped, Johnny has his brows stitched, and Diesel is leaning against the doorjamb of my office with an amused grin etched on his face.

Not willing to let any member of my crew believe this type of behavior will be deemed acceptable at Inked, I sling my eyes back with Clara and order, "Do it now or collect your last paycheck."

She inhales a quick, jagged breath as her eyes dance between mine, no doubt seeking any deceit in my statement. Although I said the job was hers as long as she wanted it, I won't be disrespected in front of my crew.

I just hope she can't see the deceit in my eyes.

Unable to determine if my threat is idle, Clara swallows harshly before marching to the counter with her head held high. She snaps open the planner and drops her eyes to it. "I contacted Clancy. He's happy to take an earlier appointment, but he has some alterations he'd like to make to his design."

I adjust the tilt of my head, forcing her eyes to connect with mine. "Have Clancy's designs already been drawn up?"

After shifting her eyes from Hugo to me, Clara shakes her head.

"Then keep him at his original time. He's fanatical about the draw-up, and it can take hours to get him to agree to a design, so he'll hold up the appointments following him. What about Riley?" I suggest while pointing to my ten o'clock booking. "Call him and see if he can get here at seven, then slot Colby in after him."

"Okay. I'll make some phone calls. Once I have everyone scheduled, I will advise you of any changes," Clara informs, her voice still high-strung.

Once she snaps the planner shut, she diverts her focus to Hugo. "If you so much as breathe a word about me working here, I will ensure it is the last breath you take," she warns in a vicious snarl. "In fact, if you even mention you saw me in this dump, I'll do far worse than ending your pathetic life."

My eyes bulge, Charity's dropped jaw gains leverage as does the grin on Diesel's face, and Johnny... well, he's simply staring at Clara in complete awe.

It's not every day you see a princess sparring against a giant.

Upon hearing the shocked gasps of her work colleagues, Clara's eyes slowly filter around the shop. The fiery anger illuminating her face with a red hue fades when she realizes her tirade has gained her the attention of half of her co-workers and a dozen clients.

Snarling, she spins on her heels and darts down the corridor. I run my hand down my face as my brain tries to work out what the fuck just happened. This is the first time in the ten years I've been working at Inked that I've had to deal with a member of my crew verbally abusing the clients.

Usually, it's the other way around.

After gesturing for my crew to get back to work, I lock my eyes on Hugo. "Sorry about that. She's a little high-strung at times," I mutter, my voice hampered with frustration at being forced to apologize for the behavior of one of my crew, let alone a grown woman who should know better.

Hugo delves his hand into the back pocket of his jeans. "It's all good. It's nothing I haven't handled before."

When he passes me one of the many credit cards housed in his leather wallet, my brows furrow. "Since when did you stop paying cash?" I jest, saying anything to lessen the awkward tension plaguing the air.

"About as long as you've been picking up rich strays." Hugo waggles his brows.

I laugh, grateful he can see the humor in a difficult situation. "A dangerous endeavor for us both, no doubt?"

"You have no fucking clue," he mutters under his breath.

After seeing Hugo out, I walk down the corridor in search of Clara. Because of the size of the shop, it doesn't take me long to find her camped out in the supply closet. Although she appears to be busy working, the feistiness that radiates out of her in invisible waves is missing, clearly indicating she's in hiding.

"I need to talk to you in my office."

Clara places a bottle of blue tattoo ink onto the third shelf before hopping off the stepladder. "Okay. Let me just finish this—"

"Now, Clara," I interrupt, my voice conveying that this is not up for negotiation.

She places the ordering clipboard on the middle shelf and shifts on her feet to face me. When her icy-blue eyes lock with mine, my furious composure slips for the quickest second. She looks more concerned now than she did when I threatened for her to collect her last paycheck ten minutes ago. I guess this is the first time I've used her real name in the past six weeks.

I nudge my head to the hallway, wordlessly demanding that she follow me. Not waiting for her to reply, I spin on my heels and stride to my office. If her rich floral scent hadn't infused the air around me, I would have assumed she wasn't following me. She's so quiet, not even the clicking of her heels on the tiled floor sounds through my ears as we make our way down the corridor and into my office.

I move to my desk, prop my backside on the edge, then lift my eyes to the office door. Clara is standing in the open doorway, looking prepared to flee at any moment. Her pupils are wide, and her face is flushed.

This is the one part of my job I fucking hate. Just like I'm not a violent man, I also loathe confrontation, but Clara overstepped the mark tonight, and she must be reprimanded for it. I warned her when I offered her a trial at Inked that if she scared away any of my customers, she'd be out on her ass quicker than I could snap my fingers. Although it will take more than a spiteful threat to scare off a regular client like Hugo, she still shouldn't have said what she did.

When Clara remains standing halfway between the hallway and my office, I request, "Close the door."

Her throat struggles to swallow before she does as requested. Once the door is closed—blocking out the buzzing of tattoo guns—I gesture to the couch.

Her eyes follow mine before she timidly shakes her head. "I'm happy to stand," she informs me as her eyes stray from the couch to me. "If you're going to fire me, Brax, can you hurry up and get it over with?"

A deep sigh spills from my lips. "You don't have anything else to say? No pleading for clemency? No begging for forgiveness?"

"No," she replies with a brisk shake of her head.

I balk, utterly shocked.

"I did nothing wrong, so why would I feel the need to apologize?" she argues to my baffled expression.

I arch my brow. "Are you fucking kidding me? You did nothing wrong?" Pushing off the desk, I walk two steps closer to her. "You not only disrespected my business, my crew, and me with the little spectacle you unleashed, you disrespected yourself."

Her eyes bounce between mine, her confusion growing by the second.

"We're a family at Inked. The instant you agreed to work here, you became one of us. Anything said or done to a member of our family is done to the *whole* family, so when you ran your mouth about my business, you were running your mouth about yourself."

She inhales a sharp breath as the fiery spark in her eyes is smothered with shock.

I cross my arms in front of my chest. "I'd always wondered why you chose to work at Inked instead of one of those fancy boutiques you buy your dresses from. Only now does it dawn on me why you showed up on this side of town. You didn't think anyone from your neck of the woods would turn up here."

Clara's tongue delves out to lick her parched lips, but she doesn't speak a peep.

"Well, I have news for you, Princess. Having tattoos doesn't make you trashy. I've *doodled* on judges, lawyers, doctors, and even stuck-up little *princesses* who have fancy-colored credit cards that cost a quarter-of-a-mil a year just to have."

The harshness of my words dulls when I spot a sheen of moisture forming in her eyes, but it doesn't completely stop my reprimand. "If your plan is to hide away from your country club friends in a place you won't be seen, the door is that fucking way." I point to the entrance of Inked. "As I guarantee you have just as much chance of being seen here as you would in some fancy dress shop on the other side of town."

After issuing my disappointment with my eyes instead of words, I walk around my desk and take a seat in my cracked leather chair. I secure a set of invoices off my desk and shuffle through them, needing something to distract my hands from the urge to take Clara over my knee and spank the sass right out of her.

Maybe that's half her problem? Perhaps her parents didn't discipline her enough?

My gaze lifts from the invoices in my hand when Clara whispers, "Am I fired?"

The roaring of blood in my ears slows as my gaze drifts between her remorse-filled eyes. "I said your position at Inked is yours for as long as you want it. I'm a man who keeps my word."

Relief swamps her eyes as she gently nods.

"But if you disrespect my crew or me again, I may reconsider."

She once again nods before pivoting on her heels and stalking to the door.

The furious twitch impinging my jaw lessens when the faintest murmur of, "I'm sorry, Brax," seeps from her lips before she slips out of my office as quietly as she entered.

Chapter Eight

Standing from my office chair, I down the glass of whiskey I've been nursing the past thirty minutes before snagging my jacket thrown over the edge of my desk. Considering it is a little after midnight on a Saturday, I don't bother checking if the premises are vacant. All the crew of Inked evacuates the instant the clock strikes midnight, more than eager to commence their two-day weekend. Clara included.

Ever since my run-in with Clara three weeks ago, things at Inked have changed. I'd like to say a majority of the change has been Clara's attitude, but unfortunately, that isn't entirely the case. Although she has toned down her prima-donna attitude, she's still coldhearted and standoffish.

You can't throw a princess into a pair of low-riding jeans and call her a cowgirl. At the end of the day, she will always be a princess. But instead of treating the crew at Inked as if they're a piece of chewed-up gum stuck under a bench seat, Clara has been treating them with more respect, as if they're members of her family instead of the enemy. It may be similar to an annoying little brother vibe, but it's better than the previous attitude she had.

After securing the deadbolts on the front door, I make my way to my Harley parked at the back of Inked. My eager steps lengthen when my eyes catch a flurry of blonde standing next to my bike.

I increase my stride as my eyes run over every inch of the fire-engine red dress clinging to the curves of the tempting female. The beat of my heart kicks up a gear as does the throb of my cock when my eyes are inundated with lavish curves on a knee-weakening body.

My excitement doesn't last long when the blonde notices my approach and twists her neck to the side to greet me. "Hey, Brax, you heading home?" asks Fallon, smiling a covetous grin that relays the question she really wants to ask, *Hey, Brax, you looking for company?*

Fallon is what I'd call a high-class bunny. With a body that brings mere mortals to their knees and the face of an angel, she could easily have her pick of any guy on the good side of Ravenshoe. Thankfully for the crew at Inked, she likes her men with a hint of roughness she can't get on her side of town. And the fact she's sprawled across my bike tells me she has her sights set on one member of the Inked crew tonight. Me.

While licking my parched lips, I run my eyes over her body for the second time. Red stiletto heels, lean runner legs, a smoking hot dress that hugs the curves of her more-than-tempting ass, and a decent rack I could easily be distracted by for hours.

Fuck it. My dick needs warmth.

After arching my brow, I stare into Fallon's bright green eyes. "You got any objections to fucking on a desk?"

"Not at all," she purrs while prancing toward me, not the slightest bit intimidated by the crudeness of my words.

* * *

My sweaty hands strengthen their grip on Fallon's hips as her body quivers through her second orgasm since we entered my office thirty minutes ago. Thankfully, her cries of ecstasy are barely heard over the slapping of skin as I pound into her. My pumps are furious as my race to climax picks up speed.

I need to come.

I need the release.

I need to get *her* out of my fucking head.

Fallon's dress slides up her waist more when I adjust her position. After flattening her torso onto my desk, I pry her knees further apart with mine before slamming my cock back into her. She groans a long, quivering moan when I take my cock to the root before drawing it back out. Her pussy ripples around me, begging for me to stay immersed in her warmth, and sweat rolls down my glistening torso when I thrust my hips forward, slamming back into her.

"Ah, Christ, Brax," she pants breathlessly as I fuck her at a ferocious speed.

Her new position has her taking more of my cock than she was earlier while also increasing my sprint to climax.

"It feels so good, baby, so deep. So... oh..." Fallon purrs.

A familiar tingle races along my spine when her pussy clamps down on my cock, her third climax coming to fruition even more quickly than the first two. Unlike the lower-class bunnies, Fallon's climaxes are void of the usual ear-piercing screams I've come to expect. If it weren't for her pussy milking my cock and her slick wetness coating my balls, I'd be none the wiser that she's orgasming.

Once the violent shudders raking Fallon's body lessen, I close my eyes, trying to block her from my thoughts. It isn't that she doesn't have a body most men would take a stake to the heart for or that her pussy isn't sucking at my cock the way I like it, it is the fact my cock has some fucked-up ideas on what it classes as a fun time.

Tonight's event, unfortunately, has become a regular occurrence for me the past three months. My cock plays his part to a T. He shows up hard and primed to go, but no matter how close my chase to climax gets to the finish line, I've failed to cross the line every single time.

It's there, right in front of me, but the final push I need to get me over the line is missing.

Fuck, I hope I find my mojo soon, or I'm going to die of sexual deprivation.

My eyes sluggishly open when the door in my office creaks.

Although shocked to see Clara, I'm not at all surprised when she walks in unannounced.

Princesses don't require permission to enter private premises.

She walks three steps into the sweat-infused space before her eyes lift from the cell phone in her hand. When she spots Fallon sprawled on my desk, one of her hands darts up to clutch her neck, stifling a scream, while the other yanks a set of earbuds out of her ears. As her eyes absorb the scandalous visual playing out in front of her, her pupils dilate to the size of dinner plates. Her lips part, and her cheeks turn a hue of pink.

Her flushed expression gives me the final push I need to cross the finish line. I close my eyes as the most intense orgasm I've ever experienced rockets through my body, shredding any concerns I had about dying of sexual deprivation. I come like I've never come before, a vision-hazing orgasm that utterly destroys me.

I'm so spent, I don't notice Clara slipping out of the room until the bells above Inked's entrance door chime into my office.

Fuck!

After pulling out of a delirious Fallon, I snag my jeans off the floor and take off after Clara. My abrupt departure has me accidentally stomping on Clara's expensive diamante-encrusted cell she left on the floor.

I drag my jeans up my thighs and tuck in my half-masted, condom-covered cock before staggering onto the sidewalk in front of Inked. My head cranks to the side when metal crunching together booms out of the alleyway. My heart thrashes against my ribs harder than it did when I was climaxing as I charge for the alley.

I take a step back when Clara's white convertible flies out of the narrow alley, missing me by the skin of my teeth. Tires squeal across the asphalt, and horns honk when she merges dangerously onto the street.

Any thoughts of jumping on my bike and chasing after her fade when my eyes lock in on my pride and joy lying on its side on the asphalt partway down the alley.

"Oh, baby, what did she do to you?" I mumble to myself as I bend down to collect the broken side mirror of my custom Harley Davidson Fat Boy.

* * *

"You owe me three grand," I declare while slapping the invoice from the panel beater who spent forty-eight hours of my weekend restoring my Harley back to her original condition onto the windscreen of Clara's BMW.

For the past hour, I've been lying in wait in the parking lot of Inked for Clara to show up. For the first time in the nine weeks she's worked here, she's arrived only ten minutes before opening.

I was getting worried I'd finally scared her off.

"I don't owe you shit," Clara replies before she opens her car door into my hip.

"Wow, Princess knows how to cuss. Did they teach you that in princess school?" My taunting words hide the grimace crossing my face from the sting her door made to my hip.

"Uh-huh. Along with how to avoid low-life scum." While glaring into my eyes, she curls out of her car all ladylike, her prim and proper composure not matching the malice of her words.

When she tries to sidestep me, I move into her path, foiling her quick getaway with my six-foot-two height.

Her nostrils flare as her icy eyes connect with mine. "If you don't move, you'll learn about another technique they taught me in *princess school.*"

"Oh, yeah, like what?" I take a step closer to her, not the slightest bit intimidated by her threat.

When she takes a retreating step, her back splays against the driver's side door of her car. Like *carpe diem*, I seize the moment by taking another step forward. The pulse in Clara's neck thrums when my body pins her to her car. I try to ignore the way her nipples are budded and pressed against my chest, how her rich floral scent has my cock stiffening, and how I'd let her smash her BMW into my

Harley again just for the chance of discovering if her lips taste as yummy as they look.

In case you didn't realize, my endeavors of being ignorant are fruitless. My body is acutely aware of every inch of her skin flattened against mine. And from Clara's wide-eyed and flushed expression, I'd say she's also mindful of my body's reaction to her closeness.

"This is workplace harassment." The hotness of her breath tickles my lips.

"If we were inside Inked, that might be the case, but since we haven't entered the premises yet, I'm perfectly within my rights to seek restitution for the damage you did to my property. Believe me. I checked," I say, quoting some of the words she flung at me during our last tussle.

Everything I'm saying is a lie. I didn't check shit.

When Clara fights my hold, I lean in even deeper, nearly crushing her tiny frame under my two hundred pounds. My movements cause my cock to brush the tempting warmth between her legs. My girth swells when a breathless moan unexpectedly topples from Clara's O-formed mouth. Her pupils expand as she snaps her mouth shut, no doubt mortified at her body's response to my closeness.

Fighting the desire to request the restitution I'm owed in a non-monetary value, I repeat, "You owe me three thousand dollars," while peering into her arctic-blue eyes.

My blood heats from the cunning grin that curls onto her lips. "As I said earlier, I don't owe you shit. Your bike was like that when I exited the parking lot."

The throatiness of her voice makes me even harder, but even if I wanted to ignore the deceit her eyes are relaying, I can't ignore the massive streak of vivid black satin paint—the color of my bike—on the right front fender of her car.

Noticing the direction of my gaze, Clara huffs before she struggles against my hold, fighting to get free. I hold my ground, refusing to relinquish her from my grasp.

Realizing she has no chance of fleeing from a man my size, she sighs. "It was an accident! I didn't mean to hit your bike." Her words come out in a hiss as she strains them through her clenched teeth.

"You didn't mean to hit it?" I quote, moving my head into her line of sight, demanding the attention of her bouncing eyes. "You dragged it halfway down the alley."

"It was an accident!" Her chest heaves against mine. "Because I was blinded by an image I'd give anything to forget, I *accidentally* clipped your bike with my car. Believe me, I was just as mortified as you were."

I don't know if the last part of her statement is referring to the damage done to my bike or the scene she witnessed in my office. While I strive to unravel the mystery of Clara, I return her determined stare. I've said previously her eyes were soulless, but the small sparks of life that have grown in them the nine weeks she has worked at Inked display she's telling the truth. So, ignoring the screaming protest of my cock, I take a step back, not only unpinning her from her car but also moving away from the warmth my cock wants to delve into.

The instant I step away, Clara runs her hands down her dress, smoothing the crinkles I caused to the material. My mind goes straight to working out a way I can get that dress creased on my bedroom floor.

What the fuck? I don't take girls back to my place.

Correction. I don't take bunnies back to my place. Since Clara isn't a bunny, technically, she doesn't count. But either way, I shouldn't be having those types of thoughts about a member of my crew.

"What were you doing at Inked at that time of the night?" I ask, endeavoring to return my thoughts to less deviant grounds.

I racked my brain the majority of the weekend trying to work out why Clara would be entering my office a little after one in the morning. Not one plausible reason was found.

"I could ask you the same thing. Haven't you heard of a bed?" She fakes a gag.

I smirk, loving not only her feistiness but the glint of jealousy firing her icy eyes. It's rare to spark a reaction out of her, so I'll take it for all it's worth. I'm not sure which look I prefer the most on Clara—the feisty little temptress or the jealous scorned woman. Both are as enthralling as the other.

"When you have an itch that needs to be scratched, you scratch it."

The rise and fall of her chest grow the longer I bounce my hankering gaze between her wide eyes. Even knowing I'm playing a game I shouldn't participate in, I add more chess pieces to the already overstacked board.

"Have you got an itch, Princess?" I mutter, no longer able to harness my curiosity on what has caused the glint of lust in her eyes.

The zipper of my jeans dig agonizingly into my cock when she murmurs, "Uh-huh," in a soft, throaty moan.

The pinch of pain turns into a full throb when she takes a step closer to me. She stands so close, the minty freshness of her recently brushed teeth fans my hungry lips.

"I have a *really* bad itch," she purrs, her voice the most provocative thing I've ever fucking heard. "It's just one a *beast* of a man like you wouldn't know how to scratch."

My conceit surges into unchartered territory. "Is that so?" I mutter, dropping my eyes to the generous swell of her curvy breasts. "Your tits are telling me a different story, Princess." I raise my eyes from her heaving chest to her face. Believe me, it's no easy feat. "They're telling me you not only want me to scratch your itch, but you also want me to fuck you hard and fast on my desk like I did to the little bunny Friday night."

Any concerns about my grandma having me lynched are left for dust when Clara's knee catches my groin unaware. Hot lava seers through my lungs as the air is violently removed from my body. I stumble backward and curl over, fighting through a torrent of pain I've never experienced before.

No grown man should ever experience this type of pain.

There are no doubts about it. Clara McGregor—Princess-Fucking-Socialite—has officially broken my cock.

"Jesus Christ, Clara. You could have just said no," I wheeze out.

"Oh. Could I? I once had someone tell me little punks don't understand the word no. So I figured I'd try a new tactic. I think it's safe to say my new ploy worked." Her words are vicious and add to the pain crippling me.

I cough, feeling my balls gargling in the back of my throat. "Yeah, it's safe."

My balls have barely returned to my stomach—let alone my sack —when Clara mutters, "Just in case the knee to the balls wasn't convincing enough, I'll spell it out for you, Brax." She spits my name out like venom. "The odds of me paying your three-thousand-dollar repair bill are nearly as good as your chances of scratching my itch."

The hot air of her breath flutters my earlobe when she snarls, "Pigs will fly before either of those things will happen."

She saunters away with her head held high and her hips swinging.

Even hunched over and nursing a set of crushed balls, my fucked-up brain tries to invent a way to get pigs to fly.

Chapter Nine

Did I get an apology from Clara for my balls being crushed beyond recognition? No.

Has Clara coughed up a dime of the three thousand she owes me? No.

Do I care? In all honesty, no, I don't.

Clara set me in my place, but I deserved it. I pushed, she pushed back harder.

Although we have spoken since the incident in the parking lot two weeks ago, we've never discussed what led to our heated exchange. If she's happy to forget I suggested fucking her like a bunny on my desk, I'll happily forget she crashed her BMW into my Harley before she crippled my balls with the same amount of intensity. Seems like a fair compromise.

I'm totally fucking pussy-whipped.

Ignoring the thoughts that would have Diesel paying out on me for weeks, I wander aimlessly around Inked. Not wanting another *incident* marked in my ledger, I now check that Inked is void of any living thing before I lock up each night.

Happy that the premises are lacking human contact, I amble to my bike. A grin curls on my lips when I enter the thick six-foot steel enclosure my bike is now protected behind. I had it installed three days following Clara's *accidental* collision with my bike.

The look on Clara's face when her BMW rounded the corner the morning it was installed was priceless. She looked a cross between amused and mortified. I've been loving all the new expressions she's been experimenting with for the past two weeks.

I squint my eyes when flashing orange lights impede my vision as I glide my bike down the side alley of Inked. Even with my vision hindered by bright lights, I can't miss the panicked expression on Clara's face as she pleads with a gentleman wearing a pair of grease-stained overalls.

I park my bike next to a tow truck that has Clara's BMW sitting on the tray and switch off the ignition. Clara's panic hits an all-time high when the second man with inky black hair clamps a set of safety chains onto the tires of her pride and joy.

Since Clara is so immersed in pleading with the middle-aged gentleman, she fails to notice me approaching. "I sent a check yesterday, I swear," she says, her begging eyes locked onto a man who has 'Jim' stitched on the upper left side of his overalls. "If they just waited a day or two, this whole situation could have been avoided."

"I'm sorry, sweetheart, I don't make the rules. I just enforce them," Jim replies while flicking the ash from his lit cigarette onto the ground. With a nudge of his head, Jim gestures for his employee to hop into the cab of the truck. "If you're going to rack up thousands of dollars in credit and cannot make a payment, you have to be prepared for the repercussions," Jim reprimands Clara while tearing out a sheet of paper from his extensively used tow slip pad. "If you can come up with the payment they're requesting by Monday, call the number at the bottom of the slip. If not, your car will be auctioned."

Jim gives Clara an apologetic smirk before he climbs into the cabin of his tow truck and drives down the street. Clara's chest thrusts up and down as she watches her beloved car become nothing but a speck on the horizon.

An ear-shattering scream expels from her lips when she spins and crashes into my chest. Snapping her eyes shut, she inhales a large breath as her hands scan the ridges of my chest and stomach.

A few inches lower and she'd discover the knee to the balls she struck me with two weeks ago didn't sustain me any permanent damage.

"How long have you been standing here, Brax?" she questions with her eyes still shut as tight as a bank vault.

I smirk. "You can tell it is me just from feeling me up?"

Quicker than a flash of lightning brightening a blackened sky, her eyes pop open. "I was not feeling you up."

"Yeah, you are." I nudge my head to her hands still plastered across the ridges of my stomach.

She freezes for a second in shock before she yanks her hands away as if scorched by an open flame. The tears glistening in her eyes prevent me from issuing a smart-ass remark to her absurd reaction. *She was touching my stomach, not my cock, for crying out loud.*

After running her sweat-slicked hands down the front of her designer dress, she turns her wide eyes to mine. "Have a pleasant evening." She cringes at her poor choice of words before she storms down the sidewalk.

It takes a minute for the reality of the situation to dawn on me.

After clenching my fists into firm balls, I hotfoot after her. "My warning still holds credit. If you get on a bus, your ass will be fired," I state.

Clara's quick strides to the bus shelter come to a dead halt halfway down the sidewalk. Her shoulders rise and fall as she inhales a large breath before she spins around to face me. "You just saw my car towed away, right?"

I nod.

"Then you know I have no other way to get home than to take the bus," she continues before crossing her arms over her chest.

The nod of my head converts to a shake. "You don't need to catch the bus. I'll take you home."

Her lips quirk as her perfectly etched brow curves high. "Do you have another mode of transportation that has more than two wheels?"

I crack a smile at the sassiness in her voice. "No," I reply with a brisk shake of my head.

Her brow arches even higher. "Then I'm taking the bus."

"Like fucking hell you are," I shoot back, my words flying out of my mouth like daggers.

All the high-spiritedness in her face drains, making way for the well-worn angry mask Clara usually wears. "You may be my *boss* when we're inside those walls," she spits out while pointing to the doors of Inked behind my shoulder. "But you have no power over me on this sidewalk."

The stern mask she's wearing slips for the quickest second when I take a step closer to her. "Are you sure about that, Princess?"

She squares her shoulders and looks me dead in the eyes. "Certain."

Not thinking of the repercussions my actions could cause to my business, I seize her elbow and drag her toward my bike. The clicking of her heels drowns out a small portion of her incessant rant on my beastly demeanor.

The angry sneer in her tone changes to panic when I snag my helmet out of the saddlebag and place it on her head. When squealing brakes shriek over her blubbering, Clara cranks her head to the side in just enough time to see bus 57 pulling away from the curb.

Realizing the next bus doesn't arrive for another forty minutes, she swings her eyes back to me. Her pupils are massive, nearly swamping her entire cornea. "I can't, Brax... oh God. I can't," she mumbles with her eyes fixated on my bike.

She shakes like a leaf when I ignore her continued protests by lifting her in my arms and plopping her onto my seat. She looks prepared to flee, but her panic has rendered her motionless. I open my mouth, planning to deliver some reassurance to the dark cloud of fear forming in her eyes, but my words fail when my eyes zoom in on the indecent amount of her smooth thighs her new straddled position has exposed. I don't think I've ever seen anything as provocative as a princess on the back of a Harley—*my Harley.*

After dragging my eyes away from the mouthwatering visual I

have no right to be perusing, I climb on my bike. "If you don't want to fall off, you better hold on tight," I warn.

Any objections spilling from her lips are drowned out by the loud rumble of my engine when I kick over the motor. As I pull into the heavy flow of traffic, Clara plasters her torso to my back and wraps her arms around my waist. It should feel wrong to have her sitting on the back of my bike—*very, very wrong*—but this feels right.

Actually, it feels fucking great.

Clara remains quiet the entire twenty-mile trip to her apartment building. There isn't much chance of holding a conversation between the warm May wind whipping past us and motorists honking their horns as I glide my bike through the densely populated roads.

When I pull into the driveway of Clara's apartment building on Hyde, she wastes no time scampering off my bike. "Are you a goddamn lunatic!" she screams after yanking my helmet off her head.

I slide down the kickstand, then dismount my bike. "I did the speed limit... just," I reply with a chuckle.

A winded grunt escapes my lips when Clara shoves my helmet into my chest with brutal force. "You could have killed me."

"I've been riding these streets for years, Princess. I know them like the back of my hand."

"You could have killed me, Brax!" she screams again, her eyes teeming with tears.

Although I've imagined for weeks what she'd sound like screaming my name, I don't want to hear it like this. "I'd never..." When her eyes stray to the ground, I grip the top of her arms, forcing her to lock her eyes with mine. "I would *never* let anything happen to you, Clara." I stare into her eyes, ensuring she can see the truth in mine. "I shouldn't have forced you onto my bike, and I'm sorry if I scared you, but I promise you, you were safer on the back of my bike than on the bus."

Gritting her teeth, she yanks out of my embrace and storms into her apartment building. I run my hand over the top of my head, vainly trying to gather some of my scattered composure. It's a fruitless effort considering the reasoning behind my skittish demeanor just stormed away from me.

After gesturing to the valet that I'll be back in a few, I take off after Clara. I only just make it into the elevator before the doors snap shut. Clara maintains a quiet front, but I can tell she has noticed my presence. Not only did she intake a sharp breath when I first entered the cramped elevator car, but her scorching eyes also haven't left mine for the past ten floors.

For each floor the elevator rises, the number of occupants dwindles. Once we reach the thirtieth floor, Clara and I are the only remaining riders. When I take a step toward her, she spears me in place with her furious gaze. Even with her composure screaming annoyance, her pupils are massive, exposing her earlier panic is still firmly clutching her throat.

"Clara—"

My words halt when the elevator dings, announcing we've arrived on the penthouse floor. My strides out of the elevator car come to a dead stop when Clara suddenly spins around to face me. "I can take it from here," she mutters, her words shaking as badly as her composure.

"I just want to make sure you don't pass out in the hallway." My tone relays the honesty of my statement. She looks beyond rattled that I don't feel comfortable leaving her unattended.

Her wide eyes bounce between mine, but not a word escapes her hard-lined mouth.

"I've come this far. What's a few more steps?" I gesture my head to a set of double doors a measly few feet from us.

Clara's eyes follow mine before she faintly whispers, "Okay, but you're only walking me to my door. You can't come in."

I gesture with my hand for her to lead the way. Although annoyed at the bitterness of her tone, I'm also grateful she's lowering some of the impenetrable walls she has placed between us.

My thankfulness is short-lived.

Any panic left on Clara's face from the ride on the back of my bike turns to absolute fury when her eyes drink in the eviction notice taped to her apartment door. After snatching the document off the polished hardwood door, her eyes speed-read the notice. "You bitch!"

Her hair smacks me in the face when she abruptly storms to a door directly across from her apartment. Her abrupt movements infuse the corridor with her rich floral scent. Loud bangs on a wooden door bellow through my ears when Clara whacks her fists on her neighbor's door. Her pounding is so hard, I won't be shocked if she turns up to Inked on Tuesday with busted knuckles.

Clara stumbles forward when the door is suddenly yanked open. I grab the top of her arms, ensuring she doesn't kiss the pristine marble foyer of her neighbor's entrance.

After gathering her footing, Clara pulls out of my embrace and locks her angry eyes with the blonde who just opened the door.

When I follow Clara's irate gaze, my eyes bulge. *Damn! I'm living in the wrong neighborhood.* With long, wavy platinum-blonde hair, fierce green eyes, and a body any man would happily spend hours exploring, Clara's neighbor is a knockout, an easy ten out of ten.

"You can't do this." Clara shoves the piece of paper she snatched off her door into the chest of her neighbor. "I still have another two months remaining on my lease."

The blonde grins a ball-clenching smile that *nearly* has the same effect on my cock as Clara's feistiness. "Chapter 83 of the Florida State landlord statutes clearly state Isaac is acting within his rights by issuing you an eviction notice," she replies, her words as strong as her stance.

Clara takes a retreating step, bewilderment evident all over her face. She isn't the only one surprised. The last time I was confronted with the name Isaac was when Clara wanted it inked on her skin nearly six months ago.

"Isaac approved this?" Clara queries, her voice hindered with shakiness.

The blonde crosses her arms under her impressive rack. "Isaac is a businessman, Clara. His priorities remain focused on his empire, leaving me the task of ensuring the trash is placed on the curb."

"Trash?"

"Yeah. *Trash*," her neighbor replies, drawing out the derogatory word in a long hiss. "You are nothing but a vindictive little bitch who is about to be taught a precious lesson."

Ouch! Even my ego got slapped by that catty remark.

Though she copped a low blow, in true Clara style, she straightens her spine and gives as good as she's getting. "Well, I have news for you, *sweetheart...*"

I grin, loving that she used a term of endearment as if it is an offensive word.

"The only person going to be taught a valuable lesson is you. You can act all high and mighty in your designer pantsuits, sipping expensive wine from a crystal flute in your fancy top-floor penthouse, but at the end of the day, you're no better than me." Clara takes a step closer to her neighbor, meeting her eye to eye. "Enjoy it while it lasts, Regan, because when Isaac finds out about the *special guest* you've been *entertaining* the past two months, it's all going to come tumbling down, one Chanel suit at a time."

After flashing a sly grin, Clara enters her apartment without a backward glance. I remain motionless, standing in the foyer with my mouth gaped open and my cock as hard as stone.

There's nothing as compelling as a feisty princess standing her ground.

I'm not the only one rendered into silence by Clara's gutsy tirade. Her neighbor stands just as muted as me.

Several seconds of dense awkwardness pass before Regan shifts her eyes to me. "You should be cautious about messing with a woman like Clara," she warns, her tone not as snarky as the one she used while tussling with Clara.

A grin tugs my lips higher. "I could say the same to you."

Regan doesn't attempt to refute my statement because you can't deny the truth.

Chapter Ten

I jerk my chin up in greeting to Penny—the nurse my grandma tried to set me up with three months ago—before I continue striding down the corridor of Caramine Care.

Although Penny has the naughty-nurse getup down pat, I'm glad I steered clear of her tempting offer. I've got enough on my plate with a certain feisty princess to be adding any more into the mix.

I knocked on Clara's door for a good ten minutes last night, only to be asked to leave through a crack the width of an inch. I only left when she guaranteed me she wouldn't take the bus to work on Tuesday. Even though she agreed to my demand, I have an inkling she won't adhere to my advice.

She better, or she will find out the hard way that I'm a man of my word.

Just as I'm about to enter my grandmother's room, the quickest glimpse of a profile stops me in my tracks. Clara just exited a door a few spots down from my grandma's room. She stops halfway down the corridor to chat with a man in a navy-blue suit and a white doctor's coat.

A woman of Clara's caliber could never be referred to as dowdy, but with her pale face and red rims around her eyes, her usually bright appearance is a little more tarnished than normal. Even tired, her beauty can't deter her male companion's longing glance at her backside as she saunters away from him.

Clara's composure is so off-kilter, she doesn't notice me gawking at her as she strides down the narrow hallway. Even stepping into her path doesn't slow her brisk pace.

"Sorry," she mumbles, her voice barely recognizable as she side-steps me and continues for the door.

Her brisk pace only falters when I ask, "Why are you in such a hurry, Princess?"

Her hands dart up to rub her face before she slowly spins to face me. I take a step back, uneased by the look on her face. Bitchy, hormonal women I can handle, but a crying one? Not so much.

Acting purely on impulse, I draw her into my chest and guide her into my grandma's room. Thankfully, the room is empty. Clara stiffens like a board the instant I curl my arms around her shoulders, but surprisingly, she doesn't fight against my hold. I expected her to shove me away or yell at me to "get my filthy beast hands off her." But she does nothing. She just accepts my comfort without a single qualm spilling from her lips.

Hell must have frozen over.

I'm confident she can hear my heart hammering my ribs, but I don't care. I continue to hold her in as tightly to my body as I can, relishing a moment of reprieve from the bickering we've endured the past three months.

My bliss doesn't last long.

"Let me just grab my coat then... oh, hello, Brax," my grandma greets me with her rheumy eyes bouncing between mine before they lower to Clara plastered against my torso.

Clara freezes before pulling away from my embrace. Her red-rimmed eyes stare into mine for numerous heart-clutching seconds before she swings them to my grandma standing in the doorway. The whiteness of her face grows when her eyes absorb my grandma's flushed cheeks and gaping mouth. "I'm sorry."

Not waiting for a reply, she bolts for the door.

"You don't need to leave, dear," my grandma advises Clara's quickly retreating frame.

Either not hearing a word my grandmother spoke or choosing to ignore it, Clara continues for the door.

"Clara!" I shout when she flees into the corridor without a backward glance.

By the time I make it to the hallway, being extra attentive not to bump into my grandma, Clara has already exited the automatic double doors of Caramine Care and climbed into the back seat of a taxi idling at the curb. Although I'm grateful she was smart enough not to take the bus, I'm not sure how her bank balance will handle the forty-mile cab fare from here to her apartment building.

Once Clara's taxi disappears from my view, I walk back into my grandmother's room. She has seen Mrs. Porter off and is sitting on the edge of her pale blue bedspread-covered bed. Her face looks as shocked as Clara's did when I told her she had secured a two-week trial at Inked.

"I didn't realize you knew the McGregors."

While rubbing the back of my neck, I take a seat on the recliner next to my grandma. "Yeah, Clara's been working with me for the past few months."

My grandma's eyes rocket to mine. "Clara works at Inked?" Her voice is smeared with uncertainty, and she looks the most dumbfounded I've ever seen her.

"Yeah." I nod my head. "Don't look so shocked, Grandma. We aren't all tattoo-covered Neanderthals."

My grandma slices her hand through the air. "It's not that, Brax. I'm proud of you and the crew at Inked. They're my family. I'm just surprised a sweet young thing like Clara would be seen over that side of town, let alone need a job."

"You're not the only one surprised. I've been asking myself the same question for the past three months." I scoot across the leather seat and rest my elbows on my knees. "Do you know who Clara was here visiting?" My voice is shaky, hampered by the guilt I feel for prying into Clara's personal life.

My grandma locks her glistening baby blues with mine. "When she wants you to know, Brax, she will tell you."

I sink deeper into my chair before running my hand down my tired face. I shouldn't have expected a different response from my grandma. She's never seen politeness in snooping.

After giving myself a few minutes to gather my strewn composure, I ask, "Do you know if Clara has any family out this way?" When my grandma's eyes thin, I add, "I'm not prying into her personal life, Grandma. I'm just trying to keep an eye on her. She had her car towed last night, and when I drove her home, there was an eviction notice taped to her front door."

The concern in my grandma's eyes intensifies with every word I speak. "Oh, Brax, you've got to help her," she requests, her words pleading.

"I'm trying, but she's the most guarded woman I've ever handled. Unlike you, she holds in her inner dialogue and protects her secrets with an iron fist... *or knee.*"

I confessed my prior run-ins with Clara to my grandma the Sunday following the knee-to-my-balls incident. It wasn't that I felt forthcoming. It was the fact I couldn't walk without grimacing that had me spilling the beans. It was only my crippled status that stopped my grandmother from issuing her own form of justice.

My grandma's lips tug into a wry grin, but the concern in her eyes doesn't dampen the slightest from my witty comment. "The McGregors were based in Hopeton up until a few years ago. When Clara's momma got sick, they moved her to a superior care facility in New York City. Since most of the children were young, they moved right along with her."

A niggle hits my chest. "Is her momma still sick?" Concern for finding out Clara's mother is unwell is evident in my voice.

My grandma nods. "There's no cure for dementia, Brax. No matter how much money you throw at the fancy doctors."

The niggle in my chest turns into a full stab. "How old is her momma?"

Clara is only twenty-five, so even if her mom had her late in life, she'd still only be mid-fifties to sixties now.

"I'm not sure, but way too young to be dealing with dementia. Some days she recognized her kids. Others, she couldn't tell them apart from the nursing staff."

I run my hand over my recently clipped hair. "Tough break."

My grandma connects her sorrow-filled eyes with mine. "Yeah, especially after everything Clara has been through. She needed her momma, but unfortunately, her momma needed her more."

The pain in my chest turns catastrophic.

* * *

As sweat rolls down my back, my head cranks to the side in super slow motion. My teeth smacking together shrill into my ears as I plummet to the ground. While I was distracted by my conversation with my grandmother yesterday, Diesel's right-swung fist connected with my left jaw. He knocked my jaw into the next century, right along with my ego.

I spit out my mouth guard before running the back of my hand across my mouth, removing a smear of blood his hit produced. Diesel stands in the corner of the ring as instructed by Hank. His grin is smug, but his eyes show his correct response—regret.

Hank, Diesel's trainer, squats down in front of me. His nearly black eyes assess my face as he runs his thumbs along the edge of my jaw. "Nothing appears broken, although you may end up with a nasty bruise in a few days," he advises.

He stands from his crouched position and offers me his hand. His strong yank on my arm has my feet lifting from the ground. For an older guy, Hank is ripped and extremely fit. He has dark afro hair clipped close to his scalp, his mocha skin is covered with a collection of tattoos Ryder inked on him, and his eyes are the darkest I've ever seen.

Hank's son, Derrick, was not only a customer of mine, but he was also a longtime friend. I was devastated when I was informed he was gunned down four years ago as he and Hank left a boxing tournament. It's one of those moments I will never forget. Derrick was set for greatness, all to have it snatched away by a man who couldn't grasp defeat. It was a truly senseless tragedy.

I'm ashamed to admit before Diesel started training with Hank, I hadn't seen him since the day of Derrick's funeral. It wasn't that I didn't want to. I just didn't know what to say to Hank. Derrick was Hank's world, and no measly words I could have offered him would have changed that fact. Although now, while scanning my eyes over the old, desolate gym we are working out at, I wish I'd taken the time to make sure Hank was doing okay.

Four years ago, this gym was the number one spot for wannabe fighters. Hank's training services were in high demand. Now, the equipment is outdated, the gym is devoid of clients, and Hank's once full-of-life eyes are bleak. I had heard his marriage was on the rocks after Derrick's passing, but I didn't realize things had gotten this bad.

My attention diverts from staring at the boxing mat when Hank cranks his neck to Diesel and asks, "Did Brax go and get himself a weak spot?"

Diesel's smug grin turns massive before he nods. I bounce my bleary eyes between Diesel and Hank, trying to work out what the fuck they're on about. They eyeball me with a glint of amusement sparking their eyes, but they fail to ease my curiosity.

Ignoring the two grown men glaring at me like imbeciles, I mumble a curse word under my breath before untying the laces of my boxing gloves with my teeth.

After pulling apart the boxing ring ropes for Hank to exit, Diesel comes and stands next to me. "I don't need to ask who has your mind, but I'm willing to play along."

Arching my brow, I stare into his hazel eyes. "I don't have the faintest fucking clue what you're referring to." My words are rough like I dragged them over a gravel road before spitting them out.

Diesel smirks. "I know boxing isn't your thing, Brax, but even you're off your game today. My first guess was you had an issue with your grandma but considering you wouldn't be here if it were a problem with Grace, I'm going to say it is a woman who has you kissing the pavement... a certain blonde member of the Inked family."

The smugness he's been wearing most of the morning increases when I attempt to shrug off his insinuation. I don't know why I bother trying to deceive him. He knows me well enough to know where my mind has wandered to.

"What makes you say it's a personal problem? You catching me in a moment of weakness might have something to do with work," I reply while running a white towel over my head to absorb the mountain of sweat running down my face.

Hank has always been a hard-assed trainer. Nothing's changed.

Diesel takes a seat on the boxing mat to unlace his shoes. "Inked is your baby, Brax, but it isn't your first love. It might keep your bank balance in the positive, but it doesn't keep the blood pumping to your chest."

I grin but don't refute his statement. Inked is my business, but at the end of the day, it is nothing but a pile of bricks and mortar. It is family and friends who keep my blood pumping. And if I'm being totally forthright, it has been pumping a little faster since my run-in with Clara yesterday.

Clara can spar with the best of them, and she can dish out scornful words like grenades, but I hated seeing her upset. Every tear shed from her eyes cut me deeper than I ever anticipated.

Even though she's icier than any woman I've ever handled, there's something about her I'm drawn to. Call it a case of machoism, but I want to wrap her up in cotton wool and protect her from the world. And if that isn't a shocking enough confession, my desire to protect her has nothing to do with my cock's fascination with her. I don't know if this revelation should have me running for the hills or running to Clara to seek confirmation on what the fuck she's doing to me. Yes, I've always been a sucker for helping a woman in distress, but it's never been this profound.

When Diesel spots the expression on my face, he smirks. "It's not just your cock she's gone and twisted up, is it?"

"What are you, a psycho? Get out of my fucking head," I mutter, throwing my sweat-soaked towel into his mocking face.

"It's called 'psychic,'" he replies while yanking my towel off his head. "But I don't need to be a psychic to recognize that glimmer in your eyes. You got it bad, man. You've let her get under your skin. I just hope you know what you're doing. There's no way to predict how chasing a woman like Clara will go. You've just got to work out if she's worth the risk of having your heart decimated."

I scoff. "Fuck, Diesel, no one is talking long-term commitment. It's all about a bit of fun. A few hours between the sheets. Nothing permanent." I keep my words strong, vying to undermine the seriousness of our conversation. My efforts are less than stellar as deceit has never been a game I can play for long. "Besides, I can't mess with a member of my crew. A few hours of fun wouldn't be worth the legal complications."

Diesel etches his brow high into his sweat-slicked hair, but he doesn't need to speak. His skeptical gaze speaks volumes without a peep spilling from his lips. He knows as well as I do that bedding a woman like Clara would be worth any hassle.

"Well, I wish you luck, brother, because you're going to need it."

Not giving me the chance to reply, he darts between the boxing ropes and hotfoots it to the outdated locker rooms at the side of the gym.

* * *

I'm straddling my bike, recalling the conversation I had with Diesel yesterday when Clara enters my peripheral vision. I was so immersed in wading my way through the massive mess of confusion muddling my mind that I hadn't noticed her exiting her apartment building and walking down the street until she stopped directly in front of me.

"What are you doing here, Brax?" she questions while shoving her hands into the front pockets of her mid-length skirt to conceal their shake. "If it's about Sunday, I can assure you I'm fine. You just caught me during a weak moment. It won't happen again." Her words are stronger than the pain in her eyes.

"It's not about Sunday."

She stares at me in shock.

"I just want to make sure you get to work safely." I keep my tone low, not wanting to spark another Jerry Springer-inspired battle between us.

Her eyes widen as she sucks in a lung-filling gulp of air. "I can't get on the back of your bike again... I-I can't."

"I know." I stop her retreating steps. "But I still want to make sure your travels are done safely."

The feared expression on her face morphs into confusion. When bus 57 pulls into the curb in front of us, I gesture my head to it. "You can ride the bus to Inked, but only when I'm following you."

Her eyes snap to mine. "You rode all the way to this side of town just to follow me to work?"

Nodding, I reply, "Yep," without a smidge of hesitation.

"Why?"

I shrug my shoulders. "Why not? You're my friend. I want to help you out."

Call me pussy-whipped or any other name you like, but this is the only solution I could come up with for Clara's predicament. Although she may be a smart-mouthed lady when she wants to be, that doesn't mean she shouldn't have someone looking out for her. Considering no one appears willing to fill that role, I've stepped up to the plate.

When Clara remains quiet, I stare into her confused eyes, wordlessly advising that my offer comes with no strings attached. It is nothing more than a friend helping another friend. No matter how much she makes my cock ache, I'm not here trying to find a way into her panties. I'm just looking out for her.

"If you don't hurry, your chariot will leave without you, Princess." I nudge my head to the bus driver, who's glaring at her as he impatiently waits for her to board.

Clara's massively dilated eyes bounce between the Asian bus

driver and me for numerous heart-clenching seconds. Her pulse is throbbing through her veins so furiously, the entire left side of her neck is twitching. I don't know if her freaked-out expression is about her upcoming bus trip or at my sudden attempt to call a truce between us. Either way, she needs to board the bus before it leaves her stranded on the sidewalk.

My heart thrashes my ribs when she snatches my helmet resting on my thigh, throws it on her head, then hooks her leg over my bike. Even though I hoped this outcome might be a possibility, I honestly didn't believe it would actually happen. Don't get me wrong, I'm beyond stoked. I'm just shocked as well.

Clara plasters her torso as close to my back as possible before muttering, "Go before I change my mind."

I tighten her grip around my waist before kicking over my bike. Even the deep rumble of my engine can't overtake the mad beat of her heart pulverizing my back. Not wanting to scare her, I keep well under the speed limit and leave a good three car spaces between the motorist in front and me. Although I can't see her, I'm fairly sure her eyes are snapped shut as tightly as her arms are curled around my waist.

Twenty miles later, the loud boom of my engine bellowing down the alley secures the attention of Charity and Diesel as they make their way from the parking lot to the employee's entrance of Inked.

When Charity notices Clara on the back of my bike, she smiles a broad grin and playfully winks. Even though Diesel bowed out on his endeavor of pursuing Clara months ago, he still looks like a kid who had his lunch money stolen. If I were as respectful as him in our little black book game we've been playing since our school years, I could inform him that his assessment of the situation is misguided. But unfortunately for Diesel, I have no intention of doing that.

If he fails to see the true meaning of my relationship with Clara, so be it. Nothing against him—he's a great employee and an even better friend—but I'm not an idiot. I'll do anything I can to ensure his greasy mitts stay off Clara. Even going as far as pretending I've sealed the deal when I haven't and have no intention of doing so.

Chapter Eleven

"Hey," Clara greets, her voice a throaty purr.

I jerk up my chin in greeting before handing her the black helmet I purchased especially for her to use when she rides with me. Her face pales as she places the helmet onto her head and climbs onto my bike. Even though she's been riding with me the past three weeks, the panicked expression that crosses her face hasn't once altered.

The only thing that has changed is her clothing selection. She no longer wears designer dresses and fancy skirts, opting instead for black trousers or the occasional pair of jeans. Although her clothing choices are more suitable for riding on a motorbike, I'd be lying if I said I don't miss watching her strut around Inked in her figure-hugging dresses.

Actually, come to think of it, I'm not the only one complaining. A handful of male customers have cited objections the past three weeks. Some even went as far as stating I should make it mandatory for Clara to wear a dress as her uniform.

I may have dug my tattoo gun in a little deeper those days.

Things between Clara and me have been following along the

same path that started when she began working at Inked, although she's a lot less bitchy now. Don't take my admission the wrong way. She doesn't hesitate to whip out her fiery tongue when needed. She can argue with the finest, but instead of unleashing a torrent of malicious words with no just cause, she reserves them for more compelling moments.

Take last week, for example. Johnny was happily accepting part of his tattooing payment in a non-monetary way. Stupidly, he decided to do the exchange in the supply closet of Inked. When Clara walked in on them, let me just say, Johnny was lucky he walked away with only a slight limp. The bunny he was entertaining... she'll think twice before she calls Clara a skanky bitch again.

When we arrive at Inked, Clara climbs off my bike and hands me her helmet. "Thanks for the ride. It should only be a few more days until my car is returned. It was all just a *huge* misunderstanding."

I nod, pretending I haven't heard the same declaration twice a day for the past three weeks. It eats away at me not knowing what's going on with her life, but no matter how badly I want to know why her car was towed the same night she got served an eviction notice, I won't force her to share. Clara is only just coming out of her shell, so I won't do anything that will risk her taking a step backward. It is also not my place to demand an explanation of her private life. Although our relationship has veered more toward the friend zone the past few weeks, I'm still her boss, so it wouldn't be appropriate for me to demand anything from her.

"Are you listening?" I mumble to my cock while shadowing Clara into the back entrance of Inked.

I'd like to say my cock's interest in Clara has waned as the weeks rolled by, but unfortunately, that isn't the case. Whether she's giving me lip or whining about the outdated computer in my office, my cock's attention has never wavered. I may not have any claim to her, but if you asked my cock the same question, I'm confident he'd tell you Clara owns his ass. He doesn't care about protocol or morals. He just wants Clara.

Clara's brisk pace slows to the speed of a tortoise when the crew of Inked breaks into a poorly serenaded version of "Happy Birthday" the instant they spot her sauntering down the hallway. She stiffens before her wide eyes bounce between her work companions and me. When she notices the triple-layered chocolate cake I asked Ryder's missus to bake for her, a single tear escapes her eye and rolls down her ashen cheek.

"I can't," she mutters under her breath as she barges past Charity, nearly sending her and her birthday cake toppling to the ground.

The crew stops singing as they follow Clara's swift bolt down the corridor leading to my office. After slipping inside, she closes the door so harshly, I'm sure the patrons dining at Betty's Burgers felt the ripple effect.

I turn my eyes toward Diesel. "Open up the shop and tell my first client I'll be out in a few."

He nods before instructing the rest of the crew to get ready for a normal workday.

Charity smiles a tense grin as she hands me Clara's birthday cake. "She's still trying to find her place in this family, Brax."

Nodding, I reply, "I know." But I'm still shocked by Clara's reaction. I shouldn't be, though. Nothing about her has ever been simple.

After placing the cake on the break room table, I stride to my office. Clara's head lifts from a barrage of paperwork on her makeshift desk on the couch when the creak of the door's old hinges announces my arrival. Even though she puts on a brave front, I can't miss the tears staining her blemished cheeks.

"We weren't going to force you to eat it," I jest, saying anything to ease the thick tension suffocating the room. "The guys just wanted to get you something for your birthday."

From her silence, you'd assume she didn't hear a thing I said, but from the way her chin is quivering, I know she heard every word.

I gather documents from the couch before taking the seat next to her. When she fails to acknowledge my presence, I place my index finger under her chin and lift her head. Her glistening glacier-blue eyes appear to be staring straight at me, but they're looking right through me.

"What's the deal? Don't the rich celebrate birthdays?"

Now her eyes are focused on me, and they're fierce enough they could cut through glass. "Does a card showing up a week after your birthday count?" she mutters ever so quietly.

I shrug. "Depends on what's in the card? A check with a million bucks, I'd happily accept years later."

Her lips twitch as she battles to hold in her smile, but she maintains her silent stance. I continue with my endeavor to force a smile on her face. Even if she can get my hackles up quicker than any woman before her, I hate seeing the dejected look her eyes are carrying, even more so since it's her birthday.

"If you thought their singing was bad, wait until you see the wilted bunch of daisies waiting for you on the counter. Oh, and don't be surprised when you open your box of chocolates to discover it's half-empty. They're an impatient bunch, but Johnny promised he saved you all the good flavors."

The heaviness on my chest lessens when the quickest smirk stretches across Clara's face. "They brought me gifts?" she murmurs ever so softly.

Her smirk turns into a full smile when I nod. "Nothing fancy, but they purchased them themselves. Well, except the flowers. Johnny stole them from his neighbor's garden."

Clara's smile enlarges even more.

I wait for it to fade before saying, "I have one final thing to give you. It was a little hard to wrap, so I didn't bother."

Her surprised eyes bounce between mine when I delve my hand into my pocket and pull out a key. The longer she stares at the car key, the more her pupils dilate.

"It's nothing like your old car, but it will get you from point A to point B safely," I advise her shocked expression.

Her lips quiver as she begins to speak. "I can't accept it, Brax. It's too much."

"You can accept it, and you will." My voice is sterner than I expected. "This isn't a gift, Clara. It is a payment for all those late nights you worked your first eight weeks at Inked."

Her eyes snap to mine. Shock is all over her face as I stare into her eyes while nodding my head, silently advising I'm aware of the work she put into the shop after hours. I only discovered her strong work ethic after going through the surveillance tapes the day following our incident in the parking lot of Inked.

For the first eight weeks of her employment, Clara stayed back a minimum of an hour every night, restocking the supply closet and preparing the invoices for the following day. She even went as far as donning a pair of fur-lined pink gloves to tackle the male staff bathroom a handful of times. I could tell from the determination in her eyes those first few weeks that she'd do anything to secure a permanent position at Inked, but I didn't realize her need for employment was so dire she was willing to scrub a urinal.

"I really needed the job," she murmurs under her breath, confirming what I already suspected.

I gently pinch her chin and lift her eyes back to mine. "I know. But you didn't need to break your back for it. Your work ethic during the opening hours already earned you your place in the Inked family." After setting the key for the piece-of-shit car the crew of Inked chipped in for into her palm, I nudge my head to the door. "Your new ride is in the lot. Take the rest of the day off and go spend your birthday with your friends. It will be a hard feat, but I will hold down the fort tonight."

Clara's teeth graze over her bottom lip. "Thanks for the offer, but I don't have anywhere to go."

"Sure you do." My eyes dart between hers. "There are at least a dozen restaurants in Ravenshoe that will happily serve vegetable scraps as if they're a main course."

A rare and genuine smile etches onto her plump lips. If that isn't rewarding enough, the little giggle that spills with her smile is worth spending my days off scouring the used car lots searching for the perfect car for her. This is the first time I've heard her real laugh. I hope it isn't the last.

When her laughter dies down, she locks her eyes with mine. "It isn't that I don't have a place to dine. I just don't have anyone to go with me." The last half of her sentence comes out in a faint whisper as her eyes stray to the floor.

My brows furrow. "What about your drunk chook-cackling friends? Surely, they would have a spare hour to help celebrate your birthday?"

Since I know Clara's momma had dementia, I forgo mentioning her family, not wanting to upset her on her birthday any more than I already have.

Clara's eyes lift from the floor and connect with mine. Confusion and another expression I can't read mars her face.

"The friends you showed up with the night you got your tattoo," I explain to her puzzled expression.

I swallow the brick in my throat when her eyes narrow into thin slits at the mention of her tattoo. *Apparently, she hasn't gotten over our first tussle in the ring yet.*

"I know who you are referring to," she replies, her tone bitter. "Unfortunately, they're too... *busy* to socialize with me today."

I scoff. "It's your birthday. Tell them to get un-busy."

She rolls her eyes before rising from the couch. "It's fine, Brax, honestly. I'd prefer to stay here anyway. Wasn't it you who said Inked is my family now? Shouldn't I spend my birthday with my family?"

Even though she's asking a question, she doesn't wait for me to reply. She just moves to my desk to gather a pile of unpaid invoices from the top.

I glare at her in a shocked, disbelieving type of way. "You'd rather stay here than hang out with your friends?" When she nods, I say, "I'm sorry, Princess, but I'm calling bullshit."

She cranks her neck to the side. "Lucky for me, your opinion doesn't bother me in the slightest."

I push off the couch and step closer to her. "What's really going on, Clara? The princess who walked in here demanding a job three months ago would never turn down the opportunity to live it up on the good side of the tracks."

Her shoulders square as she murmurs something under her breath. She's so quiet, I miss every word she speaks.

"You need to speak up. I've been told on a few occasions I have a problem with my hearing." Even though I was aiming for witty, my comment comes out a little snarky.

When Clara ignores me, I grasp the top of her arms and force her to face me. I'm taken aback when her eyes lift to mine. Gone is the vibrant spark that typically alights her fiery gaze replaced with a pair of eyes that look lost. I'd even go as far as saying haunted.

Fear grips my heart when she snaps her eyes shut, battling to hold in her tears.

Fuck, I hope she doesn't cry. The tears she shed weeks ago in my grandmother's room still haunt me.

"Clara—"

My words stop when the plumpest set of lips brush against mine. I freeze, not to give myself time to assess the situation but to investigate the unique taste of her mouth—minty-cool freshness with a hint of sweetness and warmth.

Only a woman as complicated as Clara could have her lips described as warm and cold at the same time.

Forgetting the seriousness of our conversation, I run my tongue along the seam of her lips, daring her to open her mouth for me. My hang-ups about not messing with a member of my crew are left in the dust when her lips part, giving me full access to her mouth. My cock pulses against the zipper of my jeans as one of my hands moves to her nape, securing her mouth to mine, while the other drops to the curve of her back to pull her closer.

Although I keep my lips sealed over hers, I don't take the kiss any further than an innocent game of tonsil hockey in the janitor's closet at my local high school. If she wants this kiss to go further, she'll need to make all the moves. This way, I won't fall into the trap of sexually harassing my staff. If anything, she's assaulting me, and I'll love every goddamn motherfucking minute of it.

A rough groan tears from my throat when Clara delves her tongue inside my mouth in a long, tantalizing stroke. Her kiss is robust and determined—just like her personality—but warm and enticing. For a woman whose heart appears to be carved from ice, her kiss causes a roasting fervor of excitement to scorch my veins. I shouldn't be surprised she knows how to kiss. She's no ordinary woman. Her kisses are no different.

The skin on my torso prickles with goosebumps when she slips her hands under my shirt to rake her nails against the skin of my lower back. I'm certain she can feel the effect her touch has on my body, but I don't fucking care. If she wants to touch me, I sure as hell ain't going to stop her. The only thing I'm stopping is my desire to ravish her on my desk. Why? Because Clara isn't a bunny, so I won't treat her as if she is one.

When I pull my lips away from hers and she whimpers, my strength is pushed to its absolute limit. I skim my lips along the edge of her jaw and down her delicate neck before stopping at the collar of her shirt. Just knowing my lips are near an area of her skin I've never seen has my cock throbbing furiously and my restraint faltering. It's a thrilling and torturous experience at the same time.

The throaty moans toppling from Clara's throat while I nibble on her neck have an edge of danger to them—a clear warning I'm stepping over the line of what is acceptable for an employer and his staff. But, in all honesty, I don't give a flying fuck. My cock... No. Correct that. *I've* wanted this for months.

From the very moment I laid my eyes on her going toe-to-toe with Johnny in the foyer of Inked, I've been dying to find out if her feisty personality holds the same level of intensity in the bedroom. From the way her nails are raking my back and the warmth between her legs two layers of jeans can't conceal, I'll say my answer is an unequivocal and resounding yes.

My poorly wavering constraint gets harnessed when the creak of my office door sounds through my ears, closely followed by a deep voice. "Your three o'clock is getting snarky."

My eyes shift to Diesel at the exact moment Clara pulls away from me so abruptly, a blast of warm air smacks me in the face. Pretending there isn't a massive elephant of awkwardness sitting in the room, Clara peruses the invoices on my desk while muttering, "I'll be sure to get these paid right away." She lifts her lust-filled eyes to me. "Was there anything else you needed me to do?"

She puts on a good act of being unaffected, but her blemished cheeks and wide eyes are giving away her true composure. She looks exactly how I want her to look—like a woman in the process of being claimed.

Clara's head rockets to the side when I instruct Diesel to tell my client I'll be there when I'm good and ready. His hooded gaze bounces between Clara and me for numerous seconds, his face expressing the words his mouth fails to produce. *I knew you'd be the first to break Inked's no fraternization policy, Brax.*

I glare at him, silently warning that the rules won't be the only thing I'll be breaking if he doesn't leave. With a shit-eating grin, he cockily winks and exits my office, closing the door behind him.

I wait until I hear the stomping of his feet on the tiled floor before I turn my eyes to Clara. She continues rifling through the invoices on my desk, seemingly unmoved from our heart-stopping kiss. I stand motionless in my office, unsure whether I should take the slap to my ego like a man or kiss the living hell out of her again just to ensure she's aware a kiss like the one we just shared could never be forgotten.

But even if she wants to pretend her flushed expression is from the warmth of a late May afternoon, she sure as hell can't come up with a reason for the marks on her neck the stubble on my chin created, let alone her kiss-swollen lips. Although I have no right to admit this, I fucking love seeing her body marked because of me. If I weren't concerned about my business and my crew, I'd strip her naked and mark every inch of her from the top of her disheveled locks to the tips of her expensive designer shoes, stopping only to pay careful attention to the needier regions of her body.

Shaking my head to remove the thoughts that could have me breaking another rule I swore I'd never break—fucking Clara on my desk like a bunny—I lock my eyes with her and ask, "We good?"

Clara licks her kiss-swollen lips before nodding.

"All right. I'll be finished up here by ten. We'll discuss this more then."

I canceled my last two appointments three days ago when I discovered today was Clara's birthday. Clara was so quiet about her upcoming birthday that if I weren't in the process of working out how to have her signed at Inked as a full-time employee, I would have never discovered today is her twenty-sixth birthday. I have an inkling she was hoping the day would pass with no celebration. Although I'm not a fan of getting older, I'm all for celebrating life milestones, birthdays included.

Clara's brows stitch as she stares at me in shock. "*This?*"

"Yeah, *this*." I gesture my hand between us.

Her brows become lost in her blonde hair. "There's no *this*, Brax." Her face looks stern, but her words are unsteady.

When she veers her confused gaze back to the documents in her hand, I curl my hand around her elbow. Unlike thirty seconds ago, she repels from my grasp instead of melting into it.

Here comes the pounding headache that's been plaguing me for the past four months.

"I don't know how many times I need to tell you, Brax. *This...*" she gestures her hand between us, "... is *never* going to happen." For the first time since I've known her, she keeps her voice sincere. Almost regretful.

I connect my eyes with her. "Well, I've got news for you, Princess. *This* is fucking happening."

Her eyes narrow and glare into mine. I swear I can hear her teeth grinding together. "Why? Because *beasts* just take what they want?" Her tone has reverted back to the bitchy sneer she hasn't used in weeks.

I smirk while shaking my head. "No. It has nothing to do with that."

"Then what is it?" She places her hand on her cocked hip.

"Because you're loving this game of chase just as fucking much as I am."

Clara's pupils widen to the size of dinner plates as her cheeks go even pinker, but she remains as quiet as a graveyard at midnight, abundantly proving what I said is true.

I fucking knew it.

"So, as I said earlier, we'll continue our *discussion* at ten."

I stride toward my office door, needing to exit before I kiss the shocked look right off her face.

Chapter Twelve

On the night of her birthday, I wasn't at all surprised to discover Clara had left Inked at precisely 9:55 p.m. You can't be chased if you aren't running. What I said to her that night wasn't just to soften the blow my ego took from her blunt dismissal of me, it was to prove a point. I'd like to say my point was proven beyond a reasonable doubt when she failed to deny my accusation that she's loving this game of chase we've been playing the last few months. Unfortunately, her denials came in hard and fast the following day. From her reaction, anyone would swear it was *me* who made the moves on *her* in my office that day.

I'm not going to lie, even playing in a game I swore I'd never field, my ego still got a little bitch-slapped. Not because I believed a single lie spilling from her lips, but because I've never had a woman blow me off the way Clara has. Call me conceited, but usually, I'd just flash a quick smirk to the woman I was interested in, and she'd be purring at my feet moments later.

I know half of my interest in Clara is because she will never be the type to kneel before me, so she's a challenge any guy would love to conquer. But the other half... I'm at a complete fucking loss. I seriously don't know what is happening to me.

Now don't get me wrong, Clara is no doubt beautiful. She's one of the most ravishing women I've ever laid my eyes on, and the feisty girls have always been a lot of fun between the sheets. But this little game I'm playing with Clara feels different. It isn't your standard game of cat and mouse. It's... it's... I don't know *what the fuck* it is.

It's a fucking minefield I should be retreating from, not encroaching, but no matter how much I try to pull the pin, I can't. Even though Clara denied having any interest in me, she still treats me in the same manner she did in the weeks leading to our kiss. She gives me lip, has no trouble putting me in my place, and if my whole flirting radar hasn't completely blown off-kilter, she's been laying down some solid groundwork on a bit of sexual flirting.

Every time she has entered my cubicle the last two weeks, I've had to fight the urge to pull her into my lap and resample her lips. Why? Because without fail, every time she's in my eyesight, she has something in her mouth. Just watching her slowly chew on one of the chocolates the crew gave her for her birthday had my tongue dying to discover if her mouth took on the raspberry flavor.

If that wasn't bad enough, more times than I can count, when she advised me of my next appointment, she nibbled on the end of the pencil. I swear to God, I've jabbed my tattoo gun into my thigh at least a dozen times this week alone just to keep myself seated in the swivel chair. If I didn't, her little teases would have forced her lips to become acquainted with the one part of my body she's kept firm a minimum of ten hours a day for the past two weeks. Considering I'm endeavoring not to treat her as a bunny, I refuse to have her kneel in front of me, no matter how badly my cock wants to be surrounded by her lips.

I have no doubt Clara knows the effect she has on me. If the smug grin etched on her face isn't enough proof, the glimmer of lust sparking in her eyes is a surefire indication. Thankfully, even with all the blood in my body rushing to the lower half, I can still tattoo. Don't get me wrong, it is no easy feat, but the fact all my clients over the past two weeks have been male has been a lifesaver.

I adjust the crotch of my jeans as a faint cough sounds at the door. Glancing up from the sketch in front of me, I run my eyes over the enticing physique of Clara standing in my office doorframe. Because she's driven herself to work the past two weeks, she's reverted to wearing the body-hugging dresses she used to wear. Today's dress is a fitted-to-every-single-mouthwatering-curve-of-her-body ensemble. I struggle to ignore my cock's response to her most days, but today is by far the hardest day I've had. She doesn't merely look downright gorgeous, she looks positively edible. And since I've tasted her lips, I know without a doubt her lips taste even better than the sexiness of her dress—one hundred percent.

I drag my eyes away from her cock-twitching body when she questions, "Hey, Brax, can I ask a favor?"

"Sure. What's up?"

"Is it all right if I head home a few hours early today?" she asks, her voice hesitant. "I know it is Saturday night, but we're not as busy as—"

"It's fine, Princess," I interrupt, not requiring further explanation. "I have no problem with you leaving a few hours early."

I won't lie, even saying I have no concerns, a stabbing pain is hitting me right in the chest. Even though it should have never been turned on, I can't flick off the possessive switch Diesel's interest in Clara instigated. Believe me, I've tried. Nothing works. I just really fucking hope her reasoning for leaving early has nothing to with a member of the opposite sex.

"Is everything all right?" I strive to keep my tone neutral. My attempts are borderline.

Clara grins a soft smile while nodding. "Yeah, I'm just moving into a new apartment tomorrow. That's the reason I need to leave early. I have some loose ends to tie up at my penthouse."

My brows hit my hairline. The last I heard of Clara's living situation was that she fought the eviction notice and was staying put in her luxury penthouse on Hyde, so to say I'm shocked by her revelation would be an understatement.

"My new apartment is close to work so it will save me the

commute," she blabbers out, saying anything to ease the staggered expression on my face.

I slouch deeper into my chair, battling the urge to force her to open up to me.

My fight doesn't last long.

"Who's helping you move into your new pad?" I ask, deciding to start my meddling with a less nosy question before I move on to the big hitters.

Clara's throat works hard to swallow before she faintly murmurs. "Umm... me."

I drop my pencil onto my sketching pad and arch my brow, silently demanding the attention of her fleeing eyes. "Princess," I grumble, my word as grating as my jaw is clenched.

With a huff, she turns her hard-set eyes to mine. "I don't have much stuff to move... I'll be fine," she assures me.

Her firm stance weakens the more I glare at her, but she maintains her calm approach. Not willing to holster our conversation, I push away from my desk and stand from my chair. The throb of the pulse in her neck speeds up when I stride around my desk to stand in front of her.

"What time is your moving truck arriving tomorrow?" I narrow my eyes into thin slits when a cloud of deceit filters over her eyes. "Only someone who is planning on lying takes time to contemplate a response," I remark, quoting something she's said to Johnny many times in the past four months.

"Ten o'clock," she whispers, finally grasping she's waging a battle she'll never win.

"I'll be at your penthouse at eight."

Not giving her the chance to reply, I head back to my desk to work on a set of sketches I've been designing for the past six weeks.

A grin tugs my lips higher when the faint murmur of "Thanks, Brax," sounds through my ears before my office door closes.

Chapter Thirteen

"Are you fucking kidding me?" I murmur to myself.

After yanking my sunglasses off my face, I snag my cell phone out of my pocket and check the address Clara texted me earlier. The tick of my jaw increases when I discover the graffiti scrawled on the wall of the derelict apartment building matches the address Clara texted.

My fear that this rundown block of apartments is Clara's new residence surges when her little beat-up Ford Focus pulls to the curb behind my bike. I grit my teeth together, barely swallowing the string of illicit cuss words dying to break free from my mouth. Not only is Clara's new crash pad closer to Inked, but it is also in the seediest part of Ravenshoe.

Although Ravenshoe has seen a massive growth in the past three years, the money being pumped into the good half hasn't spanned this far yet. Broken beer bottles line the gutter, tennis shoes dangle off the power lines, and the sounds of sirens wail in the distance. And don't even get me started on the condition of the hideously ugly apartment building. If there wasn't a steel gray Audi parked a few spots up, I would have said Clara was the only thing of value on this entire street.

Clara curls out of her car and saunters to stand next to me. Sheltering her face from the mid-afternoon sun with her hand, her eyes run over the rundown apartment building. Her lips quirk and the scent of fear plagues the air between us. She keeps her shoulders high, endeavoring to ensure me she isn't rattled by the ghastly sight standing before us.

While spinning a set of keys around her finger, she strolls up the cracked concrete sidewalk, her steps shaky and slow.

I hop off my bike and follow her. "You're *not* staying here."

If my abrupt statement wasn't greeted with a glaring stare, I would have assumed Clara didn't hear me over the blaring music pumping from an apartment three stories above. Clara's furious gaze silently warns me she's on the verge of snapping, but I don't care if she's about to blow her top. She can call me a brute, beast, or any other name on her wish list, but I'm not budging an inch. I wouldn't let the feral cats living in the dumpster at the back of Inked stay in a joint like this, let alone the woman my cock is infatuated with. And although I've said earlier my status as Clara's employer gives me no rights over her personal life, I don't give a flying fuck. Even if we didn't share a kiss two weeks ago and hadn't been flirting like it is going out of fashion, there's no way in hell I'd let a member of my crew stay in a dump like this. Male or female. No fucking chance.

"Call the delivery truck driver and get your furniture taken to the storage sheds on Traeter. Once we find you a new apartment, we'll have your furniture shipped there."

Acting like she didn't hear a word come out of my mouth, Clara shoves a key into a door that is hanging by a thread and enters the dimly lit apartment. Growling at her ignorance, I shadow her inside. The deepness of my growl intensifies when I walk into the mildew-scented living area.

"It's not too bad," Clara mutters while roaming her eyes around the paint-peeled walls and heavily stained carpet. "Nothing a bit of elbow grease won't fix."

"Elbow grease?" I arch my brow into my hairline. "The only thing that could fix this place is a gallon of fuel and a match."

Clara rolls her eyes before moving to the front window. Dust particles riddle the air when she draws open the mold-covered curtain. I crunch my teeth together. Adding sunlight hasn't helped the situation. This place is a fucking dump.

"You're *not* staying here," I advise again.

Seizing her elbow, I drag her to the door we only just entered. She tries to pull out of my embrace, but I stay holding on tight, refusing to relinquish her. She can dig her claws into my arm all she likes, sue me for harassment, or knee me in the balls, but I'm not leaving her here.

My quick strides only stop when Clara whispers, "It is the only apartment available in my price range."

Even knowing she has never lied to me, I can't hold in my retaliation. "Come on, Princess, cut the bullshit. Even if you weren't dripping in wealth in your thousand-dollar dresses and shoes, I know what you get paid since I'm the man who pays you."

I don't mean to snap at her, but my mind is spiraling, unable to adapt to what is going on in her life. First, her car was towed, then she got an eviction notice, and now she's moving into an apartment that is smaller than the storage closet at Inked. I don't know if this is all some fucked-up rich-person joke, but I ain't laughing. I'm all for branching out and trying new things, but this is taking it a step too far. She's not only experimenting with a new lifestyle, she's risking her safety, and that's something I won't stand for.

Clara takes on her fighting stance. Her hand is splayed on her cocked hip, her eyes narrowed. "You may pay me, Brax, but you don't pay my bills." Her words come out like hot lava spilling from a volcano. "I know what I can and can't afford." She nudges her head to the shoebox apartment we just vacated. "That is all I can afford."

"Then I'll give you a fucking pay rise," I snap back.

Anger envelops Clara's entire body, flushing her skin with a red hue. "I'm not a *charity* case," she snarls through gritted teeth, her words rickety, hampered by a sob she's barely holding back.

I scrub my hand over the stubble on my chin, giving myself some time to calm down before I say something I'll later regret. "I'm not saying you're a charity case, but you won't be *anything* if you live in this area of Ravenshoe. It isn't safe, Clara."

The anger lining her face softens when I use her real name. She knows I only ever use it in dire situations. *This is a dire situation.*

Her hand slips off her hip as the harshness in her eyes fades. "I appreciate your concern, but I can take care of myself," she replies, her words not as callous as earlier.

I ball my hands into tight, white-knuckled fists when she ambles back into the rat-infested apartment. It's the only defense I have to fight the urge to scream my frustration into the street.

I want to drag her away from here kicking and screaming, but instead, I stay standing on the graffiti-painted path. I need a few minutes to contemplate her predicament. I'll never win an argument with a woman who is as stubborn as Clara, but I have to do something.

Call me a chauvinistic pig, but just like she was wrong about catching the one a.m. express, she's wrong to believe she can look after herself in this part of Ravenshoe, and no amount of arguing will change that fact.

After a few moments of silent pondering, an idea formulates in my overworked brain. Instead of dragging Clara to a safer location, I'll bring the safety to her. With a grin, I yank my cell phone out of my pocket and call in a favor with a long-time client.

Forty-five minutes later, Hunter Kane pulls his security van onto the curb at the front of Clara's apartment building.

"Brax," he greets me, slapping his hand into mine before leaning in for a man hug. "What the hell are you doing in a dump like this?"

"Long fucking story," I mutter while returning his embrace.

Hunter's eyes assess the apartment in great detail when I gesture for him to enter before me. "What type of security system are you after?" he queries, intuiting why I requested his help this afternoon.

It wouldn't take a genius.

"The best you have." I walk over to close the door of the main bedroom.

When I saw Hunter's security van pull down the street, I

suggested that Clara start unpacking her boxes of designer clothes and shoes. For the first time ever, she did as requested without a single qualm escaping her lips. I'm not hiding her away as I don't want her to meet Hunter. It's the fact I know she will put up a fight when she discovers the amount of coin I'm going to hand Hunter to have her apartment wired with the world's most advanced security system. Considering there's no chance of me budging on this term to feel comfortable having her live here, I'd rather keep our argument on the back burner until Hunter leaves.

The fewer witnesses to my pussy-whipping, the better.

After running his hand over his scruffy beard, Hunter shifts on his feet to face me. "I've got a new system I've just designed that will be ideal for a place like this. Motion sensors, burglar alarm, sirens, voice command, but it will cost you a pretty penny. I'm happy to give you wholesale prices, but the equipment itself is expensive."

"I don't care how much it costs." I shrug. "All I care about is when can you get it done?"

Hunter smiles a broad grin. "How free is your tattooing chair this month?"

"As free as you need it to be."

His smile widens. "Then I'll have this wrapped up before the sun goes down."

The heaviness that's been sitting on my chest for the past hour lessens. "That will be great. Call out if you need any help."

Hunter nods before making his way to his van parked out front to gather some equipment while I head to Clara.

The smell of damp, moldy carpet filters into my nose when I prop my shoulder against the wall of the main bedroom. Since she is sorting through boxes of shoes, she doesn't notice my presence straightaway.

I stay quiet, relishing seeing a side to her I rarely get to see—her outside the walls of Inked.

There's no doubt Clara is a girly type of girl. If the cute dresses, high-altitude shoes, and glossy hair aren't enough of an indication, her fascination with color coordinating her shoes is a surefire sign.

I give myself a few more minutes to quietly absorb her before pushing off the wall and stepping deeper into the room. "Not enough room in your closet?" I ask when I notice she has several boxes of shoes and garment bags sprawled across her queen-size bed. Because her apartment is so small, the movers were in and out in under thirty minutes.

She screws her nose up. "Not exactly." I follow her gaze to the half-empty closet. "I was considering giving them to the women's shelter three blocks down from Inked."

My lips purse, not only shocked by her generosity but also wondering if couture dresses would be suitable for homeless women. It seems pretty pointless. I've worked in the soup kitchen numerous times over the past three years. From what I've seen, the women and children who live there only want food in their bellies and warm clothing. They don't need designer dresses worth thousands of dollars.

"But I've decided to sell them instead," Clara continues, lifting her wintry-blue eyes to me. "Half the money I make from the sale will be donated to the shelter. The other half will be put toward the security system *you're* getting installed in *my* apartment."

I balk, faking innocence.

She doesn't buy my woeful attempt at candor. Not in the slightest.

"You heard that?" I gesture my head to the living room of her apartment.

"Yeah," she replies with a nod. "Just like I knew you were stalking me for the past ten minutes."

I give her a cocky wink. "So that's why you kept bending over to reach the shoes in the furthest corner."

A hearty chuckle scuttles through my lips when she picks up one of the shoes off her bed and pegs it at my head. You can laugh. You haven't seen the size of the heels she wears. They could kill a man.

After picking up the stiletto that airport security would class as a lethal weapon, I step closer to Clara. I'm shocked when she doesn't cite an objection to me having a security system installed. My surprise only lasts as long as it takes for me to see the width of her pupils. Although she's putting on a brave front, she's just as petrified as I am about her staying here.

Nothing typically scares me, but the idea of her being hurt scares the shit out of me.

Chapter Fourteen

My brisk pace into the break room slows when my eyes are inundated with a set of curves I have no chance of ignoring. Clara has one arm braced against the refrigerator while the other is propped on her hip. The top half of her body is hidden as she seeks something in the sparsely filled refrigerator. The figure-hugging fire-engine red dress she's wearing displays every perfect curve the clients at Inked won't stop raving about—inches of luscious, soft skin, a mouthwatering ass, and a pair of legs that go on for miles. And let's not get me started on the regions of her body I can't see.

The inviting image of a bent-over Clara has a particular area of my body springing to life.

Sensing a presence in the compact lunchroom, Clara tilts her torso out of the refrigerator. The hardness of my cock turns fatal when my eyes zoom in on her painted red lips wrapped around the end of a whole carrot. Illicit thoughts slam into me on more appropriate things her plump lips could wrap around.

Just like the intense bout of flirting we'd been undertaking the two weeks prior to her move, nothing has changed. If anything, our playfulness is venturing into new territory since a few hours of our time together have been spent outside of Inked's walls.

Clara will never admit her new surroundings daunt her, but the fact she has invited me to her place for a late supper each night this week is all the sign I need to know she hates being alone in her dingy, cramped apartment even more than I hate her living there.

Don't take my admission the wrong way. Our flirting has never crossed the path it did in my office three weeks ago, but we've been cutting it close. Although I'd love nothing more than to sample her lips again, I'll never make the first move. I have a massive ego and confidence in the bucketloads, but in the back of my mind, I know a woman like Clara is way out of my league. *Hell, she's way out of my universe.* But by waiting for her to make the first move, I know she isn't being coerced into doing something—*or someone*—she doesn't want to do.

Shaking off the thoughts that will have my good mood sin-binned, I make my way to the coffee percolator in the corner of the room. Clara's eyes track me as I step toward her.

"Did you enjoy my salmon, Brax?" Her tone is a unique mix of bitchy and playful. "Probably the first time a guy of your standards has sampled something so refined."

I lift the coffee pot from the base and pour myself a generous helping before turning around to face Clara. "Salmon? What salmon?" I brace my back against the counter.

She arches one of her perfectly manicured brows high into her hairline. "I saw *my* empty container on *your* desk." Her eyes drop to a stain on the top left-hand corner of my white shirt. "Not only can I smell the garlic lemon sauce that was drizzled on my salmon leaching from your pores, but you also stained your shirt with it."

I roll my eyes. "I didn't eat your salmon, Princess. That's a toothpaste stain."

That's a total lie. When I first saw a fancy takeaway container in the refrigerator with Clara's name on it, I had planned on jabbing my finger into her food just to mess with her, but when the delicious aroma swamped my senses, my initial plan went to shit.

Although I've never eaten pink fish before, it was quite tasty.

Clara glares at me, not believing a single word seeping from my lips. I return her leering glare while taking a large gulp of my unsweetened coffee. Black liquid comes spraying out of my mouth, dousing the lunch table and my jeans when my taste buds recoil at the disgusting flavor besieging them.

I lift my shirt and run the cotton material over my tongue, doing anything to lessen the ghastly taste that has my stomach heaving. Although Clara is quick, I don't miss her eyes dropping to absorb the exposed skin of my lower stomach.

Glad to see I'm not the only one having a hard time keeping my eyes above the belt.

While running my now thickened tongue under the tap water, I spot a nearly empty box of Epsom salt sitting next to the percolator.

No fucking way. Is she pranking me?

Although the crew and I have pranked Clara numerous times during the past four months, not once has she gotten us back. If she's pranking me, this will expose a side of her I've never witnessed before.

Clutching the box in my hand, I shift on my feet to face her. Her amused eyes lock with mine as she takes a big bite out of the tip of her carrot. Even knowing it is only a carrot, my cock scampers away, frightened by the determined look in her eyes.

"Don't touch my food, Brax," she warns, glaring into my eyes. "Or things will get a lot more... *complicated.*"

After issuing me a knee-clattering stink eye, she saunters out of the room, her hips swinging even more provocatively than normal. Even though I won't taste anything for a week, I have the biggest grin stretched across my face. Not only did Clara return my prank, she did it without a single drop of blood being shed.

Finally, after four long months, the real Clara is emerging from the shadows, and I can't wait to share the experience with her.

* * *

My head lifts to the clock hanging on the wall on my right when the buzz of my cell phone clatters through my ears. Since my last client's tattoo didn't take as long as expected, I headed down to a fancy deli a few miles away from Inked to replace Clara's salmon I ate. Call me pussy- whipped, but I hate the thought of her only eating a carrot for supper because I couldn't calm my stomach's cravings.

After wiping my sweat-slicked hand down my jeans, I yank my cell out of the front pocket. My lips quirk when I peer down at the screen and notice it is a call from Inked's landline.

"Fucking hopeless," I mutter under my breath.

I only left Inked twenty minutes ago, and they're already interrupting me. Unfortunately, this is nothing new. It wouldn't matter if I were gone for five minutes or fifty, I field calls from my crew the instant I step out of the premises.

God forbid I ever have a vacation day.

I swipe my finger across the screen and press the phone into my ear. "What's up?" I try to keep my annoyance at the interruption out of my voice. My effort is fruitless.

"Hey, sorry to disturb you." Johnny's deep tone is more jittery than normal. "But some shit went down out back I thought you'd want to know about."

I grit my teeth. Probably another bunch of gangbangers brawling in the side alley. Unfortunately, that's a regular occurrence at Inked, even more so since it is Saturday night. Standing from my seat in the waiting area of the deli, I head to the far corner of the room to ensure I can hear Johnny over the hum of patrons enjoying their overpriced meals.

My head cranks to the side when the restaurant hostess calls my name. Jennifer—the bunny who stuffed up my order of a cheesesteak months ago—jingles Clara's order of salmon in her hand. I lift my chin in thanks before pointing to my ear, advising her I'll be right there after my call. She nods before sauntering into the kitchen at the back of the deli. Her hips sway even faster than her words did when she thought I'd rocked up tonight for a replay of our rendezvous in the supply closet at Inked six months ago.

I swear I let her down as gently as possible, but I'll still be checking Clara's salmon for spit before I serve it to her. No girl likes being told they'll never take the leap from cocksucker to sheet-warmer—no matter how polite you say it. Nothing against Jennifer, she's a nice girl and gives great head, but the instant she lost the interest in my cock, she also lost me.

I shift my focus back to Johnny. "Has Diesel got it handled? Or do you need me to call in Ryan?"

"Ryan's already on his way." Johnny's tone is still off-kilter. "Diesel said you'd usually want to keep this type of thing in-house, but considering Clara was involved, he told me you'd want the authorities called in…"

Although he continues speaking, I don't hear a fucking word he's saying. His deep voice is nothing but white noise as I sling open the restaurant door and barrel onto the sidewalk. "I'm on my way."

Not giving him the chance to reply, I disconnect the call and house my cell back into my jeans. Since it is early on a Saturday night, the sidewalks are populated with heavy foot traffic. My heart thrashes against my chest as I weave through a throng of people completely oblivious to the anger blackening my blood. Just the thought of any woman being hurt makes me furious, but since it is Clara, my anger is reaching levels I've never experienced.

Upon reaching my bike parked half a block down, I throw my leg over it and shoot out of the car park not even thirty seconds later. Within minutes, I've reached Inked. My fists are balled, my jaw is clenched, and red-hot fury is seething through my veins, but nothing can slow me down—not even the close call with death I had on the way here. I'm running on pure adrenaline.

As I guide my bike down the alleyway, I dart my eyes in all directions, both assessing the situation and seeking Clara. Diesel is on my left talking to three teens. Charity has her shoulder braced against the brickwork near the dumpster, and Johnny is manning the back door.

I park my bike to the side, dismount, and make my way to Diesel. My furious pace slows when, in the corner of my eye, I spot a flurry of blonde. Clara is huddled on the stained concrete ground shaking like a leaf. The furious heat scorching my veins intensifies when my eyes run over her bloody and I see scraped knees.

"Why the fuck is she still sitting in the alleyway?" I ask Charity, who is two steps up from Clara.

"She won't let anyone touch her." Charity's voice is as shaky as Clara's composure. "I think she's in shock."

I crouch down in front of Clara and lift her downcast face. The fiery spark that usually brightens her eyes has been snuffed, replaced with a haunted glint. Her lips are cracked and quivering, and her cheeks are stained with tears. Her defeated pose angers me even further.

"What happened?" I shift my gaze to Charity.

She shrugs. "I didn't get the full story, but from the marks on her neck and wrist and the fact all her jewelry is missing, I'm assuming she got jumped."

"Fucking hell. I told her to take that shit off," I mumble under my breath.

Even though my declaration was only meant for me, Clara must hear it as a painful whimper escapes her lips while a new flood of tears rolls down her cheeks.

Riddled with guilt at placing unwarranted blame on her shoulders, I seize Clara's wrists and pull her into my arms. She *must* be suffering from shock as she doesn't put up a single protest.

I stand from my crouched position, draw her in close to my chest, and amble to the back entrance of Inked. "When Ryan arrives, send him into my office," I demand, not once taking my eyes off Clara gathered in my arms, staring up at me with a pair of bleak eyes.

* * *

By the time Johnny announces Ryan's arrival, Clara's tears have created two large wet patches on my shirt. She hasn't spoken a word for the past ten minutes, but the earth-shattering shakes havocking her body have simmered to a dull vibration.

Ryan smirks an uneasy grin as he strides into my office. After removing a pile of invoices from the couch, he takes the spare seat next to Clara and me. When he locks his eyes with mine, I'm not shocked to see they're clouded with anger. He's witnessed some bad shit no man should ever see. Unfortunately, not all of it has been from his service in the police force.

It takes a bit of effort on Ryan's part to get Clara to open up, but the cocky statement he made at the strip club months ago rings true. He is a great detective, one of the best I've ever known, so with a little encouragement, he eventually gets Clara talking about what happened.

I will not lie. Over the past thirty minutes, I formulated at least a dozen ways to kill a man with my bare hands. The desire grew even more potent when Clara mentioned her assailants were carrying guns. If it weren't bad enough she got jumped in the alleyway by three men while taking out the trash, two of them were wielding weapons.

I've never been more ashamed of this part of Ravenshoe than I am right now.

"Did any of the jewelry have distinguishable markings?" Ryan queries, his eyes lifting from the notepad in his hand to Clara.

She runs a tissue under her nose before gently nodding. "My necklace pendant has an inscription on the back." Fresh tears prick in her eyes before she quietly mutters, "To C, Happy 18th Birthday, Love Remy."

Ryan snags a few extra tissues out of the tissue box on my desk and hands them to Clara. "That's all I need for now, but if you recall anything you believe may help my investigation, Brax has my number."

Clara nods while accepting the tissues.

When Ryan gestures his head to the corridor, I turn my eyes down to Clara, who is still sitting on my lap. "Will you be all right if I talk to Ryan for a minute?"

Her massively dilated eyes bounce between mine for several heart-pounding seconds before she gently nods. I stand from the couch, taking her with me. It takes all my strength to pivot around and place her back on the sofa. The only reason I do is because I want to know who is responsible for doing this to her.

"I'll be back in a minute," I advise Clara. I wait for her to acknowledge that she has heard me before stepping into the hallway.

Ryan's mouth opens, but I begin speaking before he gets the chance to say anything. "Was it the teens Diesel was talking to when I showed up who did this?"

Ryan shakes his head. "No. They saw the assailants running out of the alley. When they discovered Clara, they were the ones who sounded the alarm."

His answer removes three names from my hit list.

"Give me a chance to do my job before you step in, Brax," Ryan requests, sensing I'm on the verge of dishing out my own form of punishment.

Mine won't be as pleasant as Ryan's. Guaranteed.

"She's a member of *my* fucking crew, jumped in the alley of *my* fucking shop." My loud voice bellows down the hall. "You know I can't be disrespected like this without issuing some type of punishment. If I let it slide, you'd have to add Inked to your nightly drive-by schedule as we'd become a mockery to the community."

"She's a *member* of your crew..." His words come out a little hazy like he doesn't fully believe my anger is solely based on Clara being a team member of Inked. "So if you're genuinely worried about her well-being, the best thing you can do is take a step back from this investigation and look after her. She's in shock, Brax. You need to convince her to let the medics look at her."

I shake my head. Ryan suggested the same thing to Clara at the start of their interview. She blatantly refused his request. "She feels violated enough as it is. She doesn't want any more people prodding her."

Ryan runs the back of his hand over his tired eyes before nodding. He's been dealing with so much shit the past six months, his exhaustion can be physically seen. His eyes are plagued with dark circles, his skin is blotchy, and his hundred-dollar haircut is well overdue for a trim. "I get that. I do. But she can't be left alone like she is."

I nod. "I know. I'll look after her."

Deep down in my soul, I know Ryan won't rest until he finds out who did this to Clara. He doesn't understand the word *defeat*, but it doesn't lessen the fervent rage pumping through my veins that someone messed with a member of my crew on my watch. Let alone someone as important to me as Clara.

"I'll give you twenty-four hours, but if one of my guys finds them before you do, I can't guarantee they will call in the authorities."

"Fuck, Brax, you can't say shit like that to me," Ryan replies, his eyes drifting up and down the corridor, ensuring none of his fellow officers are listening. Happy we haven't caught the attention of any unwanted ears, he pulls me deeper down the hallway. "I'm asking friend to friend. Give me forty-eight hours before you send out your guys."

I shake my head. "That's forty-eight hours she will stay panicked like that." I hook my thumb to Clara. "I can't erase what happened to her, but I can ease her fear that the men who did this to her aren't still walking the streets."

Ryan peers over my shoulder to look at Clara. His composure alludes to the general confidence he exudes in bucketloads, but his eyes are giving away his true feelings. He's as angry as I am. "Thirty-six hours and I'll give you ten minutes with them when I bring them in," he negotiates, drifting his eyes away from Clara and locking them with me. "Alone."

I take a moment to consider his request. Although I'm sure Diesel and Johnny will locate the men responsible for jumping Clara, there's no guarantee it will happen within thirty-six hours, and although I hate entrusting the care of my crew to an outsider, I've known Ryan most of my life. He's like family to me, so I can trust he has me and my crew's best interests at heart.

While exhaling a deep breath, I hold out my hand. "I'll still send my guys out. If they find them first, I'll instruct them to call you."

Ryan looks like he wants to push the issue further, but thankfully, he leaves it as it is and accepts my handshake. "In her condition, please don't put her on the back of your bike," is the only request he makes as I walk him to the front door.

"I may have skipped the line for brains, but even I'm not that stupid." I wrap my arms around his shoulders and pull him in for a brief hug.

"When you're out seeking your revenge, stop and think about who will keep an eye on Clara when you're rotting in jail for defending her," he mutters in my ear before pulling away and strolling down the sidewalk.

I should have known he wouldn't leave the conversation as it was. Not only does he love having the last word, but he also knows how to play my weaknesses. My biggest weakness is the people left behind to fend for themselves.

After taking a few moments to ponder Ryan's statement, I return to my position on the couch next to Clara. Not thinking, I pull her back into my arms.

She doesn't protest.

She doesn't cry.

She doesn't do a damn thing.

And that worries me even more than her frightened expression.

Chapter Fifteen

"If you need anything, I'm only a phone call away," Charity offers from her crouched-down position in front of Clara. After giving Clara's forearm a final rub, she heads to the door.

"Wait up. I'll walk you out," I shout, not wanting another incident on my conscience.

Usually, one of the crew walks Charity to her car each night. Considering I'm the only remaining male member of Inked here, it's my responsibility to ensure she arrives at her car safely.

Diesel and Johnny left not long after Ryan and the rest of my crew dwindled out of Inked the past thirty minutes. Although none of them are to blame for what happened to Clara, their shoulders were still weighed down with guilt. What I said to Clara weeks ago is true. What happens to one of us happens to all of us. We're family. And whether she likes it or not, Clara is now one of us.

Clara's massively dilated eyes lift to mine before she gently nods, acknowledging my silent question if she's okay with me walking Charity to her car.

"I'll be back in a minute."

Standing from the couch, I place her down. It isn't any easier the second time.

A humid mid-June wind greets us when we exit the back entrance of Inked. Surprisingly, the parking lot is void of the bunnies who usually frequent the space this time on a Saturday night. *Perhaps they heard of the earlier incident?*

My lengthened strides slow when Charity mutters, "Diesel called an hour ago. He's got a solid lead on the guys who jumped Clara."

I arch my brow, wordlessly demanding why I'm only being informed of this now.

"We figured if you were the only one left to watch Clara, you might actually stay put," she mutters as her skittish eyes dart around the lot.

Her eyes snap to mine when a furious growl rumbles from my throat. "We?"

"Diesel, Johnny, and I." She turns her eyes to the back door of Inked. "She's not from this side of town, Brax. But even if she were, this still wouldn't have been a pleasurable experience. You need to focus on Clara and let the boys have your back for a change."

The anger bubbling my blood with furious heat simmers to a slow boil. Not only is everything Charity is saying true, but I also need to remember my advice. Clara is just as much family to Diesel and Johnny as she is to me. This ensures they will handle this situation to the same degree I would.

"Did Diesel call Ryan?" My words aren't as scratchy as earlier.

Charity shakes her head. "He said he would, just not until after he has a *talk* with them."

My right shoulder lifts into a shrug. "Fair enough."

I rub a kink in the back of my neck as my earlier conversation with Ryan runs through my head. Fuck, why did I give him my word?

Because you're a soft cock when it comes to Ryan, that's why.

"Can you do me a favor and call Diesel? If he hasn't already had a solid word with them, request that he lower the severity and contact Ryan. I gave Ryan my word I'd call him if we found them in the first thirty-six hours. Considering it's only been a few hours, I don't want to break my word."

Charity nods. "All right. I'll call Diesel on my way home." She wraps one of her tiny arms around my torso and squeezes me tight. "Look after Clara for me."

A brief chuckle spills from my lips, spurred on by the hidden innuendo laced in her words.

I wait for Charity's taillights to become a blur in the heavy flow of traffic before making my way back to Clara. I'm surprised to find her standing near the window of my office. From behind, you wouldn't have a clue about the seriousness of the situation she just went through. She looks the same as she has every other day. She's stared out that window the past four months. It is only when she spins around does the reality of the situation slam back into me. She smiles to put on a brave front, but her eyes show she's still sitting in an incredibly deep, dark pit.

"Is everyone gone?"

I nod while striding deeper into the space. Before I can comprehend what is happening, Clara jumps. One of her hands pushes me hard in the chest, sending me sprawling onto the two-seater couch, while the other moves to the buckle on my belt.

"Whoa, Princess. What the fuck are you doing?" I don't mean to yell at her, but I'm so beyond shocked by her reaction that my first response is anger.

Her icy-blue eyes rocket to mine. "What does it look like I'm doing, Brax?"

"It looks like you're about to suck my cock."

She winks before muttering, "Bingo."

What the fuck?

I stop her frantic movements with my hands. If I weren't a man who liked my woman feisty, the fierce glare she scorches me with would have made quick work of the hard-on her eagerness has triggered.

"People handle shock differently, but sucking my cock isn't the way to go."

"How do you know? Have you actually tried it?"

"No, I haven't, but sucking cock isn't really my thing, so I've got nothing to go off." I keep my tone cheeky, hoping to diffuse the seriousness of our confrontation with humor.

My optimism doesn't last long. A heaviness slams into my chest when Clara slumps to the floor and bursts into tears.

Fuck!

Crouching down, I scoop her into my arms and flop back on the couch. I run my hand down her back as the heavy shaking hampering her body earlier returns full force, as do the wet patches on my shirt.

"It's okay, Princess. You're okay. Nothing like this will ever happen to you again. I promise you," I assure her.

"You can't guarantee that." She hiccups through tears.

"Like hell I can't."

She lifts her tear-stained face off my chest before her watering eyes bounce between mine. "How?"

I remove a strand of hair stuck to her tear-drenched cheek before locking my eyes with hers. "By never letting you out of my sight. That's how."

Clara inhales a sharp, quick breath but remains as quiet as a sleeping baby. I draw her in close to my body and stand from the couch. After gathering her purse from the filing cabinet at the side of my office, I head to the back door of Inked.

Clara's eyes drift between mine as I stride down the hallway, but not a word spills from her lips. By the time we make it into the parking lot, the tears flooding from her eyes have dampened to a slight trickle, and her shakes have dulled.

I adjust her position so she's being held by one arm, before digging my hand into her purse to search for her keys. A growl of frustration rolls up my chest when I fail to find them. My excavation is hampered by the massive amount of makeup and girly shit she carries in her oversized purse.

The heaviness weighing down my chest the past two hours lightens when a giggle spills from Clara's lips before she snatches her purse out of my hand and delves her hand inside. I roll my eyes when she produces a set of keys in under two point five seconds.

Once I locate the car key I gave her four weeks ago, I jab it into the passenger side door and unlock her car. Clara's gleaming eyes lift to mine when I gently lower her into the passenger seat before securing her seat belt. After closing the door, I race around her car and glide into the driver's seat. Her second giggle of the night topples from her lips when my knees become trapped behind the steering wheel.

"What the hell? How can you drive sitting so close to the steering wheel?" I grumble, yanking on the seat mechanism.

Clara giggles again.

She must still be in shock. I've never heard her laugh so much.

After pushing the seat back as far as possible, I prod the key into the ignition and fire up the engine. The only noise heard in the cabin of Clara's car for the first two miles is the small pants of her breath.

Another mile out, I shift my eyes from the road to Clara. Although she doesn't appear as rattled as earlier, her pupils are still filling her cornea, and her face is stained with tears. When another mile clicks over, the expression on her face surges from confused to concerned.

"Where are we going?" she queries as I pull her car into the underground parking lot of my apartment building.

I park her car in my assigned parking bay and switch off the ignition. "My place," I reply before yanking open the driver's side door and stepping onto the concrete.

Any words she might speak are drowned out by the loud echo of the driver's side door slamming shut. Not giving her a chance to protest, I run around the car, swing open her door, and pull her into my arms. I'm shocked as hell when I walk through the deserted parking garage, and she clings to my chest. I expected some type of response—at the very least, a gripe about how she can walk and doesn't need to be carried—but she doesn't say a thing until I place her on her feet at my apartment door.

"Why am I here?" she asks as her eyes aimlessly float around the empty corridor.

Her eyes rocket to mine when I answer, "Because you're in shock."

Her confused gaze stops bouncing between mine when my apartment door gives out a slight creak when I swing it open. I lean in and flick on the lights, illuminating my modest but well-decorated loft apartment.

Clara takes two steps inside before stopping dead in her tracks. She stands frozen in the entryway I finished refitting six months ago. After my grandmother moved into Caramine Care, I downgraded from a two-bedroom apartment to the loft on the top floor. Although I lost the bonus of a guest bedroom, I have the same floor space and the new addition of a rooftop patio.

I track Clara's eyes as she absorbs my apartment in great detail. A double-size living room with two suede sofas sits to her right, a manly black kitchen adeptly stocked with all the latest appliances is on her left, and a four-seater dining table is directly in front of her. Her eyes circle when she takes in the black wrought iron and wooden spiral staircase that leads to my bedroom floating above the living space. The thrum of the pulse in her neck quickens when her eyes run along the wood-lined pitched roof.

Once she has surveyed every inch of my apartment, she locks her eyes with mine. "Why am I here?"

"Because you're in shock," I repeat. I curl my arm around her shoulders and guide her deeper into the space. "You're shaking and shit. I can't leave you alone like this."

To be honest, I don't know if the new shakes hammering her body are from the mugging or because she's just realized I only have one bedroom. Either way, I'm not leaving her alone in this condition.

When her shakes increase, I say, "Unless you can give me the address of a friend or family member I can take you to, you're staying here." I move to stand in front of her. "Can you give me an address?"

Fresh tears spring in her eyes before she shakes her head.

"Then you're staying here."

Her eyes continue to absorb my apartment as she shadows me up the staircase. While her eyes drink in the king-size bed in the middle of the room, I walk to a set of drawers on my left.

After yanking out a dark blue T-shirt, I pivot to face Clara. "Do you want to shower before you go to bed?" She licks her dry lips before shaking her head. "All right, then put this on and jump into bed." I hand her my shirt then nudge my head to my bed.

Her pupils enlarge to the size of dinner plates as shock makes itself known on her face. "Can you turn around?"

I arch my brow. "You were just about to suck my cock, but now you're acting all shy."

Quicker than the flash of a camera bulb, Clara grasps the hem of her dress and whips it over her head.

Holy fuck!

I knew her body would be dynamite, but mother-fucking-lord it's even better than I expected. Perky round breasts only just concealed by a hot pink fancy lace bra I've only seen on the runway, a smooth, flat stomach, and lusciously long legs spread far enough apart, her sheer panties award me the slightest peek of a pussy I have no doubt tastes sweeter than honey.

Staring me straight in the eyes, Clara drops my shirt beside her feet before sauntering to my bed. The hardness of my cock turns deadly when she slips between the sheets wearing nothing but a lace bra and a tiny pair of panties.

The rise and fall of her chest increases when I grab the collar of my shirt to drag it over my head before lowering the zipper of my jeans. Her soft pants quicken when my jeans are kicked aside two seconds later.

Just like I couldn't take my eyes off her during her provocative striptease, her eyes drink in every inch of me as I stand before her in nothing but a pair of white briefs.

"Calvin Klein?" she queries with her brow bowed high.

I shrug. "What? They're comfy," I reply before slipping into the opposite side of the bed.

I freeze, and a curse word seeps from my lips when a warm hand grips my crotch, instantly turning my cock to stone. It takes a few moments for my brain to register what's going on, but when it does, it takes all my strength—and then some—to stop Clara from stroking me through my briefs.

"Nope. Not happening." My words are rough, relaying the moral struggle I'm trudging through.

"Why?" Clara snaps back. "If this isn't what you brought me here for, why the hell am I here?"

"Because... *you're in shock!*" I hiss through clenched teeth. "And when I take you... and don't have any doubt, Princess, that is a when, not an if... it won't be while you're in shock. I made a mistake once letting you kiss me when you were rattled. It ain't happening again." Leaning over, I switch off the lights. "Now roll onto your hip, so I can spoon you."

Clara gasps in a sharp breath, astonished by my demand. She isn't the only one surprised. I don't spoon. I've never fucking spooned. But I'll spoon her if it guarantees the parts of her body I want to explore the most are facing away from me.

While grumbling under her breath, Clara rolls on her opposite hip. I splay my hand across the smooth planes of her stomach and draw her back.

What? If I'm going to do this, I'm going to do it right.

My lips quirk. This spooning shit isn't too bad. My cock is nestled between the crack of her ass and halfway up her back, my torso is being warmed by the heat of her body, and the scent of her recently shampooed hair is penetrating my nostrils. It isn't half bad. I could get used to this.

A few minutes pass in silence as I run my hand up and down Clara's forearm. If her breathing pattern had leveled out, I might have believed she was asleep, but I know she's awake, even with not seeing her face.

After another stint of quiet, Clara does a one-eighty. The moonlight sneaking into the room from the roof window illuminates half of her face. Even though I can only see half of her beautiful features I've studied in great depth during the past six months, I can see enough to tell she's struggling to emerge from the dark pit her attack pushed her into.

The warmth of her breath flutters my lips when she quietly murmurs, "Why am I here, Brax?"

I run the back of my hand down her face, removing a tear that sneakily escaped her eye. "This may be a little hard for you to believe, but you're here because I actually like you, Princess. I want to take care of you." When she gasps, feigning shock, I chuckle. "Is my revelation really that shocking?"

She sighs. "Depends. If you really knew me—"

"I know you," I interrupt.

"The real me, Brax. The before-Inked Clara," she interjects, her voice shaky and low. "If you knew *that* Clara, your opinion of me might change."

"Un-fucking-likely," I reply without the slightest hint of hesitation.

Another stretch of silence passes between us. It isn't awkward but necessary. Clara needs time to compose herself, and I need time to get over the shock I brought a woman to my apartment, and I'm not freaked out about it.

An uneasiness settles in the bottom of my gut when Clara asks, "What are the chances of my necklace being found?"

"I don't know," I reply honestly. "Depends on the value. If it's worth a lot, the chances are low." A heaviness slams into my chest when a stream of tears rolls down her cheeks. "Was it worth a lot?"

Clara shakes her head. "No." She draws herself into my torso. "It's not even valuable, but it's all I have left." Her lips quiver against my bare chest as she cries and cries until her eyes have no tears left, then she falls asleep in my arms.

Chapter Sixteen

My already brisk pace down the spiral staircase of my loft increases when three quick taps hit the front door of my apartment. I finish buttoning my jeans before swinging open the door. Diesel greets me with a broad grin and the key for my bike dangling from his index finger. "Thought you might need these," he says before attempting to enter my apartment.

I step into his path, blocking his entrance. "Clara is still sleeping," I advise him, my voice rough from just waking up. "She's not appropriately dressed for guests."

Diesel's bawdy grin turns huge. "So a shit night transformed into a good one?" He waggles his brows before curling his arm around my neck to noogie the top of my head.

I punch him in the ribs, winding him. "Not exactly, asshole. She didn't have any other place to go."

He takes a step back and peers into my eyes. "You still playing with that overstacked deck?"

I scoff. "Only as long as it takes for her shock to wear off." My tone has a smear of annoyance attached to it. "Wouldn't be much of a man if I took advantage of her while she was in shock."

Diesel's lips purse before he curtly nods. "True. Didn't think about that."

"You don't really think about anything," I quip.

His smile enlarges. "True." He props his shoulder onto the doorjamb of my entryway. "We found two of the guys who jumped Clara last night."

My eyes drop to his knuckles. I'm not at all surprised to see they're busted. "Did you call Ryan?"

Diesel bites his lip. "Yeah... after I had a quiet word with them."

"Were they locals?"

He shakes his head. I'm not shocked by this revelation either. Inked has had a not-to-be-messed-with stigma attached to it from the day Ryder opened the doors. There's also the fact most of the crew who work there are born and bred Ravenshoe residents.

Ravenshoe locals protect their own.

"Did they have any of Clara's jewelry on them?"

My heart stops beating as I wait for Diesel to reply. It feels like I'm sucker-punched when he briefly shakes his head. "I checked. They had nothing on them. For how well they kept their mouth shut, I think they're nothing but bottom feeders. When we snag the main guy, we might have a better chance of getting her stuff back." He pushes off the doorjamb. "Anyway, I'll let you get back to it. Just wanted to let you know Johnny and I are handling everything." He flicks his eyes up to my loft bedroom. "You look after her."

Nodding, I shadow him down the corridor.

"I parked your bike half a block down because I didn't know the code for the underground garage," he advises when he reaches the peak of the staircase.

I run my hand across my tired eyes. "Thanks. I'll move it into the garage later."

Diesel's brows shoot up into his hairline when I hold out my hand for him to shake. "Since when have you been a shaking-hands type of man?" he jests before wrapping his arms around my shoulders and drawing me in for a man hug. A chuckle escapes from my lips when he adds to Charity's request last night. "Take care of Clara for me. If not, step aside and let a real man show you how it's done."

He stumbles down the first three steps when I jab my fist into his right rib. After regaining his footing, he salutes me with two middle fingers before galloping down the stairs. His hearty chuckle is still bellowing up the stairwell when I amble back to my apartment.

* * *

My eyes lift from the tiled floor in my kitchen when a creak sounds through my ears. I adjust my grip on the mug of coffee I've been nursing for the past thirty minutes when Clara saunters down the staircase and floats across the room wearing nothing but my navy-blue shirt she left crumpled on my floor last night. Her face is creased from where it was pressed against my chest, her hair is a mess, and her face is void of any of the makeup she typically wears, but she still looks one hundred percent appetizing.

"This is even more embarrassing than the walk of shame." She tugs down the hem of my shirt. "Where are my clothes?"

I crack a smile. "They're in the wash." I nudge my head to the laundry room attached to my kitchen. "They should be ready in around forty minutes." *Or eighty, since I'm close to extending the wash cycle.* Seeing her in nothing but my shirt is a cock-twitching visual I want to retain as long as possible.

Clara's eyes drop to the coffee mug in my hand as she slips onto a barstool.

"Coffee?"

She smiles. "Yes, please."

After filling a second mug with coffee, I place it in front of her before moving to the refrigerator to grab a carton of milk. Unlike me, Clara has her coffee with cream.

I tilt my torso out of the refrigerator when she quietly mutters, "I'm sorry about last night."

Grabbing the carton of milk, I stand in front of her. "It's all good." I set the milk down in front of her. "Are you okay?"

Her eyes lift from the speckled black counter to me before she nods.

"Then we are all good."

Taking a step backward, I brace my back on the kitchen counter. The next few minutes are filled with quiet as we stand across from each other enjoying the pick-me-up only a healthy dose of caffeine can give. Although Clara doesn't look as tired as she did last night, she still appears restless. That probably has something to do with the little whimpers that escaped her lips while she slept.

Once her mug is empty, Clara sets it on the countertop and lifts her eyes to me. "How come you didn't take advantage of the situation last night?" she queries with her brows scrunched tightly.

After placing my mug in the sink, I cross my arms in front of my bare chest. "Because under this *beastly* exterior is a man whose grandma raised him right."

Clara smiles softly. "You were raised by your grandma?"

I nod. "Yeah. My momma died when I was little. I have no clue about my dad."

A flash of remorse passes Clara's eyes, but she remains quiet.

"You?" I query, hoping since I've shared personal information, she may as well.

Her face cringes. "I was raised by a handful of nannies." She straightens her spine and sits higher in her chair. "My mom had been unwell for a long time, and my dad was always busy."

"I'm sorry to hear that."

Clara shrugs. "I guess it's all part and parcel of being born with a silver spoon in your mouth. Not something you would have ever had to worry about."

She balks as her pupils widen. Even though I can see she wishes she could ram her words back down her throat, it doesn't stop my anger from rising.

"No, it's not something I could ever say concerned me." I try to keep the sneer out of my tone, but I fail miserably. "Can I ask you a question?" Even though I'm asking a question, I continue speaking, not giving her a chance to reply, "Where was that silver spoon when your car got towed and you were served an eviction notice? Where was it when you moved into a rat-infested dump? And where the fuck was it when you got jumped in the alley while working on the side of town you should have *never* stepped foot in?"

Clara locks her soul-burning gaze with mine. "You, *of all people,* are going to judge me?"

"Yeah, I fuckin' am," I reply, ignoring the way her little snipe dented my ego. "Because if you didn't have the crew of Inked and me stepping up to the plate, you'd be out there swinging the bat on your fucking own."

My words are callous, but now that they're unleashed, I have no chance of reeling it in. My mind is spiraling, incapable of grasping how Clara can sit before me declaring she has a glamorous life when all I've witnessed the past several months is her taking blow after blow after fucking blow.

Ignoring the anger blemishing her skin with a pink hue, I ask the question I've wanted to know for weeks, "Where's this Isaac guy you wanted to mark your skin with? You cared enough about him that you were going to permanently bear his name on your hip, but he's nowhere to be found the instant your life starts circling the toilet bowl."

Clara pushes back from the kitchen counter, sending the barstool toppling over. She glares at me with nothing but disdain tainting her arctic eyes. Her lips twitch, dying to fight back, but not a single word spills from her mouth.

"He was your daddy replacement, wasn't he? A strong, dominant man you wanted to swoop in and look after you the way your father should have."

Her nostrils flare as anger envelops her entire body. "You don't know what you're talking about." Her words fly from her mouth like daggers.

"Fucking bullshit, Princess." My voice is as vicious as my words. "You're the classic story of a poor, unloved little rich girl. When you failed to secure the love of your daddy, you went hunting for the next best thing... a man just like him."

With her fists clenched at her side, Clara charges into the laundry room. The washing machine beeps, announcing it has been opened, when she yanks the door so hard, it indents the drywall.

Ignoring the fact her dress is still wet, she throws my shirt over the top of her head before dragging her dripping wet dress up her quivering thighs. You'd think her absurd overreaction would surprise me. It doesn't. The only thing I'm shocked about is that she doesn't attempt to refute my claim.

No bitchy reply.

No snarky remark.

Nothing.

"Come on, Princess. Where's your fighting spirit? What happened to the feisty little temptress who has told me time and time again how she can look after herself? Where the fuck has that Clara gone?"

"I *can* take care of myself," she hisses, her angry words unable to hide the sob sitting at the back of her throat, dying to break free.

"Yeah, you can. So fight me. Prove what I'm saying is wrong."

She angrily shakes her head while striding across the room. My eyes track her as she makes her way through my residence searching for her belongings, the water dripping off her dress leaving puddles in her wake.

When she snatches her purse off the coffee table in my living room, I push off my feet and race to the door. I only just make it to the entryway before her.

When she lifts her eyes from the floor, the heaviness weighing down my chest since last night grows. Fresh tears leak from her over-filled eyes as the same broken look she was wearing last night returns full force.

She won't fight as she believes every word I'm speaking is true.

"Look around, Princess." I wave my hand in the air. "There's no white horse, and I sure as hell can't see Prince-Fucking-Charming, but you're still breathing, you've got clothes on your back, food in your belly, and a roof over your head. Who gave you that, Clara?" Her face crunches as she battles to settle the heavy flow of tears streaming down her face. "You did. Not your daddy. Not Isaac. You did it. You're not a damsel who needs saving. You and only you crawled yourself out of the pit that was trying to swallow your life whole four months ago."

"If I don't need saving, then why am I here? Why are you helping me?" she stutters through a barrage of hiccups.

"Because it is what a man does for the woman he's falling in love with," I reply before my brain has the chance to object. "Last night scared the shit out of me. The thought of losing you... *Fuck!* I couldn't handle that. I can't handle that." I lock my eyes with her. "Don't *ever* make me handle that."

More tears spill from her eyes. "If you knew the things I've done, the people I've hurt, you wouldn't be saying that, Brax. You would leave me to fend for myself like every other member of my family and friends have. I'm not a nice person. I am not who you think I am."

"I don't care about your past, Princess. None of it matters to me—"

"It should," she interrupts as her glistening eyes bounce between mine. "No one should get away with what I did."

"You don't think you've already been punished? You got mugged at gunpoint in an alleyway, for fuck's sake. I think your dues have been paid."

"That's nothing compared to the hurt I've caused people," she replies, her voice switching from a medium volume to a faint whisper. "Not even close."

"Then tell me what you did. Let me make my own decision."

She balks before shaking her head.

"Then I guess I'll keep running with my own opinion." I move to stand in front of her. The closer I get to her, the more she retreats. Her fleeing steps only stop when her back is plastered against a wall in my apartment, and my body is splayed to her front.

"And my opinion is one hundred percent certain that I need to taste your lips again." I lift my eyes from her thrusting chest to her face. "So unless you tell me something shocking within the next five seconds, I'm going to kiss you. And since I'm planning on kissing you until you can't speak, you better speak now while you have the chance."

Lifting my hands, I cup her jaw. "Five."

I run my thumbs over her cheeks to gather her tears. "Four."

I drop my thumb to brush the mouth I'm dying to taste again. "Three."

I adjust the angle of my head to align our lips better. "Two."

I tilt my head closer to hers. "One—"

"I snuck into a taken man's bed while he was heavily intoxicated so I could pretend we slept together," she blubbers out, her hot breath fanning my hungry lips.

Although shocked a woman of Clara's standards would need to stoop to those levels, it isn't the first time I've heard of women running those types of tricks.

It also isn't enough to stop me from tasting the lips I've been dying to become reacquainted with for the past three weeks.

"I was also the reason my brother lost the love of his life."

I pull back and peer into her eyes. They're shimmering with silent regret, undoubtedly proving what she's saying is true.

"Have you tried to fix the mistakes you made?"

A big, fat tear rolls down her cheek when she shakes her head.

"Why not?"

She scoffs. "Because I'm not who you think I am." After flinging a tear off her cheek, she locks her remorseful eyes with mine. "That vindictive two-faced bitch you met at Inked months ago, that's the real Clara McGregor. I'm a spiteful cow who doesn't think twice about steamrolling anyone standing between me and the ultimate prize. I'm not the Clara you see, Brax. Not in the slightest."

With that, she slips under my arm and throws open my front door. A waft of warm air hits me in the face when I slam the door shut before she has the chance to exit.

"I'm not even half done with you, Princess," I growl into her ear.

Chapter Seventeen

While I stand so close to Clara, her wet dress creates a large watermark on my jeans. "If you were a vindictive bitch who didn't care, you wouldn't be crying right now," I mutter in her ear. "You also wouldn't have sold *all* your designer dresses and shoes to give the profits to the women's shelter three blocks over from Inked."

She intakes a ragged breath, seemingly unaware I knew she sold every designer outfit she owned and not the half she had sprawled on her bed the afternoon she moved into her apartment.

"You did that because—"

"Because that women's shelter was where I would have ended up if you hadn't given me a chance," she interrupts, her words croaky, hampered by a sob sitting at the back of her throat. "I was two seconds from living on the streets."

Even though her admission hits me fair in the guts, I continue my endeavor to show her she isn't the woman she thinks she is. "It's not just that. You did it because under the hard shell you've been wearing the past... I don't know how many years... is a woman with a massive heart. The Clara you spoke of earlier isn't you, Princess. It is the sheltered Clara who was hiding behind a pile of money. The instant you stepped away from the lifestyle that was no doubt slowly killing you, the *real* Clara was set free."

I tap my finger on her chest that is furiously pounding her ribcage. "This didn't just start beating when you walked through the doors of Inked. It's been beating since the day you took your first breath. Just no one was listening." I cup her jaw and tilt her head back to face me. "I'm listening," I declare into her tear-welling eyes. "And I'll never stop listening."

I'm hoping my admission will have her spinning around and sealing her mouth over mine. What I'm not expecting is for her to bury her head into the crook of my neck and shed enough tears to fill a river.

Riddled with guilt that I pushed her too far, I gather her into my arms and stride to one of the sofas in my living room. I draw her in close to my chest and run my hand down her back as I whisper assurances in her ear. I tell her everything will be okay and that I will always step up to the plate for her, undoubtedly proving the words I blurted out in the heat of the moment ring true.

I'm falling for Clara. Only now am I realizing she's the reason my cock went into hiatus and why I've been so lost the past few months. And while I'm being totally fucking honest, she's the cause of my biggest worry.

Imagine finally getting close enough to something you've always wanted that you can taste it on the tip of your tongue, only to discover it might be short-lived. Although I truly believe the Clara sitting before me is the real Clara, I can't one hundred percent testify that she will stay this way if her silver spoon ever finds its way back to her mouth. I hope she will, but there are no guarantees in life, let alone for a woman who is as complicated as Clara.

Any concerns about only having her in my life for a fleeting moment shift to the back of my mind when Clara lifts her head off my chest and locks her wide eyes with mine. Just from the way she's staring up at me, I don't care if she can only give me a second, I'll take every moment I can get.

I move my mouth, preparing to continue apologizing for the

callous words fired off my vindictive tongue, but my words fall short when Clara's hand grips the back of my neck to pull my mouth to hers. The aroma of coffee filters through my nose, and the flavor of salty tears swamp my taste buds when she seals her lips over mine. Just like our first kiss, I open my mouth to accept her tongue, but if she wants this to go any further, she needs to make all the moves.

"Take what you want, Princess," I mumble against her mouth when she freezes with the tip of her tongue bracing the seam of my lips. "If you want to stop, stop. If you want to take it a little further, take it further. But you need to guide the pace."

Pulling back, she peers into my eyes. Shock and confusion are marring her face. "Don't you want me?"

A smirk curls on my lips. "Believe me, I fucking want you." I jerk my hips up so she can feel the effect her PG13 peck had on my cock. "I just want to make sure this is something you want. I'm not going down the denial road again. We've already walked down that path, and I'm not repeating it. If this is going to happen, then I'm all for it. But if you're planning on waking up tomorrow morning in my bed and pretending it was all a dream, it ain't happening. You got me?"

My brow arches when Clara bites on the inside of her cheek, struggling to hold in her giggle.

What the fuck is she laughing about? I didn't hear anything humorous in my speech.

Spotting my furious scowl, she asks, "You do realize it is only ten o'clock? So the whole statement about waking up tomorrow morning in your bed was a little overboard."

"You don't think I'm up for the challenge?"

Heat creeps across her cheeks. "Well... no... it's not that."

"Then what is it?"

She mumbles something under her breath, but she's so quiet I miss what she said.

"Speak up, Princess."

Her eyes snap to mine. "From the conversations I've overheard at Inked, you don't wake up with anyone in your bed." Her voice is surprisingly strong considering the number of tears she just shed.

I arch my brow. "Did you not wake up in my bed this morning?"

She scoffs. "Yeah, but that's different. We didn't *do* anything."

"Only because I stopped you."

Her eyes roll as she huffs. "Thanks for the reminder. I would have hated for the sting of rejection to heal too quickly," she snarls, shifting her eyes sideways.

I grip her chin and force her eyes back to me. "How bad would that sting have been if I'd taken advantage of you last night? Was it not better for me to deny you than hurt your feelings?"

"Ah, you just called me out for having a daddy complex. My feelings were still hurt, rejection or not."

"Yet here you are sitting in the lap of a guy who's far from a father figure. Maybe I was wrong?"

I'm braced and prepared for her to either flee from my lap or unleash a scathing tirade. She shocks me for the second time in under five minutes by remaining quiet.

I don't know how many minutes pass with me holding her in my arms as she stares out into space. I'm too entranced by her beautiful face to keep track of time. The silent void isn't awkward, and it doesn't feel uncomfortable. It just appears as if she needs a few minutes to gather her thoughts.

While she does that, I run my hand down her shiny locks, smoothing the frazzled pieces into place while relishing being the man she can find a moment of peace with.

After a stretch of silence, Clara mumbles, "I wasn't always like that."

I quirk my lips, pretending I don't know what she's referring to.

"I wasn't always attracted to men who could take care of me," she elaborates as the glazed-over look in her eyes fades. "I can't recall the exact moment it happened, but I'm fairly certain the switch was flicked on not long after my eighteenth birthday."

"That would make sense. The jump from adolescent to adulthood is pretty daunting."

"It wasn't that." Her words are barely audible over the mad beat of her heart. "It was so much more than that."

I hold my breath, hoping she'll open up to me.

My wish isn't granted when she leaps off my lap and declares, "I *really* need a shower."

I only just stifle the groan her sudden loss of contact spurred from my cock. He was as happy as a fish in water nestled against the soft curves of her ass.

There's no chance of holding back my second groan when Clara drops her eyes to mine. "Care to join me?"

I try to speak, but words fail me when I spot an unrecognizable glint in her eyes. Although her stance is strong and determined, something about her body language is off. I'd like to say I've witnessed a wide variety of her personalities over the past four months, but this one is leaving me wholly stumped. I can't tell if she's petrified or excited. And while I'm being entirely forthright, not being able to read her scares the fucking shit out of me. I've got enough obstacles to jump over. I don't need any more things added.

The unidentifiable sparkle brightening Clara's eyes fades by the moment, no doubt snuffed by my delay in replying. It isn't that I don't want to join her for a shower—believe me, I want that more than anything—but I want to make sure this is what she wants and she isn't acting impulsively from the mass surge of adrenaline pumping through her blood after her brush with death last night. I only denied her advances ten hours ago. *Is ten hours truly enough time to overcome shock?*

I scrub my hand over the stubble on my chin. "Are you sure this is what you want, Princess? I can't guarantee once I've had you, I'll ever stop. So if you're hoping your adventure on this side of town will be a short one, you need to step back and consider your options more thoroughly."

Any concerns clutching my throat loosen when a flash of excitement flares in Clara's eyes. "Who said my visit was going to be a short one?"

I shrug. "Just an assumption."

"A *wrong* assumption." Her words crack out of her mouth like a whip. Spreading her hand on her cocked hip, she stares me straight in the eyes. "Are you going to show me where everything is? Or am I going to figure it out on my own?" she asks, quoting the exact thing she said the first day she arrived at Inked for her two-week trial.

I slant my head to the side and return her fervent stare. It takes a massive effort to keep my feet planted on the floor when a glint I can identify ignites in her heavy-lidded gaze before my very eyes. Even a blind man would recognize it. She doesn't just want to be ravished, she wants a man to help her get back the confidence she lost last night.

So, that leaves me with two choices. I either back away and let another man step up to the plate or continue wielding the bat I've been holding the past four months. Since there's no chance in hell I'll ever let another man take care of Clara, let alone touch her, it looks like there's really only one option. I'd be lying if I said I wasn't as happy as a pig in mud to be awarded the challenge.

Chapter Eighteen

The soft pants of Clara's breath increase the further we step toward the bathroom. A crackling of energy fires the air between us, inciting a prickling of goosebumps to form on her arms. When I swing open the thick black door and switch on the light, she inhales a ragged breath before her eyes absorb the grandeur of the bathroom.

Other than my bedroom, this is my favorite room in my apartment. It is roomy, dark, and incredibly manly. Although it took a good chunk of the money I had left after downgrading from a two-bedroom apartment and a solid forty hours of my weekend, I'm glad I put the effort in. Even more so now since it's managed to shock Clara into silence.

I watch the excitement in her eyes grow when I unfasten the button on my jeans and lower the zipper. Her eyes blaze when I glide them down my thighs and kick them to the side. She tries to hold my gaze when my Calvin Kleins follow the path my jeans just made. She fails.

I'm hard in an instant, jutted and firm when she gasps in a wild breath. The heat scorching my blood turns potent when she murmurs, "Jesus," under her breath as her eyes drink in the effect her avid gaze has on my cock.

She drags her eyes away from the lower half of my body when I take a step toward her. "Your turn," I mutter, my voice laced with smugness, proud as a peacock about her slack-jawed reaction. "Wait," I instruct when her hands move to the hem of her dress. "I want to undress you."

Her eyes brighten with anticipation before she nods. The tips of my fingers float over the skin high on her thighs when I move them to grip the hem of her dress. My movements are hurried since I'm more than eager to see the skin after its scent kept me awake half the night.

A rich floral aroma floats into the air when I whip off her dress in one quick motion. Discarding it to the floor next to my jeans, I rake my eyes up Clara's body, gliding them past the velvety smoothness of her cock-teasing legs, over the flat planes of her stomach, and across the generous swell of her breasts. Her perfect body sends a jolting spasm straight to my balls.

"Fucking beautiful," I mutter more to myself than Clara.

My devoted gaze over her body only stops when I catch sight of her lust-riddled eyes. The unidentifiable glint her eyes were wearing earlier has been replaced with a gleam I know all too well. It's the shimmer of a woman preparing to be claimed. Taken. Utterly consumed.

And I know just the man to do it.

Now I just need to work out where to begin.

Should I start at her heaving breasts that are thrusting up and down with every breath she takes? Or at the glistening slit her sheer panties barely cover. If we weren't in the confines of a bathroom, I would have started with her pretty little mouth. Considering its fiery tongue was the main reason for my cock's extended stint of abstinence, it has a lot of making up to do.

When Clara drops her eyes to my lengthened rod and licks her lips, I wonder if she can read my thoughts.

"Although I'd love nothing more than to have your lips wrapped around my cock, that's not happening."

Her eyes rocket to mine as her face fills with confusion. "Why not?"

When I drift my gaze around the bathroom, her eyes track mine.

"Do you see a suitable location to host such an event?"

Clara's eyes instantly stop floating around the room and snap down to the tiled floor at my feet.

Ignoring my twitching cock, I shake my head. "Nope. Not happening."

Her eyes dart back to mine. The shocked expression on her face has increased tenfold.

"Princesses don't kneel for anyone," I mutter, answering the silent question her eyes are relaying. "When you suck my cock, it won't be while you're on your knees."

My balls tighten when a soft moan ripples from her mouth. She looks both shell-shocked by my admission and turned on. Her astonishment is about to increase.

"Beasts, on the other hand..." Her breathing turns excited when I fall to my knees in front of her. "They have no problems kneeling before princesses."

She stares down at me with her mouth hanging wide and the scent of her arousal lingering in the air. Other than her rapid breaths, she stays quiet, which makes me even harder. It's not every day a mere man can silence a fire-breathing princess.

"Do something," Clara eventually mutters when the stint of silence stretching between us becomes too great for her to ignore.

"I will when you tell me what you want."

"I want you," she immediately replies, her voice husky and ball-tingling sweet.

I don't have a chance in hell of holding in my smug smirk, so I just let it go. "You're going to need to be more specific than that."

"Why? Don't act like you don't know what you're doing, Brax. I had the unfortunate displeasure of witnessing your abilities first-hand. I can assure you that you've got this covered." Her brows scrunch together as a deadpan look slips over her face. "Please don't tell me you're one of those guys who act all macho until they step into the bedroom."

The smirk on my face morphs into a full-toothed smile. Not only has the silky softness of her voice been replaced with the tone she regularly uses, but the fiery spark that makes my cock ache is beaming from her narrowed gaze.

There's a brief flicker of the feisty temptress my cock is infatuated with.

If I weren't loving her renewed feistiness, I wouldn't hesitate to assure her my handing over of the reins is a one-time-only deal. But not wanting to snuff the impish gleam her eyes lost last night, I keep my mouth shut.

I lean back until my backside is resting on the balls of my feet before lifting my eyes to Clara. "Were you told what to do your entire life? How to sit, eat, act?"

She balks as her pupils widen, confirming my suspicion.

"That's not happening tonight. So, unless you tell me what you want, nothing is going to happen."

My attempt to boost Clara's confidence strengthens when her yearning eyes leer into mine. The heavy pants of her breaths quicken before she murmurs, "How specific do I need to be?"

My lips tug into a lewd smirk, pleased she isn't backing down without a fight. I shouldn't have expected any less. Although rattled from her encounter last night, Clara is one of the strongest and most opinionated women I've ever met, so I have faith she's got this.

"I only need to know three simple things. Where you want it, how fast, and how long."

She blinks three times in a row before she replies, "In the shower, hard and fast until my legs give out."

Ignoring my cock jumping from the hankering look beaming from her eyes, I ask, "No foreplay?"

Clara inhales a quick breath before she shakes her head. "Not yet."

The grittiness of her voice travels all the way to the base of my cock, puffing my chest high. I'm smug as hell she's considering round two when we haven't even begun round one yet.

More than eager to get this party started, I rise from the floor and band my arms around Clara's waist. A jagged growl tears from my throat when she asserts a small snippet of control I'm handing her by sealing her lips over mine and spearing my mouth with her tongue. She grunts a long, purring moan like my mouth is the most delicious thing she's ever tasted. She explores my mouth with slow, tantalizing strokes as her nails scratch my back. Her kiss is mind-hazing and lush, a promise of the greatness about to be unleashed.

Cupping her ass, I encourage her to wrap her legs around my waist. My cock hardens to the point it is almost painful when it is seared by the heat of her scorching pussy. While my tongue becomes reacquainted with every inch of her delicious mouth, I step toward the shower recess. I rock my hips along the way, ensuring she can feel the effect her kiss has on me.

Not removing my lips from hers, I lean in and turn on the shower before reaching up to bat the showerhead out of the way. I don't want anything impeding my view of her in the midst of ecstasy. I've been waiting for this moment for months, and I don't want anything between us, not even something as simple as a stream of water.

Steam curls around us as I walk through the double-size shower to the only sturdy wall. When I reach our destination, I pin Clara to the dark gray tiled wall with my body before dragging my lips away from her.

"Here?" My breathless word exposes my wavering constraint.

"Yes." She rubs her clit against my shaft. "Here. There. Fucking anywhere. Just do it already."

A ghost of a smile spreads across my face. This is the first time I've heard her say a proper cuss word.

I drop my eyes to her hot pink lace panties. "Expensive?"

Clara leans back and slithers her hand down the smooth planes of her stomach. An animalistic groan rumbles up my chest when she grips her sheer panties in her hand and tears them off her body before muttering, "Not anymore," exposing her patience is wearing thin.

She isn't the only one.

I secure a better grip on her hip with one hand while the other one guides my stiffened shaft to the entrance of her pussy. She purrs a ball-clenching moan when I rub the crown of my cock on her wet pussy, coating myself in her slick wetness. Her pussy grows wetter and warmer with every second that ticks by.

Happy she's wet enough to ease the friction she will feel from the lack of foreplay, I lift and lock my eyes with her heavy, hooded gaze. "You sure?" I ask, giving her one final chance to flee. If she agrees now, there will be no turning back. "Because my cock has a slight fascination with you that will most likely get worse once he has you."

"Your cock or you?" Although her words are breathless, I can't miss the cheekiness in her tone.

I sweep my cock across her clit, wiping the glint of cheek right out of her eyes and replacing it with the vibrant spark of lust.

"Does it matter either way?"

"No." She drawls out the short word in a long, breathless moan.

"Then let me ask you again. Are you sure?"

My cock twitches when she replies, "Yes, I'm sure."

"Then let's do this."

Clara throws her head back when I push the first inch of my cock inside her. Her pussy ripples around me, greedily sucking me in, begging for more.

I clench my teeth, vying to ignore how good it feels to have her snug slit wrapped around me. Even though I haven't climaxed in months, I want this to last as long as possible.

I've notched in another three inches when reality dawns.

Fuck!

Ignoring the begging protests of my cock, I withdraw from Clara in one swift motion, place her onto her feet, then head out of the shower.

"Where are you going?" Clara's voice is as shaky as her thighs.

"Need a condom." My words are gruff, spurred on by my stupidity of forgetting something as critical as protection. This is the furthest I've ever gone without a condom. Normally my cock wouldn't get within sniffing distance of its target without being wrapped.

Only a woman as captivating as Clara would force me to lose my rational head.

Snagging my jeans off the floor, I check the back pocket for my wallet. Even beyond annoyed with the delay, my cock is as hard as stone. The memories of Clara's heat wrapped around it is enough to hold its focus.

Failing to find my wallet in my jeans, I make my way to my bedroom. My steps are as fast as the string of illicit curse words streaming through my head.

I stare at the top of my dresser for several seconds, shocked and confused. My bike key is in its rightful place, but my wallet is nowhere to be seen. I always house my wallet and key in the same location, so where the fuck is it? Only when the events of last night run through my head does another reality dawn on me. I left my wallet on my desk at Inked.

Goddammit!

I scrub my hand down my tired face as I stride back into the bathroom, mumbling incoherently under my breath. My steps are no longer eager, weighed down by my rapidly deflating cock. Because I've never brought a girl back to my apartment, and most of the bunnies I've played with bring their own supplies, I don't have a single condom in my entire place. Not a goddamn one!

When I enter the shower, my stupidity hits me fair in the guts. Even concealed behind a thick sheet of steam, nothing can take away from the entrancing beauty of a saturated and completely naked Clara. Her body is pure perfection. Graceful and lean but designed to be fucked with mouthwatering pert breasts, long toned legs, and just the right number of curves to set my heart racing.

Her body is a promise of many restless nights and mind-shattering orgasms. And I've gone and fucked up the opportunity by not doing something as basic as stocking my bathroom vanity with condoms.

I'm a fucking idiot.

When Clara notices me entering the shower, her lips part, and her breathing turns excited. Her chest thrusts up and down as she steps deeper into the flow of water. A steady stream of water rolls down her face, removing any tearstains left clinging to her cheeks. Her inviting eyes sweet talk me into joining her without a single word seeping from her lips. When I fail to step forward, she crooks her finger and gestures for me to move closer.

"I can't." My words come out strangled since I have to fight my mouth to release them.

Clara's eyes drop to my once-again jutted and primed-to-go cock, its new bout of stiffness stirred by the ravishing visual of her naked in my shower.

"I'm pretty sure you're good to go." The soft purr of her voice makes me even harder.

I shake my head. "Can't. Don't have a condom."

She flinches, her eyes widening. "Are you serious?"

"Unfortunately, yes." A brief chuckle escapes my lips which is full of torment and despair.

"Oh my God," she mumbles, her words muffled by her hand, which shoots up to slap over her mouth.

Her eyes bounce between mine for several heart-clenching seconds before she murmurs, "Are you clean?"

"No," I mutter, my response short and swift.

The width of her eyes grows as she gasps in a ragged breath.

I stare at her, utterly confused by her shocked reaction.

"Yes, I'm fucking clean. I work with needles, for crying out loud. We get checked regularly. I meant no to your suggestion of going bareback," I growl when it dawns on me why she's looking at me in disgust. "I'm not fucking you without a condom."

In an instant, a mask of anger slips over Clara's face. "Why? Are you worried I'll try to pin a pregnancy on you or something?"

"What? No! Don't be fucking ridiculous."

She crosses her arms under her mouthwatering breasts. "Then what's the problem?" The longer I delay in replying, the redder her face lines with anger. She stares at me with her eyes glaring and nostrils flaring. "If I'm clean and you're clean, I don't see what the problem is."

"Because I don't fuck without a condom. Period." My angry voice shrills off the tiled wall and jingles into my ears.

I'm not angry at Clara. I'm furious with myself. I've wanted this for months, and now I'm the one putting up barriers. But this is a rule I'm not willing to break. Clara has already forced me to break many rules I said I never would, and I'm not willing to back down on another.

Clara reinforces her firm stance. "You don't fuck without a condom?"

I nod.

"Just like you don't mess with members of your crew? And you don't bring girls back to your apartment?"

"Exactly," I reply, nodding.

My eyes follow Clara's hand as she runs it down her naked body. "Member of your crew, and the last time I checked, I was still a girl."

"That you are," I mutter while dropping my heavy-lidded gaze to her glistening slit.

Just like its owner, Clara's pussy is prim and proper. If it weren't for the small strip of light-colored hair running down the middle, it would be entirely bare. It is pink and smooth, and I have no doubt it tastes even better than it looks.

Dragging my eyes away from the pussy I'm dying to be immersed in, I lock them with a pair of eyes I haven't seen in months. Clara's gaze has the same determined look they had when she fought for her position at Inked. They show her mind is made up, and she isn't leaving this shower until she gets what she came here for.

So I guess I'm going to have to give it to her.

Clara's throat works hard to swallow when I push off my feet and slowly stalk toward her. For every step I take, the anger raging in her eyes dulls from a fierce storm to a faint mist.

"Do you want to come, Princess?" My words are gravelly and deep as excitement thickens my blood.

She stares me straight in the eyes before unashamedly nodding.

"I don't need a condom to make you come."

Any protests spilling from her lips muffle into an erotic moan when I fall to my knees in front of her, hoist her leg over my shoulder, and suck her throbbing clit into my mouth. Her thighs clamp around my head as my tongue is swamped by the most delicious thing I've ever tasted.

"Oh, Jesus," Clara moans, gripping the back of my head with her hand to draw me in even closer. "Don't stop."

"No chance of that happening." Especially since I've now had a taste of her, there's no chance I'll give this up.

Clara's back arches, her hips thrusting forward as my tongue runs the length of her silky-smooth slit. I gather every drop of the arousal slicking her pussy with more wetness than the water pumping from the showerhead.

When I spear my tongue inside her, she grows wetter, and her groans become more feral.

"Brax," she purrs, her voice husky and strained as she writhes against me. "It feels so good..."

I suck her, lick her, devour every fucking inch of her until she screams my name in a startled cry. I growl, and my cock throbs when my tongue is coated with evidence of her climax. She quivers against my mouth as her ear-piercing cries slowly simmer to a husky moan. Hearing my name torn from her throat during ecstasy is the most thrilling thing I've ever heard. It was just how I anticipated—throaty, breathless, and ball-tighteningly sweet.

I slow down the lashings of my tongue, trying to gently bring her back from the earth-shattering climax surging through her body. Once her violent convulsions weaken, I place a final lick on her pulsating clit before standing, meeting her eye to eye. Her heavy-hooded gaze is blazing, but unlike before we entered the bathroom, her eyes are fired with nothing but lust. Just seeing her sexually satiated look has me wanting to bang my chest like a caveman.

Maybe Clara was right. Maybe I am a beast?

"Are you ready for round two?"

Her eyes flash before she nods.

"Put your foot onto the step," I instruct while nudging my head to the tiled step on my right.

A grin tugs my lips high when she does as told without a protest. Although I said earlier Clara was going to control the pace of our exchange, now that I've tasted her, the dynamic has switched. Once my natural dominance is unleashed, there's no chance of reeling it back in. Thankfully, from the impish gleam in her eyes, I don't think she's concerned with the change of power.

I lift my eyes to Clara's flushed face. "Now I'm going to fuck you hard and fast in the shower as you requested."

Her breathing pants out as her eyes brighten with excitement.

"Only using these," I continue, wiggling my fingers in the air.

She sighs—it's a disappointed sigh.

Her disappointment shifts to exhilaration when I slip two fingers inside her. A tingle races along the length of my spine when her plush tightness clamps around them. She's tight, wet, and silky soft. When my fingertips brush the sweet spot inside her, her head falls back, and she sucks in a hasty breath. I keep my eyes fixed on her beautiful face as I rub my thumb over her clit and pump my fingers in and out of her at a speed I wish I were fucking her. My cock aches, begging to be immersed in her slick wetness, but I continue my mission, not willing to give into my desire until her legs give out.

A hiss parts my lips when Clara slithers her hand down the ridges of my stomach and grips my throbbing cock. My balls clench when she matches the thrusts of my fingers stroke for stroke. With the warm water streaming out of the showerhead and the silky smoothness of her hand, I could pretend it is my cock plunging into her tight pussy, not my fingers.

Fighting the desire to replace my fingers with my stiffened shaft, I increase the speed of my pumps. I finger fuck her so furiously, her body jerks up and down with every thrust. My race to climax heightens when the generous swell of her breasts scrapes across my shirtless torso.

Her pussy's clutch on my fingers tightens as the whimpers from her mouth become more winded. "Please. Oh. God."

I stare into her eyes when her body tenses, wanting to watch her unravel in front of me, to see her quiver and shake her way through another orgasm I triggered.

"Give it to me, Princess," I hiss through clenched teeth as I battle to hold in my climax, which is rushing to the surface.

I grip her ass and pull her closer to me, aligning our bodies together so well, my cock brushes past her clit with every stroke she inflicts. Her groans become carnal, and her pussy ripples around my fingers as if she's milking my cock of the cum it's dying to give her.

"Come for me, Princess. Come for me now!" I demand.

Unlike her previous orgasm, this time she comes with a soft moan. Seeing the way her eyes flare during ecstasy sets me off. Hot cum rockets out of my knob in rapid, quick-fired hits. When the spurts of my cum hit Clara's throbbing clit, the trembles of her pussy increase as do her pleasurable cries. I obtain a better grip around her waist when her knees give way to the violent convulsions racking through her body.

Once her vicious shudders slow, I pull my fingers out of her snug canal and draw her in close to my chest. The harsh pants of her breaths tickle my bare torso as she struggles to secure a full breath.

"God. That was—"

"Just the beginning," I interrupt, my throat hoarse.

A pleased grin curls on my lips when Clara briefly nods. Her throaty pants switch to a squeal when the water pumping out of the showerhead turns colder than a witch's tit.

"Jesus," she shrieks, leaping out of my arms and hightailing it to the other end of the shower.

The satisfied smirk on my face morphs to cocky when I notice her steps are shaky and slow as she has yet to regain full control of her quivering legs.

"It could have been worse."

Clara eyeballs me, blinking and confused.

"It could have switched to cold five minutes earlier." I lock my big-headed gaze with her twinkling eyes. "Before you came for the second time."

She rolls her eyes and crosses her arms in front of her chest, feigning annoyance. I'm not buying her act. Even if I could ignore the look of bliss on her face only two mind-shattering orgasms can produce, I can't miss the glimmer in her eyes I've wanted to put there for months.

Clara looks exactly how I want her to look.

Claimed.

Chapter Nineteen

y head rockets to the side when someone knocking on my front door bellows into the bathroom. I consider ignoring the interruption until a raspy voice sounds through my ears, "Brax, are you home?"

Ryan.

I shift my eyes back to Clara. "I've got to get that," I inform her while nudging my head to the door. "There are clean towels under the vanity. Wait in here, and I'll bring you some clothes in a minute."

She huffs and crosses her arms in front of her naked chest, apparently annoyed by my request. Ignoring her white-hot glare, I rustle up my jeans from the floor, yank them up my thighs, and hightail it to the door.

Just before I open the door, I crank my head back to Clara. The lewd grin I've been wearing the last forty-five minutes turns massive when I catch her staring at my ass. My confidence hits an all-time high. Even annoyed at my request to stay put, she can't help but ogle my assets.

When she notices I've stopped walking, her gaze lifts and connects with mine. I arch my brow and stare into her gleaming eyes so she knows I didn't miss her lingering stare at my backside. A traffic-

427

stopping grin stretches across her face, undoubtedly proving she isn't the slightest bit ashamed she was busted eyeballing me.

I cockily wink at her. She winks straight back.

After closing the bathroom door behind me, I make my way to Ryan.

"Hey," he greets me, his eyes shifting around my loft with the same amount of eagerness as Diesel's did earlier. When he fails to locate whatever he's searching for, he drifts his eyes back to me. "I heard from a reliable source you had an overnight visitor. Scare her off already?"

Like a perfectly timed skit, the vanity tap in the bathroom turns on.

Ryan's lips tug into a wry smirk, exposing two dimples that sit on his top lip. "Is that Clara?" he questions, waggling his brows.

From the smug look on his face, I know he already knows my reply, but since I'm still running on a high from my bathroom antics with Clara, I nod.

Ryan shoves a white paper bag under his arm before jabbing my mid-section with a set of rapid-fire hits. "Since when did Brax let girls into his bachelor pad?"

"About as long as you've been doing house calls," I fire back, my voice a mix of gruff and playfulness. "What the fuck do you want, Ryan? You're killing my mojo."

He freezes and studies my face. "Haven't you sealed the deal yet?"

I curse under my breath before yanking him into my apartment. "Keep your voice down. Clara wouldn't appreciate her business being shared with the neighborhood."

"There isn't anything to share if you haven't done the deed," Ryan mutters under his breath.

"Jesus Christ. Do I look like an asshole? She was in fucking shock," I reply, preferring to use the excuse of her shocked state than disclose my stupidity about not having any protection in my house.

Ryan glares at me in a sadistic, jeering type of way. "When has a little shock ever stopped you?"

"Whatever. Clara isn't a bunny, so the rules don't apply to her," I hiss through gritted teeth.

His brows hit his hairline. "Diesel said you were gone. Wouldn't have believed it if I didn't see it myself."

"Yeah, yeah, you've witnessed it. Now fuck off." I jerk my head to the hallway.

Ryan laughs. "You didn't even cite an objection. You're *way* past gone." He freezes and inhales a quick breath. "Holy fucking shit. Is Brax in love?"

His laughter simmers when I glare into his eyes, warning him I'm close to blowing my top. "You've got five seconds to tell me why you're interrupting an uninterruptable moment before I throw your ass out of my apartment."

He chuckles, knowing my warning doesn't hold any threat. Ryan and I have been friends for years, and not once have we come close to blows.

Suddenly, he stops laughing and stands a little straighter. "Shit. When I caught sight of the weird look on your face, I forgot the seriousness of my visit." The anger boiling my blood last night returns when he says, "Two of the men who mugged Clara were granted bail this morning."

"How the hell did they get bail so quickly?" My voice is smeared with anger. "It's Sunday."

Ryan combs his fingers through his hair before shrugging his shoulders. "Although I'm certain they have meddled in this activity before, they had no prior convictions." He locks his glistening blue eyes with mine. "The DA was also a little lenient on them since they spent a couple of hours at the hospital having a few nasty bruises and gashes taken care of."

"Could have been worse," I mumble under my breath.

Even though Ryan heard me, he pretends he didn't and continues speaking, "Do you want me to put a unit on Clara's apartment... or are you going to keep a close eye on her?" he asks, his eyes telling me he already knows my reply.

"You worried they're not done with her?"

His eyelid twitches. "I don't know. After the shakedown your crew gave them, they might seek revenge."

"Not if they're smart," I interrupt.

Ryan huffs. "Tell me one gangbanger who is?"

I cross my arms in front of my bare chest and glare into his eyes.

"You don't count. Your grandma and Ryder whipped that attitude right out of you."

"If only it were a few years earlier," I grumble.

"Better late than never," Ryan responds to my quiet musing. He sighs loudly. "I shouldn't be telling you this, but..." My gut twists from the cloud of worry brewing in his eyes. "The guys who mugged Clara are part of the Petretti crew."

My brows stitch. "I thought that crew disbanded when Col was killed?"

Col Petretti was a notorious mob boss running the streets of Hopeton for as long as I've been breathing air. He was killed in a joint FBI and Ravenshoe police sting late last year.

"Rumors are his son, Dimitri, is trying to raise his legacy from the ashes."

"By peddling petty crimes like mugging women in back alleys?" My voice is rough as the events of last night filter back through my mind. Although Clara should have never gone into the back alley unaccompanied, it shouldn't be that way. Women should be able to walk wherever they want without fear of being harmed.

Before Ryan can answer, the creak of a door opening sounds through the room. My heart rate kicks up a gear when Clara saunters out of the bathroom with a dark gray towel twisted around her body and another wrapped around her drenched head. Her bare feet padding across the wooden floor as she makes her way from the bathroom to my bedroom can't drown out me backhanding Ryan, warning him to move his bugged-out eyes off Clara.

"What? Couldn't help but see what has your feathers ruffled," he mumbles, his words barely heard over his breathless chuckle. "I can understand your fascination."

His quiet chuckle turns to a full laugh when I whack him harder than I did the first time. Our little confrontation gains Clara's attention. She stops walking and cranks her neck to the side. My chest puffs higher when her eyes connect with mine. Even looking like a woman who's been taken to the brink and back, her eyes are still beaming with lust.

In a flash, the humorous expression on Ryan's face changes to regretful when Clara shifts her optimistic gaze to him and asks, "Did you find my necklace?"

Ryan reluctantly shakes his head. "No, not yet. I'm sorry, Clara."

The hope in her eyes vanishes. "That's okay. Thank you." With her shoulders sagging a little lower, she climbs the staircase to my bedroom and sinks deeper into the space.

I return my eyes to Ryan. "Do you have any leads on her jewelry?"

He once again shakes his head. "I don't like her chances of recovering the tennis bracelet. It's probably already on the black market."

"She isn't worried about the bracelet. She just wants her necklace back. Seems to have a lot of sentimental value to her."

"She told you about the origin of the necklace?"

I shake my head. "No. I just have a feeling."

Ryan rubs a kink in the back of his neck. That's a sign he's holding something back.

"Why? What did you find out about it?"

"Nothing," he responds with a shake of his head.

I don't even need to look into his eyes to know he's lying. I can hear it in his voice.

I stare into his eyes, silently demanding him to spill the beans.

"I'm not saying anything, Brax. I learned the hard way to keep my mouth shut," he responds to my silent interrogation.

"Chris's death wasn't your fault. No one could have predicted he would go down that road," I reply, knowing him well enough to know what his brief statement is about.

Ryan connects his remorse-filled eyes with mine. "Do you think Noah would see it like that?"

I curtly nod. "If you'd ever give him a chance, yeah, I think he would. You've been carrying the burden of Chris's death for years. Don't you think it's time to let it go?"

A thick, cumbersome silence greets my suggestion. It is always this way when the guilt of our younger years is brought to the surface. Ryan, Chris, and I were the equivalent of the three musketeers back in our high school days. Although we had uniquely distinct personalities, we were thicker than thieves, inseparable until our last days of high school.

Always knowing the path he was going to walk, Ryan joined the police academy. Chris and I... we walked down a very different road. Those bottom feeders Diesel mentioned earlier, that was Chris and me. I have no doubt my life would have mirrored Chris's if I hadn't gang-tagged the wrong man's building.

Young and stupid, I spray-painted a tag on the side of Inked. Like every young gangbanger, I thought I was invincible. I was cocky and full of attitude until Ryder tracked me down. He not only made me paint over the tag I left on his wall with the permission of my grandma, he also forced me to work at Inked for six months without paying me a dime. He said it was my penance for the injustice I did to the art world with my hideous graffiti.

Unable to knock the massive chip off my shoulder, I set out to prove him wrong. I started learning the craft. At first, I just traced pictures directly out of comic books. As the weeks went on, my drawing technique improved, closely followed by my attitude.

Although I never admitted it to Ryder, Inked became my life. I arrived hours before anyone else just to get in some sketching time, and I left hours later. I ate, slept, and breathed Inked. As the countdown to the end of my six-month sentence loomed, my devastation about leaving the Inked family grew. So you can imagine my excitement when on the final day of my punishment, Ryder offered for me to join his crew.

I was ecstatic... until he advised the stipulation his offer came with. I had to tattoo him. I'm not talking a small tat hidden away from view. He requested a highly complex tattoo to be placed on a prime chunk of real estate on his left shoulder. If he liked my tattoo,

I'd become a member of his crew. If he hated it, I was out on my ass.

I'm not going to lie, I was fucking petrified. I guess I don't need to share the rest of my story with you. The fact I'm still working at Inked ten years later is a pretty clear indication of how that story panned out. Ryder loved his tattoo.

Ryder will never admit it, but he saved me. If someone had done the same for Chris, I doubt he would have overdosed in his bathtub four years ago.

"You couldn't save Chris, Ryan, but you saved his brother from following in his footsteps," I say, breaking the silence between us.

An uneasy grin etches on Ryan's mouth before he briefly nods. The things Ryan has done for Noah over the past four years should by far outweigh any blame he harbors for what happened to Chris. Besides, if anyone should feel guilty, it should be me, not Ryan. With Ryder's help, I pulled myself out of the lifestyle that was going to kill me. Nobody helped Chris. Not even me.

"Clara will probably give me hell about it, but I'll keep her here with me until things calm down," I mutter, saying anything to move us away from our somber conversation. Nothing we can say will ever bring back Chris, so why dig up buried guilt?

Ryan cocks his brow and stares into my eyes. "If this is the Petretti crew, it could be weeks, possibly months, before this blows over. Are you willing to keep an eye on her that long?"

I try to hold in my smile. My efforts are fruitless.

All heaviness of our previous conversation vanishes when Ryan breaks into a childish song about Clara and me sitting in a tree. His hearty chuckle rumbles through my ears when I open the door of my apartment and shove him into the hallway.

I'm in the process of slamming my front door in his face when he mutters, "Think quick."

Before I have the chance to respond, the white paper bag he's been gripping the past twenty minutes sails across the corridor and smacks me in the chest. I only just grab ahold of it before it tumbles to the floor.

I shift my eyes between Ryan's snickering face and the bag as I pry it open. My cock twitches when I discover what is inside—a twelve-pack of magnum condoms. My eyes rocket back to Ryan. If I weren't sporting major wood, I'd plant a massive sloppy kiss smack bang on his grinning mouth.

"Figured you might need them since you never bring girls back to your apartment."

With a cheeky wink, he strides down the corridor. "Call me if you need me," are the final words I hear before slamming the door shut and bolting to the staircase of my loft.

My steps are hurried as anticipation scorches through my veins. My cock braces against the zipper of my jeans as I take the steps two at a time. I don't care if a hurricane roars down the main street of Ravenshoe, nothing will stop me from claiming the ultimate prize. It is time for the *Beauty and the Beast* fairy tale to turn into reality.

"Well, nothing except that," I mutter to myself when I land on the top step of the staircase, and my eyes roam over Clara lying in my bed wearing nothing but one of my T-shirts. She's rolled on her side with her hands tucked under her cheek. Her eyes are snapped shut, and the soft pants of her breath clearly indicate she's asleep.

She looks like a real princess when she's sleeping.

My princess.

Quietly striding to the edge of the bed, I secure a grip on the duvet and pull it up to cover her. She stirs when I tuck the covers in tight but stays fast asleep. After brushing a few strands of her hair off her face, I press a kiss to her temple and walk out of the room. My cock screams in protest with every step I take.

Chapter Twenty

"Hey," Clara greets me, her voice groggy from just waking up.

Just like this morning, she glides through my apartment wearing nothing but my short-sleeve tee she fell asleep in. Even without a speck of makeup, her face is fresh and vibrant. That might have something to do with the fact she just napped for two hours straight. I've been wondering the past week if she was getting enough sleep in her new apartment. It wasn't just the dark circles plaguing her eyes that had me guessing. It was the fact she couldn't stop yawning.

Anyone will tell you there's nothing more contagious than a vigorous yawn. I bet you're yawning right now, aren't you? Well, that's what it's been like at Inked the past week. Every time Clara yawned, it spread through the entire crew like an out-of-control fire.

Her brisk strides to the kitchen slow to a snail's pace when her eyes stray to a suitcase sitting at the entryway of my apartment. "Is that bag from my Tumi Alpha luggage set?" she queries, swinging her eyes back to me, her voice high and ear-piercing.

"If you're asking if that is your bag, yes, it is," I reply, having no clue what Tumi Alpha is.

I stand straighter, bracing for impact when I spot the fighting spark igniting in her eyes.

"Why is my bag sitting in your foyer?"

The confusion on her face escalates when her eyes bounce around my kitchen, absorbing her fruit bowl, smoothie blender, and a handful of cosmetics Charity rustled up from her apartment scattered across the countertops.

"Two orgasms don't equal a lifetime commitment," Clara mumbles, her concern growing by the minute.

Her eyes rocket to mine when I ask, "What about three?"

A grin curls on my lips when the concerned mask on her face momentarily slips, exposing a flare of excitement from my tease.

Quicker than I can snap my fingers, the excited gleam is replaced with anger when I mutter, "You got an itch you need scratched, Princess?"

My cock turns to stone when she replies, "You're lucky the kitchen counter is between us, or my knee would have become reacquainted with your crotch."

I smile a shit-eating grin. "Don't break it before you get the chance to use it."

Her breathing becomes excited when I nudge my head to the box of condoms sitting to my right. She tries to keep the expression on her face neutral. She miserably fails.

A smug grin curls on my lips. I've never seen her so muted. She usually spits her fiery words off her still sizzling tongue when we engage in a bit of friendly banter, whereas now, her lips twitch but not a word spills from her mouth.

I like this new look, and I can't wait to study it in greater detail when she's beneath me.

Clara's throat struggles to swallow before she mutters, "How long?" Although her question is short, her interrogating gaze adds to its length.

"As long as it takes for your shock to wear off—"

"Already gone," she interrupts, her eyes blazing with the spark our earlier union in the shower renewed.

"And…" One word is all it takes to secure her utter devotion. "Until the men responsible for your attack are held accountable."

Her brows tact together. "How long will that be?"

I lift my right shoulder into a shrug. "Could be days… or weeks."

Her eyes bug as her lips purse into a sexy pout. "Weeks?" she squeaks out. "You want me to stay here for weeks?" She gestures her hand around my apartment.

When I nod, her pupils enlarge to the size of dinner plates. She balls her hands before her eyes drift between me and the entry door of my apartment, no doubt calculating the most viable exit.

I arch my brow and glare into her eyes, warning her that if she attempts to flee, I won't hesitate to tie her to my bed. There's no chance of her leaving here before I've had my fill, and considering I've just spent the last two hours moving her belongings into my private abode, and I didn't freak out once, the chances of me getting my fill anytime soon are low. *Very fucking low.*

"Weeks of finding out how many ways you can scream my name." My voice is as wild as my desire to claim her. "Do you have a problem with that, Princess?" My words are crass, but I want to test her to see if she's only here because she's afraid of being alone or because she actually wants to be.

Clara snaps her eyes back to me. She doesn't say anything. She just stands across from me, wide-eyed and open-mouthed. I slant my head to the side and stare into her glistening eyes. The more I stare, the livelier the glint I identified last night becomes. Clara isn't here because she's afraid or lonely, she is here because she wants to be ravished. Consumed. Devoured.

And I know just the man for the job.

"If you keep leaving your mouth hanging open like that, I'll find something to fill it with."

Clara sucks in a deep breath and lets it out slowly before her eyes drop to my jeans. My cock—now hard—pulses against my zipper when she licks her lips before slowly raking her eyes up my body. Even though I'm wearing a pair of ripped jeans and a short-sleeve shirt, her eyes drink me in as if I'm standing before her as naked as the day I was born.

When her heavy-lidded gaze reaches my face, I jerk my head back and say, "Come here."

I push off the kitchen counter I'm leaning on, preparing to beat her race to the door if she attempts to bolt. She stuns me for the third time in under twenty-four hours by simply shrugging her shoulders before spanning the distance between us. I can tell by the look on her face that she wants to engage in a war of words, but since I've caught her in a moment of weakness—her libido overriding her astuteness—she appears more willing to put our game of tit for tat on the backburner for a few hours so we can undertake more stimulating activities.

If I were a better man, I wouldn't use her weakness against her.

It's a pity I'm not a better man.

My cock firms as Clara steps toward me with her eyes blazing and hips swinging. Some men would feel intimidated by the determination set in her eyes. Lucky for me, I don't have a problem with a woman who calls it as she sees it. Don't get me wrong, I can't wait to have her flushed and speechless beneath me, but I sure as hell won't cite an objection to her climbing onboard and taking herself for a ride.

Fuck! Just the thought has my cock wrangling the zipper in my jeans, dying to break free.

A jagged groan rumbles from deep in my gut when Clara slings her arms around my neck and seals her mouth over mine. Her tongue sweeps across my lips before plunging inside my mouth. I return her kiss by weaving my fingers through her silky hair and twirling my tongue around hers. The warm goodness of her mouth has my cock aching to be immersed inside her.

Curling my arms around the back of her slim thighs, I hoist her feet off the floor. She smiles against my lips when I place her on the kitchen counter on my right. Her backside dangles far enough off the edge, our crotches align.

The stubble on my chin scratches Clara's neckline as I place a succession of featherlike kisses along her jaw, making her purr like a kitten. My chest swells. There's no greater compliment to a man than being able to switch a strong, determined woman to a purring little kitty. Clara is a take-no-shit type of lady, and I love that about her, but when she loosens the tight reins she governs her life with, I feel invincible. *Like King-Fucking-Kong.*

After a few more nibbles on her jaw, I pull back and peer into her bright eyes, distracted by something rumbling louder than her erotic purrs—her stomach.

"Sorry," she mumbles, chewing on her lip. "I haven't eaten anything since the carrot last night."

I inwardly swear. I was so caught up in ravishing her, I didn't even consider she hasn't consumed a single nutrient in the past sixteen hours.

"Food first," I reply to her whimpering protest when I pull away and walk to the refrigerator. My tone relays my internal battle not to kiss her sexy pout right off her sinful little mouth.

I groan when I swing open the refrigerator. It is so empty, I can hear wind hollering through it.

Upon hearing my grunted response, Clara hops off the kitchen counter and saunters toward me. "What have you got?" she queries, bobbing her neck and peering into the refrigerator. The cutest little crinkle scrunches her nose when her eyes roam over the bare basics it is stocked with. "It isn't too bad," she mumbles under her breath, snagging the half-filled carton of eggs and a nearly empty bottle of milk.

Pushing the door closed with her hip, she steps to the cooktop. After leaning my back against the counter, I cross my arms in front of my chest, relishing the view of a princess preparing breakfast for a beast.

Clara moves along the main counter of my kitchen, swinging open each cupboard she drifts past. I tilt my head to the side and arch my brow when her search extends to the overhead cabinets. Her stretched position forces a small portion of her scrumptious naked backside into my view. I've never been one for going it alone, but with a visual that enticing, I'm fighting the urge to whip out my cock and give it a few strokes.

She grabs a glass mixing bowl I didn't even know I owned from the top cabinet before turning around to face me. "Are you going to show me where anything is? Or am I just going to work it out on my own?" She tries to keep her words sharp, but the cheeky grin tugging her lips high foils her attempt.

With a wink, she spins around and commences cracking the eggs into the glass bowl. I give my eyes a few more moments to drink in her long bare legs, sexy-as-sin body, and tousled hair before pushing off the counter and striding toward her.

I wrap my arm around her waist, pull her in snugly, and drop my head into the crook of her neck. "What do you need me to do?" The heat of my breath bounces off her skin and filters through my nose, engulfing my senses with her rich floral scent.

"Not distract me," she replies before slipping under my arm.

I try to hold back my groan. I fail.

"Do you have any paprika?" she asks after twisting her neck to peer at me.

My brows stitch. "What?"

Clara smiles before briefly shaking her head. "Do you have anything with a bit of heat I could add to the egg whites to give them flavor?"

I quirk my lips. "Chili sauce?"

She smiles a broad grin. I move to the pantry to gather the hot sauce while she pulls out a frying pan from the cupboard below the stove.

"In time, buddy, I promise," I mumble to my cock when the alluring image of Clara bending over has him springing to life.

* * *

Twenty minutes later, I'm sitting down to the most unmanly lunch I've ever eaten. Forever healthy, Clara divided the yolk from the eggs, removing all the hearty goodness a guy of my size loves. My ceramic plate is void of the regular crispy bacon and pancakes it is generally stacked with, replaced with slices of avocado and apple.

I push back from my four-seater dining table, causing a massive creak to sound through my apartment, then amble to the refrigerator. Clara's egg-white loaded fork stops halfway between her plate and her mouth when I stride back into the dining room with a chunk of cheddar cheese and a grater.

I drench every inch of my plate in the scrumptious goodness of cheese before lifting my eyes to Clara. "Cheese?" I angle my head to the side and arch my brow.

Clara chews on her lip before shaking her head.

"Are you sure?" I ask, noticing a flare of hesitation sparking in her eyes.

I scoop up a sizable chunk of cheese-covered egg whites and shovel it into my mouth. Clara squirms in her seat when my deep, throaty moan rumbles up my chest. "It is so good."

Her nose screws up as she pushes her plain egg whites around her plate.

After leaning in close to her side, I whisper, "What about if I guarantee you will burn off those calories within twenty minutes of eating them."

Her eyes snap to mine.

"There's no better cardio than sex, Princess."

I transfer some of the cheese piled up on my plate to hers. "Now eat up. You're going to need the energy."

A grin curls on my lips when she fails to sound a single protest to my demand. My grin turns into a full smile when she digs her fork into her now cheesy eggs and raises them to her mouth. Just as her fork disappears between her pouty lips, she locks her wintry eyes with mine. The huge smile etched on my mouth gets wiped right off when she releases the most provocative fucking moan I've ever heard when the eggs hit her taste buds.

I was wrong earlier. Sex isn't Clara's weakness. It is her ally.

I thought I had our whole dynamic worked out. She would be a strong and independent woman until we stepped into the bedroom—

then, she'd happily hand the baton to me. But I was wrong. *Very fucking wrong.* Not only does Clara have me over a barrel outside the bedroom, but she also has me by the throat inside as well. All it took was hearing that one little moan topple from her lips, and I'm ready to do anything to hear those noises torn from her throat in the middle of ecstasy. *Anything at all.*

The last ten minutes have felt like I'm an inmate serving a life sentence with no chance of parole. It's been torturous. I devoured every scrap of food on my plate within thirty seconds, shamefully displaying that my patience to have Clara beneath me has worn thin. Clara, on the other hand, has taken her sweet-ass time enjoying her first meal in over sixteen hours.

If that isn't bad enough, she savored every last bite with soft little moans and slow, gentle chews. If I didn't want her to know her little ploy to unravel me was working, I would have dragged her across the table and force-fed her. And no, I'm not referring to food.

Once the last smidgen of avocado is smeared off Clara's plate and popped into her mouth, I seize her wrist and yank her across the table. A limited-edition hearty giggle topples from her mouth and jingles through my ears.

Her laughter transforms into a throaty moan when her new straddled position has her feeling the thickness of my cock. Any defiance her eyes have been wearing the past ten minutes fades into the horizon when I pull my shirt over her head and discard it on the floor. Her eyes grow darker, switching from an icy blue to the color of a dark ocean. I wait for her to speak, to put up a protest about me stripping her bare without first seeking permission. Not a word seeps from her lips.

The voluptuous swell of her chest is thrust into my face—as if she's offering them to me—when she slings her arms around my shoulders and draws in nearer. I connect my eyes with hers before taking one of her taut pink nipples into my mouth. A hiss parts her lips when I swirl my tongue around her tweaked bud.

"Brax..."

Fuck, I love the way she says my name.

As one of my hands moves to secure a handful of her curvy ass, the other cups her spare breast. The tightness of her nipples firms as my mouth and fingers work her at a chaotic pace, eliciting more purring moans. My cock stirs, loving her hearty moans but hating the constraint of my jeans.

Like she can hear the silent protests of my cock, Clara slides her hand underneath my shirt and fiddles with the button on my jeans. Her throaty moans turn into a feral groan when her fumbling movements are unable to unclasp the fastener. A chair scraping across the wooden floor thunders through the room when I abruptly push my chair away from the table. I feel her smile against my lips when I undo the button of my jeans and slide down the zipper. A deep growl vibrates through my mouth as she slips her hand inside my jeans to stroke my cock.

Clara pulls her lips away from mine and stares down at me, her eyes sparkling bright, her lips swollen from our kiss. For a woman who protects her heart with an iron fist, she's open, vulnerable, and utterly unguarded. She's exposing sides to her I've hoped to see but have never witnessed. She holds my gaze as she speeds up her strokes, her focus solely devoted to taking me to the brink of ecstasy.

Her affectionate—almost loving—gaze has my chase to climax strengthening and my heart swelling. Every minute I spend in her presence makes me more beguiled by her. And from the doting blaze sparking Clara's arctic-blue eyes, I'd say I'm not the only one becoming entranced.

When the shriek of my landline sounds into her ears, Clara's strokes halt, her head snapping to the side. I ignore the interruption, not willing to harness my desire to claim her any longer. I bite down on her nipple before jerking my hips upward, trying to recapture her devotion.

My plans go to shit when a deep voice sounds over my answering machine. "Brax, it is Daniel from Caramine Care. Don't panic, but your grandma took a turn this afternoon..."

Chapter Twenty-One

The heavy stomps of my boots bounce off the walls and cluster in my ears as I stride down the narrow corridor of Caramine Care. My heart is thrashing in my chest, still panicked about my earlier phone call with Daniel. Although he downplayed the seriousness of the situation, I've still arrived at Caramine Care within twenty minutes of his call. My grandmother means the world to me. She's the woman who raised me, and the woman who owns a vast majority of my heart. *All but the little snippet enlarging to accommodate Clara.*

The instant Daniel's message sounded through Clara's ears, she slid off my lap and secured my shirt off the floor. She stood at my side biting her nails as I returned Daniel's call. I didn't need to speak for her to know the urgency of the situation. The concerned expression on my face told the whole story. I was gutted.

Although Daniel assured me my grandmother was comfortable and resting, I knew the twisted feeling in my stomach wouldn't settle until I saw it with my own eyes. That sick feeling spread from my stomach to my heart when I suggested that Clara come with me. I tried to smother the panic in her eyes by pretending it wasn't about her meeting my grandma, that it was just killing two birds with one stone. She could visit her friend while I checked on my grandmother's condition. The soulless gaze that filled Clara's eyes the night she was mugged returned stronger than ever.

She blinked back tears before mumbling, "Friend? What friend?"

Her chin quivered, exposing she knew exactly who I was referring to. Deciding to play stupid, I said, "The person you were visiting the day I bumped into you at Caramine Care."

Any walls I crumbled between Clara and me the past twenty-four hours reformed before my very eyes. She took a stumbling step backward, her retreating strides only stopping when she crashed into the kitchen counter.

"I can't visit her today," she mumbled, her voice the weakest I'd heard. "I can only visit her the first Sunday of the month. It's not the first Sunday of the month."

"Visiting hours are whenever you want them to be," I replied, my eyes drifting between her haunted ones. "You don't have to stick to a schedule."

Worry churns in my stomach when her pleading eyes stare into mine, begging for me to drop it. Her face is ashen, and her eyes are pained. I draw in a deep breath before briefly nodding my head. Relief fills Clara's eyes. Although I want her to open up to me, I know if I push her too much, her retreating steps will reach my front door. Willing to do anything to ensure she will still be at my apartment when I return from visiting my grandmother, I simply drop the conversation and act like I can't smell the fear oozing from her pores.

It is a fucking hard feat.

* * *

My grandma's rheumy eyes lift to the door when a creak announces my arrival. She sighs softly before shifting her gaze to the window illuminating her room with an orange hue from the afternoon sun beaming inside. My brows tack together when Penny—the nurse my grandma tried to set me up with—exits the bathroom adjoining my grandmother's room.

Penny smiles a greeting as she saunters to my grandmother's bedside. Any concerns about my grandma conjuring up a ruse to force Penny and me together dampen when my eyes zoom in on a bruise on my grandma's wrist while Penny carefully checks her pulse.

After completing a set of observations on my grandmother, Penny mutters something quietly into her ear before gesturing to talk to me in the corridor. I lift my index finger in the air, requesting a minute. When Penny enters the hallway, I walk to my grandma. The twisted, sick feeling in my stomach intensifies when my eyes zoom in on a bruise on her right cheek.

Being mindful not to touch her bruise, I press a quick kiss onto her cheek before muttering, "I'll be back in a minute."

When my grandma's gaze remains on the window, I spin on my heels and make my way into the hall. I cross my arms in front of my chest, hiding the shake of my hands before asking, "Is she okay? What exactly happened?"

Penny locks her green eyes on me. "We're not exactly sure. Your grandma is a very *spirited* woman—"

"Stubborn would be a more appropriate word," I interrupt, mumbling.

Penny smiles softly. "We believe she took a tumble in the bathroom a couple of hours ago."

My heart beats triple time. "Hours ago?" The shortness of my reply doesn't hide my anger.

Penny nods. "Yes. We only discovered the incident when another resident arrived at her room for an afternoon game of gin."

"I thought you had protocol for stuff like this? Isn't there an aide button installed in her bathroom?" I gesture my hand to my grandma's door.

"Yes, there is. Grace refused to use it."

I run my hand over the stubble on my chin. I shouldn't have expected a different reply. My grandmother is so determined not to grow old gracefully. She refuses to use any device with the stigma of age attached to it. Her phone? The latest fandangle device Hunter could design. Her watch? A brand spanking new Apple Watch. No,

I'm not kidding. The day I see my grandma shuffling behind a walker will be the day I announce I'm never tattooing again. It will *never* have a chance of happening.

Penny brushes her hand across my forearm. "Go easy on her. She's still a little fragile after being informed her care is being upgraded from minimum to high." My personal bubble pops when she takes a step closer to me. "We would really appreciate it if you could talk to your grandma about the possibility of having some grab bars installed in her bathroom."

I jerk my chin up. "Yeah, I'll have a talk with her now." I shrug my shoulders. "I don't know what good it will do, but I'll give it my best shot. Thanks, Penny, for all your help."

"No worries," she replies, her voice low and throaty. "If you need anything, Brax, anything at all, don't hesitate to call me."

My brow arches. Even in the seriousness of my visit, there's no way in hell I could miss the sexual ambiguity hidden in her statement. It is like seeing a pair of tits on a bull—obvious and shocking. Although Penny is no doubt beautiful, my cock didn't stir the slightest from her offer. Not even a twinge. Twenty-four hours ago, I would have been panicked my cock was broken, whereas now, I'm beyond ecstatic it wasn't riveted by Penny's offer.

My cock only has one blonde on its radar.

Penny isn't her.

After bidding farewell to Penny with a dip of my chin, I amble into my grandma's room. She tries to maintain an irritated attitude, but her composure slips the instant I sit in the reclining chair next to her bed. She quirks her vibrant, red-painted lips as her world-assessing eyes bore into mine. My brow cocks when she inhales a big, undignified whiff through her nostrils. Her eyes widen as they bounce between mine.

Before I can ask what her odd behavior is about, she blurts out, "Joy by Jean Patou."

I stare at her, shocked and confused.

"The smell of the perfume on your clothes. It is Joy by Jean Patou." She inhales a quick breath, her expression astounded. "The last time I smelled that scent was when you came to visit me months ago. When you were in my room with Clara McGregor."

I move my lips, preparing to speak. My words become trapped in my throat when my grandma cuts them off with a fierce glare.

"Don't think you're too big for me to take over my knee, young man. I may be half your size, but that won't stop me from punishing a liar."

I wave my hands in front of my body, calming the dragon. "I wasn't planning on lying," I mutter. I'm not that stupid. I have no doubt she'd spank my ass if I were ever caught lying to her. Seventy-eight or not.

"I was just going to say we aren't here to discuss why I smell like women's perfume..." I won't lie, I'm grinning like the Cheshire cat at the fact I smell like Clara, "... we are here about your turn."

"Turn, ha!" she says, spitting her words off her tongue in a malicious snarl. "The only thing that is going to have a turn is your backside when I give it a good walloping before marching you right out that door."

Her eyes snap to mine when I mumble, "Do I need to start scrutinizing your reading material? What's with your sudden fascination with spankings?"

She tries to keep her eyes stern, but the corners of her mouth tugging into a lewd smirk gives away her real composure. *There's the grandma I know and love.*

After releasing a deep sigh, she mutters, "I had a little tumble."

Scooting across the cool leather, I sit on the edge of my seat. "Have you been feeling unwell? Dizzy?"

A heavy line of worry indents her forehead before she mumbles, "A little."

I try to hold in my growl. I fail.

"Only a little bit. Nothing to worry anyone about. I'm fine. Look at me," she babbles, gesturing her hand down the front of her body.

In her head, she believes she's gesturing to a twenty-something-year-old female, but all I see is a little old lady who hates the idea of getting old. I'm all for enjoying every day life gives you, but that doesn't mean I want to see her getting hurt for being too stubborn to admit she isn't as young as she once was. Her fall could be the result of something life-threatening or as simple as a low blood-sugar count, but with her refusal to acknowledge she needs help, we'll never know.

Like she can read my thoughts, she says, "I'll have a blood test... on one condition." She connects her glistening baby blues with my eyes. "You have to tell me every detail as to why you have arrived at my room smelling like Clara McGregor."

I arch my brow. "Every detail?"

"Every. *Sordid.* Detail," she replies, her voice slow and calculated. "It couldn't be any worse than the books I've been reading," she adds on with a cheeky wink.

* * *

Forty-five minutes later, I'm leaving my grandmother's room with a less heavy heart but a more twisted stomach. Although I kept my half of our discussion on a clean and even playing field, my grandmother threw out curveball after curveball. It is lucky my grandfather passed away six years ago, or I would have never been able to look him in the eye. The only good thing about being told stories that will give a grown man nightmares is that my discussion not only has my grandmother agreeing to have the blood workup Penny requested, she will allow them to install a grab bar next to the toilet and in the shower. It isn't because she needs them. It is for any 'visitors' she may have. That statement had me vomiting in my mouth for the eleventh time in the past half an hour.

Slipping out of my grandma's room, I take a left instead of my usual right. I need to ask Daniel to have the railings installed in my grandmother's bathroom before she can change her mind. My quick strides slow to a snail's pace when I walk past the room I spotted Clara exiting nearly six months ago. I'm taken aback when my eyes zoom in on a young woman lying still in the bed. I was expecting to see someone close to my grandmother's age, not a lady in her early twenties.

My bewilderment grows when my eyes scan her room. From the technical equipment attached to the motionless female, I can easily derive she's on a life-support machine. And from her frail and withered body, I'd say she has been on it for a long time. My heart pains for the young woman. It is terrible to see someone who should be in the prime of their life more fragile than my grandmother.

My eyes drift away from the young brunette when my name is called from a deep voice on my left. Daniel is standing halfway between his office door and the corridor. Noticing my stunned expression, he pushes off his feet and heads my way.

"I was unaware you knew Sophia," he says, nudging his head to the door I'm standing next to.

"I don't," I reply with a brisk shake of my head.

Daniel seems surprised by my admission. I guess it would appear odd that I've stopped to gawk into Sophia's room without knowing who she is. The only reason I stopped was because I remembered Clara's rattled composure the day I bumped into her in this very hallway. Now her demeanor that day makes sense. I don't even know Sophia, and I hate that she's going through this. I can only imagine how hard it is for Clara.

I swing my eyes to Daniel. "Her last name isn't McGregor, is it?"

I'm filled with relief when he briefly shakes his head. "No. Her name is Sophia Remy."

My brows stitch as I try to recall the last time I heard that name.

When the reality slams into me, the twisting of my stomach extends to my heart.

Chapter Twenty-Two

"Sorry," I apologize when my thoughtlessness has me crashing into a gentleman exiting the foyer of my apartment building in a hurry.

A fit-looking man in his mid-thirties with a military-style haircut dips his chin—accepting my apology—before increasing his pace. His brisk speed from the awning of my apartment building to a steel gray Audi parked at the curb a few spots up from the underground garage exposes he's carrying a semi-automatic weapon. My brows scrunch when I notice the burly man sitting behind the steering wheel of the Audi also has the same style haircut and is wearing an identical suit.

I thought Ryan was holding off on putting an undercover unit on Clara?

Shrugging off my confusion, I adjust the bag of groceries I collected from the corner store and amble into the foyer. My mind has been working overtime since I left Caramine Care two hours ago. It could be a coincidence, but deep down in my soul, I know Sophia is somehow connected with Clara's necklace. It isn't only my intuition telling me this is the case, it is the fact Daniel advised me Sophia is Clara's age, and before she was transferred to Caramine Care, she lived in Hopeton, the town where Clara grew up.

Just remembering the bleak look in Clara's eyes when she asked about the possibility of her necklace being returned had me spending the last two hours scouring every pawn shop within a twenty-mile radius of Ravenshoe. Unfortunately, Clara's necklace hasn't been seen. Since the mugging was less than forty-eight hours ago, the local brokers believe it will be a few more weeks before it surfaces. I don't care if it takes me weeks, months, or years, I won't stop searching until I find it.

When I walk into my apartment, I'm confronted with silence.

I don't fucking like it.

I place the bag of groceries on the kitchen counter and climb the stairs to my loft. Although my room still smells like Clara, it is empty.

I don't fucking like it.

I check the laundry room, the bathroom, and the patio attached to my living area. Clara is nowhere to be seen.

I don't fucking like it.

I hated leaving her alone, but she assured me she could take care of herself and didn't need a babysitter. When I failed to see any untruth in her eyes, I left, expecting her to still be here when I returned.

Obviously, I can't read Clara as well as I thought I could.

I hate that more than anything.

The seething rage bubbling my blood simmers to a slow boil when I catch the quickest giggle. I stop frozen in my tracks and crank my neck. It is only faint, but there's no doubting who the laugh belongs to. *Clara.*

My eyes rocket to my bedroom when the soft babbling of a conversation sounds above me. Once my eyes travel from the living room to the loft, I notice the door to my rooftop garden has been cranked open.

The quiet hum of dialogue between two female voices grows louder as I climb the staircase. From the high tone and limited vocabulary of the second voice, I can easily tell it belongs to a child.

I hit the stoop of the stairs when a female child's voice asks, "Are you staying here long?"

I round the corner to discover my eleven-year-old neighbor, Clementine, sitting next to Clara on the frayed double couch. They have two half-full wine glasses of soda and a bowl of plain chips sitting on a makeshift pallet coffee table.

Clara finishes twisting a piece of Clementine's thick wavy hair into a fancy braided design before she answers Clementine's question, "I don't know. Brax said it could be days or even weeks before I can go home." A grin curls on my lips when a mask of worry slips over Clara's face during the last half of her sentence.

Clementine huffs and crosses her arms over her chest. After placing a tie in Clementine's hair, Clara adjusts her position so she's facing the girl. "Don't you want me to stay? I thought we were having fun today?"

Clementine's shoulders hunch forward. "It isn't that. It's just... just... you shouldn't get comfortable. You won't be here for long."

"Oh," Clara breathes out heavily at the same time I mutter, "Are you trying to scare off my girl, Clementine?"

Clara and Clementine's heads snap to mine in sync. Clementine smiles a cheeky grin I've seen numerous times over the past six months. It's usually worn when she's creating mischief for Ms. Hartler who lives in apartment 2B.

After shaking her head, denying my claim, Clementine turns her eyes back to Clara. Clara slants her head to the side and stares at me like she's shocked to see me standing on my rooftop garden. Her pupils are wide, and her plump nude lips are parted.

I need those lips on me. Anywhere.

"Clementine, I think I hear your momma calling you."

Clementine springs up from the sofa. "Really?" She angles her head to the side and hoists her ear into the air. "I don't hear anything."

Like the stars aligning in the sky, the faint holler of Mrs. Daphne bellows up the stairwell. If I were a religious man, I'd send thanks to God. Since I'm not, I simply thank my lucky stars.

Clementine's eyes bug before she rushes to the door. Her brisk pace slows when I say, "Clementine."

When she cranks her neck back to peer at me, I hold out the packet of Mars bars I'm clutching in my hand for her. She smiles a broad grin before she crosses the space between us. Her steps are so fast, she reaches me in less than a heartbeat. I learned early on in life that candy is my best ally in keeping any female in my life happy.

If only Clara were a fan of sugar.

Still grinning, Clementine snatches the chocolates out of my hand and presses a quick kiss to my cheek. My brow cocks over her audacity. She's always been a little showy around her friends from school, but she's never taken it this far before.

She must be trying to impress Clara.

Clementine's girly giggle is only just heard over the stomping of her feet as she gallops down the stairwell. When the front door slams shut not even two seconds later, I drift my eyes back to Clara. Her expression is even more shocked than it was earlier.

In a nanosecond, she switches the appearance of her face, changing it from stunned to forthright. "How's your grandma?"

I smile. "She's good. A hurricane couldn't slow her down."

Clara releases a deep breath before a rare and genuine smile etches onto her mouth. I'm in trouble with this woman. I've only been away from her a little over three hours, and she hasn't left my mind. I knew the day she walked back into Inked she'd be trouble. I just had no clue the type of trouble she would cause.

Clara curls her feet under her bottom when I take the empty seat next to her. "Tread carefully with Clementine, Brax," she mumbles while brushing her hand over the sticky lip gloss stain Clementine left on my cheek. "She's too young to understand the repercussions of chasing an unattainable man." Her voice comes in barely a whisper. "I wish someone had given me the same warning."

"Isaac?" I ask, even knowing I could be throwing the first grenade in World War III.

Like I could be any more shocked the past twenty-four hours, Clara surprises me again by simply nodding. "Despite what everyone thinks, I did care for Isaac... a lot."

I nod. The fact she was going to get his name inked on her hip is a pretty compelling point.

"But I didn't care about him because of his money or power. I just thought if two people with half a heart joined, they could have one whole heart again." Her voice is so weak my ears strain to hear what she's saying. "I just never considered his heart would heal on its own."

Seizing her wrists, I pull her to sit side-saddle on my lap. I fight the desire to bang my chest like King Kong when she doesn't cite a single protest.

Now is not the time for cockiness.

Clara's pained eyes lift to mine when I say, "A broken heart never mends, but it can swell to accommodate more people in it. You don't have to live your life unloved because your heart was once broken. You just have to be willing to increase its size to include the new people in your life. The people who care for you. Guys like me."

Diesel and Ryan are right. I'm gone for this woman. Completely and utterly fucking done.

The hurt in Clara's eyes softens as she quietly mumbles, "Do you really think that's true?"

I nod without pause for consideration. My heart swells when she cups the edge of my jaw and smiles a knockout grin. Her eyes bounce between mine. She looks like she wants to say something but not a word spills from her lips.

After twisting a lock of hair behind her ear, I say, "I saw Sophia today."

Clara stiffens, and her eyes widen, but she tries to keep the expression on her face neutral. She fails. "How is she? Is she okay?"

"She's good. Daniel said they have had a couple of recent developments the past month he looks forward to discussing with you at your next visit."

Clara's pupils dilate more. "Recent developments?"

I smile before nodding. "She moved her toes last week."

She sucks in a deep breath as her eyes brim with tears.

"She has also been recorded taking unaided breaths."

Tears stream down Clara's cheeks as her hand clamps over her mouth.

"These are good signs, Princess."

"I know," she replies, her tone weak. "These are happy tears."

She takes a few moments to settle her composure before locking her red-rimmed eyes with mine. My heart rate kicks into overdrive, but I remain quiet, praying she will open up to me.

"Sophia is Remy's little sister. Remy was my first serious boyfriend. His real name was Victor Remy the Second, but everyone called him Remy. Although I was only a teen, I loved him. Truly I did."

Her eyes flare as a range of emotions flash through them.

"But my father hated Remy. Remy thought it was because his parents were divorced, but that wasn't the real reason my dad hated him. It was because he didn't have any money, and he lived on the wrong side of town. Remy begged me for months to leave my family and go live with him, but I couldn't. He could barely afford to live as it was, let alone take care of me, and since I was under eighteen, I had no way of supporting myself."

Her eyes gloss over. "Remy gave me my pendant the night of my eighteenth birthday party. The night was going surprisingly well. Although Remy looked slightly out of place in a pair of ripped jeans when all the other male attendees were wearing dress pants, but I didn't care. I loved him for who he was, not what he wore."

She takes a breath before continuing, "I don't know exactly how it started, but Remy got into a disagreement with my father. After they flung a string of hateful words at each other, Remy dragged me out of the party. I pleaded for him to wait until my guests had left, but nothing I said made a difference. He was furious I didn't stand up for him. I wanted to... truly, I did... I just couldn't get my mouth to cooperate. I was still six days away from officially turning eighteen, so I feared the repercussion of going against the wishes of my father. Remy broke up with me because I refused to leave with him. I was devastated."

She stops talking for a moment and stares out into space. "That devastation was nothing compared to being informed he was involved in a motorbike accident three weeks later. He was killed on impact. Sophia has been on life support ever since."

Fuck! No wonder she was so scared when I threw her on my bike.

"I'm sorry, Princess. If I had known, I wouldn't have forced you onto my bike—"

My words stop when Clara places her index finger on my lips. "It's okay. I know you'd never hurt me, Brax."

I strengthen my grip around her waist but remain quiet. Just like there were no words I could say to ease Hank's pain when Derrick was killed, I have no words to offer Clara to lessen the hurt brewing in her eyes.

After removing a tear tracking down her face, Clara lifts her tear-drenched eyes to me. "Sophia's parents couldn't afford Remy's funeral, let alone Sophia's extensive medical bills, so I made a deal with the devil to ensure she was taken care of. By becoming the daughter my father wanted... an upstanding member of society who never spoke unless spoken to and did exactly as demanded... Sophia's medical expenses were paid. As the years went on, I became more and more like my father, a vindictive and callous human being with an ice heart." A painful whizz of air parts her mouth. "I thought once my father died, his hold over me would vanish. It didn't. I was too far gone by then. My heart was beyond repair."

"I don't believe that," I reply, speaking for the first time in ten minutes. "If you didn't have a heart, you wouldn't have visited Sophia every month for the past eight years. You wouldn't have used seventy percent of your salary at Inked to put toward her care expenses, and you wouldn't have tears in your eyes right now. You have a heart, Princess. A very big one. Don't let a man with wrong values ever let you think any different."

I run the back of my hand down her cheeks, removing her tears before saying, "Besides, you can always hold onto the piece of my heart you've already stolen until yours fully thaws." I aim to keep my tone cheeky, but my words come out with more sentiment than I anticipated.

When the pain in Clara's eyes eases from my statement, I'm happy for her to take the meaning any way she sees fit.

"I have a piece of your heart?"

When I nod, a true and genuine smile etches onto her mouth.

"I like the sound of that," she murmurs before resting her cheek on my chest.

A stretch of silence passes between us. It isn't awkward. It is comforting and necessary, and I could stay like this for hours. I don't know why, but I've had an overwhelming desire to protect Clara since the day I met her. Finding out she has suffered a loss has strengthened my desire to protect her, but it isn't the only reason I'd happily sit here for hours with her in my arms. In some ways, this type of affection is more intimate than the moment we shared in the shower this morning.

Don't construe my statement the wrong way. Our time together this morning was out of this fucking world—better than I could have ever predicted—but it's during the quiet times like this that I get to see other sides of Clara, the ones not governed by her libido.

Her outward appearance gives the illusion that she's a woman with a frozen heart, but I realize now that isn't the case. She's protecting her heart so fiercely because she's afraid one more knock may shatter it completely, permanently disfiguring it. And although she puts on a brave front, even a woman as headstrong as Clara doesn't want to live her life unloved, no matter how much she pretends she does.

* * *

Enough time rolls by in complete silence that the sky changes from a vibrant blue coloring to midnight black. My eyes shift away from the stars scattering in the sky to Clara when she lifts her head off my chest.

The crazy beat of her heart pounds the nape of my neck when she curls her arms around my shoulders. "Kiss me, Brax," she mutters, fluttering my lips with her warm breath. "I've missed your lips on mine."

My lips tug high, loving that she's becoming so forthright with her desires.

"You wish is my command, Princess."

Her mouth tastes sweet and spicy. Sweet from the soda she was sharing with Clementine and spicy from the flavor of the potato chips they were consuming. Unlike our previous kisses, this time, I control the pace. I don't mind handing over the reins on an odd occasion, but I want to prove to Clara what I said was true. Loss, heartache, and betrayal are not something you simply get over. You just have no choice but to move on and live the best life you can. Although I hate the idea of another man holding a portion of Clara's heart, she isn't sitting in his lap, nibbling on his lips. She's here with me. And if I have it my way, that isn't going to change anytime soon.

After I'm happy I've sampled every portion of her mouth, I pull my lips away from Clara. I run my thumb over the curve of her top lip before locking my eyes with hers. My chest swells, beyond smug, her gaze is hazy and brimmed with lust. I tilt my head to the side and stare deeper when sparks of the unidentifiable glint she was wearing this morning resurfaces.

It brightens before she mutters, "Make love to me, Brax."

Chapter Twenty-Three

Keeping her entrancing eyes connected with mine, Clara tugs the hem of her shirt out of her skirt then pulls it over her head. My nostrils flare, relishing the rich scent of the floral smell floating in the air. The generous swell of her breasts falls gently to her chest when she slips her hand around her back and unfastens her bra.

I'm not a man who usually makes love. I fuck—*and I fuck hard*—but I am going to make love to this woman. Not only to prove what I said was true but also to show her what she means to me.

A husky purr escapes Clara's parted lips when I cup her breast and take her rosy-pink nipple into my mouth. The muscles in my stomach tense when she slips her hand under my shirt and runs her fingernails over the bumps of my abs. My cock throbs against my zipper, dying to be immersed in her silky softness. It's had an unquenchable desire to claim her as mine from the moment I laid my eyes on her, but his pleas must wait. Clara asked me to make love to her, and I'm a man who keeps my word.

I release her breast from my mouth with a little pop, the bud of her nipple hardening when I blow hot air onto it. My plans to take it slow go to shit when she rubs herself along the hardness in my jeans.

"Oh God, Brax, please touch me. I need you to touch me."

Her soft pleas strengthen when I slip my hand between our bodies. I groan when I feel how wet she is. She's saturated.

My rough moans are captured by Clara's mouth when she covers her lips over mine and kisses me. She kisses me with so much heat and passion that before I know it, she's lying beneath me on the two-seater couch, and I'm grinding up against her.

Slow, Brax. Slow.

Ignoring the protest of my cock, I pull back and rest my backside on the balls of my feet. Clara's skirt is bunched around her waist, and her chest is thrusting up and down as she stares up at me with wild, crazy eyes. Smiling a grin I've never seen, she slides down the zipper on her skirt and glides it down her thighs. It joins her shirt on the concrete floor not even two seconds later. My eyes drink in every inch of her glorious skin as I unbutton my jeans and discard them next to her clothes.

The full moon bounces off her smooth white skin, illuminating her in a silvery glow. If I didn't already know she was a princess, I would have sworn an angel had fallen from the sky. *My angel.* I drop to my knees and drag her ass to the edge of the couch. Her giggles trail off to a moan when I spread her open with my thumbs and run my tongue along the seam of her glistening pussy, absorbing the wetness shimmering on her pretty pink lips.

"Oh," Clara garbles when I wrap my lips around the swollen bud of her clit and suck softly.

Her thighs loosen as I devour her sweet pussy in slow and tantalizing licks and nips. I work her into a frenzy at a leisured pace, making love to her with my tongue instead of my cock. My slow speed is drawing out her race to climax, but I want her to feel every stroke of my tongue, every nip of my teeth, and every suck I inflict. I don't ever want her to forget the first time we made love, so if it takes me four hours to get there, it takes me four hours.

"Brax, yes. It feels so good. Oh, so, so good."

Clara's throaty moans have me dying to slide my fingers inside her and pump her until she comes screaming my name. The only thing stopping me is her writhing against me. She's rocking her hips in a similar rhythm as my tongue, proving she wants to go at a slow and controlled pace.

I delve my tongue in and out of her before sliding it up to her clit and sucking down. Any concerns about my moderate tempo lessening Clara's pleasure shifts to the back of my mind when a long, quivering orgasm shimmers through her body. Her back arches, and a cock-twitching moan spills from her O-formed lips as every fine hair on her body bristles. Pre-cum seeps into the material of my briefs when her juices gush onto my tongue.

God, she tastes good. So fucking good.

I'm rock hard, I swear my cock is about to burst out of my briefs. He'd even go at a leisured pace if it guaranteed him the opportunity to be wrapped in her warmth.

After guiding Clara down from her prolonged climax, I stand from my kneeled position. I scrape my hand over my mouth, removing the residual of her arousal before shoving my briefs down my thighs. My cock thickens as Clara inhales a sharp breath when it springs free from its tight restraints. I love the shocked reaction she gets every time she sees my cock.

While running my hand up and down my shaft, I lock my eyes with Clara. Even though her eyes are beaming with lust, I can't miss the glint they were wearing earlier. Except now, I can recognize that gleam. It isn't lust, feistiness, or a woman being ruled by her libido. It is the glint of a woman who wants to be loved—to be cherished.

I know just the man for the job.

The gleam in her eyes brightens when I nestle the crown of my cock between her wet heat. After lubing myself with her wetness, I slowly inch inside her.

Fuck! She feels so good.

Tight.

Wet.

Mine.

If I weren't set on ensuring the glint in her eyes never leaves, I could come right now. That is how good she feels. Instead, I grit my teeth and sink in deeper.

A curse word seeps from my lips when Clara scrambles backward, withdrawing my throbbing cock from her slicked pussy. "Condom," she mutters breathlessly. "You need a condom."

Placing my hands under her ass, I drag her back to me. "I don't need a condom." I push the first inch of my cock back inside her. "I don't mess with my crew, I don't bring girls to my apartment, I don't fuck without a condom, and I don't make love."

Clara's massively dilated eyes bounce between mine.

"With anyone *but* you," I mutter, inching further inside her.

I fight the urge to thrust into her in one quick motion when her pussy protests the intrusion.

"Open up for me, Princess. You've got to let me in, or I'll hurt you." *And there's no fucking chance of that happening.*

Clara nods before doing as asked. Her pussy ripples around me, sucking me in deeper as she swivels her hips to loosen their tight hold.

"That's it, Princess. Just like that."

Her teeth gnaw on her bottom lip when I take her to the root of my cock. I still my movements, waiting for her body to adjust to the intrusion before drawing back out. Clara's eyes pop open and lift to mine when I fully withdraw my cock. Before she can protest, I thrust back in at the same leisurely speed.

I rock in and out of her over and over again until her husky moans are heard over the mad beat of my heart shrilling in my ears. Although my speed is slow for a guy who is used to fucking, it isn't slow enough to stave off my desire to come. She feels too good to ever scare off that urge.

Her French-tipped nails dig into my ass when she adjusts the tilt of her hips so I can take her deeper. Her hips rock faster with every stroke I make. I try to hold back, to keep the slow pace she requested, but the fight becomes unwinnable when she mutters, "Please, Brax. More. I need more."

Banding my arms around her sweat-slicked waist, I roll us over so she's straddled on top of me. "Take what you need, Princess."

And she does.

Her nails dig into my chest as she rises and falls above me in a tempo not fast enough to be classed as fucking but a few notches faster than my previous speed. I slither my hand down her damp body to find her pulsating clit. Her pussy grows wetter when I roll the pad of my thumb over the throbbing bud.

"Oh God. You feel so good, Brax. I'm going to come," she purrs moments later.

"Give it to me, Princess. I want it all. Give me everything you have." I cup one of her bouncing breasts in my hand to tweak her nipple at the same speed I'm flicking her clit.

Her thighs quiver as her breaths come faster. She does another four rises and falls before she shatters like glass hitting a concrete floor. Her pussy milks my cock, my name spilling from her lips in a breathless, erotic scream.

"Brax. Oh..."

I wait for the shakes of her body to settle before gripping her hips with my hands and guiding her back up and down my thickened shaft. I jerk my hips to arouse her clit with my pubic bone as my cock consumes her clenching slit.

Dropping my eyes from her spent face, I lock them with an image I'll never forget. Her pussy is red and swollen, but nothing can take away from the sight of my cock pumping into her glistening mound in long, lengthened strokes.

The harsh pants of her pleasurable moans spur on my desire to come. My cock throbs as my race to climax intensifies.

"Give it to me, Brax," Clara quotes my words, her's husky. "I want every drop."

Now I'm even harder.

Fuck, she's gorgeous.

Her tousled hair falling around her shoulders, her lips puffy and raw from our kisses, and her eyes sparked with so much life, I'm afraid she'll run out of room for anything else.

I thrust into her again, and again, and again until the walls of her pussy clench around my cock for a second time. She rides the intensity of her climax by slamming down on me so hard, her ass slapping my balls booms into my ears. Her legs shake, her words come out garbled, and her bucks turn wild.

"Fuck, Princess, you're strangling my cock with your greedy sucks," I roar, my words echoing into the quiet night. I jerk my hips up, my desire to come overwhelming me. "I'm going to come so fucking hard."

And I do.

I take my cock to the very base—giving her my all—before the hot thickness of my seed jets out of my throbbing crown.

"You feel that, Princess? Me inside you. Marking you. Claiming you with my cum."

Clara purrs like a little kitten as her pussy ripples around me, milking every drop of my cum while the wetness of her slit coats my balls. "I want it all. Give me all of it."

"You've got it all, Princess. Every fucking drop. Every fucking inch." I thrust in and out of her, smearing the walls of her pussy with my cum. "Not just my cum. You've got all of me. You hear me, Princess? I'm not ever giving this up. Tell me you understand what I'm saying?" I mutter, still pumping into her, my cock unable to stop now he has *finally* claimed the pussy he's been yearning for the past six months.

I come for the second time when Clara says, "I hear you, Brax. I hear every word you're saying."

Chapter Twenty-Four

Propping myself on my arm, I adjust my eyes to the darkness of my bedroom. My eyes drop when the same pained murmur I heard thirty seconds ago sounds through my ears again. With the moonlight shining into my room from the rooftop window, I can only make out some of the features of Clara's face. Although disoriented from the darkness, I can't miss the heavy set of wrinkles lining her forehead. She looks scared and frightened.

When she whimpers again, reality smacks into me. She's having a nightmare.

I nudge her gently with my arm to wake her. As she claws her way through the dark pit of a nightmare, her skin is clammy and warm. Guilt riddles me, hating that her safety was compromised so much it is hindering her sleep. Her face contorts as she pulls her legs up into a tight ball. I put a little oomph into my next nudge. This time, she jerks awake, springing to a half-seated position.

Remorse and maybe a twinge of jealousy twist my stomach when she painfully whispers, "Remy."

I lean over and switch on the bedside lamp when the heavy pants of her breath increase. She's gasping for air so fiercely, I'm afraid she's about to hyperventilate.

"It's okay, Princess. You're okay," I soothe when her massively dilated eyes filter around my room. She looks both lost and confused. "You're in the bedroom of my loft."

Her head snaps to the side. Confusion and another look I can't work out mars her beautiful face. The jealousy squeezing my heart eases when she feebly mumbles, "Brax," under her breath before she throws her arms around my shoulders. I catch the remaining tears from her nightmare with my thumbs before drawing her into my chest.

Several minutes pass with me just holding her. She gathers her wits while I give into the fact that as much as I'm falling for Clara, I still have so much to learn about her. I was certain her nightmare was from her mugging. Now, I'm not so sure. It isn't just her mention of Remy that has me backpedaling on my initial assumption, it's the fact her eyes lost the glint I worked so hard to put in there the last forty-eight hours.

In all honesty, although Clara said she heard what I was saying last night, I was still expecting her to flee once she came down from cloud nine. I said what I did as I knew I had her in a moment of weakness, but she continues to shock me more and more every day. Not only did she not flee, we spent all day yesterday like a normal couple. We cooked breakfast together before making love in the shower. We ate lunch on the patio of my apartment before we fucked like rabbits on the couch in my living room, and we ordered takeout for dinner before we... yeah, you guessed it, we fooled around in my bed. My cock has spent the last twenty-four hours in heaven—Clara's sweeter-than-nectar pussy heaven.

Even though I've loved our vigorous sexual activities the past forty-eight hours, I also cherish moments like this. I love being the man Clara can find comfort with. And I'm as happy as a pig in mud that she trusts me enough to spill her deepest and darkest secrets without fear of rejection.

These are the moments that will tether us closer together, the moments that will see us growing into a strong, unbreakable couple, and the moments that have me falling in love with her even more.

* * *

Several hours later, I wake up startled. It's not a nightmare waking me from my sleeping state, it is the alarm on my phone hollering loudly. Careful not to wake Clara, I slip out of bed, snag my phone off the drawers, and step onto the front patio of my apartment. I squint as my eyes adjust to the brightness of the mid-morning sun before dropping them to my phone. Reality smacks into me hard and fast when I realize why my phone was hollering. It is Tuesday. *Dammit!*

I was so wrapped up in Clara, it feels like months have passed instead of just two measly days. While scraping my hand over the stubble on my chin, I dial a number I know by heart.

Diesel answers on the first ring. "No closer to finding the third assailant yet, but we have our ears to the ground."

A car whizzing by sounds through the phone, proving he's already out looking.

"Ryan called yesterday. He got some grainy footage of the men leaving the alleyway from an ATM camera. He's going to see if Hunter can clean up the image enough to run it through facial recognition." My voice is gruff from just waking up. "Give Ryan a few days to see what he can come up with. If he doesn't get any closer, I'll call in a few favors."

Although Diesel doesn't reply, I can imagine him nodding.

"Talking about favors, I have one I need to ask."

"Anything," Diesel replies without a smidge of hesitation.

"Clara is doing well, but I don't think it'd be wise to throw her back into Inked so soon after her attack."

"That's understandable. We held down the fort months before she arrived, so I'm sure we can keep things going until she feels comfortable returning."

"I also don't want to leave her alone," I add on quickly.

Diesel is so quiet I can hear the smile etching onto his face.

"Do you think you could handle taking the reins at Inked for a couple of days?"

Diesel chuckles. "I hope so, considering I already rescheduled your appointments."

I smile. I shouldn't be surprised. He is always one step ahead of the pack.

"Call me if anything urgent comes up."

"Call me if you want a real man to show you how it's done," he replies, chuckling.

Laughing, I pull the phone away from my ear, but I return it when Diesel calls my name. "Yeah?"

"Give her an extra pound just for me," he adds, since his first tease didn't have the effect he was aiming for.

His hearty chuckle is barely audible over my furious growl. My attention is diverted from ways of seeking my revenge on him when a car honking shrieks through my ears, closely followed by crunching metal. When I walk to the end of my patio, I spot the cause of the commotion. A white sedan has run up the backside of a black truck.

I'm about to call for help when I notice a steel gray Audi parked at the curb. It is the same steel gray Audi I spotted two days ago when I returned from visiting my grandmother. A sense of dread washes over me when the occupants of the car fail to exit their vehicle to aid the people involved in the crash.

Shouldn't a police officer's priority always be helping civilians?

I stand out on my patio, watching the scene unfold for the next twenty minutes. Not once do the suit-clad men in the silver Audi step out of their vehicle. Not even when the female driver of the sedan stumbles out of her car with a massive gash on her forehead.

No longer able to restrain my curiosity, my finger slides across the screen of my phone before I punch in a well-used number.

"Ryan Carter."

"Ryan, it's Brax." My voice is gritty as concern strangles my vocal cords. "I thought you were holding off on putting a unit on Clara."

"I did," he replies with confusion in his tone. "You said you'd take care of her. Did something happen? Do you need a unit assigned?"

I grit my teeth. "No, Clara is fine. I need a favor."

Ryan delays in replying. He hates being asked a favor.

"I had my guys call you when they found two of the men who attacked Clara. That wouldn't have happened if you didn't ask me for a favor. Besides, if you can't do this, I'll call Hunter."

"Fine," he breathes out heavily, hating that I'm considering taking a non-legal approach. "What do you need?"

I adjust my position so the Audi is directly in my line of sight. "I need you to run a license plate for me…"

* * *

Two hours and thirty-nine minutes later, I'm pulling my bike into the curb of Destiny Records in Hopeton. Charity did a mighty fine job pretending she needed to speak to Clara alone for a one-on-one girl talk when she arrived at my apartment an hour ago. She was so convincing, she had Clara begging for me to give them some private time.

"Just for an hour or two," Clara pleaded, her begging eyes adding to the strength of her plea.

I acted disappointed before nodding. I'm not going to lie. A shit-eating grin etched on my face when I saw a petrified mask slip over Charity's face as Clara led her to my rooftop garden. Although I'll be kissing Charity's ass for the next six months, it will be worth it. The instant I discovered who the owner of the steel gray Audi was, there was no chance of ignoring my naturally ingrained protectiveness of Clara. And since she had a nightmare last night, I didn't want to leave her alone. Hence Charity's sudden desire for girl talk.

A pretty receptionist with unique yellowish-brown eyes greets me with a smile when I saunter deeper into the foyer of Destiny Records. She has a tight, fit body, luscious caramel skin, and dark, rich hair.

"Hello. Welcome to Destiny Records. How can I help you?" she greets me, her voice as absorbing as her eyes.

"I need to speak to Cormack McGregor."

The receptionist's eyes widen before she curtly nods. "I'll see if he's available."

She lifts the receiver of her phone to her ear as my eyes run around the space. Destiny Records' headquarters is an architectural wonder with large glass paneling and expensive features. The floors are inlaid with reclaimed wood, and I've spotted numerous expensive paintings lining the walls. The premise screams wealth.

Wealth Clara's brother is keeping to his greedy self.

My eyes return to the receptionist when she says, "I'm sorry, Mr. ..."

"Anderson," I fill in.

She smiles. "Anderson. Mr. McGregor is unavailable to speak with you at this time. If you'd like to make an appointment, I can check his calendar, or if you want to leave a CD, I can forward it to the creative artist team."

"I'm not a musician," I interrupt. "I'm here regarding his sister."

The receptionist's eyes bug. "Okay," she replies softly before lifting the receiver back to her ear. Her eyes shift between her desk and me as she speaks in hushed whispers. "I understand," she replies before disconnecting the call. "Is this regarding Cate or Clara?"

I arch my brow. "Does it fucking matter?"

She balks, shocked by my foul language. "Not to me, but to Mr. McGregor it does," she replies, her lips quivering.

Blood roars through my veins, thick and fast. Ignoring the security officer standing at the door of Destiny Records, I make my way down the corridor hidden behind the reception desk. The receptionist calls out for me, but I can't hear a word she's saying, too blinded by rage to hear anything.

My long strides have me walking the length of the hallway in two heart-thrashing seconds. I'm not at all surprised to spot a gold plaque with the name *Cormack McGregor* on a wide wooden door at the end of the hall.

The important people always make you come to them.

I swing open the door with brutal force at the same moment my shoulder is seized by a burly-looking security officer.

"You either leave of your own accord, or I'll throw your ass onto the curb."

"You have two seconds to get your hands off me before I show you that bad genetics won't be the cause of your ugliness. My fists will be."

Our little tousle is interrupted by a deep voice inside the office. "Let him in, Pablo."

The security officer loosens his grip on my shoulder, but he doesn't entirely remove his hand. I arch my brow and glare into his eyes. My stare is dark and brimmed with danger. When Pablo lifts his hand and takes a retreating step, I swing my eyes to my right. I don't need to see his identification to know the gentleman standing in front of me is Cormack McGregor. He's the spitting image of Clara, just a manlier version. Same wintry-blue eyes, same defined facial features, and same platinum-blond hair.

"When you look in the mirror every morning, do you feel remorse? Or are you too busy counting your millions to be worried about the safety of your little sister?"

Cormack cops my snide comment on the chin before gesturing for me to enter. I walk three steps into the room before stopping and crossing my arms in front of my chest. *I didn't come here to drink tea and eat cucumber sandwiches.*

"You have enough money that you can put a tail on your sister, but you don't care enough about her to make sure she's safe and well."

Cormack smiles. It is a pained and bitter smile. "I didn't put a tail on Clara. The men are there to ensure she is safe. I'm not a monster, Brax. I didn't send her out into the world completely alone."

I suck in a deep breath, surprised he knows my name, but my shock isn't great enough to leash my anger. "You're not a fucking monster? You're sitting in an overpriced leather chair in an office the size of most people's apartments while your little sister works at a tattoo parlor for minimum wage. You've got a fancy-ass mansion with a butler and a handful of maids while your sister is living in an apartment which is about as fancy as a crack house. Your security team is getting around in a brand spanking new Audi for fuck's sake while your sister is driving a piece-of-shit car that is older than she is."

He attempts to interrupt me, but I continue speaking, foiling his attempts, "And while you're out eating meals worth hundreds of dollars a plate, your sister is getting jumped in a fucking alley by men wielding guns. Yeah, I guess you're right. That doesn't sound like a monster to me. It sounds like a coward."

Cormack balks as his face goes ashen. "Clara was mugged?"

I smile a conniving grin. "Yeah. All while your men probably stood by and watched it happen. What fucked-up game are you playing that you're willing to risk your sister's life?"

"It isn't a game. It is a lesson." His words come out weak like the man he is.

"A tough fucking lesson."

"I never wanted Clara to get hurt. I wanted to teach her not to take everything for granted. To be grateful for the life she was born into. I never wanted her to get injured. That is why I put the security detail on her. But every time they were about to step in, you were one step ahead of them. The night she took the bus, they were following her. They were about to react when the teenage boy approached her. You beat them. When she moved into the apartment, they were going to have security installed. You beat them again. I didn't want Clara hurt, but I wanted her to be taught a lesson. I wanted her to be grateful."

"Then where the fuck were they the night she got jumped?" I shout, my loud voice ricocheting off the pristine white walls and shrilling into my ears.

Cormack's face goes paler. "I don't know, but I *will* find out. I guarantee you I will find out." He locks his remorse-riddled eyes with mine. "Is Clara okay? Is she safe?"

"Maybe you should ask her that yourself." I spin on my heels and amble down the corridor, needing to leave before I break the promise I made to Ryan.

Chapter Twenty-Five

My brisk strides down the hallway of my apartment building slows when the vibration of my cell phone shakes in my pocket. I'm not at all surprised when I see it is a call from Ryan. When he discovered who the Audi was registered to, he pleaded for me not to take the issue any further. My consideration of his plea only lasted as long as it took for me to remember the bleak look in Clara's eyes the night she was mugged.

Ryan's pleas settled when I promised I was only going to 'talk' to Cormack man to man, not have a 'word' with him. Considering I left without a single drop of blood being shed, I kept my word. I won't lie. It was hard. The only thing that stopped me from pounding some sense into Cormack was the look of repentance in his eyes. He was genuinely horrified that Clara had been assaulted. He was so upset, he looked physically ill.

I don't have any siblings, so I can't say I comprehend Cormack's logic of wanting to teach Clara a lesson. But even without siblings, I still think he has gone about it the wrong way. Clara's life was jeopardized. That is not something I'll ever be okay with.

Swiping my finger across my phone's screen, I press it to my ear before throwing open the front door of my apartment. "Not a drop of blood was shed," I mutter, not bothering to issue a greeting.

"Have you seen Damon?"

I throw the keys for my bike onto the entryway table before answering, "No. I was set to put a couple of hours into his back tattoo later this week, but I canceled my appointments to spend more time with Clara."

Ryan's deep sigh sounds down the line.

"Why? What's up?" My lips purse when my gaze locks in on Damon's ocean-blue eyes sitting across from Clara. "Ha. You won't believe this. He's here. Did you want to talk to him?"

"Damon is at your apartment?" Ryan's words come out in a hurry.

Even though he can't see me, I jerk up my chin. "Yeah. He's here with Clara."

Feet stomping bellows down the line before Ryan yells, "I'm on my way. Keep him calm," before he disconnects the call.

A sick feeling spreads across my stomach when I drift my eyes to Clara. She's nursing the same set of eyes she wore in the alleyway the night she was mugged. Her cheeks are stained with tears, and her face is as white as a ghost.

Hot anger boils my blood. "It was him, wasn't it? The third man in the alley."

My stomach winds all the way up to my throat when Clara nods, spilling fresh tears down her cheeks. Her confirmation means only one thing... I *am* going to kill Damon.

Clara squeals, and my quick charge to Damon comes to a dead stop when he lifts a gun I didn't notice he had until now and points it at Clara's head.

Clara freezes, her chest the only thing rising and falling as her massively dilated eyes lock with Damon's. When I take another step closer, Damon pulls back the hammer on the gun and curls his index finger around the trigger.

"I swear to God if you hurt her..." My words trail off as a wide range of ways I can kill him runs through my mind.

"I told them not to do it. I warned them your crew wouldn't stop until you found us, but they didn't listen. None of them listened to me! Why doesn't anyone listen to me?" His last sentence is only a whisper.

"I'm listening." I take a step closer. "But pointing a gun at someone to force them to listen won't get you heard. Put the gun down, then we'll talk."

Damon laughs a painful chuckle. "Like the *talking* your crew gave the other two men? They've pissed their pants the last two nights. That's how fucking scared they are that your crew will come back and finish what they started."

"This is different. You came to me. That changes everything."

"I came to see if you had any info on who the third man was. I didn't expect to have the door opened by the same face that haunts my dreams. Why is she here? You don't bring girls back to your place!"

"She's *my* girl, Damon. That is why she's here. And if you hurt her, we're going to have a problem. Is that what you want? Is that why you came back to Ravenshoe? To start trouble?"

Damon runs the back of his spare hand under his nose before using it to reinforce his brace on his gun. His hand is rattling so much, the gun is shaking like a leaf in a hot summer breeze. "I came here to get away from that life, but they followed me here. I didn't mean to hurt her. I don't want to hurt her."

"Then drop the gun." My voice hints at my wavering constraint. "Drop it before you make another mistake you can't take back."

It appears as if Damon didn't hear a word I spoke.

"How did you know it was me? I was wearing a mask," he asks with his gaze fixed on Clara.

Clara's lips quiver as she begins to speak, "I recognized your voice when you greeted Charity."

Fuck, Charity. I forgot she was here with Clara.

My heart rate climbs into dangerous territory, spurred on by the potent rage of fury blackening my blood. Just as I begin to ask about Charity's whereabouts, my eyes lock in on a pair of red leather boots sprawled on the floor between Damon and Clara. They're the same pair Charity has worn every day since she brought them two months ago.

I hold my hands out in front of my body, signaling to Damon that I mean him no harm as I slowly walk to Charity. Fury scorches my veins when I spot the welt on the top of her head. It looks like the mark a person would get when they're struck with the butt of a gun. I crouch down in front of her to check for a pulse. My heart starts beating again when I discover a pulse—it's faint, but it is there.

In a hazed blur, the front door of my apartment is kicked open at the same time Damon launches for Clara. He curls his arms around Clara's chest and plasters his body to her back. While holding his gun to Clara's right temple, he retreats deeper into my apartment. My fury hits a never-before-reached level when he uses her as a shield to protect himself from Ryan's gun.

Damon stares into his brother's eyes while declaring, "Drop your gun, or I'll shoot her." His voice is weak and pathetic like the man he is.

"If you don't let her go, I will shoot you," Ryan warns. "Don't make me shoot you, Damon. Don't put another death on my hands."

Clara's entire body shakes as her wide, horrified eyes drift between Ryan and me. New tears fill her eyes before spilling down her cheeks.

"Look at me, Princess. Keep your eyes on me," I request, my voice scratchy as a range of emotions surge through me. "You're okay. No one will hurt you."

I take a step closer to her as Ryan and Damon continue with their negotiations. I don't hear a word they're saying, I'm too fixated on calming Clara solely by using my eyes.

My ploy seems to be working as the shivers racking her body simmer to a dull vibration. She keeps her tear-filled eyes planted on me while Damon's remain glued on Ryan.

Using his distraction to my advantage, I charge for Damon. A gun being fired momentarily startles me, but it doesn't stop my pursuit. Ignoring the thick stench of fear plaguing the air surrounding me, I yank Clara out of Damon's grasp with one hand while striking his unprotected face with my other.

A bone cracking is barely audible over the deep "oomph" expelled from Clara's mouth when she lands on her backside with a sickening thud. Damon's eyes roll to the back of his head before he plummets to the concrete, his body crashing lifelessly to the floor, knocked out by one punch.

Bullets from the cylinder of his gun fall to my feet when I disarm it before sliding it into the back of my jeans. A massive surge of adrenaline pumps through my veins as I stoop down onto my knees to gather Clara into my arms. My pulse pounds into my ears as my eyes assess every inch of her. She's alarmed and highly distressed but uninjured. *Thank fuck.*

My gratefulness doesn't last long when Clara gasps, "Ryan!"

When I swing my eyes to the entryway of my apartment, a heaviness slams into my chest when I see a pool of blood seeping into Ryan's crisp white business shirt. His eyes lock with mine—they're lifeless and tormented. His gasps are wheezy and uncontrollable as he battles to secure a full breath. He mumbles the quickest apology, spraying his lips with droplets of vibrant red blood before he crumbles to the ground.

I scramble across the floor, ripping my shirt off in the process. Dropping to my knees, I wrap my shirt around my fist and apply pressure to the bullet wound in Ryan's stomach. "Stay with me, Ryan," I beg into his desolate eyes. He stares straight ahead, not blinking, not moving, not making a fucking sound. "Don't you fucking quit, Ryan. Don't you give up."

After using my cell phone I left on the floor to call for an ambulance, Clara falls to her knees next to Ryan. "What can I do?" she asks, her voice breaking into a sob.

"Hold this."

I release my hands from applying pressure to Ryan's wound and replace them with Clara's. The rattle of her hands is felt all the way up her arms, but she maintains enough pressure to slow the gushes of blood pouring from Ryan's stomach.

Fear grips my heart when I move my hand to Ryan's neck to check for a pulse and fail to find one. Acting purely on instinct, I begin the CPR resuscitation technique Ryder made all the Inked employees train in last year. I've never been more grateful for Ryder's analness for protocol as I am right now.

I continue to pump Ryan's chest when a brunette female wearing a sleek pantsuit enters my apartment. She has a government-issued gun drawn in front of her chest, and her dark brown eyes are scanning the room. When she discovers Damon sprawled unconscious on the floor, she balks and takes a step backward. "Ryan?"

"That is his brother, Damon." My words come out garbled as a range of emotions smack into me. "He shot Ryan. He shot his own fucking brother."

The brunette's eyes snap down to mine. She takes a few seconds to absorb the scene before she calls in a command over the police radio strapped to her shoulder. "We have a 10-71 at 1314 Coulson Avenue. Officer down. I repeat, officer down."

She moves over to check on Charity, who is slowly coming to while I continue pumping Ryan's chest. My heart is smashing my ribs, and tears are swamping my eyes, but I don't stop. I can't.

After helping Charity sit on one of my couches, the brunette drops to the floor next to me. "How long has he been unresponsive?"

"Five minutes," Clara responds on my behalf.

The brunette's eyes rocket to Clara, the shock on her face intensifying.

"Can you call Isaac? He will get the surgical team at Ravenshoe Private on standby," Clara requests to the unnamed police officer. "They may be Ryan's only chance."

The brunette curtly nods as her hand delves into the pocket of her black pants to retrieve her phone. Just as she begins talking into her cell, feet stomping booms through my ears, closely followed by the sight of two first responders.

"Thanks, we can take it from here," one officer advises me, replacing my hands pumping Ryan's chest with his own.

I take a stumbling step backward, landing on my ass a foot from

Ryan. As the paramedics work on his lifeless body, the realization of why Ryan feels guilt for Chris's death smashes into me. Ryan was the one who discovered Chris. He worked on him for over thirty minutes while waiting for the paramedics to arrive. Even after they officially pronounced Chris deceased, Ryan wouldn't give up. He only stopped pounding his chest when I dragged him away kicking and screaming. He didn't want to give up on Chris just like I don't want to give up on him.

Crawling across the small space between us, I bang my enclosed fist on Ryan's chest. "Come on, Ryan, fucking fight!" I roar, pounding on his chest over and over again. "You've never given up before, so don't start now!"

I pound, and pound, and pound his chest until I have nothing left to give. The stranglehold on my heart is crippling me, and my lungs refuse to secure an entire breath.

Feeling defeated, I slump to the floor, my heart beyond broken, my eyes full of tears.

I gave it my all, and I still failed.

Just as the first lot of tears escape my eyes, a ragged gasp booms through my ears. I run the back of my hand across my cheeks before lifting my eyes. Ryan's blue eyes are open and staring directly at me. They're haunted and brimmed with worry, but they're open, and that is the only thing that fucking matters.

Chapter Twenty-Six

Clara and I have spent the last two hours sitting in a little blue room at the Ravenshoe Private Hospital waiting for an update on Ryan's condition. Other than the nurse who came in to complete a set of observations on Clara, the room has been void of any other visitors.

Although Clara is clearly in shock, she refused to take the sedative offered by the nurse. Understandably, she wants to remain lucid until we receive an update on Ryan. Charity received four stitches to the welt on her head. With a prescription for a heavy sedative and pain medication, Diesel and Johnny took her home. Although she was adamant she was fine, I didn't feel comfortable leaving her alone.

Plain-clothed detectives and police officers have lined the corridor throughout the past two hours, but surprisingly, none have requested statements from Clara or me. Their priorities also remain focused on Ryan and not police protocol.

When another shiver racks through Clara's body, I sling my arm around her shoulders and pull her into my lap.

Twenty minutes later, our heads lift in sync when a creak of a door sounds through the quiet passing between us. The beat of my heart turns crazy when a small Asian doctor with a crisp white coat enters the room. Her inky black hair is pulled off her face in a twisted design, and her lovely green eyes are issuing silent sympathies.

I stand from my chair, taking Clara with me. We stare at the doctor, blinking and muted, but I release a deep sigh when she says, "He's okay." Clara squeezes my hand tightly while the doctor continues talking, "He was fortunate he had you both there. The amount of blood he was losing would have seen him hemorrhaging within minutes. By applying pressure to the wound and keeping his heart pumping, you saved his life." Her eyes drift between Clara and me. "Both of you. He has a long way to go, but he's doing remarkably well."

The doctor accepts my offer of a handshake before she runs her tiny hand down Clara's forearm. The instant she steps back into the corridor, Clara collapses to the floor. Tears roll down her cheeks as a devastating sob tears from her throat. "It's my fault. It's all my fault," she cries through a barrage of hiccups.

After gathering her in my arms, I stride to the chair I've been sitting on for the past two hours. Carefully, I pull her back and peer into her red-rimmed eyes. "This is not your fault."

"I should have taken off my jewelry. I should have listened to you."

"You shouldn't have had to listen to me. You should be able to wear anything you want. This is not your fault."

"But—"

"No, Princess. No buts. Damon pulled the trigger. Damon shot his brother. You did nothing wrong." I cup her cheeks in my hands and run my thumbs under her eyes, catching her tears. "This is not your fault."

She looks like she wants to push the issue further, but thankfully, she leaves it as is, nuzzling into the crook of my neck.

I don't know how long we stay huddled together, but it is long enough that the watermarks Clara's tears created on my shirt have dried, and she has fallen asleep nestled into my chest. Even though my ass is dead from the rock-hard chair, I refuse to move. Not just because I don't want to wake her but because comforting her is helping heal some of the cracks that chipped my heart tonight. Her touch soothes me in a way no words can.

My eyes lift from Clara when the main door of the waiting room swings open. I'm not surprised but more apprehensive when Cormack hesitantly enters the room. His eyes are restless, and his composure is distraught. The crisp dark blue suit he was wearing earlier today is disheveled, and his hair is messy like he has been running his fingers through it regularly.

The smell of expensive cologne filters through my nose when he crouches down in front of me. Sensing another presence in the room, Clara's head pops off my chest. She inhales a quick, jagged breath as her eyes glance at her brother's remorse-filled gaze.

Launching out of my lap, she wraps her arms around Cormack's neck. Cormack draws her in close before standing from his squatted position. He mutters into her ear, but he's so quiet, I can't hear a word spilling from his lips.

I give them a few moments of privacy by stepping into the corridor. Warmth spreads across my chest when I discover the number of off-duty police officers lining the walls of the ICU hallway. It is a sea of law enforcement officers for as far as my eyes can see.

I shouldn't have expected any different. Ryan is a much-loved member of the entire Ravenshoe community, let alone his law enforcement colleagues.

Ten minutes later, my neck cranks to the side when the visiting room door opens, and Cormack strides through. Spotting me standing to the side, he raises his index finger to a gentleman wearing a three-piece suit standing at the end of the corridor. When the dark-haired man curtly nods, Cormack spans the distance between us.

"Thank you for taking care of Clara," he says, holding his hand out in offering. "I'll take it from here."

I keep my hands fisted at my side. It isn't that I'm ungrateful for his praise, but he said it like I was paid to take care of Clara instead of doing it of my own free will.

"I didn't take care of Clara because she's a member of my crew. I took care of her because I wanted to." My angry sneer gains us the attention of a handful of officers in the hallway.

"I understand," Cormack replies, gently nodding. "But she needs more care than you can give her right now. She's in shock. She needs to see a doctor, take a shower, and eat a warm meal."

"I can give her that. You don't need to step in."

Cormack's icy-blue eyes spear into mine. "Can you take care of Clara and Ryan at the same time?"

A dash of indecisiveness tinges my mind.

"That's what I thought," Cormack replies, reading my internal dialogue. "If you care for Clara like you say you do, you will encourage her to come with me. A hospital waiting room isn't the best place for her to be in her condition."

While scraping my hand along the scruff on my jaw, I turn my eyes to Clara. She's sitting on the hard plastic chairs that line the walls of the waiting room. Her posture is slumped, her face is gaunt, and she looks both physically and mentally exhausted.

I swallow the bile sitting at the back of my throat before muttering, "If I step back, will you call a truce with Clara? Stop this stupid *lesson* you were supposed to be teaching her?" I try to keep my tone neutral, but my words still come out in a vicious snarl.

Cormack's lips tug into an uneasy smirk before he nods. "Yes. You have my word."

"Your word don't mean shit to me." I take a step closer to him. "The fact you sat back and watched all the crap Clara went through the past four months and did nothing doesn't even make you a man in my eyes. Let alone a man of his word."

"Everything I did, I did for Clara. You may think it was cruel and unwarranted, but you should be thanking me. The Clara you see in there..." he points to his sister's slumped figure sitting in the waiting room, "... isn't the same Clara she was six months ago. My tactics may have been harsh, but they were necessary."

I hate to admit this, but part of what he's saying is true. Not the part about Clara not being the same Clara she was six months ago. To me, she will always be the same Clara. She just needed to be shown she deserves to be loved. My agreement is the part I should be thanking him for. If he hadn't forced Clara out of her comfort zone, she would have never walked back into my life.

For that, I will forever be in his debt.

Ignoring the twisting of my heart, I say, "Give me a few minutes to talk to her."

Not waiting for Cormack to reply, I walk into the waiting room. Clara's downcast head lifts from staring at the floor when the door gives out a slight creak.

"Is Ryan okay?" she asks, wrongly intuiting the forlorn look on my face as concern for Ryan. The tightness in her shoulders slackens when I nod.

"Do you have your purse with you?"

She nods while slipping her hand into the front pocket of her blood-stained jeans to produce her all-in-one cell phone purse. I've been so embroiled in everything happening, I didn't even notice we're both wearing blood-stained clothes. That just proves what Cormack said is true. I can barely take care of myself right now, let alone Clara.

"Do you want me to have your luggage dropped off, or will someone from Cormack's staff come and collect it?"

Clara's brows stitch as she stares at me, shocked and dazed.

"Cormack is going to take you home," I advise her baffled expression.

"To your apartment?" she queries, her voice high and laced with worry.

I shake my head. "He's taking you home, Princess. To the side of Ravenshoe where you belong."

"I thought... I thought you said I was staying with you until all this blew over?"

Her confusion intensifies when I shake my head. "I said you were staying with me until the men who mugged you were held account-able. That has happened, so there's no reason for you to stay with me anymore." My words come out strangled since I had to fight my mouth to relinquish them.

"You don't want me to stay with you?" Although she could mean staying with me at the hospital, her eyes aren't relaying that.

"No. I don't." Pain hits the middle of my chest the instant the words seep from my lips.

Clara glares into my eyes, searching for any untruth in them. The only reason she fails to detect any is because deep down, I knew this day would eventually come, I just never wanted to believe it. But by manning up and stepping away from the plate I've been guarding the past four months, Clara's silver spoon will find its way back into her mouth, and she won't have to keep fighting the struggle she's been battling the past four months.

I care enough about her that I'm willing to give her up to ensure she's safe and taken care of.

Clara's lips twitch, dying to speak, but not a word spills from her mouth. Her confused eyes dart to the door when it flings open and Cormack steps into the room.

Releasing a deep breath, she turns her eyes back to me. "Are you sure this is what you want?"

It kills me, but I nod.

She gives it her best fight to hold in her hurt, but a rogue tear rolls down her cheek before she mutters, "Okay. Goodbye, Brax," before making a beeline for the door, exiting without a backward glance.

Chapter Twenty-Seven

It is a little after three in the morning before I'm striding toward the automatic double doors of the hospital. I'm beat—both mentally and physically. Ryan was in surgery for a little over three hours. After spending the next four hours in recovery, he was wheeled into a double private suite in the Intensive Care Unit. Although he was awake, he was barely lucid. But, thankfully, even with his words slurred worse than the weekend Chris and I spiked his cans of Coke with vodka, his doctor assured me he will have a full recovery.

Even being informed Ryan will have no long-term health issues from his bullet wound, the sick, twisted feeling in my stomach hasn't lessened in the slightest. I haven't been able to shake off the guilt I feel for hurting Clara. I spent the last forty-eight hours renewing the spark of life her eyes lost when she was mugged all to snuff it out by lying to her face. I know stepping back is the best thing I can do for her, but it doesn't make it any easier to do. It took all my strength—*and then some*—to keep my feet planted on the floor when she bolted out of the hospital waiting room. If it weren't for a uniformed officer arriving to take my statement, I have no doubt my fight would have been lost.

My brows become lost in my hairline when I stride out of the double doors of the hospital to discover my bike is still parked in the emergency vehicle only bay I had left it in hours ago. I already have my cell in my hand, prepared to call a taxi as I had expected it to be towed by now.

Shrugging off my confusion, I make my way to my bike.

* * *

I'm walking into my apartment twenty minutes later. The heaviness that has been sitting on my chest for the past eight hours amplifies when my eyes zoom in on the puddle of blood in my entryway. Just seeing how much blood Ryan lost makes the reality of the situation crash into me.

I nearly lost him today.

He almost died protecting the woman I love, and I thank him by pushing her away from me.

I'm a fucking idiot.

Call me a pussy, a soft-cock, or any other derogative name you like, but I'm not going to lie, tears are inundating my eyes and threatening to spill down my face at any moment. Ryan is the closest thing to a brother I have. He's my family. That is why it is even more devastating that his own brother shot him.

I don't know what is going on in Damon's life, but it must be pretty fucked-up if he thought his only way out was to harm his brother. And if all that wasn't already enough to have my mood hitting an all-time-low, knowing the gun that shot Ryan was pointed at Clara's head only seconds earlier utterly destroys me. Her frightened face when Damon held his gun to her head will forever haunt my dreams.

Ignoring the pit forming in my gut, I drag a bucket and mop out of my laundry room to clean up Ryan's blood that's soaking into my wooden floor. I run the back of my hand over my cheek, angrily removing a stupid tear that escaped my overfilled eyes before clearing away the mess.

Just as I've finished mopping up Ryan's blood, tiny feet padding down my staircase jingles through my ears. When I crank my neck to the stairs, I recoil and take a step backward.

"Princess?" I ask, certain I'm seeing things. I haven't slept, eaten, or had a clear thought in well over ten hours, so a stint of insanity could be surfacing.

Clara glides across the living area wearing nothing but one of my plain white short-sleeved T-shirts. Her hair is damp and hanging loosely, her eyes are brimming with tears, and her face is void of makeup. The only difference between the Clara who left the hospital hours ago and the one standing before me is this Clara's eyes are sparked with the gleam I thought I snuffed. They're bright, determined, and one hundred percent relaying she's not leaving this apartment until she gets what she came here for.

"What are you doing here, Princess?"

The smell of freshly shampooed hair overtakes the ghastly scent of blood when Clara stops to stand in front of me. "I wanted to clean that up before you came home, but, in all honesty, I didn't know how." Her nose screws up, and she looks genuinely mortified that she doesn't know how to use a mop and bucket.

The most inappropriately timed chuckle escapes from my lips. *Yes, I've definitely hit the insanity stage of my anguish.* I can't help it, though. Clara's statement abundantly proves she's a real-life princess. *No fucking doubt.*

Ignoring my erratic behavior, Clara removes the mop from my hand, places it into the bucket, and stores it back in the laundry room. Not speaking a peep, she encloses her hand over mine and guides me to the staircase to my loft bedroom.

"What are you doing here, Princess?" I ask again, my voice relaying my disbelief.

Clara continues walking while muttering, "You're in shock." She stops pacing when we reach the base of the stairs. "You're shaking and shit. So, unless you can give me the address of a family member or friend I can take you to, I'm staying with you. I'm going to take care of you."

I arch my brow. "You want to take care of me? That's why you're here?"

She nods without hesitation before locking her determined eyes with mine.

"Why?"

"Because that's what a woman does for the man she's falling in love with. You look out for them, even when they don't want you to," she answers, her truth-bearing eyes adding strength to her statement.

The massive weight sitting on my chest vanishes in an instant. She has no idea how much I needed to hear that right now. I was barely hanging on by a thread, and she just lassoed a rope around my waist and pulled me back in.

I knew I wasn't the only one falling.

"I want you here, Princess, more than anything, but what about your silver spoon?"

She shrugs. "What about it? I have food in my belly, a roof over my head, and clothes on my back. What more do I need than that?" She rakes her eyes over the length of my body. "Well, there's one other thing I need. But, lucky for me, it's free." Her arctic-blue eyes stare into mine as she climbs the spiral staircase. "And lucky for you, I don't have any concerns about messing with a member of my crew while they're in shock."

Keeping my eyes locked on her, I shadow her into my bedroom. My heart is beating a million miles an hour, but my mind is the clearest it's ever been.

Her gorgeous scent filters through my nose when her hands move to the hem of my blood-stained shirt to yank it over my head. She works on the belt of my jeans as she guides us across the room. Once the fastener has been unbuckled, she slides my jeans down my thighs. My cock twitches when she lifts her hankering gaze to me. Her eyes relay her intentions without a word needing to seep from her lips.

"Princesses don't kneel for no one," I mutter, my deep tone conveying my wavering constraint.

She sighs softly. "I want to take care of you, Brax, to make you forget the image you should have never seen."

Who the fuck is this woman? She just saw straight through me. Only one other woman has been able to do that. My grandma.

I cup the edge of Clara's jaw and peer into her shimmering eyes. "Just you being here is already doing that, Princess. You don't need to kneel before me."

My cock leaps in my briefs when I catch sight of the determination brewing in her gaze. "Get on the bed, Brax," she demands, her voice throaty and ball-tingling sweet.

I arch my brow, feigning shock, but in reality, I'm loving the feisty spark brightening her eyes. There's nothing as captivating as a princess in battle.

Clara watches my every move as I make my way to the bed and sit on top.

"Do you have any objections to me kneeling above you?"

The thickness of my cock grows as does the vibrancy in her gaze when I shake my head. My eyes drink her in as she slowly prances my way, her hips swinging, her chest panting. A brief chuckle rumbles from my mouth when she pushes on my bare torso, sending me toppling onto the mattress.

My laughter comes to a screaming halt when she climbs onto the bed and frees my cock from the tight restraints of my briefs in one quick motion like a woman starved of my taste, then time comes to a standstill when her lips hover over the glistening crown of my rock-hard cock.

After rolling her tongue over the crest of my stiffened shaft—gathering a drop of pre-cum beading on the end—she bores her full-of-life eyes into mine. Tonight, they're so readable. They not only expose fragments of her personality I've yet to witness they also reveal she isn't just offering me her body she's offering me her heart.

I'd be lying if I said I wasn't as happy as a pig in mud to accept her offer.

Epilogue

Six Months Later...

My head lifts from a sketch I've been working on for the past eight weeks when a set of knuckles rap on the wooden door of my office. Diesel props his shoulder onto the wall before locking his hazel eyes with me. "We have a client out front requesting to speak to the manager," he advises, his tone gruff.

I arch my brow and glare into his eyes.

"Don't even fucking ask," he mutters to my questioning expression.

I push back from my desk and stand from my chair. After gesturing to Diesel to lead the way, I shadow him down the corridor of Inked. Charity smiles a greeting before gesturing her head to the gang-related tattoo she's placing on some young punk's rake-thin bicep. I run my fingers over the top of my scalp and shake my head. Although we haven't had any more incidents occur at Inked the past six months, we've noticed an increase in gang-related tattoos.

Doing our bit for society, my crew inks the tattoo as requested by the client, takes a copy of the design, then sends the client on their merry way. What our customers don't know is that once they sit in a chair at Inked, they relinquish the rights to their tattoo design.

Any tattoo we believe to be gang-related is uploaded to a private server Hunter created specifically for Inked. If a gang-related crime occurs within the vicinity of Ravenshoe, we can scan the tattoo references into our database. If a compelling match is found, our information is handed to the Ravenshoe Police Department.

Although it may seem deceitful to our clients, I don't give a flying fuck. Women like Clara should be able to enter a back alley without fear of being jumped. Until that happens, I will continue my endeavor to clean up the streets of Ravenshoe.

When I enter the foyer of Inked, I swing my eyes around the room. A broad grin stretches across my face when my eyes lock in on a feisty blonde going toe-to-toe with another attractive female.

My cock jumps, spurred on by Clara's strong stance.

I've always loved a woman who gives a bit of lip, let alone a fiery-tongued princess.

Things between Clara and I have been staggering this past six months. Although Cormack kept his word by giving Clara back her silver spoon, nothing between Clara and me changed in the slightest. She still lives with me in my loft apartment, she still works at Inked, and she still continues to shock me every single day. The only thing that has changed is that I'm no longer falling in love with Clara. I love her. No doubts. No limits. One hundred percent fucking gone.

So does my grandma.

Although if she keeps nagging Clara for grandbabies, she may see a side to Clara she has not yet had the pleasure of witnessing.

I've not yet found Clara's necklace, but I won't give up until I do. I keep in regular contact with the pawnbrokers servicing the Ravenshoe area, and I called in a few favors so I have ears close to the ground throughout the entire state. When it surfaces, I have no doubt I'll be the first to hear about it.

Ryan's recovery, although rocky, is complete. His relationship with his brother... well, that's a whole other story. Unfortunately, Sophia's recovery is still a slow process. She continues to make advancements, but it doesn't appear that her level of care will be changing anytime in the future.

After giving myself a few minutes to absorb the beauty of Clara in her element, I make my way across the room. Her rich floral scent stirs my cock when I stop to stand next to her. "I heard someone needed to speak to the manager."

The petite blonde with a pixie-style haircut and piercing blue eyes shifts her gaze to me. "Yes. Becau—"

Clara shoves her hand in front of the blonde's face, stopping her midsentence. "We don't need the manager. We just need someone to give this *idiot* a hearing test. No matter how many times I tell her she will *not* be served at Inked this evening, this *moron* doesn't seem to understand what I'm telling her."

I sling my arms around Clara's waist, being cautious not to touch the newly inked skin on her hip and pull her in close to my side. "What have I told you about insulting the customers?"

Clara's icy-blue eyes blaze into mine. "I wouldn't need to insult her if she weren't *stupid,*" she says loud enough to ensure the blonde can hear.

The unnamed blonde's mouth hangs open. Shock is all over her face. My cock firms when Clara maintains her ground, not the slightest bit intimidated by the vicious snarl the blonde has bestowed upon her. Keeping her eyes locked with me, Clara hands me a sheet of paper. "If you tell me this isn't a design only a *stupid* person would have inked on their skin, I'll apologize."

I drop my eyes to the sheet of paper. A grin curls on my lips when the reasoning for Clara's fighting stance becomes apparent. Not only is this tattoo hideous and overly floral, but it also has a name in thick red ink smack bang in the middle of it.

"I've explained on numerous occasions the repercussion of having a person's name inked on your skin, but no matter how many times I spell it out to her, she isn't listening," Clara advises me. "There's no cure for idiocy."

She spent four hours earlier this week in my tattoo chair having her princess tattoo covered with a new tat I designed for her. I had been working on the design from the day she stormed out of Inked rambling that she would sue me for every penny I had. Although the design was finished before she started working at Inked, I never showed it to her, worried I was exposing my hand too early, but in all honesty, even if I had shown her the tattoo, it wouldn't have changed a thing. Clara has had me over a barrel from the day I met her. She knew it and so did my cock. It just took me a little longer to submit to the idea.

It was my tattoo design that brought us back together. It was the sole reason Clara was waiting for me at my apartment the night Ryan was shot. After nursing me through my shock by using only her body, Clara admitted she found it while packing her belongings through a haze of tears. I've never been more grateful for my inability to leave work at work as I was that night.

I give Clara a cocky wink before turning my eyes to the unnamed blonde. "Is this your father's name?"

The blonde places her tiny hands on her even smaller hips before shaking her head.

"Your grandfather? Brother? Deceased uncle? Any type of male relation?" I query while staring into her squinted eyes. When she once again shakes her head, I say, "I'm sorry, sweetheart, I can't do your tattoo."

"Oh, come on. Not even for a family member?"

I chuckle a hearty laugh. "Nice try, but I don't have any siblings."

The blonde scrunches her brows together. "Not your sibling. Hers." She hooks her thumb to Clara.

I drift my eyes between Clara and the unnamed blonde. Now that I've managed to drag my eyes away from Clara's mouthwatering curves, I can notice a lot of similarities between them. Same wintry-blue eyes, platinum-blonde hair, and flawless skin. The only difference is their personalities. This blonde is a little firecracker about to explode at any moment, whereas Clara is full of class and elegance, even when she's dishing out insults like they're grenades.

"Cate-with-a-C McGregor," the blonde introduces, holding her hand out in offering. "This ice queen's baby sister."

Clara rolls her eyes at Cate's snide comment but surprisingly, doesn't react to her taunt.

I accept her handshake. "Brax."

"So you're the famous Brax I've been hearing about. The man who thawed Clara's heart. What do you have? A magic heart-thawing penis?" Cate replies while indecently raking her eyes over my body.

This time, Clara reacts. If I hadn't tightened my grip on her waist, I have no doubt she would have leaped over the counter and strangled her sister.

My cock hardens more. Fiery Clara is beautiful, but jealous Clara... she's downright out-of-this-mother-fucking-universe beautiful.

Since I have a firm hold on Clara's waist, she issues her retaliation in another form. "I think you should do her tattoo, Brax." Her tone is sugary sweet, a huge contradiction to her earlier one.

I gawk at her, shocked and confused.

Clara playfully winks before turning her eyes to Cate. "If you're willing to make a few changes to your tattoo design, I think I can convince Brax to do it."

Cate eagerly nods. "Sure. I'm happy to make any changes necessary." She connects her lively eyes with mine. "Do anything you need to make this happen."

"Great," Clara exclaims excitedly as she yanks a tattoo contract out of the top drawer in front of her. I bite the inside of my cheek, fighting my hardest battle to hold in my smile when Clara slaps the contract onto the glass counter, hands Cate a pen, then says, "Just sign here, here, and here."

* * *

The next book in the Enigma Series is about Enrique Popov, son of Vladimir Popov and brother of Isabelle. *I Married a Mob Boss* is already published.

Facebook: facebook.com/authorshandi

Instagram: instagram.com/authorshandi

Email: authorshandi@gmail.com

Reader's Group: bit.ly/ShandiBookBabes

Website: authorshandi.com

Newsletter: https://www.subscribepage.com/AuthorShandi

Hunter, Hugo, Cormack, Hawke, Ryan, Rico, Brax, Brandon, Regan, and all the other great characters of Ravenshoe have their stories, and all of them are published.

If you enjoyed this book, please leave a review.

Part One

I Married a Mob Boss

Chapter One

A ragged gasp escapes my lips as I springboard into a half-seated position. While my hands dart up to rub the stabbing pain rocketing through my temples, I suck in large gulps of air, hopeful it will calm the panic scorching me from the inside out.

Goose bumps prickle my sweat-slicked skin when the coolness of air conditioning glides over my body.

Pure agony.

Gut-wrenching hell.

I'd rather die than open my eyelids is how I feel right now.

Someone, please tell me why the National School Board would ever think holding their annual conference in Las Vegas was a good idea. I swear, I only had a couple of drinks, at the very most a few, but there's no way I drank enough to suffer the side effects of a tunnel hole digger drilling through my skull.

I thought waking up the morning following my twenty-first birthday was wretched.

This is ten times worse.

After taking a few minutes to calm my pounding head, I reluctantly open my drooping eyelids. My lips quirk when I drink in my elaborate room. For a school district that can't afford to buy kindergarten students coloring pencils, the hotel they booked is extravagant. Monstrous vaulted ceilings, white wood-paneled walls, gorgeous dark wood furniture, and one of the largest beds I've ever seen confront me.

As I slide across the pristinely crisp three-thousand thread count sheets, another confronting fact dawns on me. I'm naked. Not slightly nude. Naked-*naked*.

Oh, Lord, what did I do?

I swing my eyes around the room while my sluggish brain struggles to gather my bearings. My heart wildly beats, matching the thumping twinge between my legs when the typical Vegas lifestyle reflects back at me. Casino chips line the highly varnished wooden floor, my clothes are strewn from the door to the bed, and black polished dress shoes sit at the edge of a mattress that smells of hot, raunchy sex.

Nothing out of the ordinary here.

Not a single thing...

Wait a minute... black polished dress shoes?

After scampering off the bed, I fall to my knees next to the shoes. I assess them carefully like they're a bomb set to detonate in two point five seconds. The soles are well-scuffed, but the leather on the size thirteen shoes is so thoroughly polished I can see my disheveled appearance in them.

I cringe after taking in the travesty.

I don't recall using a spatula to apply my makeup last night.

Ignoring the fact I look like I've returned from a moonlighting job, I continue inspecting the shoes, seeking any sign of who their owner may be.

"Like grown men write their name on the soles of their shoes, Blaire," I mumble to myself.

Upon finding no signs of ownership, I stand from my kneeled position then drift my eyes around the vast space.

A silent squeal ripples from my parched mouth when a door creaking open booms through my ears not even two seconds later. I dive for the bed, only just making it beneath the scrumptiously thick covers when a female with a heavily wrinkled face enters my room.

While grumbling in a slurred accent, she retrieves my clothing from the floor and tosses it into a woven basket balancing on her ample hip.

"Oh... umm... excuse me. I didn't order housekeeping," I strangle out, my voice weak with embarrassment.

When the elderly lady's narrowed gaze connects with my light green eyes, I sink deeper into the mattress. Her nearly black gaze is fierce, and it has my heart pumping. "You no want me to clean your room?" From the depth of her accent and poor wording, it's easy for me to derive her first language isn't English.

After peeking my head out of the sheet I'm clutching for dear life, I shake my head.

"You want to live like pig?" Her words are spat out of her mouth in a malicious slur, right alongside some real-life spit.

Now I need housekeeping.

While muttering in a language I'm not familiar with, the silver-haired female scuffles to the door. I'm eager for her to leave, but she can't just yet.

I hold my hand in the air like my kindergarten students do when seeking my attention. When my efforts to secure her attention fail, I say, "Umm... excuse me." My voice is low, hindered by the pounding of my hungover head.

The elderly lady's cotton skirt flares out when she spins around to face me. "Yes?"

The longer she stares at me, the more my heart palpitates. "Ah... I'm going to need my clothes." I point to the clothes she collected off the floor. "Unless you can get the concierge to bring up my suitcase?"

She glares at me with flaring nostrils and protruding veins in her chunky neck. "Concierge?" When I nod, she spits out, "You want *concierge* to bring your bag to your room?"

I arch my brow, shocked by the maliciousness in her tone, before nodding again. "Please?"

She smiles. It isn't a friendly grin. It is scary and life-threatening. "I'll be sure to ask *concierge* to bring up your bag," she says in a thick, heavily drawled accent.

"T-thank you."

The crazy beat of my heart weakens when she places the basket onto an antique dresser sitting by the door. After issuing me a final reprimand solely using her eyes, she exits the room. The instant the latch on the door lock clicks into place, I slip out of bed and make a mad dash for the door.

Since my bare feet can't grip the overly polished floor, I crash into the door with an almighty thud. The winded rattle of my brutal blow bellows up my heaving chest before leaving my mouth with a huff.

After brushing an unruly strand of hair off my cheek, I secure the lock on the door, snag my clothing out of the basket, then make a beeline for the only other door in the room.

My quick speed slows to a snail's pace when I walk into an extravagant bathroom. I scan my eyes around the room, drinking in the black marble countertops, artisan glass sinks, and a ginormous clawfoot tub.

If I weren't concerned about receiving another visit from the Wicked Witch of the West, I'd be tempted to drown my hangover in that heavenly-looking tub. But since that is more a hope than a certainty, I ignore the pleas of my aching muscles and head for the double vanity to splash some cold water on my inflamed face instead.

Confusion muddles my brain when sunshine bounces off my blonde locks. If the brightness beaming through the rooftop window is any indication, I only have mere hours until my scheduled flight home.

My first visit to Vegas was planned as a fly-in-and-out one-night affair. My odds of winning Teacher of the Year were small, but the privilege of being nominated saw me cashing in my parents' frequent flyer miles for a whirlwind weekend.

From the swirling of my stomach and thumping of my head,

whirlwind is an extremely adequate word to describe my once-in-a-lifetime solo getaway.

While clutching the sparkling marble counter, I drag my heavy eyes over my reflection in the mirrored wall behind the vanity, eager to discover what has caused my muscles to be taut with the odd combination of agony and pleasure.

Deciding to start my assessment at a less risqué part of my body, I drop my eyes to my pastel yellow-painted toes. The fiery heat gifting my face with a pink hue hasn't extended to the lower extremities of my body. Other than my legs being bronzed with the effects of a desert sun, the lower half of my body is in the same condition it was before I arrived in Vegas.

I munch on my bottom lip while continuing my in-depth perusal. My scan doesn't get far, stopping mere inches from the lower half of my body when my eyes lock in on an accessory I didn't have Friday night.

Oh, sweet Jesus. What in the Lord's name is that?

As I stumble backward, I scrub my hand over the thick black ink scrawled across the curve of my right hip. My heart rate surges into dangerous territory as I scrub, scratch, and scour my skin.

Even with my hip on the verge of bleeding, nothing works.

The four-letter word scrawled across my skin won't budge.

"Who the hell is Rico? And why is his name tattooed on my hip?" I mumble to my wide-eyed reflection.

After planting my backside on the edge of a black marble tub, I bury my head in my hands. This is not me. I'm the safe friend. The good girl. I'm a kindergarten teacher, for crying out loud! I don't go to Vegas and get a man's name tattooed on my hip. I grade papers, hunt garage sales every Sunday for low-cost books for my students, and knit booties for the babies in the NICU at my local hospital. I don't get drunk and most definitely do *not* get tattoos.

Maybe I'm dreaming, and I haven't arrived at Vegas yet? Maybe those sleeping tablets I guzzled down with a wine spritzer while squeezed between a man whose body odor smelled like a cat's food bowl and the lady who had an extra toe are messing with my mind.

Yes! That makes perfect sense. This is all just a big bad dream.

Ouch!

Nope, I'm not sleeping.

Rubbing my leg, I soothe the sting of my nasty pinch while I struggle to unscramble the confusion muddling my brain.

Minutes pass in silence as nothing but a sea of blackness greets me. There's one thing my over-fried brain can decipher—I need to get out of here.

After yanking my knee-length floral skirt up my thighs, I fasten my cotton push-up bra around my back. My movements are unsteady, inhibited by my thumping skull. Once I snag my dusty pink cotton blouse off the vanity, I sling it around my shoulders, then run my fingers through my ratted hair. The number of knots in my hair gives my usually straight design a bolder, much more risqué look.

"Ha! Who are you trying to kid? You look like you've just arrived home after starring in an eighties music clip for Bruce Springsteen," I mumble to my disheveled reflection.

While pretending I didn't wear any panties yesterday, I make my way back to the main part of my suite. The elderly maid found my clothes with ease since they were left where they fell, but my shoes are proving to be quite the challenge.

After searching every inch of the floor space, I drop to my knees and crawl under the bed. I inwardly gag when I find a strip of condoms stuck to the satin bed ruffle. My pounding temples drop to a lower region of my body when I notice the three-strip of bare-skinned condoms is empty, then my heart rate kicks when the quickest memory filters through my brain.

I ripped open one of those condoms with my teeth while... while... *darn it!* My memories have converted back to black.

I flick the used condom packaging to the side before stretching my arm to reach for my orthopedic sandal wedged in the furthermost corner. Don't judge. Have you ever walked the entire strip of Vegas before? I did for three hours solid!

Comfortable shoes are not a recommendation.

They are a necessity.

I freeze before sucking in a big breath. That was my first recollection of arriving in Vegas. Other than recalling portions of the plane ride over, my memories of the last twenty-four hours are best described as hazy.

After snatching my second sandal from its hiding spot in the middle of the enormous bed, I fasten them to my feet then head for the door. Hazy memories, drunken mistakes, and googling how to have a tattoo removed without your parents finding out can wait until my feet are safely back on my home turf of Ravenshoe.

While exhaling a nerve-cleansing breath, I push down on the gold embossed handle and swing open the door. My brows hit my hairline when a second bout of elegance smacks into me. However, for an elegant hotel, they have a laid-back approach to security. None of the rooms have the swipe locks most hotel chains have, and not a peephole can be seen.

The more I take in the chandeliered hall, the more my heart restricts.

This isn't a hotel, is it?

Dammit!

My feet pad along the chunky woolen rug in silence as I make my way down the hallway. Renaissance paintings line the walls, and the aroma of garlic lingers in the air. The pounding of my pulse in my ears reaches deafening status when I hit the end of the hall. Two men with shoulders as wide as my height are standing at the stoop of the stairwell, talking to each other in a foreign language.

"Hello," I squeak out when my approach stifles their conversation.

While snubbing their imprudent stares, I race down the stairwell. The gallop of my heart matches the stomping of my feet as I charge through the massive unknown residence. My tornado pace comes to a shrieking halt when a handful of women suddenly bombard me only seconds later. Lace and satin materials are shoved in my face as they fire a range of questions at me.

Well, I'm assuming they are questions because I don't understand a word they're saying.

Their approach reminds me of my backpacking adventures in Bali, Indonesia. If you haven't experienced the craziness of a street market in Bali, you haven't lived. It's the equivalent of shopping at Walmart high on crack.

That's another assumption, as I've never touched a drug in my life.

Not understanding a word the ladies are flinging at me, I spin on my heels and scuffle down a dark and dingy corridor on my right. Their hair-raising battering is left for dust when I creep deeper into the hall. My stomach gurgles when the women stop at the end of the hall and eyeball me with a snick of panic in their eyes.

Anyone would swear I just entered the gates of hell.

Taking no notice of their odd reaction—*and my brain pulverizing my skull*—I continue striding down the dark, dingy hall. Just like the hallway my room is in, this corridor is lined with doors, but unlike that hall, this corridor isn't elaborately decorated, and these rooms have locks—big clunky deadbolt locks.

I stop dead in my tracks and furrow my brows. *Why would there be locks on the outside of the doors?*

Oh, God.

My retreating steps out of the stuffy space halt when the faint murmur of voices tinkle down the bland corridor. When I slant my head to the side, I level my breathing and prick my ears. My regular breathing pattern returns when the distinct noise of men talking sounds into my ears.

Pretending the twisted feeling in my stomach is from my raging hangover drilling my skull into the next century and not fear, I pace toward the collection of deep, masculine voices. The swirling of my stomach eases when I catch the occasional sentence spoken in English between the heavily accented voices.

"If you just give me a chance..."

"As I said earlier..."

"It wasn't as your men are saying..."

After stopping outside the door the voices are coming from, I inhale a deep, calming breath. *"You can do this, Blaire,"* I chant to myself.

I clutch the handle for dear life before throwing open the heavily weighted door.

Just as it gives out a creak, pleading pummels my eardrums. "Please. No. I'm begging you. I have children. Small, precious little children."

Chapter Two

With my heart clutched in fear, I float my eyes up from my feet. Men in midnight-colored suits are huddled around something in the middle of a poorly lit room. Just like the men in the hallway, they're tall, wide, and their snarling faces set my pulse racing.

I take a stumbling step backward when black smoke loiters through my nose. It burns my eyes and suffocates my throat. I try to hold in the cough the thick waft of smoke instigates. I try to smother it until I'm in the safety of the hall, but no matter how much I plead with my brain that now is not the time to protest about the disgusting habit of smoking, my efforts are fruitless.

The instant my measly cough splatters through my snapped-shut lips, the group of men shift their attention to me. I take another retreating step, alarmed by their fuming glares, and dread-induced chemicals pump through my body when my eyes zoom in on their original devotion.

A balding man in his mid-fifties is bound to a rickety chair in the middle of the room. A nasty gash across his right brow is trickling blood down his pale cheek, his eyes are wide and terrorized, and a wet patch goes from the crotch of his dark blue trousers until it joins a puddle sloshed around his shoeless and bloodied feet.

My pupils widen as my heart drops from my ribcage. I beg for my feet to move, but just like the man bound to the chair, I'm frozen in fear. The only remaining functioning part of my body—my eyes—swing to the side when a deep, rumbling voice vibrates through my chest. "Kitten?"

My head thumps for a completely different reason when my wide gaze is met with a dark, mysterious stranger sitting in the corner of the room. He has thick black hair, bleak sable eyes, and a few days of stubble hiding his well-carved chin.

If I weren't currently immersed in a scary rendition of *The Godfather*, I would say he is handsome—perhaps even deliriously gorgeous—but since I'm on the verge of peeing my pants like the man bound to the chair, I harness my perving gaze for a more suitable occasion.

My pulse quickens when the dark-haired stranger stands from his chair. His aura demands my attention, and his stature alludes to his power. Even in a room filled with scary men, there's no doubt who the alpha of the room is.

It is him.

Unlike the other half a dozen men gawking at me in shocked anger, this handsome stranger looks at me with a sense of familiarity, and if I'm not mistaken, *ownership*.

Blinking to break the trance he has trapped me in, I squeak out, "Wrong room," before spinning on my heels and charging for the door.

Thick, accented voices yell for me to stop, but I barely hear a word over the mad beat of my pulse in my ears. I race down the corridor remarkably fast for someone on the verge of wetting their pants.

Unfortunately, my fast-moving legs are not quite quick enough.

A window-shattering squeal tears from my throat when a broad arm wraps around my torso. His powerful hold has my feet lifting from the floor and my heart smashing my ribs. I thrash and kick out wildly, fighting with all my might. After clawing the suit-covered arm with my nails, I attempt to bite the hand moving to cover my shrieking mouth while struggling to keep haunted memories buried.

My vicious attack only diminishes when my name comes barreling out of a deep voice, the same voice that called me Kitten mere seconds ago. "Calm down, Blaire, or you'll gain unwanted attention." Since I'm frozen in shock, he drags me into an unlocked room on our right without protest. "You're safe. No one will ever hurt you."

Air hisses through the small cracks of his hand covering my mouth as I battle to fill my heaving lungs with oxygen. With the fear of hyperventilating surfacing faster than my anger, I decrease my wails and shift my focus to breathing. The last thing I want to do is pass out in a house full of scary men and non-English-speaking females.

Upon realizing I'm no longer fighting, the stranger removes his hand from my mouth, dropping it to the curve of my neck. Every hair on my body bristles when he rubs his thumb over the dip in my collarbone. Now instead of suffering the crippling clutch of panic, I'm overcome by the frantic rush of desire. Insanely, my nipples bud and my lips part, my body choosing its own response to the closeness of the spicy-scented stranger.

"That's it, Kitten. Nice big breaths."

The carnal rasp of his tone tightens the coil of my womb even more. His voice is sophisticated and smooth, the type that could sell ice to Eskimos. It switches the mad beat of my heart from a frightened gallop to a leisured trot in an instant.

After a few more cavernous breaths, my regular breathing pattern returns, and some normality takes hold. When the unnamed stranger places me on my feet, I run my sweaty hands down the front of my skirt before swiveling around to face him. My blood pressure skyrockets again. He's even more alluring up close—defined nose, dark, edgy eyes, and cheekbones any sculptor would love to carve. He's a true masterpiece.

I peer into his eyes, unable to look away for fear of missing something magical, while asking, "How do you know my name?" Not giving him the chance to reply, I add, "Have we met before? You seem so familiar." My words come out hoarse, strangled by both arousal and alarm.

The handsome stranger's eyes flare with a vast range of emotions before his lips tug high. The quickest flash of a smirk freezes my heart. My god this man is beautiful.

When he runs his hand across the scruff on his tanned face, a shimmer of platinum wrapped around his ring finger captures my attention.

"You're married!" I cringe when my nasally high voice bounces off the walls and jingles into my ears.

Since I'm locked in an enthralling daze of idiocy, I thought there was something greater than fear between us.

Obviously, I was wrong.

Masking my disappointment with a neutral look, I return the married stranger's rousing stare. "Is your wife here? Does she speak English?" I question when my inquisitiveness gets the better of me.

His brows knit, but he remains so quiet only my heart drumming against my ribs can be heard.

Astonishment and another unreadable glint brighten his nearly black eyes as he begins to speak, but before a syllable escapes his mouth, the door I was dragged through seconds ago flies open. The trance the sable-haired man's beauty placed on me lifts when a burly-looking thug in a full-length trench coat steps into the room. His hollow eyes bounce between the mysterious stranger and me for several heart-thrashing seconds before he locks them on the gentleman standing beside me.

Mimicking the direction of his gaze, I turn my eyes as well. My heart sinks into my stomach. The captivating specimen I was entranced by seconds ago has vanished, replaced with the man who confronted me in the room earlier. The same room with an injured man bound to a chair.

Oh, my God, I'm a terrible person.

I'm standing in a room eyeballing a man as if his body parts are on a dessert menu while another man sits helpless only doors up from me.

The despair digging a hole in my heart deepens when the man at the door says, "Rico, it's time." His voice is heavily drawled with an accent I don't immediately recognize.

"Do as requested. I do not need to be present," responds the handsome stranger standing next to me.

The gentleman at the door bows his head. "Yes, boss." He shuffles backward like a dog afraid of getting a newspaper whacked across his disobedient nose.

When he closes the door, I stand quiet for a minute, giving my scattered brain a chance to run the events from the past ten minutes through my blurry mind.

It's only when I reach the first half of the intruder's statement does my dazed state end.

While trying to ignore the room closing in on me, I stammer out, "You're Rico?"

Dizziness plagues my senses when Rico nods. I splay my hands across my hips and gulp in large breaths, shocked at discovering the mysterious stranger standing before me is Rico, the owner of the name tattooed on my hip.

When my swirling stomach becomes too much to handle, I slap my quivering hand over my mouth and battle to hold in the contents threatening to break free. The fiery heat scorching my veins unveils another discovery, a crisp coolness tingling on my parched lips.

Heavily panting, I pull my hand away from my mouth. Giddiness clusters in my head when my eyes zoom in on a sparkling platinum band wrapped around the third finger of my left hand. The twisting of my stomach extends to my heart when I realize its ruby and diamond design is an exact replica of the ring on Rico's hand.

I stumble backward as my pupils widen, and my heart falters.

Oh. My. Lord.

I married a mob boss.

Chapter Three

White spots dance in front of my eyes as the room spins. This can't be happening. There must be a mistake. I'm a good girl. I wouldn't wake up married to a stranger, let alone a mob boss.

Stumbling, I make my way to a wooden chair similar to the one the gentleman three rooms over is bound to. Upon noticing my unsteady movements, Rico places his hand on the crook of my elbow. His touch is electric and it sends a surge of awareness over every inch of my body.

After plopping into the seat, I drop my head to my knees and draw in big breaths. My chest rattles as I battle the impulse to faint. The efforts of my heaving lungs double when the warmth of a hand spreads across my back. My brain screams for me to yank away from Rico's touch, but my heart pleads for me to accept his comfort.

Unable to concentrate on anything but the panic havocking my body, I take the comfort he's offering with a grain of salt.

Over time, the heat of his hand soothes my shakes, and the smooth grittiness of his voice swallows the violent ringing in my ears. After giving myself a few moments to settle the crazy beat of my heart, I lift my head from between my knees.

Giddiness swamps my brain again. It isn't from my sudden incline. It's from the deliriously handsome specimen crouched in front of me.

"Are you all right?" Rico's tone is a unique mix of commanding and nurturing.

Unable to speak through my fire-scorched throat, I simply nod. He takes two retreating steps, then props his backside onto a wooden chest a few feet from me. When his dark eyes run over my body, my shoulders instinctively roll, and I straighten my slouched posture. Unlike the chill I got when his eyes raked my body in the other room, this time, his long perusal causes the temperature in the room to become stifling.

I inhale a shaky breath when he returns his eyes to my face. His gaze is commanding, primitive, and strong, and it sets my pulse racing.

Upon spotting my heated cheeks, a smirk curves on his plump lips. "Did you not see the sign at the start of the hall, Kitten? Women are not allowed in this area. And where are the men stationed outside your room?"

My brows stitch, mindful of the authoritativeness in his voice. "Women aren't allowed down here?"

His powerful gaze burns into mine, charring my soul from the inside out before he nods.

"Was the sign in English?" I mumble, my voice incapable of hiding the insanity of the situation.

Rico smiles a lazy smirk that has my veins boiling. "No. It's in Russian."

My shocked eyes meet his. "Russian?" My pupils widen as reality dawns. "As in Russian, *Russian?*"

When he nods, the wooziness inflicting my head over the past twenty minutes travels to my stomach. I sit still in shock, watching him in silence, hopeful he'll fill in the blank gaps in my mind.

When he remains quiet, I stutter, "You're Russian?"

A mouthwatering smirk carves onto his mouth before he dips his chin. Even entranced by the lazy smile stretched across his handsome face, I drop my head to my knees again before fighting through a second battle of keeping the contents of my stomach where they belong.

Unfortunately, my attempts this time are fruitless. Nothing can stop the uncontrollable swirls. Even certain my stomach is empty, I clamp my hand over my mouth and straighten my spine. "Is there a bathroom close by?" I ask Rico, mumbling through the cracks of my hand.

A speck of blood on the cuff of his light blue business shirt becomes exposed when he gestures his hand to a door on my right. Seeing evidence of his corrupt life firsthand hinders any chance of containing my flipping stomach.

Springing to my feet, I bolt to the door as fast as my quaking legs can take me. I only just make it into the poorly designed bathroom when the slosh in my stomach makes its way into the world. My throbbing temples scream in pain as my back violently bends.

Despite the brutal heaves racking my body, I can't help but notice the way Rico's hand rubbing down my back causes every fine hair on my body to bristle.

Once all the throat-burning contents of my stomach have been expelled, I lean back on the balls of my feet. Tears of confusion well in my eyes, and my heart is a muddled mess of turmoil.

I've never engaged in a battle as vicious as the one my brain and heart are in right now.

How could one man incite such a contradictory set of emotions? My brain is begging me to leave this room before I walk so far into the darkness I'll never find my way out. But my heart is pleading with me to ignore the protests of my brain, and for once, let it have a chance to prove its decisions are as gripping as its astute counterpart.

Warmth engulfs me when a set of broad arms band around my body and hoist me from the floor. The stomach-calming smell of spices filters into my nose when Rico pulls me into his chest and strides out of the room. My first reaction is to repel from his grasp, but with my mind nothing but a hazy blur, my heart wins this battle.

When I press my cheek against Rico's well-formed chest, the wild beat of his heart tames the furious thump of my pounding skull. If I closed my eyes, I could pretend I'm not in the midst of one of the scariest dreams I've ever had.

Unfortunately, I lose any shot of normality when he strides past the room I scampered out of minutes ago. The door is only open a mere inch, but it's wide enough for me to see the immoral act playing out before my very eyes. I'm a kindergarten teacher, but I've seen enough Hollywood movies to recognize the weapon a man standing in the room is holding.

Like he can sense my snooping stare, the man clutching a black pistol with a silencer screwed on the end turns his gaze to me. His eyes are a vibrant icy blue, but they are lifeless and hollow.

With a conniving grin etched on his face, he winks at me before swinging the barrel of his gun to the now gagged and bound man I saw earlier.

I shoot my eyes to Rico just as quickly. "Are they... is he... are they going to..."

My words trail off when the faintest pfft of a silencer filters through my ears. It doesn't matter how much the manufacturer claims it's silent, there's no mistaking that sound. It's heart-shattering and devastating.

Dread strikes my heart as wetness floods my eyes. Rico doesn't flinch, balk, or even acknowledge he heard a thing. He continues moving through the vast residence without a single reaction crossing his face.

Who is this man I married? Only a monster could ignore the quiet screams of death.

Fighting my trembling muscles, I crawl out of his embrace just as we hit the door of my room. His eyes convey his protest to the loss of my contact, but his lips remain locked. My body is uncontrollably shaking with fear, but thankfully, my legs are in functioning order.

After entering the room, I force my eyes to lock with Rico's. "Did they kill him?" My words come out strained since they're coerced through the bile lodged in the back of my throat.

He holds my gaze, his eyes blazing with a range of emotions I can't read. "Don't ask questions you don't want the answer to, Kitten." Although his tone is clipped, the remorse concealed by his sharp eyes answers my question.

I throw my hand over my quivering lips. "Why? Why did they kill him?"

He slants his head to the side and stares at me with bleak, desolate eyes. "Why what? As far as anyone is concerned, you heard and saw nothing. Do you understand what I'm saying, Kitten?" My lungs become winded when he takes a step closer to me. "You saw nothing." His eyes relay the importance of his words. This isn't a request or a suggestion. This is a demand. "Tell me what you saw, Kitten?" His face is emotionless, his tone low.

Tremors rake through my body as I say, "Nothing. I saw nothing," through a sob. The indents lining his forehead smooth the instant the words seep from my lips.

No longer trusting my legs to keep me standing, I pace to the monstrous bed and sit on the edge. Rico's eyes track me, but his feet remain planted in their original position as he watches me with reserved silence.

Pain shreds through my heart when the man's pleas sound through my ears on repeat. Did he have small children like he said? Did Rico's men just make them orphans?

Several minutes pass in silence as I search his impassive face for answers to my inaudible questions. They are full of turmoil and despair. I don't know what's more disturbing, the fact I don't know the man in front of me, yet, he is my husband, or that I discovered him sitting in a room with a man who was just killed. Rico nor I pulled the trigger, but we didn't stop it from happening either. Doesn't that make us just as callous as the man who did?

After running my hand under my nose—removing the contents spilling there—I return my eyes to Rico. A frown line mars the space between his brows as he watches me like a hawk, but he has not spoken a syllable since he warned me to remain quiet.

"Can I go home?" My voice is rickety but full of silent begs. "I want to go home."

Rico's brows scrunch as the quickest flash of antagonism fills his eyes.

Even with the scent of fear encroaching our small gathering, I continue, "I shouldn't be here. I don't want to be here." My words fly out of my mouth before I have the chance to stop them. "Please let me go home."

The small flare of anger in Rico's eyes expands to a raging tornado, but even rattled beyond comprehension, I hold his gaze as he spans the distance between us. He carries himself with a confident poise that not only demands respect but trust as well. And for some reason unbeknownst to me, I already trust him enough not to be scared of him.

His hand fills the side of my face when he places it on my jaw and peers into my watering eyes. For someone whose stern gaze alone could terrify any man, I find comfort in his gentle touch and glistening eyes.

"What do you remember about last night?" His tempestuous voice lowers to a more intimate tone.

My eyes bounce between his while I murmur, "Nothing."

His thick brows slant, his gaze searingly intense. "Nothing?"

Tears dribble from my eyes when I nod, confirming his question.

He runs his thumbs over my cheeks to gather my tears before asking, "From when?"

Sick gloom spreads through me as I admit, "I don't remember stepping foot off the plane."

Rico yells a foreign word. From the harshness of his tone and the rage brewing in his eyes, I'm going to assume it was a Russian curse word. "You were sipping on a spritzer, Kitten. You had three at the most. How can you not remember anything?"

His deep timbre sends a shiver down my spine. Don't ask me if it's a good or bad shiver as I wouldn't be able to tell you.

When I fail to answer his question, he scrubs his hand over the stubble on his chin before crouching down in front of me. I only just hold in my gasp when we meet eye to eye. His dark eyes are captivating from a distance, but up close, they're soul-stealing. "You're my wife, Kitten. Do you understand that?"

When I nod, relief fills his eyes.

It's short-lived.

"But not because I remember marrying you. I put two and two together when I saw our matching wedding bands." *And my tattoo...* but I keep that snippet of information to myself.

With a furious storm raging in his eyes, he asks, "Do you regret marrying me?"

I balk, utterly shocked by his question. He can't be serious? He just walked me past a room where a man was murdered without a spark of remorse in his eyes. If I didn't regret meeting him, I'd be as much a monster as he is.

Furthermore, I don't know anything about the man standing before me. I don't even know if Rico is his full name or how old he is. I don't know him any better than the man who delivers my mail. He's a stranger. A scary stranger who can make my heart race in alarm and excitement, but still a stranger, nevertheless.

I can tell the exact moment Rico reads the silent response in my eyes. The anger in his fear-provoking gaze grows, and the scruff on his jaw cannot hide its manic tick.

Standing from his crouched position, he extends to his full six-foot-plus height. With his eyes facing straight ahead, he says, "Collect your belongings. I'll have one of my men take you to the airport."

With that, he turns on his heels and stalks out of the room without a backward glance.

Chapter Four

Forty-five minutes later, a gentleman of medium build and short stature gathers my bag that was left dumped by the door within minutes of Rico fleeing it. Other than the clothes I'm wearing, I have no other personal stuff to collect, so I've spent the remaining forty-three minutes staring at the ceiling rose surrounding the crystal chandelier, silently pondering.

Forty-three minutes of reflecting only awarded me with forty-three minutes of blank memories and a lifetime of haunted ones.

Dozens of eyes track me when I follow the balding middle-aged man through the large residence. Unlike an hour ago, the women with thick accents don't accost me when I enter the main living area of the house. They eyeball me with curiosity, but remain quieter than the front row of churchgoers during Sunday mass.

My eyes shift sideways when the heat of an imprudent stare captures my attention. The man I spotted earlier with the icy blue eyes has his shoulder propped up on the curved wall of the corridor that saw me walking into the gates of hell. His hair is dark and slicked back, his eyes are mocking and full of evil, and his chin holds less stubble than Rico's.

When he issues me a conceited wink, I hold my head high and turn my gaze to the front, trying to display he doesn't scare me.

If only I could stop my knees from wobbling, then my attempts would be more believable.

The blue-eyed stranger's mocking laughter shrills in my ears when I step out a set of double doors. The warmth of a late afternoon Las Vegas sun reddens my cheeks when I stop on the front stoop of an elegant yet highly-guarded mansion.

I scan my eyes over the manicured grounds, absorbing the rolling turf that goes as far as the eye can see. A stream of elegant cars worth millions of dollars and beautiful floral displays make it feel like I'm not in the middle of a desert. If I could look past the heavily armed men in every corner, it would be a spectacular view.

Ignoring the gawking stares of the numerous men with guns strapped to their chests, I shadow the unnamed gentleman down the steps of the private residence. A thankful smirk curls on my lips when he holds open the back passenger door of a black Escalade.

"Thank you," I mumble while sliding into the car.

My heart leaps out of my chest when he unexpectedly slams the door shut.

After gathering my heart from the floor, I attempt to latch my seat belt. My fiddling with the uncooperative latch stops when the door opposite me swings open, and Rico slides inside. The veins in my neck twitch when he leans over, yanks my seat belt out of my grasp, then latches it into place in one swift motion.

I try to issue him my thanks, but just like the seat belt fastener, my mouth refuses to cooperate.

Once he has secured his belt, Rico turns his eyes to the window. I stare at him, gawking and confused. He said he'd have one of his men drive me to the airport, not himself.

When a gentleman in a cream checkered suit enters the escalade, Rico dips his chin in greeting before raising his eyes to the rearview mirror. Not speaking a peep, he signals to the driver to leave.

Confused and nursing a bruised ego, I keep my eyes rapt on Rico.

If I were holding my breath waiting for him to acknowledge my presence, I would have been asphyxiated by now.

My eyes stray away from Rico when a deep voice calls my name.

"Sorry, were you talking to me?" I say to the gentleman sitting across from me.

The corners of his lips tug high, exposing his perfectly straight teeth. "Yes, Blaire. My name is Erik Monstrateo, I'm Rico's lawyer." He offers me his hand to shake.

Masking my shock that he knows my name, I accept his handshake before shooting my eyes to Rico. From the way he keeps his gaze planted straight ahead and his subdued mood unwavering, anyone would swear he hasn't noticed my intrusive stare. Anyone but me. I can feel his scorching glare burning a hole in my soul.

I drift my eyes back to Erik when he says, "Rico has been very generous with his settlement offer. Once the annulment forms are signed—"

I wave my hand through the air, stopping Erik mid-sentence. "Settlement offer?" I interrupt as my confused eyes bounce between Erik's light blue gaze.

Erik is a handsome man in his early thirties with sandy blond hair and sharp facial features, but just like Rico, he has a snip of danger in his eyes that sets me on edge.

Erik smiles. It's a warm smile in a callous and vindictive confrontation. "Yes. When you sign the annulment papers, a transfer of two million dollars will be wired into your account within twenty-four hours..." He continues speaking, but I don't hear a word he is saying. I'm too busy staring at Rico, slack-jawed and muted.

Throughout Erik's legal jargon on the terms of our annulment, Rico taps his index finger on his trouser-covered knee while his gaze remains fixated on the heavy flow of traffic whizzing by the window. Anyone would swear he is being informed of the lunch specials at a fancy restaurant on the strip, not a life-altering decision.

The only time Rico's attention is won is when I drift my eyes back to Erik and say, "I don't want Rico's money. All I want is to dissolve a drunken mistake and return to my normal life." My brows scrunch as bile crawls up my windpipe. "Well, as normal as it can be after what I've experienced this weekend."

A grin stretches across Erik's face as he scratches out the excessive monetary amount in the alimony section of our annulment documentation.

His smile is wiped right off his face when Rico commands, "Leave the figure as stated." He turns his hard-set eyes to me. "We had an agreement. The amount will remain. This is not negotiable."

"I don't want your money," I fire back, my voice surprisingly strong considering how fast my heart is racing.

"Then don't sign the annulment papers." Rico glares at me. "You either leave with the figure stated or remain married to me. Only you can decide which is the lesser of two evils."

When he returns his narrowed gaze to the window, I stare at him, blinking and confused. Why would he agree to hand over such an extravagant amount of money to a stranger? He has only known me for twenty-four hours. It honestly doesn't make any sense.

After adjusting the figure back to two million dollars, Erik hands the five-page document to me. I shift my eyes away from Rico to scan the densely worded form.

My heart squeezes when my eyes roam over Rico's full name— Enrique Julies Popov.

It's a beautiful name for a handsome but cold-hearted man.

My heart gets squashed for the second time when I spot the reason for our annulment. "Plaintiff lacked understanding of his/her actions to the extent that he/she was incapable of agreeing to the marriage because she was..."

"Severely inebriated," I read aloud.

Ignoring the swirling of my stomach, I snap my eyes to Rico. "I thought you said I only had a spritzer or three?"

He appears to be paying me no attention, but he can't fool me. I can feel the heat of his gaze on me. It's even more scorching than the blistering sun hanging in the sky. But no matter how long I glare at him, he never acknowledges my presence.

That hurts even more than a failed marriage under my belt before I turn twenty-five.

With my heart clutched in my chest, I scribble my signature across the forms before passing them to Rico. He doesn't read the document or pause for hesitation, he merely signs his name beside mine before handing the papers back to Erik.

I grit my teeth when absurd tears prick in my eyes. I was married for less than twenty-four hours, so I have no clue why I'm being so dramatic. But, I guess, at the end of the day, I always thought when I married, it would be to a man I love, and it would last a lifetime. I never considered the prospect of a quickie Vegas wedding.

While keeping my snivels to a bare minimum, I persevere with keeping my eyes locked on the scenery flying by. Famous Las Vegas landmarks stretch as far as the eye can see. It's a beautiful landscape, but nothing can ease the pain crippling me from the inside out.

It isn't just the freshness of an annulment maiming my heart or the coldness Rico is directing at me. It is the desolate look I saw in the eyes of the unnamed man bound to the chair shortly before his untimely death. He looked broken and defeated, similar to how I'm feeling now.

My eyes move away from the architectural wonder of Vegas when the Escalade suddenly stops at the side of the highway. Cars roar past the stationary vehicle, rattling the heavily tinted windows, and motorists beep their horns and yell obscenities, completely oblivious to who they're unleashing their vicious road rage on.

I bounce my dilated gaze between Erik and Rico when Rico demands he leave immediately.

Shocked and frozen in place, my brows hit my hairline when Erik exits the Escalade without a single protest. Warm, muggy air blasts into the car when he steps onto the road, adding to the outrage swirling in my stomach.

"It's a busy highway in the middle of a desert," I protest on Erik's behalf, my high voice conveying my utter disbelief.

I won't witness another untimely death without citing an objection.

Either not hearing a word I said—or continuing to ignore me—Rico signals for the driver to continue with our journey.

With my heart walloping my chest wall, I crank my neck back to Erik. He's standing at the side of the blistering asphalt with a cell phone attached to his ear and a complacent look on his face. Unlike me, he doesn't seem the slightest bit bothered by the one hundred-plus degree temperature beaming down on him.

Obviously, this is nothing new for him.

"One of my fleet drivers will collect him," Rico explains to my appalled expression, his tone deep and heart-clutching. He turns his blank eyes to me before asking in a more subdued tone, "Why are you crying, Kitten?"

The simplicity of his question causes a fresh batch of tears to trickle from my eyes. At a guess, I'd say he's a similar age to me, in his mid-twenties. So it makes me wonder how much darkness he's witnessed in his short life that knowing a man was killed has no effect on him whatsoever.

Rico is no doubt a handsome man, but as he's sitting before me now, he's hideously ugly.

There's nothing uglier than a human being without compassion.

"Did that man have children like he said?" My words are brittle like cracked glass.

Rico adjusts his position so he faces me front-on. His thigh muscle twitches in sync with his jaw. "Does it matter?"

I nod. "Yes. He was a human being, Rico! How can you be so callous? You sit here demanding a woman you hardly know to take your money, but you can't have sympathy for a man who lost his life!"

His dark eyes glare into mine, his gaze an odd mix of anger and interest. "I know you," he cites without a snick of hesitation. "And he was not a man. He was an errant coward who had to pay for his actions." His angry tone exposes a slight twang of a Russian accent.

"By death?" I blubber out.

He holds my gaze, his stern composure unyielding. "Yes. By any means I saw fit."

I balk, both flabbergasted and disgusted. "Who made you judge, jury, and executioner?"

"My birthright, my title, and my morals." His voice gets louder with every word he speaks. "You're convicting me, judging me, and sending me to execution all to defend a man you don't even know."

I run my hands across my cheeks, angrily removing the tears tracking down my face. Even knowing I'm waging a war against a man who clearly has no morals, I can't holster my campaign. I would have never married a soulless man, drunk or not, so I know there's more to this man than what I've witnessed this morning. My moral compass would have never blown so far off course.

"Nothing deserves a death sentence." I stare him dead set in the eyes. "*Nothing.*"

My breathing shallows to a wheezy pant when he asks, "Not even a child molester?"

My mouth falls open as a brutal pain hits the middle of my chest. "W-what?" The tremor of my heart echoes in my voice.

"Or what about a murderer? Or the man who laced his drugs with cheap chemicals, resulting in the death of fourteen teens in one night? What punishment would you give them, Kitten? A slap on the wrist? A stern talking to?"

I return his stare, but I don't speak a word. I'm silenced by my heart sitting in my throat, and honestly, I don't know how to reply. I've never believed in the death penalty, but that was easy for me to preach when I wasn't confronted with a flurry of heinous crimes. Child molesters and murderers are the lowest of the low, but how does that give Rico the right to deliver justice?

"Two wrongs don't make a right." My softly spoken words point to the uncertainty of my reply. I'm at a loss on which direction I want to take our conversation.

"No, it doesn't. But justice isn't about what's right or wrong. It's about equitableness."

Our conversation comes to a shrieking halt when the Escalade pulls onto the curb of McCarran International Airport. When the driver exits the vehicle, Rico closes the small gap between us. Just like when we were together in the dingy bedroom, a vibrant, electric current fires between us. But it doesn't heal the damage my heart sustained in our volatile discussion. This man is technically a stranger. I've only known him for hours, but something deeper in my soul is telling me this isn't true.

The muscles in my cheek twitch when Rico brushes away the leftover tears that slide down my face. His gentle touch and the cloud of sorrow in his eyes are a vast contradiction to the man debating who has the right to deliver justice mere seconds ago. It's like he is two completely different people. In front of others, he's a callous, cold-hearted monster who can dish out cruel punishments, but when he's with me alone, he's a man who appears caring—almost loving.

Once my tearstains have been removed, Rico connects his dark gaze with mine. "I'm the son of a monster, Kitten. Not a monster myself," he mutters like he can hear my internal dialogue.

My chance to reply is lost when the driver of the Escalade gathers my suitcase from the trunk and opens my door. Hot, muggy air streams into the cabin of the car, adding to the giddiness of my swishy stomach. The blaring desert heat of Las Vegas will always be stifling, but it's nothing compared to the roasting temperature building between Rico and me.

I curl out of the vehicle before my queasy stomach decides to act. My fast exit halts when a warm hand curls around mine. I sink deeper into my seat before swinging my eyes to Rico, discounting the way his simplest touch caused a shiver of euphoria to run the length of my spine.

The stern mask Rico was wearing earlier has slipped back into place, and his jaw is tense, but his eyes are still carrying the heaviness of remorse. "This is as far as I can go," he explains, his tone flat and brimmed with anger.

I swallow the brick in my throat. "Okay. Thanks for the lift." I catch my eye roll halfway. I met and married a man in less than twenty-four hours, yet I'm acting all modest and cordial.

My mother would be so pleased.

Overlooking the hammering of my heart, I lean in to press a kiss on Rico's cheek. He twists his neck, forcing my kiss to land on the edge of his mouth instead of his cheek. I stop frozen with my lips attached to his. It isn't just the shock of excitement dashing through my veins that have my movements stiffening, it's the quickest snippet of a memory flashing through my mind...

"I want to kiss you, Enrique," I declare, peering into a pair of soul-capturing eyes.

My heart stops beating when the quickest flash of a smirk freezes time. "Nothing is stopping you, Blaire."

After closing my eyes, I rest my hands on his well-formed pecs and tilt my head to the side to align our mouths better. Just as my lips brush his soft, sensual mouth, I open my eyes. His dark, beautiful gaze is staring dotingly into mine.

"You're supposed to close your eyes." My minty breath bounces off his lips and filters into my nose.

"I don't want to close my eyes," he replies as his heavy-hooded gaze dances between mine.

A grin curls on my lips. "Why?"

"Because I don't want to wake up and find out you were a dream." He runs the back of his hand down my flustered cheeks, causing every hair on my body to bristle.

I smile. "If it's a dream, it's the most beautiful dream I've ever had."

"Me too," Rico confesses, smiling a lazy grin that surges my heart into dangerous territory...

I pull back and peer into Rico's eyes. He's watching me with the same amount of intensity he bestowed on me in my memory, but his eyes are void of the tender spark that brightened his dark gaze last night until I mutter, "It was the most beautiful dream."

Not giving him the chance to react, I curl out of the car, snag my suitcase, and become lost in the heavy foot traffic on the terminal sidewalk.

In a muddled haze, I weave in and out of the bustling airport on my endeavor to reach my gate. The nicks in my heart enlarge with every step I take. My mind is scrambled, trying to recall any other events buried beneath the rubble of my drunken state while also ignoring the insane hope my statement might force a reaction from Rico.

I need to leave Vegas as soon as possible. This place is messing with my head. I only signed annulment papers twenty minutes ago, and now I'm praying my soon-to-be ex-husband will track me down and beg me not to leave.

Vegas doesn't just steal your morals, but your sanity too... and perhaps even your heart.

Chapter Five

"Come on, Care Blaire, the water is beautiful," my best friend, Lacey, shouts while splashing me with the refreshing coolness of the inground swimming pool at our apartment complex. My skin is so sun-kissed, the water sizzles when it hits the skin high on my bare thigh.

Lacey cocks her brow and stares at me. "What's the deal? You've always been a water baby."

I rise from the daybed I'm lazing on, fling off my sunglasses, then gaze into her blue eyes. She is right. I've always loved the water, but after researching ways to have a tattoo inconspicuously removed, I discovered a range of new facts a tattoo virgin is naïve about. The most compelling, you can't swim in chlorinated water for two to three weeks after getting a tattoo. Considering my tattoo was only inked on my skin five days ago, I'm not willing to risk getting an infection on my newly open wound, even if I'm melting on a ninety-six-degree afternoon.

"I'm fine here," I lie, my tone as low as my hydration levels. "I thought I'd add a few more hours to my summer tan before school returns."

Lacey arches her brow into her drenched hairline. "Fine, but it's your loss."

I screw up my nose and stick out my tongue. After returning my snicker, Lacey dives into the holy-looking water. People may construe our little banter as bickering, but there's no maliciousness in our exchange. Lacey is straight to the point and calls it how she sees it, but she doesn't have a malicious bone in her body. She's my very dear friend and my closest confidant. That's why I find it so shocking I've managed to hide my Vegas antics from her for the past five days.

Don't take my admission the wrong way. Lacey was onto me like white on rice the instant my plane landed in Ravenshoe, but since I've always been the straight-laced friend, her interrogation never went further than asking what food was served at the conference and if there were any hot male teachers she could use to fulfill her naughty teacher slash student fantasy.

Her interest in the boring life of a kindergarten teacher only lasted as long as our ten-mile trip to our apartment building. By the time we walked into our two-bedroom unit, my adventures in Vegas were a forgotten memory to Lacey and, unfortunately, me too.

No matter how hard I try to unlock my memories, the only snippets I've unearthed the past five days are the quickest flashes of Rico's beautiful, tormented eyes and lazy smirk. The flashbacks are short enough to keep my Vegas memories hidden but long enough to tether my heart to a man I don't know.

This is incredulous for me to say, but I never thought it was possible to miss a man you only knew for hours. Rico defies that logic. Most of our time together is lost in the background of my mind, but when I'm lying in bed, I miss him—the stranger I married.

I stop staring into space when Colt from Apartment 4A charges across the shimmery pool tiles and does a cannonball into the pool. "It's Friday, baby girl!" he shouts at the top of his lungs before the pool water swamps his words.

His playful antics force a smile on my face while also saturating my one-piece swimsuit. Leaping up from my sun chair, I snag a towel off the table next to me and pat my vibrant red one-piece swimsuit dry. Since I'm so immersed in drying my swimsuit, I don't notice Colt sneaking up on me until it's too late. Goose bumps prickle my forearms when he wraps his thick arms around my torso and hoists me off the ground. I squeal an ear-piercing protest. My pleas to be put down are barely heard over Lacey's boisterous giggle.

"Do it, Colt! Throw her in the water!" Lacey yells through a barrage of laughter.

I scamper up Colt's torso—climbing him like a monkey climbs a tree—before locking my eyes with his mischief-filled gaze.

"Don't you dare," I warn, my voice low and crammed with false anger.

I've always been a sucker for Colt's mischief-filled eyes and cheeky grin. Normally, he just flashes me the quickest smirk, and I do anything he requests. But today is different. I'm not the same Blaire I was five days ago. *Not even close.*

"Don't you want to go for a swim, baby girl?" Colt smiles so broadly, the dimples in his bronzed cheeks become exposed.

"No." My reply is quick and resolute. "I'm happy tanning."

Colt stops striding when we hit the edge of the pool, then drops his gaze to me. The afternoon sun beaming off his blond locks shrouds him in a golden halo, making him look more angelic than his mischievous composure.

"Tanning?" His quick reply can't hide his laughter.

I return his sassy glare before nodding. Chlorinated skin, sunscreen, and the scent of a burly male filters through my nose when we face off in an intense, sweat-producing staredown. Lacey doesn't pay us any attention. This type of bantering is nothing out of the ordinary for Colt and me. Every time we're together, flirtatiousness hangs thick in the air. We've been flirting pretty heavily for the past seven months, but it's never gone any further than two friends toying around.

"What are you willing to give me not to throw you in the water?" Colt barters with his green eyes locked on me.

I narrow my eyes into thin slits, pretending I'm annoyed by his banter. "Nothing, because you're going to put me down as I'm requesting."

My grip on his thick biceps tightens when he straightens his arms and dangles me over the water as if I'm a weightless child. This is no hard feat for Colt. He works as a personal trainer at the local gym. He can bench press two hundred and fifteen pounds, so my five-foot-six, one-hundred-twenty-pound frame is easy-peasy for him.

"Colt! Don't you dare!" I squeal, praying to the Lord he doesn't dump me into the pool.

Colt's smile broadens when I wrap my legs around his waist and clamp his hips with my thighs. "Do you have your phone on you?" he asks, obviously recalling the time he threw me into the pool fully clothed while I had my cell phone in my pocket. His wages were stretched to the absolute limit when he replaced my phone with the latest model the very next day.

"Yes!" I lie. "I have my cell!" I'll say anything if it saves me from being thrown into the deep end.

My lie is squashed when he turns his eyes to the lounge chair I was lying on and spots my cell phone sitting on top of my beach towel.

"Nice try, baby girl." He chuckles, returning his blazing eyes to me.

I dig my nails into his biceps. "Please, Colt. I'm begging you."

This time, my voice comes out sounding like a plea instead of a demand. I'm not below getting down on my knees at this point.

"Three, two, one..." Colt counts down, ignoring my begging protests.

"I have a tattoo!" I scream when his shakes loosen my death-tight grip on his waist.

Colt freezes.

Time freezes.

Everything freezes.

Feeling an indiscreet stare burning a hole in the side of my head,

I swing my eyes to my left. Lacey is staring at me, open-mouthed and wide-eyed. "No way. You'd never get a tattoo." The veins in my neck thrum when she scampers out of the pool and stands next to Colt in less than a heartbeat. "Bring her in. She has some explaining to do," she demands, her voice stern.

I gulp loudly.

Lacey only brings out her bossy boots during dire situations.

Obviously, she feels this is a dire situation.

Colt draws me away from the water's edge before placing me on my feet. A new type of awareness prickles my skin when every inch of his rock-hard body glides past mine in the process. Normally, his playfulness would have caused the pulse in my body to redirect to my pussy, but today his tease is less effective.

Don't construe my admission the wrong way. My nipples are budded, and euphoria has thickened my blood, but his appeal is nowhere near what I felt standing across from Rico in the dungeon-like room five days ago.

"Ms. Blaire Williams... cardigan-wearing, has never said a curse word in her life, kindergarten teacher got a tattoo? I knew there was a rebel hiding in there somewhere," Colt jests, lazily raking his eyes over my body. "What did you get? A cute little heart? A butterfly?" He locks his lust-filled eyes with mine. "Come on, baby girl. Are you going to show me? Or am I going to go on a treasure hunt?"

Lacey bumps my hip, her eyes wide, her jaw hanging. Even she can't miss Colt's innuendo-laced flirting. I'm not surprised. He has no trouble ruffling up any woman's interest. He just smirks, and they all flock to him. But this is different. Normally, our flirting is an acceptable notch over the friendship line, but this feels more like a gigantic leap.

After returning Lacey's hip bump, I cross my arms in front of my chest, ensuring my body's reaction to Colt's avid gaze remains concealed.

Unable to locate any ink on my scarcely covered body, Colt lifts and locks his eyes with me. "Where did you get it?" The waggling of his brows doesn't hide the eagerness in his words.

I tighten my arms under my chest, hoisting my moderate-size bosoms higher into the air. "Not in any place you'll ever see."

His smirk enlarges to a full-toothed smile, not believing a word I'm saying. He knows as well as I do, if given a chance, I'd climb him like a jungle gym.

Well, I would have before Vegas.

Now, I'm not so sure.

Colt's real name is Marshall, but we all call him Colt because... well... he's hung like a horse, that's why. And from the noises Lacey and I regularly hear bellowing from his apartment, he has no trouble bucking for hours.

Ignoring my flaming red cheeks, I say, "I'm... *leaving.*" After snatching my phone and towel off the chair, I bolt for the exit.

"But the fun is only beginning, baby girl," Colt jests, his tone low and tempting.

I've just hit the pool gate when Lacey catches up with me. "You have a lot of explaining to do, young lady." She weaves her arm around the crook of my elbow. "But I don't know where to begin. With the fire-sparking showdown I just witnessed? Or that you got a tattoo on an obviously *private* region of your body that you failed to update your best friend on?"

After guiding me into the elevator, Lacey snags the towel out of my hand and commences drying her light brown hair. The elevator ascends to our apartment in absolute silence. She doesn't need to speak. Her questioning eyes are more interrogating than her mouth ever could be. If the elevator car wasn't air-conditioned, I might have melted under her stifling gaze.

Her quiet approach lasts as long as it takes for us to walk into the front door of our modest apartment. "Spill. Now."

Throwing my house key onto the glass and wrought iron entry table, I pad into the living room. My steps are lazy, weighed down by the confusion still muddling my heart. I sit on a red wing-backed chair while Lacey props her backside on a stark white loveseat, not at all concerned her dripping wet two-piece bikini is soaking into the expensive material. She eyeballs me but has reverted to her silent stance, her gaze a unique mix of intrigue and shock.

"I got a tattoo in Vegas."

She huffs and rolls her eyes. "Duh."

The arch of her manicured brow increases when I blubber out, "And a husband."

Her mouth gapes as her eyes bulge. "Wait. What?" The shock of my admission has reduced a woman who can talk underwater to one-word sentences.

I gulp, washing away a lump in the back of my throat. "I don't remember exactly how it transpired. All I remember is waking up with a wedding band on my finger and a man's name tattooed on my hip."

"Wow." She breathes out heavily, then scoots across the double-seated sofa to sit closer to me. "No half-baked Vegas experience for you. You went straight for the complete package."

I throw my hands over my eyes and slump into my chair. "That's not even the whole story."

Lacey gives herself a few moments to settle her shock before she sits on the edge of my chair and pries my hands away from my face. "Okay. We can handle this. First thing first... did you use protection? If not, there's a pharmacy half a block over. I can go get—"

"Yes," I interrupt, my words weak. "Although I have no recollec-tion of the actual *deed,* empty condom wrappers were in my room."

Her lips quirk as a glint of curiosity fires in her expressive eyes. "*Wrappers?* How many are we talking exactly?"

I munch on my bottom lip before raising three fingers into the air. Her bugged-eyed expression grows, and the corners of her lips twitch, but she respectfully holds in her smile. Lacey knows me well enough to know the finger signal I'm holding in the air is the combined number of times I've done the *deed* the past two years, so to achieve that in one night is a record-breaking achievement for me.

"Okay. Good. Protection was used." Her voice is high with shock and excitement. "Second... was your husband still present the following morning, or did he do the Las Vegas hightail escape?"

Even in the intensity of the situation, her statement causes a smile to stretch across my face. Lacey can bring any girl down from the ledge, no matter how dire the situation may seem.

"He was still present."

I keep my reply short, deciding not to elaborate on where Rico was when I woke up.

"Huh. Must not be a Vegas local?" Lacey jests, her tone crammed with wit.

I laugh. It's laced with torment. "From what I witnessed, I'm fairly certain he's a local." *Judge, juror, and executioner local.*

Lacey takes a few moments to gather her bases. "So we have a name, a town, and a non-drunk description. Given to the right people, we should have enough info to track down your husband and file for an annulment," she advises, her mannerisms quickly reverting from life-long friend to third-year law student.

Her eyes rocket to mine when I mutter, "Already done."

"Tracking down your husband or the annulment?" Her words fly out of her mouth in quick succession.

"The annulment. Rico had his lawyer serve me papers during our trip to the airport."

She scoffs. "Wow! What a jerk. Did you seek alimony or request compensation for him being an asshole?"

"No." I shake my head.

Her eyes narrow into tiny slits. "It doesn't matter if you were married for two minutes or two years, Blaire. Alimony terms should have been included in your settlement."

"They were." I say anything to lessen her furious scowl burning into me. "Rico stipulated an amount he was willing to pay. Even though I didn't agree with the amount he was offering, I signed the forms."

She stands from her seated position and rests her hands on her tiny hips. "You never sign a legal document without having a lawyer present, Blaire. How many times have I stated this?" She crosses her arms over her chest and bores her eyes into mine. "What amount did you agree to?"

She falls back into her seat when I breathe out, "Two million dollars."

"Who the hell did you marry?" Her disbelieving eyes bounce between mine. "A prince from Saudi Arabia?"

"He seemed like a prince. Just not one from any fairy tales we've read."

Chapter Six

The remainder of my weekend was spent holed up in my apartment. Although Lacey was apprehensive about my short replies to her grilling set of questions, she agreed that the dissolution of my Vegas wedding was handled in the best manner for both parties involved. It was quick and resolute, just like every Vegas wedding ends.

If only the nicks in my heart could be handled as swiftly.

After adjusting the heavy book satchel on my shoulder, I continue sauntering down the corridor of Ravenshoe Primary School. The chatter of little voices sounds through my ears, and the smell of dirty faces lingers in the air. I enjoyed summer break, but I can't wait to get back to work. This may sound a little geeky, but I missed seeing the smiling faces of my students the past few weeks. There's nothing more beautiful than the innocence in a child's wide gaze.

My strides down the hallway slow when I notice Timothy Jamison leaning in the doorjamb of his third-grade class. He's staring at me in a bemused, disarrayed type of way.

My heart rate quickens. I really hope I didn't make a fool out of myself in front of him last weekend. Timothy was nominated beside me for the Teacher of the Year award. We flew on the same flight to

541

Vegas but were seated several rows away from each other. Due to my failing memory, I don't know whether to offer him my commiserations, congratulations, or an apology.

Deciding that avoidance is the best remedy for Las Vegas idiocy, I smile a greeting to Timothy before slipping into my classroom three doors up from his. Warmth blooms across my chest when I spot a large red apple sitting on the corner of my desk next to several hand-picked daisies from the school's front garden. I'm certain the children in my class this year will be absolute sweethearts. I'm always smitten with my class members. I don't care if I have to wipe smelly bottoms for the next sixty years, nothing beats seeing the smiles on my students' faces when they arrive for class every Monday morning.

My mom was a teacher for over thirty years. She loved each of her students as much as I do. Watching the way she nurtured her rebellious teenage students to become upstanding young adults made me want to be a teacher as well. But unlike my mom, I want to shape their minds before they are affected by outside influences.

Kindergarten students don't understand violence, hate, or racism. All they care about is whether Peter Rabbit is ever caught by Mr. McGregor and how many minutes remain until lunch. Seeing the innocence in a child's eyes is a truly magnificent sight, and I want them to hold onto that innocence for as long as possible.

I'm halfway through my first lesson of the day when the excitement on my students' faces grows exponentially. Smiling at their pleased reaction, I shift my eyes back to the book I'm reading them. My lips quirk. Although the story about the fluffy penguin seeking a new set of friends is riveting, I'm still surprised by my students' wide-mouthed responses.

Shrugging off their odd behavior as excitement for the upcoming lunch break, I continue reading. I lose sight of the words scribbled across the page when all twenty-three of my students crank their necks back to peer at something behind my shoulder.

After swallowing to relieve my parched throat, I place the book on my lap and twist my body around. My students' shocked expressions morph onto my face when I discover who's holding their interest. Rico has his backside propped on the edge of my desk, grasping my red apple in his hand.

Despite the weather being considerably warm, he's decked out in a full suit and black trench coat. His face has been recently shaven, but his five o'clock shadow remains even though it's not even noon. His eyes are rapt on me, and he looks deliriously handsome and dangerous at the same time.

A handful of girls in my class squeal when Rico takes a big bite of my apple, sending a crunching sound bouncing around my class.

Clutching my chest to ensure my pounding heart doesn't escape my chest cavity, I shift my eyes to Mina, my teacher's aide. "Can you please continue reading the story to the children? I'll be right back."

Not waiting for her to reply, I scamper out of my seat, grasp Rico's hand in mine, and dash into the corridor. The children's eyes track Rico and me the entire time, their expressions a mixture of confusion and excitement.

The instant we step into the corridor, I release Rico's hand. From the throbbing ache between my legs, you'd swear I wasn't simply holding his hand. Just like last week, sparks of energy bounce between us, bristling the fine hairs on my nape and swelling my heart.

"What are you doing here, Rico?" I ask, incredulity heard in my tone.

He doesn't respond. He just runs his eyes over my outfit, absorbing my knee-length floral skirt, fitted lemon-colored blouse, and modest white sandals. If I didn't know he'd already seen me naked, I'd swear he was wondering what I'm trying to hide under my goody-two-shoes outfit. He wouldn't be the first man to accuse me of 'hiding my appeal with dowdy clothes.'

"Ah, Kitten, you're every teenage boy's naughty teacher fantasy."

My pulse quickens when his heavy-hooded gaze connects with mine. His eyes are dark and dangerous but innocent and beautiful at the same time. Don't ask me how that's even possible as I wouldn't be able to answer.

The throb between my legs intensifies when he mutters, "You look fuckable and sweet at the same time. Two complete contradictions."

"I could say the same thing about you," I reply before my brain has the chance to voice a protest.

A flash of excitement brightens his dark eyes and makes me hot and needy.

Striving to lead our conversation back into chartered waters, I say, "I meant the two contradictions part. Not that you look *fuckable.*"

The excitement flaring in his eyes doesn't waver. He knows as well as I do there's no truth in my statement. He wouldn't wield the type of confidence he has without having the reputation to back it up. He knows he's so gorgeous, he merely needs to snap his fingers, and women would flock to his feet. That's why I find it somewhat surprising he's standing in the hallway outside my classroom, looking at me in a way I've only ever dreamed of—like I'm his savior.

Talking through a lump in my throat, I ask again, "What are you doing here, Rico?"

I can feel the heat of his tense gaze studying my profile before he mutters, "I need you to come back to Vegas with me."

Speaking through the shockwaves rocketing around my body, I protest, "What? No! I can't... *why do you want me to come back?*" I roll my eyes when the last sentence comes with too much neediness clinging to my words.

"You witnessed an *event* last weekend." His eyes darken with every word he speaks. "In my industry, there are no witnesses."

I balk. "W-what d-do you mean there are no witnesses?"

I'm a stuttering idiot, but I can't help it. My heart was last seen somewhere in the region of my shoes, and even with my brain stuck in a lust-crazed haze, I felt the air shift between us. It's gone from steaming with yearning to roasting with danger.

My heavy breaths increase when he tilts in close to my side. Even frightened, I can't deny my body's signals. It's riveted by the man standing in front of me. In absolute awe.

My body's desire to overrule my astute brain flies out the window when Rico explains, "You either come back with me to Vegas as my wife, or they kill you." His words are straightforward and direct, ensuring there's no way I can misinterpret what he's saying.

"They?" I squeak out, my voice as high as the hairs on my forearms.

"My *family*," he replies, the timbre of his tone lowering.

When he lifts his eyes to peer past my shoulder, I follow his gaze. Two men in matching black suits stand side-by-side filling the double fire doors at the end of the corridor. The width of their combined shoulders is enough to block the late morning sun beaming into the hall.

I swing my eyes back to Rico. "If they're your *family*, why can't you call them off? Why can't you—"

"I've already tried." He glances at me with the same vivacity I saw in my flashback last week. "This is the only option I have left. If you're my wife, they won't touch you. But if you refuse to come with me, my hands will be tied."

My nose tingles as fresh tears prick into my eyes. Even if his eyes weren't relaying the truth, I've watched enough *True Crime America* to know I should believe him. Witnesses are the most critical element in any case. Without them, there's no case. But I can't just pack up and leave. I have commitments, a life... *an ex-husband.*

A thick cloud of despair hovers over my head. "We already signed the annulment papers. Your money was wired into my account first thing Monday morning. We're no longer married."

"The money was transferred, but the paperwork has not yet been filed."

I take a step backward, flabbergasted. "Why didn't you file the paperwork?"

I try to keep excitement out of my voice. My attempts are borderline. My reaction can't be helped. With his eagerness to have our annulment papers signed, I assumed he would have filed them the very next morning.

His dark eyes dance between mine before he mutters, "For the same reason you didn't let your *friend* throw you into the pool. If you were planning on having your tattoo removed, any concerns about it fading wouldn't have been an issue."

My heart beats triple time, equally shocked and excited. "You've been watching me?"

"I've been protecting you." A shiver runs down my spine from the edge of danger in his tone. He takes another step closer to me, engulfing my haywired senses with his delicious spicy scent. "I'm trying to keep you safe, Kitten, but this is as far as I can go. You either come back with me to Vegas or die. The choice is yours."

"What type of choice is that? I either go with a murderer or be murdered," I blubber out before I can stop my hurtful words.

When Rico's face lines with anger, I wish I could ram my callousness back down my throat.

"I'm sorry," I apologize, my tone sincere. "But you have to understand, this is all a little bit crazy. I'm a kindergarten teacher, and you're a..." My words trail off when I fail to find a word to explain who he is.

"If you want to live, as far as anyone is concerned, I'm your husband."

My stomach flips. I can't tell if it's from concern or because he's still my husband. I can barely breathe, let alone work out my body's crazy prompts.

"Are you sure there's no other viable option?" I ask, refusing to acknowledge the absurdity of my excitement.

Despair clouds his eyes before he shakes his head. Leaning against a stack of lockers on my right, I gulp in large breaths of air. My nostrils flare as they fight to fill my burning lungs. If I don't secure a full breath soon, I'm going to pass out.

I spread my hands across my hips and bend over. After saying something to the gentlemen standing at the end of the hall in Russian, Rico places his hand on the curve of my back and crouches down in front of me, meeting me eye to eye. Any chance of regaining my composure is lost when I look into his beautiful yet dangerous eyes.

"If I had any other choice, Kitten, I'd take it. I don't have any other option." His words are gruff, but his eyes relay the truth of his statement.

After sucking in a deep breath, I quickly mumble, "I understand, but I can't just pack up my life and leave with you. I have obligations, an apartment, my students."

"Everything has been taken care of." He removes a handkerchief from his pocket and hands it to me. I use it to soak up the sweat beading on my nape as he continues speaking, "Mr. Rodchester was happy to grant you an extended leave of absence. The rent for your apartment has been paid in full for a year, and your parents just discovered they were the fortunate winners of an all-expenses paid three-month tour of Europe."

My jaw muscle slackens as my heart rate skyrockets. "How did you get Mr. Rodchester to give me time off?"

The rest of his statement makes sense. They seem like an easy fix. But Mr. Rodchester governs Ravenshoe Primary with an iron fist. When I called in sick with the flu last semester, he couriered a mountain load of papers to my apartment for me to grade. He does not believe in sick days and never approves time off outside the standard school vacation schedule. He's such a stiff, I was only given a measly two hours off to attend my great aunt's funeral last year.

The swirling of my squishy stomach escalates when Rico replies, "My men are very persuasive."

I straighten my spine when he shifts his gaze sideways. The man standing at the end of the hall doesn't speak a peep, but his eyes must be forthcoming as Rico nods before turning his dark gaze back to me. I inhale a sharp breath, unnerved by the blackness filling his eyes.

"We have to leave now," he instructs, his monotone voice conveying the urgency of his statement.

I nod, giving in to the fact there's no other option. If I want to stay alive, I have to place my trust in a man who equally intrigues and intimidates me.

"Can I say goodbye to my class?" I ask Rico, my chin quivering.

His eyes drift between mine for several heart-clutching seconds before he nods. A grateful sigh spills from my lips as I run my hands across my blemished cheeks. I don't want my students to see me upset.

The hum of young voices dulls to a slight buzz when I swing open my classroom door. My strides into the room fumble when my eyes lock in on Mr. Rodchester standing at the back of the room. His eyes are wide, his pupils massive, and his entire composure screams of nothing but fear. I would not normally condone an act of violence, but I'm glad to see karma finally caught up to Mr. Rodchester.

Overlooking the fact a man who typically shows no emotion looks like a frightened child, I lower my eyes to my students sitting on the carpet in front of my desk. Twenty-three tiny faces peer up at me, gawking and shocked. Like they can sense a change in my composure, they stand from their seated position and swarm around me.

A barrage of emotions slams into me as I bid farewell to each member of my class with a brief cuddle and an assuring word that I'll be back as soon as I can. My last embrace with a little boy named Jeremiah goes a bit longer than the ones before him. Jeremiah holds a special place in my heart after the rough start he has endured this year. His mom was arrested for conspiracy to commit a crime just after Christmas. Although her day in court has not yet happened, the events leading to her arrest have taken their toll on him.

"I'll be back soon, Jeremiah." I peer into his ocean blue eyes.

"Okay, Ms. Williams."

After running my finger over the dimple in the middle of his chin to remove a smudge of dirt, I stand from my crouched position. Rico has gathered my handbag and book satchel from the bottom drawer of my desk, so there's nothing left for me to do but walk out of my classroom.

Why does the simplest act have the greatest impact on my already pained heart?

Chapter Seven

The twenty-minute trip to my apartment is made in silence. The mask Rico wears in front of his crew members slipped into place the instant we entered the back of a black Escalade. The mood is somber, but there's still a weird crackling of energy in the air adding to the confusion of my pained heart.

The only good thing about the lack of ambiance is that it gives me plenty of time to study the man seated next to me. Taken out of the life-and-death situation I've been placed in, I can wholeheartedly understand my attraction to Rico. He has gloriously thick hair, a straight and defined nose, and lips that are too beautiful to ever spill the vicious words he has no doubt spoken in his short twenty-four years. And his eyes... *my goodness!* They are dark and beautiful but look like they are guarding a lifetime of secrets. He's night and day rolled into one strikingly handsome and complicated man.

When the Escalade pulls up to the curb of my apartment building, I run my hand down the front of my blouse. Two scantily dressed women with blown-out hair flock in close to the vehicle. They twist chewing gum around their fingers as they rake their sullied eyes down the length of Rico's body when he curls out of the Escalade's back seat.

After securing the button on his suit jacket, Rico dips his torso back into the vehicle to offer me a hand. His kind gesture reinforces what I already know deep down in my soul—there's something more to this man than just cloaked darkness.

The women stare at me, bitter and shocked when Rico ignores their lewd propositioning as he guides me into the lobby of my building. The way he moves with such grace and animal arrogance, his allure demands the attention of every pair of eyes milling in the lobby, both male and female.

Snubbing the inquisitive stares rapt on him, Rico steers me into the elevator. The two men who have been shadowing us since we left my classroom move to the stairwell without a peep needing to be spilled from Rico's lips. Our ride in the elevator is made in silence, but a vibrant buzzing sensation infuses the air surrounding us.

When the elevator dings open on my floor, Rico directs me down the corridor without stopping to gather his bearings. With his splayed hand hovering near the curve of my lower back for the past five minutes, my body is achingly aware of the loss of his contact when he delves his hand into the breast pocket of his suit to produce a freshly-cut key.

Shoving the key into the front door of my apartment, Rico turns his gaze to me. "You have twenty minutes to pack."

"How did you get a key to my apartment?"

He removes the freshly-cut key from the lock and places it back into his pocket. "Nineteen minutes now, Kitten," he advises, rudely ignoring my interrogation. "Do you want to lose another minute?"

My body instinctively jumps to his command before my mind has time to object. Following the same routine I do every day, I gather the mail off the floor, place it on the entry table, and hit my answering machine button. While pacing into my bedroom, the mature voice of my dad sounds down the line.

"Blaire! You won't believe it. My raffles paid off. Your momma and I hit the jackpot! An all-expenses-paid holiday to Europe! Three months! Can you believe it?"

I roll my eyes. "No, I can't, and neither should you, Dad," I mutter under my breath.

"The only catch is we leave tomorrow. Your mother's gone crazy. She'll be lucky I don't take her out back and shoot her before we leave. Anyway, darling, with your school schedule and our windfall, we won't see you before we leave."

A smile stretches across my face when my mom's voice chimes into the background. "Don't forget to tell her about the postcards, Norm."

"Postcards. Yes, yes, I'll tell her," my dad says. "We'll send you and your class postcards from each location we visit. We thought they could mark them on the big world map you have in your classroom."

Heat creeps across my chest at the same time a stabbing pain hits my heart. Last year, my class spent the three months before summer vacation discussing which regions of the world we would like to visit the most. Surprisingly, the chosen locations varied significantly.

"All right, darling, I have to go and help your mother pack before she leaves without me. Talk soon, sweetie. Bye," my dad says before disconnecting the call.

My heart slithers into my gut. How long will it be until I see my parents again? Is this arrangement with Rico just temporary or permanent? Will I ever see my friends and family again?

"You will see them again, Kitten. I promise."

I jump, startled. Rico's movements are so agile I didn't notice him standing in the doorway of my room. Pushing off the doorjamb, he paces closer to me. I watch him cross the room, riveted just by the way he walks. Graceful yet authoritative.

"What can I do to help?" His tone is still commanding but not as gruff as it usually is.

You'd think my first thoughts would be to plead for my release, but for some strange reason, I hand him my empty cosmetics bag and point to the small washroom next to the entryway of my apartment.

"Anything marked with a B is mine."

Rico smiles a lazy grin that surges my pulse to the lower half of my body before spinning on his heels and ambling to the bathroom.

Pretending I can't feel an odd pain twisting my heart, I grab a handful of my clothing off the overflowing racks in my closet and pace to my suitcase sitting in the middle of my bed. My brisk strides slow when the answering machine switches on, announcing it's about to record a new message.

After dumping my clothing into my open suitcase, I lean on the doorjamb of my room just as Colt's deep voice barrels out of the answering machine speakers. "Still trying to work out where you placed your new tattoo, baby girl. I haven't stopped thinking about it all weekend. Might need a private, in-depth search, starting at the cute little dip you have in your collarbone—"

The remainder of his message is lost when the answering machine sails across the room and smashes into a wall. It shatters into dozens of tiny pieces while also leaving a dent in the drywall of my living room.

With my heart hammering my ribs, I drift my eyes from the mangled remains of my answering machine to my entry table. Rico stares straight at me, unwavering and calm, a complete contradiction to the maniac who just demolished my retro answering machine in a rage of jealousy.

"What?" he asks, seemingly unaffected by my confounded stare.

When a trace of a smirk forms on his plump lips, the ache between my thighs has me grateful I'm leaning against a wall. Is it wrong of me to say his aggressive nature turns me on? Even having no recollection of our time together in Vegas, I know it would have been better than anything I've ever experienced. You can't have his arrogance without skills to back it up, and the way he holds himself reveals he'd be exceptional in bed. I bet he has the type of control that would make even the most rational woman go wild to unleash it.

Wild enough they would marry him in a matter of hours.

My attention snaps back to the present when Rico mutters, "We only have fifteen minutes, Kitten, nowhere near enough time to work through your fiendish thoughts."

My cheeks heat from his bold words as my brows scrunch. I am in the process of packing my bags as I'm being forced to leave my hometown against my will, yet I am getting hot and bothered by the wicked smirk of a man who is the equivalent of a stranger to me.

While grumbling to myself about my newfound stupidity, I set back to work on packing my belongings. I've always been the cautious, safeguarded member of my inner circle, but one glance into his dark gaze has me throwing caution to the wind. Even knowing I shouldn't be, I'm fascinated by him.

I should have heeded my grandmother's advice. Vegas made me lose my mind.

Ten minutes later, I hand my overflowing suitcase to a burly-looking man standing on my door stoop. When he exits my apartment, I scribble a quick note to Lacey, begging for her not to panic and that I'll call her as soon as possible.

After a final glance around the apartment I've lived in for the past two years, I shadow Rico outside. The instant I step onto the tiled floor, my regular breathing pattern turns into ragged pants. From the corner of my eye, I spot Colt emerging from his ground-floor apartment.

Sensing my snooping stare, he cranks his neck and locks his eyes with mine. My heart beats triple time when he smiles a roguish grin before he hotfoots it to the lobby.

I stop walking, muted and in fear. "I forgot something," I stammer out, saying any excuse I can to stop Colt and Rico from meeting.

With Rico's overreaction to Colt's playful message on my answering machine, I don't think a face-to-face meeting would come highly recommended. And considering there's no other viable exit from our building than to cross the lobby, I need to delay our departure.

"We need to go, Kitten. My men will collect anything you need later." Rico places his hand on my lower back and guides me into the open elevator two men are guarding.

Just like our first ride together, this one is infused with a shocking current—it isn't only filled with lust. I chew on my nails and fidget on the spot. My squirms make it look like I'm one of my students busting to use the bathroom.

When the elevator doors ding open, my eyes scan the room. I breathe a sigh of relief when Colt is nowhere to be seen.

My thankfulness is short-lived.

An unexpected squeal parts my lips when a set of arms wrap around my waist and hoist me off the floor, scaring the living bejesus out of me. Not just from Colt's sudden grabbing but from the livid glare that sparked in Rico's eyes the instant I was yanked away from him.

"Ready for round two, baby girl," Colt croons into my ear.

The temperature in the lobby becomes stifling when a deep, cavernous growl shreds through my ears. Like he can sense he's in imminent danger, Colt places me back onto my feet and drifts his eyes in the direction of the loud growl.

Rico glares at him, veins pumping, nostrils flaring. His eyes are black, haunted, and look like they could kill a man with only a stare.

Aiming to tame the beast, I stand next to Rico and sling my shaking arm around his waist, where I stop frozen, held captive by a sudden flashback...

Rico stares at me with blazing eyes, his attitude laid back, his smile lazy. "My beautiful Kitten. My light in a world full of darkness."

I roll over and balance my chin on his sweat-slicked chest. "Always. You'll not spend one more day living in blackness. Not while I'm by your side..."

Pain claws at my chest, leaving my heart open and exposed for all to see. That was one of the most beautiful memories I've ever had. Not just because of the words spoken but also from the loving gleam brightening Rico's dark gaze. He looked peaceful, and if I'm not mistaken, happy.

I snap back to reality when Rico's pulse surges through my arm wrapped around his waist. Pretending my spur-of-the-moment memory had no effect, I lock my eyes with Colt.

"Marshall, this is my... *husband,* Rico," I introduce, my words as uneasy as my facial expression.

Colt's brows become lost in his hairline. I don't know if his shock originates from calling him Marshall or my declaration that Rico is my husband.

"Rico, this is a friend of mine, Co... ah... Marshall."

Sweat forms on my top brow when the two men undertake a sweat-producing showdown. Colt's face is a mix of confused and amused. Rico's is nothing but blatant fury.

My heart recommences beating when Colt smiles hesitantly before offering his hand to Rico to shake. "It's a pleasure to meet you, Rico. I'd love to hear how you swooped in and stole Ravenshoe's most valuable asset." Colt's tone overflows with egotism. "As far as I was aware, baby girl was still on the market last week."

Rico growls. I'm not talking a slight rumble. I'm talking a full, pussy-quaking growl.

"I can assure you *Kitten* was not on the market last week." His gaze is as dangerous as his deep tone. "Unless this *market* you're referring to is my bed. Because that's where she was. *For hours.*"

My eyes bounce between Rico and Colt, beyond shocked two ridiculously handsome specimens are undertaking a pissing contest right in front of me—let alone *over* me.

The belligerent expression on Colt's face vanishes the instant Rico accepts his offer of a handshake. For every second that passes, the bronze coloring of Colt's face decreases, as does the size of his pupils.

When Colt's hand turns so white it looks like his fingers are about to drop off, I yank Rico's hand away from him. "We really must go."

I attempt to drag Rico toward the entry doors. My efforts are fruitless. His stance is so stable, a crane wouldn't budge him.

I peer up at his stern expression. "Come on, *honey*, we wouldn't want to miss our flight."

Colt's eyes snap to mine. "Flight? Where are you going?" The furious pace of Rico's pulse surging through his body wallops my hand when Colt takes a step closer to me. "What's going on, Blaire? Are you okay? *Are you safe?*" He whispers his last question.

My head rockets to Rico when he sneers. "She has never been

safer, *Colt.*" He spits out his name like venom. "I can't make the same guarantee about you."

Spinning on his heels, Rico walks toward the double doors of my apartment building. His rough yank on my arm ensures I fall in step beside him. I briskly shake my head when Colt attempts to follow us out of the lobby. His exchange with Rico has already gained him the devoted attention of two of the men who have been flanking Rico and me for the past forty minutes. I don't want the spotlight to shine on him any more than it already has.

"I'm fine, Colt. I'll be back in a couple of weeks. Look after Lacey for me," I squeak out before Rico's fast speed has us hitting the sidewalk in under five seconds.

The two women who were roaming their gazes over Rico earlier hover in close the instant we step onto the cracked concrete sidewalk. I run my unclutched hand down the front of my blouse when their malicious words insult my already faltering composure.

"If you ever want a real woman, sugar, look me up."

"I thought trannie dressing was the latest fad, not grannie dressing."

"Bag it before you shag it, honey. Her head, not your cock."

Rico opens the back door of the Escalade and gestures for me to enter. When I slide across the cold leather seats, he turns his narrowed gaze to the gentleman manning the driver's door.

"Deal with them," he requests before sliding into the car next to me and slamming the door shut.

My heart rate climbs into dangerous territory when the man in the suit approaches the double doors of my building. I try to force words out of my mouth, but my fear has rendered me speechless. The blood pressure returns to a safe zone when Rico's goon stops upon reaching the two women who just insulted me. I suck in a grateful breath. I thought he was going after Colt.

With his hands clenched at his side, the man holds a conversation with the two women. Even though he's only speaking, the more he interacts with them, the more their expressions change from playful to scared.

After a few more silent words, the man in the suit gestures his head to the Escalade. My eyes dart between the two scantily clad women approaching the back-passenger side window Rico is sliding down.

With my heart in my throat, I tilt my head to the side and peer out the window.

"We're sorry if our words caused you any harm. We were only teasing," says the blonde wearing a hot pink sequin top.

Rico's furious growl rumbles through my chest.

"But we shouldn't have teased you. What we said was wrong and disrespectful, and we're very sorry." The brunette's words fire off her tongue before they have a chance to be fully developed.

Several seconds pass in uncomfortable silence before Rico's deep voice breaks the quiet. "Do you accept their apology, Kitten? Or should they be served a more severe punishment for their malicious jealousy?"

Two pairs of panicked eyes snap to mine, their expressions spooked and frozen.

They sigh loudly in sync when I shakily say, "I accept their apology."

With a wave of Rico's hand, the women are removed from the side of the Escalade. When the vehicle lurches into the dense flow of traffic that always impedes the streets of Ravenshoe, I glance back to my building. A pair of concerned green eyes reflects back at me.

"*I'm fine,*" I mouth to Colt.

My words don't seem to reassure him, but they are all I have to offer.

Shocked—not only at the events that just transpired but the entirety of my day—I keep my eyes planted on the scenery whizzing by my window for the next ten minutes. It feels like I've emerged into a parallel universe. Everything looks identical, but somehow, it's all different.

My attention shifts from scenery gazing when Rico's low-timbre voice jingles through my ears. "Stop here," he demands to the driver.

I scan my eyes over the building we've pulled in front of. It's a nightclub Lacey and I have frequented numerous times the past year called The Dungeon. It's owned by the same gentleman who is the landlord of my apartment building, Mr. Isaac Holt.

After scribbling a saying onto a blank square of cardboard, Rico swings open the back passenger door of the Escalade and walks toward a flashy-looking sedan parked at the side of the club. He twists his neck to the right before cranking it to the left. Happy he hasn't caught the attention of any curious eyes, he slips the card under the sedan's windshield before walking back to the Escalade and curling inside.

"Who was the note for?" I ask, incapable of harnessing my curiosity.

Rico turns his dark eyes to me before he mutters, "My sister, Isabelle."

Chapter Eight

"Your sister lives in Ravenshoe?"

Rico presses his index finger to my lips before he does a single nod of his head.

"How did your sister leave your *family* without any... *repercussions?*" I ask through his finger zapping my lips. I keep my voice calm even though my composure is anything but.

When Rico lifts his eyes to the rearview mirror, I follow his gaze. The driver doesn't hide the fact he's eyeballing us. I wouldn't be surprised if we veered off the road, considering his dark gaze is paying more attention to the rearview mirror than the heavy flow of traffic surrounding us.

A startled squeal rolls up my chest when Rico seizes my wrist and drags me across the dark leather seat. His endeavor of bridging the gap between us doesn't stop until I'm straddled in his lap. My eyes widen when his sudden movements cause the thickness in his trousers to brush the heat between my legs. I don't know if he's aroused, but try as I may, I can't ignore the... umm... girth of his... umm... penis.

Grow up, Blaire! You sound like one of your students!

Penis, penis, penis, I chant to myself as I struggle to settle the erratic beat of my heart. Once I've gained a small sense of composure, I drop my eyes to Rico. He's staring straight at me, eyes blazing, heart thumping.

Any chance of calming the wild beat of my heart flies out the window when he says, "Undo the buttons on your blouse, Kitten."

I bounce my massively dilated eyes between his. "What?"

He runs his hand up my back, only stopping when he reaches the nape of my neck. His touch forces a breathless moan to ashamedly spill from my lips. From a man who is a stranger, he seems to know all the erogenous zones of my body. The most obvious, the portion of skin between my collarbone and neck.

He drags his thumb along my collarbone while asking, "Do you want to know how my sister left my family?"

I nod, a little overeagerly.

I can't help it.

Just the warmth of his hand on the nape of my neck has my usually noble persona weakening. When he's close to me, it's like I'm in a trance, stuck captive by his intoxicating eyes and alluring aura.

"Open your blouse, Kitten," he repeats, his words less demanding than earlier.

Ludicrously, I do as instructed without another protest spilling from my lips.

With teeth-shattering shakes impeding my hands, it takes a little longer than normal to undo the five buttons of my blouse. I'm wearing a fitted white cami beneath my shirt, but I feel naked when it drapes open at the front.

My unease has nothing to do with Rico's absorbing eyes drinking in every inch of my skin and everything to do with the driver's imprudent gaze scorching a hole in the back of my head. The only way he could be more involved in our intimate gathering is if he placed himself in the small section of air left between Rico and me. That's how enthusiastic his spying is.

Keeping his captivating eyes planted on my flushed face, Rico cups one of my breasts in his hand, while his other hand on the nape of my neck draws me in close to him.

"Kiss me, Kitten," he murmurs against my lips. "I need your lips on mine."

I stare into his eyes, trying to force my mouth to cite a complaint to his request. Nothing comes out. So, operating purely on the desires of my heart, I cup the edge of his jaw and seal my mouth over his.

His lips move sweetly under mine, the strokes of his tongue controlled and gentle while his fingers send a jolt of pleasure down my spine when he firms his grip on my neck and strengthens our kiss. I part my lips more, surrendering my mouth to his mind-hazing talent. His kiss is sweet and tender while also dominating and controlling. He really is the equivalent of night and day, blackness and light... *enemy and lover.*

The roughness of his five-o'clock shadow scratches the skin below my ear when he drags his lips down the side of my neck. "You can't trust anyone, Kitten. Even when they don't appear to be watching you, they are." I can only just hear his faint whisper over the mad beat of my heart when he adds on, "Especially me."

Suddenly, the reasoning behind his brash approach smashes into me. Because of our closeness, the driver can't hear a word spilling from Rico's lips. And since we look like every other newlywed couple who can't keep their hands off each other, he'll be none the wiser to the private conversation we are undertaking right under his snitching nose.

My heart rate climbs into coronary failure territory. I don't know if it's from Rico's admission that I can't trust anyone—not even him— or from the way his fingers have tweaked my nipple into a firm bud in mere seconds. For a man who can appear cold and heartless, his touch causes a burning heat to scorch every inch of my body.

I'm panting, wet, and waging one of the hardest battles I've ever fought not to rub myself against him like a crazed woman who can't control her libido. The only thing stopping me from carrying out my desire is when Rico continues talking. With how quiet he is, all my energy must be reserved for listening only.

As Rico nips, licks, and kisses my neckline, he tells me the story of how his oldest sister, Isabelle, was sold after the death of their mother. My heart clutches in my chest when he informs me his sister was only six years old when she was placed on the black market. That's the age of half the students in my class.

When Rico finishes his story, I take a second to gather my bases. It's no easy feat with every nerve in my body solely dedicated to Rico's lips still attached to my neck. But even with my brain muddled with fear and excitement, my conclusion about the information handed to me never alters. If the only way a blood descendant can leave Rico's family is by being sold, what happens to someone who doesn't have a drop of Popov blood running through their veins? What happens to people like me?

Like he can hear my private thoughts, Rico mutters, "No one will *ever* hurt you, Kitten. Not while you're with me."

Before I can ask if his statement includes himself, the Escalade pulls into a private airstrip on the outskirts of Ravenshoe. After speaking to Rico in a foreign language, the driver climbs out of the car and stands guard at the side. The stern mask Rico wears in front of his crew slowly slides down his face as he adjusts my disheveled blouse back onto my shoulders and fastens the buttons.

Once I'm semi-respectable—*my outfit, not my mind*—Rico locks his dark gaze with mine. "Is Colt going to be a problem?"

My tongue grows thicker from the blackness forming in his sable eyes. "No." Strands of blonde locks fall into my eyes when I shake my head. "Colt has only ever been a friend." *Not through any choice of my own,* but I'll keep that snippet of information to myself.

Rico's Adam's apple bobs up and down. "Okay. Good. Because I don't share."

"Duly noted," I reply, my voice disgustingly chipper considering the circumstances of our exchange.

What the hell is wrong with me? I'm being forced to leave my hometown against my will, yet I'm pleased my husband is refusing to share me with another man.

Screw my mind. A lifetime of morals was lost the instant I stepped off the plane in Vegas.

I'm not the only one stunned by my reply. Rico stares at me, his face a cross between shocked and delighted. With a predatory smirk etched on his mouth, he curls out of the Escalade. Since I'm still sitting on his lap, he takes me right along with him.

The vileness of my predicament smacks back into me when Rico sets me onto my feet and walks into a heavily manned airport hangar. When I'm with him one-on-one, I forget he's shrouded by an impenetrable cloud of darkness. It's just me and him—the stranger I married.

While keeping my nosy glare hidden, I scan my eyes around the premises. At a quick guess, I'd say there are at least a dozen men with weapons strapped to their chests and another half a dozen dressed similarly to Rico. For a man more than capable of protecting himself, it seems a little dramatic for him to have so much excessive protection.

Rico stops at the end of a set of stairs that climb up to a private jet before cranking his neck back to face me. I almost swallow my tongue when he mutters, "The security detail is not for me, Kitten. They are here for you."

Ignoring my gaped mouth at the fact he read my mind twice in under a minute, he places his hand on the curve of my back and guides me onto the plane. As we enter the opulent space, my eyes shoot in all directions, unsure which fine feature to absorb first—the rich, opulent seating area that looks like it belongs in the middle of a mansion, not a plane, or the crystal and dark wood bar that's stocked with every bottle of alcohol you could imagine.

For men who live in the cloak of darkness, they sure have world-class standards.

Upon noticing the direction of my gaze, Rico asks, "Would you like a drink?"

My lips tug into a lewd smirk. "Why ask what I want when you can read my mind?"

While smirking a grin that sets my pulse racing, Rico gestures for me to sit in one of the two white leather chairs in the central area of the plane. Not trusting my thrumming-with-excitement legs, I plop into the closest leather seat.

Rico removes his suit jacket and throws it over the chair beside me before shifting on his feet to face the pretty brunette flight attendant. I'm not at all surprised that her cheeks turn a vibrant hue of red when she's awarded Rico's alluringly dark eyes. "I'll have a double shot of whiskey, and Blaire will have a sparkling apple cider."

Huffing, I cross my arms over my chest before muttering, "Not even close."

Smiling, Rico slots his backside into the seat next to me. "I know it isn't what you wanted, Kitten. But considering what happened the last time you had a wine spritzer, I altered your request. Your drink will still have the apple flavor you're after, but without the alcohol content." When I stare at him with shock and disbelief tainting my face, he leans back in his chair and rests his ankle on his opposite knee. "You did want an apple martini, didn't you?"

The smugness lining his face advises he's aware of my reply. He is one hundred percent correct. I pinch myself—hard. I must be dreaming. Otherwise, how would he have known that? There are millions of drinks in the world, so there's no way he could have known I was going to order *that* particular drink.

Rico accepts his double whiskey from the flight attendant before resting it on the table between us. I mutter a quick "Thank you" when she hands me an apple cider. After placing it on the table next to Rico's glass, I look back at him. It is the fight of my life not to shoot my hand up to clutch my chest when I discover he's watching me with a poignant stare, but I keep them fisted in my lap—barely.

After a heart-clutching staredown, Rico mutters, "You really don't remember anything about the night we got married, do you, Kitten?"

A range of emotions flares in his eyes when I shake my head. Relief. Confusion. Anger. It all pumps through his dark gaze. "I feel like I know you, I just... don't."

With knitted brows, he nods, then adjusts his position so he can peer out the arched window at his side, my confession ending our reunion on a somber note.

Chapter Nine

As soon as the plane is thirty-five thousand feet in the air, Rico unlatches his seat belt and stalks toward a varnished door at the back of the plane. He still walks with commanding power, but his shoulders hang a little lower.

Once he passes through the door, I lower my gaze to my lap. I've never been on a private jet before, but I'm fairly confident that's the bedroom. Considering I don't want a rerun of my shameful response to his touch in the Escalade, I keep my backside planted in my seat and my hands flicking through a wide variety of magazines the flight attendant keeps handing me.

* * *

Two hours later, when my bladder's protests become too great for me to ignore, I dump a gossip magazine onto the table in front of me then head for the flight attendant who served me my drink earlier.

"Excuse me, where's the bathroom located?"

My heart sinks to my stomach when she points to the door Rico entered hours ago.

"Are you serious?" I gasp out in surprise.

After smiling to hide her shock, she bobs her chin. "The only bathroom in this jet is in the main bedroom, Mrs. Popov."

"Then where do you pee?" I blurt out before my brain can stop me or fathom that she just called me Mrs. Popov.

While staring straight in the eyes, she mumbles, "I hold."

If her eyes weren't relaying the truth of her statement, I might have laughed. The flight is five hours long. No one can hold it that long. *Can they?*

When my bladder kicks up a stink about the delay, I smile a thank you before sauntering to the back of the plane, my steps hurried. I knock three times before opening the door. Rico is sitting behind a chunky wooden desk, speaking in a foreign language into the cell phone attached to his ear.

Upon noticing my presence, his head lifts, and his dark eyes connect with mine. I hook my thumb to the frosted glass door on my right, advising I need to use the restroom. His flow of conversation continues without pause as he nods, soundlessly granting my request.

I slip into the space, close the door behind me, then dash into the bathroom.

"Oh, Lord," I mumble under my breath when I enter the extravagant washroom. Such opulent surroundings shouldn't be reserved for peeing.

After doing my business, I wash my hands and exit the restroom. I freeze halfway out the door when I notice Rico is no longer sitting behind the chunky desk. He's near the edge of the bed. His suit jacket has been removed, and the top two buttons of his crisp white shirt have been undone, exposing inches of his smooth, tanned torso.

Unlike when I entered the bathroom, his gloriously thick hair is rustled like he's been running his fingers through it, and his composure is a stark contrast to the man he was moments ago.

I'd be lying if I said his fierce gaze isn't scaring me.

"Come here, Kitten," Rico demands, his voice gritty. When my feet remained rooted in place, he releases a deep exhalation, infusing the space with his whiskey-scented breath before saying, "I'll *never* touch you against your will."

Even frightened, just like last week, my intuition tells me I can trust him. Furthermore, our time together has been an awkward dance routine—two steps forward, one step back—but I've always been a willing participant.

After unclenching my fists, I slowly step toward him. As I glide across the room, he shifts his head to the side and watches me in silence, categorizing every movement my body makes. The fear clutching my heart intensifies when I see nothing but anger clouding his beautiful irises, but then I remember the words I spoke to him last week.

You will not spend one more day in darkness. Not while I'm by your side.

Eager to keep my promise, I increase my speed. When I hit the edge of the bed, Rico lifts a single piece of A4 glossy paper I didn't notice he was holding until now. I was too focused on working out a way to lighten the darkness swamping his eyes to notice anything else.

"Do you know this man?"

When he hands the paper to me, my eyes widen while taking in the image. "That's Timothy Jamison. He's a teacher at my school."

It's a grainy surveillance camera image, but there's no mistaking Timothy's thick-rimmed glasses and wonky smile. I've also worked with him for two years, so I'm confident with my assessment.

"Was this taken in Las Vegas?" I ask upon seeing a bank of poker machines in the background of the highly pixilated photo.

When Rico nods, I gasp in a quick breath. I'm snitching on an acquaintance to a man who governs Las Vegas.

After raising my eyes from the photo clutched in my hand, I ask, "Why do you want to know who Timothy is? He's a good person. He wouldn't have done anything illegal. He is a teacher at my school and a father. A well-respected—"

My blubbering halts when Rico announces, "He is the reason you can't remember your trip to Vegas."

I glare at him in shocked silence for a moment. "What! How?" I blurt out once my shock subsides.

"He drugged you," he replies like it's everyday news.

I take a step back, dazed and confused. "Why would he do that? He wouldn't do that. That doesn't make any sense."

Rico walks to a laptop sitting in the middle of the desk. After hitting the space bar, a heavy flow of chatter booms out of his laptop speakers. Through wobbly legs, I move closer to the desk when the video on the monitor zooms in on a round table with a dozen people seated around it. Even having no recollection of my time in Vegas, I can tell this image is from the Teacher of the Year awards luncheon because I recognize a few faces sitting around the table, drinking wine and laughing.

The most familiar face belongs to Timothy.

He's seated next to me.

Blood roars to the surface of my skin, illuminating it with a pink hue when Timothy drops a small pill into my drink as I stand from my seat to say goodbye to a lady I met at a joint school camp last year. After stirring my half-consumed wine spritzer with a butter knife from the table, he slouches low into his chair and joins a conversation with two gentlemen sitting on his left.

I remain motionless as the unethical scene unfolds before my very eyes. After bidding farewell to Darlene, I retake my seat next to Timothy. He smiles before gesturing his head to the half-filled glass of spritzer in front of me, encouraging me to finish it.

Within five minutes of consuming the laced drink, I excuse myself from the table. Even watching the video from a bird's-eye view, I can see my eyes have a little more sheen than normal, and my mood is surprisingly chipper.

The camera angle shifts multiple times as it follows me through the facility where the event was held, but no matter which direction I take, Timothy is a few steps behind me in every frame.

When the image freezes upon me exiting a set of double doors, I snap my eyes to Rico. "What happened? Did he..." I can't force the words out of my mouth.

Luckily for me, Rico has no qualms filling in the gaps. "No, Kitten. He never got the chance," he replies, staring at me with angry eyes.

"How do you know that? How can you be so sure?" I ask while rubbing my chest, trying to erase the pain stabbing the middle of it.

"Because this happened."

Rico sits on the edge of the bed, seizes my wrist, then pulls me onto his lap. Before I can react, a hidden memory rushes to the surface of my muddled brain...

"Oh, I'm so sorry. The heel of my shoe caught the carpet pile," I apologize to the gentleman whose lap I just stumbled into.

Dark, beautiful eyes stare down at me, holding me captive by their unique beauty. The sable-haired stranger doesn't speak. He doesn't need to. His eyes share a lifetime of stories without a word spilling from his lips.

After giving myself a few moments to register every unique speckle in his mesmerizing eyes, I snap back to reality. I'm sitting in a stranger's lap after tumbling into his arms. Can anyone say, 'cliché?'

"Sorry about the intrusion."

Cringing at the weakness of my words, I continue my endeavor of locating a bathroom. Ever since I finished my wine spritzer ten minutes ago, my tummy has been unsettled and my mind woozy. I'd also like to say it is the cause of my inflamed cheeks, but unfortunately, that isn't the case. The blame for my blemished appearance solely belongs to the handsome stranger eyeballing me as I step away from him.

My pulse quickens when, in the corner of my eye, I catch sight of the dark-haired stranger throwing a casino chip into the middle of a poker table. After gesturing his head to a group of men dressed in black suits lounging at the side of the poker table, he races to catch up with me. His long, efficient strides have him reaching me in three captivating heartbeats.

A jolting spasm rockets up my arm when he places his hand on the crook of my elbow. Muted by my body's insane reaction to this mysterious stranger's touch, I allow him to guide me through the vast throng of people milling about the space without a word spilling from my lips...

When I lift my eyes to Rico, my heart squeezes from seeing the same dark, beautiful eyes from my memory staring back at me. "Where did we go?"

A grin curls on the edge of his lips, sending my heart rate skyrocketing. It's the first genuine smile I've seen etched on his face, and it is nearly as striking as his dark eyes. "We went to the bathroom."

He tucks a strand of my hair behind my ear, stands from the bed, then places me on my feet. I try to hold in my disappointed groan, but it escapes my lips involuntarily.

"One memory at a time, Kitten," Rico responds to my whine, believing it was only based on my interest in unraveling my lost memories.

It wasn't.

The Rico standing before me intrigues me just as much as extracting my lost memories.

My brows scrunch when he strides to the bedroom door, opens it, and gestures with his head for me to leave. "I have some business to take care of before we land."

My heart smashes my ribs when the first half of our conversation dawns on me. I span the distance between us, my steps shaky, hindered by a pair of wobbly legs. "You're not going to do anything to Timothy, are you?"

"Don't ask questions you don't want an answer to, Kitten," Rico replies before slapping me on the backside, his spank so hard it pushes me into the central section of the private jet.

Defying my Jell-O legs, I pivot around to face him. Just like in my memory, his eyes relay his intentions without a word needing to flow from his plump lips.

My mouth twitches, dying to spill the objections my brain is screaming, but no matter how hard I fight, not a word escapes my parched lips.

Taking my silence as confirmation I want him to execute revenge on Timothy for drugging me, Rico winks before shutting the bedroom door.

Oh. My. Lord.

What did I just do?

Chapter Ten

Guilt consumes the next hour of our trip. Do I believe what Timothy did was wrong? Yes, without a doubt. Do I believe he should be punished for what he did? Yes, more to stop it from happening to another woman than anything else. Do I want that punishment issued by a member of the Las Vegas mob? No, not at all.

With my stomach twisted in knots, I stand from my seat and make my way back to the main bedroom of the private jet. My beliefs the past hour have never altered. It has merely taken me this long to build the courage to go against a man who equally frightens and intrigues me. However, I must do this. If I ever want the chance to rescue Rico from the blackness, I can't let him make heinous decisions no man has the right to make.

Timothy will one day meet his maker, but until then, there are legal ways justice can be served.

Not bothering to knock, I enter the room. Rico is sitting back behind the desk, speaking into his cell phone. Even not understanding a word he's saying, I can tell his temper is short-fused. The veins in his thick biceps are bulging, his jaw is clenched, and his entire composure screams blatant fury. My hesitation to approach him only lasts as long as it takes for me to recall Timothy's youngest son only turned two last month. He's a baby.

Just like earlier, Rico's eyes follow me as I cross the room to stand in front of him, except this time, his eyes aren't filled with anger. They're brimming with downright fury.

Overlooking the feverish agitation beaming out of him in invisible waves, I remove the cell phone from his grasp, disconnect his call, then toss his phone onto a stack of papers on his desk.

The furious tick impinging his jaw amplifies when I lower onto my knees and peer up into his eyes. "Please, I'm begging you, Enrique. Don't do this. I may not remember you, but my heart does. It knows there's more to you than this lifestyle. It knows you're a good man. Don't break its confidence."

If I thought his eyes were violent before, it's nothing compared to how they look now. I don't know if his anger originates from me pleading to him on my knees or from the fact I called him Enrique for the first time.

"You're willing to fall to your knees and beg for mercy for the man who drugged you?" he snarls out, his voice the most malicious I've heard.

With tears welling in my eyes, I nod.

They almost topple when Rico shouts, "He was going to rape you, Blaire! Do you understand that?"

"Yes. I'm aware of that," I reply, gingerly nodding. "But he has a wife and three small children—"

"Children he doesn't deserve to have!" His angry roar startles me so much I jump.

After pushing his chair back from his desk, he stands with his fists clenched at his sides and his face lined with anger. Fear unlike anything I've ever felt races through my veins. It isn't because I believe he will hurt me. For some reason unbeknownst to me, I truly believe he means me no harm. My worry is for Timothy and his family.

"I'm not saying he doesn't deserve to be punished for what he did. He does. But not like this. Not unlawfully."

"You wouldn't be saying that if you knew what he was planning to do to you!" The bite of agony in his voice sets me on edge. "If you hadn't fallen into my lap, you would have fallen into a shallow ditch."

Dread clutches my throat, squeezing so hard, I can't inhale an entire breath. "What?"

Rico runs his hand across the scruff on his chin before snatching a pile of papers off the printer sitting on his desk. His dark, haunted eyes stare into mine for many seconds before he hands the printouts to me.

I hesitate, wary of the concern beaming from his eyes before I eventually drop my eyes to the photos I'm clasping for dear life. My spare hand shoots up to cover my mouth when my stomach lurches in protest of the ghastly images reflecting at me. Although each picture has a unique backdrop, the theme of the photographs is horrifyingly similar. They all contain the body of a woman in her early to mid-twenties lying lifeless in a shallow grave.

When I raise my eyes to Rico, I notice he is watching me cautiously. Although his face is lined with anger, I now realize his anger isn't directed at me. It's for the monster who did this heinous act to these poor defenseless women.

"Who did this?" I ask, my voice quieter than a hushed whisper.

"Timothy," Rico replies without pause, his voice deep and teemed with anger.

Refusing to acknowledge that a family man could ever be responsible for such atrocious acts, I shake my head. This is not something a married father of three would do. This is the deed of a horrible person with a black soul.

Rico crouches down in front of me then removes the papers and photographs from my hand. He lays the pictures out in a pattern similar to a timeline on the varnished wooden floors.

My heart breaks when my eyes roam over six beautiful ladies who lost their lives way too early.

"Annie Rogers was killed on May tenth last year." Rico points to a police image of a lady with long caramel hair buried in a shallow grave in front of a mountain landscape. "Timothy attended a conference in her hometown the same weekend." He taps on the second image. "Clarissa Enrode was killed July thirtieth. Timothy was a guest speaker at her university the same weekend."

For each name he goes through, my heart cracks more.

"Could it be a coincidence?" I lock my moisture-filled eyes with his. "There has to be some explanation. Some..." My words drown out when I fail to find a legitimate reason as to why Timothy would be at each location on the exact dates the women were killed.

Panic roars through my veins when Rico says, "There are surveillance tapes matching yours for each girl in each town. He drugged them, raped them, then killed them." His dark eyes settle on mine. "If you didn't fall into my lap, he would have done the same thing to you."

My heart stings when the undeniable facts he has displayed crash into me. I sit on the floorboards, my stomach churning with fear and grief. I had danced with the devil and once again escaped with my life. These beautiful women weren't as lucky.

My throat tightens painfully as I struggle to hold in my devastating sob dying to break free. My efforts are fruitless. Nothing can keep in my despair. I thought life as I'd known it ended when I stumbled into Rico's lap. Little did I know it was only just beginning.

The instant the first whimper escapes my parched lips, Rico scoops me into his arms. I cling to his white dress shirt when he moves us to sit on the edge of the bed. Tears flood my cheeks as the disturbing images play on repeat in my mind. I know why Rico had to show me the photographs—I would have never believed him otherwise—but now I wish I'd never seen them. It's another set of memories I'd give anything to forget.

Rico doesn't speak a word over the next several minutes. He simply runs his hand over my back in a circular motion until I eventually give in to unconsciousness.

* * *

Several hours later, I wake up startled and confused, and for the first time in years, without the body-havocking effects of a nightmare. I'm lying in bed with my back pressed against the warmth of a body. Just from the spicy scent alone, I know it's Rico sleeping next to me, but the way every nerve in my body has sparked is another clear indication.

Unlike when I entered the room earlier, it's void of any light, natural or unnatural. Since the shutters on the windows are closed, I can't tell if it's night or if the plane is sitting in a dark airport hangar.

After giving myself a few minutes to gather my bearings, I carefully roll onto my opposite hip, not wanting to wake Rico. A breathless squeal squeaks between my lips when I'm met with his dark and beautiful gaze. He's awake and staring straight at me.

"How long have you been awake?" My voice is scratchy from the rawness of my throat.

He brushes a bunch of unruly hairs off my face while replying, "I didn't sleep."

My brows furrow. "Then why are you lying in bed with me?"

A flare of emotion passes through his eyes, renewing my hope that I didn't lose all rational thoughts when I was drugged. Although I'm sure my laced drink impeded my usually astute brain, while peering into the eyes of the stranger lying across from me, I realize it wasn't just drugs ruling my decisions last week. Part of it was my heart.

What I said to him earlier was true. I don't know him, but my heart does.

Rico takes his time configuring a response to my question. Just when I think he isn't going to answer, he mutters, "You whimpered every time I moved."

I have no chance of holding in my grin, so I let it break free. "You stayed with me so I wouldn't wake?" Disbelief and a small dash of glee are evident in my tone.

While peering into my eyes, he nods.

"How long?" When he looks at me, confused, I add, "How long did you stay with me?"

He checks the time on his watch before announcing, "A little over four hours."

My heart skips a beat. Dark Rico intimidates me, but knowing he stayed with me for four hours exposes a side to him I don't think many people have witnessed—the light side.

After a short beat, I ask, "Why does this feel so familiar?"

Rico smiles a vain grin. "Because it is," he replies before tugging on a strand of my hair.

Although hazy, the faintest memory creeps into my mind from his playfulness...

My heavy eyelids slowly flutter open before drifting around the opulent room to absorb the rich antique furniture and beautiful chandelier hanging from the ceiling rose. My observant gaze has me stumbling onto an even more beautiful sight—a pair of dark and alluring eyes.

"I fell asleep again, didn't I?" My words are lazy and hoarse.

Rico's lips tug into a grin as he nods. "Only for twenty minutes this time," he replies before pulling a strand of my hair playfully.

While stretching out, a glimmer of light captures my attention. Smiling, I lower my left hand to inspect my newly added accessory—a ruby and diamond platinum wedding band. "It's so beautiful."

Rico props himself onto his elbow and peers down into my light green eyes. "Not as beautiful as you."

Even with a broad smile stretched across my face, I can't stifle a big yawn. I'm exhausted.

"Sleep if you're tired, Kitten." Rico runs his hand down the side of my face, doubling the heaviness of my eyelids. "I'll be here when you wake..."

I prop my elbow onto the satin pillowcase and rest my weighted head on my open palm. "Did you sleep at all the night we got married?"

Rico smiles a similar grin to the one in my memory before shaking his head.

"Why not?" I grimace when my overly girly voice bounces around the quiet room.

"Because I didn't want to wake up to find out it was all a dream." His voice is so faint, I barely hear what he says.

Heat expands across my chest, filling some of the cracks that formed in my heart the past week. I want to say something to ease the confused look on Rico's face, but I can't think of a single phrase that would be appropriate in this situation. It's so odd. Although the man before me is technically a stranger, he also seems so familiar. *Is that even possible?*

"Other than the snippets of memories you unearthed tonight, how many others have you had?" Rico tries to hold in the eagerness of his words. He fails.

I slip my hand under the satin pillow and rest my inflamed cheek on the cool softness before killing his excitement with one short word. "None."

I'd like to elaborate on my response, but there's no need.

All my disappointment was expressed with that one paltry word.

"Why don't I have any memories?"

In less than a nanosecond, the smile on Rico's face vanishes, and a new expression settles in its place. It's the same unapproachable look he wore when deciding Timothy's fate. "Because Timothy gave you a drug known on the black market as 'club drug.' Because of its strong amnesia-based product, most victims have limited recollection of their assault."

I twist my lips. "If he was planning to kill me, why would it matter if I had any memories?"

"The drug isn't just used as a date rape drug. It's also distributed as a party drug. Rohypnol is regularly taken by teens to get high. To some individuals, it has the same effect as heroin or cocaine. It's the reason you were more... *carefree* the weekend we married. Your insecurities vanished." His words are informative and clear until the end. His last two sentences come out heavily laced with confusion.

Since I am also confused, I seek clarification for part of it. "Can you see a difference between the Blaire you met last week and the one before you now?"

Rico's tongue delves out to replenish his lips before he murmurs, "No. But it's not a drug steering your decisions now. It's fear."

"I'm not scared of you, Rico," I splutter out, allowing my heart to overrule my head.

"You should be, Kitten." He's so quiet. If I didn't see his lips move, I wouldn't have known he'd spoken.

A stretch of silence crosses between us. I wouldn't say it's awkward, more necessary. The flight over this side of the country was only five hours long, but it feels like five months have passed. So many life-altering decisions have been made during our trip. But my biggest worry is that the most imperative one wasn't made by me. It was made *for* me.

"What will happen to Timothy's family?"

Rico's dark eyes stare directly into mine as he replies, "Nothing. As far as his family is concerned, Timothy will merely vanish without a trace."

My eyes burn as a new batch of tears well into my eyes. My tears are not for Timothy. They're for his wife and children who will be left wondering what happened to him. For some people, that can be more upsetting than learning the ill fate of their loved ones. When a life is lost, you never forget, but you get to grieve and try and move on. But not knowing what happened, you can't get closure. You spend your entire life scanning strangers' faces wondering if one day you will spot them in the crowd, or every time the phone rings, you ponder if it will be the call you've been waiting for the past ten years.

The people who are left wondering what happened have no chance of closure and no chance of healing.

"What about the victims' families?" I ask, incapable of reining in my desire to lessen their grief.

Rico's heavy brows stitch. He looks angry or perhaps even stumped by my question. "What about them?"

His tone is knee-shaking low, but it won't stop me from asking, "Don't they deserve to know justice was served?"

Rico's lips set into a firm, straight line before he shakes his head.

"Why not? They deserve to know. They have the right to know." My voice gets louder and angrier with every sentence I speak, and although I see the same amount of anger brewing in his dark eyes, it doesn't dampen my pleas the slightest. "Someone they loved was killed. They've suffered enough, so they shouldn't have to live their life wondering if they are walking amongst a killer. Give them peace, Rico. Give them closure."

"That's not the way it works in this industry, Kitten. It's not my job to—"

"Why? Because the mob doesn't have a heart? They don't understand compassion!"

"No, they don't." His loud roar vibrates my heart right out of my chest. "They'll slit your throat without a second thought and dump you in an acid bath before sitting down to enjoy a meal. Their stomachs won't twist. Their hearts won't feel pain. They will feel *nothing*. That's the type of men you're dealing with, Kitten, and believing any differently will only get you killed."

His chest heaves up and down so violently, it competes with mine with every breath he takes. "If you want any chance of coming out of this alive, you need to learn your place. Women are seen, not heard. Your body is a valuable commodity, not your mind, and you should *never* voice your opinion unless asked. And even then, your replies should echo your male counterpart." He stares into my eyes, ensuring I'm aware the words he speaks are nothing but gospel.

Once he's satisfied I've absorbed his warning, he rolls out of bed and puts on his suit jacket. In seconds, the man who spent hours comforting me is replaced with a cold-hearted, emotionless stranger. His eyes are bleak, his jaw clenched, and the stern mask he wears when surrounded by his crew has slipped back into place.

After fastening the button on his suit jacket, Rico nudges his head to the washroom. "Tidy yourself up before meeting me in the hangar," he instructs, his words clipped.

Not waiting for me to reply, he paces to the door, his steps fast and efficient. Before he exits, he cranks his neck back to peer at me.

When his gaze zooms in on the moisture forming in my eyes, his stern mask slips for the slightest second, exposing an emotion I was certain he didn't know—fear.

Although regret is by far the highest emotion in his voice, his next set of words leaves me on edge. "I'm trying to protect you, Blaire. Please don't make it harder on me."

Chapter Eleven

After splashing cold water on my face and using a napkin to remove the mascara stains tracking down my cheeks, I roll my shoulders, lift my head high, then exit the bathroom.

My brisk strides falter when I sense a presence in the room. Unlike the weird buzzing sensation that fills me when Rico is close by, this isn't a rush of excitement.

It is unbridled fear.

With my heart dropped past my shoes, I spin on my feet to face my unwanted welcomer. Glacier blue eyes on a ruggedly handsome face reflect back at me. The backside of the unnamed man who confronted me last week is propped on my suitcase, and his eyes are trained on me.

Upon noticing he has gained my attention, he angles his head to the side and mutters, "One little bag for a week worth of packing." His voice is gritty and colored with a Russian accent.

My heart finds its way to my throat when he pushes off my suitcase and paces toward me. He walks with an air of authority, but his commanding swagger isn't as refined as Rico's. Wearing ripped jeans rising from black military boots and a buttoned-up dark navy shirt, his clothing showcases his body in eye-catching detail, not even the evilness beaming from his eyes can detract from. The blue-eyed stranger is a similar size to Rico, but I'm dwarfed by his height when he stands next to me.

When he circles me like a shark homing in on his prey, a vein in my neck thrums. During his slow trek, he drinks in every detail of my face before he eventually drops his eyes to my body.

Mere seconds pass, but it feels like hours.

You'd think my first thought would be to dart for the door mere feet from me, but I'm frozen in place, incapable of thinking, let alone fleeing.

When the mysterious stranger leans in to sniff my hair, I balk. It isn't a quick, dignified whiff. He takes his time, soaking in every strand of my wavy blonde hair.

I breathe for the first time in almost a minute when he murmurs against my skin, "Rico has always had an eye for quality." His breath fans my sweat-beaded neck when he snickers about my whitening face. He moves into eyesight before muttering, "He knows what you haven't even worked out yet. That's why he married you before fucking you."

My eyes slit as a hiss ripples through my lips. I don't know the man standing before me, yet he believes he has the right to disrespect me.

Loving my feisty response, the stranger's eyes flare in excitement. "There it is. I knew it was hiding in there somewhere." He tilts in closer. "Oh, *Ahren*, you'll be a lot of fun... if only Rico would loosen your collar. A little kitty should be free, not restrained."

Even the most naïve person in the world couldn't miss the sexual innuendo in his reply, which prompts me to something Rico said earlier in the Escalade. "Rico doesn't share."

I snap my eyes to the stranger when he asks, "Not even with his little brother?"

As my eyes scan his face, I seek any similarities between Rico and him. Although they both have dark hair, tanned skin, and gorgeous facial features, there are no distinct similarities between them.

"You're Rico's brother?" I try to mask the shock with a friendly tone. I fail.

His lips curl into a smirk that sets my heart racing, but unlike Rico, it isn't a good heart flutter. "Yes. I am Nikolai. But you, my sweet *Ahren*, can call me *Cataha*."

Before I have the chance to ask what *Cataha* means, a new type of awareness prickles my skin. I feel as if I am being watched, and the recollection as to why I could be freezes both my feet and my heart. *'You can't trust anyone, Kitten. Even when they don't appear to be watching you, they are. Especially me.'*

The already insane beat of my heart kicks into overdrive when my eyes lift to the doorway and connect with a pair of eyes that are teeming with anger. Rico's head is tilted to the side, and his stern gaze is fixed on his little brother. His six-foot-plus frame swamps the room, and his edgy composure suffocates the room of air. Even seeing him standing behind his brother doesn't conjure any similarities between them to form in my muddled brain.

Either unaware of his brother's furious gaze or ignoring it, Nikolai leans into my side and whispers, "You're ninety-nine percent angel, but oh how I can't wait to unearth the other one percent. There are devilish thoughts in the most angelic minds. I can't wait to hear yours."

I'm torn between feeling safe and worried when Rico snaps out something in Russian. I settle on relieved. Even not understanding a word he's speaking could have me missing the authority in his words.

He's reminding his brother of the pecking order, and mercifully, Nikolai disclosed earlier that he is the younger of the two.

After flashing me a teasing grin, Nikolai spins around to face his brother. While rubbing his hands together, he rocks on the balls of his feet. "There's no need for rudeness, Rico. I was merely welcoming your *kitten* to the family."

He turns his gaze back to me, wordlessly requesting I back up his claims. I stand muted, not only refusing to acknowledge his demand but also unsure what our exchange was about. Although he intimidates me, he wasn't threatening or welcoming.

My frozen stance ends when Rico barks out, "Come, Kitten."

Like a dog being called by its owner, my feet leap into action before my brain can register its disgust. I could say my obedience is solely to smooth the thick grooves lining Rico's forehead, but, in all honesty, it isn't. I can barely breathe with how much testosterone is suffocating the air, so if jumping on cue for my husband is a way to escape the throat-clutching awkwardness plaguing the air, I'll take it.

My eyes dart to Rico when Nikolai starts singing a song as we exit the bedroom. From the flow of the words and the softness of his voice, it sounds like a nursery rhyme.

I double-guess myself when I catch sight of Rico's haughty expression.

He looks less than impressed.

"What is he singing?" I ask Rico as we merge onto the steps of the private jet. Even though it's late, humid Las Vegas air smacks into me, adding to the swirling of my stomach.

While he guides me down the small steel steps, Rico advises, "It's a rhyme our father recited to us when we were younger."

So my original assumption was correct. It is a nursery rhyme.

Then why did it cause such an adverse reaction from Rico?

Too curious for my own good, I ask, "What nursery rhyme is it?"

Rico drops his dark eyes to me. "Not now, Kitten."

Not speaking another word, he directs me toward a long motorcade lined up outside the hangar. A gentleman with silver hair and a kind smile dips his head in greeting while opening the back passenger door of a four-wheel drive.

Other than advising the driver to take us to the Popov compound, Rico doesn't mutter a syllable the thirty minutes of our trip. I don't mind. It gives me time to run the foreign words Nikolai sang through my head. Although it was in a foreign language, it has an addictive rhythm I can't help but repeat.

Отправить ангел в дьявола кровать, удерживайте ее, ценить ее, затем отрежьте ее головки блока цилиндров. Она дебютировала с сатаны и в настоящее время она является мертвой точки для всех лежа в дьявола кровать.

It only dawns that I'm humming the words out loud when Rico roars, "Enough!"

When my eyes snap to him, I swallow the brick his demand lodged into my throat. His nostrils are flaring, and his chest heaves. "You're singing a song about sending an angel to her death."

Shock ripples through me. "What? You said it was a nursery rhyme. They don't include death."

"They do when the devil sings them," Rico fires back, his tone deep and knee-quaking. "Send the angel to the devil's bed, hold her, cherish her, then cut off her head. She danced with Satan, and now she's dead, all for lying in the devil's bed." He sings the song in the same low tone Nikolai used on the plane but hearing it in a language I understand doesn't lessen its impact. It's just as spine-tingling.

"Why would a father sing a song like that to his children?"

"Because to him, all *ahrens* must pass Satan's test."

"*Ahren?*" I query, recalling Nikolai calling me that.

My heart stops beating when Rico replies, "*Ahren* is Nikolai's version of angel. He couldn't pronounce *Ангел* when he was a child, so he said it how it was spelled instead of how it sounded. For some reason, it stuck."

Although his story is cute, I can't settle the nerves twisting in my stomach. "What does *Cataha* mean?"

My breathing shallows as I wait for Rico to reply. Considering *Cataha* was only used once in the nursery rhyme Nikolai sang, I'm reasonably sure I know what it means, but I still want Rico to spell it out for me. I don't want to get worked up over a simple childish rhyme. I've got enough on my plate with an unknown husband, barely escaping a murder attempt, mob-like activities, and unearthing my lost memories to add an immature threat into the mix.

Any chance of sweeping Nikolai's taunt under the rug slips away when Rico says, "*Cataha* is Satan, Kitten."

Everything blurs when the last part of the rhyme runs through my head—*She danced with Satan, and now she's dead, all for lying in the devil's bed.*

I sound as tormented as I feel while asking, "Aren't Satan and the devil the same person?"

Dark strands of hair fall into Rico's eye when he shakes his head. "Not in this rhyme. Satan sends his angel to the devil's bed to test her. If she fails, Satan cuts off her head."

"How does the angel fail?"

He runs his index finger across his top brow, removing a bead of sweat formed there. "By sleeping with the devil."

"Who's the devil then?" I snap out so fast I startle the driver.

Rico shrugs. "Whoever Satan decides to test his angel with."

After sinking deep in my seat, I take a moment to work through the information I've been bombarded with. Why would Nikolai request that I call him Satan after calling me angel? It doesn't make any sense. Unless he thinks I'm going to sleep with the devil?

My pupils widen. *Was that Nikolai's way of warning me that I am sleeping with the devil?*

The cruel twist on my heart weakens when I turn my eyes to Rico. He's watching me with the same tenderness he did when he comforted me on the plane hours ago. Even shrouded by darkness, there's something in his eyes that exposes he isn't the devil I need to be wary of. He's the man who saved me from the devil, not the one testing me.

Confident in my assessment of the situation, I advise, "Nikolai called me *ahren.*"

Rico's jaw tightens, but he doesn't appear totally shocked by my admission. "Nikolai calls all beautiful women *ahren.*" Even with his composure not altering, his tone is low, exposing that my disclosure still agitated him.

And that angst doubles when I blubber out, "He also told me to call him *Cataha.*"

Now he looks shocked.

Actually, it's more like fury is beaming out of him.

After removing his seat belt, he slides across the small section of leather between us then gathers my hands in his. "Stay away from Nikolai, Kitten. Do you understand me?"

Although I could construe his words as aggressive, his eyes aren't relaying that.

All I see is genuine concern.

Relief empties his lungs with a big sigh when I say, "I understand."

* * *

The remaining ten minutes of our trip are made in silence. Rico held my hand the entire time, and it said more than any words ever could, but I'd be a liar if I said dread didn't wash over me when the six-car motorcade pulls into the ginormous mansion I fled from only a week ago.

I truly thought my long walk of shame through this residence would be the last time I stepped foot onto this property.

How wrong was I?

After opening the back passenger door and sliding out, Rico dips down to offer me a hand. Tension hangs thick in the air as we climb the stairs leading to the main entrance of the house. A tall gentleman with slicked-back hair, cold blank eyes, and an evil smirk blocks the entry into the mansion. I can tell the instant Rico notices him as his grip on my hand tightens and an expressionless mask slips over his face.

"Maya, come," Rico demands, his tone deep and brusque.

A young woman with long brown hair tied back in a ponytail peeks her head out from a group of women on our right. She bows her head at the gentleman hogging the entrance before locking her dark eyes with Rico.

"Take Blaire into her room and get her settled," Rico instructs.

After dipping her head again, Maya waves her hand to the elegant staircase behind her.

Although desperate to escape the awkwardness cracking in the air, I'd rather not walk the gallows alone. "Are you not coming with me?" I ask Rico, my voice panicked.

His pendulum-swinging moods startle me, but I'd choose to be

588

attached to his hip than be left to defend myself in a house of horror with a lady who is so waif thin, a slight breeze could blow her away.

"I'll be up in a few, Kitten." Before I can plead with him, he peers past my shoulder to Maya and says, "Take her now." Unlike his earlier tone, this time his request comes out with the nasty bite of demand.

I'm not the only one noticing Rico's new superiority. Maya jumps to his command by intertwining her arm with mine and lugging me toward the stairwell. For a girl who has twigs for arms and legs, she has a lot of gusto in her core. She drags me through the lobby as if I'm the one missing twenty pounds on her frame.

As we climb the first step, I crank my neck back to Rico. He's standing toe-to-toe with the gentleman everyone seems frightened of. *Everyone except Rico.* He looks him directly in the eyes as they speak in Russian, not the slightest bit intimidated that their exchange has caught the attention of over a dozen pairs of eyes. It's a scary yet riveting confrontation.

When we reach the landing of the stairs, I shift my focus to Maya. "Maya, who is the man Rico is speaking with?"

Her throat works hard to swallow before she whispers, "Father."

My head rockets back to Rico so fast, my neck screams in protest. "That's Rico's father?" My question comes out tainted with disbelief. Fathers are meant to nurture and protect their children, but that man emulates the traits of a tyrant.

Maya doesn't need to answer my question, but I reach my own conclusion when Rico's eyes lock with mine for a fleeting second. Even though his lips don't move, I hear his silent plea. "Go, Kitten, before you once again dance with the devil."

Chapter Twelve

Maya accompanies me to the room I woke in last week, supplies me with a hearty Russian dinner of a Reuben sandwich, and attempts to teach me how to play a Russian card game, Durak. However, three hours tick by on the clock, and I haven't seen hide nor hair of Rico.

Although Maya's English is best described as poor, it isn't her lack of vocabulary that has our girly night ending. It is my heavy eyelids.

After bidding farewell to Maya, I head to the bathroom. Upon entering, I stare at the gorgeous clawfoot bath, hoping it will garner me the energy to draw it. A few hours soaking in a tub sound like heaven.

Although the temptation is strong, I don't think my eyelids will remain open long enough to enjoy it, so instead, I turn on the double shower at the side of the tub then shed my clothes, leaving them where they fall.

Have you ever been so tired, you wonder if you're awake or dreaming? That's how I feel right now.

I am beyond exhausted.

Once my clothing is removed, I step into the steam-filled space.

Hot water bombards my body, waking me from my sleeping state. When I lean further into the spray, water pours down my cheeks and rolls over my heavy breasts, triggering a hidden memory to rush to the surface of my muddled brain...

With a lavender-colored shower puff, I lather my body with soap-suds, being extra cautious not to touch my newly inked skin. When I step into the spray, blissfully hot water heats my front at the same time a warm body molds my back. My heart doubles in size when a large hand with a ruby and diamond wedding band wrapped around the third finger curls around my stomach. Even with the shower filled with muggy dampness, goose bumps follow the trail the hand makes when it slithers up the smooth planes of my stomach to cup my desire-heavy breast.

"I thought you didn't want a shower?" My voice comes out throatier than normal, giving it a sexy edge.

"I didn't..." His Russian accentuated voice does even more wicked things to my insides. "Until I realized it was ten more minutes I could spend with you."

A ghost of a smile stretches across my face as I lean into him deeper. It turns into a full-toothed grin when his erection presses into my back. He's thick and long, swelling halfway up my spine.

"Only ten minutes," I jest, my tone a unique mix of playfulness and seduction. "Feels like a whole lot more than ten minutes."

The deep richness of his laugh quickly fills the room. It's a beautiful chuckle that sees my head following my body's desires for a change.

I spin around...

"No!" I slant into the water, hoping it will bring back my memory. "You can't end it there."

Even knowing in my heart that the man in the shower was Rico, I want to see it, recall it, and cherish it. It doesn't matter if I'm unearthing two seconds of memories with him or two minutes, a range of emotions wallop into me with every one I discover. And no, they aren't all solely based on my libido. Unveiling my memories is like working on a Rubik's cube. It seems like a complicated waste of time, but once I achieve the seemingly impossible, I'll have a better understanding of the square box with the six unique colors.

Rico is my Rubik's cube. I didn't marry him because I was drugged, so I want to discover what else drew me to him that night. Behind his cloaked-in-danger façade, Rico is insanely gorgeous, but deep down inside, I know his good looks wouldn't have made me agree to marrying a stranger. Until I discover the other reasons, I won't stop hunting until every lost memory is unearthed.

After switching off the shower, I curl a fluffy towel around my body then use another to secure my wet hair in place. Because I forgot to turn on the exhaust fan, the floor-to-ceiling mirror attached to the double vanity is covered with steam.

It's probably for the best. I don't need to see myself to know how wretched I look.

I can feel it.

My lazy steps stop halfway out the door, closely followed by the beat of my heart when an awareness of being watched smacks into me. My heart rate—although agile—returns when I discover a pair of dark eyes peering at me from across the room. Rico is sitting on a high-backed chair. His suit jacket has been removed, and the sleeves of his dress shirt are rolled up to his elbows.

After his eyes finish raking over my body, he locks his heavy-hooded gaze with mine. Unnerved by the darkness of his eyes, I take a retreating step. They are the blackest I've seen them.

"Come here, Kitten." His voice is throaty and spine-tingling deep.

With my heart walloping in my chest, I shake my head, denying his request.

Rico strengthens his glare before repeating, "Come here, Kitten," for the second time.

His authoritative tone has me pushing off my feet before my brain can register a complaint. I've never been a confrontational person, and tonight is clearly no different.

Even though I'm following his command to a T, every step I take alters the power between us. Not only do Rico's eyes reveal I'm not the only one confused by our weird kinship—he's just as baffled as me—they also show there was something more than a laced drink guiding my decisions last week.

I'm in a house that makes the burliest men quake in their boots, but with Rico looking at me like he is now, all my insecurities fade into the horizon. It's just me and him—the stranger I married.

When I stand in front of him, he grips the end of my towel and pries it open. My hands shoot down, endeavoring to maintain my modesty the best I can in a skimpy towel, but my abrupt movements halt when I realize he only opened the towel far enough to uncover his name inked on my hip.

Although there's still a scandalous amount of my skin exposed, it isn't sufficient enough to warrant an overreaction.

"Is it itchy?" Rico questions with his eyes fixed on the flaky skin on my hip bone.

I shrug. "A little." When his truth-absorbing eyes connect with mine, wordlessly demanding an honest answer, I mumble, "A lot."

I followed the advice posted online about caring for newly-inked skin, but no matter how stringently I adhere to the guidelines, my tattoo is blotchy, scaly, and painstakingly itchy. I try my hardest to ignore the desire to scratch, but just like my ability to deny Rico's attention, I have the occasional slip-up.

My chances of having another relapse grow when Rico secures a tube of hydrocortisone cream from the drawer beside him. He unscrews the cap, squirts a small portion of lotion onto two fingers, then carefully applies it to my hip.

I stare at him, utterly dumbfounded. He is dutifully attending to me like a caring husband would his wife. I won't lie, my nose is tingling, and sentimental tears are pricking my eyes. It's a sweet thing for him to do even with it seeming out of character.

"If you keep it well-moisturized, the itching sensation will lessen." Rico screws the cap back onto the tube then lifts his eyes to me. "But no matter how uncomfortable it gets, don't pick at it."

I nod before handing him the towel wrapped around my

drenched hair so he can dry his slicked fingers. Upon noticing my wound is already less itchy, I say, "Thank you."

His dark eyes glance into mine before his chin balances on his chest. "Maybe next time you'll heed my warning on an impromptu tattoo session."

My mouth gapes, shocked and blinking. "Me? Wasn't my tattoo your idea?"

When he throws his head back and laughs, my shock intensifies. He has a beautiful laugh, the type that shreds through my body and warms my heart.

It also makes my stomach do a stupid fluttery thing, but we will keep that between us.

Once Rico's laughter settles down, he answers, "No, Kitten. The tattoo was all *your* doing."

"But... *are you sure...* I thought it was some ownership slash branding kind of thing."

The laughter lining his face vanishes, replaced with an emotion I find a little hard to decipher. "Hmm... is that why you chose my chest?"

My eyes bug, then they almost bulge out of my head when Rico unfastens the top three buttons on his shirt. I swallow harshly to relieve my burning throat when he pulls open his shirt to expose my name in thick black ink swirled on his left pectoral muscle.

It isn't solely the six letters of my name raising my body temperature but also being awarded the visual of his smooth, muscular torso. From his build alone, I knew he'd have an impressive body, but seeing it up close... *Jesus.*

Now I wish even more that my flashback of our time together in the shower went a few seconds longer.

My heart threatens to break out of my chest when Rico seizes my wrist to run my fingers over his chest. The muscles on his pecs contract when he runs the tips of my fingers over the peeling ink. Although his tattoo doesn't look as scaly as mine, there's no doubt it's fresh ink.

Talking through the lump in my throat, I mutter, "I branded

you." Disbelief, and if I'm not mistaken, a little bit of honor dangle off my vocal cords.

"You can't brand someone unwilling, Kitten," Rico replies, staring up at me. "Memory?"

The hope in his eyes dampens when I shake my head. "I had a flashback earlier, though."

His heavy brow cocks as he waits for me to continue.

"It was in the shower."

He smiles at the flustered state my confession causes my cheeks before asking, "Was it a good memory, Kitten?"

"It was a little short," I blubber out, honestly.

Now it's my turn to smile at his shocked expression.

"My memory, not your..." I stop talking as heat floods my cheeks.

I don't want to be, but disappointment clouds me when Rico removes my hand from his chest. "You look tired, Kitten. Let me shower, then you can go to bed."

"Okay." I catch my eye roll halfway from the neediness of my voice. I've never been a clingy type of girl, but for some unknown reason, Rico incites a side of me I didn't know existed.

Maybe it is because I've always been the girl who plays it safe? Marrying Rico added an edge of danger to my life I've never been brave enough to explore. Meeting him forced me out of the safe box I have been living in the past ten years. He isn't just a challenge for me to unravel, he challenges me as well.

"Your sleeping clothes are on the bed." Rico nudges his head to the ginormous bed on my left.

A smile etches onto my weary face when I follow his head nudge and notice he has laid out my pajamas—a satin slip and a three-quarter length silk negligee. When I shoot my eyes around the room, the warmth spreading across my chest flourishes. Not only did he remove my sleeping garments from my suitcase, but he also unpacked my bag.

Suddenly, my happiness evaporates. *Does that mean he intends for my stay to be a long one?*

My heart rate hits an all-time high, but if I were honest, I'd admit I don't know if it's beating faster in exhilaration or alarm.

After pressing a quick kiss to my temple, Rico ambles into the bathroom. Once he slips behind the door, I hurriedly get dressed and hop into bed, vainly trying to disregard the breakneck speed of events.

Seconds have never felt like hours until I'm in Rico's presence.

Chapter Thirteen

I've been tossing and turning for approximately fifteen minutes when the creak of a door jingles through my ears. Although I'm beyond tired, sleep is evading me after my exchange with Rico. The entire day has been nothing but a blur of confusion. In a matter of hours, I went from being surrounded by twenty-three grubby faces to trying to ignore the affections of a man who equally intrigues and intimidates me.

Any chance of ignorance is lost when I twist my head to the side and spot Rico entering the room wearing nothing but a pair of skimpy boxer shorts. His hair is wet and flat, his naked torso is shimmering with droplets of water I'm suddenly envious of, and his plain blue cotton boxers have no chance in hell of hiding his yummy six-pack or the defined cut of his oblique muscles.

When he spins around to face the dresser, my mouth falls open. A large tattoo covers a majority of his left shoulder blade and twists halfway down his back. It's an intricate design that weaves through muscles I didn't even know existed. And his ass... *oh*... there should be rules against a man having an ass that fine.

Failing to notice my ogling stare, Rico undoes the latch on his gold watch, places it on a tray on top of the dresser, then turns to face the mirror on the dressing table. He runs his fingers through his gloriously thick hair, giving it that sexed-up look usually achieved through bedroom antics.

Like the first time I viewed an original Monet painting, I can't stop staring at him, both riveted and confused. His body is truly spectacular—a fine piece of art.

After tussling his unruly hair into place, Rico throws a plain shirt over his head then spins to face me. In silence, I watch him stride across the room. Just the way he moves his body with such fluidity and ease, I know he'd be extraordinary in bed. Sheet-clenching, I'll-never-forget-being-claimed-by-him, mind-hazing sex.

The heat in my cheeks doubles when my mind wanders to the time I discovered a three-pack of empty condom wrappers under this very bed.

That was a mere week ago.

Seems more like a lifetime.

The fiery warmth clogging my veins diverts to another region when Rico pulls back the sheets. Not saying a word, he slips into bed next to me.

While springboarding into a half-seated position, I stammer out, "W-what are you doing?"

He adjusts two pillows behind him before connecting his dark eyes with mine. "Getting ready for bed."

"In *my* bed?" I splutter, my voice high and cringeworthy.

"Kitten," Rico draws out in a long, husky moan that causes the hairs on my arm to stupidly bristle. "This is not *your* bed."

I peer around the room, confused. This is the room Maya brought me to. Doesn't that automatically make it mine?

My eyes stop aimlessly floating when Rico continues, "It is *our* bed."

I speak slowly, still shocked. "*Our* bed?"

He smiles a lazy grin that sets my pulse racing. "Yes. *Our* bed."

Annoyed at my body's reaction to his playful grin more than the way he says 'our,' I mutter, "And how many other women have you slept with in *our* bed?"

I'm not going to lie. A stabbing pain hits the middle of my chest just from thinking about him with anyone but me.

Is that inconceivable for me to say? I don't know him—he's practically a stranger—but I'm jealous about any prior relationships he may have had.

Yeah, that's inconceivable.

My shock multiplies tenfold when Rico answers, "Not one."

I arch a brow, demanding further explanation. There's no way a man with looks like his wouldn't have women falling at his feet, so I find it extremely doubtful no one has slept in his bed before me.

Upon noticing my skeptical gaze, Rico explains, "We purchased this bed an hour after being married. At your request, it was delivered before we arrived here."

I release a long-winded breath. "*Ohhh.*"

He smiles at my ambiguous reaction before tilting in close to my side. "I've never had so much fun breaking in a bed." His breath on my ear causes goose bumps to race to the surface of my skin.

That isn't the only response his closeness instigates, though. It also causes a new memory to rush to the forefront of my mind...

Not the slightest bit embarrassed, I yank down the zipper of my floral skirt, step out of it, then charge for a monstrous bed in the middle of the room. A girly giggle explodes from my mouth when the softness of new sheets engulfs me.

"Oh my goodness, it's huge!" I squeal before fanning my arms and legs out like I'm making a snow angel in the high thread count sheets.

My nostrils flare, relishing the scent of new bedding, but that isn't the sole cause for my quickening pulse. It is the distinct aroma of spices on sweat-slicked skin.

My darling husband is close by.

Immature laughter switches to a needy purr when Rico presses a kiss on the edge of my ankle, closely followed by one on the back of my knee. I squirm when his beard scrapes the skin high on my inner thigh. Fighting my body's desire to pull my knees inward, I loosen my thigh muscles and sweep them open.

I'm on the bed my husband purchased for us to christen on our wedding night. Now is not the time for modesty.

My breathing pans out when the softest pair of lips graze past my longing core. I gasp, incredibly turned on when Rico places a gentle peck on the middle of my satin panties. Acting purely on instinct, my hips swivel, soundlessly pleading for more direct contact. I only just hold in my disappointed moan when Rico's sinful lips continue their journey, denying my body's silent pleas.

Every kiss placed on my skin as he leisurely travels from my ankles to my torso has my excitement growing. I'm incredibly aroused while also reveling in his tenderness. I've never had a man treat me with so much compassion before. Every kiss he gives is filled with silent promises that he will always love and protect me, keep me safe, and never break my heart.

My heart swells, incapable of accommodating the massive surge of blood pumping into it when a final peck is pressed on the dip in my collarbone. It isn't the softness of the kiss that has my heart defying logic. It's the beautiful pair of dark eyes staring down at me.

Rico's hair has fallen into his face, framing his chiseled cheekbones and shaped brows. His lips are swollen from our kisses shared in the back of the car during our travels, but his most exquisite feature is the look beaming from his eyes. Nothing but admiration reflects back at me, abundantly proving I'm not the only one who has fallen head over heels in a matter of hours.

He loves me too.

Rico presses a kiss to the edge of my mouth, drawing my sole devotion back to him. "Are you sure this is what you want, Blaire?" he asks with his gorgeous dark eyes dancing between mine. "This is your last chance to back away. Once this happens, I'll never give you up, so I need you to be sure."

I cup his jaw and return his devoted watch. "I've never been more sure of anything in my life," I reply, only just concealing my smile at the way his jaw twitches under my touch. "I love you, Enrique. From the tips of your toes to the top of your gorgeous head."

Blood surges to my heart, making it swell even more when the most captivating smile stretches across Rico's handsome face...

As I merge out of my memory, I gasp in a quick breath, shell-shocked by my admission in my flashback. I've never spoken those three words to another man before, but I gave them willingly to Rico within hours of meeting him.

What type of drug was I given that it knocked down my walls so quickly?

My eyes stray to the side when a cold hand gives relief to my flaming cheeks. Rico's dark eyes are rapt on me. His gaze is primal, dominating, and strong, and it adds to the heat hueing my skin.

"You remembered."

Although he appears to be asking a question, his powerful gaze isn't reflecting that. He seems to know me well enough to know where my thoughts strayed to.

That adds even more astonishment to the giddiness clustered in my brain.

When I nod, the first splash of a tear spills from my eye. Rico intakes a sharp breath before the back of his fingers slides across my cheek, catching my tears in one swift motion.

"If you remember, Kitten, why are you crying?" His voice is gravelly and crammed with worry.

When I notice his eyes are wearing the same tender look they had in my memory, my worry fades for hope. Even digging through the mountain load of darkness suffocating his beautiful eyes, I can tell he cares for me.

I'd be lying if I said he was the only one harboring unexplainable feelings.

Even knowing Rico isn't a man I should fall in love with, I can't deny the weird sensation my heart gets every time he is near. I've tried to ignore it. It isn't possible. Although he is technically a stranger, in my heart, I feel like I've known him half my life.

While I'm being forthright, I'll admit the idea of falling in love with a man who equally thrills and terrifies is a truly petrifying notion. When I'm with Rico, it feels like I'm standing at the crest of a large waterfall. It's beautiful from the high vantage point, but if I jump off the edge, what's hidden beneath the water waiting for me? Am I plunging into a sea of blackness? Or something magical?

A stormy cloud forms in Rico's tempestuous gaze when I fail to answer his question. I try to get my mouth to cooperate with my brain, to say something to ease the hurt in his eyes, but nothing comes out. I'm stunned into silence.

When more stupid tears unwillingly spill from my eyes, Rico scoops me into his arms and pulls me into his chest. "Shh, Kitten, shh. You're okay." His deep tone is as rickety as my composure.

I'm balancing precariously on the crest of a steep waterfall, but I nuzzle into Rico's chest to accept his comfort without protest, throwing my wariness to the side for a few moments with the hope of gathering my scattered composure.

We sit in silence for several moments. I feel like my world has been upended. It might seem a little dramatic to outsiders, but that doesn't mean it isn't true. In a matter of a week, everything I knew about my life changed—my career, my marital status, my heart. In the blink of an eye, I went from a kindergarten teacher to mob wife—two vastly contrasting roles.

While wallowing about being forced into a family I would have never chosen to become a part of, a new reality dawns.

Rico never had a choice, either. He was born into his role.

I had a normal upbringing with two loving parents nurturing me.

Rico was raised by a monster.

My pupils widen when the veracity of my statement smacks into me. I've heard those exact words before, and no, I'm not referring to the time Rico said it in the Escalade after signing our annulment papers.

As my brain labors over the last time I heard that statement, I close my eyes.

When another memory smashes into me, I inhale a quick, jagged breath...

"No, Blaire, you do not belong in this lifestyle. I will not drag you into the darkness."

I tighten my grip on Rico's hand before digging my heels into the carpet. Even though a man of Rico's size could easily yank me across the pristine marble floors, he stops walking and spins around to face me. Excitement mingled with anxiety lines his face.

"You're not a monster, Enrique. You were just raised by one," I mutter as my glistening eyes dance between his.

"We've only known each other for three hours. You're not qualified to make that assumption," he replies. Although his tone is aiming for stern, it comes out with more sentiment than he is aiming for.

"I only needed thirty seconds to see the real you." I peer into the eyes that captured my soul in under a minute. "Now I want a lifetime to show you what I already know."

After taking a few moments to register his shocked expression, I drift my eyes to the chapel on my right. I feel Rico's gaze slide over my face before he too shifts on his feet to face the chapel. "If we do this, Blaire, I can't promise you a lifetime of sunshine, but I can promise to always protect and cherish you."

I don't even need to look at him to know what he's saying is factual. The truth is evident in his voice.

"I can't promise to always protect you, but I promise you a lifetime of sunshine." I drift my loved-up gaze back to Rico. "I'll be your light in a life full of darkness."

We recited similar vows to each other when we wed in that very chapel an hour later...

My overworked heart slicks my skin with sweat as my newly discovered memory plays on repeat. No matter which way I play it—backward, forward, or in reverse—the facts never alter. A drug wasn't leading my decisions last week. Although I acted a little riskier than normal in my flashback, I was lucid and capable of making my own decisions. I'm not slurring my words, and I don't seem intoxicated. I was merely the carefree version of me that usually comes out when Lacey and I share too many glasses of wine. I also seemed happy— truly and utterly happy.

After swallowing down the bile tarnishing the back of my throat, I pop my head off Rico's chest and peer into his eyes. "It was all me," I mumble, still shocked by my audacity in my flashback. "Our tattoos, our wedding, everything was my idea." I bounce my eyes between his while asking, "Why did you go along with it? I was a stranger to you mere hours before."

He scrubs the back of his hand across my cheeks, removing the last of my tear stains before saying, "When an angel falls into your lap, you don't make her wait. You grant her every wish."

Even in the awkwardness of the moment, he reassures me it wasn't the drugs in my system steering my moral compass last week. It was him.

He's a stranger, and at times, he scares me more than any man before him, but there's something about him I'm drawn to. I don't know if it's love like I declared last week or because I have the urge to protect him as he guards me, but deep in my soul, I know there's something greater between us than a drunken mistake.

Snubbing the shake encroaching my hands, I cup his jaw and align our eyes. "I wish for us to leave this lifestyle," I mutter, allowing my heart to talk for the first time in a week.

The quickest flare of emotion brightens Rico's dark gaze before he snuffs it. "If that were possible, Kitten, you wouldn't be here. But I can only grant wishes, not miracles."

My shoulders slump as a new upwelling of tears flood my already swamped eyes. The only thing that holds them at bay is when the entirety of his reply replays through my muddled mind. "Me or us?"

He locks his hard-set eyes with me. "You, Kitten. I can't leave until I get answers."

I fall backward until my backside is resting on the balls of my feet. "When you get the answers you're seeking, will you leave then?"

Fear curls around my throat when he shakes his head, then it almost asphyxiates me when he says, "There's only one way I can leave this family, Kitten. I wouldn't be breathing."

Chapter Fourteen

My groggy head lifts from the pillow when the creak of a door sounds through my ears. My half-asleep eyes widen when I scan the unfamiliar room. Unlike last week, it doesn't take me long to gather my bearings. It isn't the familiarity of the room or the fact I've once again woken with a thumping skull, it's the smell of a delicious spicy scent lingering in the air.

When the distinct noise of a shower turning on sounds through my ears, I crank my neck back and peer toward the bathroom. Not surprisingly, the door is closed. My lips quirk when my eyes catch the time on the bedside clock. It's a little after six.

I didn't realize Rico was such an early riser.

After our heart-strangling discussion last night, Rico gathered me in his arms and held me until I fell asleep. His thumbs caught my tears, and his warm body soothed the shakes impeding mine.

I'm not going to lie. I liked being wrapped in his strong arms. On the surface, Rico seems like a complicated man, but when I look past the hard shell he wears in front of others, I understand the desire to marry him on sight. The man I was with last night was heartfelt and enduring, a complete contradiction to the man I met the previous week.

Hoping a few more hours of sleep will dull the furious thump of my skull, I flop my head back onto my pillow. I jump out of my skin when a final sweep of the room detects another presence. The lady who entered my room last week is standing by the door, scowling at me. Just like our first confrontation, her hard-hearted eyes set my pulse racing.

"Hello," I greet, my voice apprehensive. It's only a little after six, so I'm surprised she's entering my room so early, let alone unannounced.

"You. Take." She thrusts two folded towels balancing on her open palms my way.

While rubbing my tired eyes with my palm, I slip out of bed and pad toward her. My steps are slow and shaky. Not just because I'm tired but because I'm wary of the anger pumping out of her in invisible waves. I'm unsure why she doesn't like me, but it doesn't take a rocket scientist to read her signals. It's clear this lady is not a fan of mine.

I accept the lavender-scented towels from her grasp while mumbling, "Thank you."

"You. Take," she grunts again, her voice heavily slurred by a thick Russian accent.

I draw the towels into my chest. "Yes, I take."

Even with her eyes narrowed into tiny slits, I can't miss their roll. "Not you take. You. Take."

I stare at her, utterly confused. "I did take." I swallow the brick lodged in my throat when my words come out stronger than I'm anticipating.

Returning my glare—except with more viciousness—she says, "Not you take. You. Take. Rico." She gestures her hand to the closed bathroom door.

"Oh." *Ohh.*

I shake my head so fast I make myself dizzy. "He's in the shower." *Naked.*

A silent squeal bubbles up my chest when she shoves me toward the door. Just like Maya, she has a lot of gusto hidden in her small frame. Her push is so strong, I cross the expansive bedroom in three heart-pounding seconds. "You. Take. Rico."

"I can't go in there. He's naked. You. Take. Rico." My heart stops beating when I impersonate her accent to perfection—throaty gargle and all.

My mouth gapes, shell-shocked by my rudeness. Even not being able to see her, I feel her anger growing from the pit of her stomach to her face. She's so mad, her hands scorch my back when she continues shoving me toward the bathroom.

After rolling my shoulders and wiping the fear from my face, I spin around to face her. My attempt to pretend I'm not intimidated by her furious composure is left for dust when her livid gaze spears me in place.

"Sorry." My tone is as weak as my pathetic apology.

The hair on her chin wobbles when she sneers, "You. Take. Rico. You. Wife!"

With my heart clutched with worry, I nod. "Okay. I'll take these to Rico." I take two measly steps toward the bathroom before turning back around to face her. "I don't have to hand them to him? Right?" I query, my voice quivering. "I can just leave them on the vanity?"

She looks at me like I'm an imbecile. "You. Take. Rico."

"Okay." I breathe out slowly. "I can do this." *I hope.*

I swear I'm on the verge of hyperventilating when I push down the door handle. Steam seeps through the gap in the door when I swing it open, but my breathing pattern returns to a safe level when I remember how badly fogged the mirrored wall was when I showered last night. Add that to the bathroom's configuration, and I should be able to place the towels onto the vanity without incident.

Keeping my gaze lowered on the floor, I step deeper into the bathroom. I think I'm in the clear, then the stupid door shuts loudly, announcing my arrival.

I almost make a run for it when Rico instructs sternly, "Anna, leave the towels on the vanity."

Grimacing, I squeak out, "Okay."

I stomp my feet like a five-year-old when my attempt to impersonate Anna's accent this time around comes out sounding like I'm a twelve-year-old boy in the midst of puberty.

While releasing a deep breath, I scuffle across the tiled floor as quickly as my quaking legs will carry me, only lifting my eyes when the empty wastebasket enters my peripheral vision. Holding my hands out in front of me to gauge the distance, I place the towels on the vanity without peeking at the mirrored wall.

I'm not going to lie. It's a tortuous feat.

A silent squeal bubbles up my chest when the towels slip off the vanity and flop to my feet. Grumbling, I bend down to gather them back up. The veins in my neck thrum when my crouched position awards me with a mind-hazing visual. Although the top half of the mirror is covered with a dense layer of steam, the bottom half is void of any vision-impeding fog, meaning I'm graced with the reverent view of a completely naked Rico.

Oh, for the love of God, the man is a masterpiece.

My eyes gobbled up every inch of his torso last night, but they run over it again like they're assessing the authenticity of a priceless painting. Water is sloshing down the side of his face, flattening his dark hair around his temples, and his body is carved with rock-hard muscles hidden under creamy smooth skin. He's dark and dangerous rolled into an undoubtedly beautiful package.

My lips part to draw in ragged breaths when the scene switches from awe-inspiring to scandalous. After adjusting his position so the heavy flow of water can remove the suds coating his back, Rico commences *cleaning* another region of his perfect physique.

After spacing his feet to the width of his shoulders, he wraps his manly hand around his fat cock and pumps it in long, controlled strokes. My ethically motivated brain screams at me to respect his privacy by leaving the bathroom, but my lust-driven heart keeps my feet firmly planted on the floor.

When the tempo of his thrusts increases, any possibility of me leaving is a lost cause. I'm too busy studying how every muscle in his body constricts with each pump he does to consider leaving. I'm riveted and insanely turned on watching such a beautiful man in a raw and carnal position.

It's a sight I'd line up to witness time and time again.

A pleasurable jolt rockets through my body when Rico closes his eyes and his lips separate. My nipples are budded and aching, my pussy is slicked with dampness, and my morals are wavering so considerably it's taking all my strength to remain hidden. I want to enter the shower like Rico did in my flashback last night.

A familiar tingle runs the length of my spine when my eyes lock in on the wide head of Rico's cock sliding in and out of his hand. I know you shouldn't call a penis beautiful, but his is. It's beautiful, manly, and large.

I squeeze my thighs together when a hot trickle of desire puddles between them. I never thought I could climax just from watching a man please himself, but Rico is unearthing many sides I didn't know existed. The moral, upstanding kindergarten teacher I was yesterday would have never entered the bathroom, where my Vegas morally lost self can't tear my eyes away from the womb-clenching visual playing out in front of me.

As the minutes tick by, his race to climax speeds up. I've never seen anything so captivatingly raw as a man bringing himself to ecstasy. This man is a machine, his body built solely to give pleasure. He's so wondrous, he doesn't even need to touch me, and my orgasm is begging to be released.

His thrusts into his suds-covered fist quicken, forcing the muscles in his stomach to flex with every grind. A soft groan whizzes through my gaped mouth when his teeth drag over his bottom lip. His face shows his race to release is intensifying as much as mine. The glistening bead on the end of his knob increases along with his pants of breath.

I pant right alongside him, unable to hold in my excitement. My body is coated with a dense layer of sweat, my eyes are wide and heavily dilated, and an orgasm is lingering deep in my core, dying to break free.

Several strokes later, the most animalistic growl I've ever heard tears from Rico's parted lips at the same time a stream of cum rockets out of his swollen knob.

My hands dart up to secure a death-tight grip on the vanity as I struggle to contain my excited moans. Even battling to keep my crouched position unknown, my eyes remain focused on Rico. Considering he is the sole cause of the pleasurable shimmer revitalizing my body with renewed hope, he deserves my dedicated devotion.

Rico continues stroking his cock until every drop of his cum is released while I fight to keep my pleasurable groans to a hum. It's one of the hardest battles I've ever fought.

My grip on the vanity loosens when his pumps on his cock slow from a manic to a gradual pace. When he releases his still-firm cock from his grasp, reality smacks into me. I just hid in the corner of a bathroom to watch a man bring himself to ecstasy.

Oh. My. Lord. I'm a horrible person.

Beyond embarrassed about my appalling behavior, I scamper off the floor and charge across the room as quickly as my shaking legs can take me. My heart thrashes in my chest, matching the insane pulse surging through my pussy, and blood rushes to my skin, coating every inch with a vibrant red hue.

I've barely slipped out the door when the shower being switched off sounds through my ears.

I lean against the door and gasp in quick breaths, grateful that it was only a close call.

Chapter Fifteen

After taking a moment to calm the mad beat of my heart, I push off the door and amble to the chair in front of the dressing mirror. My steps are heavy, weighed down by the guilt maiming my heart. I can't believe I did that. I've never been so bold... *or disturbing.*

Vegas should come with a warning label.

"Life as you know it will become nonexistent," I mumble while waving my hand in the air dramatically.

When I plop into the chair, I catch my reflection in the mirror. My eyes are wide and bright since my natural beige coloring is accentuated with rosy cheeks, and my lips are plump from my teeth dragging over them.

I'd like to say my rouged appearance is solely based on the stifling Las Vegas heat already pumping into the room, but that would be a lie. Even a stranger could read the signs my body is relaying. I'm the most sexually aroused I've ever been.

Who wouldn't be after witnessing an event like that?

Ignoring the gnawing pit in the middle of my chest for invading Rico's privacy, I snag a concealer stick out of my makeup bag and set to work on hiding the bags plaguing my drooping eyes. Nothing but a few hours between the sheets will fix the flustered look on my face, so I may as well start at the least complicated part of my unsightliness.

Within seconds of applying the first layer of concealer, Rico enters the room. I continue with my mission, pretending I haven't noticed his presence.

My ignorance lasts only seconds when I spot his reflection in the mirror.

His *stark-naked* reflection.

The concealer stick drops to the dresser with a clatter as my eyes drink in every inch of his gloriously naked frame. I try to tear my perverted gaze away, but just like in the bathroom, my morals have been left for dust. It would be like taking a girl to Tiffany's and telling her to only look at the earrings. That will *never* happen. When there's something beautiful to admire, you devour every inch of it, giving equal devotion to each admirable asset.

And that's what I do to Rico's body as he gathers clothing from the walk-in closet and commences getting dressed. By the way my eyes refuse to blink for fear of missing something, anyone would swear he was doing something more riveting than getting dressed. But like everything he does, he dresses with a sense of confidence and stature. He moves with such gracefulness you can't help but be entranced.

Even though I've seen him shirtless numerous times in the past twenty-four hours, my eyes roam over every spectacular ridge and dip of his muscular physique. His biceps aren't brawny like weightlifters, but they're thick and veiny and clearly show he works out, and the six bumps in his stomach constrict when he bends over to step into a pair of blue boxer shorts.

Not wanting to miss the opportunity to see his spectacular package once again, I slowly drop my eyes to the lower half of his body. A trail of dark hair flows from his flat inner belly button to a small patch of curly hair. Just like his facial hair, his pubic hair is trimmed, but it still has an edge of manly roughness to it.

The throb of my pussy overtakes the pounding of my head when my eyes drop to his glorious cock. Even flaccid, his penis is thick, long, and mouth-wateringly beautiful.

When his cock twitches, a dash of desire thickens my blood, and my eyes rocket to his. The tingling of my pussy intensifies when my heavily dilated eyes meet with his heavy-hooded gaze. He clearly noticed my avid assessment of his body. His grin is smug, and his eyes are blazing with lust. He is the cockiest I've ever seen him, which is saying something for a man with as much confidence as Rico.

With a cheeky wink, he slips his cotton boxer shorts up his thighs, covering the core-clenching visual from my devious eyes. Not the slightest bit annoyed that I'm ogling him from across the room, he throws a plain white cotton tee over his head and tugs a pair of dark blue jeans up his legs before pushing off his feet and heading my way. My clit thrums with every prowling step he takes, but like a deer trapped in headlights, I remain frozen and muted, rendered immobile by the massive surge of euphoria pumping through my veins.

He locks his dark gaze with mine in the mirror before muttering, "Good morning, Kitten." His raspy voice adds to the warm slickness coating my panties.

"M-m-morning."

When he stands behind me to run his fingers through his hair in the mirror, the heat of his elongated cock scorches my shoulder blade. My breathing increases to rapid-fire pants as I struggle to ignore the pleas of my body.

Once his fingers have wrangled his dark locks into the sexed-up look he regularly wears, he locks his eyes back to me.

I dart my gaze away, pretending I wasn't daydreaming about replacing his hands with my own.

"Did you sleep well?"

"Uh-huh," I mumble through the lump in my throat, the huskiness of my voice exposing my excitement at his closeness.

He leans over my shoulder to snag his watch from the dresser, bringing his lips super closer to mine when he asks, "Why are you up so early?"

Air traps in my throat when my senses are bombarded with the delicious smell of his body wash. It's unique, virile, and adds a sweet aroma to his spicy scent. "Couldn't sleep. You?"

After fastening his flashy-looking watch on his wrist, Rico returns his eyes to mine reflecting in the mirror and says, "I needed to work off some restlessness, so I went for a run."

Heat creeps across my cheeks as the image of him in the shower plays through my mind.

Obviously his run didn't have the outcome he was aiming for.

Rico glides the back of his hand down my flushed cheeks, the same hand that was earlier wrapped around his cock.

Every fine hair on my body bristles as excitement sparks through my throbbing sex. If I weren't frozen in place with desire, I'd beg for an encore of his performance in the shower, but since my eagerness has muted me into silence, I merely return his lust-filled stare.

After placing his hands on my shoulder, Rico spins me around to face him. "Are you okay, Kitten? You still look a little restless yourself. Flustered even."

I lick my dry lips before forcing out through the dryness, "I'm fine. Nothing a hot shower won't cure." My lips part as my pupils widen. *Could I have chosen a more pathetic set of words?*

The corners of Rico's plump lips twitch as he struggles to hold in his smile. "A hot shower is a wonderful cure for any edginess, but I don't know if it will be enough for you. You seem like you need something more. Something *deeper.*" The low tone of his voice sends a thrill of pleasure through my body. It rockets through every inch of my skin before clustering deep in my aching-with-need pussy.

Incapable of going down without a fight, I turn back to face the mirror, needing to look at anything but his deliriously handsome face before I lose all rational thoughts. My efforts to act unaffected are fruitless. I look even more aroused now than I did when I fled the bathroom.

Ignoring the shaking of my hands, I lift the concealer stick to my face and get back to work on tackling the black rings under my eyes while wishing there was a way I could remove the lust-filled glint in my eyes just as quickly.

Rico stands behind me in silence for several minutes, watching me work my magic on the tiredness even the world's most perfect shower wouldn't have the chance of erasing. Even though he doesn't speak, my awareness of his closeness is paramount. Just the scent of his body wash ensures my wicked mind never strays too far from him.

Happy I've camouflaged a night of restless sleep and ignoring the fact I've put on my makeup before showering, I return my makeup to my cosmetic bag, then stand from my seat.

Thirty minutes have passed since Rico's fire-sparking display in the bathroom, but the intoxicating scent of lust is still thick in the air.

"I'm going to grab a quick shower," I mumble before making a beeline for the bathroom door. I don't know why I felt the need to update him on my happenings, it just naturally flowed out of my mouth.

My quick steps to the bathroom slow when the deep rumble of "Kitten" comes out of a voice with an edge of invincibility. Rico's tone is so smooth and sexy, I think I could come just from listening to him recite the phone book.

After rolling my shoulders, I turn around to face him on a wobbly pair of legs. My knees curve inward when I meet his blazing-with-lust eyes. He watches me for a few seconds, categorizing every feature of my face before he mutters, "I forgot to thank you."

My brows squeeze together in confusion. "For what?"

Sweat coats my palms when he paces toward me, his grin smug, his eyes firing. I can barely breathe when he tilts in close and whispers, "For the towels."

I freeze, panicked at how he'll react to me invading his privacy. Panic is a waste of time. When I shift my gaze sideways, I catch the impish gleam brightening his dark eyes, undoubtedly proving he knew I was watching every scandalous minute of his performance.

My panic recedes more when his lips curve into a heart-fluttering smirk. He knew I was watching. That's why he thoroughly *cleaned* that region of his body. His performance was a show. A pussy-tingling show I'll never forget.

My knees clash together when Rico says, "Enjoy your shower, Kitten. I'll be waiting for you when you've finished."

Chapter Sixteen

Allowing my vicious heart-versus-mind battle to run the gauntlet of my tired brain, I take my time in the shower. My body is begging me to give Rico a chance to prove how good he could make me feel, but my head is telling me there's too much murkiness lurking behind his eyes to trust him.

My heart—that's an entirely different story altogether.

After switching off the shower, I wrap a heavenly soft towel around my body and slowly trudge toward the bathroom door. My steps are heavy, not just weighed down by the dilemma muddling my tired brain but also from the climax clustering in my core, begging to be released.

Even the world's most scalding shower couldn't dampen my excitement the slightest. I'm so wound up I can't think straight. I'm sure it would only take the meekest touch from Rico to send my climax sprinting past the finish line. I just have to decide if I'm willing to give myself fully to the stranger I married because, for some reason unfamiliar to me, it isn't just my body up for barter with Rico. It's all of me—heart, body, and soul.

When I exit the bathroom, my lazy steps stop. Just like he said he'd be, Rico is sitting on the same chair he was in last night, waiting for me. His hair is still damp from his shower, but the rivulets of water that soaked into his shirt have dried.

Though I'm still fighting confusion, his steely eyes show he isn't waging the same battle. He knows what he wants, and he is determined to get it.

After snagging the hydrocortisone cream from the drawers next to him, Rico connects his dark eyes with me. He doesn't need to speak to issue his request. His candid eyes tell the whole story. He wants me. Wholeheartedly.

Deciding I'm running a race I will never win, I push off my feet and amble toward him. With every step I take, the air shifts between us. There's no doubt I have a sexual connection with Rico. It's as obvious as the sun hanging in the sky, but there's something greater than my libido that has me sidestepping the massive obstacles placed between us. He truly intrigues me, more than any man before him, and to such a degree, I appear to have lost all my common sense.

The thrum of my pulse intensifies when my leisured strides stop in the exact spot they did last night. Just like the last time we danced this intricate two-step routine only hours ago, Rico clasps the edge of my towel and pries it open. The only difference this time around is I don't protest.

My heart wallops in my chest when he rubs cream into his name inked on my skin in careful, devoted strokes. The air is fired with lust. It's so electric it sets my pulse racing.

A shameful moan topples from my lips when his finger dips a little lower on the curve of my hip. His simplest touch can cause a feverish heat to scorch my veins.

My lips part to accommodate more needy gasps of air when he lifts his eyes to me and asks, "Did you take care of your restlessness in the shower, Kitten?"

Even blinded by lust, I can't miss the hidden innuendo in his question.

Unable to speak through my dry, parched throat, I shake my head.

A flash of gratitude passes through his eyes. "Do you want me to take care of you? To make you feel better?"

Before any words can spill from my lips, his long index finger runs over another erogenous zone in my body—the area just above the heated ache between my legs.

I open my mouth to protest, but in all honesty, it's just a ploy to convince myself that unbridled hankering isn't clouding all my shrewdness. Considering my lips parted, I'd say my theory has been proven. It isn't lust keeping me standing here. It's him, Rico—the stranger I married.

When he lowers his finger down my quivering core, objections roll out of my mouth hard and fast. They aren't what you're thinking. They are disgruntled protests when his finger fails to stop at my pulsating clit.

"Shh, Kitten, I'll take care of you."

Any hostility lingering in the back of my mind becomes a distant memory when he lifts and locks his heavy-hooded gaze with me. His eyes are dominating and forceful, and they make my pussy pulse with desire. He stares at me for several moments as if waiting for permission.

When I nod, allowing my body to win this round in the debilitating mind versus heart debate, Rico slowly inches his finger inside my shuddering core in a long, mouthwatering thrust. My pussy grows wetter when he says, "Ah, my naughty little Kitten. I've only just touched you, and you're already wet for me."

A whimpering groan flows from my gaped mouth when he withdraws his finger at the same tortuous pace he entered it. The walls of my vagina quiver around him, begging him to stay, to make me come, but their pleas are left unanswered.

I groan when he fully withdraws his finger. It switches to a moan when he pops his glistening digit into his mouth. A flicker of light fires through his dark gaze, closely followed by a carnal growl. "You taste exactly how I remember."

When his arms curl around me, I arch into his embrace, surrendering to the power he holds over me. As he steps toward the bed, he seals his lips over mine and spears his tongue into my mouth. Just like our kiss in the Escalade, he explores my mouth in slow and controlled strokes. He savors every inch of me like he's afraid I may soon vanish.

I float into the softness of high thread count linen when he lays me down in the middle of the bed. I'm splayed before him naked, quivering, and wet while he is fully clothed, but not the slightest twinge of modesty encroaches me. I don't have time to be modest when I'm battling a ferocious out-of-control wildfire in the pit of my stomach.

He cups my breast in his large hand, kneading and caressing it with gentle squeezes while I rock against him, wanting to feel him on every inch of me.

"Enrique..."

"Shh, Kitten. I've got you."

My teeth comb my bottom lip when he lowers his mouth to my aching-with-need breasts and tugs my nipple with his teeth. It sends a jolt of pleasure through my soaked pussy. My nipples are usually not an erogenous zone, but every tug of his teeth tightens my coil more.

Inaudible purrs ripple through my lips when his long, dexterous fingers work one of my nipples into a hard bud while his mouth bites, licks, and sucks the other. When he lifts his head and looks at me, I'm confronted with the same set of eyes that blessed my dreams every night the past week. They are beautiful and innocent, causing my heart to swell.

Prickles sprout on my skin when he places a trail of kisses down my misted-with-sweat stomach. My legs squeeze together, vainly trying to lessen the insane throb between them when his tongue delves out to lick the salty substance slicking my skin with moisture. I watch him, panting and incredibly turned on as he makes his way to the region of my body, paying careful attention to every move he makes.

He kneels beside me, still fully clothed. "I've never seen a pussy as pretty as yours."

When he brushes his hand down my soaked sex, a tinge of vulnerability clouds my perception. This man who obviously has extensive knowledge of the female anatomy eyes me, but when he thrusts his finger back inside me, I push my weakness to the side, deciding now is not the time to evaluate my husband's sexual conquests.

My pussy ripples around him greedily, sucking him in deeper when he switches from one finger to two. I arch my back as a needy moan purrs through my lips. My brain is mindless, stuck in a trance of chasing an orgasm.

Rico sucks my throbbing clit into his mouth, boosting my race to climax. I dart my hands down to entwine my fingers through his hair, needing something to tether me down as I begin floating toward orgasmic bliss.

He rolls his tongue around my clit as my pants become labored and breathless. "Oh... God... Enrique."

Every muscle in my body tightens as his tongue works on my clit while his fingers pump in and out of me in precise, effortless thrusts. My back arches further off the bed with every flick of his tongue. I can feel my orgasm building, but something is holding it back, stopping it from being released.

"Stop fighting me, Kitten. Give me what I want, then I'll give you the same."

When the tension scorching through my body becomes too much to handle, I slump into the mattress and let out a long, throaty purr, surrendering not just my body to the man kneeling before me but my heart as well.

"Good girl," Rico mutters against the quaking lips of my pussy. "Now you'll get what you need."

He increases the pressure of his tongue on my clit, and the pumps of his fingers become unyielding, switching my sprint to climax from a leisured walk to a hundred-yard dash. Sweat slicks my skin as a massive rush of euphoria blazes through every nerve of my body.

While gripping the sheets in a white-knuckled hold, I climax while whispering "Enrique" into the early morning air on repeat. I shudder and shake beneath him, not the slightest bit ashamed that he brought me to climax without removing an article of his clothing.

He gradually brings me down from orgasmic bliss by using a gentler approach than he used to take me there. He slows the thrust of his fingers while keeping pressure on my throbbing clit with his teeth. His bite is firm enough I'll never forget he was there but soft enough to guide me down from the haze of climax.

Once every orgasmic shudder has been exhausted, Rico presses a kiss on my right inner thigh before locking his eyes with my weary gaze. From the exulted gleam in his eyes, anyone would swear it was him who just endured the strongest climax of his life, not me. He looks smug, cocky, and, if I'm not mistaken, pleased, whereas my earth-shattering climax took the last portion of energy I had left in my body, making me limp, incoherent, and drained—mentally and physically.

When the lengths of my blinks grow longer, Rico rolls onto his side and gathers me into his arms. His thick, hard body heats my back and spreads warmth across my chest, adding to the breakneck speed of events that are already tethering my heart to him.

After pulling the blankets out from beneath me, he covers me with their heavenly softness before muttering, "Sleep, Kitten. I'll be here when you wake."

Chapter Seventeen

"*Run, Katie, run!*" I scream through the sheet of tears streaming down my cheeks.

My stomach lurches when a stained white handkerchief narrows in on my face, protesting the strong waft of chemicals lingering from it. I kick the shin of the person whose arm is wrapped around my torso, fighting to break free. Even in my endeavors to escape the clutches of the person dragging me across the cracked concrete sidewalk, my eyes remained locked on Katie, my next-door neighbor and best friend since kindergarten. She wouldn't have been in this predicament if I hadn't convinced her to walk to the corner store against our parents' wishes on a late Friday afternoon.

"Nooo!" I cry in a blood-curdling scream when Katie's lifeless body is thrown into the back of an unmarked white van. Her pleated skirt bunches around her waist when she's pulled deeper into the van by a set of hairy, tattoo-covered hands...

I wake up in Rico's bed screaming. As my lungs heave for oxygen, my wide eyes scan the room. Sweat beads on my temples as tears slosh down my cheeks. I flinch when an arm wraps around my shoulders and drags me backward. Just like in my dream, I fight with all my might, kicking and screaming.

"Blaire, it's me. You're okay."

Even recognizing Rico's voice doesn't dampen my panic in the slightest. I lurch away from him so violently I fall onto the floor with an almighty thud. After kicking off the sheets entwined around my legs, I scamper across the highly polished wooden floor on my hands and knees.

My attempt to reach the wastebasket in the corner of the room before the contents of my stomach see daylight is bolstered when Rico climbs out of bed and brings it to me. He holds back my hair as the memories I've tried to keep buried for ten years resurface in the most ghastliest way.

"Shh, Kitten. You're okay. You're safe." He runs his hand down my spine as I heave into the bin.

Once every portion of slosh in my stomach has been expelled, Rico aids me in getting dressed before he pulls me into his arms and rocks me in his chest. Even during the middle of summer in a disgustingly hot climate, shivers havoc my body. I try to get my mouth to cooperate so I can offer some type of explanation to Rico as to why I've awoken screaming like a lunatic in the middle of the day, but nothing but painful sobs spill from my lips.

Over time, the warmth of Rico's body curled around mine dampens my shudders, and the rhythmic beat of his heart has my eyelids growing heavy...

The roughness of a concrete sidewalk scratches my knees as I crawl away from the man I kicked hard enough in the shins he threw me to the ground. When my ankle is seized, my chin hits the ground with so much force I freeze momentarily, dazed and disoriented. The blood from my grazed knees lines the sidewalk in vibrant red streaks when I'm dragged toward a van parked in an alleyway.

I lie lifeless on the concrete, no longer having the strength to continue my vicious fight. My vision is blurry, hampered by the massive number of tears welling in my eyes, but it isn't blurry enough that I fail to notice an unresponsive Katie lying inside the van. She looks like she's sleeping with her head lolled to the side and her lips slightly parted.

My heart snaps in two when my bleary eyes lock in on a man seated behind her. His evil gaze alone is enough to make my skin crawl.

"I'm sorry, Katie," I mumble through a sheet of tears flowing down my face.

I don't know if I've reached hysteria or if Katie is conscious, but an upwelling of energy pumps into me when the faintest whisper of, "Don't give up, Blaire," sounds through my ears.

Fighting against the pain roaring through my body, I roll onto my side, crawl onto my knees, then stand on a pair of shaky legs. I barely make it three steps out of the alleyway when my body is pinned to a chain-link fence on my left. My lungs heave when my attacker's clutch on my throat becomes so firm, I can no longer breathe.

Not even two seconds later, the brute of a man holding me against the fence is tackled from the side. He and another unknown man land on the concrete path with a sickening thud. I stand frozen, rendered motionless with fear as my savior throws his clenched fist into my attacker's face, momentarily dazing him.

I snap out of my tranced state when my dark-haired savior turns his eyes to me and says, "Run! Blaire! Run!"

I ran and ran until my legs gave out.

Katie was never seen again...

"Wake up, Blaire!"

The authoritativeness in the deep male voice has me snapping to his demand. My eyes pop open to scan the room as I gasp for air, struggling to replenish my heaving lungs. Although the setting of the room is familiar, it takes me several moments to gather my bases since I'm absorbing it from a different vantage point. My frantic breaths pan out when I grasp that I'm still sitting on the floor of my bedroom in the Popov compound, nestled in Rico's strong arms.

"You're okay, Kitten. I promise you're okay," assures Rico, his voice raspy.

The aftereffects of my nightmare dampen when my eyes swing to the window, and I notice the sun has shifted from east to west. Heat blooms across my chest, filling some of the cracks formed there. Rico stayed sitting on the floor with me for hours solely to comfort me.

I knew there was more to this man than just darkness.

After lifting my groggy head off his chest, I peer into Rico's eyes. Even though his backside must be hurting from sitting on the hard wooden floors for hours, nothing but genuine concern beams from his eyes.

"I'm sorry—"

"Shh." He places his index finger on my lip. "Don't ever apologize for having a nightmare. You can't help what happened to you."

My brows knit in confusion. "You know what happened to me?"

A flicker of hesitation flares through his eyes before he nods.

"I told you what happened?" I squeal in surprise, shock evident in my voice.

Guilt has stopped me from sharing my story with anyone not in my inner circle. Even Lacey doesn't know the entirety of what happened that day, so I'm somewhat surprised I voluntarily shared it with Rico. Either the drug Timothy laced my drink with was stronger than anyone could have predicted, or the power Rico has over me is substantial.

When I peer into his remorseful eyes, I'm fairly sure the latter is a more accurate assumption.

Rico stands, taking me with him. From the agility of his movements, no one would suspect he'd spent the last three hours sitting on a rock-hard surface. He holds me close to his body as he walks toward the bathroom.

His long strides have us reaching the edge of the double shower at a record-setting pace.

My wide eyes dart to his when he says, "Let me look after you, Blaire. Let me wash away your pain."

When I peer into his worried eyes, there's no possibility my mind will ever win this battle, so I nod with my teeth grazing my bottom lip.

The hotness of his breath tickles the strands of hair clinging to my sweat-drenched forehead when he releases a relieved breath. After switching on the shower, he flicks off his black polished dress shoes before setting to work on the belt wrapped around his waist. I stand muted, grateful his riveting striptease is pushing my haunted memories to the back of my mind.

I follow the trail his fingers make as he undoes the buttons on his dress shirt before slinging it off his shoulders. My eyes absorb and categorize every inch of his torso. His muscles are so well-defined that his skin is pulled tautly over them, but he isn't overly musclebound in a bulky bodybuilder type of way.

When he slides his trousers down his thighs, I'm not at all surprised to see that his penis is flaccid. This isn't about relieving sexual tension. He's comforting me as the aftershocks of my nightmare cling to my sweat-slicked skin.

Kicking his trousers to the side, he curls his arms around my neck to unlatch the fastener of my dress. Scenes from my nightmare rush to the forefront of my mind when his hand brushes past my neckline. He's barely touching me, but I swear I can feel my assailant's hand wrapped around my throat, strangling me.

"No one will ever hurt you, Blaire. Not while you're with me," Rico assures me as he lowers the zipper on my dress.

Once the zipper has been pulled down to the two dimples in my lower back, my dress slips off my hips and puddles around my feet. Steam curls around us when we enter the shower. As the heavenly hot water sluices down the front of me, Rico's body heats my back. His fingers lace together around my stomach as the stubble on his chin scratches my neck. He doesn't speak. He just comforts me by solely using his body. I close my eyes, allowing the water and Rico to chase away the remnants of a nightmare still playing havoc with my body.

When the violent shudders tormenting me have eased, Rico steps away from me. I inwardly sigh. My disappointment doesn't last long when he snags a shower puff from the tiled shelf and loads it up with body wash. My nostrils flare when the spicy, intoxicating scent graces my senses. The smell is virile and manly, and it pushes the ghastly odor of blood and sweat to the background of my mind.

Remaining quiet, Rico lathers my skin with suds. His dutifulness causes new tears to well in my eyes. I should relish being so loyally cared for, but my mind continually wanders to Katie and her present situation. Is she being taken care of by the man she married, or is she...

A sob tears from my throat, my body choosing its own response to the life Katie is most likely living.

"Kitten." Rico sounds as pained as my heart feels.

He slings his arms around my torso and draws me into his chest. Salty blobs flow from my eyes as steadily as the water pumps out of the showerhead.

"I should have never begged her to come with me. She didn't want to go. She said it was nearly dusk. But I pushed and pushed," I sob, my voice a quiver. "It's all my fault."

Rico pulls me back by my shoulders and glances into my eyes. "It was not your fault. None of it was your fault." When I shake my head, his fingers flex on my shoulders as his demeanor switches from consoling to stern. "Nothing that happened that day was your fault." He stares me straight in the eyes as I did during our tussle in the Escalade last week and quotes, "Nothing."

When he reaches for the shampoo, I close my eyes and let the words he spoke play on repeat in my head. I've been told the same phrase time and time again for the past ten years, but for some reason, hearing them from Rico has a much greater impact.

I was only a child the day I begged Katie to walk to the corner store with me to get an ice cream, but it doesn't lessen my guilt. When she said she didn't want to go, I should have respected her decision. Instead, I insisted. I was a teenager, and I didn't want to be strangled by my overbearing parents for a minute longer.

I was wrong.

So very *very* wrong.

My thumping head lessens under the magic of Rico's fingers as he washes my hair without a peep spilling from his lips. Once all the suds have gurgled down the drain, he shuts down the water and steps out of the shower recess, carefully taking me with him. He pays the same dedicated attention to drying my hair as he did washing it before he steps to the vanity. My brows furrow when a fluffy bathrobe magically appears in his hands.

"Maya brought them in while you were sleeping," he informs my shocked expression.

He wraps me up in the heavenly softness of cashmere before scooping me into his arms. I'll be honest, even in the heart-strangling situation we are immersed in, I love the way he can carry me with such ease. He makes me feel guarded and safe.

"Bed or food?" he asks when we enter the main area of our bedroom.

I bounce my eyes between the silver serving tray stacked with breakfast delights on my left and our bed on my right several times before answering, "Bed."

I'm not tired. My tummy is just too swishy to handle any food right now.

Rico pulls down the bed covers and places me inside before heading to the drawers to dress in a pair of boxer shorts and a short-sleeve shirt. After running his fingers through his hair to remove the excess droplets of water, he slips into the bed beside me, then gathers me in his arms.

Chapter Eighteen

We've been lying in bed for nearly twenty minutes before Rico breaks the silence. "Have you been suffering nightmares this whole time?"

Usually, this type of question fills me with shame, but because it's coming from him while he's looking at me with nothing but remorse in his eyes, I don't feel as embarrassed admitting I'm an adult who suffers from debilitating nightmares.

I nod. "Yes. They aren't normally as bad as the one today. This one felt as if I was back in the alleyway. It was one of the most realistic dreams I've had in over ten years."

He runs his index finger under my eyes as if he's preparing to catch my tears before they have the chance to fall. Mercifully, his finger leaves my cheek unscathed. "Is it because of the *situation* you've been thrown into?"

"I don't know..." I shrug. "Maybe?"

Another stretch of silence crosses between us. It's long enough that the color of the sky slowly switches to the color of his eyes, but the silence isn't awkward. It strangely feels right.

A possible reason for the silence makes my lips dry, so I lick them before asking, "Did I have a nightmare the night we got married?"

Rico smiles before shaking his head. "No, but we didn't get much sleep that night." He may have been aiming for an informative tone, but it comes out witty.

His deep chuckle rumbles through my body when I punch him in the chest. "I gathered that when I found the strip of condoms hidden under the bed last week."

The heart-fluttering smile stretching across his face grows. "I was wondering where those went."

I roll my eyes, pretending I'm not a fan of his playfulness, where in reality, I'm loving it. Although the aftermath of a nightmare is still clinging to my skin, his cheekiness is easing the pain crippling my heart.

"Who keeps a strip of condoms joined anyway? That's just weird." My mouth gapes, shell-shocked I mumbled my inner dialogue out loud.

Rico doesn't seem to mind. "Not as weird as my wife showing me her balloon twisting skills while she's lying next to me naked."

I stare at him, slack-jawed and blinking. "I showed you my balloon-twisting skills?"

Smiling, he nods.

I inwardly die a thousand deaths. "With *condoms?*"

"You take what you can get and run with it." His smirks does wicked things to my insides. "Although I wouldn't recommend showing the same trick to your students."

I playfully punch him again. "And here I was the whole time thinking we'd done the..." I stop talking to swallow away a lump in my throat, "... *deed* three times in a night."

"Oh, we *did* that." He scoots closer so we share the same breaths. "And so much more."

My eyes light with excitement, and I swear the panties I'm not wearing combust. The mood shifts. It's quick and resolute. Gone are the debilitating effects of a nightmare replaced with nothing but unbridled lust. Nothing else matters but unearthing those lost memories of our wedding night and recreating them.

I don't need to speak for Rico to notice the change in my demeanor. He can see it beaming from my hankering gaze.

Like he could lessen the space between us more, he scoots even closer. My heart hammers my ribs as my palms sweat, but I meet his stare while feeling the most desired I've ever felt. Rico's eyes are sleepy, his hair is a tousled, sexed-up mess, and his lips are curved into a mouthwatering smirk, but the optimism beaming from his eyes makes him the most handsome I've ever seen him.

The carefree look on his face alone is worth the sacrifice of having my heart broken. I'd give anything to see that gleam in his eyes time and time again.

Desperate to hide my stupid sentimental tears, I burrow my head in Rico's chest. When my lips press against his pecs, his heartbeat goes from a leisured pace to a wild thump. A grin curls on my lips. Even knowing I shouldn't admit this, I love the way his body responds to my touch. So much so, I can't stop my hand from sneaking under his shirt to caress the skin on his lower back.

The lazy smile stretched across my face enlarges when his muscles constrict under my faintest touch. They bunch more with every slither of my fingertips.

Upon feeling the incline of my cheeks, Rico places his hand under my chin and lifts my head. I bite the inside of my cheek, trying to hold in my immature smile, but nothing works. I shouldn't enjoy being wrapped in his warmth, but nothing can take away a woman's feelings when she's caressed in a pair of strong arms. I feel protected nestled against his big body. Like no one could ever hurt me. Which is utterly ridiculous considering the man caressing me is the same man who causes my greatest worries. He is the sole reason I'm living in an unknown environment, but he's also the reason my heart is beating so fast.

I've never felt more alive than I do right now.

The heat creeping across my chest amplifies when Rico mutters groggily, "There's my Blaire."

"Blaire, what happened to Kitten?" I jest, my tone witty.

With a mind-hazing orgasm still surging through my blood and the disappearance of the headache that's been riddling me the past week, my attitude has taken a swing toward the positive.

My eyelids twitch when Rico runs his index finger over the curve of my brow. "This set of eyes belongs to Blaire."

My breathing quickens when his index finger leisurely travels down my body, only stopping when it hits a snippet of my breasts peeking out from my dressing gown. When his thumb brushes over my nipple before his index finger joins the party, I draw in a shaky breath. His talented hand soon works me into a frenzy by doing nothing more than tweaking my now sensitive nipples. It shows his skills in the bedroom, a natural dominance I've only just scratched the surface of. Pair that with the confidence he exudes in bucket-loads, and he has an aggressive set of skills that wildly turn me on.

I only just hold in my disappointed groan when he moves his hand from my breast to run his index finger over my beaded-with-sweat brow once again. "These eyes belong to Kitten," he mutters while staring into my massively dilated eyes.

"But why Kitten? It doesn't make any sense."

Before I have the chance to react, Rico pounces. My back is consumed by the softness of a cloud, and my front is assaulted by ripped muscles belonging to a tall brute of a man.

When he rocks his hips, the crown of his thickened cock rubs my pulsating clit. Shockwaves dart through my body at the same time a purr escapes my O-formed lips. Beyond mortified by the erotic groan that just rumbled through my lips, I straighten my spine and snap my mouth shut.

I've never moaned like that before.

Not once.

My eyes snap to Rico when he croons, "That's why I call you Kitten."

The deep timbre of his voice spurs goose bumps to prickle my forearms. He stares down at me as he did in my flashbacks, his hair falling around his chiseled face, his lips slightly parted, and his delicious scent filling every inch of my aching-with-desire core. He's breathtakingly beautiful and thigh-shakingly dangerous at the same time.

"Who are you?" I whisper before my brain can cite an objection.

The corners of his lips curl into a heart-fluttering smirk. "You already know. You just need to remember." He stares down at me with the same eyes that stole my heart in less than a minute while demanding, "Kiss me, Blaire."

Ignoring the dangerous beat of my heart, I cup his jaw with my shaky hands and kiss him.

For a man with a rough exterior, his kisses are nothing but gentle. I sink into the mattress when he slides his tongue into my mouth in long, tempting strokes. He rocks his hips in a rhythm matching the pace of our kiss, allowing me to feel the effect our kiss is having on him. He's hard—*very* hard.

After weaving my fingers through his hair, I pull his head nearer to mine, not only deepening our kiss but strengthening our odd relationship. Rico growls at my assertiveness, then switches the intensity of our embrace, shifting it from soft and gentle to needy and urgent.

We kiss for several long minutes, sending the room's temperature from comfortable to roasting.

Just like every kiss we've shared, when Rico pulls away, I'm completely and utterly breathless. His eyes stole my heart in under a minute, but his kisses are capturing my soul.

I keep my fingers knitted through his hair, not willing to let go just yet. I've only just come to terms with the expeditious speed of our relationship, so I need a few more minutes to bask in this beautiful surreality before tiptoeing back into the Amityville Horror House.

The reasoning behind Rico's sudden withdrawal becomes clear when a loud knock bellows on our bedroom door. My bottom lip drops into a pout, disappointed my trip to Pleasantville didn't last as long as I was hoping.

I won't lie. When Rico rolls over—unpinning me from his heavenly warmth—my body screams in protest. Although my every want, desire, and need weren't fulfilled, one thing crystallized.

I do know this man.

I just need to remember him.

My heart continues swelling when Rico ensures I'm covered before he walks to the door. I tuck the sheets under my chin when the door swings open, and I spot Erik, Rico's lawyer, standing on the other side. Erik is a handsome man, but just like Rico, his true intentions are a little hard to read. Today, his expression looks both torn and passive.

After handing Rico a flat sheet of paper, Erik shifts his gaze to me. I hesitantly smile. I'm sure I look like an utter wreck. I've always been an ugly crier, and I doubt even the brilliance of a mind-altering orgasm could hide the puffiness my eyes get after a good dose of crying.

My heartbeat kicks up a gear when the mask Rico wears in front of his crew slips onto his face before my very eyes. My concern grows about his swift shift in demeanor when the carefree glint in his eyes fades into the blackness of his dark and dangerous gaze. Just like the man I confronted in the gloomy basement room last week, the Rico standing in front of me is once again a stranger.

After shaking hands with Erik, Rico closes the door and spins on his heels to face me. I freeze when I catch the quickest flare of emotion passing through his eyes as he walks back to bed. Like a man with two heads, his eyes relay two very contradicting emotions—tenderness and anger.

I throw off the sheets and crawl across the mattress when he sits on the edge and pats the bed beside him. Although I'm behaving like an obedient dog, my desire to unravel the mystery standing before me is guiding my decisions. It may make me seem submissive, but from the memories I've unearthed the past twenty-four hours, I know this hasn't always been the case in our whirlwind relationship.

Remaining quiet, Rico passes the sheet of paper Erik handed him to me. After bouncing my eyes between his unreadable gaze, I drop them to the document. Only six small words are printed in plain black ink, but they cause a significant impact to my faltering heart.

Timothy Jamison was arrested this morning.

I snap my eyes to Rico, searching his truth-bearing eyes for the confirmation he gives me with words. "Someone slipped the local authorities the information I obtained on Timothy before the Popov crew could *attend* to the matter. If the justice system prevails, I'll consider the matter closed."

Blood surges into my heart as a smile stretches across my face.

I knew there was more to this man than just darkness.

A small snippet of my happiness is sideswiped when he mutters, "Don't become complacent, Kitten. There's a long way to go before this is over. If I feel appropriate justice isn't served, I'll have no other choice but to become reinvolved in his case."

"I understand," I reply with a concise nod. "But that doesn't mean we can't celebrate the small victories. The victims' families will be so grateful you did this, Enrique. They will now have closure."

A spark of sentiment flickers through his eyes. "I didn't do it for their families, Blaire. I did it for you. To prove I am the man in your memories."

I smile through my tears threatening to spill down my face. "Thank you." Those two small words don't seem enough to express the surge of emotions pumping through me, but they are all I have to offer, so they are all I can give.

My eyes lift from the paper to Rico when he says, "Now I need you to do me a favor, Kitten."

I search his eyes, seeking an indication that he only did this for me for a favor in return. Failing to find any deceit in his eyes, I mutter. "Anything."

He appears relieved. "I need you to call off your friend before she stumbles into a life she doesn't belong in."

Chapter Nineteen

U tterly dumbfounded, I stare at Rico before my lungs lose the ability to fill with air. "Lacey isn't taking the news of your departure from Ravenshoe well. She's creating ripples. Ripples my family will soon discover. If you want your friend to stay safe, you need to force her to back away from her inquiries."

Bile twists its way from my stomach to my throat, but even feeling sick, I nod, agreeing with his terms. Lacey is my best friend, so I'll do everything in my power to protect her. I failed once before protecting Katie. I refuse to let it happen again.

Pretending there aren't tears praying to streak my cheeks, I lock my eyes with Rico and say, "What do you need me to do?"

He steps to a set of drawers on his right. After pulling out a plain black phone, he moves to stand in front of me. The torment in his eyes is even more compelling than it was earlier. "Call Lacey and ask her to back off."

My eyes dart between his, my confusion growing by the second. "Why can't I use my phone?"

"Lacey called in the authorities. There's a team of detectives stationed at your apartment. They will be tracing the call."

My heart slithers into my gut. "So I have to make my call quick? Like they do in the movies?"

Rico smiles. It doesn't match the despair in his dark gaze. "No, Kitten. That's nothing but a Hollywood ploy. Maybe back in the eighties they took sixty seconds to trace a call, but with technology today, it can be done instantaneously. Lucky for us, the compound has numerous signal jammers installed, but for extra caution, I'd prefer you use a dump phone. They'll have a hard time tracking it when it's buried under a pile of rubble."

Ignoring my trembling hands, I stand from the bed and accept the cell phone he's holding out. Thankfully, even in a day of modern technology, I have a knack for remembering phone numbers.

After dialing Lacey's cell into the outdated phone, I press it close to my ear.

She answers not even a full ring later.

"Hello?" The concern in her tone makes her greeting come out sounding more like a question than a greeting.

I exhale a deep breath. "Lac—"

"Blaire! Oh my God. Are you okay? Where are you? Are you safe?" she blubbers out in quick succession.

"Lacey, calm down. I need you to listen... I don't have long." I shift my eyes to Rico, who is watching me with caution from the side of the room. "Did you call the police?"

"Yes, of course I did! Colt said you were dragged out of here by a man claiming to be your husband." She stops talking and inhales a big breath. She's obviously rattled as I can hear the shaking of her ribcage through the phone. "He also said two of the men flanking you were carrying guns."

The truth of Rico's statement rings true when Lacey's confession causes a flurry of activity to sound down the line. The most obvious evidence is the inclusion of two male voices I don't recognize.

"Blaire, are you there?" Lacey asks when a stretch of silence passes between us.

"Yes, I am here." I breathe out.

My heart is a twisted mess of confusion. Half of me hates that Lacey is upset while the other half wants to do everything in my power to protect Rico from the authorities. Don't ask me why. I wouldn't be able to answer. If I'd been held captive for longer than twenty-four hours, I could have used the defense of Stockholm Syndrome, but deep down in my soul, I know that isn't the case.

I'm truly not scared of Rico.

Startled, yes.

Scared, definitely not.

"What's going on, Blaire? Was it your husband?" Lacey asks, drawing my attention back to the present.

"Yes," I mutter faintly.

Lacey gasps in a ragged breath, shocked by my reply. "I thought your marriage was annulled?"

"I thought it was too, but the papers were never filed. We're still legally married."

"So you thought you'd just up and leave with him on a whim? Your Vegas experience was as cookie cutter as they come for Vegas, but that craziness is supposed to stop the instant you step foot in the plane." Her words come out in a flurry, her tone a mixture of anger and bewilderment. "You don't continue with the idiocy once you return home."

Pain strikes my heart when her quiet sniffles resonate down the line. "This isn't you, Care Blaire. You've always been the safe, smart friend. You wouldn't have just packed up and left of your own free will. He's hurting you, isn't he? Holding you against your will?"

I shake my head, soundlessly denying her accusations. My brisk movements cause tears to trickle down my ashen cheeks. Spotting my upset composure, Rico pushes off his feet and ambles toward me. The concern beaming from his eyes adds to the restrictive hold strangling my heart.

"Is he threatening you? Are you in danger?" Lacey asks through a barrage of hiccups.

"No, Lacey, he'd never hurt me."

My confession clears away the painful haze in Rico's dark gaze. He stands behind me and slings his arms around my torso, the heat of his body easing my shuddering shakes.

"Lacey, I'm begging you, please drop this."

"I can't." Her heartache is unable to be hidden by those two little words. "You're my best friend, Blaire. I won't sit back and watch you make a stupid mistake you can't take back."

My heart squeezes painfully. "I'm not asking you to sit back and watch me fail. I just want you to give me a chance to make my own decisions. Please don't make me feel guilty for finally living my life how I want. I don't want to be the *safe friend* anymore. I want to live. Please let me live."

Most of my statement is to keep Lacey safe—if she believes I'm here of my own free will, she will drop this—but part of it comes from deep within my soul. I've always been the *safe friend*. I never went to college parties, never stepped over the line that balances precariously between tipsy and drunk, and I never did anything that had an edge of danger or adventure attached to it. Although I wouldn't recommend waking up married to a mob boss with no recollection of your time together. My heart has never beaten so fast.

"Lacey?" I mutter into the phone when I'm greeted with nothing but silence. "Are you still there?"

"Yes," she replies, her voice jittery and weak.

"Please don't hate me," I mumble, sickened by the thought I've hurt her feelings.

A door sliding open sounds down the line, closely followed by the faint hum of the traffic that always impedes the streets of Ravenshoe. She must have stepped out onto the patio attached to the living room of our apartment. "I'd never hate you, Care Blaire. I just want to make sure you're safe."

Even though she can't see me, I nod. "I am."

A length of silence stretches between us, crammed with stifling heaviness. If it weren't for Lacey's panicked breaths sounding down the line, I would have assumed she had hung up on me.

"Why did it have to be a suit-wearing thug who *finally* cracked your shell?" Lacey jests a short time later, her tone not as pained as it was. "I've been chipping away at it for years, but I didn't even cause a hairline crack. You spent a day with him, and all your insecurities crumbled."

Rico must hear her as he stiffens during the 'suit-wearing thug' part and tightens his grip around my torso during her last sentence.

"Promise me you're safe," Lacey pleads into the phone. "If you can, I'll tell the detectives sitting in our living room that this was all a big misunderstanding. And don't even think about lying to me, Blaire. Even over the phone, I'll tell."

A smile stretches across my face. What she's saying is true. She knows me better than anyone.

While exhaling a deep breath, I spin on my heels the best I can in the protective cocoon Rico has wrapped around me. When I lift my eyes to his face, my breathing sharpens. The same set of beautiful eyes from my memories stare down at me. Gone is the haunted, bleak look his eyes generally wear, replaced with the eyes of a boy lost in a world full of monsters.

I freeze as another lost memory is found...

"I'm not a good man, Blaire. I've done terrible, horrible things... way more than I can count. I don't deserve a woman like you. I don't deserve an angel."

I peer into Rico's eyes, seeing nothing but remorse reflecting back at me. We both know his words are true, but when I look deeper, past the guilt blackening his eyes, all I see is a little boy who grew up unloved. He's flawed and damaged but has one of the most beautiful souls I've ever seen. He simply needs to be shown how to look past the blackness. To be taught how to love.

"I'm not here to save you, Enrique. We are here to save each other..."

Now some of my decisions last week make sense. Rico wasn't a man I feared. He was the man I swore to protect. The vulnerability that flashed in his eyes the thirty seconds following my tumble into his lap had me pledging I'd stop at nothing until he walked through the darkness unscathed.

He truly did capture my soul in less than a minute.

I turn my attention back to the phone pressed against my ear before locking my eyes with Rico. "I'm safe. I promise you. I'm the safest I've ever been," I declare to both Lacey and Rico.

When a broad grin etches on Rico's face, I'm tempted to add, *physically, not mentally.*

Chapter Twenty

"Are you ready?"

After flattening down the front of my cotton dress, I nod. My heart is thrashing against my chest, and nervous sweat is slicking my skin, but I am ready, nonetheless.

"Remember what I told you, Kitten. Stay by my side at all times and don't trust anybody." From the way Rico's words are laced with warning, anyone would swear we are about to meet Jack the Ripper, not have brunch with his family.

As I prepared for our outing, Rico gave me a brief rundown on how things in the Popov compound work. Usually, the women of the house serve the men, but since I hold the prestigious role of his wife, I'll be seated beside him during brunch.

Although shocked at the inequality of women in this faction, I'm not completely blindsided by it. The fact Rico's father sold his daughter on the black market is all the evidence I require that the Popov clan is a group of callous and cold-hearted men.

No further explanation needed.

After applying a dusting of blush to my already rosy cheeks, Rico wraps his hand over mine and exits our bedroom. Things between us have been oddly normal the past five days. Our routine hasn't altered from the day I arrived. I spend my days holed up in our room like a prisoner in a minimum-security facility, reading and playing card games with Maya while Rico 'works.'

It doesn't matter if I go for a shower at eleven in the morning or ten at night, Rico is always waiting in the high-backed chair to apply cream to his name inked on my hip. When his 'working' day is over, he showers, then we spend the rest of our night together in bed, where thankfully, Rico's protective cocoon keeps my nightmares to a bare minimum.

We are like an everyday couple, our coexistence melding together surprisingly quick. The only difference between us and every other newlywed couple is our conversations aren't based on how his day at 'work' went or what china we'd like to purchase for our new house. The entirety of our discussion is if any of my hidden memories were unearthed and if I've had any more nightmares.

Unfortunately, other than the flurry of memories that were unleashed my first twenty-four hours here, I've not had any fresh memories revealed since.

I'll be honest. Even being held captive in a mansion full of gun-toting men, I'll happily pledge that the man I see in my flashbacks is the same man I wake up curled around every morning. Away from others, Rico is attentive and sweet. A man I could wholeheartedly marry on sight. It's just the air of danger surrounding him that causes my greatest worry.

While I'm being totally forthright, I'll disclose another powerful point separating us from other newlywed couples—our lack of sexual contact. Don't construe my statement the wrong way. I'm not at all expecting the band on my finger to come with the agreed stipulation of sexy time. I'm just surprised I've spent the past five nights in bed with a man who appears sexually ambitious but have not once been propositioned. Lust is no doubt firing between us, but nothing more than an affectionate cuddle has been shared the last five nights.

I won't lie. My ego is suffering the brutal sting of rejection.

My grip on Rico's hand tightens when our brisk stride down the corridor has us reaching two burly-looking men at the end. Just like last week, their conversation ends the instant they catch sight of me. They don't speak. They just eye us with caution as we saunter by.

I lean into Rico's side when a group of suit-clad men at the end of the stairwell rake their sullied eyes down my body. Considering they are several years older than me and have partners attached to their hips, I find their gaze demoralizing and nauseating.

"*Po'shyol 'na hui*," Rico growls at them, his words vibrating right through my body.

Their eyes snap to Rico in sync. "*Zashchishchat' shlyukhu?*"

Rico's pulse pulverizes my hand. "*Nyet. Moya zhena.*"

The men's eyes widen before they drop to their shoes.

"What was that about?" I ask Rico as he guides me across the opulent entry of his home.

"Nothing."

With every step I take, my legs quake, but I play my part as wife accordingly. I smile greetings at the curious stares of women eyeing me with wonder, and I redirect my eyes from the men whose avid gazes make my skin crawl.

"Who are all these people?" I query, shocked by the vast number of people mingling throughout the residence.

"Most are family members... brothers, sisters, cousins." Rico gestures his head to the group associated with each title. "The rest are *associates* of the Popov entity." Just from the way he says 'associates' indicates they're people I should avoid.

"What about the women in the den?" I nudge my head to the sunken lounge we are gliding by that's filled to the brim with attractive ladies.

Rico stiffens for the quickest second before he mutters, "They are mistresses?" The unsureness of his voice makes what should be a statement come out sounding like a question.

My heart falls out of my ribcage. "Mistresses? Whose mistresses?" I grimace when my question is delivered louder than I intend.

He releases my hand from his grasp and places it on the curve of my lower back while answering, "Once Vladimir is finished with them, anyone who wants them."

My first reaction is disgust. Most of the women in the den would be in their mid-twenties to early thirties, way too young to sleep with a man Vladimir's age. My second reaction is jealousy—sick, twisted jealousy.

After taking a moment to settle my swishing stomach, I ask matter-of-factly, "Do you have mistresses?" This time, my voice comes out level and calm, even though I'm anything but.

After dipping his chin at a man standing guard near a concealed door, Rico guides me down an incredibly long dining table. Just like our room, this space is decorated with priceless paintings and opulent antique furnishings, but it isn't enough to dampen the queasiness passing through me.

Even with no knowledge of mob-related activities, I know Rico is moving us to the higher-ranked seating. It isn't merely the fact that the hum of conversation dulled the instant we entered the room, it is also the fact every set of eyes in the room is centered on Rico and me —even with them sneakily peering up from the floor. But even being eyed like I'm a circus act and having a queasy stomach, I can't harbor the vehement jealousy heating my blood.

"Do you?" I ask again, ensuring I keep my tone as low as possible.

Rico drops his eyes to me. "Do I what?"

I snarl, bearing teeth. The gleam in his eyes exposes he knows what I'm referring to. He's just choosing to be ignorant.

My scowl deepens, leaving a heavy set of wrinkles on my forehead. Spotting my angry snarl, Rico's lips curl into a panty-wetting smirk. "Are you jealous, Kitten?" He leans in close, gaining us the curious glance of a dozen people surrounding us. "Does my little kitty have her claws out, ready to pounce on any woman who dares get close to her man?"

His words jolt through me like I've sustained a physical blow while also adding to my worry that there's been no sexual contact between us since my first morning waking up in this compound. It's inanely ridiculous for me to be jealous, but I can't help it. Drugged mistake or not, Rico is my husband. Just thinking about him with another woman triggers merciless jealousy to sear through me.

Sensing my usually carefree composure slipping, Rico murmurs, "You have nothing to be jealous of, Kitten."

His words don't offer me any reassurance. If anything, they make me even more irate. If he has nothing to hide, why skirt my question? Why not just be honest?

My irritation switches to trepidation when he pulls out a chair second from the end and gestures for me to sit.

"Exactly what rank are you in this industry?" I stammer out before I can stop my words.

Before Rico can answer, his father enters the room from a concealed entrance on my left. He walks with a sense of arrogance like Rico, but his demeanor doesn't merely invite inquisitive stares of rapacious women. It demands resolute silence.

For his age, Vladimir is a fit-looking gentleman of tall height and average build. His hair is dark brown and slicked back, and his face is void of the wrinkles most men his age have. If I could look past his cold-hearted eyes and unapproachable demeanor, I'd say he is handsome.

When Vladimir saunters deeper into the room, the attendees react similarly as they did when Rico entered. Half stare at him in awe while the other half—the mainly female half—bow their heads.

Following the vibe of the room, I tuck my chin into my neck and stray my eyes to the tabletop. "No, Kitten," Rico growls before pinching my chin and lifting my head back to its original position. "You do not bow to him."

Ignoring the fact I'm shivering like a bag of nerves, I lift my chin and swing my eyes to Vladimir. I'm taken aback when I discover the cold, depraved gaze running over my body isn't from Vladimir. It's from the elegantly dressed lady standing beside him. Even with her eyes thinly slit, she has flawless facial features, plump lips, and a straight nose. Her dark hair is pulled back in a low ponytail, and her petite frame is draped in priceless silk and jewels. If I had to guess her age, I'd say she was early to mid-forties.

Dropping her green gaze to me, the unnamed female asks,

"*Pochemu shlyukha sidit za stolom?*" Although I don't understand Russian, I can't miss the callousness of her tone.

"If you wish to address Blaire, you need to speak English." Rico shifts his eyes sideways to the unnamed lady. "She doesn't understand Russian."

"And yet you still married her," the dark-haired beauty retorts. "Spitting on your father's grave before he's even stepped foot in there."

Rico's jaw gains a tick, but he remains tight-lipped. After reassuringly squeezing my hand, he gestures for me to sit. When I do, he secures a white napkin onto my lap. I twist it in knots, needing something to settle the sick feeling in my stomach.

I swallow away a horrible bitterness in the back of my throat when Vladimir affixes his gaze with mine. His face is impassive, his eyes from the devil himself. He watches me for several uncomfortable moments, assessing me from the inside out. My stomach churns with both fear and grief. Fear for Rico striving to be just like him. Grief for Rico being raised by him. It must have been horrible, worse than the deepest pit of hell.

I jump when Rico unexpectedly places his hand on mine, stopping my fidgeting movements. I've twisted the napkin so tightly around my fingers, it's cutting off my blood supply.

With Rico breaking our horrifying connection, Vladimir takes a seat at the head of the table, then gestures for the dark-haired woman to sit. No words are needed to issue his request. His stern gaze is demanding enough for her to jump to his command.

I only just hold in my surprised gasp when she takes the chair opposite me. I assumed she'd sit beside Vladimir, considering they are husband and wife. How do I know they're married? They have matching wedding bands like Rico and me.

"*Shlyukhas* don't belong at this end of the table," she snarls at me.

My eyes shoot to Rico, seeking translation. His nostrils flare as his face lines with anger, but he maintains a quiet approach. Before I can ask what *shlyukha* means, the reasoning behind the dark-haired lady being seated away from Vladimir becomes apparent. Just like our meeting last week, Nikolai swaggers into the room with both an air of authority and a snip of fear. But unlike Rico and Vladimir, the female eyes in the room don't drop to the floor when graced with his presence. I don't know if that's because they see him as more approachable than his predecessors or because he has not yet earned their reputation. Either way, my eyes immediately dart down to the table when he issues me a cocky wink.

"Ah. My beautiful *Ahren* blushes too. If only you had fallen into my lap instead of Rico's," Nikolai jests before sitting in the chair across from Rico.

The heat on my cheeks grows as does the grip of Rico's hand curled around my thigh. Snubbing his brother's furious glare, Nikolai smiles a smug grin before he lifts his fingers to his lips, pretending to lock his mouth.

After slouching into his chair, he turns his eyes to his father sitting on his left. From the untroubled look on Vladimir's face, it appears this type of bickering is nothing new for Rico and Nikolai.

Or perhaps he doesn't know how to change his deadpan expression?

With a wave of his hand, Vladimir demands his staff to commence serving brunch. Unable to tolerate the evilness beaming out of numerous pairs of eyes in the room, I drop my gaze to my empty plate and concentrate on keeping my breathing patterns level.

Within minutes, my plate is loaded with a vast variety of food. Bread, sausages, eggs, Russian pancakes, and tea are plentiful. It smells delicious, but my stomach is too twisted to risk sampling any of it, so instead, I push my food around my plate with a fork while sneakily scanning the room.

While sipping a glass of sweetened tea, my eyes anchor on a familiar face entering the dining room from the other end—Erik, Rico's lawyer. The women pay him the same amount of attention as Rico, but they don't hide it beneath lowered lashes.

I can understand their fascination. When he isn't cloaked in darkness, Erik is a handsome man. Not as handsome as Rico, but that would be a hard feat for any man to conquer.

After taking his seat three places up from Nikolai, Erik addresses my gawking stare with a hesitant smirk before accepting a plate of food from Maya. After returning his greeting, I return my devotion to sneakily assessing the room.

Over the next forty minutes, the tension in the air never leaves, and the flow of conversation increases. Although most of the discussions are in Russian, I've noticed one word being used on repeat—*shlyukha*. If the sneer of their tone isn't enough of an indication it's a derogative word, the fact numerous pairs of eyes glare at me while saying it is a surefire sign.

Unable to harbor my curiosity any longer, I turn my gaze to Rico. The stubble on his jaw cannot hide its relentless tick, and his eyes are narrowed into thin slits.

Obviously, I'm not the only one noticing the thick stench of hostility in the room.

I keep my tone low, ensuring no one within earshot will hear my inquiry. "What does *shlyukha* mean?"

Rico stiffens for the quickest second before wiping his mouth with a white napkin. "Nothing. Finish your breakfast, Kitten."

Anger unlike anything I've ever felt boils my blood. He didn't even look at me while speaking. He just dismissed me without so much as a sideways glance.

Strangers' ignorance I can tolerate, but from my husband? No, that's something I will not stand for.

Gritting my teeth, I stand from my seat and excuse myself from the table.

I've reached my quota of dealing with ill-mannered men for one day.

Before I push away from the table, my wrist is seized, and I'm yanked back into my seat.

My unladylike topple ends with a bang, not just to my backside but my pride as well.

"Sit down and eat." Rico's angry sneer shudders through my chest.

I stare at him, dazed and confused. Although the maliciousness of his words doesn't match the remorse beaming from his eyes, anger still bombards me. Who is this man? He isn't the man I've awoken to the past five mornings, and he most definitely isn't a man I'd marry on sight.

Battling against threatening tears, I direct my eyes away from the cold-hearted stranger sitting next to me. While diverting my eyes, I catch the leering grin of the unnamed lady sitting across from me. Humor lines her heavily made-up face, and her eyes are brimmed with amusement.

Noticing she has captured my attention, her evil grin enlarges. "Do you want to know what *shlyukha* means?" she asks me, her words laced with vindictiveness.

Not willing to participate in the belittling games of this corrupt family, I shake my head before lowering my eyes to my barely touched plate of food. With my stomach swirling from the tension in the air, my usually robust appetite is waning.

Any chance of easing my squishy stomach falters when Nikolai remarks, "*Shlyukha* means whore, *Ahren.*"

My heart drops into my stomach as my eyes rocket to Nikolai. I don't need him to repeat his explanation. All the evidence I need projects from the amused gaze of every set of eyes gawking at me. They're mocking and full of torment.

"If you had fallen into my lap instead of Rico's, I would have cut out the tongue of every man who dared speak of you with such disrespect," Nikolai states before drifting his narrowed eyes to his brother. "I wouldn't sit by and watch my wife called a whore without reprimand."

"*Zatknis'*," Rico spits off his tongue, his eyes fixed on his brother. "*Ili ya zakroyu yego dlya vas.*"

Rico's words are obviously vicious as the room falls into silence. It's thick and tangible and has my pulse quickening.

The smug grin Nikolai has been wearing all morning enlarges, clearly pleased he has sparked a reaction from his brother. After kissing the cheek of the lady seated beside him, he excuses himself from the table and walks out of the room with his cocky swagger on full display.

Ignoring the pain stabbing the middle of my chest, I wait for the hum of chatter to once again fill the room before shifting my eyes to Rico. "You knew they were calling me a whore, but you said nothing?" My words come out in a hiss, strained through a sob sitting at the back of my throat. "Why didn't you stand up for me?"

"Now is not the time," Rico replies, his words abrupt.

"They called me a whore, Rico. When is that ever appropriate?" My voice gets louder as I battle to leash my anger, but even knowing I'm attracting stares, I can't stop my onslaught. I'm hurt that the only person who defended my honor was the man who wants me to call him Satan. "Why would you let them call me that?"

His ticking jaw gains momentum. "We'll discuss this later."

"No! Tell me now," I shout, gaining me the attention of every pair of eyes in the room.

I balk like I've been physically slapped when Rico snarls, "Because that's what all women are. Whores."

Chapter Twenty-One

Before I can comprehend the repercussions of my actions, I raise my hand and slap it across Rico's face. The callousness of my hit forces his head to sling sideways and for my palm to set on fire.

While nursing my injured hand, I push back from my seat and make a beeline for the double doors at the end of the room. My heart wallops my ribcage, and tears loom in my eyes, but I refuse to let them fall. I will not give anyone in this room the satisfaction of thinking they've made me upset.

My quick exit is halted when two large men block my path. When I try to sidestep them, they move back into my way.

After exhaling a nerve-cleansing breath, I raise my eyes from their boot-covered feet to their faces. I gulp harshly when I see their furious scowls, then bile creeps up my windpipe as the severity of the situation smacks into me.

I just slapped a head honcho in a Russian mob in front of his goons.

Can I be any more stupid?

When one of the wide-shouldered goons grabs the tops of my

arms, I grimace. His hold is so rough, panic zips through me as fragments of my past clash with my present.

Flashes of being grabbed in the alleyway momentarily daze me, but when the goon shakes me—knocking my back molars together—my fighter instincts kick in. I claw at him viciously and thrash out my legs, not willing to go down without a fight for the second time.

My battle seems to irritate him more. He firms his clutch, and the redness lining his face intensifies, but his fingers stop digging into my bicep when a deep voice from behind me growls, "Let her go."

Rico's voice is so gravelly it shakes my heart right out of my chest.

Cranking my neck back, I watch him urgently stride toward me. His gaze is fierce, and it sets my pulse racing. When the goon fails to acknowledge his request, he snarls, "This is your last warning. Get your hands off my wife before I slit your throat and watch your body shiver as you take your last breath."

I barely hear the collective gasps of the guests seated at the dining table over the ringing of my pulse in my ears. Rico's eyes display his threat is not idle. He intends on following through with his pledge if the goon doesn't adhere to his warning. His composure is dangerous and menacing, and it sends my heart rate skyrocketing.

His gaze is so toxic, the henchman drops his hands and takes a retreating step, his pupils large, his eyes wide. He looks even more frightened than I do.

After speaking to the two gentlemen accosting me in a deep Russian tone, Rico curls his arm around my sweat-slicked back and guides me out of the room. Friction plagues the air, making it hard for me to breathe while also adding nicks to my already damaged heart.

I suck in deep breaths as I tell myself on repeat that I'm safe and no one can hurt me. I'm stronger than I was ten years ago. I've got this. *I hope.*

By the time we reach the landing of the stairs, I've gathered back a small sense of normality. I'm still quivering like a bag of nerves, and hot, salty tears are threatening to roll down my cheeks, but my survival mode mechanism has kicked in.

Spotting the tears dying to stream down my face, Rico mutters, "Kitten."

Paying no attention to the lurking glares from the two men stationed at the end of the hallway, I pull away from Rico and angrily stride to our room. As my normal composure emerges from the thick cloud of despair, the events leading up to my frightened state steamroll back into me, particularly the part when Rico allowed me to be humiliated in front of dozens of spectators.

"Keep the corridor clear," Rico instructs the men before increasing the length of his steps to catch up with me.

When he reaches me, he places his hand on the crook of my elbow.

I yank away from him.

"Kitten—"

"Don't Kitten me," I interrupt, standing up for myself for the first time ever. "You lost the right to call me a nickname when you let people call me a whore!"

His eyes drift around our surroundings before he murmurs, "I did that for you."

I stare up at him, shocked and disgusted. "Do I look like an idiot?"

My chest is heaving, and wetness is bombarding my eyes, but I hold his gaze, trying to display I'm not as weak as he thinks I am.

Rico scowls but maintains the quiet approach he exhausted during brunch.

It angers me further, drying my tears. "How could letting people call me a whore be for my own benefit?"

When Rico steps toward me, I hold my hand out in front of me, demanding for him to stay away. I need to keep a safe distance between us because even teeming with anger, an excited tingle ran the length of my spine when he grasped my elbow earlier.

Clenching my teeth, I glare into Rico's eyes, not only disgusted he let people belittle me in front of him but also at myself. What type of sick, twisted person gets turned on by the same man stabbing a knife into her chest?

I blamed Vegas for my foolhardiness last week. But it wasn't Vegas.

It was me. I am just as sick and twisted as the man standing before me.

Noticing my irate gaze, Rico growls, "Goddammit, Blaire, don't look at me like that."

"Like what? How am I looking at you? Like you're a monster? Because that's what you are!"

Overlooking the way my callous words caused a brutal pain to hit my chest, I fling open our bedroom door and storm inside. I wait until I hear Rico enter before I spin around to face him. My fists are clenched at my side, my body poised to fight.

He attempts to speak, but I beat him to it. "What type of man are you if you allow your wife to be ridiculed directly in front of you?"

Anger lines his face. "When the time is right, they'll suffer the consequences of their actions. Their stupidity will not go unrebuked. Their punishment alone will ensure no man will dare speak of you with such vulgarity again."

His anger makes his words come out with a heavy Russian accent. They also have an edge of danger to them that sends a shiver through me.

"It isn't about punishment, Rico. It's about decency. They belittled me as if I were nothing but a worthless whore right in front of you. That means you agree with what they were saying. I thought I meant more to you than that?"

"You do!"

My brows knit into a frown. "Well, you have a very funny way of showing it." I cross my arms over my chest, my heart heavy, my pulse escalating. "I stupidly told myself that it wasn't the drugs in my system last week that made me agree to marry you. But I was wrong, so very, *very* wrong."

The expressionless mask Rico wore throughout brunch slips, momentarily revealing a blaze of emotions. Regret, sorrow, guilt all radiate from his beautiful eyes. But the biggest one—the one that causes the most impact to my heart—is the look of hope.

"You were not wrong, Blaire." He steps closer to me, his tone less heated, his eyes less pained. "It was not the drugs influencing your decisions. It was you. It was us. Together."

The brief shake of my head forces a tear to tumble from my eye. I angrily swipe my hand across my cheek, loathing that it makes me look weak. "That man out there..." I point to the door leading to the corridor, "... I would have never agreed to marry that man."

"You didn't marry that man." He pounds his fist on his heaving chest. "You married me, Blaire. You married Enrique."

"It's the same man," I yell, my voice cracking with emotions.

Rico shakes his head. "No! They're not the same. Rico is an act, a role I must play. The man here, the one standing in front of you, this is Enrique, the man you married. Me. You married me." My pulse quickens when he pushes off his feet and spans the distance between us. "You know this, Blaire, you just need to remember."

I shake my head, sending tears rolling down my face. "I don't know you. You're a stranger."

My chin quivers from the torrent of pain surging through his beautiful eyes. "No, Kitten. You know me. The real me."

I try to shake my head to deny his claims, but no matter how hard I fight, my heart refuses to acknowledge the pleas of my logical brain. Even though I realize I've only known him for two short weeks, my heart disagrees.

"You know me," he mutters again, staring me straight in the eyes. "You just need to remember." His hands curve the edge of my jaw, and he stares into my eyes as he painfully whispers, "Remember me."

The pain crippling my heart triples when his lips kiss away my tears. The sorrow in his eyes as he battles to clear away the evidence of my disappointment in him causes more tears to well in mine. These tears are sentimental ones, not anguished.

The reasoning behind my sudden change of heart becomes apparent when Rico drops his lips to the shell of my ear and mutters, "Remember, it's the darkness, Kitten, not me," ever so quietly.

Just hearing the repentance in his voice tells me what he is saying is true. It doesn't ease the sting my ego copped, nor soothe the ache tingling in the middle of my chest, but it silences the screaming protests of my brain telling me to run away from him before I lose all my scruples.

After his thumbs ensure his lips didn't miss a tear, he pulls back and glances into my eyes. I return his benevolent stare in utter shock. I'm not surprised by his sudden shift in demeanor—he can switch from night to day in an instant—I'm surprised at myself. How is it possible I've gone from steaming with anger to riddled with guilt from just one glance into his dark and dangerous yet innocent eyes?

"Trust me, Blaire. I was trying to protect you," he says with his sorrow-filled eyes boring into mine. "If they discovered you were my weakness, they would have used it to their advantage, which would have put you in harm's way. By them believing you were nothing more than a drunken mistake, I could have protected you better." The darkness in his eyes deepens. "But it's too late now. Our cards have been shown."

"They're your family, Rico, so why would they want to hurt either of us?"

His eyes grow wider. "They're not my family. This may be the life I was born into, but that does not make them my family."

He runs the back of his hand down the side of my face, removing a rogue tear that spilled from his statement. My heart is pained, hating that he grew up in such an unloved environment. The children in my class are so young—they are only babies. Rico was younger than them when his mother died, leaving him no other choice than to be raised by a monster in a house of horrors.

"I couldn't promise you a life of sunshine, Blaire, but I promised to always protect you." He quotes part of the vows we recited to each other two weeks ago. "That was what I was trying to do today. I wanted to protect you."

I stare into his forthright eyes, seeking any untruth in them.

I fail to find any.

My lips quiver when I begin to speak, "I understand, but just like you promised to protect me, I promised to *always* be your light in a life full of darkness. I can't do that if you shut me out."

The muscles in my cheeks twitch when he runs his thumbs over them. "I know, Kitten." His tone is less distressed. "I'm not purposely trying to shut you out. There are just... *aspects* of my life I can't disclose to you."

My brow arches. "Can't or don't want to?"

He takes his time configuring a response before he mutters, "Both."

Not letting me reply, he presses his lips to mine and slides his tongue along the ridge of my gaped mouth. I stand muted for several seconds, knowing he is exploiting my sexual attraction to him but unable to fight it.

I'll never be strong enough to deny his advances.

I'm not the only one helpless in this relationship, though. From the memories I've unearthed and the past five days we've spent together, I know Rico is as smitten as I am in this tumultuous relationship we've created. I never used to believe in love at first sight, but truly, when you look deeply, we are surrounded by it every day. You fall instantly in love with a child when he is born. Who's to say the same thing can't happen with a stranger? It may seem instant and extreme, but ultimately, it could be a long-lasting attraction that spans a lifetime. Should I ignore what could be the greatest love of my life just because it's happening in the blink of an eye?

Giving in to my heart's desire, I return Rico's kiss with as much passion as he's bestowing. I rake my fingers through his hair and stroke my tongue into his decadent mouth.

His kiss sparks a carnal desire in me I've never felt before. A desire I'm willing to do anything to unleash—heart, body, and soul.

Within seconds, my hands are all over him—stroking the girth growing in his trousers, running along the bumps of his six-pack, and fiddling with his shirt buttons.

Rico's hands are just as adventurous. One of his hands cups my breast, squeezing it until it's aching with desire while the other one places feathery touches to numerous erogenous zones in my body.

In no time, I'm panting, wet, and more than eager.

When my hands wander to the belt of his trousers, Rico abruptly pulls away. I stare at him, wide-eyed and confused. It's only when I see a black cloud filter over his shimmering eyes do I realize why he has reacted so fiercely.

We're not alone.

Vladimir is standing in the doorway of our room with his evil eyes fixed on me and a mean, unapproachable demeanor. A sick feeling twists into my stomach like something awful is about to happen. It intensifies when Rico snatches my wrists and pulls me behind his big, protective body.

He must also feel the change in the air.

A callous smile carves onto Vladimir's face as the evil gleam in his eyes brightens, thrilled he forced Rico to respond.

While Rico and Vladimir speak to each other in Russian, I send a prayer to God, praying that the consequences of my actions during brunch aren't too severe. Rico only warned me hours ago about the inequality of women in this compound, and I went and stupidly struck him in front of the very man who sanctions the formidable rules.

Any hope I'm holding for a reduced penalty vanishes when Vladimir leaves the room, and Rico drops his dark gaze to me. His eyes are crammed with uncertainty, and his usual confidence is subdued. "I need to go sort some things out."

Unable to speak for fear of sobbing, I shake my head and tighten my grip on his hand. My eyes plead with him, expressing all the things my mouth can't.

"I don't have a choice," he murmurs, his voice growing raspier.

Acting like he can't smell the dread permeating from my pores, he loosens my grip on his hand and enters the walk-in closet.

I hold my breath for several terrifying seconds when he emerges not even two seconds later with a suit bag in one hand and a semi-automatic pistol in the other. Fear consumes me, adding to the swirling of my stomach.

Not trusting my legs to keep me upright, I sit on the edge of the bed and lower my eyes to the floor. I refuse to watch Rico's evolution from day to night, especially since I'm the reason he's transitioning.

I've told myself numerous times that he has a double-sided façade, so why did I foolishly forget about it during the most imperative moment?

Once he's dressed, Rico crouches down in front of me and lifts my downcast head. Panic holds me captive when I notice the darkness of his narrowed gaze. His eyes are as black as his tailored suit and relay his every intention.

Bile swarms the back of my throat.

I did this. I caused him to switch back to his cloak-and-dagger lifestyle.

"Lock the door behind me, Kitten, and don't open it for anyone but Maya," he commands, his low tone ensuring I understand this is not a request.

"Please," I barely whisper, falling onto my knees so I can meet him eye to eye. "This isn't you, Enrique. My heart knows this isn't you."

My pleas fall on deaf ears when his impenetrable mask slips over his face. "I don't have a choice. It's the only way I can keep you safe," he replies, his tone a mix of remorse and anger.

Tears pool in my eyes when he stands from his crouched position and exits the room without a backward glance.

Chapter Twenty-Two

After wrapping a towel around my body, I exit the steam-filled bathroom. My steps are slow, weighed down by the guilt hanging heavily on my shoulders. I've been sick out of my mind with worry all day. I paced the floors for hours, ate more chocolate than I'd consumed my entire childhood, and begged Maya to disclose if she knew of Rico's whereabouts.

Nothing worked to calm the uncertainty twisting my stomach.

Not even the world's hottest shower.

My breath catches halfway between my lungs and throat when I step out of the bathroom. Rico is sitting in the same high-backed chair where he's always waiting for me. A potent rush of yearning slams into me just from the sight of him, and the desire to cry overwhelms me, but I manage to hold it in. *Barely.*

When he lifts his eyes from the tube of moisturizer in his hand to me, I rush to him before he has the chance to dip his chin.

My frantic speed slows when the quickest flash of a smirk has me stumbling over my feet. Rico's smile enlarges over my clumsiness, which only makes my movements falter even more.

As I slowly saunter toward him—hips swinging, heart rate surging

—my eyes run over him, seeking any indication of the repercussions of my foolish actions.

Thankfully, none are found. He appears as he did before he left. The only difference is his suit jacket has been removed and slung over the back of the dressing table chair, his gold watch has been placed on a crystal dish on the antique dresser, and the smell of cheap floral perfume is permeating off him.

Huh?

My speed slows even more, closely followed by the beat of my heart. When I stop in front of him, Rico's hands move to my towel to pry it open, whereas my eyes scan every inch of him. I'm no longer searching for evidence of my stupidity. I'm seeking signs of betrayal.

Panicked is switched to enraged remarkably quick, completed in under a second, when my eyes zoom in on a red smear on the collar of his dress shirt. If I'm not mistaken, it's the vibrant smear of lipstick.

Blood roars to my ears, and my back molars smash together.

"What?" I stammer when Rico's deep voice breaks me out of the jealous trance the red mark on his shirt forced me into.

He lifts his eyes from my tattoo to me. "It's looking much better today. Is it still itchy?"

Catching my lower lip between my teeth, I shake my head. I've lost the ability to talk as our interaction this morning regarding the Popov mistresses runs through my blinded-with-jealousy mind. Rico neither denied nor agreed that he had mistresses. He merely skirted my questions like any criminal mastermind would.

The room spins as the swirling of my stomach amplifies.

Rico once again smiles at my wobbly composure.

It doesn't have the same effect on me as it did earlier.

"We'll give it a few more treatments with the hydrocortisone cream before switching to a standard moisturizer."

After closing my towel, he stands. Upon noticing the switch in my composure, he eyes me curiously, his eyelids growing heavy as he scans my face. I roll my shoulders and force an expressionless look to mask my furious appearance. Until I've had time to assess the situation properly, I can't jump to conclusions, no matter how much my brain cites my reasons to. Accuse now, ask questions later is the tactic it wants to use.

Not buying my attempts to veil my anger, but apparently not wanting to push the issue, Rico presses a kiss to my temple and ambles into the bathroom. "I'll be out in a few."

His usual alluring composure still beams out of him in invisible waves, but his shoulders are slumped a little lower, and his cockiness isn't as paramount.

Even with his demeanor askew, I go looking for trouble, unable to harness the voice in my head telling me it isn't just his composure that's changed.

I smell a rat from a mile away.

After waiting for the shower door to open, I carefully pry open the bathroom door. Wanting to ensure it doesn't announce my arrival, I embrace its closure, meaning it only gives out the slightest click when it shuts. With my heart walloping in my chest, I slant my head to the side and prick my ears. Once I'm happy I haven't attracted Rico's attention, I quickly span the distance between the door and the linen basket sitting at the side of the double vanity.

Just like every other time I've showered in this room, the mirrored wall is thick with steam, but it isn't dense enough to fully conceal the visual of Rico in the shower. He's standing with his feet planted the width of his shoulders and his head hanging low. Water is pelting out of the showerhead, squashing his normally tousled locks into smooth wisps of hair.

With his palms flattened on the white marble tiles, he steps further into the spray, allowing the steaming hot water to run down the length of his spine. His posture looks defeated, but it doesn't stop the vehement jealousy pumping through my body.

When I snatch his dress shirt out of the basket, fiery rage adds to the pink hue blemishing my cheeks. There's no doubt the red mark smeared across the cuff on his collar is lipstick. It's as obvious as the sun hanging in the sky.

Pain twists my heart and swirls my stomach.

Dropping the shirt onto the floor, I stumble out of the bathroom, my steps wobbly and unsure. My brain is telling me not to be so dramatic. It's just a little bit of lipstick on the collar of a stranger's shirt. My heart, though. It's not even functioning right now to articulate a response to my soul-shattering discovery.

Fighting through the tears pricking in my eyes, I throw one of my short-sleeve shirts over my head and yank a pair of cotton panties up my quivering legs. Numerous scenarios explaining how the mark could have gotten on Rico's shirt run through my mind as I'm dressing, but not one acceptable reason is found as to why there would be a pair of female lips sitting intimately close to his neck.

Unless he was...

I slap my hand over my mouth to stop my stomach's vicious heaves. I thought Rico was waiting for me to feel comfortable around him, and that was why he hadn't put any moves on me the past five nights.

Obviously, I was wrong.

When the creak of a door sounds through my ears, I drag my hand over my cheeks, ensuring no sneaky tears have trickled from my eyes before climbing into bed. I hear Rico moving around the space, but since my stomach is so queasy, I refuse to look at him.

I don't think I could stand the sight of him right now.

When he slips into the bed and curls his arms around my waist, I stiffen like a board. Just like he has done every night we've been together, he draws me into his chest, surrounding me with his scent and warmth, a smell still doused in rich floral perfume.

Incapable of battling the jealousy eating away at me, I push away from him and scamper to the furthest edge of the bed. I'm dangling so dangerously on the edge that one more inch would have me sleeping on the floor.

The mattress dips when he moves over to my side of the bed and gathers me back in his arms. "Don't fight me, Kitten. Not tonight."

I kick and wail against him, devastated and inconsolable. My fight is so vicious, one of my wildly flung legs kicks him in the shin while breaking free.

The deep growl torn from his mouth puts a stop to my wailing. I freeze absurdly in equal parts fear and arousal. I've never heard such a provocative noise.

"I need my light. I need to hold you."

His words pain my heart, but it doesn't ease my anger.

Pretending he hasn't noticed my cold demeanor, he caresses me like he does every night. His hand runs down my forearm, and his warm breath tickles my neck. The only difference tonight is I don't melt into his embrace.

I repel from it.

After a few minutes of stiffened silence, Rico releases a deep exhalation of air. It expresses way more than any words ever could.

He's hurting as much as I am.

"It's not what you think." His tone is flat and brimming with uncertainty.

I scowl. "How do you even know what I'm referring to? Unless guilt is on your conscience."

When he growls again, it rumbles straight through my body before clustering in my stupidly excited core. "You left my shirt on the floor, Kitten. I'm well aware of your reason for being angry."

He moves back to his side of the bed before pulling on my shoulders, forcing me to roll over. Even with the room shrouded in darkness, the moonlight shining through the cracks of the curtain is bright enough I can see all the fine details of his face. His eyes are full of torment and shadowed in darkness.

He stares me straight in the eyes before muttering, "It isn't what you're thinking."

Seeing the hurt in his eyes doesn't lessen mine. "Don't insult me, Enrique. How else could lipstick get on the collar of your shirt unless it was put there by female lips?"

My anger accelerates to never-before-reached levels when he throws back his head and laughs. "You think I cheated on you?" he mutters between vigorous bouts of laughter. "I thought you were angry because..." I can't hear anything he's saying over his hearty chuckle.

Gritting my teeth, I throw my clenched fist into his chest. "It's not funny, Rico. Stop laughing."

He laughs even harder. "I can't help it. I love seeing my little kitten with her claws out," he says, still laughing.

The only thing that simmers his body-shuddering laughter is when he spots wetness welling in my eyes. He runs his hand down his face as he struggles to regain his usual composure.

His efforts are fruitless. Nothing can wipe the glint of happiness sparkling in his glistening eyes.

"Let's see who is laughing when I return the favor," I sneer under my breath, my tone callous. "In a house full of men, I'm sure I can find a suitor for the night."

All the laughter on his face vanishes in an instant as does my ability to breathe when his body pins me to the mattress.

His pulse rages through his body as he stares down at me with his nostrils flaring and his eyes blazing with anger. "I don't share, Kitten."

"Well... *neither do I!*"

I move my fists to pound his chest, only to have them snatched and clamped to my side.

Normally, his hold would frighten me, but even dealing with the wrath of jealousy, I know he'd never harm me. My heart? That's an entirely different story.

No longer able to hold in my devastation, I scream my anger into the silent night. My heart is beyond shattered, my body inconsolable.

Upon being alerted of my devastation, the fire raging in Rico's eyes switches from angry to remorseful. He stares at me, seemingly at a loss on how to handle my weeping.

"Kiss me, Blaire," he requests a short time later, his tone less angry, his eyes shimmering with hope.

I inhale a ragged breath, beyond shocked. "What? Are you insane? No!"

When he smiles a seductive smirk that sets my heart racing, I twist my head to the side, needing to look at anything but his sinfully handsome face. I'm not strong enough to deny his advances with his cock pressing against my aching core, let alone when he smiles at me like that.

The nape of my neck prickles with goose bumps when the stubble on his chin scratches my jawline as he mutters again, "Kiss me, Blaire."

When his teeth graze my earlobe, an erotic purr topples from my lips, and my walls crumble. Giving into the fact I'll never be strong enough to reject his attention, I lick my lips, preparing for our kiss. Like he can sense my submissiveness, he slants his head to the side so our lips are better aligned.

With my arms pinned to the side of my head and his body gloriously pressed into mine, I kiss him with everything I have, showing him what he has lost by playing me for a fool. Although his hold is rough, his kiss is nothing but gentle. He kisses me with so much passion that when he pulls away, I can barely remember my own name, let alone what we were fighting about.

A tightness spreads across my chest when he stares down at me with lust-filled eyes. The tightness has nothing to do with him pinning me to the bed—he's holding his weight with his elbows—it's the peace in his dark and stormy eyes that causes my heart to stutter.

After releasing one of my wrists from his hold, he runs the back of his hand down my blemished cheek. "Perfect, Kitten. Why would I settle for anything less?"

Even though I can see the truth in his eyes, I can't leash the pain slicing my heart in two. "Then why is there lipstick on your collar?" My breathlessness is unable to hide the pain laced in my words. I am devastated.

A flash of hesitation sparks through Rico's dark gaze before he murmurs, "It isn't lipstick."

All the anger his heartfelt kiss washed away returns in an instant. "Don't treat me like an idiot, Rico! I know a lipstick stain when I see it," I fire back, my loud voice gaining momentum.

An involuntary moan ripples through my lips when he rocks his hips forward before he reconfirms, "It isn't lipstick."

While snarling at him for using my sexual attraction to him to his advantage, I kick and buck against him, endeavoring to get free. Stupid tears well in my eyes, hating that he can make me feel special and worthless within seconds of each other.

Not the slightest bit intimidated by my vicious fight, Rico leans harder against me, leaving not even an ounce of air between us. My squirming comes to a shrieking halt when I feel the heat of his solid cock halfway up my belly. Even with my heart cut open and bleeding, if he mauled me right now, I wouldn't put up a fight. I'm defenseless to his touch.

The damp mess between my legs eases when Rico mutters, "It's not lipstick, Kitten. It's blood. The red smears on my shirt are bloodstains."

I freeze, certain I haven't heard him right.

It's only when I see the truth in his remorseful eyes do I realize my hearing didn't fail me.

"But you smell like women's perfume."

His pupils grow so large they fill his entire cornea. "Our industry doesn't discriminate between genders."

I glare at him, knowing he's lying.

"Not when handing out punishments."

My stomach churns as my mind tries to contemplate how he could get blood on the collar of his perfume-scented shirt in a humane way.

Unable to find a reasonable explanation, dread overwhelms me.

"Did you..." I can't force the words out of my mouth. Even my brain agrees that the man who comforted me after my nightmare and has awoken in my bed the past five nights couldn't be so callous. He would never harm a woman.

"No," Rico replies sullenly.

I suck in a relieved breath.

It's quickly redrawn when he mutters, "But I didn't stop the man who did."

My heart shatters as horror floods my eyes.

Rico releases a deep breath before he rolls off me. "This is why I didn't want to tell you about my industry. I didn't want you to look at me differently."

"I'm not looking at you any differently." My words are weak and pathetic, matching the sluggish beat of my heart.

My slow heart rate gets a boost when I catch sight of his livid gaze. His narrowed eyes call me out on my deceit without a word needing to spill from his lips.

I swallow the lump in my throat before confessing, "I'm not looking at you differently. I just don't want the darkness to win. This isn't you, Enrique. My heart knows this isn't you."

"You don't understand, Kitten. I was raised in this lifestyle. I don't know any better."

I roll onto my side and glance into his eyes. "Don't know any better or don't *want* to know any better? As those are two completely separate entities. You might have been raised by a monster, but you don't have to live like one."

An indecisive storm builds in his eyes. "In this industry, your value is measured by your callousness, not your morality. The more ruthless you are, the more respect you gain."

"Fear is not respect, Rico. They're not even close to being the same thing."

He scrubs his hand over the stubble on his chin. "I know. But I have a reputation to live up to. I'm Vladimir's son. His firstborn son. That title comes with expectations. Expectations I was filling. I was a terrible man, Kitten. A parodist of my father." He locks his beautiful eyes with me. "Until I met you. Then I realized what I was craving wasn't power or respect. It was you. I wanted you."

Heart hammering, I cup his jaw and peer into his eyes. "You can have me." I scoot closer to him so our hot pants of breath intermingle. "You just need to fight through the darkness."

A flare of emotion brightens his gaze for the tiniest second before it once again becomes swamped by blackness. "I can't."

"Why?" I shout through a sob. "Why can't you?"

"You don't understand how things in this industry work, Blaire, so you're not qualified to pass judgment. This is the only way I can protect you. They know you're my weakness, and they're using it against me." Anxiety strangles my heart when he mutters, "They'll kill you the instant I step out of line."

He scoots up the bed and leans his back on the headboard before running his hand down the side of his face. Just like earlier, his posture is slumped, and he looks genuinely defeated.

From his stance alone, I know my concerns about him fading completely into blackness will never reach fruition.

A soulless man doesn't feel regret.

They don't feel anything.

For the first time in over a week, I act on the instincts of both my heart and mind. After pulling Enrique's hand away from his tired face, I crawl into his lap and stare into his remorseful eyes.

The murky cloud in his gaze clears away when I say, "Let me be your light." I rock my hips forward, dragging my soaked sex along the length of his stiffened shaft. "I may not understand this industry, but that doesn't mean I can't guide you through the darkness."

Chapter Twenty-Three

Heavy sentiment fills the air when I grasp the hem of my shirt and pull it over my head. The mood is so thick it's almost palpable. As my breasts fall gently to my chest, Rico devours me with passionate dark eyes. I arch toward him, my aching breasts thrusting out in offering.

A shiver runs the length of my spine when the back of Rico's hand runs over my inflamed cheeks before tracing the curve of my heaving chest. "Are you sure this is what you want? I've been waiting for you to be sure."

I sigh in relief before a broad grin stretches across my face. "And here I was thinking you didn't want me."

"I've never wanted anything more in my life." He locks his entrancing eyes with mine. "You're my light in a world full of blackness."

A faint purr topples from my O-formed mouth when he runs his finger across the pebbled bud of my nipple, sending a zing of pleasure straight to my pussy. "Are you sure?" he asks again.

When I see the darkness in his eyes fading, I nod. I've never been more sure of anything in my life.

He grows heavy beneath me, getting thicker and wider as my belly flutters with butterflies.

"Please, Enrique," I shamelessly beg when his hands remain fisted at the side of his hips. "I need you. Please."

"That sounds more like someone who is sure than a simple nod," he replies to my shameful plea.

When he shifts his hips upward, I quiver above him, wild and free of any doubt. "I'm sure. Very, very sure," I purr.

My words turn into a gargle when his tongue circles my nipple before he sucks it into his warm, inviting mouth. I draw him in closer, my aching core tightening with every swirl of his tongue. As he licks my nipples, my hands are all over him, unable to resist feeling the softness of his skin pulled taut over his brawny muscles. The roughness of the stubble on his chin adds to the excitement clustering in my pussy when he devours my breast with long licks, playful bites, and teasing gropes. As my pussy grows wetter, I rock against him, needing something to quench the insane throb between my legs.

Every thrust of my hips has my mind spiraling, incapable of thinking of anything but the hard ridge in his cotton boxers. I need to taste him. Desperately. My nipple pulls out of his mouth with a pop when I draw my chest away from him. I don't need to speak to announce what I want to happen next. The hankering in my eyes relays the whole story.

With a seductive smirk etched on his face, Rico mutters, "Be my guest, Kitten."

A groan tears from his throat when I run my hand along the extended length protruding from his boxer shorts. As I work him through his undergarments, he places his hands on the side of his hips before lifting his glorious backside off the bed so I can slide the cotton material down his thighs.

When his cock pops free, I freeze for a moment, giving my eyes time to absorb the enormity of his glorious package. His cock is jutted and hard as stone, the tip glistening with evidence of his arousal. Desperate to taste him, I circle my hand around the base of his fat cock before adding another, unsure if one hand will be adequate to handle so much man.

Rico chuckles at my unsureness. Normally, any hint of amusement in a bedroom would have me cowering, but his laughter spurs on my pursuit. It isn't malicious or vindictive. It's heartwarming and kind.

Any humor left lingering on his mouth is swiped straight off his face when I run my tongue over the crest of his cock, eagerly gathering up his drop of pre-cum.

While I stroke his heated flesh with my hand, my mouth and tongue work his swollen knob. I take him deep in my mouth, all the way to the back of my throat as guttural hisses escape his lips.

"Don't choke yourself, Kitten. Only take as much as you can," Rico mutters through a groan.

Fighting through my gag reflex, I take him even deeper, goaded by the raspy moans rumbling up his chest and the lust brightening his eyes. His thumbs stroke the heavy grooves in my cheeks from my greedy sucks as I devour him. It aids in soothing the ache of my muscles as I give it my all.

I work the smooth velvet crest of his cock in and out of my swollen lips over the next several long minutes, loving the weight of his dick in my mouth.

His hands move to my hair when I run my tongue down the vein nourishing his glorious penis. A ghost of a smile creeps onto my lips, relishing in discovering one of his weak spots.

It's a rare treat to find vulnerability in a man as controlled as Rico.

"The desires of my cock aren't my weakness, Kitten. You are," Rico mutters, once again reading my inner dialogue.

Still pumping his silky-smooth shaft with my hand, I lift my hanker-filled eyes to his. "Show me."

Not needing any more encouragement, he bands his arms around me and pulls me toward him. With one hand on the nape of my neck and the other on the curve of my back, he kisses with so much passion my libido soars to never-before-reached levels. It is primal and urgent and shreds any chance of walking away from our relationship with my heart intact.

I melt into his embrace, fully surrendering to the man who can wipe away every insecurity I've ever had with a simple kiss.

By the time his lips move to my neck, I'm totally lost in the desire burning through me. "Enrique..."

"Shh, Kitten."

He adjusts our position so my back is resting against the softness of the mattress while he is kneeling. The damp mess between my legs grows when he snaps my panties off my body before pinning my wrists above my head. When he trails his beard across my silky skin, marking every inch of me with his spicy scent, I squirm beneath him, both ticklish and turned on.

His natural dominance oozes out of him in bucketloads, but I'm too caught up in the thrill of chasing a climax to care, and in all honesty, his strength and assuredness calm me. He will never intentionally hurt me, so I feel safe with him even while being held aggressively.

When Rico's scratchy beard reaches my aching-with-need core, he stops and stares unashamedly at my bare mound. "Pretty and pink and dripping with wetness. My little kitten is ravishing."

He presses an intimate kiss on my clit, forcing me to call out and arch my back. My legs instinctively pull together, unable to stay still when a surge of desire puddles between them.

I watch him, beyond enchanted, when his dark eyes bore into mine as he slowly inches his finger into my quivering sex.

"So tight."

I clench around him, begging for more.

"And greedy."

I throw my head back and snap my eyes closed when his beard scrapes the most sensitive area of my body. Inaudible words tumble from my parched throat when his tongue rolls over my pussy before it spears inside me. It feels insanely good, and in a short period of time, I'm lost in the throes of ecstasy.

My orgasm hits me by surprise, steamrolling me into an incoherent, blubbering mess. I writhe against Rico's tongue and mouth, blindsided by the strength of my mind-hazing climax.

With his smile felt by my thighs clamped around his head, his fingers stroke the sensitive spot inside me, drawing out the length of my orgasm while his tongue flicks the throbbing bud of my clit. His speed is relentless, unwilling to give me a moment of reprieve until I come for the second time.

A familiar tightening rapidly builds deep in my core, but I fight against it, not believing it's possible to have two earth-shattering climaxes so close together.

"Stop fighting me, Kitten," Rico mutters against my drenched lips.

The deep timbre of his voice pushes me over the edge for the second time. I close my eyes and yield to the brilliance of ecstasy, shouting Rico's name in a long, guttural groan as I take everything he's willing to give me.

My fall is blessed and long.

I've only just finished riding the crest of orgasmic bliss when a packet being torn open sounds through my ears. My excitement builds again when I watch Rico roll a condom down his thick cock. Even stuck in a trance only two mind-blowing orgasms can incite, nothing can dampen my readiness to be claimed by him again.

Rico runs his hand down my flushed cheeks. "Fuck... I love seeing you flushed... you're so beautiful. So, so beautiful."

I have no chance of holding in my smile, so I set it free.

Mimicking my giddy expression, Rico's hands slide over the wetness slicking my skin when he curls his arms around my back and draws me to his overheated body. Warmth blooms across my chest when he rests his sweat-drenched forehead against mine and stares into my eyes. The heat of his thickened rod sits hard and ready between us, but it isn't the only reason lust sparks through every inch of me. It's the look of content in his beautiful dark eyes.

"Are you sure, Blaire?" he mutters again, his warm breath fluttering my hungry lips.

My heart swells as I cup the edge of his jaw. "I'm sure, Enrique.

I've never been more sure of anything in my life," I quote, speaking directly from my heart.

The rest of the sentence I quoted to him the night we married is sitting on the edge of my tongue, but my mouth refuses to relinquish the words.

One step at a time, Blaire, my brain mutters to my heart.

Rico's thumbs clear away the sweat careening down my cheeks before he adjusts our position so the tip of his engorged penis rests against the entrance of my soaked sex.

With his eyes arrested on mine, he sheaths me one glorious inch at a time.

"Ah, Jesus, Kitten, so tight."

I swivel my hips, my body naturally trying to ease the uncomfortable intrusion. Pain rockets through my core from taking a man as well-endowed as Rico all the way to the root, but it is also pleasurable.

Rico keeps his movements still, giving my body the chance to adjust to his girth as his lips kiss away my pain. I taste myself on his lips as he strokes his tongue in my mouth in slow, dedicated licks, and my pussy grows wetter with every caress of his tongue.

Once the sting of invasion has eased, I squeeze the walls of my vagina around him, advising I'm ready for him to move.

"I'll go slow for as long as I can—"

"Don't hold back, Enrique. Take what you need. Give me your all."

"I won't hurt you, Kitten. I can't."

I stare straight into his eyes so he can't miss their honesty when I say, "I know. You'll never hurt me, so there's no reason to hold back."

The words I couldn't force out earlier nearly topple from my mouth when the most heartfelt smile I've ever seen graces Rico's sinfully handsome face. I bite the inside of my cheek, swallowing my absurd declaration of love for a man I'm only starting to know when he slowly rocks back out of me.

Any ludicrous thoughts in my mind vanish when he thrusts back in.

His movements start at a slow and controlled pace, but with every stroke, he slowly increases his speed. I sling my arms around his sweat-slicked neck and hold on for the ride of my life when his pounds become unforgiving. His cock pummels into my soaked pussy, thrusting another climax to the forefront of my mind. When he spreads his knees wider, opening my hips more, I purr an erotic moan. He takes me even deeper, pumping every glorious inch of his thickened shaft into me.

The veins in his neck throb nearly as furiously as the one feeding his cock as he pounds into me at a frenzied yet precise pace. My coil tightens as my sprint to climax gains momentum. The buildup is frantic—almost blinding.

"Give it to me, Kitten," Rico growls, his voice vibrating all the way through my drenched sex. "You're fighting a battle you'll never win."

Sweat rolls down his cheeks as he strengthens his pumps, ensuring every stroke hits the tender spot inside me. He fucks me like an out-of-control animal, unwilling to give me an inch of leniency until I give him my all—until I give him everything.

I become lost in the blessedness of an orgasm for the third time when Rico runs his thumb over the erogenous zone of my collarbone. I choke his name out of my mouth with a string of incoherent garbage as a surge of passion sparks through my exhausted body.

I'm barely lucid from the devastating effects of three life-altering orgasms, but there's one statement during my blinded-by-lust rant I hear loud and clear—my declaration of love.

Rico's dark eyes blaze into mine as the thickness of his cock increases. Not removing his beautiful eyes from mine, he slows the brutal pounds of his cock, slowly bringing me down from the haze of climax.

When every pleasurable shudder shimmering through my body has been exhausted, Rico locks his heavy-hooded gaze with me. All the indecisiveness in his eyes has vanished, replaced with nothing but optimism.

"Say it again." His deep voice is husky with his arousal strangling it.

My nose tingles when I mutter, "I love you, Enrique," in the faintest whisper.

A throaty purr rumbles through my lips when Rico's cock throbs inside me, my declaration of love alone enough to make him come.

Chapter Twenty-Four

My lazy steps to the bathroom stop when a knock rattles through the wooden door of my bedroom. I freeze, mindful of Rico's regular warnings about not opening my door for anyone but Maya.

Considering Maya only left here ten minutes ago, I'm doubtful it's her.

My assumptions are left for dust when Maya's voice projects through the thick door. My steps to let her in are slow as my body is still reveling in the orgasms Rico awarded me with last night.

Shockingly, I've been on a high the past five days. I thought once the aftershocks of our intimate gathering wore off, I would have backpedaled on my declaration of love, using my blurry state as a plausible defense, but not once has uncertainty entered my mind for the past five days.

I feel the most content I've ever felt in the midst of a loved-up haze.

Rico and I have spent the last five nights in bed kissing and fondling each other for hours before our lightning-paced union joins in the most earth-shattering way. I never thought sexual contact would be a way I'd feel comfortable expressing myself, but everything about me is different when I'm with Rico. He brings out parts of me I didn't even know existed.

He truly does make me wild with desire.

There isn't a shadow of doubt in my mind that the man I wake up with every morning is the same man I married nearly three weeks ago. Rico is attentive and sweet—a man I wouldn't hesitate to marry on sight. And thankfully, as our oddly compelling union grows strong, the more the blackness in Rico's eyes recedes.

I never thought I'd be strong enough to guide him through the darkness plaguing his life like I promised in our wedding vows. Now, I'm thinking differently. If things keep following this path, I have no doubt I'll always be the light in his life.

Ignoring the sentimental butterflies taking flight in my stomach, I pull open the heavily weighted door and greet Maya with a smile. Although Maya barely speaks a word of English, we've become close since I arrived here over ten days ago. She's the only female confidante I have in this house, so I relish the hours we spend together.

The happiness making my stomach a jittery mess eases when I notice a cloud of concern filtering over her usually expressive eyes. "Maya, are you okay?"

I run my hand along her forearm. My concern grows when I feel the clamminess of her skin. Maya is a small-framed lady, but she has the heart of a dragon. Normally, nothing frightens her.

Keeping quiet, she hands me a slip of paper I didn't realize she was holding until now. After bouncing my eyes between her evocative gaze, I drop them to the folded-up piece of paper. The tremble of my hand rattles the cream-colored document when I unfold it. Since there's only a one-line sentence on the paper, it doesn't take me long to recite the message.

Kitten,

Meet me in the servants' quarters.

Rico.

My heart rate soars. Rico mentioned earlier today that he had a surprise for me, but no matter how much I pleaded with him for a hint, he remained tight-lipped, only disclosing that I'd find out more when he returned later this evening.

This is obviously part of his surprise.

I return my eyes to Maya. "Where are the servants' quarters located?"

My head slings to the side when she stretches her arm and points to a door marked with *'sluzhashchiy'* halfway down the hall.

"Okay. Thank you."

Maya bows her head then spins on her heels and walks down the hall.

Her head flings back to me when I ask, "Did Rico say what time?"

Her pupils widen before she shakes her head. I wait until she reaches the crest of the stairs before shutting the door. Although I'm concerned about Maya's odd reaction, I can't hold in my excitement about Rico's note.

I rush to the mirror to check my hair and makeup. My cheeks are rosy from the stifling Las Vegas heat that graced my face when I sat in the window seat for hours reading this afternoon, and my eyes are full and bright.

Deciding to wear my aroused look with pride, I place Rico's note on the dressing table before exiting the room. My knees clash together with every step I take down the long hall. I've only walked this corridor once since arriving here five days ago when I attended my disastrous brunch with Rico.

It's amazing to think how much has changed between us in so little time. But I guess time has no place when I'm with Rico. It just stands still.

My heart rate speeds the further I move away from my room. Although this side of the Popov compound is elaborately decorated, nothing can take away the ghastliness plaguing the air. Just like a cemetery, no amount of potted color can hide the ugliness of death.

I stop frozen halfway down the hall and gasp in a quick breath when I spot the same two men from last week guarding the stairwell. Since they are engaged in a deep conversation, they fail to notice my quiet approach.

Not wanting to place myself on their radar, I carefully open the servants' quarters door and slip inside the narrow stairwell. The muggy Las Vegas air adds to the giddiness swishing in my stomach as I wind down a set of rickety spiral stairs. My eyes shoot in all directions, taking in what would have been a servants' quarters back in the day. White and yellow wallpaper covers the antique corniced walls, and gorgeous cedar hardwood lines the floors.

I'm so immersed in staring at an old set of service bells hanging in the middle of the room I don't notice another presence sneaking up on me until it's too late.

Pain sears across my cheek when a man backhands me with so much force, my head flings to the side. The taste of copper engulfs my taste buds as I fall to the floor with a sickening thud, my wrist jarring painfully when it hits the hardwood floor.

Blood trickles from the side of my mouth as I lift my frightened eyes to my attacker. A large brute of a man who would easily be the height of Rico and two times wider sneers an abhorrent grin as he takes a step toward me.

I shake my head, then scramble backward, ignoring the screaming protests of my limp wrist. Pleas for help sit on the tip of my tongue, but my frightened composure has once again frozen me into stiffness.

My temples scream when the stranger fists my hair and yanks me off the floor, his roughness causing the roots of my hair to pull away from my scalp. After gritting my teeth to ignore the tortuous pain rocketing through my skull, my hands dart up to claw him. I dig my nails into the skin on his hands and scratch him hard enough I draw blood.

My battle angers him more. He pushes me backward until my back is splayed against the wallpaper I was admiring minutes ago. He glares at me with a set of malevolent, morally bankrupt eyes as he lowers one of his hands to clutch my throat. My mind spirals, unable to separate the past from the present.

When images of my attack in the alleyway flash before my eyes, I shift my gaze sideways, expecting to see my savior running toward me.

The frantic beat of my heart kicks into overdrive when I discover no one is within eyesight.

I drift my frightened gaze back to the man pinning me to the wall. He keeps one of his hands wrapped around my throat while the other painfully squeezes my breast through my dress. My lungs heave as violently as my stomach, sickened at the glint of lust forming in his eyes.

Not willing to lay down without a fight, I kick my legs out wildly, fighting with all my might. When one of my kicks hits him with enough force to loosen his grip around my neck, I suck in lung-filling gulps of air.

Using his stumbling composure to my advantage, I crash my knee into his groin, then push him hard in the chest. His hand darts down to protect his crotch from another vicious attack as he takes a fumbling step backward. "You fucking bitch," he sneers in a thick Russian accent.

I slip under his arm and race to the rickety stairwell on my right. Tears flood my cheeks as I fight to keep my hidden memories from ten years ago buried in the back of my mind.

My fast speed to the stairs comes to a halt when my ankle is snagged, and I'm yanked backward. I land on my knees, and a harsh puff of air parts my lips. My mind is frantic, drifting between the present and future, but I kick my way out of my attacker's grasp, then scamper across the wooden floor.

I put up a similar fight the last time I was attacked, but this time is different.

This time, I'm not at the mercy of a dark-eyed stranger.

I throw out my leg, kicking my assailant in his despicable face. I may not weigh half what he weighs, but I'm not a fourteen-year-old girl unable to defend myself anymore. I'm a strong woman who refuses to lie down willingly.

Any life left in my assailant's hollow eyes vanishes the instant the heel of my sandal smashes into his crooked nose. Red hot anger lines his face when a trickle of blood dribbles out of his nose.

"Now you will pay," he snarls viciously.

The back of my head hits the bottom step of the stairwell hard, temporarily dazing me when my legs are pulled out from underneath me. My vision blurs, melting the images that frequently haunt my nights with my newest nightmare.

My confused state only lasts as long as it takes for my brain to register my attacker's filthy hands roaming over my body.

"No!" I scream, grateful my scared state has finally lifted when his hand slides under the hem of my skirt and inches toward my panty-covered core.

My head rockets to the side when the faintest, "Blaire," comes sounding from the top of the stairs.

Before I can respond, just like in my memories, my attacker is brutally hit from the side.

I crawl backward, pushing down the hem of my shirt as Rico and my attacker slam into the wooden floor with bone-crunching force. The hard impact does nothing to lessen Rico's fury. He pummels his fists into my attacker's face repeatedly until his knuckles are covered in the same vibrant red coloring lining his face.

"Stop, Rico," I mumble when the man he's beating stops fighting against him.

I scramble onto my knees and crawl across the floor when his manic onslaught continues on the lifeless man. Just like in the bedroom, he's a machine, frighteningly unstoppable, designed to issue punishment.

Unable to inflict any more damage to the man's bloody face, Rico's lowers his fists to his body, where he strikes him with blow after devastating blow.

I squeal and stumble backward when my hand touching his shoulder causes him to yank away from me violently.

Like he can recognize my touch, he stops swinging his fists and cranks his neck to the side. The fury in his eyes vanishes the instant he sees me cowering on the floor beside him. His eyes roam around the room. He looks frightened and confused. He runs his hand down his face, removing a stream of sweat pouring down his cheek.

When he returns his eyes to me, the swirling of my stomach gains intensity. The same set of eyes from my nightmares are staring back at me.

I stagger backward, my whole body shaking. "You're... you're..."

Panicked shock overwhelms me when Rico dismounts the man he's beaten into unconsciousness and slowly approaches me. Blood drips from his hands more quickly than remorse fills his eyes.

I stare at him, more confused than ever.

"Shh, Kitten, shh," he croons, his voice cracking with emotion.

Speaking through the sob in the back of my throat, I stutter, "Y-you're the man... t-t-the man from the alley."

Rico's eyes blaze into me, full of emotion and turmoil as he mutters, "Yes, Kitten. That was me."

Then my entire world crumbles.

Chapter 25

———

Enrique

Blaire stares at me in shock, her pupils wide, her beautiful light green eyes gloss over. Her whole body is shaking, mimicking mine to a T. I'm generally fearless, but seeing the way Blaire is looking at me now, frightened and timid, I'm truly scared. I've once again become the four-year-old boy lying next to my deceased mother for three days waiting for my 'uncle' to discover her death.

When I reach out to touch her, my heart stops, praying she doesn't pull away from me.

My prayers remain unanswered when she shakes her head, begging for me not to touch her.

I can't, though. I'll never stop. I love her. I have from the moment I laid my eyes on her.

I've lived my life at a speed double the rate of everyone surrounding me. After my mother's death, I lost contact with my sister and was thrown into a makeshift family of servants and Popov whores. Everyone in the Popov compound hated me. At first, I thought it was because I'd shown weakness by crying when they laid my mother's body to rest with only three people by her graveside— me, the priest, and my father, who stood three steps back from the unmarked grave her coffin was being lowered in. But as the years moved on, I realized my assumptions were wrong.

I wasn't hated.

I was feared.

I, Enrique Julies Popov, am the firstborn descendant of the world's most ruthless empire.

Although my father's mistresses have birthed many children over the years, I'm Vladimir's firstborn son, meaning I'm the sole heir to the Popov empire. My father's values are traditional, based on principles that stretch back as far as the seventeen hundreds when the Popov empire was created by a short, stout man named Anatoly Popov. He started the Popov empire as a cloak-and-dagger business— killing for hire. As his reputation grew, so did his ruthlessness and his crew.

Over the centuries, the Popovs' beliefs have rarely altered—men are powerful, women are weak.

Most kids my age grew up in households that encouraged their children to have their own beliefs. My upbringing was far from that. Discipline became a game to me. How many lashings did it take until the sting of the whip was no longer felt? How many droplets of my blood would spill onto the floor over the thirty minutes of my punishment? And how many ways could I exact my revenge on the man yielding the whip marking my skin?

To others, it may seem cruel.

To me, it was my life.

I knew nothing different.

By the time I was fourteen, I'd already lived most of my life. In this industry, you barely make it past your teens. I'd done countless hideous things, stuff I'll never mention again until I meet with my creator. I was ruthless, believing nothing could stop me until I saw her, my little kitten...

We were driving through a small town a few hours out of Florida. I couldn't say where as I'd spent the last seven weeks on the road, and my bearings were slightly adrift. My attention diverted from the scenery streaming past the heavily-tinted window when I noticed a beautiful teen walking on the cracked sidewalk, laughing and talking with her redheaded friend.

The late afternoon sun bounced off her hair, shrouding her in a golden halo. She had the kind of beauty that captured you and didn't let go. The face of an angel, lightly tanned skin with the smallest gathering of freckles on the bridge of her nose, and a body more mature than her years.

Even the way she skipped down the path had me in a trance. I watched her for only seconds, but it felt like the moon had circled the globe numerous times.

My eyes only left the entrancing blonde when a deep Russian voice at my side snapped me out of my imaginative state. "You like, Rico? You want to get out your tackle and have some fun with the little girlies?"

I lifted my narrowed eyes to Sergei, my cousin and goon. The mocking grin on his face irritated me. I stared him in the eyes and sniffed, purposely goading him. Sergei was double my age, but we were of similar size and build. For what he lacked in stature, he made up for in arrogance. He too was raised in the Popov compound, but since he failed to have the legacy of the Popov last name, he was nothing more than a paid goon.

Sergei slapped the chest of Timur, sitting on his left. "Veroyatno, ne znayet, kak yego ispol'zovat'!" he mocked.

"You won't be able to use your cock again when I cut it off," I snarled back, lowering my stern gaze to the crotch of his pants.

Sergei swallowed away a lump, then stared at me in surprise, shocked I understood what he said. To start with, I don't know if it was stubbornness or reverence to my English-speaking mother, but I rarely spoke a word of Russian. As the years went on, I discovered there's an immense amount of power being seated in a room with a group of men who don't realize you're bilingual.

As the seconds ticked by on the clock, the look in Sergei's eyes changed, going from scared to a gleam I'd only seen in his eyes a rare handful of times.

"Stop," he demanded the driver of the Escalade we were traveling

in. He banged his hand on the privacy partition to add strength to his request.

I turned my eyes to my brother, Nikolai. His icy-blue eyes drifted between Sergei and me for several seconds before he shrugged his shoulders. In the reflection of the mirrored privacy partition, I saw the dirty white van that had been following us most of the day pull in behind our stationary vehicle. The men inside I hadn't met. All I knew was that they were from another Russian entity that was run by a counterpart of the Popov empire. After we aided them in a business transaction taking place in a small town called Hopeton, they were to return to their station, and we were to travel back to Vegas.

The beat of my heart surged when Sergei pulled a two-way radio out of his pocket and said three short words. "Secure the assets."

I sat motionless with my heart thumping against my ribcage when two large Russian men curled out of the van and approached the blonde I had been admiring.

My stomach lurched in silence when one of the men wrapped his arm around the blonde's friend and placed a white cloth over her mouth. Even though the fabric muffled her words, one distinct word was clear—Blaire.

I moved to the edge of my seat when the second man with a snake tattoo wrapped around his wrist and halfway up his forearm approached the blonde. My hand moved to the door handle, my mind running purely on instinct. The only thing that stopped me was when Nikolai placed his hand on my shoulder and squeezed.

Drifting my eyes away from an immoral act I'd seen played out time and time again in my fourteen years, I peered into my brother's eyes. He shook his head, advising me not to respond. He knew Sergei was testing me, ensuring my loyalty remained to the Popov empire.

I continued watching the scene with my gut twisted in a knot. I didn't understand why my reaction was so fierce. I had witnessed that and far worse things numerous times in my short life, but there was something different about me that day.

Something inside me snapped.

When Blaire laid lifeless on the concrete sidewalk, her body bloody and bruised, I whispered into the air, "Don't give up, Blaire."

Like she could hear my pleas, she rolled onto her side and leaped to her feet. She had more strength than any man I'd ever punished.

My back molars smashed together when her dash down the alleyway was stopped by the Russian who had thrown her unconscious friend in the back of the van minutes earlier. Blood roared in my ears when he pinned Blaire to a steel fence by her throat.

Before I could contemplate the severity of my punishment, I threw open the Escalade door and charged at the man double my weight. My speed was unchecked as I rammed into the side of him with all my might. He let out a loud "oomph" when we smashed into the concrete with a sickening thud. I felt no pain. All I felt was fury.

I threw my fists into his face, dazing him long enough that I could turn my eyes back to Blaire. She stood motionless against a steel-chained fence, her knees bloody, her eyes wide.

"Run! Blaire! Run!" I screamed at her.

She stared into my eyes for a fleeting second before she ran down the alleyway as fast as her trembling legs could take her. When her original attacker hot-footed after her, I scrambled off the man lying half unconscious on the cracked asphalt and threw my arms around his ankles.

As he plummeted to the ground, I saw the quickest flash of blonde running into a busy street.

Relief engulfed me.

That was the last time I saw Blaire until she fell on my lap weeks ago...

Ignoring the shake that has encroached my hands, I undo the buttons of my dress shirt. The creak of the rickety stairwell at my side gains my attention. Maya is standing at the foot of the stairs, her eyes rocketing between a shocked Blaire and me.

"*Prosti*," she whispers, issuing her apologies in Russian.

She moves to a stack of shelves in the corner of the room to gather a bunch of towels as she mumbles under her breath. Although her rant is a mixture of Russian and French, it follows a similar path.

That she knew something wasn't right, and she should have trusted her intuition.

After removing my dress shirt covered with specks of blood, I yank my white undershirt over my head. Blaire stares up at me, clearly in shock as I place the shirt over her head before pulling her blood-streaked hair out of the collar. Tears roll down her cheeks unchecked as her entire body quakes.

Her tears I can handle, but the vacant look in her eyes—I don't even know where to begin.

After wiping off the smears of blood covering my hands with a towel Maya gave me, I crouch closer to Blaire. With my heart walloping against my ribs, I once again raise my hand to her face. She blinks several times in a row but, thankfully, doesn't repel from my touch.

Glancing into her eyes so she knows I mean her no harm, I brush away a bunch of unruly hairs clinging to her sweat-drenched neck. Her skin prickles with goose bumps when my soft touch runs over the sensitive skin on her collarbone.

My eyes shift sideways when the man I beat to an inch of his life makes a gagging noise as he chokes on his own blood. He should be grateful he's still breathing. If Blaire's welfare weren't my utmost priority, he'd have a bullet wound between his eyes.

Deciding Blaire doesn't need anything added to her shocked state, I return my gaze to her. She's still staring at me, wide-eyed and quiet. Her pupils are massive, filling her entire cornea, making her eyes the darkest I've ever seen.

I peer into her eyes with the same amount of sincerity she usually awards me with. "Let me take care of you, Blaire. Let me wash away your pain."

There's no greater gift than the one I'm given when she nods, accepting my assistance.

Careful not to touch the scrape marks marring her beautiful skin, I band my arms around her body and pull her to my bare chest. She whimpers into my neck as she clutches onto me for dear life. Her nails digging into the scarred skin of my back is a cruel reminder of the world I forced her into when I failed to give her up a second time.

I knew who Blaire was from the moment she tumbled into my lap hours after I'd returned from Russia. Blaire's beautiful golden hair, angelic face, and seductive body are features any man would have a hard time forgetting. But it was her light green eyes peering up at me that unveiled her. It was the same set of eyes that blessed my dreams every night for the past ten years, and the same eyes that weathered me through my darkest storms.

When she walked away from me that night in Vegas, slightly stumbling, I tried to let her go, but just like my desire to protect her ten years earlier, something greater had me pushing away from the poker table and walking toward her.

One sideways glance was all it took. She recognized me too. Although, three weeks ago, she handled the discovery of my real identity in a much calmer fashion. It was only when I discovered she'd been drugged did the reasoning behind her serene approach make sense.

We sat in a VIP booth in Omnia Nightclub for nearly three hours talking. I told her everything, disclosing things I've never shared with anyone. The murder of my mother. How I killed a man to protect my sister. Every bad thing I'd done in my life was laid out for her to see. In all honesty, half of my confession was to ease the burden I'd been carrying on my shoulders for the past twenty-four years, but the other half, the bigger half, was because I was trying to scare her. I wanted to show her the man she was staring at in awe was nothing but a monster. But the more I shared, the greater her wonderment grew.

She wasn't the only one entranced.

I was addicted to her.

She was my light in a world full of blackness.

She is my light in a world full of blackness.

As I walk through the Popov compound with a quivering Blaire in my arms, the usually robust atmosphere is smothered with despair. The elderly women who transitioned from whores to maids stare at me with concern while a snick of fear sets in the eyes of the men wary of what my reaction will be.

When I enter the foyer, my stern gaze connects with Erik, who is exiting the den. His pupils widen as his eyes drift between Blaire and me.

"The servants' quarters," I inform his questioning eyes. Erik nods when I continue, "Make sure he pays his penance, or I'll return and do it myself."

Chapter 26

Blaire

My eyelids slowly flutter open when the smell of fresh-cut flowers lingers through my nostrils. The silkiness of high thread count sheets caresses the weary muscles of my naked body when I pull my arms out of the comforter and have a leisured stretch.

When my tongue delves out to replenish my parched lips, a pinch of pain throbs in the corner of my mouth. My brows stitch in confusion when the tangy flavor of copper engulfs my taste buds. I jackknife into a half-seated position as memories of my attack two nights ago trickle back into my mind. The events after the attack are nearly as hazy as my recollection of my Vegas trip three weeks ago, but there are portions I remember as clear as day—the way Rico carried me through the residence to an Escalade parked at the front of the stairs of the Popov residence, how he held my hair out of my face when my haunted memories became too much for me to bear, and how he wiped away every tear that fell from my eyes with nothing but remorse reflecting from his beautifully tormented gaze.

He guided me through my darkest days—when the blackness tried to swallow my life whole.

Now I need to do the same thing for him.

I've awoken in an empty room, but I don't need to feel Rico's presence to know he is close by.

I can sense him.

Gathering the bedsheets around my body, I walk through the large residence. As my feet pad down the long corridor with floor-to-ceiling windows, my eyes absorb the spectacular views I was too shocked to appreciate when we first arrived at this penthouse two nights ago. The dazzling view of the Las Vegas strip stretches as far as the eye can see. It looks so beautiful from this vantage point, concealing the cesspool of crime and inhumanity that occurs there every minute of every day.

Although I'm still shocked from the aftereffects of my attack and discovering that Rico once again saved my life, I feel the calmest I've ever felt. My heart has always known he was a good man, and now that my mind wholeheartedly agrees with it, the tiresome mind-versus-heart battle I've been enduring the past three weeks has vanished, leaving me free to pursue a relationship with Rico without fear of repercussion.

It's an invigorating feeling.

I walk past a ten-seater wooden dining table located next to a small but functional kitchen. The furnishings show this apartment is owned by a man with substantial wealth, but it still has a homey feel to it with a small range of potted greens and hand-selected artwork accenting the opulent decor.

With the rawness of my throat, I'm tempted to stop by the kitchen for a refreshing glass of water, but I continue walking past the double-door refrigerator without a break in my stride. My desire to find Rico is more fervent than the requests of my thirst.

My brisk pace only slows when I reach a high-glossed door on my left. Even though the door is closed, my intuition is telling me to stop. Trusting my gut, I place my hand on the door handle and push down. My perception of Rico's presence is proven dead on point when the deep timbre of his voice sounds through my ears the instant the door cracks open.

Mimicking the time I interrupted him in the private jet, he's sitting behind a wooden desk with a cell phone attached to his ear. His tone is clipped and authoritative until he notices me leaning in the doorjamb.

"Kitten."

The urge to cry overwhelms me from the pain displayed in his one simple word. He shuts down his phone, shoves his chair away from his desk, then stands. I push off the doorjamb and race toward him. He catches me in his arms as the first lot of wetness splashes my cheeks.

"Shh, Kitten. You're okay. No one will ever hurt you," he promises, reciting the words he said to me on repeat the last forty-eight hours.

He tightens his grip around my shoulders, adding more of his spicy scent to the bedsheets curled around my shaking body. I push into him harder, needing more direct contact, wanting the warmth of his body to take away the shakes impeding mine.

My thigh muscles bunch when he tucks his hands under the grooves of my knees, and he hoists me off the floor. He moves to a double-seated sofa in the corner of the room and sits down. The cotton material of his shirt catches my tears his thumbs miss. He holds me close to his chest and confirms his promise over and over again.

Once my tears have settled to a slight trickle, I lift my head off his chest and peer into his remorseful eyes. "What happened to Katie?" My voice is croaky but full of hope. I've barely been lucid the past two days as Rico guided me through my shock, so I've only just realized he could have answers to questions I've been asking for the last ten years.

Panic squeezes my heart when Rico shakes his head. "I don't know, Kitten. She was still in the van when it shot out of the alleyway shortly after you." He cups my jaw and stares into my eyes. "Just like you, I've been looking for her every day. I'll find her for you, Blaire. I'll never give up."

Call it blind faith, hysteria, or insta-love, but I know what he's saying is true. My heart knows it, and so does my mind. Just like me, Rico won't give up until he discovers what happened to Katie.

We sit huddled together in his office for what feels like hours, but it's more like minutes as I play the events of my life over the past ten years. Having Rico's arms around me makes me feel safe as if no one will ever hurt me again, not even him. It's a feeling I've craved for years but never thought I'd achieve.

He makes me feel invincible.

I draw myself closer to his chest and slip my hands under his shirt. I flatten against him, trying to mold us into one person. I need more, so much more of him, it makes it hard for me to breathe.

"What do you need, Kitten? Tell me what you want."

"You, Enrique. I need you," I reply in an instant.

He hesitates for a fleeting second with his confused eyes bouncing between mine, assessing my face for any signs of distress. I made a similar demand the past two nights, but with my mind still trapped in shock, he refused to oblige me.

That made me fall in love with him even more.

Upon failing to find a morsel of anguish on my face, he jumps to my command. I listen to the mad beat of his heart as his long strides follow the path I took thirty minutes ago. With every step he takes, the turmoil in his eyes changes, switching from tormented to yearning, not just to protect me but to satisfy me as well. A tingle of excitement rushes down my spine, stirring the heated ache between my legs.

When he places me on the bed, I lace my fingers through his hair and pull him down with me. He growls, concerned his weight falling on me may have added to the small collection of bruises mottled across my skin.

"You didn't hurt me. You never would."

The groan of concern rumbling up his chest is swallowed by my mouth when I seal my lips over his. I kiss him tenderly, expressing my gratitude for everything he did and still does for me. He returns my kiss with the same amount of rawness, accepting my thanks while also issuing his own. My chest puffs high, creating room for my swollen heart.

As we kiss, lick, and fondle each other, my fingers make quick work of Rico's clothes. I gasp in delight when I feel his warm skin on mine. The muscles in his back twitch when I run my nails down the length of his spine, tracing the swirly pattern of his tattoo. Then a squeal topples from my mouth when he flips us over, so I'm straddled on top of him—his seemingly favorite position.

Small white lights flicker in front of my eyes when the heat of his swollen flesh nestles between my soaked sex. I grind against him three times before leaning over and resealing our lips.

The temperature in the room increases with every rock of my hips and stroke of my tongue. He suckles my bottom lip into his mouth before he playfully bites it.

I yelp and pull away from him, laughing. "No biting. What are you, an animal?"

He cocks his head to the side and arches a brow. "A tiger playing with his little kitten." His words come out so rough, they sound like a growl, and they send an electric current straight to my core.

The heated ache between my legs grows so exponentially, I'm tempted to scissor them together to ease the pain. I'm hot, wet, and needy.

A flare of excitement crosses Rico's heavy-hooded gaze as he watches me squirming above him, but he does nothing to ease the discomfort his seven little words created.

"Please..." I aim for my pleading word to come out strong. My effort is borderline.

A purr escapes my parted lips when Rico thrusts his hips upward, dipping the first inch of his heated cock into my aching core. I arch my back and snap my eyes shut, giving my body time to adjust to the spark scorching through my veins only his touch can produce.

When he notches in another inch, my pussy contracts around him, urging him deeper.

With his hands on my hips, carefully guiding me, Rico takes his time, delivering every inch of his cock in painstakingly slow installments.

By the time he fully sheaths me, my first orgasm is already lingering deep in my womb. Seemingly sensing my climax is close, Rico lowers his thumb to my clit, then flexes his cock.

With his thumb placing the perfect pressure on the swollen bud of my clit and the devoted look in his eyes, my climax hits fruition.

I hold the gaze of the man who has saved me time and time again as the blessedness of an orgasm revitalizes my drained body. My pussy clamps around him as a cold sweat coats my skin.

My orgasm isn't the strongest I've had, but mentally, it's the most powerful.

"This. I don't want to see any other look on your face but this." He runs his spare hand across my pink-hued cheeks.

Once my pleasurable quivers ease, he moves his hand away from my clit and places it back onto my hip. He adjusts my position so I am more open to him before slowly withdrawing his cock. The wetness of my climax soothes the sting from taking a man as wide-girthed as him.

I cry out in pleasure when he thrusts back in one fluid stroke. He goes so deep, he bottoms out at my cervix.

After flattening my palms on his sweat-slicked pecs, I meet his thrusts pump for pump. My heart rate surges when my spread hand cannot hide my name swirled across his chest. Just like every time my eyes scan his name on my hip, a smile stretches across my face.

If any name belongs marked on my body, it's his—my savior.

When he ups the tempo of his thrusts, I gyrate my hips and contract the walls of my vagina.

"Again," Rico demands, his words breathless.

He screws me in a rhythm fast enough that my chase to climax matures with every thrust he makes but slow enough there's no chance he will hurt me.

That will never happen—physically or mentally.

Every grind of his cock increases the pressure building low in my pussy. As my coil tightens, so does my grip on his pec muscles. When he adds a flick to his pumps, I claw his chest, accidentally drawing blood.

Regret clutches my throat when a droplet of vibrant red blood follows the rivulets of sweat sliding down his torso. I snatch my hands away, mortified that I've maimed him. Rico seizes my wrist and places them back onto his chest before he continues pummeling inside me, seemingly unaware of the injury I inflicted on him.

Tears prick my eyes as the heaviness on my chest outweighs the climax brewing in my belly.

"No!" Rico shouts, startling me when a sly tear escapes my eye and trickles down my flushed cheek.

He glares into my eyes unyieldingly, his gaze so scorching, it dries my tears before they have the chance to fall.

Remaining hilted in me, he rolls us over so he is now on top of me. The weight of his body adds to the heaviness on my chest but in a soothing way. He stares down at me with sweat-damp hair falling around his face like a dark curtain before he slowly thrusts inside me. His pace is more controlled as is the storm clouding his beautiful eyes.

He gathers my hands with his and runs them over the little indents my nails made on his skin.

"These scars I'll wear with pride," he mutters, his truthful eyes adding to the strength of his statement.

He places my hand on his left shoulder, and while maintaining eye contact, he runs my hand down the side of his back, following the pattern of his tattoo.

My lips quiver when my fingertips run over a jagged surface hidden beneath his dark swirls of ink.

"Just like these," Rico continues, peering into my moisture-filled eyes. "Every scar holds a story, Kitten. As long as that story includes you, I'll wear them with pride."

Chapter 27

Enrique

Silk running across my tattoo, tracing the scars marking half of my back wake me. Usually, I repel from anyone touching the marks that converted me from a boy to a man, but this person isn't anyone. It's Blaire—my little kitten.

"I did this, didn't I?" Her voice is so soft it matches the beauty of her angelic face.

I remain quiet as her fingertips follow the grooves hidden by a tattoo designed specifically to conceal the mottled skin on the left half of my back. It isn't that I don't want to answer her question, but the story behind my scars has never been shared because it's simply that —a story. The scars define me as a man. They made me a man. A better man. Others see them as weakness, but I don't. They are my ally, a reminder of when an angel fell from the sky and brightened my miserably bleak life.

Ever since that day in the alleyway ten years ago, I changed. I stopped being the ruthless man who could claim a life without a skerrick of remorse passing through me. I evaluated scenarios and formulated my own response, ensuring I was only instilling punishment to men who deserved to be punished. Cowards like the men who attacked Blaire and her friend.

I'm not saying what I've done over the past ten years has been lawful, it's far from it. I was raised in a life cloaked in darkness, yet my actions have been tamer than my counterparts.

Well, until it comes to protecting Blaire. I'll stop at nothing to ensure she is safe. Even throwing myself into the line of fire, I'll protect her until my very last breath.

"Did you get those scars from protecting me?"

"No, Kitten." My voice is low as I struggle to mask my deceit. "They were given as a reminder of my journey. A life I chose to live."

When she sniffles, I roll onto my hip, letting the bedsheet fall away from my body in the process. If I can use the unmarked side of my body to distract her, I will. I hate seeing her cry. I saw enough tears spill from her eyes last week to last me a lifetime. I don't want to see any more.

She peers into my eyes, her beautiful face looking tired and worn before her gaze suddenly drops. My cock goes from flaccid to painfully hard in an instant when a hue of pink adorns her cheeks. Even tired, nothing can take away from her natural beauty—plump pink lips, an angelic face, and eyes that imprinted my soul with just one glance.

Like I have every night we've shared a bed, I pull her into my arms and run my hand down her forearm. As much as my cock would love to spend a few more hours wrapped in her warmth, she needs rest. Although the small injuries she sustained in her attack have healed well the past week, she still looks exhausted.

Her tiredness is understandable. Struggling out of the depths of hell is a brutal fight for any person to battle. It was one of the cruelest battles I've ever endured.

Over time, her breathing levels out and the tightness in her shoulders relaxes. I wait a few more minutes to ensure she's sound asleep before pulling back. I like to watch her when she's sleeping. She truly looks like an angel trapped in the depths of hell. A place she doesn't belong.

I should have heeded the warnings screaming in my brain three weeks ago when we stood at the foot of the chapel we married in. I should have walked away from her without a backward glance. But I was stuck, stupidly believing that fate had brought Blaire to me, and she was a gift for changing my life full-circle. I was reckless, and now Blaire is suffering the consequences of my stupidity.

Although I love Blaire, I'd give anything to go back to that day and save her from this lifestyle. An angel doesn't belong living in the blackness of hell, no matter how much I want to keep her.

When my endeavor to sleep becomes unachievable, I slip out of bed, careful not to disturb Blaire. Sleep has never been an ally of mine. I'm lucky to get three to four hours a night. Usually, I'd stay awake for as long as possible before crashing days at a time, but I can't do that with Blaire here. I need to be on guard and alert. Luckily, when she is in my arms, my quest for sleep is more successful. That might have more to do with sexual exertion than anything.

After pulling a pair of trousers up my legs and throwing my shirt over my head, I exit my bedroom, carefully closing the door behind me.

* * *

I've been working on some developments in my industry for nearly two hours when my awareness of Blaire's closeness activates. I lift my eyes from my youngest sister's kindergarten enrollment forms to the door of my office. Blaire has her shoulder propped against the doorway. Her face still looks restless, but unlike hours ago, the torment in her eyes has vanished. She's wearing a knee-length floral skirt and a three-quarter sleeve shirt I laid out for her earlier. She looks innocent and fuckable at the same time. Two complete contradictions.

When I push away my chair from my desk, a smile slowly creeps across her flushed face before she pads toward me. Completely unaware of her appeal, every step she takes naturally seduces me. I'm sure that over the years, other men have overlooked Blaire's natural beauty as they preferred women who dressed more scantily.

They were foolish men.

I relish Blaire's choice of clothing. It means only those privileged get the opportunity to see the skin her modest clothing hides. I just wish it wasn't fear that altered her clothing selection.

Blaire wasn't attacked in the alleyway because of her short, pleated skirt and midriff top she was wearing. She was attacked because she caught the eye of a man who shouldn't have been looking, a man who should have known better. Her clothing wouldn't have changed anything that happened that day. I know it, but Blaire hasn't worked that part out yet.

When Blaire reaches the end of my desk, I catch her by the waist and pull her to sit on my lap. Her faint giggle is replaced with a throaty purr when she discovers how her closeness soothed my hesitation and traded it for desire. The scruff on my chin scratches the silky-smooth skin on her neck when I nuzzle in close to savor her refreshing scent. Her smell reminds me of daisies on a dewy winter morning. Don't ask me how I know what that smells like, as I wouldn't be able to answer you, but that's what Blaire smells like, I'm certain of it.

"Why aren't you sleeping?"

She lifts her eyes from the paperwork on my desk and locks them with me. "I couldn't sleep without you."

My chest puffs high, beyond smug. Like my entire life, my relationship with Blaire has matured at breakneck speed. Although the expeditiousness of our relationship is daunting, I wouldn't change a single thing that has happened in the past five days. It has been perfect. *Almost too perfect.*

"I had a few things I had to take care of, but it can wait. You need your sleep." I brush a few stray hairs away from the pillow crinkle mark on the side of her face.

She screws up her nose. "I'm not tired." She drops her eyes to my desk. "What are you working on?" Her eyes suddenly rocket to the side as she gasps in a quick breath. "Is that..."

She doesn't finish her sentence. She just slides off my lap and pads over to a free-floating bookshelf on our left. My chest grows tight when she gathers the mandatory Las Vegas quickie wedding photo off the shelf and stares down at it.

I inwardly smile when she says, "Darn it. I was kind of hoping we had an Elvis impersonator as our celebrant." From the lowness of her tone, I can't tell if she's being serious or witty.

I stand from my chair and amble to stand next to her. As I peer over her shoulder at the photo, reality dawns on me. I should have known she was drugged that night. Her outward appearance is an exact replica as she stands before me now, but the sparkle of life in her eyes that held me captive from the moment she glanced at me ten years ago is missing. Her eyes are still bright and full of life, but they just aren't as vibrant as they are now. With how carefree her eyes look now, it has me wondering if I ask her to marry me again right now, would she?

"Hmm?" I ask when Blaire's soft voice breaks me out of my daydream.

"Who's this?" She hands me a faded Polaroid picture in a wrought iron frame.

I accept the photo from her grasp and roam my eyes over the lady I only remember in hazy memories. "That's my mom."

My mother's death is the main reason I returned from Russia three weeks ago. For years, I was told my mom died of a drug overdose. The older I got, the more rumors circulated throughout the compound that her death wasn't an accident, that a man took her life. A man well-known to the Popov entity. My father is an abhorrent man—a reincarnation of the devil himself—but he loved my mother. She was his *ahren*, his gift from heaven.

When the rumors about the uncertainty of my mother's death reached the pillar of the Popov entity—my father—he awarded me free rein. I could use any means necessary to find out if the rumors were true. I used them, and I discovered the truth. My mother was murdered right under my father's nose. It was the ultimate betrayal.

People assumed that when I killed the man who strangled my mother to death, the story would end there. It didn't. Before his death, Col Petretti disclosed that members within the Popov compound knew of my mother's murder and hid it from my father. Spineless snitches who needed to be punished before they met with their creator. That's why I came home. To serve justice for the people who aided in my mother's death.

Well, I thought that was the case until Blaire fell into my lap. Just like ten years ago, our chance meeting ended with me saving her life for the second time, before I ultimately claimed it.

"She's very beautiful." Blaire runs her index finger over the frame to clear away the dust that settled on the glass during the six months I was in Russia.

I purchased this apartment months before I was sent to Russia by an associate of my sister's fiancé. Contractors related to the Popov entity have been remodeling the main living areas over the past six months. I was planning on surprising Blaire with news that the renovations had been finished the night she was attacked. I had planned on us moving in this weekend. I knew Blaire living in the Popov compound was dangerous, but I assumed my reputation would have been sufficient enough to protect her. Obviously, I was wrong. *Terribly wrong.*

"She looks a lot like your sister," Blaire murmurs, dragging me away from my thoughts. She nudges her head to a photo I placed on the mantel the day I drove her to the airport.

I'd never expected my investigations into my mother's death to lead me to my sister. With the number of mistresses my father has, I have many siblings, more than I could count, but Isabelle is my only true sibling. We share the same blood. Just like my memories of my mother, my memories of Isabelle as a child are best described as cryptic. But the instant I saw her, I knew she was my sister. She's identical to our mother in every way, except for her eyes.

I hated using Isabelle to seek the answers to our mother's death, but she was the only leverage I had. Although frightened, she was never in any danger when I kidnapped her to lure Col Petretti out of hiding, despite what Isaac claims.

Blaire places Isabelle's photo back onto the bookshelf before shifting on her feet to face me. "The picture of the little girl on your desk. Is she your sister... or your..."

A smirk etches on my face from the uncertainty in her voice.

She's even more beautiful when she's ruffled by jealousy.

"She isn't my daughter. That's my sister, Callie."

Relief fills Blaire's impressive eyes. "I wasn't sure. Her eyes are identical to yours."

A smirk etches onto the corners of my mouth. "All the Popov children have Vladimir's eyes. Scorched from the ashes of hell we were born in."

She screws up her nose. "Not all of you. Nikolai doesn't have dark eyes."

Jealousy slashes me open just from her mentioning Nikolai's name. Nikolai and I were close when we were younger, but after the incident in the alleyway, things changed between us. He became a shadow of our father—a ruthless and coldhearted man—where I strived to become my father's opposite.

"Who does Nikolai get his blue eyes from?" The confusion on her face grows. "I'm assuming the lady who called me a whore at brunch is Nikolai's mother?"

Knuckles popping is the only outward appearance of my anger at Blaire being taunted. It still kills me that I didn't stand up for her that day, but I was truly trying to protect her. Lessons were taught that day—no man will ever speak of Blaire with such disrespect again— not if they have a fondness for breathing.

"Yes, Oskana is Nikolai's mother," I confirm with a precise nod.

"And Vladimir is his father?"

I nod again.

"Are you sure?" Her voice is full of uncertainty.

She shifts her eyes to the photos on the mantel piece. "You said it yourself. All Vladimir's children have the same eyes." Her gaze drifts back to me, her demeanor more askew. "Nikolai doesn't. His eyes are icy blue."

I peer into Blaire's eyes and shrug, unsure what she is referring to.

"Oskana's eyes are green. Vladimir's are brown. The chances of them having a blue-eyed child are low, Enrique."

My heart rate kicks into overdrive as a million rumors I've heard over the years run through my head. "How low?"

Blaire holds my gaze, ensuring I can see the truth in her eyes. "Not impossible, but very unlikely. Both parents would need to hold a recessive blue-eyed gene."

Our conversation ends when a doorbell ringing shrills into my office. My head rockets to the side as my urge to protect Blaire kicks into overdrive. Only those in my inner circle know this apartment exists, so I find it surprising that someone is knocking on my door a little after six in the morning.

Blaire remains quiet as I gather my pistol from the hidden drawer in my desk. Although there are numerous ways you can kill a man without a weapon, a bullet is a lot less messy.

"Stay here," I instruct her before moving into the corridor.

Frozen in fear, she nods. My steps down the corridor are soundless. Not even Wolverine would hear me coming.

I release the breath I'm holding in when the faint voice of Maya squeaks through the door. Housing my gun into the back of my trousers, I unlatch the numerous deadlocks on my door and swing it open. Blaire must have recognized Maya's voice as well, as she arrives at my side not even two seconds later.

Blaire releases a deep sigh as she rushes to Maya's side. "Oh Maya, what happened?"

Fury blackens my blood when I discover what caused Blaire's skittish response. A nasty bruise circles one of Maya's brown eyes, her lip is busted open, and her wrists have welts only rope burns create.

As Blaire continues to fuss over Maya, I step into the hallway of my apartment building and run my eyes down the length of the hall. The exact set of eyes I'm expecting to see greet me from the end of the corridor. Erik.

Erik is my one and only confidant in the Popov compound. I trust him with my life. He shares the same sentiment. I duck my head back into my apartment to make sure Blaire and Maya are occupied before closing the front door behind me.

Erik meets me halfway down the hall.

"What was Maya punished for?" I question, recognizing the injuries Maya has suffered. I've seen them numerous times the past twenty-four years on Vladimir's mistresses. I'm just shocked to see them on Maya, considering she is his daughter.

Erik hands me a folded-up piece of paper. "Confronting the man responsible for this."

I dart my eyes between Erik's before lowering them to the piece of paper. My veins turn black when my eyes roam over the document.

"They orchestrated Blaire's attack?" I ask, already knowing his reply.

He nods.

I didn't even consider why Blaire was in the servants' quarters the night she was attacked. I just assumed her curiosity got the best of her. I never fathomed she was set up.

"Who did this?" My words come out strained, strangled through the fury pumping my veins.

Erik hesitates before muttering, "Nikolai."

Chapter 28

Blaire

As I pass Maya a handful of ice wrapped in a tea towel, a door slamming bellows through my ears. Rico moves down the corridor so quickly he's nothing but a blur of black. After placing Maya's half-drunk glass of water and a bottle of pain medication on the coffee table, I tell her I'll be back in a minute, then take off after Rico.

I find him five minutes later in the walk-in-closet of the spare bedroom. I can barely breathe when my eyes lock in on a black mat he has rolled out on the floor. Knives, tweezers, clamps, and other stainless-steel instruments I can't stomach to mention are stuffed into the pockets lining the leather material. It looks like an ideal setup for the creator of Frankenstein.

Sensing my presence, Rico lifts his head from the ghastly set of instruments in front of him to me. Tears pool in my eyes when I see the blackness swamping him. I hold my hands out in front of my body and take a step closer to him, hesitant to approach him while he's stuck in the depths of despair.

Rico angrily shakes his head, urging me to stay away.

"Don't do whatever you're thinking of doing, Enrique. It isn't worth it. Maya wouldn't want you—"

"He set you up, Blaire," he interrupts, the pain in his eyes growing. "He sent you down to the dungeon so that monster could kill you."

I gasp in shock. "Who?" I ask through the bile lodged in the back of my throat, my stomach as squishy as my mind.

My stomach lurches when he replies, "Nikolai. He sent you the note to meet me in the servants' quarters. He orchestrated your death."

After rolling the mat up in front of him, he stands from his crouched position. I move closer to him, ignoring the threatening glare he is issuing me, cautioning me to stay away.

"He may have organized it, but it didn't happen, Enrique. You saved me."

"What happens when he tries again, and I don't hear your cries? What happens if I'm too late?" he roars, startling me.

I shake my head, sending strands of hair into my eyes. "That will never happen. You will *always* be there to save me, Enrique. You will *never* let anyone hurt me."

Fear greater than anything I've ever felt blazes through my veins when I see the pain in his eyes. My fear isn't for Nikolai or myself. It's for Enrique. He has walked so far into the blackness I don't know if I can drag him back out.

Ignoring the shake of my hands, I curve them around his jaw, which ticks so furiously, it pounds against my palm. "Let me be your light," I plea, staring into his dark eyes.

He stares at me impassively, his whole demeanor off kilter.

"I need you, Enrique." I tilt my lips closer to his. "I love you."

My heart shatters when he mutters against my lips, "Then you understand why I need to do this."

After pressing a brief peck to the side of my mouth, he stalks out of the room without a backward glance.

Chapter 29

Blaire

I sense Rico's presence before I feel him.

The stranglehold that's been clutching my heart the last two days loosens when he slides into our bed and gathers me into his arms. I've been sick with worry the last forty-eight hours, but when I saw the grim look on Erik's face when he collected Maya this morning, my anxiety grew. I was barely functioning as it was, but the concern lining Erik's face activated a self-preservation mode I haven't used in years.

I've spent the entire day operating on autopilot. I haven't cried. I haven't spoken a word. I just sent numerous prayers to God for Rico to be returned home safe and uninjured.

Thankfully, my prayers appear to have been answered.

Blood rushes to my heart when Rico mutters in my ear, "Be my light, Kitten. I need my light." His deep voice is low and brimmed with uncertainty.

As I roll onto my opposite hip, the air is forcefully removed from my lungs when my eyes are met with his beautifully tormented gaze. His pupils are wide, his eyes the blackest I've ever seen them.

They look utterly soulless.

My shaky hands cup the edge of his jaw as I move my lips closer to his. My mouth swallows the deep sigh expelled from his lips when I seal it over his. He kisses me like he never has before—a heart-tethering kiss that soothes the nick in my bleeding heart. He savors every inch of my mouth in long, controlled strokes like I am truly his savior.

Within minutes, I go from the depths of despair to wildly turned on. Nothing is on my mind but enjoying every precious moment with the man in front of me—the stranger I married.

Only Rico's kisses can do that.

Only his touch can make me fully forget.

When his strong hands move up my back, a gathering of goose bumps follows their trail. As his tongue slides around my mouth, he hauls me so close to him that not even air exists between us. I gasp, incredibly aroused, when the heat of his thick cock presses against my aching core. When his spicy scent lingers in my nostrils, the movements of my hands become needy. They are all over him, touching, stroking, and groping.

I can't get enough.

I'll never get enough.

When Rico slides his hand down to my ass and grips it tightly, I purr, loving the bite of his fingers on my skin.

He stills my movements when I buck against him, soundlessly urging for him to do it again. "No, Kitten." His words are clipped and dangerous, adding to the excitement raging in the pit of my stomach.

"Please," I beg unashamedly. "You'll never hurt me, but I want to feel you, Enrique. I need to feel you. On me. In me. Everywhere."

Two lithe movements have my position switched from lying on my side to balancing on my knees. My bare ass is thrust high in the air, and the coolness of the air conditioning blows on the heated ache between my legs.

"You want to feel me?"

I nod a little overeagerly.

"Everywhere?"

"Yes," I beg with excitement evident in my voice. "Everywhere."

He slaps my ass—hard. I cry out as my knees slide across the crisp sheets, trying to lessen the furious throb between my legs.

Rico stops my efforts by cupping his hand over my pussy. "Ah, my naughty kitten. Saturated." His tone is lower than I've ever heard. "You like to be punished? You enjoy the roughness?"

I don't answer his questions. I've lost the ability to do anything but surrender to the man stroking the bud of my throbbing clit.

Blood rushes to the surface of my skin as the heat of desire blazes through my veins when Rico inflicts another perfect smack to my tingly backside.

"Not yet, Kitten. When you come, it will be on my cock," he demands, sensing the upwelling of desire scorching my blood.

The arrogance in his low tone bolsters my eagerness. Although he's always been a dominant lover, this morning, he has a blood-pumping edge of unbridled assertiveness attached to his natural dominance.

He adjusts the tilt of my hips, erotically exposing me even more. My race to climax speeds up when he runs his thumb up and down my pussy, coating it in my juices. His meekest touch has my orgasm precariously balancing on the edge of a very steep cliff.

When he removes his thumb from my slicked sex, he slides it across the puckered hole of my rear. I stiffen and crank my neck back to peer at him.

"You said everywhere, Kitten." He stares at me with a set of eyes I don't recognize as he adds pressure to his thumb circling my back entrance. My body puts up a protest to the intrusion. Although I've experienced a vast range of sexual positions with Rico the past five days, I've never participated in *this* type of situation.

Sensing my body's reluctance, Rico moves his spare hand away from my hip and strokes my clit with perfectly precise flicks. His thumbs roll in sync, stimulating both entrances in slow tantalizing swirls.

In no time at all, I once again become lost in the chase of a climax.

My eyes snap shut, and a jolt of pleasure and pain rockets through my body when Rico's thumb slowly slips into an area no man has been before. I press my damp face into the pillow to muffle the erotic purrs rumbling up my chest. While perched on the crest of orgasmic bliss, I wait for Rico's next move.

He does nothing.

He remains completely still.

I want to scream in frustration. Every muscle in my body is pulled taut, waiting for release. My skin is slicked with sweat, and his thumb is in an area I never considered an erogenous zone, but surprisingly is, yet he remains completely motionless.

Unable to stand the heavy tension weighing down my pussy, I push back and grind against Rico. My legs quiver when my movements cause his thumb to slip deeper inside me. I moan, then rock my hips again. My pussy grows slicker, loving the feeling of him in my back entrance while also knowing this is something I'll only ever experience with him.

"Good girl, Kitten. Now that you've stopped fighting, you'll enjoy it more."

I jerk violently when he slowly withdraws his thumb before slipping back inside. I've always thought this region was a no-go zone, but it's driving me wild. So much so, I rock back and forth, meeting the thrusts of his thumb stroke for stroke. My toes curl as the furious fire in my stomach becomes uncontrollable.

"Wait," Rico commands when the muscles in my rear clamp around his thumb.

"Please. Oh, God. Please," I sob, my voice exposing how close my orgasm is.

While keeping his thumb inside me, Rico mounts me from behind. I scream into my pillow when he slams his cock into my drenched pussy in one quick thrust. My nails dig into the sheets as I try to crawl across the sweat-damp mattress, needing to get away from the man pounding into me with brutal force.

It's too much.

I'm too full.

I can't handle both holes being assaulted at once.

"You wanted to feel me, Kitten. Feel me!" Rico grunts, his strokes quickening. "Take all of me. Everything I'm giving. Then you'll never forget what it feels like to be claimed by me."

I scream without shame as the most ferocious orgasm I've ever endured crashes into me. Rico's name is torn from my throat as my legs buckle from its brutal force. My earth-shattering climax steals all the strength from my muscles, causing me to sink deeper into the mattress with every vicious quiver my body does.

Rico uses his knees to spread my legs wider, so he can take me even deeper as I slump against the mattress, utterly exhausted. I don't notice the removal of his thumb from my rear until the sting of his fingers hits both sides of my waist.

He grips onto me before continuing with his furious pace.

"Can you feel me, Kitten?" He growls, his deep, vibrating tone adding to the tingling of my pussy.

A bead of sweat runs down from my drenched hair when I nod. "Yes. Everywhere. I can feel you everywhere."

He increases his thrusts, claiming every inch of me. "Don't forget what this feels like. Don't ever forget."

Distress grips me from the pain laced in his words.

"Never," I mumble through a sob. "I'll never forget."

I don't know why, but it feels like he's saying goodbye.

When I lift my head from the pillow and look back at him, pain shreds through my heart.

I'm too late.

He's already gone.

He has walked too far into the blackness, and I can't lure him back out.

Chapter Thirty

While admiring how the fake diamonds sparkle in the bright lights of the vanity mirror, I run my hand down my silver drop earring while praying the fake smile I'll be wearing tonight will have the same effect. The Rico who screwed me into oblivion until the wee hours of this morning is the same Rico taking me out to dinner tonight.

I don't know why I agreed to go. I've spent most of my day in a trance, trying to work out where I'd gone wrong. Nothing Rico did to me this morning hurt me, but from the way he's been cold and distant, anyone would swear he stabbed a knife into my heart.

Rico walks out of a closet on my right, stealing my focus. "Are you ready?"

After ensuring the clasps on my earrings are fastened properly, I nod. A faint smile unwillingly sneaks onto my mouth when my eyes absorb the fitted dress Rico laid out for me in the vanity mirror. It's a beautiful mint green color, matching my eyes perfectly. The knee-length skirt ensures my modesty is kept, but the V-drop neckline adds a dash of sexiness I'm comfortable with.

When I spin around to face Rico, the heaviness sitting on my chest doubles. He's wearing his usual attire of a black suit and light dress shirt, but he has paired it up with a tie that has green stripes in it—stripes that match my dress to perfection.

To outsiders, we look like an unbreakable couple. It's only the crippling pain in my heart stopping me from believing the same thing.

Rico holds my hand as we walk out of his apartment and down the corridor, but he's still distant. Even his hand is ice cold. Lust fires the elevator with electricity as we travel down multiple floors, but it isn't enough to ease the ache in my heart. When the elevator car stops at the lobby, Rico places his hand on the curve of my back and guides me through the bustling space. People stop to stare, delighted at seeing such a beautiful man up close.

Ignoring the fascinated stares of numerous women, Rico walks us to an Escalade parked at the curb.

"Thank you," I mutter when he opens the door and gestures with his head for me to enter before him.

My breathing turns labored when my eyes lock in on a man seated in the seat across from me. Erik—Rico's lawyer.

"Why is Erik here?" I mumble to Rico, my voice unable to hide the sob sitting in the back of my throat.

As the events of the last time the three of us rode together play through my mind, sick gloom spreads across my stomach.

Rico remains quiet, acting as if he didn't hear a word I spoke.

Thankfully, the drive to the restaurant is short, but it's long enough for Rico's eyes to be completely swamped by blackness. His stern mask has slipped into place, and his composure is brutish and reserved.

Bulbs flash in my eyes when I exit the Escalade and walk into the restaurant on Rico's arm. My knees clash together with every step I take as he guides me to the back of the bustling space. It is full to the brim with the same people who attended brunch last week. A lump forms in my throat when he strides down a very long table and pulls out the second chair at the end for me.

I cough, clearing the nervousness from my throat before whisper-ing, "What's going on, Rico? I thought we were dining alone."

Before he can reply, the chatter in the room dulls to a faint hum. I don't need to look up to know Vladimir has entered. The ice-cold fear sliding through my veins is the only indication I need to know the devil is walking the gallows.

My brows knit in confusion when Rico stands from his chair and greets his father with a kiss on each of his cheeks. Then dread clutches my throat when Vladimir peers down at me and says, "Hello, Blaire."

Who knew two words could sound so threatening?

When I turn my gaze away, refusing to peer into the eyes of a monster, Rico retakes his seat, then leans over to intertwine our fingers together. With a wave of his hand, Vladimir gestures for the remaining attendees left standing to take their seats.

My chest rises and falls when I notice the two seats opposite Rico and me remain vacant, the seats that belong to Nikolai and his mother, Oskana.

Oh my Lord. What did he do?

My regular breathing pattern returns when a commotion at the front of the restaurant secures my devotion. Nikolai and Oskana are pushing their way through a gauntlet of paparazzi guarding the restaurant doors.

After slinging off her lightweight coat, Oskana saunters into the room with a vibrant smile stretched across her face. She places a kiss on the edge of Vladimir's mouth before taking the seat across from me.

My stomach winds up to my throat when I notice a range of fresh bruises on Nikolai's face. But even battered and bruised, his cockiness is still paramount.

After giving me a sneaky wink, he takes his seat next to his mother.

"*Shyulakas* don't belong here," Oskana snarls at me, glaring.

"Neither do old *sukis*," I fire back.

Nikolai coughs, only just holding in his laughter. Rico's response isn't as reserved. His beautiful laugh fills the silence when he throws his head back and laughs.

Oskana's furious gaze scorches into me before she shifts her eyes to Vladimir, soundlessly demanding justice for me calling her an old bitch, but Vladimir's expression remains unchanged. He looks as hideous as he always does.

Rico leans into my side. "Maya?" he mutters so only I will hear.

I nod. It took me hours to explain the term I wanted to say to Maya, but we eventually got there.

A lazy smirk stretches across Rico's mouth as his glistening eyes stare into mine. His new carefree approach fills me with hope that he hasn't fully succumbed to the darkness surrounding him.

Sparks of the man I've fallen in love with leans over and places a kiss on the edge of my mouth. They combust low in my stomach when he mutters, "Never forget me, Kitten," against my lips.

Before I can respond, Rico stands from his chair, produces a gun from the back of his trousers and points the barrel at the small portion of skin between Oskana's green eyes.

Fear overwhelms me when over half a dozen men push back from the table and aim their weapons at Rico. I shake like a leaf, and my lips twitch, but not a peep escapes my mouth as I watch a series of stomach-churning events unfold before my very eyes.

My eyes bounce between Oskana and Rico when Rico sneers, "First, you murdered my mother, then you tried to kill my wife."

Oskana viciously shakes her head, sending tears rolling down her cheeks.

Rico's jaw tightens. "You can deny it all you like, but don't underestimate me. I know more than I say, think more than I speak, and notice more than you realize. It's usually the people you least suspect who are your biggest enemy."

Oskana's eyes rocket to Nikolai. Shock and disbelief are tainting her face. Nikolai keeps his gaze planted straight ahead, refusing to even acknowledge her presence.

When she returns her gaze to Rico, he demands, "Tell Vladimir what you did. Tell him how you scheduled my mother to meet with a monster because you knew she wouldn't give herself to him."

Vladimir sinks deeper into his chair as he drifts his eyes between

Rico and Oskana. His eyes show his interest, but his composure remains calm.

"Tell him how you set her up!" Rico startles me with his loud voice. "You may not have strangled my mother, but you still *murdered* her. You knew she was Vladimir's *ahren* and that he would never love you like he loved her."

Oskana's pupils widen, and the veins in her neck thrum, abundantly proving Rico's accusations are true.

"You killed my mother so he wouldn't leave you for her. Then you tried to do the same thing to my wife because you knew she would take your place!"

When Oskana shakes her head, Rico's index finger squeezes the trigger of his gun. My chin quivers when dots shimmer on the black material covering Rico's chest—the same area my name is inked on.

"Tell him!" Rico roars, not the slightest bit intimidated by all the guns pointed at him. "Tell him you killed his *ahren*."

My eyes shoot in all directions when the men with their guns drawn step away from the table and move in on Rico. I'm full of fear but frozen, my brain incapable of formulating a way Rico and I can get out of this situation still breathing.

When Oskana's lips remain tightly shut, Rico mutters, "Tell him, or I'll kill your son." His voice is dangerously low—a stark contradiction to one he was using ten seconds ago.

Oskana gasps when Rico turns the barrel of his gun to Nikolai.

Unnerved, Nikolai holds his brother's gaze, his stature composed, his facial expression deadpan.

"Three... two... one," Rico counts down in a tone I've never heard before.

"Okay," Oskana shouts, her voice jittery. "Okay. I'll tell him. I'll tell him everything, but please, Rico, don't hurt Nikolai. Don't kill my son."

I pant, unable to secure a full breath when Rico ignores her pleas and squeezes the trigger of his gun even more.

"No!" Oskana shouts. "Have a heart, Rico. You have to understand. I had four late miscarriages. All boys. Then Felicia had you. A son. Vladimir's firstborn son." She shifts her eyes to Vladimir, who is still seated at the table, seemingly unmoved by the devastating events happening around him. "Felicia ruined everything. I wasn't going to let her take my place as well. I earned it. It belonged to me. I loved you. I still love you. But you only cared about her. Even when she wasn't with you, I could tell you were thinking about her. If that weren't bad enough, *her* son took the title *our* son deserves to have. Nikolai deserves to rule the Popov empire. Nikolai deserves—"

"Nikolai is not my son!" Vladimir's low tone sends a chill down my spine.

A collective sigh sounds around the room as my eyes rocket to Nikolai. He appears as unmoved as Vladimir was earlier.

Clearly, today is not the first time he's been confronted with this news.

My massively dilated eyes shift back to Vladimir when he stands from his chair and signals for his men to stand down. I inhale my first full breath in over ten minutes when the red dots shimmering on Rico's chest disappear.

"You knew?" Rico's voice is as shocked as his facial expression. My heart starts beating again when he lowers his gun to the side of his body.

Vladimir smiles a vindictive grin before muttering, "Yes."

A chair scraping across the wooden floor booms into my ears when Nikolai stands abruptly from his chair. "You knew? This whole time you knew?"

Vladimir doesn't need to answer his questions.

The callous grin etched on his face tells the whole story.

"Then why did you pretend I was your son?" My heart squeezes painfully from the hurt projected in Nikolai's voice.

"Because you were the ultimate pawn," Vladimir snarls. "My plan was to nurture you into a born killer, then I was going to make you kill your father. It would have been the sweetest revenge for your mother's betrayal." Vladimir turns his lifeless eyes to Rico. "But Rico beat you to it."

Another collective gasp bellows around the room, the majority of it from me. I know Rico was forced to do some terrible things in his life, but hearing it firsthand is still shocking.

Taking advantage of Vladimir's honesty, Rico questions, "Then why did you sell Isabelle? If you loved my mother so much, why sell her daughter?"

My jaw muscle slackens when Vladimir's impenetrable mask momentarily slips, exposing a flare of emotion I was certain he didn't have. Remorse.

"Because I couldn't look at her without seeing your mother's betrayal," Vladimir spits out in disgust, his stern mask firmly back in place.

Rico shakes his head. "She never betrayed you! That's why Col killed her," he replies, his anger rising. He turns his eyes to Oskana. "Tell him how Col strangled my mother because she refused to give herself to him. Then tell him how you helped Col cover it up."

Oskana's throat works hard to swallow, but she doesn't attempt to refute Rico's claims.

Fear unlike anything I've ever felt blazes through my blood when I catch sight of the threatening glare Vladimir issues Oskana. "You said Felicia betrayed me! You said you saw it with your own two eyes."

"She played you for a fool," Rico sneers before drifting his eyes back to Vladimir. "Everything she ever told you was a lie."

Oskana's vow of silence continues, proving what Rico is saying is true.

"I did what you asked," Rico says, speaking to his father. "I brought you the person responsible for killing your *ahren*. Now you need to keep your side of our agreement."

Time comes to a standstill when Vladimir and Rico undertake a heart-strangling staredown. It's steaming and full of palpable tension.

The red-hot anger lining Rico's face softens when Vladimir nods. "One wish," Vladimir mutters while holding his index finger in the air.

"Let Blaire go," Rico responds immediately, not even taking a second to deliberate. "Full sanction. She can't be touched."

I jump to my feet, my body responding before my brain has the chance to register an objection. I slip my hand into Rico's sweaty half-clenched fist and turn my eyes to Vladimir. "*Us.* Let *us* go. Rico meant to say *us*," I mumble, my shallow words barely heard in a room quieter than a graveyard at midnight.

I tilt into Rico's side when Vladimir swings his barren eyes to me. "That would be granting two wishes, Kitten, not one. Besides, Rico and I discussed the terms of our arrangement. No mention of his pardon was ever debated."

Rico's hand tightened around mine when Vladimir called me "Kitten."

It firms even more when Vladimir steps closer to us, his demeanor frightening, his eyes lifeless.

After he finishes assessing every inch of my face in skin-crawling detail, Vladimir turns his desolate eyes to Rico. "I'll let your kitten go, full sanction, if you agree to the terms we discussed last night. You stop this nonsense of equity and go back to the man you were before your *ahren* misguided you. Become a true Popov. One worthy of the name." Vladimir's eyes flick to me for a fleeting second when he sneers, "*Ahren.*" When Rico remains quiet, Vladimir asks, "Do we have an agreement, Rico? Your soul to set your kitten free?"

I squeeze Rico's hand, begging him to deny Vladimir's demands. My heart falls from my ribcage when the conceited grin on Vladimir's face tells me he already knows Rico's answer.

He's going to accept his offer.

The thick stench of panic leeches from my pores when Rico does a single nod as he mutters, "Yes. We have an agreement."

Fear spreads through me like brittle ice, shredding my heart with tiny, invisible nicks, then it suffers more damage when Vladimir smiles a grin no woman should ever have to witness.

It's the smile nightmares were created from.

"Good. Start with her." Vladimir jerks his head at Oskana. "If you handle this *situation*, your kitten will be given full sanction. You have my word, no one will ever touch her." A chill runs down my spine when Vladimir turns his evil eyes to Oskana and sings the rhyme Nikolai sang in the plane two weeks ago. "Send the angel to the devil's bed, hold her, cherish her, then cut off her head. She danced with Satan, and now she's dead, all for lying in the devil's bed."

Anxiety paralyzes me when Oskana remains quiet, absorbing Vladimir's cruel taunt without the smallest switch in her composure. I glare at her, urging her to fight, begging for her shocked state to lift, but no matter how much I stare, she maintains a dignified approach, either accepting her fate with quiet poise or stuck in the trance of denial.

After clearing the room with a wave of his hand, Vladimir spins on his heels to face Nikolai. "Are you coming, *son?*"

My astonishment grows when Nikolai dances his eyes between Vladimir and his mother before he stands from his chair and follows Vladimir out of the room.

Oskana appears as mortified as me.

My pupils widen to the size of dinner plates when Rico lifts his gun dangling at his side and points the barrel at Oskana. The veins in his neck are bulging, and his lips are set into a hard, determined line.

"Enrique, don't, please," I plead, my voice weak.

He glances over my shoulder for the quickest second, his eyes dark and bleak. "Erik, take Blaire back to Ravenshoe," he demands, his voice as lifeless as his narrowed gaze.

"No!" I scream when Erik attempts to pull me away from Rico's side. "This isn't you, Enrique. Don't do this."

"Take her now!" Rico roars, the vein in his neck protruding.

When Erik wraps his arms around my torso, I kick and thrash against him. Dread scorches my veins, but I fight with all my might, unwilling to give up. If Rico does this, I'll never bring him back. He will merge too far into the blackness.

"This isn't you, Enrique," I scream at the top of my lungs as Erik drags me across the restaurant floor. "You're not a monster. You were just raised by one."

The refreshing wind from the air conditioning does nothing to settle the sick fear creeping up my windpipe when Erik swings open the restaurant doors and drags me outside.

"Don't, Enrique! Don't do this," I yell with tears streaming down my cheeks.

"Don't forget me, Kitten," is the last thing I hear before the restaurant doors slam shut.

Then my heart shatters into a million pieces when a bullet being dislodged from a gun booms into my ears, proving there is no noise more devastating than the crippling sound of death.

Chapter Thirty-One

One Month Later...

"**H**ey, you look nice," Lacey greets me when I walk into the kitchen of our modest two-bedroom apartment.

"Thanks." Smiling, I run my hands down my floral knee-length skirt, clearing away the invisible wrinkles I believe are in the dead-straight material.

Lacey puts an extra dash of vodka into the dirty martini she's mixing before pouring half of the contents into two salt-rimmed glasses. "You've got this, Blaire."

When she hands a full-to-the-brim martini glass to me, I nod, even though my heart is screaming *no she doesn't*.

"To getting my life back on track." I clink my glass against Lacey's.

She returns my gesture before running her hand down my arm in a comforting manner. "Two weeks doesn't equal a lifetime, Care Blaire," she replies, reiterating what she has said to me numerous times over the past month. "But even if it did, you've got this. Just remember what Dr. Avery taught you. One step at a time."

I try to issue her a genuine smile, but my heart isn't into it. Not yet. It's still struggling to piece itself back together after it was shattered into a million pieces last month. I thought I missed Rico the days following our Vegas quickie wedding, but it's nothing compared to my yearning for him the past month.

My heart is barely functioning, it's been so distraught. Like all people in mourning, my emotions have been put through the wringer. First, I couldn't stop crying. Then, I got angry, not just at Rico but also at myself for not being strong enough to pull him out of the darkness. Now, I'm carefully wading through the final stage of my grief—acceptance.

I only reached the acceptance stage half an hour ago. It's been such a longwinded process as my heart is trapped between a rock and a hard place. Half of it is yearning for Rico while the other half is stuck in debilitating confusion. My heart was certain it knew the real Rico—the man behind the veil he wore in front of others. But when news of Oskana's death circulated on every news channel in the country the days following my return to Ravenshoe, my heart began to wonder if it was duped by Rico's charm as badly as my astute brain. Did I misread him completely? Or is he more cunning than I ever predicted?

When I first arrived home, I vowed to keep myself occupied so I wouldn't stew over every nanosecond of the two weeks before our disastrous dinner date, searching for clues on where it had all gone so terribly wrong, but with Mr. Rodchester refusing to let me return to my teaching job until after the stipulated time Rico's men requested, I had no choice but to evaluate every second I spent with Rico.

Even after weeks of deliberation, I'm genuinely at a loss as to what happened.

The Rico who risked his life to save me ten years ago wasn't the same Rico I was torn away from last month. I know he can switch from night to day with a flick of his fingers, but I thought the days we spent together changed him. He felt responsible for my attack, but I truly thought we'd moved past that. I thought it made us stronger as a couple.

Obviously, I was wrong.

Lacey slings her arm around my shoulders and draws me in close to her side. "Come on, Blaire, just one night with no tears," she murmurs against my temple.

I nuzzle into her neck and inhale a large breath of her freshly washed hair. Lacey has been my savior this last month. Understandably, I arrived home a blubbering mess. Lacey said nothing. No reprimand, no lecture on my stupidity, she just held me while I cried until I had no more tears left to shed.

Most people don't understand the unique bond Rico and I formed in the two weeks we were together. They don't believe such a strong relationship could be achieved in a matter of days. I normally would have agreed with them until I met Rico. He has proven time and time again what I think I know isn't always the case. He made me see the bigger picture.

At times, it was beautiful.

Other times, it was hideously ugly.

That night in the restaurant was a combination of both.

I've encountered a riot of emotions the past month. It's been a truly challenging time, both physically and mentally, but Lacey is determined to guide me through the tumultuous storm battering my life. She's so strong-willed, she has forced me out of holey, food-stained pajamas for the first time in a month.

After ordering my heart into lockdown, I lift the martini glass to my mouth. My sole focus tonight is to push myself out of survival mode. Because as much as it kills me to admit this, Lacey is right. I need to start living again. I need to move on to the next stage of my life.

That would be a whole lot easier to do if I didn't have so many unanswered questions.

I chug down the entire martini in one hit, more than eager to get our girls' night off to a roaring start. Lacey arches her brow and eyes me curiously when I help myself to a second serving of the delicious drink.

"Taxi?" she queries with raised brows.

The smile I award her with this time is genuine. Normally, I'm the designated driver for our monthly dance-like-the-floor-is-on-fire get-togethers, but tonight, I need to let my hair down. I'm not saying I'm planning to get drunk, I just don't need to stress about whether two martinis would put me over the legal limit to drive.

* * *

It's lucky Lacey called a taxi.

Even with most of the alcohol in my system being pumped out onto the dance floor, there's no doubt I'm intoxicated. My words are slurred, my skin is a sticky mess, and I feel the most carefree I've been in the past month. If I'd known alcohol was the cure for the world's worst heartache, I would have started drinking the instant Erik dumped me onto the very plane that delivered Rico and me to Vegas only two weeks earlier. I don't know if that private jet is Popov-owned, but it was a cruel joke on a demented and twisted day.

After lifting my sweat-drenched hair off my neckline, I close my eyes and let the music overtake my body. There are attractive men as far as the eye can see, but I'm not interested. I'm here solely to wash away what's been one of the worst months of my life using nothing but great music and the vibrancy of a bustling environment.

Over the next forty minutes, that's exactly what I do. The pain inside my heart is still there, it just isn't as paramount as it is when I'm lying in bed with nothing but time on my hands.

Several songs later, the hairs on my arm prickle to attention. I flutter open my eyes and swing them around the space. It takes three long blinks for my eyes to adjust to the blinding strobe lights bouncing around the decadent space.

A smile curls on my lips when my heavy-lidded eyes absorb the area surrounding me. There's nothing as captivating as a group of cheerful faces having an enjoyable time.

Well, except one thing.

Nothing in the world is as captivating as Rico's beautiful dark eyes.

When the song pumping out of the speakers switches from a

heart-thumping beat to a slow and steady pace, I head to the bar. On my way, I spot Lacey on my left, grinding her backside on a handsome dark-haired gentleman. Sensing my snooping stare, her dilated eyes lift to mine. I flash her a smirk, grateful I succumbed to her relentless nagging the past six days. She was right, dancing won't cure my heartache, but it's a great way to relieve tension.

When Lacey cocks her brow in silent questioning, I gesture that I'm going to grab a bottle of water. I wait for her to nod before continuing with my endeavor.

The smell of sweat on heated skin lingers in my nose as I weave in and out of the densely populated dance floor. With the club's popularity and it being a Saturday night, the floor space is crowded with sweaty patrons.

Just as my flat-soled sandal steps off the mahogany floor, my long strides freeze, closely followed by the beat of my heart. Although it was quick, I swear I saw a profile a thousand whiskeys couldn't erase from my mind. *Rico.*

Disregarding the twinge of pain hitting the middle of my chest, I push through the throng of sweaty bodies in the direction I saw him. When I hit the end of the bar I swore he was standing at, I stretch onto my tippy-toes and swing my head to the right before slowly drifting it to the left. The sweat slicking my skin amplifies when I spot a flurry of black ducking down the hallway where the restrooms are located.

Adrenaline surges my heart rate to a never-before-reached level.

The blaring music booming out of the speakers dulls to a hum when I enter the hallway. Due to the club being at capacity, the hall is lined with patrons waiting to use the restroom.

After wiping my sweaty hands on my skirt, I pace further down the hall. Once I've walked past the long lines, the vibrancy in the air shifts. My heart is still pumping, but it's more from fear than exhilaration.

I barely hold in a swear word when a clearly intoxicated couple stumbles out of a supply closet. They giggle loudly while smoothing their crumpled clothing. My wide-eyed expression watches them as they stagger down the hall. Once they become lost in the crowd, I gather my heart off the floor and continue my endeavor. I could be completely off the mark, but I'm operating purely on instincts, allowing my intuition about Rico's presence to guide my steps.

The further I saunter down the hall, the greater my perception of Rico grows. Just as I take a sharp left at the end, my wrists are seized, and I'm yanked into a hidden nook on my right. The window-shattering squeal rumbling up my chest is suffocated by a hand when it splays over my mouth. I suck in deep breaths as I fight through a torrent of emotions bombarding me at once.

Joy.

Despair.

Hope.

It all smacks into me.

The tightness spreading across my chest weakens when I lift and lock my frightened gaze with a pair of eyes I recognize.

Colt.

"Jeez, Colt, you scared the living *hell* out of me." I breathe out heavily when he removes his hand from my mouth. He scared me so badly, the curse word screaming through my head nearly came out of my mouth.

The regret in his eyes grows. "Sorry, baby girl. I thought you saw me." He glances into my eyes curiously. "You were following me down here, weren't you?" Add his slurred words to the scent of alcohol on his breath, and it appears I'm not the only one who's been drinking tonight.

"No. I thought I saw someone I knew."

I lean out of the nook and peer down the corridor.

The hope thickening my blood thins. Other than a fire exit door at the end, the hallway is empty.

"You know me," Colt states matter-of-factly, dragging my attention back to him. The playfulness in his tone causes a smile to stretch across my face.

"Yes, I do know you, but I thought you were someone else. Did you see anyone come down here before me?"

Disappointment dampens my alcohol-fueled good mood when Colt shakes his head. "Only you." He taps his index finger on the tip of my nose. After dropping his finger to run it over the curve of my top lip, he murmurs, "You look good tonight, baby girl. You look happy."

Arching a brow, I retort, "I look drunk." *And heartbroken.*

"Then you should get drunk more often," he jests, his smile enlarging so his dimples become exposed. "Drunks a good look for you."

The curve of my brow arches higher. "Drunks?"

My heart rate I've only just settled down beats a little faster when he mutters, "I may be a little drunks myself. We're a couple of good-looking drunks. Especially you. You're a real pretty drunks."

Even though he's under the influence, Colt's compliment gives me back some of the confidence I lost while seeking Rico in a crowd. I can't believe the first time I've left my apartment in a month had me going on a wild goose chase. If that isn't already disturbing enough, finding out my perception of Rico's presence isn't as stellar as I first thought is another low blow to my already crippled ego.

Not wanting my foolhardiness to end my night on a sour note, I loop my arms around Colt's elbow and step back into the hall. "How about us two drunks go and get some water?" I pull him into the packed corridor.

"Water? Oh, no, is Ms. Cardigan-Wearing Williams back? I kinda liked the naughty Blaire better."

I elbow him in the ribs, pretending his snide comment didn't dent my pride. "I didn't say we would *only* drink water. We'll do shot for shot."

"Yeah! Shots!" He cheers, startling a group of girls in line for the bathroom.

As I guide a stumbling Colt down the packed hall, I ignore the pleas of my heart to peer over my shoulder. My heart truly believes it can distinguish the closeness of its mate in a crowded space, but I can't risk disappointing it. With how many cracks my heart has sustained the past month, that little nick of disappointment may completely shatter it.

Chapter Thirty-Two

When I stumble out of my bedroom a little after noon on Sunday I have a vicious hangover. It serves me right. I lost count of the number of shots Colt and I did by two o'clock this morning. As instructed, we did a shot of water for every shot of liquor we had.

For future reference, it doesn't have the same effect as glass for glass.

Lacey giggles into her coffee mug when she notices my disheveled appearance staggering into the kitchen. My heavy steps aren't just weighed down by the furious thump of my skull but also from the guilt I'm feeling. When I'm hiding in my room, eating crap and sleeping way too much, I never feel guilty. But waking up with overly exerted muscles from hours of dancing and my finger void of the heaviness of my platinum wedding band, guilt has made itself comfortable in the place my heart used to belong.

Last night, I pretended to be someone who wasn't heartbroken.

Today, I'm back to the miserable Blaire I've been the past month.

Lacey props her hip onto the kitchen counter then asks, "Coffee?"

"Please." I cringe when my tongue hits the roof of my mouth. It tastes like I ate roadkill for breakfast.

Lacey hands me a double-strength coffee before running her hand down my forearm. "You think you feel bad now, imagine what you'll feel like after Colt's self-defense class this afternoon."

I wince when the coffee burns my mouth. "Defense class?"

"Oh, no, does Care Blaire have a case of drunkenitis?" She laughs with a waggle of her brows.

While nursing my mug of coffee, I rack my throbbing head for the events that occurred last night. Although nothing is overly vivid to me, small fragments of Colt giving me an impromptu self-defense lesson in the lobby of our building crashes into my blurry mind.

"Twelve lessons?" I squeak out when the entirety of our night filters through my brain. "I agreed to twelve self-defense lessons?" The pounding in my head intensifies when my overly nasal voice bounces off the kitchen cabinets and shrills into my ears.

Lacey's broad smile expands. "Yep! And you were so eager you paid up-front." She nudges her head to the now empty swear container housed on top of our refrigerator.

With her fondness for profanity over the past two years, the swear jar was overflowing.

Now, only a few nickels remain.

* * *

After finishing my coffee, I shower and get changed. Three headache tablets have eased the furious pounding of my skull, but the niggling pain in my heart remains. The smile Lacey has been wearing most of the morning grows when I walk into the living room of our apartment wearing a pair of borrowed gym shorts and a crop top.

"How can you work out in these?" I mumble while digging the tiny shorts out of my backside and attempting to yank them down my thighs. "I can't even walk in them, let alone bend over."

Lacey laughs but maintains a quiet front.

Since my father raised me to be responsible about money and

commitments, I will attend my self-defense class this afternoon. My dad's rules are simple. Don't ever buy something unless you intend to use it more than ten times a year, don't fall for quick money-making schemes, and never make a commitment you aren't planning to keep.

If I hadn't already paid for the self-defense lessons at Colt's gym, I might have attempted to back out of our agreement, but since my hard-earned money has already been handed over, I'll honor my commitment.

And if I'm being honest, I'm willing to give anything a shot if it will help ease the constant dull ache in my chest.

"Blaire!" Lacey snickers when I throw a super baggy shirt over my head, swamping the scandalously skimpy gym attire.

"I don't want to get arrested for public indecency," I argue before snagging my car keys off the coffee table.

She laughs but doesn't refute my claim. She knows as well as I do this outfit can't really be called an outfit. I swear my swimsuit has more material in it.

"Wish me luck," I plead before pressing a kiss to Lacey's cheek.

She returns my gesture. "You won't need it."

* * *

Nervous butterflies take flight in my stomach the instant I pull open the heavy glass door of M.S. Gym. The smell of sweat mingles through my nose as blood-pumping music filters into my ears. There's so much testosterone thickening the air, the environment has an invigorating feel to it.

A small smile cracks on my lips when I spot Colt in the corner of the room. He waves a greeting before finalizing his conversation with a blond gentleman working out on a leg press machine. I swing my eyes around the space, taking in the state-of-the-art gym. It's over two levels, and nearly every piece of equipment has a body attached to it. Whoever owns this gym must be pleased by the high attendance rate on a late Sunday afternoon.

My hand automatically darts up to smooth the frazzled pieces of my hair when Colt steps toward me. Colt is no doubt attractive—*not as appealing as Rico, but who is*—but that's not why I'm fluffing my hair like a woman fishing for a compliment. I've seen Colt shirtless numerous times, but not normally when I'm suffering the severe effects of a hangover.

I look like I've been dragged a quarter-mile under a bus.

Colt looks like he's just returned from being photographed for the cover of *Men's Fitness Magazine*.

I snort. He probably has.

"Hey, baby girl, you ready?"

Colt swoops down to place a kiss on my cheek. Even his breath smells fresh.

Not wanting to kill him with my skanky roadkill breath, I nod. "All right, let's get this show started."

He places his hand on the curve of my back and guides me through the gym. Numerous women's eyes track his every move, no doubt admiring the way the muscles in his cut arms flex with every stride he takes.

My disheveled appearance becomes even more apparent when I take in my female counterparts gawking at me in surprise. They are working out in body-hugging gym clothes, perfectly up-swept hair, and a full face of makeup. I don't have a speck of makeup on my face, my shirt is three sizes too big, and my hair is limp since it's still carrying the effects of the sweat-infused club last night. I look as wretched on the outside as I feel on the inside.

When he walks us into a room at the side of the gym, my heart rate kicks into overdrive. "Where is everyone?"

Colt closes the thick glass door, blocking the endorphin-pumping music blaring through the gym before shifting on his feet to face me. "Everyone?"

"For the defense class." My voice is as unsure as my facial expression.

He smiles a boyish grin that makes my pulse surge a little faster. My reaction can't be helped. Even hungover and nursing a broken heart, he has a wonderful smile.

"Everyone who needs to be here is here, baby girl."

I swallow harshly. "Umm... are you sure? There are only two people here. Me and you." I roll my eyes at the dimness of my voice. After squaring my shoulders, I straighten my spine and stand taller. "I thought I agreed to a self-defense class?"

"You did," Colt confirms. I wave my hand over the vacant room that's clearly void of any other gym patrons. My hand gesture freezes halfway when he mutters, "You requested one-on-one defense classes, Blaire."

I drop my hand to my side. "I did?"

"Yes, you did." He moves to a set of protective mats housed on shelves near the glass-paned window at the front of the gym. "And since you're a good *friend* of mine, I wanted to ensure you got the best instructor." He puts on a set of square black pads before spinning around to face me. "That means you get me all to yourself, baby girl, for an hour, three times a week, for a whole month."

My mouth falls open. I should have listened to the pleas of my brain. Shots are never a good idea. No matter how heartbroken you are.

As Colt walks back toward me, his eyes absorb my baggy shirt hanging halfway to my knee. "Didn't have any gym clothes to wear?"

Gritting my teeth, I shake my head. I hate lying, but with the way his eyes are beaming into mine like he wants to ravish me, I'll let my little white lie slide. It's funny. Before Rico, I would have done anything to have Colt looking at me like that. Whereas now, I want to go back to us being friends.

I wonder if my logic will change as the months continue to fly by.

Or will I never move on from Rico?

My heart squeezes. *I'll never forget him.*

After placing his hand on the small of my back, Colt directs me to a section of floor that's covered with a bouncy material similar to a gymnastics mat. It's squishy and reminds me of a trampoline, and forces a genuine smile onto my face. I loved gymnastics when I was younger. Katie and I practiced our routines on the trampoline in her backyard for hours every weekend. That was what we were doing before our attack in the alleyway. Understandably, I haven't done gymnastics since that day.

Trying to keep my focus on the task at hand and not the burning hole in middle of my chest, I yank a hair tie off my wrist and secure my hair into a ponytail. "All right, let's do this."

Colt smiles a full-toothed grin while waggling his brows. I flinch and stumble backward when one of the pads covering his hands whizzes past the tip of my nose. Although the pad didn't connect with any region of my face, my first response is to drop to the floor and cower. Thankfully, I hold my ground even with ice-cold fear lacing my veins.

Panic wells in my stomach as the memory of my attack in the servants' quarters races to the forefront of my mind. I shift my eyes to the side, anticipating seeing Rico magically appear.

The pain shredding my heart in two amplifies when I fail to locate anyone standing next to me, let alone the man who promised to always protect me.

"Blaire." Colt's voice sounds distant. I blink three times in a row when he yanks off one of his pads and touches my cheek, drawing me back to the present.

When I see the confusion marring his face, I pretend my knees aren't clanging together. "Sorry, my reflexes are a little slow today. Probably shouldn't have drunk so much last night."

I can tell by the concern clouding his usually mischievous gaze that he isn't buying my explanation, but mercifully, he doesn't push the matter further. Colt is one of the people who doesn't understand my unique bond with Rico. To him, I was the naughty school teacher having a two-week bender in Vegas. He doesn't comprehend that I can barely breathe without Rico in my life.

"When the pads move in front of you, Blaire, you need to block them. Strike. Block. Strike. Block." Colt sweeps the pads on his hands across the front of me but at a slower pace than he used earlier.

"Okay." I breathe out slowly, my one word shaky.

Over the next hour, Colt teaches me basic self-defense moves. How to block a direct hit, how to execute an open-hand punch, and how even someone with my small stature has enough strength to throw a man Colt's size over my shoulder.

The last part of our training was theory, not practical. Since I had to fight the urge to flinch every time he grabbed me, he said we'd slowly build up to that level of training.

Although I was apprehensive when I first arrived, I did enjoy our one-on-one training session. Actually, I really enjoyed it. Colt took his time, never pushing me further than I felt comfortable, and for the past hour, my mind moved away from my heartache. That, in itself, is worth the burning ache of my weary muscles.

"I'll see you on Tuesday?" Colt asks while guiding me to the gym's main entrance door.

I swallow down half a bottle of water before nodding. "Wouldn't miss it. Thanks."

Forgetting we are at his place of employment, I instinctively lean in to kiss his cheek.

When a collection of wolf-whistling and catcalls sounds through my ears, my cheeks turn a hue of pink.

"See you Tuesday," I mumble before spinning on my heels and fleeing the gym.

* * *

Lacey's head lifts from her laptop balancing on her knees when our front door gives out a creak, announcing my arrival. "Hey, how'd you do?"

She shuts her laptop screen as I throw my keys onto the entry table. "Good. Although I think my muscles might have a different opinion tomorrow."

"As my father would say, 'at least you know you're alive.'" She places her laptop on the coffee table and stands from her seat. "There's a registered letter on the kitchen counter for you."

My lips quirk. "On a Sunday?"

Lacey shrugs. "Might be important."

After grabbing a bottle of water from the refrigerator, I lift the envelope off the counter. The heaviness Colt's workout cleared off my chest comes steamrolling back in when I see the return address—The Office of Erik Monstrateo.

I dump my water bottle onto the counter so hard it falls over, sending water dribbling down the cabinets of our modest-size kitchen. I don't bother cleaning up the mess. I'm too curious as to what is in the envelope to do anything.

This is the first contact I've had in a month from anyone associated with Rico.

Sensing my rattled composure, Lacey joins me in the kitchen. I register her lips moving, but I don't hear a word she's speaking as I tear open the envelope and scan my eyes over the heavily documented forms inside it.

Any pathetic attempts I made at healing my heart the past month come undone when I read the title of the forms—Petition for Dissolution of Marriage.

"He's divorcing me," I mumble through a sob sitting in the back of my throat. "Rico filed for divorce."

Just like the day I arrived home a little over a month ago, Lacey cradles me in her arms and holds me until I have no more tears left to shed.

Chapter Thirty-Three

When my back hits the mat with brutal force, I gasp in a shaky breath. Pain rockets through my body, but instead of cowering away from it, I embrace it.

Lacey's dad is right—feeling pain reminds me I am alive.

Ignoring my winded composure, I crawl onto my knees and lift myself from the floor on a shaky pair of legs.

Colt is standing across from me. His eyes are remorseful, but his grin is arrogant. "Get your head in the game, Blaire. We've done this routine every day for the past month, and you're still not doing it right. An attacker won't wait for you to get your balance. You have mere seconds to escape his clutch."

The words Colt speaks are way too familiar, but I nod anyway, pretending his knowledge is informative.

I know far too well that seconds can feel like hours when you're attempting to escape the clutches of an attacker.

"Let's do it again."

I run a towel over my face, removing the beads of sweat rolling down my cheeks before turning my back to Colt. We've continued our self-defense classes as agreed upon the past month, except I increased the number of lessons from three a week to five. The burn my muscles felt the days following Colt's training session was the only thing reminding me I was alive.

Soon to be divorced, but alive, nonetheless.

If my muscles weren't burning from the exhaustive activities we did that afternoon, I may have never crawled out of bed to soothe them with a long soak in a tub.

Although I was served divorce papers a month ago, I still haven't signed them. Don't ask me why as I wouldn't be able to answer you. Lacey placed them on the denial shelf in my room the day I received them. I haven't touched them since. Avoidance isn't the solution for any issue, but when you're running on empty, you use anything you can.

My mind snaps back to the present when Colt suddenly grabs me from behind. Even though my first thoughts go to panic, my body reacts according to the lessons he's been teaching me for the past four weeks. I jam my heel into his toes before inflicting a brutal elbow to his ribcage. I throw my head back so it connects harshly with his nose before seizing his wrist with my shaking hands. A long, guttural moan tears from my throat when I pull down hard on his wrist and attempt to throw him over my shoulder.

My pupils widen when Colt lands on his back with a sickening thud.

Pushing aside the desire to scream out in victory, I straddle his hips and throw a set of fake jabs into his face. When he flops his head to the side, announcing defeat, I can no longer hold in my excitement.

"I did it!" I squeal loudly, throwing a fist pump into the air. It has taken me over a month to perfect that move, but Colt is one hundred percent muscle, so it's a feat I'll celebrate.

Colt pokes his index finger into my belly. Even it isn't as squishy as it was last month. "You did, baby girl. I'm so proud of you."

"I don't deserve all the credit." I roll off him. "I have a wonderful teacher."

My eyes squint when the overhead fluorescent lights blind my vision.

When I twist my head to the side, my nose screws up. The sky is completely black.

"Did our session run over?" I scan my eyes over the room, seeking any type of time-telling contraption. Normally, our sessions run until seven, but with the blackness of the sky, it seems a lot later than that.

"Yeah, around an hour. But I could tell you were close to mastering the move, so I didn't want to break your focus." Colt climbs onto his feet before extending his hand in offering.

"Only you could make an hour of torture sound like you're doing someone a favor."

Colt laughs. "Learning how to protect yourself isn't torturous, baby girl. Besides, other than one other strenuous activity, exercise is the best way to relieve tension."

"With how much I'm sweating, I'm seriously considering taking up the other option you're offering."

My pupils widen when the entirety of our combined statements smack into me.

Did I just flirt with him?

Although Colt and I have spent a lot of time together the past month, we've never flirted the way we did before my trip to Vegas. Colt has maintained a professional front during our lessons while I kept my heart in lockdown mode.

My theory is proven to be dead on point when Colt's eyes flare with excitement. The air is rife with muggy sweat, but a new scent slowly streams through my nose.

My pulse quickens when I realize what the smell is. It's the unmistakable aroma of lust.

I stand still, rendered motionless with alarm and excitement as Colt slowly prowls toward me. My heart is begging for my feet to move, to walk away before I lose the chance. My brain—it's completely switched off, deciding it's no longer strong enough to continue the vicious battle it's been fighting against my heart the past four months.

When Colt places his hand on the side of my face, I shockingly lean into his embrace. Even with my heart still debilitated from losing Rico, it wants Colt to take away its pain.

Maybe he can force me to forget memories that both haunt and excite me?

Colt's extremely soft lips catch my breathy pant when he seals his mouth over mine. Just like I knew it would be, his kiss is enthralling and sets my pulse racing. He smells manly and tastes like the energy drink he was guzzling down earlier.

When he cups his hands on the back of my thighs, my legs instinctively lift and wrap around his waist. A husky moan seeps from my lips when the hard ridge of his cock rubs the ache between my legs. Although my outfit is more modest than the clothes Lacey lent me last month, they still expose a scandalous amount of skin.

As he walks us toward the locker rooms, I grind myself along the long length of his stiffened shaft. From what I can feel between two layers of gym pants, I can happily testify that his nickname is very fitting.

With the late hour, the gym is empty. Not that I'd care either way. I'm too entranced by the way Colt's skillful kiss is breaking through the negativity surrounding me to care if we have an audience.

When Colt reaches the locker rooms, he places me on my feet. I lean my back against the steel lockers that line the walls of the modern space as I gasp in shocked breaths.

The coolness of the steel material gives relief to my overheated skin while the intoxicating scent of male body wash adds to my excitement.

"Fuck, baby girl, I knew your mouth would taste good, but I had no idea," Colt murmurs while rubbing his thumb along my top lip.

I slant my head to the side, exposing my neck to his sinful mouth when he trails his lips along the edge of my jaw. As he suckles on the sensitive skin of my collarbone, my hand lowers to the hard ridge in his pants. His throaty groan sends a thrill of excitement down my spine, so I increase the speed of my strokes, loving the feeling of him in my hand. When Colt squeezes my aching breast, a husky purr rumbles through my parted lips.

My eyes snap open at the same time my heart painfully constricts. Sick gloom spreads through me when the memory of why Rico called me Kitten slams into my hazy mind.

I snatch my hand away from Colt's crotch as guilt overwhelms me.

Sensing the sudden shift in my demeanor, Colt stops lathering my neck with affection and pulls back.

"I can't," I barely mumble when his confused eyes bounce between mine. "I'm sorry for leading you on, but I can't do this." I adjust my disarrayed clothing while making a beeline for the door.

"Blaire, wait!" Colt shouts, his voice rattled with anxiety.

I pretend like I can't hear him as I charge onto the packed sidewalk.

People eye me with curiosity as I weave past them, but thankfully, they don't approach me. I don't know how I'd react if they did. I've never behaved so erratically before, but since I married Rico, my emotions have become a devastating rollercoaster ride with awe-inspiring highs and life-altering lows.

A logical reason for my pendulous moods becomes evident when my brisk strides down the sidewalk have me scrambling past a drugstore. My frantic pace slows to the speed of a tortoise when a sign blowing in the refreshing fall wind catches my eye.

Are you trying to get pregnant?
Talk to one of our specialists about the latest range of prenatal
vitamins.

"No," I mumble to myself as my brain frantically tries to recall the last time I had my period.

My heart rate speeds up, and my palms grow damp when I fail to recall having a period since my trip to Vegas.

In a trance, I stumble into the drugstore and buy one of each pregnancy test on the shelf.

"No," I mutter for a second time when the test strip I've just peed on in the public restroom turns the color of Nikolai's eyes, ensuring there's no way I can deny the results.

Oh. My. Lord.

I'm pregnant.

Chapter Thirty-Four

"I'm good, thanks, Dad. How are you guys doing? Are you enjoying your trip?"

My dad sighs happily. "It's wonderful, darling. You should consider traveling yourself. Do it while you're young enough to enjoy it."

Smiling, I accept my order of a rye-crusted peanut butter and jelly sandwich from a pretty lady serving behind the counter of my local bakery.

"You're sixty, Dad. You're not even close to being too old to travel." I issue a silent thank you to the bakery employee before walking outside.

My dad chuckles. "True. Probably best to get as much traveling in as we can now before we get laddered down with grandbabies."

A stab of pain strikes the middle of my chest. "Yeah, sounds like a good idea," I push out through the tightness wrapped around my throat.

My dad has made similar jokes over the past three years. They never hurt until today. The handful of positive pregnancy tests I collected two weeks ago have been placed on the denial shelf in my room right alongside the divorce papers I still haven't garnered the strength to sign.

If I'm being honest, I'll admit I've been sitting on the denial shelf myself for the past two weeks.

When I first went home from the drugstore, dazed and confused, I had every intention of sitting down and working out what I was going to do about my *situation.* My good intentions were left for dust when I realized I didn't have a way of contacting Rico. I don't have his cell phone number, private address, or any personal information whatsoever.

So, like all good exes, I stalked him on social media.

I found nothing.

Rico Popov is practically a ghost.

I've called the number supplied with our divorce documentation a minimum of three times a day for the past two weeks. Either Erik is avoiding me as skillfully as Rico, or his voicemail service provider isn't passing on my messages.

After exhausting all avenues, I went about my day-to-day life. I've been forcing myself to pretend everything is fine. I've started teaching again. I went to the movies with Lacey twice last week, and I even apologized to Colt for running out on him two weeks ago.

To everyone surrounding me, I seem to have resumed my normal pre-Rico existence. It's just the empty feeling in the middle of my chest stopping me from believing the same thing.

Exhaling a deep breath, I push my phone closer to my ear. "Listen, Dad, I have something important I need to tell you and Mom."

"I'm listening, honey," my dad replies.

I swallow away a lump in my throat. "I'm..." My brows stitch when my eyes lift from the ground and I see a profile I'd never forget in a million years.

"I'll have to call you back," I stammer out to my dad.

Not giving him the chance to reply, I disconnect my call and step closer to the gathering of people mingling around a dark-colored SUV. My heart is walloping against my ribcage, and nervousness slicks my skin with sweat, but I keep moving forward, more determined than ever.

"Katie?" My one word is unable to hide the hope in my voice.

When the lady with hair as molten as lava cranks her neck to the side for the quickest second, I take a step backward. *It's her.* I know it is. It wouldn't matter how many decades slip by, I'd never forget her steely blue eyes and turned-up nose.

When I attempt to close the distance between Katie and me, two burly men wearing stained jeans and misbuttoned shirts step into my path. Even frightened at their standoffish composure, nothing can dampen my eagerness. I stomp on one of the brute's feet and sidestep the second man before rushing to Katie. My movements are so agile, I slip by the two men before they have the chance to formulate a reaction.

"Katie!" I call out again when a man with platinum blond hair and a wonky nose hurriedly guides her into the back of an SUV idled at the curb.

Dust kicked up from the roadside burns my eyes when the driver of the SUV slams his foot on the accelerator and dangerously merges into the heavy flow of traffic surrounding us.

Ignoring the fear spurring on my furious pulse, I dart into the street and signal for a taxi. Thankfully, with it being midafternoon, my request is filled remarkably quickly.

I crawl into the back seat of the cab and instruct the driver to follow the dark SUV. As I fasten my seat belt, I turn my eyes back to the two men who accosted me on the sidewalk. The crazy beat of my heart weakens to a gallop when I fail to notice them anywhere.

Over the next ten minutes, the taxi driver follows the SUV through the streets of Ravenshoe, going from the newly built-up areas to a side of town that isn't as well maintained.

"Don't get too close," I instruct the driver while touching his shoulder. My shaky hand ruffles the collar on my crisp white dress shirt. "I watched reruns of a seventies-era cop show with my dad for years. Even back then, the biggest mistake the person tailing made was announcing their interest."

The taxi driver tightens his grip on the steering wheel before nodding. His eyes are as wide as mine, but he has an edgy grin stretched across his face like he appreciates the unexpected action I've forced into his life.

"Pull over here," I request the taxi driver when the SUV stops in front of a poorly lit nightclub.

After scanning my eyes around the less-than-stellar surroundings, I shift my dilated gaze to the cab driver. "Can you keep the meter running?"

Relief engulfs me when he nods without a moment of hesitation.

After handing him a selection of bills from my purse to express my appreciation, I exit the cab and walk toward the club I saw Katie and the blond-haired man entering. My legs wobble with every step I take, but my poise is determined.

As I walk past a group of men eyeing me with zeal, I give myself a mental pep talk that I'm stronger than I've ever been and that I've got this. *I hope.*

I clutch my purse close to my chest when my goody-two-shoes outfit gains me the attention of a large beast of a man guarding the nightclub doors. He takes a few moments running his eyes over the length of my body before he lifts his hardhearted gaze to my massively dilated eyes.

With a belligerent grin, he opens the cracked wooden door for me. I force a neutral expression onto my face before walking into the premises like I've always belonged here.

Clearly, I don't belong here.

Considering my clothing has ten times more material than every scantily dressed woman mingling in the dingy club, I stand out like a sore thumb. I look like a kindergarten teacher walking into a biker's bar.

I get eyeballed by people with every step I take, but I continue with my mission, not willing to wait until I've built up enough courage to tackle this task head-on.

It's taken ten years to find Katie, so I can't give up now.

My steps become shaky when a dark-haired man in a booth on

my right lifts his chin, inviting me to join him. I shake my head before changing the course of my direction. My wobbly steps come to a dead halt when the strobe lighting shackled to the roof bounces off Katie's vibrant hair.

Tucking my clutch under my arm, I rush toward the fiery redhead.

"Katie," I call out, fighting hard to raise my voice above the horrid techno music booming out of the speakers.

When I reach the redhead, I grab her by the shoulder. Disappointment smashes into me when she turns around to face me. Her eyes are brown in color, and her face lacks Katie's turned-up nose.

"Sorry," I apologize to her annoyed expression.

When the unnamed redhead returns to dancing with her friends, I roam my eyes around the space, seeking any indication of which direction Katie went.

I freeze when my eyes lock in on a figure moving quickly toward me. Then blood roars to my ears as the man whose foot I stomped on thirty minutes ago briskly strides toward me. His steps are unhindered as everyone surrounding him moves out of his path when they see him coming. His lips are set in a hard line, and his nostrils are flaring.

My brain screams at me to run, but I instinctively loosen my muscles as my body prepares to assert the maneuvers Colt has been teaching me for the past six weeks.

Just as the large brute grabs ahold of my forearm, a gun being fired shrills through the filled-to-capacity club. Panic overwhelms me as patrons of the club scramble, pushing and shoving past me as they scamper to get out of the firing zone. I stand frozen, unable to move out of fear. Flying fists I've learned to dodge. Bullets, though, I don't stand a chance against them, and neither does my baby.

My fear switches to confusion when my eyes lock in on my attacker lying in the middle of the now- isolated dance floor. His face is scrunched. His eyes are tightly shut. While muttering obscenities under his breath, he holds his right knee with both his hands. From his squirming movements alone, I can tell he's in an immense amount of pain.

The thump of my heart turns wild when I notice blood seeping between his interlocked fingers.

With my heart dropped out of my ribcage, I shift my eyes to the direction the smell of gunpowder is coming from. I gasp, beyond shocked, when I spot the cab driver standing near the club's entrance with a gun braced in front of his body. He lifts his right hand to his mouth and mumbles something into the sleeve of his white dress shirt before he houses his gun into a holster wrapped around his waist.

My eyes grow wider with every stride he takes toward me. "We need to leave before the authorities arrive." He slings his arm around my shoulders and drags me toward the exit. Panic rages in my stomach when I recognize his accent.

He's Russian.

"Who are you with?"

My eyes frantically shift in all directions, soundlessly requesting aid from the people gawking at me with a snick of fear in their eyes. When my silent pleas fail to secure any assistance, I lift my eyes back to the man beside me.

"I have full sanction." My words are hoarse, strangled by dread.

Acting like he can't hear a word I'm speaking, the unnamed man ushers me to his taxi idling at the curb in front of the club. After opening the back passenger door, he places his hand on top of my head and assists me inside. His eyes scan the premises as he slips behind the steering wheel and lurches the cab into the heavy flow of traffic.

My shocked state amplifies when I notice the taxi identification hanging on the glass partition doesn't match the man driving. The picture resembles a man in his mid-sixties with a receding hairline and a round tummy. The man driving has slicked-back black hair, a fit body shape, and couldn't be older than thirty.

"Who do you work for?"

When he fails to answer my question, I keep my eyes planted on the rearview mirror as I lift my shaky hand to the door handle. Upon discovering the door is locked, dread curls around my throat, but I refuse to succumb to it.

I've spent the last ten years of my life on high alert, always trying to spot the bad guy in a crowd, but the fear I've lived with the past ten years is nothing compared to the broken look Katie's eyes had when she glanced at me for a fleeting second.

I need to do this for her. I must fight through my fear if I want any chance of finding her.

When the taxi pulls into a derelict building on the outskirts of town, the driver exits the vehicle and walks around to my side of the car. Because he's too busy sheltering his eyes from the rapidly setting sun, he fails to notice me adjusting my position.

The instant he opens the back passenger door, I wildly kick out my leg, smashing my running shoe into his nose. When he stumbles backward, I scamper across the seat and lurch out of the taxi. I complete the maneuver Colt has demonstrated to me time and time again when the unnamed man wraps his wrist around my ankle.

Adrenaline surges through my veins when I execute the move to perfection, not only disarming myself from my attacker but adding another kick to his already bruising face.

After scanning the area for a suitable location to hide, I charge toward the derelict building. It resembles a warehouse I've seen in many horror movies, but it's the only place that will shelter me while I work out my next move.

Gravel kicks up around my feet when I slide behind the rusted framework at the side of the warehouse to hide.

"Dammit!" I curse when I turn my eyes back to the taxi and notice my purse sitting in the back seat. "There goes my chances of calling for help," I mumble to myself.

When my assailant gingerly rises from the dirty ground he's writhing on, I scuttle further into the shadows. My heart leaps out of my chest when I crash into something firm—something that feels distinctively like a broad set of thighs.

Using the adrenaline pumping into my veins to my advantage, I leap to my feet and take off running for a cracked-open door to the warehouse. I make it halfway across the leaf-riddled concrete before my wrist is seized, and I'm yanked backward.

Spinning around, I execute an open palm to the nose technique before bracing myself in preparation to knee my attacker in the balls.

I inhale a sharp breath when I lift my eyes from the cracked concrete to my attacker. With the sun setting behind a low-hanging cloud, most of my assailant's face is hidden, but there's enough light illuminating from the warehouse for me to recognize one distinct feature—a pair of dark and beautifully tormented eyes.

"Enrique?" I query, my mind spiraling, unable to differentiate between the past and the present.

I maintain my braced approach, prepared to strike at any moment when the shadowed figure takes a step closer to me.

My brave façade of the past two and a half months crumbles when the deep rumble of "Kitten" sounds through my ears from a voice I immediately recognize.

Chapter Thirty-Five

"Sorry," I apologize for the fourth time the past thirty minutes when I catch the curious stare of the man I kicked in the face—twice!

He continues holding a wad of tissues to his bloody nose as he talks to Erik in the corner of a dingy office in the back of the warehouse.

Ignoring the way every hair on my body is bristling, I move to stand next to Rico. He's shuffling through a range of surveillance photos of Katie displayed across a table. He's barely spoken to me for the past thirty minutes, but I've felt his heated gaze on me the entire time.

I've spent the past half an hour struggling to grasp the reality that the man in the taxi is an *associate* of the Popov entity and that he's been tailing me for the past two months to ensure Vladimir's request for full sanction was fulfilled.

I don't know if that means Rico is aware of the kiss Colt and I shared two weeks ago or not, but I'm not game to ask. And, in all honesty, it isn't an appropriate time to question if my soon-to-be ex-husband suffers from the same jealousy issues that plague me.

Even with my body acutely aware of every move Rico makes and my brain begging for the chance to have some of its unanswered questions resolved, my focus must remain on Katie. I've waited for this opportunity for ten years, and I can't risk another ten years passing because my heart yearns for an unobtainable man.

"It is her, isn't it?" I ask Rico as my eyes roam over the large selection of photos of Katie.

When Rico and I reach for the same photo, our fingers connect. I gasp in a sharp breath when his meekest touch sends a surge of electricity up my arm. Even after two months apart, nothing has changed. The vibrancy between us is so intense, it's electrifying. I know Rico can feel it too. The stern mask he wears in front of others is still in place, but I witness the quickest flare of emotion spark his eyes from our slight touch. He appears as helpless as I am in this volatile relationship.

After coughing to clear his throat, Rico lifts a surveillance image of Katie being clutched firmly by the blond-haired man I saw pushing her into the SUV earlier before nodding. "We've been tracking Katie the past month, waiting for an appropriate time to get her out. With the contacts I have in this area, it's an ideal time for my crew to move in."

Some of the little nicks on my heart heal when he locks his beautifully tormented eyes with me. "I promised I'd get Katie back for you, Blaire. I'm going to keep my promise."

I exhale a relieved breath, making the weight on my shoulders ten times lighter in an instant. "When can we do that?"

Rico's heavy brow slants. "There's no *we*, Kitten. You're *not* a part of this team."

I balk like I've been physically slapped. Although I could construe his statement as solely referring to Katie's situation, the raging storm in his eyes doesn't relay that.

"We..." Rico gestures his hand between Erik and himself, "... will get Katie out tonight. You're going home with Brent."

"No!" I shout, my reply quick and resolute. I cross my arms over my chest and lock my eyes with Rico. "Katie is my friend. I put her in this situation, so it's my responsibility to bring her home."

"No, it isn't." His loud voice bellows through the isolated warehouse, gaining him the attention of numerous members of his team gathered in the derelict space.

His throat works hard to swallow as he battles to contain his anger. I stare at him, shocked and muted. Just from looking in his eyes, I know the past two and a half months have been as torturous to him as they have been for me, but that doesn't stop me from standing my ground. I've waited for this day for years, and I'm not backing away without a fight.

"Katie wouldn't be in this situation if I hadn't forced her to come with me. She didn't want to go, Enrique, but I stupidly begged her to come."

Rico drops his hand from running along the scruff on his chin. "Katie is in this predicament because I was looking at someone I shouldn't have been looking at. If I'd just kept my mouth shut to Sergei's taunt, none of this would have happened. Not to you and not to Katie. It isn't your fault, Blaire. Nothing that happened that day was your fault."

"We both take blame for what happened that day. Then shouldn't we both have the chance to exonerate ourselves?"

He steps closer to me, surrounding me with his spicy scent. "I gave up everything I've ever wanted to save you from this lifestyle, and now you expect me to let you back in?"

I shake my head. "No. I'm not asking you to let me back in. I'm merely pleading for you to understand the guilt I harbor from that day. I feel responsible for what happened. This is the only way I can ease the guilt I've been carrying the past ten years. It will give me the chance to move on."

"To move on from this? Or us?" he sneers before he has the chance to stop his callous words.

From the anger projected in his voice, I know he's aware of the kiss Colt and I shared, but now is not the time to discuss the stupid mistakes we've both made in our tumultuous relationship. Katie needs to remain our utmost priority.

I hold his vehement stare, striving to display I've matured a lot over the past three months. I'm not the same Blaire he married within hours of meeting. I'm stronger and more determined.

When the silence becomes too great for me to ignore, I mumble, "I'm not the one who filed for divorce." I cringe, loathing that my voice comes out with a quiver. "I would have never given up on you like you did me." I keep my tone low, ensuring his crew won't hear my painstaking confession.

"I did that for you," Rico mutters. "Every terrible thing I've done the past three months, I did for you. But I *never* gave up on you. I *saved* you from a life of misery."

An ache hits my chest when a cloud of pain filters over his beautiful eyes, but it's nothing compared to the agony I've been harboring the past two and a half months. "We made promises to each other the night we got married. You never gave me the chance to uphold my vows."

Rico's eyes bounce between mine for several heart-clutching seconds. They're still the darkest I've seen, but I know the real Rico is hiding in there somewhere. A man can't walk the earth without a soul, and his beautiful eyes show his soul is just as remarkable as his outer shell.

"I loved you enough to save you from my lifestyle," he murmurs, his voice low and pained.

"And I *love* you enough I would have chosen to stay." My voice cracks with a range of emotions. "But you never gave me the chance to prove it. You took away my right to choose who I can or cannot love."

His stern mask slips, exposing a flare of emotion. Although his appearance makes him seem like an emotionally detached person, I know that isn't true. He's a deeply emotional man who would do anything to protect the people he loves.

"Please don't take this away from me as well, Enrique. I need closure for what happened to Katie. This will give me closure."

The dark cloud in his eyes fades as he considers my plea. Regret. Hope. Worry. They all blaze through his beautifully tormented eyes as he stands across from me muted in silence. When he takes a step closer to me, Erik attempts to speak, but Rico raises his hand into the air, cutting him off. Anxiety spurs on my furious pulse. It isn't just concern that he will deny my pleas that has my heart rate quickening, it's my body's reaction to the closeness of its mate. Even in the most heart-strangling situation, his closeness still incites a carnal desire to run ravenously through me.

The past three months of despair disappear in an instant when he places his hand on the curve of my jaw and locks his glistening eyes with mine. It won't matter if it's endured two months of heartache or two years, his touch will always heal my maimed heart.

"Please, Enrique," I beg, returning his ardent stare.

His smoldering eyes stare into mine as he finally gives in. "You're to stay in the car with Brent the entire time."

I sigh in relief before issuing him my gratitude with a smile.

His spicy scent adds to the giddiness in my stomach when he tilts into my side and mutters, "But if you so much as touch your seat belt latch, that spanking I gave you the last time we slept together will be the least of your worries."

Ignoring the way his threat both scared and thrilled me, I nod a little overeagerly.

A little after midnight Monday morning, I'm seated in the front passenger seat of a black Escalade three doors up from the house where they believe Katie is being held captive. Over the past several hours, Rico and Erik gave me a general rundown of the conditions Katie has been living under.

I'm not going to lie, it was hard listening to all the details. After Katie was snatched from Ravenshoe ten years ago, she was to be placed on the black market. But when she caught the eye of one of the head honchos of the Petretti crew, he decided to keep Katie as his pet. In all honesty, I haven't worked out yet if that was a good or bad thing for Katie.

The blond-haired man seems to have taken a fondness to Katie.

He has kept her fed, clothed, and safe the past ten years, but if he truly cared for Katie, wouldn't he do everything in his power to get her out of his corrupt lifestyle as Rico had done for me?

It was only during my discussions with Rico and Erik did the reality for what Rico did for me finally dawn on my tired brain. I've been devastated the past two and a half months, believing Rico didn't love me. Where, in reality, he loved me so much he sacrificed his own happiness to save me.

Once Katie is safe, I'll find a way to do the same for him.

I jump out of my skin when my cell phone unexpectedly dings, announcing I have a new text message.

"Sorry," I apologize to Brent when my startled reaction alarms him. Once Brent swings his irate gaze back to scanning the street, I drop my eyes to my phone.

LACEY:

How's the date going? Need me to call in backup?

A grin curls onto my lips. The only way I could get Lacey off my back when I called to say I wouldn't be home tonight was by pretending I was going on an intimate date. I thought she would have heard the deceit in my voice, but with my emotions still running high from being in Rico's presence, no deceit could be found.

ME:

It's going well. Now, shush, I'm busy…

LACEY:

Don't forget protection!

Her text is aiming for playful, but it causes a stabbing pain to hit the middle of my chest. It's my own fault. No one is aware I'm pregnant—not even Rico. For some inane reason, I wanted to tell Rico in a non-volatile environment. Considering our last four hours had been spent surrounded by members of a dangerous mob, I kept my mouth shut tight.

After rubbing my knuckles over the tightness in my chest, I quickly type out a message.

ME:

I've got it covered.

LACEY:

Good girl. TTYL.

ME:

Bye.

I shut down my phone and shove it into my clutch purse thrown on the floor.

"How long do these things normally take?" I ask Brent, my words garbled with suspense.

He turns his eyes from the poorly lit street to me. "It would be a whole lot quicker if I wasn't stuck babysitting my boss's girlfriend."

Okay. Apparently, he isn't happy with Rico's decision.

Before I have the chance to respond to his snide comment—or correct him that I'm Rico's wife—the brightness of headlights illuminates the cabin of the Escalade.

My already agile heart rate kicks up a notch when the SUV with gun-wielding men hanging on the side mounts the curb and pulls into the front yard of the house where Katie is held.

Time comes to a standstill when Rico curls out of the passenger seat with two semi-automatic weapons clasped in his hands. He's wearing his regular attire I saw him leave for *work* in every day I was at the compound—a crisp black suit, but he's minus the tie he was wearing earlier.

Even with tension hanging thick in the air, the sight of Rico hampers my ability to secure a full breath. Tonight, he's the very definition of dark and dangerous rolled into one undoubtedly beautiful package.

Like I'm sitting front row at an action flick, the scene unfolds before my very eyes in slow motion. Guns flare, bullets are dislodged, and men fall to the ground. Normally, this type of incident would have my stomach twisted in knots, but tonight I feel different. I don't know if it's because revenge is finally being served to the men who hurt Katie and me ten years ago or because Vegas did truly screw with my mind. But since now is not an appropriate time to evaluate my sudden shift to the dark side, I leash my feelings for a more fitting time.

As Rico moves closer to the residence, I keep my eyes locked on him while the same prayer plays on repeat through my mind—that both he and Katie get out of this alive and in one piece.

The awful anxiety I felt when I first saw Katie returns the closer Rico gets to the heavily manned residence. I push aside the uneasiness swirling in my stomach, downplaying it as my pregnancy playing havoc with my emotions.

Seconds feel like hours when Rico and his men enter the derelict house. Although the scene is nowhere near as ghastly as it was when they first arrived, the air has an eerie feeling to it that makes my skin crawl.

Ignoring the niggling feeling in the back of my head that something bad is about to happen, I focus my attention on scanning the face of every man emerging from the house, seeking Rico amongst the group.

I inhale my first full breath when Rico walks out of the property moments later with a wide-eyed and clearly startled Katie in his arms.

Gratefulness swells my heart and tears well in my eyes.

Not thinking, I throw open the door of the Escalade and race toward them. My fast speed causes tears of happiness to trickle down my cheeks.

I hear Rico scream my name, but nothing can slow my brisk pace.

Nothing but a bullet...

Chapter 36

Enrique

"Blaire!" I roar when I spot her racing down the cracked sidewalk.

Concern strikes my heart when the moonlight bounces off the tears rolling down her cheeks. A smile stretches across her face as she sprints toward me.

Clearly, her tears are tears of happiness not sadness, which eases my anxiety.

Although her breathtaking smile is something I've craved seeing for weeks, the area isn't secure enough for her to be out here yet. Normally, lurkers are lying in wait for a prime opportunity to take down a major player in our industry. That's the reason I made her stay with Brent. I shouldn't have let her come at all. It isn't safe, but I'm completely lost to this woman.

Even being separated from her for two and a half months didn't dampen my feelings the slightest. I love her, without a doubt, but that's the reason I gave her up. She doesn't belong in my industry, so I did everything in my power to save her from it. I sold my soul to the devil to ensure my *ahren* didn't have to live in the depths of hell. I became a man by doing what I should have done the moment she landed in my lap three months ago.

I set her free.

It was only during our heart-strangling confrontation earlier tonight did I realize I hadn't fully saved Blaire from the pits of hell. I partly pushed her into it. I thought I was saving her from a life of misery when I accepted my father's offer of a full sanction for her. In reality, I made her life miserable.

The pain in her eyes when she told me I stole her right to choose who she can love felt like sustaining a direct hit to my heart. It gutted me even more than seeing her kiss Colt. But in my defense, the hurt Blaire has experienced the past two and a half months is nothing compared to the life she could have faced if I hadn't forced her decision.

I know she's hurting—so am I—but I'll never stop protecting her. I'll do everything in my power to keep her safe.

Even sacrificing my own happiness.

When I spot Brent coughing and wheezing as his three-packs-a-day lungs struggle to secure a full breath, I realize he doesn't have the speed to reach Blaire before she enters a world she doesn't belong in.

Cursing in the night air at Brent's incompetence, I hand our target, Katie, to Erik.

When I spin back around to face Blaire, the air in my lungs is forcefully removed. Her brisk sprint down the cracked sidewalk halts mid-stride when a bullet rockets through her stomach.

"Blaire!" I roar before executing the man who shot her with a direct hit between his eyes.

He drops to the ground, his eyes still open wide but void of any signs of life.

I run to Blaire, only just catching her in my arms before she hits the concrete sidewalk. Bile rises to my throat when the blood gushing from her wound covers my hands in under a second. Her breaths are wheezy and slow as she fights through a torrent of pain rocketing through her body.

When I lay her down on the dew-covered ground, I apply pressure on her stomach. Panic engulfs me when her warm blood gushes between my interlocked fingers. I know all too well that she's mere minutes away from bleeding out.

A gargled groan whimpers through her lips when I increase my pressure on her stomach while yelling, "Get a medic!" at the top of my lungs. "Where's the fucking ambulance?"

Blaire peers up at me with glistening, tear-filled eyes. Her lips twitch, but not a word leaves her blue-tinged mouth.

"Shh, Kitten. You're okay. I've got you," I murmur when she continues trying to speak.

I crank my neck to the right when a first responder breaks the eerie silence enveloping us. Relief washes through me when the visual of an ambulance gliding down the street greets me.

Returning my eyes to Blaire, I murmur, "Help is on the way. Just hold on."

Tears trickle down her temples as she continues moving her mouth. I slant my head to the side and lean in close to her as my ears struggle to hear the faint word she's whispering on repeat.

Sirens wail, intermingled with whimpers of pain, but the most devastating thing I've ever heard shrills through my ears and issues my heart with another direct hit when Blaire murmurs, "Baby."

I pull back and glance into her eyes, certain I haven't heard her right.

Keeping her dilated gaze on me, she moves one of her shaky hands to the bottom of her flat stomach while her other hand covers my hands vainly trying to stop the blood gushing out of the open wound.

Dread encroaches me when I feel how cold her hands are.

They feel like ice.

Small droplets of blood splatter her lips when she whispers, "Our baby."

"Baby? You're pregnant?"

My blood blackens and scorches my veins with furious heat when Blaire dimly nods. My chest heaves in turmoil as my eyes absorb the amount of blood that has seeped into her shirt. I don't know anything about pregnancy, but Blaire's life is already precariously dangling on the edge of a very steep cliff from the amount of blood she has lost, so I can't stomach what the odds are for our baby to survive such a traumatic injury.

Any chance to ease the lingering fear that our baby has been harmed is lost when her blinks lengthen and her head lolls to the side.

"Blaire!" I shout through the nausea circling my windpipe. "Stay with me, Blaire. Fuck. Please. Stay with me."

I'm so focused on Blaire I don't notice the blackness creeping up on me until it's too late.

Chapter 37

Blaire

Just like it had following my attack ten years ago, my brain has been operating in lockdown mode the past five days. I've drifted in and out of unconsciousness, confused between what is reality and what is a dream. I can't recall the events leading up to me lying in a hospital bed, but from the ghastly smell and the constant prodding I've endured, I know that's where I am.

Fighting against my body's pleas, I slowly flutter my eyes open. My assumptions are proven accurate when my blurry eyes lock in on an IV stand with one and a half bags of fluid dangling off it. The beeping of monitors filters through my ears, and the swirling of my stomach grows as I scan the sanitary-scented room. From my lowered position, I can see numerous floral arrangements covering every surface and the smallest tuff of inky dark hair resting near my right wrist.

"Rico." My word comes out hoarse, hampered by the scratchy rawness of my throat.

I cough to clear my throat before attempting to speak again. My brittle wheezing through my pained lungs announces my awakened status before another word can seep from my lips. The dark-haired man lifts his head off my bed and swings his eyes around my room. He appears dazed and confused.

Against my wishes, disappointment clouds me when the worldly eyes of my dad lock on my confused gaze.

I was hoping he was Rico.

"Blaire, honey. You're awake!" His loud voice adds to the giddiness clustering in my blurry mind.

He shoots out of his chair and races to the corridor more quickly than a sixty-year-old man should move. "Hurry! She's awake. Blaire's awake."

Not even two seconds later, my mom bursts into the room, infusing the ghastly smelling space with her rich wildflower scent. After dumping two vending machine coffees onto a side tray, she stops at the side of my bed. Lacey enters the room soon after my mom but respectfully gives my mom some space so she can issue her motherly smothering she does every time I'm in her presence.

"You've had us worried out of our mind," my mom mumbles into my hair as she curls her arms around my torso and squeezes me tightly.

I hide the grimace attempting to cross my face from her firm hold when she draws back to peer into my eyes. My confusion deepens when I roam my eyes over her face. I've not seen my mom for three months, but she looks like she aged three years in that time.

As tears form in her eyes, she runs her hand down the side of my face. When she glances into my eyes like she can't believe I'm in front of her, it takes all my strength to give her hand a reassuring squeeze.

Once my mom props her backside on the edge of my bed, I drift my eyes between the three sets of eyes staring at me with concern. "What happened?" I ask, my voice croaky.

My dad moves to the side table to pour me a glass of water. After sipping on enough chilled water to ease the scorching burn in my throat, I bounce my eyes between my parents and Lacey. My brows knit together. They all appear to have aged so much in a short time.

My confused eyes rocket to my hospital room door—adding to the giddiness in my head—when it suddenly swings open. An Asian-looking doctor with a kind smile and bright green eyes enters the room carrying a stainless steel clipboard.

"Hello, Blaire, my name is Jae," she greets me, her voice a unique mix of accents. "I'm the head of surgery at Ravenshoe Private Hospital. It's great to finally talk to you in person."

After returning her smile, I ask, "What happened?" I'm not meaning to be rude. I'm just seeking answers to my questions.

Lacey pushes off the door and stands next to Jae. "Blaire's having a little bit of difficulty with her memory."

Jae smiles a contrite grin. "That's understandable. We have had you heavily sedated the past five days."

Although shocked at her admission I've been in hospital for five days, I'm not completely astounded. I feel the most rested I've ever felt.

While removing a light from her crisp white doctor's jacket, Jae moves to the left side of my bed. When she flashes a bright light into my eyes, I inhale a sharp, ragged breath. My mouth falls open as all the events leading up to me being shot flashes before my eyes.

Panic consumes me as my hands dart down to my stomach. "The baby. Is my baby okay?" I ask Jae, dread in my tone.

My parents stare at each other in shock. Their mouths wide, their brows stitched.

When her shock wears off, Lacey squeals, "You're pregnant?"

Tears almost dribble down my cheek when I nod at the three sets of eyes staring at me. Although their mouths don't utter a syllable, their eyes are questioning enough.

"Well, I was..." *Oh god. Please let my baby be okay.*

Dr. Jae places her small hand on my forearm, drawing my attention back to her. "Because you're only a little bit over three months along, the fetus is burrowed deep within your pelvis, happily nestled away from the area the bullet entered your stomach. Since the medics were advised of your condition on arrival, we ensured only pregnancy-approved drugs have been administered since you've been here. I'll schedule another scan in a few days, but everything appears to be following the path it should be."

I snap my eyes shut as sweet relief engulfs me.

My happiness is short-lived when the air shifts so dramatically, a shiver racks through me. Clutching my chest to ensure my wildly beating heart remains in my chest, I slowly open my eyes. A numbness spreads across my chest when I'm met with four sets of eyes staring at me in alarm.

"But..." I want to say more, but I can't force any more words out of my mouth. The tension suffocating the air of oxygen thickens as my concern grows exponentially.

"What aren't you telling me?" I force out through the painful lump in my throat.

Heaviness slams into my chest when Jae turns to face my parents. "I'll give you a few moments of privacy. Please be aware Blaire has just awoken after major trauma."

The beat of my heart merges into dangerous territory, sending the equipment on the side of my bed into alarm. They are the exact words spoken to my parents when they advised me Katie didn't escape our attackers' clutches the first time.

After switching off the wailing alarm, Jae exits the room, and I lock my eyes with my dad. "Katie?" My one word is rickety, coerced through the sob sitting in the back of my throat.

Keeping his worldly eyes connected with my wide gaze, my dad moves to sit in the chair next to my bed. When he curls his hand around mine, the rattle of his hand vibrates all the way up my arm. His eyes glisten with unshed tears as he says, "Katie is okay. She's safe." I sigh in relief as tears of joy roll down my cheeks, but my breathing turns labored when my dad adds, "But Rico..."

My eyes rocket to my dad. "No... oh, God, please no," I beg when his eyes relay the entire story without another word needing to escape his lips.

My dad scoots to the edge of his chair and stares me straight in the eyes while saying, "He saved you, honey. Rico put himself in the line of fire to save you."

Pain shreds through my heart, tearing it in two. "No, Daddy, no." I sob, not wanting to believe the truth beaming from his truthful eyes.

Standing, he bands his arms around my shoulders. "I'm sorry, honey. I'm so sorry."

My heart shatters.

Not partly.

Not slightly.

Wholly.

Epilogue

Four weeks later...

News of Rico's untimely death circulated on every news channel in the country the two weeks following his death. Hysteria broke out from the fear his murder would start the equivalent of World War III within the Russian mob. Even the governor urged calm. The only thing that eased the tempestuous waters was when the man who was arrested for killing Rico was found hanging in his jail cell the morning of his arraignment. Suspicions ran high that he too was murdered, but with the surveillance cameras in the local county jail on the fritz, they were only that. Rumors.

Just like the months following my return from Vegas, I've been slowly wading my way through the stages of grief. I cried. I got angry. Now, I'm in denial. I'm not just talking about Rico's death, I am talking about every part of my life that included him in it.

All I want to do is crawl into my bed and forget the world exists.

That would be a whole heap easier to do if I weren't lying in a hospital bed with an ultrasound wand gliding over the small curve in the bottom of my belly.

I've spent the last four weeks recovering in the hospital from my gunshot wound. The nursing staff and doctors have been wonderful. They didn't even bat an eyelid when my frightened screams in the middle of the night bellowed down the corridor or when they would find me huddled in the corner of the room crying like a blubbering mess. They took my drastic mood swings in stride, giving me space when needed and occasionally a shoulder to cry on.

They have been a godsend.

But with my injuries now manageable, I can go home—after they check on the little miracle nestled safely in my stomach.

Lacey's squeeze on my hand tightens when my baby's heartbeat fills the silence in the hospital room. It's a bittersweet sound.

Bitter, because Rico never got the chance to hear it.

Sweet, because a part of him will forever live on in his baby's memory.

"Do you want to know the sex?" the ultrasound technician, Jennifer, asks.

"Isn't it too early to tell?"

Jennifer smiles a tight grin. "Depends on the baby. Your baby is very obliging today." Her cheerful tone forces the first genuine smile onto my face in weeks.

"Okay. I want to know," I inform Jennifer, nodding.

I hold my breath as I wait for her to issue me the news I already know. It isn't because I can tell an arm from a leg in the images on the monitor at the side of my head, I can just feel it deep in my soul. I know I'm carrying Rico's son, a little boy who will have eyes as beautiful as his father's.

Jennifer clicks on the keyboard of her ultrasound machine before zooming in on the black and white image. "Can you see that?"

Blood surges into my heart as I nod. Even without having a degree in radiology, I can't miss the long dangling thing sitting between the baby's legs. *Rico's son's legs.*

After wiping the gel off my stomach, Jennifer helps me sit before handing me two black and white printouts. The weight on my chest doubles when I peer down at the images of the little miracle I created with Rico.

"After you empty your bladder, you're free to go." She wraps her arms around my torso. "Best of luck, Blaire. If you ever need anything, don't hesitate to call."

"Thank you." My voice is barely a whisper.

Throughout the day, the nurses and doctors who cared for me the past four weeks have expressed similar sentiments.

Putting on a brave front, I tell Lacey I'll be out in a minute before stepping into the bathroom. Although my injuries have healed quickly, a twinge of pain still rockets through my body with every step I take.

I manage to make it inside the bathroom before the first devastated sob tears from my throat. I bite on the side of my palm to ensure Lacey won't hear my heartbreaking howls as the final stage of my grief reaches fruition.

Acceptance.

I grip the edge of the vanity in a white-knuckled hold before crouching down, no longer trusting my legs to keep me upright. My cries are loud and gut-wrenchingly long. In these walls, I could hide away from reality and pretend nothing happened, but the instant I step foot out of this hospital, I'm being forced into a world where I have to start living again.

In a cruel, tormented world without Rico.

I don't know if I can do that.

The two and a half months following my return from Vegas was painful enough, but knowing I'll never see Rico again utterly destroys me.

After splashing water on my tear-stained cheeks, I exit the bathroom and shadow Lacey to her car. She can tell I've been crying, but thankfully, she pretends she can't. She's been great the past four weeks—the only person I could truly talk to—but I still don't think she fully understands the crippling pain I'm feeling. How can I explain that I lost the love of my life to a group of people who think

Rico was nothing more than a drunken mistake? It's not possible. I've tried.

Remaining quiet, I keep my eyes planted on the scenery whizzing by as we make our ten-mile trip home. Just like the day Rico collected me from Ravenshoe, everything looks similar, but it feels different. The heavy clog of traffic is still on the roads, the sky is still blue, but something is missing.

Someone is missing.

Acting purely on instincts, I follow the same mundane routine I always do when I come home. I gather my mail off the floor and hit the button on the answering machine.

"I'll make coffee." Lacey stops halfway into the kitchen and spins around to face me. "Can pregnant ladies drink coffee?"

I laugh, but it's full of despair. "I don't know. This is all new to me too."

Lacey twists her lips. "I'll do tea just in case. Chamomile tea," she says with a slight nod of her head.

I force a fake smile onto my face, grateful she's taking my pregnancy in her stride. "None for me. I'm going to jump into bed. I'll see you tomorrow?"

Her bottom lip drops into a pout, and she looks like she wants to plead with me, but thankfully, she just nods. "One step at a time, Blaire. It will slowly get better."

After kicking off my shoes, I press a kiss to her cheek and walk down the hallway to my room. Even though I've spent the past four weeks in bed, mine is still calling me. I don't know if it is my pregnancy making me sleepy or the heavy grief sitting in the middle of my chest.

Either way, I'm exhausted.

I stop halfway down the hall when my answering machine announces the timestamp of a message, one recorded within hours of Rico's death.

"Blaire, it's Katie..." She swallows before she continues, "Thank you. I know what happened, and I'm sorry, but I just wanted to say thank you for never giving up on me."

Pain twists through my chest. I've talked to Katie a few times over the past four weeks, but our conversations were quite brief. Understandably, we both have a lot of issues to work through. But, hopefully, one day, we'll both be strong enough to arrange a face-to-face meeting.

I run my hand across my cheeks, removing the tears tracking down my face before continuing with my mission. My steps are slow and sluggish. Although I faked a chipper personality throughout the hospital mandatory counseling for victims of violent crimes, I'm fairly certain I'm sitting on the cusp of depression. I've lost weight, I constantly feel restless even doing nothing but sleeping, and no matter how hard I try to ignore it, I feel dead on the inside.

After flicking on the light in my room, I lower the dimmer so it's dark but not completely black.

I can't stand the thought of sleeping in a completely darkened room.

My sluggish steps to my bed stop—closely followed by the beat of my heart—when I detect I'm being watched. I blink several times to clear my blurry vision when my eyes lock in on a dark shadow standing at the side of my bed. My lips twitch, dying to spill the screams running through my brain, but my mouth fails to cooperate.

I'm once again rendered mute by fear.

Even frightened, my naturally engrained fighter instincts kick in.

It's not just me I'm protecting anymore. It's also my baby.

I'll protect him until I take my very last breath.

Any chance of leaving my room with my heart intact flies out the window when the shadowed figure steps out of the darkness and mutters, "Hello, Kitten."

Goose bumps rush over my skin as a dash of disbelief taints my blood. I shake my head, certain my eyes are playing tricks on me.

When the brisk shake of my head fails to clear the image in front of me, I take a step closer to the denim-clad man. With my composure balancing precariously between insanity and lucidity, my eyes scan every inch of Rico's body, seeking any type of morbid injury.

I fail to find any. Other than his hair being clipped close to his scalp, and his dark eyes concealed by a pair of thick-rimmed glasses, he looks the same as he always has—dark and dangerous rolled into one unbelievably handsome package.

"How?" I want to say more, but I've been rendered speechless. I can barely grasp what is and isn't reality, let alone speak.

When Rico removes his glasses and places them on my dresser, tears fill my eyes. "There was only one way I could leave my family, Kitten."

"Not breathing," we quote at the same time.

"But... it can't... you're..." Nothing I'm saying makes any sense. It can't be helped. I'm staring at a ghost.

When Rico moves closer to me, his spicy scent engulfs my senses, adding further confirmation that my imagination isn't playing tricks on me.

Rico is standing before me—alive and well.

You'd think my first reaction would be to throw my arms around his neck and never let him go.

It isn't.

My palm sets on fire when I strike him hard across the face.

"How could you do that to me?"

Unable to hold back the desires of my heart any longer, I throw my arms around his neck. I seek deeper contact, needing more, always wanting more when it comes to him. I bury my face in his neck and breathe in his scent, my mind spiraling, my heart shut down.

He scoops me into his arms and moves us to sit on my bed. I cling to his plain white shirt, certain he'll vanish at any moment. Holding my jaw in his shaking hands, his riddled-with-remorse eyes dance between mine, relaying his sympathies for the horror I've been living the past four weeks without a word needing to trickle from his lips.

"You broke my heart," I whimper with heartache in my brittle tone.

The pain in his beautiful eyes grows. "I know, Kitten, but we needed it to look real. We knew they'd be watching you. Your grief added to the belief of our story."

I frown in confusion. "Our?"

He brushes a tear off my cheek. "Erik and me. Erik isn't a lawyer. He works for the FBI." My confusion skyrockets when he adds, "So do I."

"What?" It's hard to get my words out with how tight my throat is.

He peers into my eyes so I can see the truth relayed in his. "I've been working alongside the FBI the past six years."

"You've been working *undercover* in the Popov compound for six years?" I ask through the bile sitting in the back of my throat.

I feel sick. My stomach is twisting so badly I feel physically ill.

When I attempt to scamper off Rico's lap, he holds on tight, refusing to let me go.

"You lied to me. This whole time you've been lying to me?"

I'm stuck halfway between angry and grateful.

Angry he never told me.

Grateful he can tell me now.

I freeze and gasp in a quick breath. "Is Vladimir even your father?"

Rico places his hands on the edge of my jaw and glances into my eyes. Just seeing the torment in his gaze dampens the anger raging in my stomach. Only he can change my moods more quickly than he can convert from day to night.

"Everything you witnessed and heard about my life is true, Blaire. I've never lied to you. I'm Vladimir's son. His firstborn son. I may have been raised by a monster, but I'm not a monster myself. You know this, as you know the real me."

My brows stitch. "You've said that to me before, haven't you?"

The corner of his lips tugs high before he nods. "Yes, the night we got married. I told you every detail about my life. *Everything.*"

My mouth falls open. "I've known the entire time you're an FBI agent?"

His eyes dance between mine. "I'm not an agent... more of an *associate.*" His expression is as unsure as his words.

I take a few moments to let the information be absorbed by my exhausted brain.

The silence only creates more questions in my already over-worked mind.

"Why did you wait so long? Why didn't you fake your death years ago?"

"After you were attacked in the alleyway ten years ago, my life changed in an instant. I wanted to be a better man," Rico replies before lifting and locking his dark eyes with me. "I wanted to be a better man for you. But Vladimir is very cautious. He knew he was being watched. The FBI has been undercover in the compound for years, but they had nothing on him. The information I obtained on him the past two years alone outweighs the last forty years of undercover work. I did more good from inside the compound than I ever could have from the outside because he never thought to suspect his own son."

He runs the back of his fingers along my cheeks to gather my tears before dropping them to the curve of my mouth. The wetness of my tears relieves the dryness of my lips. "I requested to leave when you were attacked in the servants' quarters, but the FBI wouldn't let me go. They needed more intel on Vladimir. That's what I did during our separation. I gathered as much evidence on Vladimir as I could."

His jaw gains a tick as he draws me in closer. He holds onto me like I'm truly the most valuable thing in his life. "When you got shot and told me about our baby, I knew I would never return to the Popov compound. I told Erik he either had to get me out or I'd find my own way out."

"How did Erik handle that?" I query, my rickety words unable to hide the mad beat of my heart.

Rico smirks. "Not very well, but he soon saw the benefit of it. My death means Erik is now ranked number three in the Popov empire. That's the deepest the FBI has infiltrated the compound."

"Except you," I mumble.

His smile enlarges. He looks part cocky, part smug.

After swallowing down the harsh bitterness in the back of my throat, I ask the one question my heart wants immediately answered, "Oskana? What happened to her?"

His thighs tense beneath me as he clears his throat. "I had every intention of bringing her in. She killed herself before I had the chance." He stares into my eyes, ensuring I can see the truth conveyed by them. He's being honest.

I inwardly sigh. My heart knew he could never harm a woman. His soul is too beautiful to harbor a monster.

"Oskana knew her fate."

Rico nods. "She didn't know life outside the Popov compound. It was her entire world."

"Do you?" I interrupt. "Know life outside the Popov empire?"

"Yes," he replies without a pause for consideration. He connects his eyes with mine. "Especially when I'm with you."

His comment eases some of the nicks my heart has been beaten with the past three months. Don't construe my statement the wrong way. My heart still has a lot of healing to do, but I can see that process will be a whole lot easier now.

Although I still have many unanswered questions I want resolved, my brain is too overloaded with everything that has happened in the past thirty minutes to continue with our life-altering discussion. My heart? It only wants one thing. Him—Enrique—the stranger I married.

I run my hand over his clipped hair. "I like this," I mumble, my composure still sitting halfway between insanity and reality.

Rico smiles. "Good. It was either clipped or blond."

He scoots us up the bed until his back is resting against the headboard. I nuzzle into his chest, loving his thumping heart booming into my ears. It was a noise I never thought I'd have the opportunity to hear again so I relish every precise beat.

We sit in silence for what feels like hours but is only mere minutes.

Once the silence becomes too great to ignore, I murmur, "Where do we go from here?"

I don't need to look at him to know he's smiling. I can feel it in my bones. "I've heard from a reliable source that Europe is nice this time of year. Although, he did warn me that I may need to take my wife out back to shoot her if it isn't planned well."

Lifting my head off his chest, I peer into his eyes. "Have you been talking to my dad?"

That's one of my dad's favorite sayings for when my mom's feathers get a little ruffled. Any time she gets flustered, he threatens to take her out back and shoot her. It's odd to think that in the family I grew up in, that type of bantering is perfectly acceptable, but for someone like Rico, he'd have to wonder if it was a simple joke or an actual threat.

That must have been a terrible environment to be raised in.

It makes me so grateful our son won't grow up in that atmosphere.

My pupils widen to the size of dinner plates. "Oh my God, I forgot to tell you. We're having—"

"A son," Rico fills in, smiling.

I stare at him, shocked and confused.

He tucks a strand of my hair behind my ear before locking his eyes with mine. "You can't trust anyone, Kitten. Even when they don't appear to be watching you, they are." He tilts his head closer so his minty fresh breath bounces off my lips before muttering, "Especially me."

Cringing, I sink deeper into the mattress. I'm already aware that he knows about the kiss Colt and I shared, but I don't have the energy to deal with that *situation* right now.

Another small stretch of silence passes between us. It's healing and most definitely required.

When Rico tightens his grip around my torso, I lean into his chest and breathe him in, grateful we are getting a second chance in our tumultuous relationship. The past four months have been a teeth-clattering rollercoaster ride, but I'm sure now that the darkness has been vanquished, we will be unbreakable—a force to be reckoned with.

There's only one greater dynamic than a man protecting the

woman he loves—a man protecting his family. So, although there's a niggle of doubt in the back of my mind that this isn't the last we'll hear of the Popov empire, I have no doubt Rico will stop at nothing to keep our son and me safe. Just like I'll always be his light in a life full of blackness.

As the minutes tick by on the clock in silence, my eyelids grow heavy.

When I'm unable to stifle a yawn, Rico mutters, "Sleep if you're tired, Kitten. I'll be here when you wake."

He was.

That day.

And the next day.

And every day that followed.

Enrique

"We have a twenty-four-year-old pregnant Caucasian female with a gunshot wound to the upper right quadrant of her stomach, unresponsive on arrival but resuscitated on site. ETA to Ravenshoe Private is ten minutes," announces one of the paramedics into a radio strapped to his shoulder as his partner pushes an unconscious Blaire into the back of his ambulance.

I stumble backward when a third medic slams the ambulance doors shut before climbing into the driver's seat.

While running my fingers through my hair, my eyes scan the area. Dead bodies are sprawled across the compound of the recently reformed Petretti crew, and a few of my crew have sustained life-threatening injuries. But nothing compares to the lifeless look in Blaire's eyes when she peered up at me and told me she was pregnant. I've seen some bad shit in my life—stuff no man should ever have to witness—but her bleak eyes will forever haunt me.

I feel the blackness closing in on me, but I'm not strong enough to fight it anymore. I did everything I could to save Blaire from this lifestyle, yet she is still suffering the consequences of my actions ten years ago.

When is enough going to be enough?

I'm tired of this fucking life.

I'm tired of the game.

I'm tired of pretending to be someone I'm not.

Adrenaline surges through my body as I grab one of the many guns left lying on the blood-soaked lawn. I storm past the men in my crew, eyeing me with caution, my pace unchecked. Burning rubber lingers in the air when I dive into the black SUV mounted on the curb and shoot out into the street.

Ignoring the shake of my blood-covered hands, I check that my pistol is loaded and the safety is off as I make a short three-block trip.

I'm out of the SUV and storming toward a white surveillance van before the SUV comes to a complete stop. Numerous faces lift from the bank of monitors in front of them when I throw open the surveillance van's door and step inside. Their mouths gape open, and their eyes widen, clearly shocked at seeing the carnage they are witnessing first-hand on a computer screen, but they remain seated, either scared or unsure of what to do.

FBI agents jump from their seats when I move through the surveillance van, but I don't pay them any attention. There's only one man I came here to see—Agent Alex Rogers.

Because he's so immersed in evaluating the massacre that just occurred, he doesn't notice me sneaking up on him until the barrel of my gun is pushed up against his right temple.

"You'll be dead before you even remove your pistol," I warn when his hand slides toward his gun holstered at his side.

"Rico—"

"I want out," I interrupt.

Like a man who has no concerns for his safety, Alex turns around to face me, pretending he can't feel the barrel of my gun pinching the skin on his temple. "We still have so much information we need to get before I can approve that."

"I. Want. Out!" I roar again before pushing the barrel of my gun to the small portion of skin between Alex's eyes.

I hear several guns being removed from their holsters to no doubt be pointed at me, but I don't back down. I've walked too far into the blackness for fear to stop me now. A soulless man can't feel anything, let alone something as weak as fear.

"Enrique," says a voice to my side. "We've discussed this. You know what we need."

I drift my eyes to Erik. "I've given your agency six fucking years of my life. Not anymore. I'm done."

I wasn't joking when I said my life changed full circle when Blaire was attacked in the alleyway. The FBI has been infiltrating the Popov empire for years, way before my mother was killed. The years following Blaire's attack, I tried to gain the trust of the men I believed were deep undercover in our compound, but none of them trusted me. They all thought I was hunting snitching rats. Erik was the only one who trusted me enough to fully disclose himself and his operation. He's been sheltering me under the FBI banner for the past six years.

"I've spent the past three months living in the deepest pits of hell. I became a man only a monster like my father would be proud of. I've given all I can fucking give. I'm done."

As Erik steps closer to me, his remorse-crammed eyes request that I lower my weapon without a word needing to seep from his lips. "Heads will roll," he warns when I refuse to lower my gun.

"Not as much as they will when I disclose every agent in the Popov compound to Vladimir." I swing my eyes back to Alex. "Starting with your brother."

Alex holds his ground, vainly trying to act unaffected by my threat. Little does he know, I know way more than he thinks I do. You don't spend years walking amongst the dead not to learn how they operate.

"I can arrest you right now, and you would never see daylight again," Alex snarls, his words vicious.

I laugh. It's a laugh that displays how far I've walked into the blackness that's been swallowing my life the past twenty-four years. "You really think four walls will stop me? Your agency was left scrambling when I was snatched right under your nose after I killed Col Petretti. This is way above your pay grade, Alex. It's time for you to step back and watch how the big boys play."

As much as it kills me to do, I lower my gun from Alex's head and turn my eyes to Erik. "I'm done. You either get me out, or I'll find my own way out."

With that, I turn on my heels and walk out of the surveillance van, trusting that Erik will have my back as he has for the past six years. He knows too well the hell I've endured the past ten years as he was standing right beside me. Erik was the one who sought medical attention when my back was burned with acid as punishment for helping Blaire. He was the one who helped me ensure my sister's fiancé was the winning bidder when my youngest sister, Callie, was auctioned on the black market, and he was the one who stopped me from killing Nikolai when I found out he orchestrated Blaire's attack.

Erik has guided me through some of my darkest days. And since today is the blackest day I've endured, I need to trust he will continue to have my back as I've had his these past six years.

* * *

Several hours later, I'm walking into a recovery room at Ravenshoe Private Hospital. The heaviness on my chest intensifies when my eyes lock in on Blaire lying in the middle of the bed. She looks so tiny and frail swamped by the medical equipment surrounding her.

"I'll keep the staff occupied for ten minutes, but I can't give you any more time than that." Jae runs her hand down my arm before gesturing for me to the enter the room.

Just before she exits, I call out, "The baby?"

Jae smiles. "They did a quick ultrasound during surgery. Everything looks okay."

The stranglehold clutching my throat weakens. "Thanks."

Jae nods before exiting the room.

I remove the cap hanging low on my head and place it on the side table attached to Blaire's bed before moving to stand next to her. Other than the medical equipment surrounding her, you wouldn't know she's injured. She just looks like she's sleeping. She has the same peaceful look on her face she was wearing when I saw her dancing at a nightclub six weeks ago.

The weeks following Blaire leaving Vegas, I tried to stay away from her. But just like my ability to deny her requests, I couldn't. I needed to know she was safe.

The night I followed Blaire to a bustling nightclub in Ravenshoe was a bittersweet night. I was glad she was safe and happy but also devastated she appeared to be moving on. Even though I wanted to save her from my lifestyle, I always hoped I'd be saved one day too and that we could be together.

Although seeing her enjoying life outside the compound hurt, it also reinforced I had done the right thing. After everything she'd been through, she deserved to be happy.

That was why I filed for divorce. I thought it was what she wanted.

My mind snaps back to the present when Blaire mumbles something in her sleep. Her eyes are moving rapidly under her eyelids, and her face is scrunched up. When her hand creeps across the sheets to grab at the IV line inserted in her opposite wrist, I curl my hand around hers.

"Shh, Kitten, you're okay. I've got you," I mutter as I glide my thumb over her hand.

Over time, her jittery movements still, and the heavy grooves in her forehead smooth. I sit with her for several minutes, comforting her in silence. Jae said Blaire's parents have been called, but with them in Europe, they won't be here for a few more hours. And since Lacey isn't related by blood, she can't see Blaire until she's wheeled out of recovery.

Several minutes later, when a door creaks, I shift my eyes to the side, expecting to see Jae.

I'm taken aback when I see Erik's six-foot frame filling the doorway.

He walks two steps into the room before saying, "If you want to do this, we need to do it now, and we need to do it right."

The heaviness on my chest clears away. It's time for me to finally go home.

I nod at Erik before leaning over to press a kiss on Blaire's cracked lips. "Don't forget me, Kitten," I whisper against her mouth. "I'll be home soon."

* * *

"Just do it already!" I shout, glaring at Erik.

He has the barrel of his gun pointed at me but is failing to pull the trigger.

I take a step closer to him. "You said we need to do this right, so let's do it. You know the areas to avoid. Your aim is nearly perfect. Shoot me."

"Nearly perfect isn't fucking perfect," Erik replies, his words as uneasy as his facial expression. "I could kill you, Enrique. One millimeter in the wrong direction can be the difference between life and death."

I shake my head. "That's not going to happen."

"How can you be so sure?" Erik's voice is laced with uncertainty.

"Because I trust you. You have my back like I've always had yours. Do it. Shoot me!"

Sensing Erik's hesitation, Alex hands the mobile device recording the incident of my 'death' to a blond-haired agent at his side. Without a moment of indecision, he yanks the gun out of Erik's grasp, points it at me, and fires three times.

Pain rockets through my right shoulder, my left thigh, and the upper right quadrant of my stomach. Bitter-tasting bile surges to the back of my throat as dizziness plagues me. I remain standing for mere seconds before the pain tearing through my body becomes too great for me to handle. I crash to the ground hard while clutching the wound in my stomach. Blood splatters my lips as I wheezily battle to fill my lungs with air.

The dew-covered ground cools my back when I roll over and face the stars scattered in a brilliant, dark sky. It reminds me of the shimmering in Blaire's eyes every time she's about to smile.

Looking into her eyes when she's happy is like staring up at a million stars brightening a pitch-black night.

It's so beautiful.
She's so beautiful.
My light.
My life.
My everything.
As the blackness slowly rolls in, my thoughts go to her—my little kitten.

THE END...

The next book in the Enigma series is about Hawke. Widower, soldier, and bodyguard of Rise Up. His book is called Second Shot

Did you know **Nikolai**, Enrique's brother, has his own series? It is called Nikolai: A Mafia Prince Romance

Facebook: facebook.com/authorshandi

Instagram: instagram.com/authorshandi

Email: authorshandi@gmail.com

Reader's Group: bit.ly/ShandiBookBabes

Website: authorshandi.com

Newsletter: https://www.subscribepage.com/AuthorShandi

Also by Shandi Boyes

<u>Perception Series</u>

<u>Perception Series</u>

<u>Saving Noah </u>(Noah & Emily)

<u>Fighting Jacob </u>(Jacob & Lola)

<u>Taming Nick </u>(Nick & Jenni)

<u>Redeeming Slater </u>(Slater and Kylie)

<u>Saving Emily </u>(Noah & Emily - Novella)

<u>Wrapped Up with Rise Up </u>(Perception Novella - should be read after the Bound Series)

<u>Enigma</u>

<u>Enigma </u>(Isaac & Isabelle #1)

<u>Unraveling an Enigma </u>(Isaac & Isabelle #2)

<u>Enigma The Mystery Unmasked </u>(Isaac & Isabelle #3)

<u>Enigma: The Final Chapter </u>(Isaac & Isabelle #4)

<u>Beneath The Secrets </u>(Hugo & Ava #1)

<u>Beneath The Sheets</u>(Hugo & Ava #2)

<u>Spy Thy Neighbor </u>(Hunter & Paige)

<u>The Opposite Effect </u>(Brax & Clara)

<u>I Married a Mob Boss</u>(Rico & Blaire)

<u>Second Shot</u>(Hawke & Gemma)

<u>The Way We Are</u>(Ryan & Savannah #1)

<u>The Way We Were</u>(Ryan & Savannah #2)

Sugar and Spice (Cormack & Harlow)

Lady In Waiting (Regan & Alex #1)

Man in Queue (Regan & Alex #2)

Couple on Hold (Regan & Alex #3)

Enigma: The Wedding (Isaac and Isabelle)

Silent Vigilante (Brandon and Melody #1)

Hushed Guardian (Brandon & Melody #2)

Quiet Protector (Brandon & Melody #3)

Twisted Lies (Jae & CJ)

Enigma: An Isaac Retelling

Bound Series

Chains (Marcus & Cleo #1)

Links (Marcus & Cleo #2)

Bound (Marcus & Cleo #3)

Restrain (Marcus & Cleo #4)

The Misfits (Dexter & Megan).

Russian Mob Chronicles

Nikolai: A Mafia Prince Romance (Nikolai & Justine #1)

Nikolai: Taking Back What's Mine (Nikolai & Justine #2)

Nikolai: What's Left of Me (Nikolai & Justine #3)

Nikolai: Mine to Protect (Nikolai & Justine #4)

Asher: My Russian Revenge (Asher & Zariah)

Nikolai: Through the Devil's Eyes (Nikolai & Justine #5)

Trey (Trey & K)

The Italian Cartel

Dimitri

Roxanne

Reign

Mafia Ties (Novella)

Maddox

Demi

Rocco

Clover

Smith

<u>RomCom Standalones</u>

Just Playin' (Elvis & Willow)

<u>Ain't Happenin'</u> (Lorenzo & Skylar)

<u>The Drop Zone</u> (Colby & Jamie)

Very Unlikely (Lennox & Summer)

False Start (Cash & McKayla)

<u>One Night Only</u>

Hotshot Boss (Mr. Carson & Octavia)

Hotshot Neighbor (Caleb & Jess)

<u>Bobrov Bratva</u>

Wicked Intentions

Sinful Intentions

Devious Intentions

Deadly Intentions

<u>Short Stories</u>

Christmas Trio (Wesley, Andrew & Mallory -- short story)

Falling For A Stranger (Short Story)

Acknowledgments

Thank you to the following individuals who, without their contributions and support, this book would not have been written.

First to my husband, Chris. When I said I wanted to write a book, he simply replied with, "Okay, great." No hesitation, not even a small amount of consideration, he just offered his full support. This is very much in tune with exactly how my husband has been our entire marriage. I have an idea, and he supports me one hundred percent. I'm so grateful to have him in my life, and I wouldn't want to have it any other way. He is my most valued gift in life.

Second to my darling Mum. She reads the entire first draft of every novel I've penned while attempting to assist in editing. I have never been good with anything grammatical-related, but she assists me where she can. For this, I will be eternally grateful.

Third but not at all least, to my readers. I appreciate each and every one of you. You're the reason I write something every day. It might only be a paragraph, or it may be ten thousand words in a day, but it is your encouragement and support that keep me writing.

So THANK YOU!

Please remember to leave a review of my book.

Shandi xx